Destiny's Quartet

Destiny's Quartet

BARBARA KNIGHT

Library of Congress Control Number: 2011908525
ISBN: Hardcover   978-1-4628-7662-4
                 Softcover   978-1-4628-7137-7
                 Ebook   978-1-4568-9382-8

To order additional copies of this book, contact:
Xlibris Corporation
0800-891-366
www.xlibris.co.nz
Orders@xlibris.co.nz
700129

Dedication

To my husband for his unwavering support and love

PART ONE

OVERTURE

1976-1988

CHAPTER 1

At nineteen years old, Graeme Stuart McKenzie and his best friend, William (Billy) Watson, caught the train going 'up North' to begin their service careers with the Royal Air Force.

They were off on the greatest adventure of their young lives happy, excited—and perhaps just a little nervous at what lay ahead. Although neither would ever admit the latter in a month of Sundays!

Scurrying away to seek relief from the cold wintry wind, a small crowd of other shivering well-wishers soon dispersed. The lone figure of a dark-haired girl stood on the now deserted, litter-strewn train platform, fighting back tears.

As Julie Smith watched the rear end of the train rapidly disappearing, the words Graeme had spoken so earnestly a few weeks earlier filled her thoughts. "Julie, I've received my acceptance for the RAF. Luckily, Billy and I are going to the same 'square basher.'" He had sighed, "It's going to be the way for me to get somewhere in life. Maybe I'll even get to fly . . . that's my secret ambition. Julie, I'll only be away for twelve weeks at first."

Julie sighed, only twelve weeks! She blew her nose, dried her tears and walked back home. Her Gran would be there with a warming cuppa and a sympathetic shoulder.

Walking quickly to stave off the bone-chilling wind that wickedly whipped her clothing and viciously nipped her bare ears and hands, she reflected how, until now, they had been just a normal average family. Home consisted of her parents, Gran, Julie and her younger siblings, brother Don, and sisters Lisa and Carole. Then, unexpectedly, Graeme McKenzie had entered and brought turmoil into her life.

It had all started just weeks ago when, after leaving High School, she began a new social life by joining the local Youth Club. When the club announced a 'Grand Christmas Party Dance' Julie enlisted the help of her Gran to make her first formal gown.

The waltz-length dress she had designed herself was in a deep, dusky pink silk. It had long bell sleeves and a full circle skirt, which swished alluringly around her ankles. To complete the ensemble, she bought her very first pair of high-heeled, gold strap sandals.

Maureen Watson, Julie's long-standing friend and neighbour, had recently begun her hairdressing apprenticeship and offered to fix Julie's hair. Maureen also suggested, "Why don't you come with my brother, Billy, and me tonight? Don't go on your own."

As she entered the hall for her very first adult dance, Julie became aware that the tall figure standing at the entrance was her other neighbour, Graeme McKenzie.

Although he lived in the house backing onto Julie's home, he had attended the Boys College and Julie the Girls College, in opposite directions. Consequently their paths had rarely crossed.

Now here he was, smartly dressed in a dark blue suit, white shirt and a very snazzy, red bow tie. To Julie it seemed he had always been around. He was just Graeme, the blue eyed, blonde boy from over the fence, someone she had known most of her life.

Yet tonight . . . somehow . . . something . . . did feel different. She felt something stir within her, a strange feeling of anticipation, of hoping that he would find her attractive.

Whoa! Back up screamed her brain! That was much too scary a track to be going down.

As they walked towards Billy and Graeme, Maureen stage whispered behind her, "Gee, he's sure become one handsome dude. Hey! You've gobsmacked him, girl. Look at his face!'

Julie became aware Graeme was admiring her—and only her. His face broke into a warm, welcoming smile as he asked, "Hi, Julie. Would you care to dance?"

Without saying a word, Julie blushed and nodded. He led her towards the dance floor. Julie's heart began skipping beats, she felt as though she was floating in a trance, a cocoon of space occupied by just the two of them.

Behind them, Billy said to the empty space beside his sister, "Hello, Julie, great to see you." He answered himself, mimicking a female voice, "It's great to see you too, Billy."

Turning to his sister, he exclaimed, "Wow! Did you see that! They didn't even notice us."

As Graeme held Julie in his arms ready to dance, their bodies made contact and Julie felt an electric current race through her body from head to toe.

She felt a heady dizziness at being held so close to him. Her heart began to race, her throat felt constricted. She found it difficult to speak. Even in her new high-heeled sandals, the top of her head only just came above his shoulder. He was so much taller.

Julie could feel that his heart was beating as fast as her own. She looked up at him and, as their eyes met, both were startled by the intensity of the magnetism, and the new, powerful feelings they saw mirrored there. With great willpower, Julie pulled her gaze away from his.

Turning her head to one side, she looked right into the idiotic, grinning faces of Maureen and Billy as they danced by.

Maureen was mouthing, "I told you so! Gobsmacked!"

Blushing, Julie looked up at Graeme and saw that he too had reddened.

But the spell was broken.

They swung away into the dance, talking nineteen to the dozen, catching up with each other's news, all awkward restraints gone.

They were completely oblivious to the handsome dance pairing they made, not noticing the many envious glances they were receiving.

"I think it's so romantic," sighed Maureen to her brother, "I only hope I get someone, someday, who'll look at me the way he does at her."

That night, Julie had lain awake for a long time. She was just too excited to sleep. It had been a very special evening, her confused thoughts focused on how, so suddenly, she'd discovered her new feelings for Graeme.

The next morning . . .

Julie gazed down from her upstairs bedroom window on to the tall figure standing under the stately, but winter bare, sycamore tree, on the back boundary between their two gardens. He seemed deep in thought.

Opening the window, she called, "Penny for them?"

Graeme looked up and his whole face lit up in a smile, which made Julie catch her breath at how handsome he was.

She ran down to talk to him. He greeted her warmly, nodding towards the sycamore tree and saying, "I've always considered this a special tree. To me it somehow joined our two families . . . It has grown up with us. You planted it—about 1970, wasn't it?"

Laughing, Julie retorted, "It's grown, yes, almost as quickly as you have! Yes, I do remember, it was the day you moved here. I was just ten and I'd picked up the seed in the park earlier that day. My Mum warned me to plant it well away from the house. Nobody expected it to grow—least of all, me!"

His face became serious as he explained how he was about to begin his career in the RAF. "I'd like to write to you. Would that be okay?"

Julie blushed as she answered, "I'd love it if you'd write . . . I do hope you get your secret wish to fly, Graeme . . . I also have a 'secret ambition'. For as long as I can remember I've wanted to design clothes. I'm about to start classes to learn the basics. Then I can apply for an apprenticeship."

Julie bought Graeme a leather-bound writing compendium for Christmas and he solemnly vowed to write to her. Graeme gave Julie a sandalwood trinket box, lined with dusky pink velvet, the same colour as her first formal gown. What also made this gift so special to them was the sycamore leaf design carved on the lid.

On Julie's seventeenth birthday, St. Valentine's Day 1977, Graeme hung a golden, heart-shaped locket around her neck, saying, "I'll leave this part of me with you—for now."

CHAPTER 2

Graeme had been gone for a month and Julie enjoyed getting his letters. He had described his 'square bashing' life as harder than he expected, 'tough but fair'.

Julie wrote how, with her sister Lisa and Billy's sister, Maureen Watson, she was learning the tango from Felix, the Youth Club Latin dance tutor.

Lisa soon dropped out, complaining it was too hard. Maureen screamed with laughter, yelled that it tickled, when Felix made her bend low, or do a 'freeze' turn. She was soon banned from any further classes. Julie didn't overly like Felix, thinking him a good tutor but a hard taskmaster.

So it was on that fateful Saturday afternoon . . .

The music of the classic tango 'Jealousy' was booming out. Julie's skirt was swirling, twisting, revealing her bare legs under the layers of stiffened, tulle petticoats.

Felix swung her around, forcing his pelvis hard against hers. Gripping her waist he bent her backwards in a particularly suggestive movement of the torrid 'love dance', twirling her as though she were a matador's cape. Once more the rapid movement sent her skirts flying, before Felix brought her tight against his chest, and kissed her fully on the mouth.

The music ended with a typically Spanish crescendo of raucous, clashing cymbals, and the rapid 'click click' chatter of castanets.

Trying to catch her breath, Julie turned and saw Billy and Graeme standing at the back of the hall.

On Graeme's shocked face was a look of pure, angry thunder. Billy's mouth gaped open.

Then Felix, to her utter astonishment, bellowed an oath and ordered them out of the studio.

Graeme, now white with anger, turned on his heel and stalked out. Billy recovered to retort, "Don't worry drongo, we don't want any part of your lewd dancing."

Julie, shaking with anger and embarrassment, hissed between clenched teeth at the gloating Felix, "Who do you think you are!" She slapped his face soundly, gathered up her bag and coat and went to report his conduct to the Youth Club Manager.

She was totally devastated that Graeme had so readily assumed she had consented to Felix's suggestive approaches.

Graeme and Billy never set foot in the Clubrooms again. Even Maureen kept away.

Shattered by these events Julie decided it was time for a change. Using her evening class qualifications and good college results, she applied for and got an apprenticeship with the up-market fashion house called, Maison Chevalier. It was a dreams-come-true position. She was surrounded every day by well-groomed principals and their glamorous models draped with gloriously rich fabrics of every hue.

As a junior apprentice, she attended daily classes, learning fashion design, pattern making and fabric selection. She soon became a popular younger member of the staff and to her delight, occasionally she was invited along as a 'gopher' on photo shoots.

Julie had told her Gran what had happened on that terrible afternoon. Gran saw a haunted, pained look in Julie's eyes that almost broke the older woman's heart.

Gran tried to reassure her, "Now, now, Graeme is too sensible a lad to hold a grudge for long. He'll soon come around."

But he didn't. The rift between them had become a gulf too wide to bridge. Word filtered back that he and Billy had applied for duty in Cyprus.

The night he was due to fly out, Julie cried herself to a restless sleep . . .

The painful, lonely summer passed.

Julie was pondering a significant decision. She was about to bury the locket Graeme had given her on her seventeenth birthday.

Sitting resting against the trunk of the sycamore tree, she wrapped it in a blanket of cotton wool, sealed it in a tin, dug a deep hole and gently dropped the small package down. She gave the earth one more determined pat, firmly stating; "Now I am going to start a new phase in my life with a new man."

Julie had met John Field nearly three months previously when she had accompanied her bosses, Michael and Denise Armstrong, to a major fabric showing. He was six feet tall, had dark brown wavy hair and almost black eyes. He was twenty-five years old, well groomed and ambitious.

John Field had been in London for several months representing a New Zealand wool company, selling fine wool fabrics to the leading Fashion Houses. At the dinner that night, Julie and John found themselves sitting together. Right from the start they found that they had much in common, both being vitally interested in their respective jobs and in the fickle, fragile world of high fashion.

Suddenly John clicked his fingers. "Now I remember where I have seen you before!"

He described the magazine photo he had spotted on the flight to London. "It was you in that photo by Tony Prentice, wasn't it?"

Laughingly, Julie admitted, "Yes, I was the 'gopher'. I was taking the props, bolts of silks, back to the van when . . . whoosh, a breeze sprung up from absolutely nowhere. It whisked the rolls loose and unravelled them as though I had cast out a fishing line. I didn't want the ends hitting the ground, so I tried catching them by twisting myself around to hold them up. That's when they wrapped themselves all around me . . . the tails flew skywards just like a kite taking off. It was such an incredible sensation—it felt as though I was floating up with the silk. T.P. was just passing by and snapped off the shot."

"Care to dance?" John asked.

"Why yes, I love dancing," was her reply, although a fleeting shadow seemed to pass across her face.

Watching the young couple dancing, laughing and talking animatedly, Michael hoped that, although he didn't want to lose Julie from his successful team, she would find a happy distraction in the young New Zealander.

Now, some three months later, on Graeme's twentieth birthday, almost eighteen years of age herself, Julie knew that John Field was getting serious about their relationship. He was fun to be with, mature, good looking, dressed impeccably and was reliable. He liked dancing as much as she did, and was always good company.

"What is missing then?" she asked herself.

She sighed; Graeme was no longer in her life. Could John be the answer? Looking up into the rustling leafy branches of the sycamore tree, she asked her old confidante, "Well, what d'you think?"

As if to answer, the tree swayed in the breeze and gave a long, rustling, soughing sigh. It trembled, shaking glorious, autumn coloured leaves down around Julie.

"Yes, I know," she whispered back, "but life goes on. Next spring you'll be back to your former glory, new leaves, new growth, new hope. I've got to look forward too." She gave one last, reluctant look at the spot where she had buried the locket . . . and walked away.

John and Julie were soon recognised as a couple, both in their places of employment and around Julie's neighbourhood.

Maureen, looking out just as they were passing, saw them smile happily at each other. She indignantly cried, "It's not right! Julie and Graeme belong together!"

That night she wrote to her brother Billy, urging him to 'get into Graeme's ear,' warning him, 'do something before it's darn well too late!'

On her 19th birthday, Julie comfortably passed the first of her major apprenticeship examinations.

That same evening, John proposed and she accepted.

John telephoned his parents, Naomi and George Field, in New Zealand. As John finished his call to his delighted parents, Julie saw her tearful mother being comforted by Gran and her father.

"All of a sudden, New Zealand seems such a long way Julie, love," murmured Gran.

The realisation was also beginning to seep into Julie's consciousness. The reality of leaving her job, her family, her country of birth, and of going to live on the other side of the world, with complete strangers, produced a frightening and recurring nightmarish dream for her.

In it she was running down a long, straight road, lined with faceless people, all calling out, "No! No! NO!", getting louder and louder. Behind her, Julie could hear other voices, urging her to stop. She ran on, her chest heaving as her lungs gasped for air. As she stumbled and fell, a tall, shadowy figure loomed out of the darkness ahead. A bright white searchlight beam illuminated the outline of the figure from behind. With its arms outstretched towards her, in the voice of Graeme, it softly called, "Hurry Julie! Just a little further."

The figures running behind her, urging her to stop, were almost upon her . . .

At this point she awoke, covered in perspiration.

After several exhausting nights when the dream constantly repeated itself, she went to the one place where she had always found peace, serenity and solace, beneath the sycamore tree. Protected by the overhanging branches of the beautiful tree, she opened her heart. Tears welled up and ran down her face in a waterfall of sorrow. Heart-breaking sobs wracked her body for several minutes as she attempted to forcibly evict the grief of a lost, young love.

CHAPTER 3

The late afternoon sun fired the diamonds in Julie's engagement ring, catching her attention. She quickly checked her wristwatch. John would soon arrive to escort her to the hospital.

Gran had been ailing for several weeks. Finally being persuaded to visit the family doctor, it came as no surprise when she was admitted to the local hospital.

Gran and Julie were close as she had always been Julie's comforter. When Gran had witnessed the despair in her favourite grandchild's eyes after Graeme's departure, she had become more than ever 'a good listener'.

She had encouraged Julie to accept John's proposal, saying, "He's a good man and he will always be there for you. You could do worse, my girl. Marry your John, get on with your life. If in the future something else occurs . . . well . . . just make sure you don't hurt anyone else in the process."

"It's not that I don't care for him, Gran," Julie explained. "Oh! I don't know, perhaps I want too much."

"Tell me about your wedding dress, love," Gran said, discreetly changing the subject.

"Oh Gran, Michael and Denise have been so generous! For my engagement present they gave me the run of the fabric stock. I had such a choice! Well, we decided today to go with a terrific blushed, moire grosgrain silk from Switzerland. Blushed, instead of ivory, because of my 'Anglais coulore' Monsieur Alexandre said," Julie chuckled. "He's the one you reckon sounds like Maurice Chevalier, remember? Anyway, he's sending my veil straight from Paris. Gran, I am going to feel like a princess."

"Aye, and you'll look like one too, my girl," said her Gran, wiping happy tears from her eyes.

In just two more weeks, Julie and John were to be married. Their honeymoon cruise trip was booked to New Zealand aboard the luxury liner Ocean Queen. Michael Armstrong looked across the office at Julie and read again the letter that had arrived from his own 'best man', Andrew Martin, his New Zealand manager.

"When should we expect to see the fabulous Julie?" the letter asked. "If she is only half as bright as you have described, we want her here A.S.A.P.—on our side. Ask her to give me a ring when she gets here."

Michael Armstrong called to Julie, "Here's a letter from Andrew Martin in Auckland. They want to see you when you arrive," he smiled, adding, "especially now you have almost completed your apprenticeship. Just one final exam to go, Julie, lass."

"Yes, thank goodness. Hey! This will be super, Michael," she replied reading through the letter, "and I know John already works with them."

"Ah ha! Hello, methinks the bridegroom cometh," he called with a thespian leer, as John entered the office.

Julie greeted her fiancé, with a happy smile, "Hey! I've got some good news. Okay for him to read Andrew's letter, Michael?"

"Be my guest, good lady," Michael said with a theatrical flourish.

"Take no notice, John," Julie giggled, "he's been like this all day. He's getting in the mood for the Shakespearean play he and Denise are going to tonight."

With a big grin, she left the room to put away the fabrics she had been working on.

Michael turned to John. "God! I'm going to miss having her around, old boy. She's a breath of fresh air."

Michael escorted the young couple out of the office.

To himself he surmised, 'Now, Will Shakespeare, time to do me duty by thee, methinks. I often wondered, old chap, if you believed 'the entire world was a stage' where you thought your dammed audience would be sitting! On those rock hard wooden seats I'll be perched on tonight, I suppose.' With that, jamming his hat on his head, Michael let himself out the back door.

Arriving at the hospital, John and Julie were met by the Ward Sister.

"Your Grandmother is not so good, I'm afraid," the Sister told them. "I think you'd better get your parents to come in. You can use my telephone."

John looked at Julie's stricken face. "You go and sit with Gran, Julie. I'll get in touch with your parents."

As if in a dream, Julie walked down the ward to Gran's bed. She looked so small and shrunken. Julie took the wrinkled, careworn hand in hers, and softly said, "I'm here Gran. It's me, Julie."

With a weak smile, her Gran opened her eyes and squeezed Julie's hand. "Hello, my love. I'm so glad you are here as I'm feeling really tired. I may not be there in the flesh, but I'll dance at your wedding in spirit. I'll always be there for you, Julie." She closed her eyes.

They were her last words.

She died in her sleep that night.

Julie was devastated by her Gran's death, but relieved it had happened before she left for New Zealand. She had been able to say 'good bye' in person, to the dear grandmother who had been always so lovingly supportive.

Julie was also to learn what a tower of strength John was to her in her hour of need. His arms were strong, comforting and always there for her to hide in. They became closer and her respect for him grew even deeper.

For Julie it was the closing of an era in her life.

But as one door closes, another opens . . .

. . . Michael related to her, in detail, about his experience at the Shakespearean play. But, what really interested him was the young woman from New Zealand, who had been sitting alongside him that night.

"We found out that she is Kate Reynolds, married to Harry. She has the reddest of red hair I have ever seen, and she bounces around like a human dynamo," Michael told Julie. "I was complaining to her about getting a square sided derriere from sitting on the hard seats. It apparently tickled her fancy and she burst out laughing, right in the middle of a very serious scene, much to the annoyance and disgust of all of the stuffed shirts around us. She has a laugh that automatically makes you want to join in, whatever the joke is." He paused, remembering.

"But, the strangest coincidence of all, she works for Andrew in Auckland. They were coming here on an overnight stopover, but had to change their plans at the last minute and flew direct to Los Angeles, straight after the play.

Anyway we took the liberty of telling her about you. She's your type of person, Julie, she'll be a big help in getting you settled."

"She sounds great, Mike," Julie smiled, "it will be good to have a female friend. You said her name is Kate Reynolds?"

He nodded and then, with a big grin, handed her a handsome box, decorated in the silver and white livery of their Paris office.

Julie gently separated the many layers of tissue paper, and gasped at the delicate, full-length, filmy bridal veil lying there. Carefully extricating it from its box, she found a small card within its folds, which said, "To Julie, a very special colleague, with our very best wishes, from all of us in the Paris office."

Lying in the bottom of the box was another smaller package. Julie opened it to find an exquisite blue and white satin 'Can Can' garter, and a cheeky personal card from Monsieur Alexandre that said, "Something blue, cherie. I envy the lucky man who gets to take this off!"

As Michael and Denise guffawed at the typical and very continental Monsieur Alexandre quip, Julie blushed a bright beetroot red.

Lifting the veil from its box, Denise gently draped it over Julie's head. With a flourish, Michael produced the headdress the bridal accessories department had made especially for Julie. It was a delicate tiara, consisting of lustrous creamy drop pearls intertwined with blush pink, miniature orchids and orange blossom.

Julie managed to stammer out her thanks, as she choked back the tears that were threatening to come.

Her mother came in from the dressmaking room where she had been having a final fitting for her Mother-of-the-Bride outfit.

Her eldest daughter grinned weakly at her. "What d'you think, Mum? Will I do?" she asked.

Her mother hugged her and proudly said, "Julie love, you'll look like a princess, just as Gran predicted." Crying and laughing all at once, she clasped Julie tightly in her arms. "Oh, if only she could have seen you."

CHAPTER 4

Graeme McKenzie saw the tactical and technical radar course in Cyprus as an opportunity to gain some worthwhile qualifications. It was over two years since the 'lewd dancing' incident, as Billy Watson had labelled it.

Graeme and Billy had just driven into the old city in a ramshackle ex-American Army jeep, euphemistically known as 'the transport', in R.A.F. station parlance. It was hot, hotter than it had been for days, so when Billy suggested that they stop for a beer at the local excuse for a pub, Graeme didn't need any second bidding.

"Come on," Billy urged, "I'm as dry as a wooden god."

It was cooler inside, with ancient, noisy ceiling fans doing their best to keep it that way. Billy headed for the bar and Graeme found a couple of seats. Selecting one of the London papers from the rack he was soon engrossed in the football pages.

Billy returned with two frothing glasses of beer.

Clumsily putting them down on the table in front of Graeme, he slopped a dash of the brown liquid over a magazine lying there. "Watch it! Careful! Don't waste good beer," Graeme admonished, with a broad grin.

Billy took out a grubby handkerchief and began to mop up the small puddle. The glossy magazine paper stuck to his handkerchief revealing a full-page coloured photograph of a pretty girl holding several bolts of silk material. The smile on her face was one of pure joy.

"Julie?" he croaked.

"What?" Graeme dropped his newspaper and snatched up the magazine.

The caption read, "Mme Julie Eve Smith. A new and lovely employee of Maison Chevalier."

Graeme turned the photograph over and saw it was in a well-known fashion magazine. He surreptitiously tore the page out and tucked it inside his shirt.

Finishing their drinks, Graeme went to a nearby shop and had the picture mounted in a silver frame. Back at their billet, he lay staring at it.

His thoughts turned back a couple of months when he and Billy had gone to the local cinema. As they waited for the main feature, a short film from one of the film festivals was being shown. Billy was not paying any attention because he was eyeing up the audience, seeing if there was any local 'talent' he could 'chat up'.

Graeme had suddenly cried, "My God! Look!"

On screen a couple dressed in the Spanish national costume were dancing a fiery tango. The male dancer bent his partner over in a backwards movement and then swung her around in a complete circle, before holding her tightly to his chest and kissing her passionately on the mouth.

The cinema audience broke into cheers and applause, much to Graeme and Billy's surprise.

"Wow! So that's what Julie and Felix were dancing!"

Billy had murmured. "It wasn't lewd after all. Er . . . Graeme, I think we owe her an apology, mate."

Graeme sat through the main feature as though made of stone, blind to everything around him. Hammering in his brain and raging through his mind were some painful questions. What had he done? Why hadn't he listened to his heart, instead of being led by his stupid hot head!

He decided he would write to Julie, try to make amends and he resolved he would learn the tango steps himself!

Fate . . . as it invariably does . . . stepped in.

The weekly letter from his parents arrived the next morning. It wasn't until the second page that the lines blurred, and he had difficulty reading the words. 'We have some local news. It seems Julie Smith is going steady with a young man, there is even talk of them getting engaged, it's apparently that serious.'

Graeme's immediate thoughts were that somehow he had to get back home in a hurry. He had to explain to Julie that he loved her. There had to be a way for him to get home. Anyhow—even AWOL!

When Billy saw and heard the anguish in his best friend's voice, he felt deep compassion for him, but no way was he going to condone Graeme going AWOL!

Billy clicked his fingers. Compassionate leave! That's it! I'll go and see the Chaplain.

He explained to the Chaplain, "I've known him since we were kids. I know how he feels about her. I've tried to warn him if he does anything illegal he'll ruin his life and hers. But, honestly padre, it's like talking to a brick wall!"

"I'd better see the C.O.," mused the Chaplain.

"Perhaps get him home on one of the shuttle transports. Leave it with me, Billy."

Billy gave a sigh of relief. "Don't get me wrong, Julie is one helluva great girl. Graeme was the one that cocked it up last time when he didn't give her a chance to explain." He hung his head. "I'm just as stupid. I also jumped to the wrong conclusions."

The Chaplain immediately telephoned the Commanding Officer's adjutant.

Two hours later Graeme was summoned to his C.O.'s office. A discreet knock on the door roused Group Captain David Peters from where he was studying Graeme's service records. Issuing a gruff, "Enter," he faced the man in question.

Graeme fidgeted with his uniform cap. "Sir, I know the Chaplain has already told you the facts. I must get home, I am really desperate," The young man beseeched the older man. In anguish he asked, "Sir, what can I do?"

"Well, I think I have something to offer you," answered the C.O. "I've been studying your record and it's all good news. Your Flight Lieutenant has only just recommended you be offered the opportunity to apply for an aircrew selection course." He paused to let his words sink in. "Apart from your immediate problem, what are your long-term aspirations in the R.A.F?"

Graeme, startled by these revelations, responded, "I want to fly, that's my one passion. I believe I can bring my tactical radar expertise to an aircrew position. I'm already taking flying lessons at the local Aero Club."

Pursing his lips, giving both ends of his bushy R.A.F. moustache a twirl, the C.O. nodded his head. "I'm prepared to recommend that you go to H.Q. for an aircrew selection course, forthwith. It is an intensive seven-day series of tests. No outside contact is permitted, no personal contacts, no telephone calls."

The Group Captain paused. "Do you understand? I emphasise, personal issues must be left completely behind for those seven days. Your fitness to be considered for aircrew and officer training depends greatly upon the attitude and dedication you display whilst at the selection centre. I propose to convene a special board here within the next twenty-four hours. They will make a decision on your suitability. Well?"

Graeme gaped at his C.O. and could only nod.

The Commanding Officer smiled at the dazed but talented young man in front of him. "I gather that's a 'Yes'? Well, I'm going back to H.Q. myself in a week's time, got to keep up my own flying hours. You can fly with me, if the Board agrees. It will give me a chance to pass on some tips to help you. I'll be there for about twelve days. That'll give you a chance to complete the course and perhaps a couple of days afterwards to sort out your personal problem. But, remember, for the first seven days you let your head rule, and not your heart, m'lad!"

Graeme's delighted face said it all. "Yes sir! Thank you!"

Before he could blurt out his news to Billy, he saw that, like himself, Billy was dressed in his best uniform, and not looking so well.

"The C.O. wants to see me, now," Billy managed to gulp. "Gotta go. See you later."

Graeme collapsed on the nearest chair, stunned by what the C.O. had offered him. So deep was he in his own thoughts, he hardly took note when Billy staggered into the room twenty minutes later.

Flopping down heavily on Graeme's bed, Billy squeaked, in an almost emasculated voice, "Graeme, old son, pinch me, will you! I can't believe it! We are both going back to Blighty next week, trying out for aircrew. You and me, we are going with the C.O. Naw! I musta got it wrong, old son."

Suddenly, the realisation hit them. Graeme's face lit up as the two of them hugged each other and proceeded to dance a wild, crazy dance around the tiny room.

Graeme shook his head soberly, as he said, "Believe it mate, but first we have to convince the special Board here. So 'spit and polish' everything you have my friend. No alcohol and Billy . . . for God's sake, get your hair trimmed! We two have to look like the best officer material this Board has seen, since the R.A.F. began."

He rubbed his hand in a disbelieving gesture across his face, as he added, "Oh dear God! I'm even going to get the chance to see Julie afterwards."

The special Board, consisting of several local senior R.A.F. Officers, duly convened two days later. Graeme and Billy were subjected to intensive interviews, including a technical interrogation when their work records were analysed and dissected. An equally severe questioning followed as to their personal aspirations within the modern Air Force.

At the end of the Board hearings, their Commanding Officer was invited to address the Board. After he had spoken of their unblemished records and added that he wholeheartedly recommended their applications, the Board unanimously agreed on their suitability.

A short time afterwards, Group Captain David Peters beamed as he gave the two men the good news, saying, "How will that do?"

Their faces conveyed their total delight as their Commanding Officer continued, "Right, to business. We fly direct to the U.K. tomorrow. Your course starts the next day, and we are due back here in twelve days time. Give it your very best, gentlemen."

Graeme and Billy stood stunned before Graeme recovered and vigorously shook the officer's hand.

CHAPTER 5

The noise in the aircraft cockpit droned in Graeme's eardrums. Everything around him seemed to be vibrating and shuddering in a giddy, dizzy 'dance macabre'. Voice contact with Billy was virtually impossible.

When the C.O. offered him the chance to join him in the cockpit, he gratefully accepted. Since taking his initial flying lesson, he had come to terms with the realisation that, for him, flying was truly a kind of freedom, a passion. He fully understood the meaning of the pilot's favourite poem that began, 'Oh, I have slipped the surly bonds of Earth . . .'

Breaking through his reverie, he heard the voice of his C.O. chuckling over the intercom. "You've really got the 'bug' haven't you? You are smitten. Well, let's see what those 'cowboys' back at the airfield have taught you. Take over the controls, son."

After a delighted grin at his C.O., he flew the plane the rest of the way to the U.K.

Billy, waking up with a jaw-dislocating yawn, realised Graeme was actually flying the plane!

They landed late in the afternoon, checked in with the duty officer and were given their instructions.

On arrival at their billet, they found they were the only two candidates from an overseas posting. They were soon surrounded by their fellow aspirants, answering numerous questions. Graeme was surprised at how young, even naïve, some of the others were. He and Billy were the two longest serving men in the room. Billy was soon stringing them along with stories extolling the talents of the girls of Cyprus.

Cocking a quizzical eyebrow at Billy at one stage, warning him to tone it down, Graeme discovered, for the first time, the responsibility of being the senior ranking man.

His maturity and calmness under stress was noted by several of his examiners over the next gruelling week. So was Billy's ability to smile, make a jocular remark and bounce back from adversity.

The days and nights during that week passed as a blur. The aptitude, coordination, educational, health and physical gymnastics tests left each man totally drained. Some were occasionally too tired to even eat a meal before falling into their beds. Not least of the tension building up was the mental anxiety of whether they were going to pass.

Then, as suddenly as it began, it was all over.

One by one, in alphabetical order, they were invited into the Wing Commander's office. The success, or otherwise, of the young men as they emerged from the room was easy to assess. It was also evident that, out of the group of twenty hopefuls, there were going to be a very small number passing the strict criteria required.

Alphabetically McKenzie comes before Watson, so Graeme expected to be the first to front up. The Wing Commander's assistant approached him, asking him to step aside as the Wing Commander wanted to see him last.

Catching his eye, Billy mouthed, "What's up?"

Graeme shrugged, as puzzled as Billy.

When it was Billy's turn, Graeme showed him that he had his fingers crossed on both hands!

Billy emerged, the smile on his face saying it all! Clenching a fist, he punched the air before momentarily closing his eyes, as he whispered a relieved and heartfelt, "Yes!"

Then it was Graeme's turn.

The Wing Commander invited him to sit and looked down at Graeme's open file in front of him. "Young man, I have never seen such a high aggregate of points as you have received this week. First, let me congratulate you and put you out of your misery . . . you are 'in'."

Graeme released the breath he hardly knew he was holding.

The Wing Commander smiled, "Great feeling, isn't it?

Enjoy the moment, for although there will be others, this is the first, the very first." He paused before referring to the file in front of him with a chuckle. "I have a foot-note here from one of your task masters that states, 'Watch Out! This man will be our boss one day, treat him VERY nicely!' Prophetic words? Well, Corporal McKenzie, you are to be invited to attend an Officer Cadet Course at Cranwell immediately. I understand you are already undertaking private flying lessons? Fine, but it is your tactical and leadership qualities that have impressed your examiners during the past week. In plain language, McKenzie, you have the all of the abilities we are seeking. Congratulations!"

Billy saw the stunned but happy look on Graeme's face. Clapping him on the back, a delighted Billy said, "A quick drink with the rest of the group and then home, eh?"

Graeme looked dazed as he murmured, "We have a future, Billy. We are going places. All of my wildest dreams have come true . . . . What? Oh yes, let's go and commiserate with the unlucky devils. They must be feeling devastated."

This sad duty done, they mutually decided that, as they were potential 'Officers and Gentlemen', they deserved to treat themselves to a taxi for the rest of the journey.

As the taxi stopped, Billy chortled with glee and told Graeme, "Give me half an hour, I'll try and find out from our Maureen where Julie might be."

Letting himself in through the front door, his mother clutched her chest in shock.

"It's okay, Mum," Graeme hastened to reassure her, "I'm not AWOL. I'm here legit, honest."

It took him the next ten minutes to tell his parents and his older sister, Beth, the full story of his unexpected arrival home. He proudly told how he had gained the chance to be an Officer Cadet and of spending the last week on a course from which he could not communicate.

Excitedly he explained how his career dreams had come to fruition, and next he had to go and make his peace with Julie. He talked non-stop, not allowing them to get a word in edgewise.

"She has always been special to you, hasn't she?" asked his sister Beth. "Even when you were kids, you always looked out for her."

"I think I must have loved her most of my life," Graeme replied. "Thank God, I'm home before she gets married."

At this declaration of love his sister burst into tears and rushed from the room.

His parents looked sadly at him, amazement on his father's face, sorrow on his mother's. Graeme looked from one to the other, "What's wrong, Mum, Dad? What am I missing here?"

His mother hid her face in a handkerchief and his father clasped his son's shoulder, saying slowly, sadly,

"Son, Julie gets married tomorrow. We thought you knew."

"Julie, married . . . tomorrow? Oh dear God, no!"

The pain and anguish in his voice sent his mother into another burst of sobbing. Hurrying from the room, Graeme bounded up the stairs to his old bedroom, wanting to be alone. A tight band of pain encircled his heart, restricting his breathing and causing his head to throb.

Standing at his bedroom window, he looked across the adjoining gardens to Julie's home. He was surprised at how tall the sycamore tree had become. He had always believed that the tree linked their lives together.

When they saw him coming downstairs half an hour later, all three members of his family looked anxiously towards him, their faces full of compassion.

"What are you going to do now, son?" his father gently asked.

"Billy is waiting for me. No doubt Maureen would have filled him in on the situation. I'd like to go for a walk, be on my own for a bit, if that's okay with you, Mum, Dad?"

"Graeme, whatever happens we are so proud of what you have achieved," his father beamed at him. "Our hearts are bursting with pride, son, at your news. We'll always be here if you need us."

Billy and Maureen were waiting at their front door. Maureen threw her arms around him. "I can see by your face that your parents have told you," she said sadly.

"Well, Graeme. What now?" Billy asked.

"I can't upset her life the night before her wedding, Billy. I'll just keep out of the way. Please, both of you, respect my wishes, and don't let on that I'm here."

"Graeme! She's not married yet!" groaned Billy. "Don't be so pig-headed, go there, sweep her off her feet."

"No, I can't do it. I've no proof that she cares for me in any way. What will I achieve? All I'll do is upset what, to most women, is the most important day of their lives. No, I can't do that to her."

Maureen was in tears as she nodded, agreeing to keep quiet. Eventually, Billy, somewhat reluctantly, acquiesced.

With that, Graeme quickly jogged away down the road.

Burning tears stung his eyes and sobs wracked his chest as he turned into the dark avenue of trees leading to the local park.

He sat on a park bench and poignantly asked, "Dear God, you have unexpectedly granted me my lifetime dream, my ambition, the opportunity to fly. But, dear Lord, did the sacrifice have to be the girl I have loved and cherished for so long?"

Sheltered and almost enveloped by the ancient trees towering over him, he sat for many hours, a lonely dejected figure coming to terms with the devastating knowledge that he had lost her again.

This time it seemed . . . for good.

CHAPTER 6

Wedding Day!

The Smith house was a hive of activity. Everyone was hustling and bustling, coping with the little things that go to make up the whole for a family wedding.

Sadly, John's parents had been unable to undertake the long flight as his father was still not sufficiently recovered from his recent heart attack.

Michael and Denise Armstrong readily agreed to stand in as his 'support' family.

Maureen had offered to do Julie's hair and to help her dress. To Julie's surprise she looked red-eyed, as though she had been weeping.

"What is it, Maureen? What's happened?" she asked anxiously.

"People always weep at weddings!" Maureen protested, blowing her nose loudly, and in a very unladylike manner.

Maureen helped Julie put on her wedding gown and stood back, gazing in admiration. The gown was simply, but not severely cut in the Princess line. The bodice fitted closely with a scooped neckline, and the semi-fitted sleeves fell elegantly to the wrist. A full-circled gored skirt swirled in a graceful cloud of the heavy silk. The neckline, sleeve cuffs, and the skirt hem were edged with intricate scallops of exquisite Chantilly lace. A separate over-bodice, which gave a sleeveless waistcoat effect, was heavily encrusted with creamy, pink lustre, drop pearls.

Maureen was speechless. She had reluctantly promised not to tell anyone that Billy and Graeme were home from Cyprus, now looking at the beautiful vision of her friend, she was having some difficulty in keeping up the pretence.

Maureen angrily thought, "It should have been Graeme!"

"Ouch! Maureen that hurt!" Julie yelped as Maureen vehemently wielded the hairbrush through her hair.

She lifted the exquisite filmy French veil and the masterpiece of a tiara into place on Julie's head.

With a sharp intake of breath and yet another massive gulp, Maureen managed to stifle her tears. Standing before her, Julie looked as though she belonged in a fairy tale. The gossamer veil floated around Julie's head in a bouffant, misty cloud, as fine as any spun by a spider, before trailing several yards behind her in a filmy web train.

The overall effect was just as Monsieur Alexandre predicted. The tint of pink had given her skin the right amount of colour. On her dressing table lay the glossy, shell-pink, pearl lipstick he had chosen to complement the gown.

Glancing down at her feet, Julie could see the toes of her white satin, high-heeled shoes peeping out from the front of the skirt, just as the dowager seamstress, Madame Bouvier, had planned.

"You don'ta wanta to treep and fall flata on you face!" Madame Bouvier explained in her heavily accented French voice.

"Julie, it's breath-taking! I've never seen anyone look so radiant." Maureen loudly blew her nose again, forcing the tears away. "Now. Have you 'something old, something new, something borrowed and something blue'?"

With a smile Julie nodded. "My dress is the 'new'. Monsieur Alexandre's garter is 'something blue.' See," she lifted her skirt to show Maureen the very saucy can-can styled garter. "I have borrowed a lace handkerchief from Mum and the 'something old'—my Gran's pearl earrings."

As Julie took the earrings from the trinket box, with its lid engraved with a sycamore leaf design, Maureen saw her wistfully, gently, stroke the lid. Then she firmly closed it with a gesture that had all the hallmarks of some sort of finality.

Her father gave an appreciative gasp as Julie descended the stairs towards him with Maureen holding her veil clear of her shoes. "Julie, love. You take my breath away. Young John has got himself a Princess."

"Dad, that's such a lovely thing to say, thank you . . .

Dad, before we go . . . I am going to miss you all, you know. I'm a little bit scared about what I'm taking on."

As she sounded more like his little girl, rather than the grown-up sophisticated young woman he saw before him, a lump came to her father's throat. Huskily he told her, "You are made of stronger stuff than you realise, Julie. You will make a go of anything you attempt. New Zealand may be at the other end of the earth, but we shall always be here for you." He paused and shook his head before continuing.

"Your mother and I thought you and young McKenzie would make a go of it at one time, but no, it wasn't to be, was it? You always were and will always be your Gran's pride and joy. She'll be up there somewhere, watching over you. Come, my beautiful daughter, let's get this wedding under way."

Smiling happily, they left the house to be greeted by applause from all the neighbours gathered to see one of their own on her way. Following closely behind, Maureen settled Julie and her veil into the back seat of the car and, as she turned away to close the wedding car door, she glanced up at her own home. All of her family were crowded around the front door to catch a glimpse of Julie's departure, but Maureen also saw the lounge curtain twitch.

She knew it would not take much of a guess on her part to know who was hiding there with an aching, breaking heart.

With her long, floor-length veil trailing behind her and the front piece decorously covering her face, Julie glided towards the tall, handsome figure of John waiting nervously at the altar rail.

When Julie stepped up beside him, he whispered, "Darling, you look fantastic."

The ceremony over, Julie and John Field walked back down the aisle to the triumphant Mendelssohn Wedding March. The old bells high in the steeple rang out, and it was agreed by everyone present that Julie and John made a truly handsome couple.

Still with great difficulty, Maureen kept her painful secret to herself as she watched the people photographing and congratulating John and Julie.

Julie looked down at the golden ring on her finger.

There it was, she was now Mrs John Field, 'for better or for worse, for richer or poorer, in sickness and in health.'

At eight o'clock that evening, Maureen whispered to Julie that the car was waiting outside to take them back to her parents' home, to change from her wedding finery. The newly-weds were due to board the liner Ocean Queen by midnight.

Maureen slipped the wedding gown back onto its hanger. "It seems a shame to have to take it off so soon. Did I hear Mr Armstrong say it was going on display in their next Fashion Fabric Show?" she asked Julie.

Julie nodded. "That's right. The complete outfit will be in Sydney, Australia, in time for their Spring Showing. But, I'll get another chance to wear it when John's parents arrange our New Zealand 'wedding'. Not many brides get that opportunity."

Maureen carefully folded the gossamer veil, putting it with the tiara headdress into its own hatbox. "Right, I think that's all," she said. "When are you throwing your bouquet for some lucky girl to catch?"

"I'm not throwing my whole bouquet, only a few pieces," Julie explained. "We are calling in to Gran's grave on the way to the boat and I'm leaving most of it with her." Maureen had already gone into raptures over Julie's trousseau. The whole collection was of fine woollens from New Zealand for her outer clothes, down to the smooth silks, delicate laces and shimmering satins from Europe for her evening and undergarments. Michael Armstrong had been overwhelmed with offers of the finest fabrics from his contacts all over Europe. All of them wanting to give the Mademoiselle Julie 'a good send off.'

CHAPTER 7

The sound of the sea swishing, hissing, in a constant monotonous rhythm against the side of the liner caused Julie to be lulled into a sleepy, relaxing doze. As she lay full length upon a deck lounger, her thoughts drifted back over the past couple of weeks.

Leaving their wedding reception, Julie had tossed part of her wedding bouquet flowers backwards over her head, as was the custom. Amidst loud, raucous cheers, a blushing Maureen caught them.

Giving her parents a last emotional hug, Julie bade them farewell.

At her Gran's grave, under the oak tree in the little peaceful cemetery, Julie left the core of her wedding bouquet and John gently placed his white carnation buttonhole beside Julie's flowers. They stood silently, hand in hand, saying their final goodbyes to Gran.

Julie's first ever experience of being on board a ship of any kind meant she was excited, wide-eyed, but feeling just a little out of her depth. To her delight, she found the cabin to be spacious, not at all cramped as she had wrongly surmised.

Even now, two weeks later, Julie reflected it had been a difficult farewell. Seeing her homeland disappear over the horizon breaking her family ties, while going forward into the virtual unknown, had brought forth a torrent of tears. The luxury liner had sailed blissfully on, taking her away from all that she had known in her young life.

Julie was roused from her reverie by the slight noise beside her as John slipped into the lounger next to hers.

"Hello, darling," he whispered, bending over to kiss her. "Sorry, did I wake you?"

She gave him a lazy, languorous smile, studying him through half-opened eyes. She saw her tanned, very muscular, broad shouldered ardent lover. She remembered how, as she first unpacked on their first evening aboard ship, he had shown an out of character twinge of irritation and surprise when she had unpacked the sycamore trinket box. He was obviously not best pleased that she had brought it with her. She had soothingly protested that she hadn't packed it and thought perhaps Maureen had included it by mistake in her luggage.

He soon recovered his composure and had surprised her with his gentleness on that first night. He had been patient with her, letting her arousal come slowly as he explored her body. He knew it was her first sexual experience and that he needed to temper his ardour.

Julie found to her surprise, it was indeed a most pleasurable experience. She discovered she was happy to fully respond to John's caresses and become an active, innovative sexual partner. Now it had only been an hour since they had been again locked in each other's arms, their bodies demanding satisfaction from each other. John had surprised Julie in the shower. He stood watching her admiringly as she washed her hair before stepping into the shower with her, soaping her body, arousing her as he did so. Towelling her dry, he had been butterfly kissing her breasts, as their joint arousal grew.

Finally, he had lifted her bodily onto the bed, in a passionate union that ended with them experiencing a mutual, breath-taking burst of erotic pleasure.

Lying in this public place, Julie blushed as she recalled her own primitive response to his passion.

The day-long journey through the Panama Canal fascinated both of them. They sat on deck for most of the day, even taking their meals al fresco, rather than miss any of the exhilarating, exotic landscape. They marvelled together at the intricate canal lock system which manoeuvred their huge liner from one level of water effortlessly on to the next.

When the liner docked in Panama City, they were amongst the first ashore, eager to explore. They found the bright, almost primitive colours of the Central American city irresistible. The bold, glaring fabrics displayed in the market place drew Julie's eyes. She could not resist buying a dozen yards of fabric. The dazzling variety of heady hues would forever remind her of the flowers and vegetation of the Panama Canal.

That night their lovemaking entered a new, more carefree phase. It was as though, at last, Julie was beginning to totally trust him with her feelings. During the first week or so of their marriage, John felt that, although Julie was always responsive to him whenever they made love, she also seemed to be holding back from him. This new responsiveness from Julie resulted in a complete sensual and sexual fulfilment for them both.

Julie had enjoyed the stress-free sojourn alone with John. It had been a time of learning, for showing tolerance, of sharing, of being part of a joint partnership. But tomorrow it would be a new country—new home—a new family. Quite a daunting experience for any woman, let alone a newly married one hardly out her teens.

Julie lay beside John in the gently rocking cabin. Her stomach felt cramped, tight, almost as though she was having a panic attack as she contemplated leaving what had become her comfort zone. The ship was her last link with her homeland. Once she stepped ashore the umbilical cord to England would be cut. The prospect of going ashore and having to face John's parents was frightening.

What if they did not like her?

What if she didn't like them!

Finally, unable to sleep, she dressed and went up onto the deck. She was surprised to find that they were already at the entrance to Auckland Harbour.

The harbour was a vast, unspoiled panorama, so uncrowded, so uncluttered. Julie could see the houses were not built close together, in the way she had always known them in England. Here they all appeared to be well separated, standing alone. Though she had been told this was the largest city in New Zealand, even from this distance, Julie could see that it abounded with trees and greenery. It almost sparkled. It looked so clean out there. There appeared to be space for everyone to stamp his or her mark on the landscape.

John soon joined her and she saw on his face and in his eyes there was a soft, happy glow as he scanned the harbour of his hometown. "Boy! It's sure great to be home again!" he said, with a boyish grin. "I didn't realise how much I missed this old place. Look, Julie, see the building with the blue glass windows, there, just along the waterfront. That's my office. I look out at this glorious Waitemata Harbour every single day. Translated from the Maori it means 'Sparkling Waters', wai, being the Maori word for water."

A ships announcement broke into their conversation, inviting all passengers to hurry along for breakfast.

"That's us, my darling. Come on, let's eat and be ready to go ashore soon as we can. Mum and Dad said that they would be here at nine. I can't wait for them to meet my beautiful wife."

As soon as the gangway was lowered, John began anxiously scanning the small crowd waiting on the dock. Then, with a whoop of joy, he waved his arms frantically. "Mum! Dad! Up here!"

A tall man in a grey suit and a white panama hat, standing beside a slim, tallish, grey haired woman in a pale blue suit, looked up and began to wave furiously. "There they are, darling." John put his arm around Julie's shoulder, using his other hand to point at Julie mouthing 'Here she is' to his parents.

CHAPTER 8

All too soon for Julie's trembling knees and nervous hands, they made their way down the gangway.

Introductions over, John's father held Julie at arms length. "Boy! You've picked a beauty here, son. Look at her lovely English skin, Naomi," he said.

"We'll have to look after you, m'dear," Naomi told her kindly. "Our sun is tough on young skins. George, you're right, she's beautiful."

"Come on, the old jalopy is over here." George rattled the keys. "You take Julie over, Naomi, John and I'll round up the luggage."

The older woman gently asked, "What would you feel comfortable calling us, my dear? Do you prefer Mother and Father, Mum and Dad, or Naomi and George?"

"Mum and Dad would be nice," Julie, replied, somewhat tremulously.

"Then that's settled, Mum and Dad it is. Now we thought we'd get you settled, have some lunch and then John can show you around this afternoon."

Warming to this woman, Julie replied, "That sounds wonderful . . . Mum."

Taking Julie's hands in hers, Naomi Field looked at her very young, very new daughter-in-law. "It's going to mean a great deal of tolerance, adjusting to being a couple, instead of 'lone rangers'. If I can help in any way, please call upon me. I've so looked forward to having you with us.

Welcome Julie, my dear, thrice welcome to our family." Smiling warmly, she kissed Julie's cheek.

Julie gave her new mother-in-law a wan smile, "Thank you . . . Mum. I do feel a bit out of my depth."

Naomi Field suggested, "John, you sit in the back with Julie. I'll drive, George, you mustn't get overtired."

Julie clutched John's hand, her feelings hard to describe, even to herself. She felt overwhelmed by John's parents' kindness to her, but the panicky feeling persisted, it felt like being a wild animal caught in a trap! The happy, chatty conversation flowed over her head. The three of them laughed easily, their distinctive New Zealand accents seeming broader, more pronounced to Julie's ears. She had become used to John's accent, now she felt 'left out', a stranger in their midst. Even their terms of endearment were different—no one called her 'luv' any more.

Julie could see the happiness on John's face as he occasionally squeezed her hand. Julie sat numbly, watching the unfamiliar scenery of the city speeding past her window.

When the car turned on to a narrower rural road, John put his arm around her and let out a happy sigh of relief. "Not long now, darling. That's the city left behind, now for some pure New Zealand rural scenery."

Julie looked around at peaceful green hills, dotted with tall pine trees. The fields were stocked with many black and white cows, several brown horses and flocks of snowy white sheep. There were very few houses.

To Julie's eyes, although it was a peaceful, unhurried landscape, she suddenly felt a deep longing, for cramped terraced houses, grey skies, and crowds and crowds of noisy people! This place was so isolated!

The panicky feeling worsened the happier John sounded. 'What am I doing here?' her insides silently screamed, trying valiantly to hold herself together.

John, oblivious to her panic, suddenly yelled, "There it is! See, Julie, you can just spot the homestead over there. Gee! It's good to be back, Mum, Dad!"

Swallowing hard, Julie could see, snuggled at the base of a green hill, a large, rambling, U-shaped, single storey homestead. It was a white wooden structure, with a green tiled roof and enormous windows, surrounded on all sides by many trees and shrubs.

It took up the space of about ten terraced houses!

As the car stopped, two dogs came clambering out, barking excitedly. One, a black and white Border Collie, headed straight for John as he held out his arms. The collie jumped ecstatically into them, nearly knocking him over. It then proceeded to furiously lick his face, whilst its tail wagged furiously.

"Hello, Toss, you haven't forgotten me, then. Gee, that's a great welcome, boy," his said, his eyes aglow as he turned to where Julie was kneeling.

She had her face buried into the neck of the other dog, an elegant Golden Retriever. In contrast to the Border Collie, this one sat quietly, wearing a look of pure joy as it snuffled Julie's hair.

"Well, I dunno," declared George Field, "look at that, Naomi. Sandy's always friendly, but I think she has just found a soul mate in you, Julie, lass."

"Come on, let's go inside. I'm dying for a cuppa," suggested Naomi Field. "Yes, Sandy, you can, just this once," she told the dog, which followed close to Julie as they entered the spacious house.

John picked up a ball lying on the steps and tossed it for the collie to bound after it. He laughed and put his arm around Julie, "Come on, darling. Welcome to 'Greenfields'. Are we in the guest wing, Dad?"

The guest wing proved to be the entire right-hand wing of the U-shaped house. Julie clapped her hands in delight at the spacious bedroom, with a full sized bathroom leading off it and another small room as a dressing-room-cum-wardrobe. Through French doors she saw a covered balcony with a cane wicker suite and a table.

As they ate lunch on a covered veranda, several birds, which were strangers to Julie's eyes, visited the garden. George Field was soon regaling his new daughter-in-law with wild and woolly tales about tuis, wax-eyes, cheeky fantails, keas and the dreaded, 'possum that wreaked havoc, amongst the native trees behind the homestead.'

He soon had her in fits of laughter and a bond that had had its beginnings as soon as he had set eyes upon her that morning, rapidly strengthened.

Naomi Field, speaking quietly, told John, "He has been so ill, thank goodness the worst is over. She's good for him, John. She makes him laugh."

After lunch, Julie clambered awkwardly up behind John onto the pillion seat of the farm bike. John described which sheep breed they were raising for the fine wool and which of the black sheep were big favourites with the local spinners, weavers and knitters.

John also explained that, since his father's illness, the farm manager, Bob East, his family, and his staff saw to the day-to-day running of the farm.

"Dad and Mum still keep their hands in, by doing the books and the buying and selling of the animals. We all muck-in for shearing, lambing and the like." He added, with a chuckle, "Even a city slicker like me!"

Eventually he drove up a gentle hill and stopped beneath a grove of huge old trees at the top. They dismounted and Julie took in a sharp breath at the wonderful vista. Below, a wide, swift river snaked through a fertile valley, bordered by an impressive grove of olive trees with their distinctive grey-green foliage.

Just below the brow of the hill, nestling amongst mature camellias, rhododendrons and hydrangeas, was a large, modern house built of a warm, golden apricot brick with a chocolate-brown tiled roof.

Julie experienced an extraordinary feeling. Somehow the house was beckoning to her, a strange feeling almost of recognition flooded Julie's body. She asked, "What a special place. Who's the lucky owner, darling?"

"It's mine, well officially now it's also yours," John said softly, "plus twenty acres down as far as the river. What d'ya think, Julie. Could you live here?" He gathered her in his arms and gazed into her eyes.

Julie was overwhelmed as she whispered, "It's so beautiful, so quiet, and so peaceful. How far are we from the city? It seems a world away."

"About an hour. For me it's close enough for commuting, but you are right, it's a different world once you get out here. I had the house built just below the rise of the hill, so it's protected from any wind, yet still has this marvellous view. It was the site of my grandparents' cottage, when they first bought the property, Mum and Dad's land and this block were on one title then. They transferred the deed over to me on my 21st birthday. I demolished the old cottage as I had always dreamed of living on this site. That's why the gardens are so well grown—my grandmother planted them."

He paused. "Julie, it's all brand new. When we became engaged I had it locked up, hoping one day you'd come and finish the interior the way you'd want it to be. It's my wedding present to you, my darling. Your own personal slice of New Zealand—given with all of my love."

Holding him tightly, and with tears of joy in her eyes, she kissed him. "John, darling, thank you, from the bottom of my heart, my dearest."

Grinning down at her, he added, "Oh, one more thing, the school bus trundles past the gate at the bottom of the hill—just in case we need it one day." Holding her tightly again in his arms, he said fervently, "Dear God! I do hope so . . . Come, my darling, let's explore the inside."

CHAPTER 9

For the next couple of weeks, life seemed to be a hectic round of plumbers, electricians and painters.

Selecting a cool, soft avocado green as the interior background, Julie felt this was the perfect hue to complement the magnificent gardens. The conservatory faced an exotic flowering shrub garden and it soon became her special place. She decided to furnish this room with a natural cane wicker suite, using the dazzling tropical fabrics bought in Panama City for the cushions.

In between all the chaos, John and his father took turns at teaching Julie to drive. The bond between George Field and Julie grew stronger by the day. George knew he would miss her when she started her new job, but for now, he was always ready to give an impromptu driving lesson.

Early one morning a large crate was delivered containing Julie's wedding dress, their English wedding presents, and a large box of their wedding photographs.

Gently fingering Julie's wedding dress, Naomi shed a few tears as she asked, "Will you still consider having a small ceremony here?"

Hugging her mother-in-law, Julie replied, "We haven't forgotten, we just wanted to get the house finished first. Make it any weekend that suits you, Mum."

With the arrival of the wedding ensemble, Julie knew it was time for her to contact the Auckland office of Maison Chevalier.

"Hello, Julie! At last!" a man's voice echoed down the telephone line. "All settled in yet? When can you and John come in for lunch with me and Kate?"

It was all hands on deck when the brass bed and John and Julie's personal bits and pieces were all moved up to the new house.

Julie sighed, "I feel so good. I love this house, John, darling. It's a life I never knew existed . . . You surely have opened my eyes. Darling, there is something we should discuss. We should be thinking about some sort of birth control. You know how I feel about starting a family just yet, and I do have an obligation to start work for Andrew Martin."

John frowned. "Julie, I don't want you to go back to work. We don't need the money . . ."

He stopped and, after a few moments, he continued, "Julie, darling, I'm sorry I'm being selfish. How about we make a pact. We'll make an appointment with Doc Matthews. You go to work for six months and then we'll see how things stand."

Dressing the next morning for their lunch appointment with Andrew Martin and Kate Reynolds, John groaned about being collar proud and of having to wear a tie again.

Julie retorted, "You're getting off lightly, I've got to struggle into stockings AND a business suit."

Immediately forgetting his own discomfort, John offered, with a suggestive leer, "I'll gladly take them off as soon as we get home again."

Standing side by side, they looked at each other in the full-length wardrobe mirrors. Julie had got used to seeing John around the place dressed just in a paint-splashed shirt and a pair of almost indecent ragged shorts.

Meanwhile he had only seen her in the skimpiest of tops and the briefest of shorts for weeks.

Julie admiringly told him, "I've almost forgotten how handsome you are in business clothes!"

Putting his arms around her, John chuckled, "You look gorgeous, my darling."

The modern décor, the elegance and the warm ambience of the Maison Chevalier offices impressed them both. Andrew Martin was a Scot in his late forties, of average height, blue eyed and sandy haired. When he offered Julie a position as Design Consultant, she accepted without hesitation.

But, right from the outset, it was Kate Reynolds that impressed Julie. Kate was in her late twenties, tall and willowy. A red head with the greenest eyes Julie had ever seen and a bubbly personality to match. They immediately formed a rapport, almost knowing what the other was thinking, or going to say, before it was said.

When Kate unpacked Julie's wedding gown, she gasped, "It's gorgeous, Julie. The tint of pink is so right for your colouring."

The wedding photos were spread over the desk as they gauged the overall effect of the full ensemble. Julie gazed at the faces of Michael and Denise Armstrong, her parents, her siblings and her other relatives, smiling up at her from the group photos. It suddenly seemed so long ago and so far away.

John saw her fingers trembling as she picked up a photo of her parents. Kate also witnessed the poignant, emotional moment and softly said, "Come on, time for lunch."

Gazing around the restaurant, Julie's fingers itched to begin designing suitable clothes for this warmer climate. Involuntary thoughts flew around in her head and began to gel. They must be lightly structured, brighter colours than for the Northern Hemisphere, washable, yet crease resistant . . .

"Julie, darling, come back," John's voice cut through her thoughts.

"Oops, sorry," she apologized, "I've just had some great ideas."

"Here, use my sketch pad, show me," urged Kate.

With a few quick strokes of the pen, Julie transcribed her thoughts to paper and drew a simple dress with classic lines.

"In linen, of course," said Kate, as she looked over Julie's shoulder. "Perhaps with two different necklines, see like this." She sketched in her ideas.

The two young women looked at each other, seeing mirrored in the other's eyes a perfect understanding of their intentions.

A lifetime friendship had just begun . . .

As she entered John's personal office, Julie could not help but marvel at the phenomenal and expansive vista John had of the magnificent Waitemata harbour from his windows.

A short while later, John declared, "That's enough, darling, let's go and see Doc."

Julie found Doctor Reuben Matthews a slight, balding, pleasant man in his late forties.

After Julie had broached the birth control subject, John was taken aback when Doc totally agreed with her. He then cautioned John, "Remember what I advised you and your parents after you had that rugby accident . . . you were what . . . twelve? Now, Julie, m'dear, any female problems? No, okay."

Doc then decided, without hesitation, to issue her with a prescription for the contraceptive pill.

The next morning, Julie waited until John had left before ringing her mother-in-law. After chatting with her about their experiences at Maison Chevalier, Julie, rather shyly asked, "What exactly did happen to John when he was injured in a rugby tackle?" She hesitated, "Mum, I haven't got anyone else I can ask."

"Oh Lord! Julie dear, you have every right to know." Naomi hesitated for a moment, gathering her thoughts.

"Let me see now . . . He was twelve, playing school rugby, he took a pass just in front of the goal posts. He dived across the line, the opposing fullback tackled him, and trapped John's legs either side of the goal post. He had scored the winning try, saving the match, but he couldn't get up."

Naomi paused. "Doc Matthews told George that, although there appeared to be no apparent serious damage apart from the terrible bruising, when John was ready to start a family he should have a full medical and possibly sperm count tests. Julie, my dear, confront him again . . . soon. It's important for both of you."

Julie returned to the guest-room where she had set up her work desk. First things first, she needed to concentrate on her latest official assignment from the United Kingdom Apprenticeship Board. That accomplished, her design ideas began flowing with ease . . .

When Julie showed John the designs, he studied them with a practiced eye, before declaring, "Andrew will jump at them, darling. You've captured just the right touch for our summer. Well done, my clever girl."

"Right, I need to know something, Mr. Field. No more shenanigans. Have you had any sort of medical examination regarding that injury you had years ago?"

"What's brought that up again?" John huffed and puffed, trying to bluster his way out of answering.

"I want a straight answer, John. You owe me that," Julie said firmly, holding her ground.

"Yes. I went to a specialist in London and yes, I have a very low sperm count. Everything else seems to be in order, as we have already discovered, don't you think? I have to have a prostate exam, sometime. Yes, sometime. That's all, Julie, Scouts Honour!"

He looked so embarrassed, so hurt, like a small schoolboy. Julie grinned as she said, "Now, that wasn't so difficult, was it? I do have a brother, you know, and Billy, Graeme and the rest of them took a great delight in teaching us girls the differences between boys and girls when we were about ten!"

"That Graeme . . . you were pretty keen on him?"

"Yes, we were pretty close for most of our lives. After that tango fiasco I missed them, especially Maureen, it was ages before she would talk to me again. Billy and Graeme never did, they joined the RAF." She smiled, "Maison Chevalier opened up a new world for me. Best of all, I found you, my dear husband."

That evening Julie looked at the brilliant Southern Cross constellation of stars shining down on her as she sat at her favourite spot on the hillside above her house.

Speaking of Graeme earlier had evoked such a raw feeling of homesickness. A wet nose was pushed into her hand as Sandy, the Golden Retriever who had became her constant companion, came and stood beside her. "You understand, don't you girl," Julie whispered. "I'll never totally get over him, will I? One minuscule spot inside me will forever be his."

Suddenly the dog pricked her ears and wagged her tail.

There was nothing visible but a peaceful, pleasant sensation passed through Julie. The ache around her heart evaporated and she could feel Gran, comforting her, as she had done so many times in the past.

CHAPTER 10

Julie's first working weeks in New Zealand were a personal triumph. Andrew and Kate greeted her fresh and innovative design ideas with enthusiasm. Kate and Julie made a convivial team and the office echoed to their peals of laughter as the affinity between them grew.

When Andrew announced, "I've decided a sample collection of Julie's designs should be entered in the Young Designer Show," he hardly expected the response.

Kate squealed with excitement, whirling a stunned Julie around the office in a madcap polka.

Julie quickly became busily engrossed with all the ramifications of designing the garments for the competition. So she was taken by surprise when one day she got a call from Naomi Field, asking if she and John could come and discuss the final arrangements for the 'family wedding'.

It was decided John and his best man, Harry, Kate's husband, who was an old school friend of John's, would stay at his parent's house on the night before the 'wedding.' This prompted Kate to offer to stay with Julie, which she joyfully accepted.

That evening the two friends decided to walk to the top of hill in the moonlight. Julie seemed pensive so Kate asked, "A penny for them?"

Julie smiled and shook her head, saying, "John calls it my 'natural enough homesickness'. Sometimes I look up at the stars and the moon, knowing they are in the same sky as the one over my family, and I wonder what they are all doing." Her voice dropped almost to a whisper. "There's also one special person . . ." She sighed deeply. "I'll tell you about it one day. We parted in such an unfriendly way because of a misunderstanding . . ." Her voice faded, but Kate heard a note of yearning in it.

Next morning, Kate helped Julie dress for the lunchtime ceremony. Seeing Julie in the flesh, dressed in her bridal finery, Kate exclaimed, "Julie, you're breath taking! The colour, the fit, I dunno, just the whole combination. It's about perfect. Had you thought of modelling it yourself in Sydney? Wait until Andrew sees you, he's sure to come to the same conclusion. We couldn't get a better model than the bride the gown was especially made for, now could we?"

There was a 'Wow!' from Andrew Martin, as he stood in the doorway.

"Can you hear the penny dropping?" Kate stage whispered.

Andrew Martin appraised the lovely bride with a professional eye. "The gown fits you like a glove, the colour tint is perfect for your skin tone, and the style makes you look statuesque. Kate's right, you are the ideal model for the gown, Julie."

"Toldya!" said Kate, triumphantly. "You're too late, boss. I've already told Julie that."

"But . . . hang on a mo. I haven't had any catwalk experience," Julie protested.

"That's okay, we'll teach you," Kate told her. "You already walk and carry yourself well. The bridal walk is always slow, elegant and regal, to give the clients and customers time to either bawl, or to cheer."

Andrew looked at his pocket watch. "I agree. We'll talk about it next week. But now, my lovely ladies, it's time."

The driver sounded the horn, sending a triumphant trumpet rallying call reverberating around the valley. Hearing it, the assembled guests made their way to the beribboned bridal bower, set up in Naomi Field's pride and joy, her formal rose garden.

Now standing beside Harry, John had time to reflect on the short time they had been married. Julie was a vibrant, vivacious person. He knew she got homesick and sometimes briefly she showed signs of loneliness. He mused, if only she would agree to have a child, but no, she was adamant she wanted to wait a while.

A buzz of anticipation amongst the people waiting in the rose garden brought him out of his reverie.

They could hear the car purring its way up the drive . . . and then . . . there she was!

A murmur of appreciation filtered around the gathering guests as Andrew and Kate helped Julie from the car. A royal princess could not have made a bigger impact on the gathered assemblage.

Julie had refused to take off her original wedding ring, stating emphatically it would be bad luck. John had sided with her, and it was agreed that the ceremony should take the form of them reaffirming their vows, not a re-marriage, as such.

Andrew Martin scrutinised Julie carefully, absolutely convinced he must persuade her to model her own wedding ensemble at the Bridal Show. He could virtually see WINNER written all over her.

After just a few weeks, Andrew Martin was already aware of her potential impact on the Australasian market, and very possibly way beyond. She possessed a rare insight into what women of her age group were looking for in their world of fashion.

Kate was also observing her newly found friend. Julie was her junior but their friendship had already become very much of the sisterly kind. But, Kate had already felt and seen that, although Julie was trying to put on a brave face, especially for John, she could not help wondering who was Julie's 'special' person.

To cheers and applause, the happy couple returned down the garden aisle, cameras clicking from every direction.

Looking over at his son, George saw John give him a nod, their prearranged signal. George walked behind the house to fetch the wedding present the three of them had decided upon for Julie.

Julie and John were still being congratulated by their wedding guests when John, taking her hand, led her through the guests to where his father and mother were standing beside a brand new, scarlet red, sporty two-seater car.

George dangled a small bunch of keys, tied with a huge white bow. "Here you are, Julie, with all of our love, from John, Naomi and me."

Julie was stunned and rushed to kiss her husband and his parents as their wedding guests crowded around, admiring the racy new car. "Wow! Thank you, thank you. I've always dreamed of owning one of these beauties. So you think I'm ready to be trusted to take my license?"

"More than, my darling. We'll make a time next week.

Meantime, you'll need these to start with though," John laughed as he handed her a pair of 'L' plates.

This gesture caused howls of hilarity from their guests, who had not heard the context of the conversation and thought John was calling his new wife a learner! Julie blushed beetroot red as John suddenly realized the innuendo and the double entendre he had triggered.

By seven o'clock their guests had departed, leaving just Julie, John, Naomi and George Field sitting relaxing with a last glass of champagne.

Julie pointed to the table, overflowing with gift-wrapped parcels. "We are so lucky! I can't wait to try out my car. I think I'll call her . . . Scarlet O'Hara. Thank you both, most sincerely, from the bottom of my heart."

Julie drove around the joint driveways of the two homes, before finally, reluctantly, garaging it for the night.

During the next three full days of their short second honeymoon in Rotorua, John and Julie recaptured the closeness that they had first found after their original wedding.

When they returned to their home, it was with a deep sense of belonging, melded together as a couple.

CHAPTER 11

A formal letter arrived, inviting Julie to take her final apprenticeship examinations, but she found she had little or no spare time to do any pre-study. She and Kate were up before dawn and were still working until late most nights on the Sydney collection.

At the imposing Auckland Fine Arts building she was shown into a large airy room.

"This is my own workroom and teaching studio," said her examiner, a very elegant middle-aged woman. "I thought you'd be more comfortable in here. Once you begin I'm not permitted to speak with you, of course."

Julie gathered her thoughts and to her profound relief discovered she was adequately experienced to complete the tasks required of her in the examination. Afterwards, her examiner told her that she had watched her working and considered she showed considerable potential. But she stressed that the papers would now be returned to the examining institute for marking.

Because of her workload, it had been a while since Julie and John managed an evening out together. The only exception came when she passed her driver's license test, at her first attempt.

Often John would groan as he heard her sneak out before dawn and of 'Scarlet O'Hara' speeding away, taking Julie to her office. When Julie eventually arrived home, she was so tired that she immediately fell into a deep, exhausted sleep.

One day, over lunch at their club, he bemoaned this fact to Harry. His old friend shook his head as he responded, "John, she has a God given talent that even I can see. The designs and colour schemes are all Julie's creations. She needs be on hand for any emergencies," Harry had argued. "Julie is, after all, the natural choice to model her own wedding gown. Remember this, John, if we're lucky enough to win an award, what a huge feather it'll be in the cap for Maison Chevalier."

Eventually all was ready for Sydney.

At the airport John embraced Julie, "I'll miss you. Go get 'em darling."

Julie also felt a sense of loss at parting so soon from her new husband, but there was also a sense of . . . freedom. It was an exhilarating sensation, a chance to prove something to herself, an opportunity.

In Sydney, Kate looked into Julie's happy face, warning her, "It's going to be jolly hard work, my girl. You might not be so enthusiastic once the bickering and the in-fighting starts! It can become murder with some of the more hoity-toity models. Still our clothes are worth it." Spinning gleefully around, she exclaimed, "Oh, look, there's Tony Prentice."

Julie and the famous photographer recognised each other at the same moment. He rushed over and swung her off her feet in a mighty bear hug.

"Hello, poppet!" T.P. cried. "It's so good to see you. Michael told me you might be here. Hello, Andrew, me old mate, and who do we have here then?" he asked, his photographer's eye appraising Kate's auburn hair and green eyes.

"Are you doing a shoot? I'd be happy to come along," T.P. offered. Andrew rubbed his chin, "We do need open-air shots, preferably countryside, gum trees, red earth, that sort of thing. Got any good location ideas?"

"Just the place, old thing. A vineyard, two hours north. The grapes are ripe, the colours are rich, and the sunset is to die for."

Two days later, Julie, Kate and Andrew loaded the collection on board a hired bus. Tony Prentice gave the directions to the driver . . . and they were off.

Julie studied their four models, all in their mid-twenties. This was her target age group. Old enough to be grown women, yet young enough to want a range of clothes which were too youthful for their mothers to wear!

The collection was to be known under the label 'Flowers of the Field'. An inspiration of John's. He had assured her, "Incorporate your surname in your label. Look at Chanel, Dior, YSL . . ."

The bus grunted and groaned its way up a steep hill until at the top T.P. asked the driver to stop, saying, "Julie, you must see this."

He led her down a small track, and there before them was the most glorious, breath-taking, picture postcard valley Julie had ever seen.

The air was ripe with the smell of eucalyptus gums and wood smoke. The raucous calls of kookaburras, cockatoos and lorikeets were the only noises to break the heavy silence around them.

Endless columns of grapevines marched over the hills, interspersed with banana palms and pineapple bushes. Way down below them they could just see a large, sprawling, Mediterranean styled homestead.

The tranquil hidden peace of the place gave Julie the impression she had stepped back in time. "Aaaah . . . 'Shangri-La'," she whispered. "It's so beautiful."

As the bus wound down the hill, Kate's head swung from one side to the other. "No wonder T.P. suggested coming here," she exclaimed in an awestruck whisper. "It's magical! Look at the light, look at that riot of colour."

"It's perfect for our bright, bold colours," Julie responded. "It'll show them so sharp, clean and vibrant. Gee! I can't wait to get started!"

T.P sighed, "Wait until you see the château up close, and you meet Maria and Giovanni Martini. They're as special as the wine they produce."

The breath-taking, picturesque château emerged into view. Sitting as though posing for a picture postcard, the white stone, Mediterranean style building, with its orange tiled roof, lay snuggled in a natural amphitheatre.

Magenta bougainvillea flowers ran in a riotous, glorious rampant state, while the loggia, the full length of the building, was vine covered. A multitude of dark black bunches of grapes hung lusciously ripe and tempting from its boughs, an exquisite sight.

Julie was enchanted with the whole ambiance of the place. She felt she had come home, that somehow she belonged here.

A soft voice behind her said something in Italian.

Turning, Julie saw a handsome middle-aged couple, both dark-haired, olive-skinned and with huge, dark brown eyes. They were dressed in country-styled clothes—check shirts, corduroy trousers, a homespun cotton skirt and natural straw sun-hats.

The woman held the man's hand as he spoke. "Puo aspettarmi, cara mia." (Wait for me, my darling).

The man doffed his hat to Julie. "I am Giovanni Martini. My wife, Maria, would like to speak with you on your own, Signorina. Would you mind?"

"No, of course not . . . but I cannot speak Italian, Signor," Julie replied.

"That'sa okay, I canna speak Inglese, cara. Come, letsa go into the chapel," the woman replied, smiling kindly at Julie.

They walked along a flagstone path and through an ancient lych gate. There, hidden from the house, in a bower of its own, and surrounded by a hedge of white blossomed camellias, sat an ancient, small grey stone church. It had a square Norman tower with a clock set in its front. Long, narrow, stained glass windows completed the picture, Julie was awestruck.

Yet another surprise was to come for Julie, for there, growing in front of the church was a majestic, sycamore tree. It was the first of its species she had seen in the Southern Hemisphere.

Suddenly, momentarily, as she pushed open the lych gate, Julie found herself unable to move. Welded to the spot, held by an invisible force, she saw a misty, dreamlike vision of a bridal couple come out of the front door of the church.

Her eyes blurred . . . she felt a warm pleasant presence surround her . . . the visionary couple disappeared. Immediately the holding force dispersed, releasing her from its power.

Mystified and somewhat shaken by her experience, she walked groggily into the cool stone chapel. Maria indicated for Julie to join her in the front pew.

Taking Julie's hands in hers, Maria asked, "You feela it, eh? You seena something? You are a sensitive girl. You looka troubled, unhappy, you yearning for someone, perhaps?"

Feeling the power and strength flowing from this woman's hands, Julie realized this was the same rapport she used to have with her Gran.

She knew instantly Maria was someone to be trusted, someone wise, caring and understanding.

Her voice sank to a whisper as she asked, "This place, it feels like I have come home, Maria. What is it? Outside . . . the sycamore tree . . . what did I see?"

"Thata tree, it come from the 'old country'. It's notta your new life thata you are troubled for, or, marito, the husband. You no have children with marito, husband. You have a true love. You knowa, il mio ragazzo . . . er . . . si, boyfriend. Your destiny isa later. You hadda angry words, eh? But perhaps he stilla love you?"

Julie sat stunned.

"Me, Maria, willa always be here for you. You called Julie, eh? Julie, Maria looka after you. You come here when you needa me, eh? Anytime."

Maria gathered Julie into her arms. In the ensuing embrace Julie experienced a strange emotional flow throughout her body.

"Come, letsa find Giovanni. He willa wanta know about you." Taking Julie by the hand, Maria led her back to the château's sunny courtyard.

Giovanni rose from his chair in the shade. "She tell you? Maria spots you as you get off the bus. She tells me you troubled. Maria has great knowledge from the old country, you listen good to her, she knows!"

"Well, yes," Julie smiled wistfully. "I just know there is something special about this place."

Maria took Julie's face in her hands and softly said, "Mi cara, you come anytime, anytime you needa to, capisco?"

For the next six hours the frenetic rush to catch the good light took over. T.P snapped shot after shot as the models whisked in and out of the bus in different garments.

Suddenly, the sun dropped low in the western sky, the whole area was bathed in a mystical golden-orange light. T.P quickly yelled for the four models to don every white garment that was available. Running from one girl to another, he posed them against the sun-kissed backgrounds in his haste to catch the magic light of the sunset.

Just as suddenly, it was dark, the short, sharp sub-tropical dusk was over in minute. The exhausted crew made their way wearily back to the City.

CHAPTER 12

It was the awards evening.

Standing backstage, hidden behind the gold lame stage curtain, Julie and Kate were finding it increasingly difficult to keep still, keep focused and to stop trembling!

The collection had received rave reviews from local and international media. Reports had appeared, gushing in their praise, using phrases such as 'a new young star is born' or, 'a brand new concept for the young business woman'. One fashion reporter, of some repute, even used just a two-word headline, 'About time!' Kate's favourite was, 'Flowers of the Field, A New Blossoming In The Marketplace.'

For Julie it had been a mind-boggling experience. Kate had watched with admiration as her younger colleague had blossomed. She had handled all of the publicity and fuss with a dignity well beyond her years.

T.P.'s capture of the magical glow of the golden-orange sunset in his photographs had been widely praised and published during the week in many newspapers and magazines. The reviewers had, without exception, strongly stressed how this collection had been made in heaven for the younger Australian woman.

Unbelievable pre-sales had filled Andrew and Kate's order books. Every item had thus far exceeded all of their expectations.

Julie glanced nervously at what was happening on stage as Kate beckoned her closer. A disembodied voice was saying, "Our first award is for Daywear . . . and the winner is . . . 'Flowers of the Field'—designer, Mrs Julie Field, from Auckland, New Zealand!"

Kate gave Julie one tearful hug before gently pushing her through the gap in the gold lame curtain. A thunderous roar of cheering and applause from the huge audience greeted Julie.

The prestigious award took the form of a large abstract golden cotton reel, with a golden needle and thread as an arrow piercing the cotton reel.

While they continued to admire their award backstage, the excitement outside seemed to be growing again. Then, the Master of Ceremonies called for the entrants in the 'Casual Wear' category to come on stage. Once again a longish wait ensued before they heard the words 'and the winner is' echoing around the now silent audience . . . "Flowers of the Field, designer, Mrs Julie Field, of Auckland, New Zealand!"

They had agreed that if there were to be a second trophy, Kate would be the recipient. Looking glamorous in her green-grass trouser suit, crowned by her glorious burnished copper head of hair, Kate was close to tears making her acceptance speech. "At last, clothes for a younger woman's lifestyle! Thank you, Julie."

They were nearly blinded by the photographers flash bulbs as they stood smiling, holding aloft the two supreme awards. Tony Prentice joined Andrew. "Just wait until they see her wedding gown tonight. So much love went into the making of it by the London and Paris staff. When I took that photo of her with the bolts of silk, she was what, seventeen? The camera loves her, it eats her up, her whole face glows. Well, that dress has the same effect—it simply oozes love and romance. All the weddingy things women love. I'll put money on it, I predict she'll win the award, hands down, the others won't stand a chance."

"She nearly didn't come, y'know," grumbled Andrew. "John wasn't that keen. Thank God, Harry managed to change his mind."

T.P shook his head. "He's a bit too possessive, too intense is our John Field. He's a hard drinker, not a good sign, my friend."

T.P looked towards Julie as she smiled graciously for the hordes of news media. "Maria and Giovanni were very taken with her. They treated her like a long lost daughter. I also know certain music can really get under Julie's guard, seen it myself. She's such a sweetheart, so special, so talented. I hope nothing comes along to hurt her. I find myself looking out for her all of the time."

"Me too. I think I look upon her as a young niece," sighed Andrew. "Well, in that case she has two middle—aged, doddery old guardians, even though we are no angels."

"Come, let's rescue the girls and have a drink to celebrate," suggested T.P. with a happy laugh.

A drum roll interrupted their departure. "Ladies and Gentlemen, we have one final award to make; it is a very special award, the 'Personality of the Year'. It gives me great pleasure to introduce our President, Mr Emile Anzanour, to make the presentation."

He was a well-respected Frenchman, but Julie whispered to Kate, with a giggle, "My Gran used to say, 'just another one with a Maurice Chevalier bedroom accent'."

Emile Anzanour began, "This week we have seen the emergence of a new star in our midst. A young lady of such tender years, who has shown us what the younger women of the world want to wear. And . . . as we have seen by her own example today, one who can look simply delicious, wearing her own feminine designs. English doesn't do the words justice, so in my own language then, Vive la Difference!"

A roar of applause rang around the auditorium.

Emile Azanour continued, "Mesdames et Messieurs, it gives me the greatest pleasure to present the 'Young Designer Personality of the Year', to a most worthy recipient . . . Madame Julie Field!"

There was almost a riot in front of the stage as people thronged forward, wanting a closer look at Julie.

Julie was virtually speechless as she clutched the precious award to her chest. This award, from her peers, said it all. They had judged her as much for her personality and demeanour during the show, as they had for her talent and artistic ability.

Feeling slightly dazed by their good fortune, Julie and Kate returned to their hotel, bubbling over with excitement. Kate expressed it, in her own inimitable way. "Now I know how a scrambled egg feels, 'cos that's about the status of my brain right now!"

Later, as Kate helped Julie dress, she sighed, "Jules, you are the epitome of what every bride wishes she could look like on her wedding day."

Answering a knock on the door, Kate found a young Naval Officer standing there. He was Julie's officially designated escort. Resplendent in his naval uniform, he politely introduced himself.

"Good evening, Ma'am, I'm Lieutenant Peter Grossmith.

I'm here to escort Mrs Julie Field . . ." he gulped, staring as he spotted Julie, and blurted out, "Weeow! Ma'am, you sure look bloody gorgeous! It'll be my very, very special pleasure to escort you—anywhere!"

Kate and Julie broke into peals of laughter at his very Australian expletive, and his strong accent.

As they made their way to the waiting white limousine, they heard admiring comments from hotel guests and staff alike.

Aesthetically, Peter, tall, dark and handsome in his naval uniform, was the perfect foil for Julie's blushed bridal finery. It came as no surprise to him when Julie was amongst the six semi-finalists.

When Julie made the final three the audience erupted.

Peter whispered to Julie, "No contest, Julie honey, you have won it. Listen to that crowd!"

The judges handed the Master of Ceremonies their decision. Dramatically, he waited until the drum roll stopped, then without further ado, called "First Place . . . Maison Chevalier of London, modelled by someone we've already got to know fairly well . . . Julie Field!"

The audience noise was deafening as Peter proudly escorted Julie on her triumphant winner's parade along the catwalk.

"Good heavens! This is what it must be like to be a pop star!" Peter shouted in Julie's ear, trying to make himself heard above the cheers of the audience.

Several hours later, the sound of Julie crying woke Kate. She heard, "No! No! Graeme, wait for me!"

She padded over to Julie's bed but found she was still asleep. Shrugging, Kate went back to her own bed.

Next morning, Kate asked, "Hey, you had a bad dream last night, Jules. Who's the Graeme you want to wait for you?" Julie blushed a deep red. "Graeme! Did I say his name?"

Kate nodded, but as she saw the discomfort on Julie's face, quickly added, "It's okay, all you said was, 'No, no. Graeme, wait for me' nothing too incriminating there, Jules."

"It's a recurring dream," Julie explained. "When we went to Maria's she said something which has weighed upon my mind."

"But . . . ?" queried Kate. "What did Maria say? What's the dream all about? Is he the one you parted from after a big misunderstanding?"

Resignedly Julie revealed, "Graeme is someone I grew up with. We parted after a hideous incident. Well, he went off to join the RAF and I married John." She explained how in the dream she was always running towards the shadowy figure with Graeme's voice, but how she could never reach him.

Kate's jaw dropped open. "No wonder you're having nightmares. Don't discard out of hand what Maria says though. Those old country women can be mighty prophetic."

Kate and Andrew were deep in conversation when Julie joined them at the breakfast table. Kate looked at Julie with a shocked, startled look on her face.

"What's wrong, Kate?" Julie asked, concerned at Kate's stunned expression.

It was Andrew who answered, "Actually it's me, Julie, love. But, before we get on to that, I rang Harry about other matters . . . M'dear you have passed your finals, with honours. Well done, my dear Julie, you are now a fully accredited Fashionista!"

Kate cried out with her usual exuberance, "Oh Julie, congratulations, my dear, dear friend. What a fantastic climax to a memorable few days . . . Yet, after Andrew's news, I'd believe anything!"

Andrew took hold of Julie's hand. "Your exciting news is another reason that adds sense to what I have just told Kate. I'm staying on in Sydney. Michael and I have been planning to expand the Sydney branch for some time. Michael has asked me to offer the Auckland franchise to the four of you."

Julie now understood the flabbergasted look on Kate's face. She imagined her own face must also reflect startled surprise.

Kate asked anxiously, "Well, what d'ya think? Can we?

I'd love to give it a try, wouldn't you, Julie?"

Julie exclaimed, "Why not! If Harry and John agree, let's give it a go. Yes, Andrew, tell Michael we'll definitely be in touch . . . ASAP!"

CHAPTER 13

The clock chimed seven o'clock on Julie and John's fifth wedding anniversary. Julie added the finishing touches to a celebratory dinner while she waited for John, due home from a fabric-buying excursion in Japan.

As she worked, her mind drifted back in time; back four years to winning the awards in Sydney. Awards that had been vitally instrumental in launching their fledgling company.

Those precious awards were still prominently and proudly displayed in the reception area of their office suite, alongside Julie's Fine Arts Diploma.

Julie sighed; the diploma ceremony was for her a truly memorable affair. She recalled how she had been congratulated for achieving such high marks, with the words, "Do keep up the good work, Julie Field. The younger women in our world need you. Well done."

Five years had passed so quickly. So much had happened. So much had been achieved. "Well, almost," she murmured, "No babies, yet."

Deep in thought, her mind went back to the company beginnings and to the all-important roundtable conference, which had included the company accountant and John's parents.

They had all whole-heartedly accepted the exciting prospect and the challenge of becoming the new Auckland franchise holders of the prestigious Maison Chevalier.

It was amicably decided that Kate and Harry would run the office and the workshop and Julie and John would head up the design and buying departments.

It had taken them several weeks to fill the orders received in Sydney, even after taking on extra staff to cope. The orders just kept rolling in, with repeats following closely. It didn't seem to matter what garment they turned out, there was always an eager market waiting for more.

Her simple, clean lines were a hit. 'Still are,' she mused, 'I'm now a financially independent woman.'

Ideas were always buzzing around in her head, even as she looked up into the heavens at silver stars shimmering against the velvet vista of a blue-black sky. 'If only I could capture that on fabric,' she murmured under her breath, 'what a magnificent gown it would make.'

John's car swung into the drive. With a deep sigh he walked over to her, but she could tell by his body language, he was not in a good mood. He gave her a perfunctory peck on the cheek, and grunted, "I need a drink. I have something to talk about that can't wait."

Almost pushing her out of his way, he headed to the drinks cabinet and poured himself a large glass of neat whisky. He took it out to the conservatory, slumped down on a chair and held his head in his hands.

Julie looked at him in alarm. "John, what's wrong?"

"Bad news I'm afraid, darling," his speech was slurred. "Well, bad news, for me. You'll probably be over the moon, the way things are around here."

"John, do stop speaking in riddles! Please, what is it?" Julie pleaded.

"Well, to cut a long story short, I'm sterile! I went to that Japanese specialist Doc Matthews recommended in Tokyo, he confirmed it. No babies from me, sweetheart," he sneered cynically. "I only fire blanks! God, I'm tired, I'm going to bed. I'll sleep in the other room. See ya."

Placing his glass into the dishwasher, he noticed the food preparations and saw the festive table setting.

Realization hit him! Oh God! Our Wedding Anniversary! Because of the time zone differences, the interminable airline delays, numerous drinks, he had mixed the dates up. Stricken with guilt, he turned to Julie. She was still standing in the lounge with a shocked expression on her face.

Muttering, "I'm sorry, Julie, I forgot, let me sleep it off. We'll talk in the morning." He stumbled to the guest room and noisily closed the door.

Feeling hurt and sad, Julie closed down the kitchen, changed into jeans and a warm jacket and headed to the top of the hill.

Reaching her favourite spot, she sat on the stile overlooking her special piece of land.

John's medical tests were not hopeful. Julie had not been taking the contraceptive pill for some time and although Doc Matthews had tried explaining there was nothing wrong with Julie, John had stormed off on one of his now frequent fishing trips.

He usually stayed away for one or two nights before coming home, reeking of fish and alcohol, apologetic and remorseful. Until something trivial would again upset him and the pattern would repeat itself.

Now sitting alone in this haven of her own, after several minutes it was Maria's words that she heard. Her prophetic prediction several years ago, "you no have children with marito, husband . . ."

Now how did the rest of it go? Something about a childhood friend . . . and . . . my destiny?

With an aching, heavy heart, she stumbled down the hill, resolved that something had to done about John's mood changes and his heavy drinking. As much for his own good—as for the sake of their marriage.

That night, Julie's recurring nightmare returned.

Just before dawn she had her usual, frightening awakening, finding herself covered in perspiration.

In the morning John, thoroughly contrite, asked for her forgiveness. But, Julie knew she had to take a stand.

"John, I cannot go on like this," she told him gently. "We are going to have to talk this through and come to an understanding. We both have a lot of people depending upon us."

John sat subdued, not at all his usual, full of confidence self. In a husky voice he began. "When I first arrived in Tokyo I went to that chap. He physically examined me. My count was virtually non-existent. It also looks as though I may have a prostate problem coming up."

"Did he advise you about us going to a fertility clinic, the one Doc Matthews spoke to us about?" Julie asked.

"Yes, they do have some success in cases like mine." He shook his head despondently. "But, Julie, it's such a rigmarole and there's no guarantee it will work."

"We've got to try. John. Please let's try," she pleaded in a whisper. "We have so much to offer a child."

In the weekly exchange of family letters from her family, Julie read between the lines of their disappointment. She knew Naomi and George Field had also hoped to be grandparents by now.

For several traumatic months, keeping it strictly to themselves, Julie and John went through all of the routines, suggestions and recommendations from the local Fertility Clinic. Julie had embarked on an experimental hormonal programme, John was given medication and Julie took her temperature daily to decide when the 'right' time was. They made love to rote on the 'right' days; they only ate certain recommended foods, and drank no alcohol.

Then early one evening John was watching as Julie took her temperature yet one more time. He held up his hands.

"Enough is enough, Julie. Okay, we have tried it all. Julie, making love like this it's . . ." He shrugged his shoulders, with an exasperated movement, "it's so mechanical!"

Julie immediately put the thermometer away and sighed with relief. "I agree, John. I can no longer think straight when I'm working. I can't concentrate on anything for any length of time. The hormonal programme is making me so emotional."

A few days later, looking around at the cramped space Julie was working in, John suggested that it was time to build her a proper workroom.

Six weeks later, a large sunny room with a glassed roof had been added to the house. It also meant she need only to go into the office once a week.

Although John still strictly guarded their privacy, when a women's magazine approached them to write Julie's story, he agreed to let it take place. He theorised, the magazine article could only bring them valuable publicity by putting their label and their franchise in the forefront of the fickle fashion market.

The magazine was published the week of Julie and John's sixth wedding anniversary. They were delighted when the article depicted a hardworking crew of young people producing quality, affordable and attractive clothing.

Kate, though, was a little uneasy at John's dominance of Julie, and confided her concern to Harry. "Do you think John is getting just a bit too possessive again about Julie?"

Harry reluctantly agreed, "There's been some concern around the club that John drinks too heavily. Julie was pretty young when they married. She virtually had no one else close to her, until you came along, my love."

"Well, perhaps he's just being over protective," Kate suggested, with a worried tone. "I'll make sure I'm always there for her, just in case."

Kate handed Harry an elaborate circular letter. "We'd better have a company board meeting soon to discuss these World Fashion Awards."

Harry read: 'The World Fashion Awards are coming back to Sydney for the autumn of 1989. This will be the biggest Fabric and Fashion Show that Australasia has ever seen . . .'

Over dinner a few evenings later, they all four agreed this would be the most opportune time and place for them to expand the 'Flowers of the Field' label. In particular, their continuing target was their ever growing and lucrative North American market.

Julie wholeheartedly accepted the challenge, pointing out to Kate, "Golly! Do you realise it'll be nearly a decade since we won our last awards!"

CHAPTER 14

It was exactly one year to the Sydney World Fashion Awards Week.

Julie was transferring the ideas in her head onto the paper in front of her. Ideally she wanted to have a completed structured concept to present to her partners. The eventual selection, as usual, was a group decision.

Checking the official guidelines again, Julie read: For the purposes of these particular awards a maximum of twelve garments represent a collection. 'Perfect, we can handle that,' she murmured.

John, always a constructive critic and an expert judge of fabrics, arrived home. She revolved the design easel, enabling him to leaf through her sketches.

"Wow! That blue evening gown is very striking, it's magnificent! 'Blue Heaven', eh? A definite yes I reckon our Kate would say."

He scanned through more of her preliminary sketches, they were definitely Julie's best ideas ever. He particularly liked the innovative design of a Highwayman's cloak, instead of a top coat, and whistled admiringly at a simple, feminine day dress.

"Come on! Speak to me. What?" She playfully dug him in the ribs. "I need your input. Did you bring the new samples home, John?"

"Julie, they are breath-taking!" John fanned the sketches out on the desk. "Look, I've an ideal fabric for this business suit concept, and I've also found a very special lightweight cream wool you wanted."

Even as he congratulated her, John experienced a sudden realisation she was rapidly moving away from him. She had become a mature, confident woman, and her creative talents were world class.

Jostling the sketches, he dislodged a letter, and a photo of a woman holding a baby, fell to the floor. John saw it was Julie's sister, Lisa, with her newest child. Such photos always upset Julie. A child, of course! That would be the ideal answer, keeping her at home and dependent upon him.

John lifted her face. "Julie, it's time to talk about it again, isn't it?" he softly reminded her. "Doc Matthews told us six months ago a sperm donor was our only answer. You have my unequivocal permission to go ahead. At least that way, half of the baby would be all ours."

Julie wondered, with surprise, at his sudden change of heart. "No man wants his wife to carry another man's child," he had yelled when Doc Matthews first broached the idea.

"John, I'm fully committed to the awards right now.

I'm going to be tied up with this work for the rest of the year."

"Okay, but let's think hard about it, Julie." He kissed the top of her head and left the room whistling.

The next day, Andrew Martin rang from Sydney, urging Julie, "If you are seriously considering an entry in the big promotion, come over fairly promptly and stake your claim. Categories and accommodation are filling fast."

"I suppose you could go, Julie," John conceded, a bit grumpily. "Spy out the land, get a feel of the venue. Actually, Mum made a suggestion the other day. They have a Country Club membership on the coast outside of Sydney with some holiday villas on the complex. Mum reckons, make it your base, there's tons of storage room for the garments and it's a short commute to the venue. It would also give privacy and security against any 'leaks'. We know only too well what a problem that can be in our business!"

Julie suggested, "How about two weeks from today? I'll give Andrew a ring."

So it was arranged.

Andrew Martin gleefully swung Julie off her feet at Sydney Airport. As usual, she was impeccably dressed in a style of her own design, suited to her age, her colouring and her build. Today it was a trouser suit in a light woollen mix material that had tones of sky blue, baby pink and lilac. It was softly feminine, and so very flattering.

"Let me look at you, young lady." Andrew held her at arm's length. "That's a good colour for you, Julie, my love. Is it the new Heather mix?"

"Can't fool you, can I? Yes, its part of the range John scooped from the U.K sales. It should sell well this coming winter," Julie laughed. "Well, my dear friend, we have quite a challenge with these new awards."

Andrew ruefully nodded agreement. "Still, they are the World Awards, and it will be feathers in all our caps, if we are successful, m'dear."

Julie was anxious to see the awards venue, but wanted to spend the next day with Maria and Giovanni. So her first call was to the Chateau Cornacchia.

Maria answered the telephone. "Come sta, how are you, ma cara bambina? Quando, when you come here?"

"Tomorrow, Maria. I'll be there by eleven o'clock. I can't wait to see you and Giovanni again."

"Si, we missa you too. We see you domani, si? Ciao for now."

As always, the strength and love that seemed to flow in a natural abundance from Maria was evident, even via the telephone line.

She rang Andrew, arranging to go to the Country Club for dinner together, so that she could inspect one of the villas. He agreed to collect her later.

At the Events Centre, a smiling young woman introduced herself, "Hello, I'm Polly Adams, your escort. This is a complicated place, you'll waste valuable time getting from one point to another, if you don't know the layout."

"Polly, I can see by the outside what a huge building it must be. I'm impressed! I'm in your hands. This list will outline what I need to know."

"Right, let's start right here." Polly indicated, "This is the Main Entrance and car drop off area . . ."

For nearly two hours, Polly guided Julie who explained that she needed to clarify exact details as to where her models would dress and change. How long it took them to enter and walk the catwalk, leave the main auditorium or, hopefully, enter the stage for the award presentations.

At the completion of their tour, Julie was grateful to accept Polly's invitation to join her for coffee. It was a pleasure to sink into a comfortable chair and peruse her notes.

Polly shyly commented, "Mrs Field, you are the first designer to reconnoitre the whole complex."

"Polly, so much capital money is tied up in a competition such as this. So much depends upon winning an award. The big houses have large expense accounts, smaller establishments, like ours, must do their homework. For example, your building has natural wooden interior walls . . . they are lovely . . . they absorb unwanted sound and are acoustically wonderful. But, they are deadly for any brown fabrics; they make a garment look nondescript, drab, and unattractive. Do you follow what I mean? I won't give you any other examples, they are trade secrets. This is why, as the designer, I must come and see the place for myself."

Polly gave Julie an admiring look, "Mum's the word, I won't tell a soul. When you were in Sydney in 1980, you won all the top awards and you modelled your own fabulous wedding gown. I was there that night, my brother, Peter Grossmith, was your naval escort. He didn't come back to earth for days, he so kept raving on about you. His girlfriend . . . well, she's his wife now . . . got so mad at him that she threatened to break up with him. They are stationed in Singapore now, with their two children."

Julie exclaimed, "Polly, I'm delighted to hear about Peter. He was so considerate and sensitive—he really helped me to win that Bridal Award. I've often wondered what had become of him. Please send him my regards. Thank you so much, Polly, I'll look forward to seeing you next year."

Back at Julie's hotel, Andrew ordered cocktails while Julie changed into an elegant, black sheath dress for the evening. The classic, sophisticated style, with its black and white print over-jacket, a chunky, African styled black and white necklace with matching earrings, had Andrew giving her an appreciative wolf whistle.

As she sipped her cocktail, Julie curiously asked, "Andrew, why have you never re-married? You are such good company, I always enjoy being with you."

"Honestly, I've never found anyone to take Ellen's place. When she died . . . so did part of me. Anyway, my two favourite girls, you and Kate, are already happily wed. How are things—still no luck in the baby stakes, I see."

"No, we've been told officially now that our only chance is a sperm donor. We are going to make a decision after the awards next year."

Andrew took her hands in his. "Julie, my sister is a specialist physician in that field, here in Sydney. If you'd like an introduction, you only have to ask."

He smiled and said cheerily, "Anyway, m'dear, let's go and check out the Country Club cuisine. You're really going to be blown away with the place."

CHAPTER 15

Her first impression of the Country Club had Julie uttering appreciatively, "Goodness, Andrew, it's truly magnificent!"

The two storey stone building was built as a large, spacious rotunda. Sparkling mirror glass gave the front entrance a spectacular three-dimensional effect. The foyer was lit in opulent brilliance by several huge chandeliers.

Andrew returned from the reception dangling a bunch of keys. "Here we go, Villa Number Two, 'Renata'."

The Mediterranean styled villas, 'Renata' and 'Rosa' were right on the shoreline, separated by fifty yards of a pristine golden sandy beach and judiciously planted gardens. Parking the car, they walked down a boardwalk path to the Villa Renata's covered patio.

Julie was already sold on the whole idea but, when she saw the cream and white décor, and the state-of-the-art kitchen, she needed no second look.

There were four double bedrooms, each with its own en suite bathroom and a separate spa bath. The combined living dining area was furnished with cream sofas and white wicker cane chairs and table. The floors were tiled and had colourful, Spanish type scatter rugs, placed in strategic places.

"It's just lovely, Andrew. It'll be heaven to stay here next year." Julie clapped her hands together like a schoolgirl. "No wonder my dear in-laws suggested it. I'll book it now, before anyone else discovers this piece of Paradise."

They returned along a beach boardwalk connecting the villa to the main building. This gave direct entrance to the dining room from the beach. It was divided into two parts, one for 'al fresco' dining, the other was a larger, more traditional buffet dining room, including a dance floor.

"Well, Mrs Field, will we do?" asked the smiling manager. "Mrs Naomi Field reckons you'd be pleased with our new facilities, was she right?"

Julie could not believe her luck and, when she returned to Andrew, she was almost beside herself in glee!

"I've done it! I've booked the number one villa 'Rosa', she enthused.

They talked 'shop' as they enjoyed a meal before Andrew took Julie back to her hotel, promising to take her to the Chateau Cornacchia next morning.

Julie told Andrew how she called the Chateau Cornacchia her own 'Shangri-La'. Reaching the summit of the long steep hill, he stopped the car. The silence was as deafening as before, and the air was heavy with the smell of the eucalyptus gums. But the silence lasted just for a few seconds. Then, as Julie remembered so clearly, the birds resumed their singing, calling and screeching in a cacophony of sound.

Julie inhaled deep breaths and cried in pleasure, "Thank God! Nothing has changed."

As they rounded the last bend, the charming setting unfolded and brought tears to Julie's eyes. This time in a whisper, she breathed, "Thank God, this also hasn't changed."

"Julie, Julie, ma bambina," cried Maria, running towards them, enfolding Julie's body tightly within her buxom embrace.

The years had not left their mark on Maria, she looked just as Julie lovingly remembered her.

Maria stroked Julie's face as she said, "There has beena sorrow, cara? You are no longer a young girl, but a beautiful woman now, si. We talka in Chapel. Giovanni is in the wine cellar, Andrew, you go finda him. We see you on loggia, il pranzo, for lunch. Say trenta, thirty minutes? We needa talk awhile, come cara."

Walking along the flagstone path, through the white painted lych gate, Julie suddenly remembered, with crystal clarity, her last visit here. She looked warily at the towering sycamore tree, half expecting to experience the invisible force to stop her in her tracks. This time nothing mysterious occurred.

Sitting beside Maria inside the cool chapel, Julie could feel the peace of the holy place seep through her body. Maria took Julie's hands in hers, saying, "Itsa beena a longa time, mio cara it's notta beena easy time, eh? The husband, il marito, John, he is difficult, si? Youra star it shina too bright for him, perhaps? He no like you to shina without him?"

"Yes, si, there have been rough moments, Maria. Gran is with me during the worst of them—I can still feel her presence. Strange, I don't feel stupid telling you, because you understand." She sighed deeply. "Just as you foretold, John cannot give me a child. We have to make a decision soon, whether or not to have a child using a donor."

"You notta needa a stranger, my Julie. I tella you truth. You wait justa little longa. I know these things. Be patient. Next year you come here, gooda things are going to happen, mio cara. Your Karmic tella me this."

"Maria, I have this wonderful feeling of coming home whenever I come here. I'll be here next year, late April to early May."

As Maria cuddled her, Julie experienced the enormous power and strength flowing from this unique woman.

They ate a lunch of Maria's freshly made foccacia bread, olives and cheese, followed by Giovanni's good wine.

Andrew studied Julie fondly. Even to his rheumy old eyes she definitely was a special person to the Martini family, and was treated like a daughter.

Since T.P. had voiced his unease at John's obsessive behaviour, Andrew had heard even loyal Kate remark that Julie hid a lot of John's unsociable habits. Kate admitted that she worried sometimes that Julie spent too much time alone in her beautiful, but remote house.

All too soon it was time to return to the City.

Maria whispered to her, "Be patient, donta do anything yet. Promise me, cara. Next year all willa be fixed, all willa be, migliore, better, giusto, right. Ciao!"

When they reached the outskirts of the City, Andrew suggested, "Well, young lady, how about you join me for dinner at my Club, or have you other plans, perhaps?"

"A quiet dinner with you will be just fine, Andrew, thank you," Julie replied with a happy smile.

It was still dark next morning when the repetitive beep of the telephone woke her. Groggily answering the call, she was surprised to hear a very grumpy sounding John.

Julie looked at the bedside clock, seeing it was just five o'clock. Having explained she had dined late with Andrew after a day at the Chateau Cornacchia, she was puzzled by John's surly attitude.

With a sudden change of tone in his voice, he replied, "Oh heck, I was just worried. I had visions of you being hurt on that long trip to the vineyard. Forgive me? What are you up to today?"

Breathing easier, Julie told him of her plans to check in with the button maker, and various other allied trades people. When he eventually hung up, she lay in her bed, troubled by his call. Was he checking up on her?

Julie invited Andrew to dine with her that evening. Arriving promptly, Andrew was shown to her table by the Maître d' himself. "Madame Field has just gone to take a telephone call," he advised. She sends apologies and will be here directly. Aah, here is Madame now."

As he stood to hold her chair for her, Andrew chuckled at the small stir she was unaware of causing. More than one head had turned admiringly to follow Julie's progress.

Tonight she was wearing a 'little black dress', but it was the panache with which she wore it that caused heads to turn. Andrew knew that he was receiving sly looks from many men present, who would be thinking, 'Lucky old devil!'

Giving him a peck on the cheek, Julie saw the amusement in his eyes. "Hello you. Sorry about that, it was John, again. What's the joke? Have I missed something?"

"No, no. I'm just basking in your reflected glory. I am enjoying the envy of many a gentleman in this room," Andrew told her with a happy grin. "What's that you said, about John, again? Is something up?"

"Would you believe he rang me at 5 a.m. this morning!" Julie explained. "He'd got into a right stew, thinking I'd had an accident or something. He's just rung again, checking if I'm still catching the plane tomorrow. I don't know whether to laugh or cry at him being such a worry wart."

CHAPTER 16

Julie looked up from the fabric she was draping over a dressmaker's model as the sound of a car's engine broke the peaceful silence in her workroom. The cheery voice heralding Kate's entrance brought a smile to her face. Just the person she wanted to see.

"Hello, Jules, brought you some fresh bread rolls, and your favourites—squashy doughnuts! Come on, time to stop for a break, honey." Kate breezed into the kitchen, putting on the coffee maker.

Julie had been working on samples for the Fashion Week, now only five short months away, she took Kate over to a covered model. With a flourish, she whipped the covering sheet off, "Trala . . . It's finished. What d'you think?"

The shop mannequin was dressed in a Highwayman's styled cloak in Black Watch Tartan, a brilliant scarlet red woollen dress, and on its head a matching tartan tam-o'-shanter. A pair of soft black leather knee-length boots completed the ensemble.

"Oh, yes," breathed Kate, "I'll put money on this becoming the 'in thing', darling, for next winter. It will be a runway hit on both sides of the Tasman, Julie. There's what, a four way colour range?"

"Yup, we have the four different tartans that John has snaffled from Scotland. But, come and see 'Blue Heaven', I'm really, really pleased with the way it is coming together."

She went over to her pet project, the evening-wear section, and removed the dust cover from the dress, 'Blue Heaven'.

Kate exclaimed in awe, "Oh my!"

Held up by two slim, silver chain shoulder straps, the gown consisted of layers of various blue shades of Chantilly lace, interwoven with silver thread. The lovely gown shimmered in the sunshine as though it was alive.

Julie held up an intricately worked silver belt with long silver tassels. "This arrived this morning from Doug. Isn't it exquisite? It's just what I envisaged for the dress."

"My God, Julie, It's fabulous. Look at how it shimmers, it'll catch every light in the place. You have come up with another winner, girl." Kate reverently stroked the material.

"Can we do a 'reccy' on what's completed and what's still to do, once we have eaten your delicious food?" Julie asked. "I'm pretty sure everything is on target, but I'd rather not get any nasty late surprises."

"Okay, but let's go up the hill first. Dr Kate prescribes fresh air and light exercise for her genius of a partner."

It was pleasantly sunny with the temperature hovering around 20C. It was so clear that they could see for miles.

"I love it up here," Julie said, taking in another deep breath of clean, sweet air. "I come up here most days and think about all sorts of things. It's so therapeutic."

"Julie, where's John?" Kate asked in a soft, low voice. "He hasn't been around the last couple of times I've come here."

"No, he's on one of his fishing trips," Julie admitted sadly. "We've been trying to sort out the sperm bank option. One day John is all for it, and the next he's vehemently changed his mind. I'm finding it so unsettling. I try to bury myself in the work . . . to a certain extent I'm succeeding, but . . ."

Her voice drifted off and Kate saw the pain and worry on her face. Harry had already told Kate how John had made an ass of himself at the Club several times of late, by drinking too much and becoming obnoxious.

"Julie, we have a lot at stake here. We have invested a lot of capital and time getting it right." Kate held Julie's hands in hers. "What you've already accomplished is absolutely marvellous. The 'Scottish Highwayman' and 'Blue Heaven' are real winners in my eyes. Can you face going on with the full collection?"

"John doesn't interfere with my work. He's brilliantly sourced all of the fabrics we need," Julie explained protectively. "My detailed draft designs are all finished, so we only need to make them up. No, we can still make the date, Kate dear."

Kate put her arms around Julie. "Come on then, back to work. You are a genius, you know that, don't you, Jules?"

Close to tears, Julie replied, "Thank you, Katie. You are the boost my ego needed just now."

The work in earnest began as they started their detailed assessment. At the end of two hours of solid work, Kate stretched her back and her cramped leg muscles. "Whew, that's it, Jules," she sighed. "Some of the accessories are still to be decided, but, honey child, we are over the hump!"

"Right, I'm on my way. Jules, promise me you'll give me a call if ever you want me to come out. If you feel lonely . . . or anything else. Okay?"

As Kate was about to leave, John came roaring up, skidding to a screeching stop in front of the house. He got out of the car quite unsteady on his feet. Kate's mouth dropped open at his unkempt appearance. His clothes were creased, he had several days' growth of beard, and he looked grubby and very bleary eyed.

Julie looked in despair at her husband and flinched when he approached as if to kiss her. His breath reeked of alcohol and his clothes stank of fish.

Kate looked sympathetically at Julie, so obviously embarrassed by John's demeanour. Waving a cheery farewell, she decided to leave discreetly, and not add to Julie's distress.

Julie looked at John in disgust. "Perhaps you'd better clean yourself up, John, and then sleep it off in the spare room. I'll be working late."

With that she returned to her workroom and locked the door behind her. She rang George Field, she explained the state John was in and her father-in-law assured her he would come straight away.

She met him in the driveway with tears in her eyes. "He's at the back, Dad. He's getting worse and I don't know how to handle this situation."

George Field put his arms around his daughter-in-law and comforted her, before quietly saying, "Leave him to me, I'll get him cleaned up and into bed. Don't forget to lock your workroom. You have too much at stake in there for any accidents to happen."

George Field's suggestion to lock her workroom was good advice. The last time John came home from one of his binges, he had angrily knocked her easel over and thrown her pencils and sketches out of the window, accusing her of being a workaholic. No real damage had been done, but it had dismayed and alarmed Julie so much that she had confided her concerns to his parents.

George Field had promised to come each time John returned home in such a state, just to make sure Julie was safe. He had also tried to counsel his son.

Julie knew John was getting worse. Something was eating at him, but whatever it was, she felt unable to help him. It was as though a demon within him surfaced every now and then.

Now sitting on her usual seat on the stile, her thoughts went to Maria's words. "Be patient, donta do anything yet, promise me, cara."

'Well, there's nothing I can do until after the awards, we have sunk too much into it now,' Julie told the night sky.

Down below her, the outside light of her house was switched on, George Field's signal that he had put John to bed and it was safe for her to come home.

When she reached the house he was waiting for her. "This can't go on lass, he must seek help. I'm going take John to see Doc Matthews myself. Go into the factory tomorrow for a few hours. Ask Kate to be with you, Okay?"

He put a reassuring arm around her shoulder as she nodded her agreement.

CHAPTER 17

As George Field proposed her twenty-eighth birthday toast, Julie reflected that her marriage had undergone a dramatic change during the past three months.

She let her thoughts drift back . . .

John had visited Doc Matthews and there had been no more drinking binges. He had thrown himself into his work, undertaking more trips to Asia on his own. Julie was fully absorbed with getting the collection ready, so had, to her surprise, not really missed him.

Julie recognised she had become professionally more self-confident and much less emotionally dependent on John. But it also seemed that the more she succeeded, the more morose John became.

John now seemed to accept the inevitable, that he would never father a child, appearing sexually disinterested, detached and resentful.

Doc had reiterated that the only hope for Julie to have a child was by sperm donor, or adoption. Previously John had shown a strong reluctance to the latter suggestion.

Julie, recalling her conversation with Andrew Martin, asked Doc for his opinion of Dr Andrea Martin.

"She is excellent, one of the best in her field," enthused Doc Matthews. "I'd highly recommend you consider visiting her."

John had commented, "If that's what you want, Julie, set up an appointment when you are in Sydney."

Julie let the idea ferment before ringing Dr Andrea Martin's office in January. She tentatively asked did John need to be present and was relieved when the answer was not for the first visit.

⌐—*HJ/L*—꙳

Kate broke through Julie's reverie. "Hey! Birthday Girl, time to blow out your candles. Don't forget to make a wish now."

Julie blew out all the candles in one long breath. A phrase in Maria's voice kept echoing through her mind, 'be patient, wait justa a little longer.'

"Well, I bet I could guess what you wished for," sneered John, cynically, downing a full glass of wine.

Taking their birthday cake out onto the patio, Kate said softly, "A penny for them, Jules. You seem a bit unsettled tonight, my friend."

"Silly old homesickness blues I'm afraid, Kate, dear. I had birthday cards and letters from my family today," explained Julie. Forcibly changing the subject, she smiled, "We should be arranging a full dress rehearsal by next month. Catwalk, timing, full changes, the whole works."

Kate responded, "I was about to suggest it to you. I found out today that we can use the old local ballroom anytime for a practice."

Julie sighed in satisfaction. "I'll give Harry the floor plans and the notes I made of the Events Centre. Remember how massive I said it was?"

Over the next three weeks, everything fell into place like clockwork. Garments were finished, accessories arrived on time, and the models were fitted, with dire threats issued to not gain any weight!

They had contemplated hiring Sydney models for the show but Kate and Julie decided their local Auckland models were familiar with the garments. Thus knowing the way the fabric draped and worked would give the clothes a much better showing.

Using tapes and chalked lines, Harry and his crew had marked out the ballroom floor so that it simulated the floor plan area of the Events Centre. Harry walked everyone through the runway floor layout, pointing out where there were entrances, exits and which corridor led to where. Once he was satisfied they were familiar with the complex layout, Kate and Julie began rehearsing in earnest.

Each of the four models had a dresser. Each being given a detailed list itemising everything her model was to wear, from her bare skin outwards.

Harry and John timed everything to the split second. Two Wardrobe Mistress kept track of the sequence in which the garments were to be presented. Two hairdressers worked frantically, brushing loose curls and fixing ruffled hair.

Kate had cajoled a friend from the local radio station to act as the music technician for them. She had made the initial music selection and waited anxiously to hear if her choices were working. Barney, her technician friend, was even coaching the girls, getting them to swing a little more here, or to slow their pace there, as the music demanded.

The coup d'etat—their finale, were the two 'Evening Wear' gowns. There was an audible sigh as the two models appeared in the 'Night Sky' and 'Blue Heaven' gowns. As Kate had predicted, 'Blue Heaven', modelled by Gloria, to romantic soaring string music, shimmered as the gown absorbed every twinkle and sparkle of light from around the room.

Model Serena, wearing the black and silver 'Night Sky' gown, depicting Julie's magnificent vision of the astral Milky Way, was accompanied by an arrangement of outer space music.

Kate hugged Julie, saying, "We've done it! Oh! I'm so proud of us. It works and it is so . . . so . . . just wonderful!"

Kate and Julie were reviewing their notes when two models shyly approached them.

"Serena and I particularly love the two evening gowns." Gloria hesitated. "We have a suggestion to make about them."

"Let's hear it, we are open to anything constructive. After all, you're the professionals," said Kate.

"Well, we wondered . . . could we wear silver wigs for the finale? We think it would give an extra zest to the gowns."

"Wow! Yes! Yes! Brilliant! Why didn't I think of that," cried Julie.

When the box, containing a selection of silver wigs, arrived it caused great hilarity. Harry and John did an impromptu-exaggerated sashay down the catwalk, wearing two of the more outrageous wigs, before Gloria and Serena both opted for a close fitting helmet style.

So that Gloria could judge for herself the shimmering effect of the 'Blue Heaven' gown, Julie slipped it on one afternoon. Harry sighed, "Julie could model that just as well as Gloria," he said to John. "Perhaps even better. She has a fuller figure than Gloria, more rounded, more womanly. She has put her own heart and soul into that gown. Aren't you proud of her, John?"

"Yes, of course," retorted John sharply. "Isn't she everybody's darling? She does everything right, doesn't she?" He stalked away.

Harry raised his eyebrows quizzically at Kate. "Methinks I do detect a little bit of the green-eyed monster there."

Kate nodded. "It's not the first time Master John has shown it lately. She's doing so well, holding everyone together, we all love her. That's what's upsetting John. She isn't dependent upon him."

"I've warned him about it. He'll lose her if he carries on like this," retorted Harry.

Reflecting on this later to herself, Kate wondered how much more of John's shenanigans Julie would put up with.

The penultimate day arrived! Tomorrow 'The Team' would depart for Sydney. John and Harry were to stay and run the day-to-day affairs of the company.

"Anyway," as Harry had voiced privately to his wife, "Julie is better off without him. He only intimidates and restricts her . . . and frankly I don't trust him to stay off the sauce. The last thing we need is the spectacle of him tying one on. We have a huge financial investment riding on this show. No, Katie love," he ended firmly, "he stays here, and I'll stay to keep an eye on him."

CHAPTER 18

Julie and Kate found Andrew Martin waiting for them at Sydney airport. Arriving at the Villa Rosa, Kate went as 'gaga' as Julie had done, uttering increasingly louder and louder "Wow's!'" as she explored every room.

Andrew told them, "You have been allotted a two hour rehearsal time, tomorrow afternoon at 2.30."

He paused, to give them time to digest his next piece of news, "The Country Club has kindly loaned you two vans for your transportation and some of you are in adjoining rooms in the hotel complex. You're going to have a huge advantage over other competitors being here, away from other spying prying eyes. So keep it 'mum' as to where you are staying." He raised his glass, "Now cheers and here's 'Good Luck' to us all!"

Andrew took Julie to one side, "How are things, poppet?" Julie replied, "John still agrees with my keeping my appointment with your sister. I'm really looking forward to meeting her."

Andrew took her arm. "Julie, I spoke to Maria last week. Their grandson is being christened. She was most adamant you came, wanting to know the exact dates you would be here. She kept saying, something very good is going to happen for you, very soon."

"Oh, Andrew, I'd love to be there for a real Italian family christening." Silently in her thoughts she added, 'How I hope Maria's predictions come true.'

Later that evening Julie telephoned Maria and, on hearing her voice, immediately felt a peaceful presence surround her and . . . something else . . . something she could not explain. But she knew it was a good omen of some kind when Maria lovingly said, "Something really gooda, extra special, is about to come, Julie, cara. You do wella in your competition, I know. You be happy, Julie, cara, it isa going to happen. You are going to be so happy, cara mia. Ciao, mio bambina."

The team arrived at the event complex for their rehearsal to find the sheer size of the arena overwhelming. Even Julie, who had already seen it, found it awesome. She was most relieved when she saw Polly Grossmith had been designated as their personal guide.

Polly led them into the massive foyer of the building, decorated with Aboriginal paintings, Australian flags, kangaroos and, of course, koala bears. They followed her through to the auditorium, which seemed to be the size of a football pitch, divided down the middle by the catwalk runway. They straggled through this colossus of an arena, eyes wide open in astonishment at the sheer size of the place.

The length and height of the catwalk drew the four models in for a closer look. This was where they would be 'strutting their stuff' from tomorrow.

"Dear God! It looks long enough to launch a plane!" cried Gloria.

"I see what you meant about the natural timber walls," whispered Kate to Julie. "They'll kill anything brown, or even black. 'Night Sky' will need tons of spotlights."

Climbing onto the stage, Kate turned to face the junction where the catwalk projected from the stage. She peered into the gloom, trying to see the end of the structure. "Jeez! It's gianormous!"

Without spotlights or a live audience, the auditorium had a ghostly atmosphere. "It's dangerous without adequate lighting," grumbled Andrew. "Don't let the girls onto that catwalk, Julie, until I can organise more lights." He disappeared into the gloom.

He soon arrived back with a satisfied grin on his face. "All fixed. I've thrown out all the 'hangers on' and locked the doors. We now have complete privacy for the rest of our rehearsal time. So let's go, girls!"

For the next hour and forty minutes, they rehearsed with some very precise timing taking place.

When a bell rang, Kate clapped her hands. "That's it! Our time is up girls. Mum's the word from now on!"

The doors all around the auditorium sprang open and hordes of people streamed back into the complex. The team could not stop themselves bubbling with excitement at the prospect of being a part of the prestigious World Fashion Awards.

According to their timetable schedules, they had four parades each day for the first three days. Each day a 'Best in Category' was to be awarded, culminating on the Sunday with a glamorous dinner and the presentation of the top awards, plus the supreme award for the 'Overall Winner'.

So it began . . .

At one o'clock the next afternoon, the courtesy vans pulled into the Events Centre. Here, like a well-oiled machine, the team swung smoothly into action, preparing the four models for the first parade.

There was an intercom loudspeaker in the dressing room so Andrew, watching proceedings backstage, could relay the progress of their competitors. Kate and Julie began the detailed scrutiny, ensuring each girl was wearing the correct accessories.

Andrew's voice crackled over the loudspeaker, "We are 'Go', girls."

Julie looked at Kate, they hugged each other, words were not needed. Julie got a unanimous 'thumbs up's' signal from the wardrobe mistresses, helpers, dressers and hairdressers.

Andrew gave Barney the 'start up' signal and the soft, soothing lilt of an Scottish air began to play. Kate glided to the dais, clicked on her microphone and announced, "Ladies and Gentlemen, Team Maison Chevalier proudly presents its label, 'Flowers in the Field' and 'Winter Casual Wear' designer, Mrs Julie Field."

Gloria, resplendent in her Black Watch tartan trews, sleeveless jerkin and a cream Aryan sweater, sashayed down the catwalk—closely followed by Serena, Didi and Eve, in the other variants. The tartan colours were rich against soft woollen sweaters, giving the overall appearance of easy to wear, yet fashionable and affordable ensembles.

The applause was continuous, growing in volume.

Andrew hugged Julie and whispered, "They liked 'em."

There was no time to rest on their laurels. The models hurried to change into the 'Summer Wear'.

The lively music of Sir Cliff Richard's, 'We're all going on a Summer Holiday' rang out.

The summery split skirts, matching jerkins and bright camisole outfits, plus Julie's deliberate clash of colours, Seagrass Green with Cambridge Blue, Melon Pink with Sunflower Yellow, Vanilla Ice with Coffee 'n Crème, and Jamaican Lime with Seville Orange, all added to the wonderful feeling of summer.

The infectious beat of the music soon had the whole audience clapping in unison. Julie gave an involuntary gasp as her models, sensing that they had the full attention of audience, ad libbed a few extra 'bumps and grinds'.

Andrew murmured to Julie, in astonishment, "Will you look at that! Look! Even the judges are smiling and beating time to the music!"

Back in the dressing room, it was all giggles as Gloria repeated her 'bumps and grinds'.

Polly reminded them of the evening timetable. "You are due back here at 7 o'clock and on stage at 8 o'clock. I'll be waiting for you. Okay?"

At Villa Rosa, Julie and Kate asked if they had any queries. Did anything need changing, adjusting?

"What, with the reaction we got! No way," laughed Barney. "Keep it just as it is. They love it."

The ever-helpful Country Club management organized a light dinner before the team set off to do battle again.

Following the now familiar routine, Kate introduced the first of the tartan 'Winter Daywear' ensembles. All four models boarded the catwalk, taking up their rehearsed poses.

The music played soothingly, hauntingly, conjuring up visions of heather covered hills, misty mountains and clear babbling brooks and burns. Ambrosia to anyone with Scottish heritage.

Using the same four tartans as the 'Winter Casual Wear', Julie had incorporated the timeless Scottish designs of kilt, waistcoat and fringed scarf over the shoulder.

The audience clapped profusely. Kate and Julie exchanged hugs. The vibes were extra good.

A change of music introduced the 'Summer Daywear' section. Colourful, halter-necked, full-skirted sundresses were worn with matching bolero jackets. The models wore white high-heeled strap sandals, white lace gloves and carried a white, boxy handbag.

It was Serena this time who had the audience in her in pocket. With her body language, firstly coquettish, then brazenly flirtatious, she provocatively dropped a lace handkerchief. It was picked up by a handsome, Gaelic gentleman who, much to the delight of the audience, gallantly kissed Serena's hand, before handing it back.

Kate stole a glance sideways to Julie and Andrew, her eyebrows rose quizzically. Once again the applause was loud, warm and appreciative.

Later, as she squeezed in beside Julie in the van, Kate suggested, "Let's ring Harry and John and give them an update."

"It's after midnight at home. John will be asleep, so will Harry," Julie reminded her ebullient friend.

"Then let's wake them up," bubbled Kate.

"No, I'd better leave it until the morning, Kate," Julie said, looking guilty. "John gets a bit grumpy if he gets woken up."

As she lay in her bed, almost too excited to sleep, Julie ruefully thought that, once she would have eagerly rung John to share her success. Sadly, that was no longer the case. A lonely, empty feeling filled her heart.

A warm breeze drifted through the open window and Julie remembered there was someone with whom she could share her success.

"I did it, Gran," she whispered. "I did it!"

CHAPTER 19

Relishing her Sergeant-Major routine, Kate beat a saucepan with a wooden spoon and yelled, "Day Two! Up and at 'em! Breakfast!"

When everybody had assembled, she read over their timetable. "Today first up winter 'Business Wear', followed immediately by summer." She gave one of her infectious, bubbly chuckles as she said, "Then, time off for good behaviour."

They were all aware that today they would face an audience principally comprised of important trade buyers from all around the Pacific rim.

Sophisticated melodies from the Bert Kamfoert Orchestra rang out as Didi led the way in the Wavy Navy Blue, calf-length skirted version of the business suit.

Kate reeled off the colour options and the availability of three skirt lengths, plus a trouser option. The other three models followed, wearing the optional versions. To complete the 'business look', each girl was wearing heavy, black-rimmed spectacles and carrying smart, snappy black briefcases.

Julie, smiled happily, "Great work, Katie," she enthused, "Even when Didi stumbled, you never missed a beat."

"I watch them like a hawk, believe me," laughed Kate, as Barney restarted the music and cued her.

This time the melodies featured a slower, lighter, gentler orchestral beat.

Kate began, "As a contrast to the dark winter outfit, the classic summer 'Business Suit' is lighter in colour and overall weight. It is a feminine, practical and hardwearing option for the working girl."

Giving an almost imperceptible nod, she signalled Didi. "The suits come in four colours. Here we have Didi, in Cambridge Blue, Serena, in Seagrass Green, and Eve in Vanilla Ice. Finally, Gloria, in Coffee 'n Crème. Their jewellery is appropriately named 'Lustre Pearl', a natural pearl necklace and matching earrings."

Kate paused momentarily. "It is important to note that this range is made in a crease-resistant, wrinkle-free washable fabric. We feel the ensembles depict a cool, sophisticated, well-dressed and well-groomed young businesswoman."

As the knowledgeable audience showed their appreciation with enthusiastic warm applause, Julie hugged Kate and asked. "Did Andrew tell you about Zena . . . somebody, from Melbourne? She's booked a special viewing on Buyers Morning."

"That must be Zena Bentley. Wow! She controls ninety per cent of the Australian market, and also has contacts in the U.S.A.!"

⌒⌁⥲⥲⥲⌁∽

That evening Kate looked around at the packed house. This was the fullest the auditorium had been all week. There was not a spare seat anywhere; people were even standing at the back. When Barney started the lone piper music, an expectant hush fell over the audience.

Suddenly, dramatically, a lone spotlight revealed the tall, slim figure of Eve, swathed in a cloak of Black Watch Tartan.

"This, Ladies and Gentlemen, is Team Maison Chevalier's 'Scottish Highwaywoman'," announced Kate, as the lone piper faded, and a Scottish marching tune echoed around the large arena. Eve began her walk, swishing the cloak theatrically to reveal the scarlet red woollen dress underneath. Her Black Watch Tam O'Shanter was set at a jaunty angle upon her head, and the heels on her knee-length black leather boots clicked in time with the music.

The audience broke into thunderous applause. The other three models joined Eve. Gloria clad in Clan MacDonald and a Royal Blue dress; Serena, in Clan Gordon and a dress of Forest Green; Didi, in Clan Bruce, and a navy blue dress.

The audience clapped enthusiastically in time to the stirring music. When all four models walked side by side down the catwalk for their final showing, it was difficult to hear Barney's music above the cheers and clapping.

Kate rushed off stage and threw her arms around Julie. "See, I told you way back when, that I'd put money on the outfit becoming a 'hit'. Listen to that applause!"

Kate, could sense the air of expectation amongst the audience when she mounted the podium for the final time. Barney had Italian mandolin music playing softly, as Kate named the outfits they were about to present as 'Cappuccino'.

Eve walked on in the cream, lightweight wool suit. The sheaf skirt calf-length, with a coatdress draped to mid-thigh and fastened with one button at the waist. Her coffee-coloured silk blouse, tied at the neck with a huge, floppy artists' bow, shone with lustre under the lights. Gloria and Serena paraded the suits with the trouser options, Didi brought up the rear in the above-the-knee length skirt.

Back in the dressing-room the excitement knew no bounds. They all realised they had done well.

Day three and Julie and Kate decided the team deserved some free time, "Until four o'clock, sharp," Kate cautioned. "We need to leave at six o'clock. So, please girls, no sunburnt faces, and no accidents!"

Julie and Kate were strolling the shopping mall when Kate quietly asked, "Have you been sleeping okay since we have been here, Jules? I thought I heard you crying in your sleep."

"Did you? I thought I'd slept right through," Julie sounded surprised. She had woken at one stage when the nightmare started, but a strange, calming, warm presence had sent her straight back to sleep.

"Jules, I'm always here for you if you need to talk,"

Kate told her friend.

"Oh look, Kate! Look at all those baby 'goodies' in that shop over there. I must buy a present for Maria's grandson, Rico. I've been invited out there for his christening."

Browsing around the nursery shop as she selected a gift she decided it was time to confide in Kate.

Over lunch, she broached the subject and her words tumbled out in a rush. "Kate, I have an appointment next week, with Andrew's sister, Doctor Andrea Martin. She's a fertility specialist . . . We . . . well, me really, have decided to try for a baby again. Doc says a sperm donor is the only way for us now."

"Oh, so that's why you've taken the villa for the extra week." Kate frowned, concern on her face. "Jules, are you sure? Is John okay with the idea? Well, you never know, if you have a baby, I might get 'clucky' and join you! It could be fun, both of us the size of barrels around the office for a few months!"

Sharp at four o'clock, the two hairdressers 'tut, tutted' fussily at the state of the four models' hair, and set about repairing the supposed damage. A tasteful, light meal arrived, courtesy of the Country Club kitchen.

Six o'clock came around almost too quickly. Kate clapped her hands, calling, "Here we go, for the final time. I'm convinced we have a brilliant evening ahead of us. So go, 'break-a-leg' to us all!"

The traffic around the complex appeared to be extremely heavy.

"Hey look!" Julie exclaimed, pointing to a sign, which read, 'House Full/Sold Out'.

Andrew discovered they had been drawn number three out of eight for the Day/Evening and tenth, last place, for the big one.

Finally their call came. Taking her customary place on the podium, Kate drew in a sharp breath as she saw the size of the audience. The auditorium was even more congested than the previous evening, with extra seating placed right up to the edge of the catwalk. Also, the noise level was considerably higher.

Kate quietly called Julie, "Warn the girls it's crowded out here, much bigger audience, much closer to them!"

Barney commenced the smooth, big band dance favourites, and Kate opened her commentary with her customary identification of the team.

She continued, "We invite you to view our collection of glamorous outfits for those romantic dinners, special anniversaries, or that extra special occasion. We see Gloria first, in a winter weight cream silk suit. Her ankle-length skirt is slightly flared, while her jacket has a self-embroidered shawl collar, and is fastened at the waist with an embroidered 'frog'. Under her jacket you will see a sleeveless camisole in an enchanting pure Guipure lace in a delicate, contrast colour, 'Coffee 'n Crème'. Eve wears the trouser version of the suit, and a camisole in pastel 'Seagrass Green'."

Peeking from behind the stage curtain, Julie could see that the two suits looked exquisite. The bright spotlights gave the shining cream silk fabric a pearly lustre.

Kate grinned confidently at her. "Next we have Didi, who is wearing a classic dusky pink, short-sleeved dress in pure silk, with a flattering scooped neckline and a very full mid-length skirt. Surely a 'dancing' dress if ever I saw one, and what better to keep you warm for that cool romantic walk home under the stars than a soft pink mohair stole?"

Kate paused as Didi reached the end of the catwalk and twirled around, pouting prettily to the sound of many wolf whistles. Serena waited for Kate's signal. "Serena wears the same pure silk dress, but with a different skirt. This is knee-length with a rouched hem, giving an almost 'harem' look when worn over its matching 'stove pipe' trousers."

Both girls walked the usual side-by-side dual finish, to a noisy chorus of wolf whistles and rousing applause.

Back in the comparative quiet of the dressing room, everyone was talking about the size of the audience.

Julie looked nervously at Kate and suggested, "How about everyone not needed for the 'Haute Couture' going out to the wings to watch the show?"

The room emptied fast.

It was time to prepare their finale—the piece de resistance.

CHAPTER 20

Hairdresser Ellen fitted Gloria's silver wig in place, whilst her assistant Wendy did the same for Eve. The simple accessory transformed their faces completely, giving the impression that they were beautiful creatures from outer space. The illusion was further enhanced when Ellen painted their lips with pearlised silver lipstick, and the same colour as an exaggerated eye shadow.

Barney started up his stellar, astral theme, soft, soothing mood music that rose into black space.

The stage lights were extinguished as Kate began. "Ladies and Gentlemen, Team Maison Chevalier presents the 'Haute Couture' exclusive, one-off selection, designed by Julie Field . . . 'Night Sky'!"

Six super strong spotlights sprang on, all focused on Eve. She stood at the head of the catwalk, her black and silver gown shimmering upon an embroidered backcloth of glittering stars, representative of the night sky.

A collective, audible gasp emerged from the audience. Then the applause began. It rolled around the auditorium, building into a great roar of sound.

Barney faded out the music and turned Kate's microphone fully up. Her voice took on an eerie, echoing pitch, as though it was also coming from outer space.

She told her audience, "'Night Sky' consists of a softly draped, georgette fabric sheath dress, interwoven with a silver thread. The matching edge-to-edge, three quarter sleeved jacket being held at the waist by a crescent moon shaped frog, in solid silver."

As Eve slowly walked down the catwalk, the spotlights emphasized her every move. The cleverly woven silver thread sparkled and twinkled, replicating the heavenly, astral 'Milky Way' over their heads, the original divine inspiration for Julie's design.

As Eve reached the stage end of the catwalk, the spotlights dramatically and abruptly switched off. The audience were left gasping and blinking in the half-light, absorbing the magic they had just witnessed.

Without giving them time to recover, Barney started up the music again, a montage of soaring strings and romantic orchestral tunes, all containing the word 'blue'.

Kate recommenced, "This final gown, Ladies and Gentlemen, is aptly named 'Blue Heaven', designed once again by Julie Field."

The brilliant spotlights sprang into action again.

This time they illuminated Gloria as she stood at the top of the catwalk. With another collective, indrawn gasp of breath, the audience was beguiled as Gloria stood with her arms stretched above her head, allowing the shimmering dress to capture every wink of available light, giving the impression of a silver blue goddess.

Barney started the sensuous, haunting, blue theme music, as Gloria sashayed down the catwalk, her sparkling dress shimmering in the spotlights. The audience watched in a stunned silence.

Kate quietly described, "This unique gown, literally one of a kind, is a semi-sheath, and aptly named 'Blue Heaven'. It falls in several layers of various blue shades of Chantilly lace, interwoven with silver thread. This gives us that beautifully elusive shimmering effect. The solid silver belt is tied with a pair of long silver tassels. As you can see, Gloria is wearing matching tasselled earrings."

Gloria drew out the time she took strolling along the catwalk to the hypnotic strains of the atmospheric music. She paused at the end and slowly rotated, so that the spotlights hit one glittering spot on her gown after another. All the while the cheers and wolf whistles continued to grow in volume.

Barney abruptly turned the music volume up for five seconds, and then suddenly, equally dramatically, all of the spotlights were extinguished. The music stopped dead, leaving a black space, a void, and an abyss where Gloria once stood.

There was a moment of hushed silence, as though the audience was afraid of breaking a spell. Then with a rush, the applause erupted, reverberating around the auditorium as the house lights came on.

Returning to the Villa Rosa, Julie and Kate were exhausted but delighted with their success. Kate sighed, "Julie Field, you are a genius, I don't know how I am going to get any sleep tonight. I feel as though I am walking on Cloud Nine."

"Me too," Julie agreed. "It has been a dream come true, Katie. We are just about guaranteed a full order book after the Buyer's Morning. The capital expense we put into this trip has been more than justified, hasn't it?"

"You're so right! Harry told me they've been fielding heaps of inquiries at home," stated Kate excitedly. "Look at this pile of business cards." She fanned out a large fistful of various cards, of all shapes and sizes.

"It's a phenomenal response," agreed Julie. "We are on our way to fame and fortune, Katie Reynolds."

They had arranged to meet Andrew at seven o'clock for the official awards dinner, the celebratory end to the Fashion Week. Natural choices for this glamorous evening were their 'Haute Couture' gowns. Julie chose to wear 'Blue Heaven', and Kate, 'Night Sky'.

During the pre-dinner socialising, Julie, in Kate's view, was as vivacious and alive as Kate had ever seen her. At one stage she caught a fond look on Andrew's face as he laughed at a remark Julie made. 'That's how she affects us all,' Kate mused. 'I hope John's problem doesn't destroy that sparkle in her!'

A drum roll announced that the awards were about to be presented.

For the next hour Kate and Julie were ecstatic. They had entered garments for seven specific categories during the weeklong event and now, in an unprecedented, never heard of before occasion, they'd won awards for all seven.

"Gee, Jules, I don't know about you but I can't think straight!" Kate stammered as they admired the astonishing haul of trophies sitting in the middle of the table. "I'm staggered, happy, overwhelmed and darned weepy—all rolled in one!"

Julie could only nod. She felt utterly and emotionally drained, but was also—totally elated.

At the conclusion of the dinner, the Master of Ceremonies introduced the Chief Judge, Monsieur Henri Dupont.

In a softly modulated voice, with his charming French accent, he began, "Thank you, my friends. This week has been an eye-opener for both my fellow judges and me. I can honestly say that the Southern Hemisphere designers have given the Northern Hemisphere visitors a—'ow do you say?—a wake-up call."

"We also have, this evening, some special surprise awards to make. These awards have not previously been publicised. My fellow judges and I have been, what do you say? . . . 'sneaky'. We must confess that we have been quietly appraising all of the entrants, without their knowledge."

Monsieur Dupont continued. "I am holding here a Gold Medal for Best Fabric Selection. In the unanimous opinion of all the ten judges, the winner is . . . Madame Julie Field!"

Julie's surprised face was a picture!

The Chief Judge then announced, "The next Gold Medal is for the best descriptive fashion commentary. One young woman, we felt, met all of the criteria through an arduous week. Mesdames et Messieurs, the winner is . . . Madame Kate Reynolds."

Kate's mouth gaped open in an unladylike and inelegant manner. Kate, for once, was speechless.

The Chief Judge adjusted his reading glasses. "Well, my friends, we come to the final presentation. This award is presented to the person who was judged the overall winner of the World Fashion Week 1988. All judges unanimously felt there was no contest. The decision was clear-cut."

"Mesdames et Messieurs, it is with the greatest of pleasure I invite back to the stage one of the most exciting new stars in our world wide industry. Wearing her unique 'Haute Couture' winning creation, the overall winner is . . . Madame Julie Field!"

With her cheeks blushing at the compliments given by the Chief Judge, and with her 'Blue Heaven' gown shimmering in the spotlights beaming down on her, Julie clasped Andrew's arm tightly as he led her to the stage. She was received with tumultuous audience applause, and affectionate kisses and hugs from all ten judges.

Accepting the prestigious overall award, Julie, speaking quietly and sincerely, said, "Monsieur Dupont, eminent judges, distinguished guests, ladies and gentlemen, I am both honoured and humbled by this award. I'd be lying if I said it had come easily. It has not . . . It is the result of a lot of hard work by a very loyal and very supportive team. I sincerely thank every member of the Team Maison Chevalier for his or her total and unselfish team contribution."

As the applause rang around the room, Julie paused to give emphasis to her words. "We call ourselves a 'team', and that, Ladies and Gentlemen, is what we are. So on behalf of them all, I proudly accept this award. Thank you."

She raised the award high above her head and left the stage to a standing ovation . . .

Andrew had telephoned Michael and Denise in London, Kate had excitedly rung Harry and, although Julie had dialled her home many times, it was always engaged.

The next day, after a final happy, hilarious lunch the courtesy vans arrived to take the team members to the airport.

For the next three days life became just a blur for Kate, Julie and Andrew. They worked at a frenetic pace through buyer meetings, photographic and media interviews.

Before Kate left that final morning she helped Julie select a small sample range to use for any further last minute buyer viewings.

Kate's parting words of advice were. "Just shut down for a while. Have a seriously relaxing dinner, listen to the music. That's Doctor Kate's orders!"

Julie decided to take Kate's advice and go to the Country Club for dinner. A decision that was about to change her life, forever . . .

CHAPTER 21

The clock struck six o'clock as Julie selected a dress to wear. Quite inexplicably, a warm draught of air rushed through the open window and caused the 'Summer Wear' dusky pink dress to slip from its hanger and fall at her feet. She shrugged, well it was as good a choice as any.

In the near distance a string of fairy lights blinked invitingly in their coloured lanterns along the balcony of the Country Club and soft music drifted through the window.

She hesitated, thinking perhaps she would forgo dinner, but she realised she was hungry and resumed her walk to the Country Club restaurant. She was warmly greeted by the maître d' and was shown to a corner table overlooking the sea. Selecting a salmon salad, she authorised the waitress to add it to her account.

As she ate, she idly gazed around, her thoughts on the marvellous week she had just been a part of, when suddenly a woman sat down at the table next to hers. "I see the flyboys have arrived, Julie," she drawled in a broad Australian accent.

Julie recognised the woman, "Oh hello, Zena. How are you? What was that about flyboys?"

"Actually, I have just come to pick up my husband Kevin and we are leaving directly. That's my husband Kevin over there, talking with the big brass. They're staying here at the club until Monday. The management has extended them member privileges, or so Kevin tells me. Kevin knows a couple of them . . ." she stopped mid-sentence. "Oh Lord! He's bringing them over!" Rapidly grabbing her purse, she was soon checking her lipstick and finger combing her hair.

Julie picked up the large wine list and hid behind it, trying to hide her amusement.

"Hello darl', sorry to be so long," said a male voice, with his back towards Julie. "Look chaps, I'd like to introduce my wife, Zena. Darling, this is Wing-Commander Pryce Crawshaw, Squadron Leader Kingsley Hall, and two chaps from the British RAF, Squadron Leader Graeme McKenzie and Flight Lieutenant Bill Watson."

Julie's wine list dropped from fingers that suddenly seemed to have become as weak as jelly, while her legs and feet appeared to have turned to lead. Her heart began racing and thumping like a two-ton hammer in her chest. She found herself gazing at two very familiar faces, now politely shaking hands with Zena.

Her heart turned over and her insides seemed to have gone into meltdown as she saw the tall, handsome figure of Graeme, in his blue RAF officers' uniform. As though from a great distance, she heard him greeting Zena courteously, his voice mature, soft and cultured, befitting his commissioned rank.

Then she heard Billy echoing Graeme's courteous greeting. Billy's voice, like Graeme's, had matured, but still had its usual appraising tone that he had always used for anything female. With an extra flourish, he bent to kiss Zena's hand and, as he straightened up, his eyes met Julie's.

An unbelieving look of astonishment struck his face, his jaw slackened and he hoarsely cried, "Julie?"

Graeme spun on his heel towards where Billy was idiotically gawping like a floundering fish.

She managed a weak smile. "Yes, it's me. Hello Billy. Hello Graeme."

"I say!" said Kevin, the dinner suited male, "Do you three know each other?"

Zena rose from her chair. "Darling, let me introduce Mrs Julie Field, from New Zealand. She is the 'Top Dog' around here this week. Her company took ALL of the top awards at the Show!"

The RAAF men shook Julie's hand, and Billy and Julie hugged each other. Graeme stood dumbfounded, staring at the vision in front of him. He took both of her hands in his and just continued staring at her. As their hands made contact, Julie could feel that hers were trembling, and she became aware of the electrical charge that ripped right through both of their bodies.

Graeme's whole being filled with the vision of her, she was even more beautiful than he remembered. He just could not speak. The other people, the surroundings, everything around him faded into oblivion. Only the beautiful woman he had always loved and who was now, like a miracle, standing in front of him, came into focus.

Julie was overwhelmed by the sheer magnetism of his physical presence. His deep blue eyes seemed, as in the past, to be piercing her very soul. His skin was deeply tanned, his hair still as blonde. He was tall, broad shouldered and muscular and so, so handsome in his Air Force uniform.

With a realization that hit her like a bolt of lightning, she gazed into his eyes, thinking, 'I've known him most of my life, he is still the only man I'll ever completely love.'

Billy, seeing the immediate chemistry reaction between the two of them, groaned to himself, 'Oh no! Here we go again. Here's trouble with a capital 'T', Billy boy!'

He drew the conversation away from Julie and Graeme, giving them the chance to pull themselves together.

He loudly and enthusiastically explained to the others how they all grew up together in England. "Actually right next door to each other. What a coincidence, eh?" He managed to surreptitiously nudge Graeme in the back. "We're going to have heaps to talk about and catch up on. Ten years of our lives in fact. Aren't we, Sir?—Graeme!" Desperation entered his voice, as he tried to break the spell around Julie and Graeme.

Graeme blinked, reluctantly tearing his gaze away from Julie, trying valiantly to call his military training and discipline to the fore. "Sorry. It's a bit of a surprise, I guess." He smiled gallantly at Zena and Kevin. "We haven't seen each other, for ten years or more. I certainly didn't expect to see Julie in Australia. Forgive my rudeness."

"Look, old chaps," said Kevin, glancing anxiously at his wristwatch, "Zena and I have got to love and leave you, got to catch a plane to Melbourne. Been great catching up with you all again. Enjoy your weekend."

The two RAAF men, realising that the other three wanted to talk, quickly and politely excused themselves, leaving Julie, Billy and Graeme alone on the balcony.

With her heart still galloping at a very fast rate, Julie managed to stammer, "Look at you. You are both senior officers. What are you doing in Australia?"

Billy answered her, for Graeme still seemed to be in a trance. "Well, we're here on a joint exercise with the RAAF We've been in Australia for a week, we leave for the U.K. on Monday. The Country Club have given us a suite and made us honorary members." He glanced around. "Is your husband here?"

"No. John is at home in Auckland. I'm here until the end of next week."

"No kids?" Billy asked very pointedly. Graeme still had not spoken, but continued to gaze longingly at Julie.

"No, not yet." She shrugged her shoulders. "How about you?"

"Gee, well none that I know of!" Billy cheekily responded. "I'm not married, yet. I haven't taken the plunge, like you two." The last words were spoken with a pointed note of warning to them.

Graeme still grasped Julie's hands, overwhelmed that she was miraculously here. His need for her, which had been suppressed for so long, now surfaced as strong as ever.

"Billy, I'm staying next door, the villa 'Rosa'." Julie murmured, not taking her eyes off Graeme. "I'm here alone. I'll take Graeme there, if he wants to come."

Billy knew it was no use arguing, what will be, will be. He looked from one to the other, saw the raw longing in Graeme's eyes, and the soft loving way Julie was looking at Graeme.

"Right, in that case I'll drop his Nibs' gear off there." He ran his fingers through his hair and pleaded, "Well, we have the weekend to ourselves here at the Country Club. You are two grown people. Let me know when you want me, or the Staff Car, to pick you up, Sir.

"You have a Group 'check in', at oh eight hundred hours, tomorrow morning. Savvy? Julie, make sure he makes his call tomorrow. He's our senior ranking officer, and there'll be hell to pay and panic in the streets if he doesn't call in," said Billy, in a resolute voice. "Look, it's great to see you, Julie. Here's my contact number. Right, I'm outa here."

Graeme still looked shell-shocked as he gave Billy a wan smile. "I'll contact you later, Billy. For now, give us some time alone to catch up."

After Billy left, Julie and Graeme just sat holding hands, looking and drinking in the sight of each other.

Graeme softly said, "Oh, my God, Julie, you look so wonderful. I just cannot believe it really is you."

Julie was the first to realise what a scandal it would cause if they were recognised. "Graeme, we have to get out of here, too many people know me."

Gathering up her stole and evening bag, she quickly headed for the beach exit, hoping that Graeme, so conspicuous in his uniform, did not attract any unwanted attention.

Once in the comparative privacy of the beach boardwalk, Julie slowed, allowing Graeme to walk beside her. Hidden in the shadows, under the canopy of a large tree, he gently touched her arm and she turned towards him. Julie was shaking all over as he tenderly took her in his arms and, as their bodies met, she felt his heart beating as rapidly as her own.

As the soft moonlight filtered through the branches of the massive tree over them, he murmured against her lips, "Dear God, Julie, I have missed you so much."

As their mouths touched, gently at first, but soon deeply demanding, with a passion that stunned and staggered them both. The intensity of the chemistry between them was such that their mutual need, hidden for so long, was instantly rekindled. It became a magical ember of fire, fanned to a fever heat of desire, which could no longer be denied.

He held her very tightly against him for a long, long moment, as he murmured, "I have waited so long for this, Julie, my darling."

Returning his kiss with equal fervour, Julie clung to him. A sob escaped her throat as she whispered, "Dearest Graeme, I have also missed you, so very much."

Both of them knew in their hearts that Fate had brought them together again, for whatever purpose, and that neither of them was going to come out of this encounter unscathed.

CHAPTER 22

As soon as they were inside the villa, she turned towards him and he clasped her in his arms, murmuring against her lips, "Dear God, Julie, you'll never know how much I've missed you."

Julie touched his face and tenderly told him, "I still can't believe you are really here."

A thump against the door startled them but Graeme huskily suggested, "That must be Billy with my gear. Are you sure you want me here? If I stay, we both know where it is going to lead. We are not children any more. I want you, as only a man can want a woman." Looking into her eyes, he saw her desire for him mirrored there.

Tremulously, Julie whispered, "Oh, Graeme, that's what I want too. For far too long I've kept up the pretence, of how I felt about you."

Graeme brought his service holdall inside. Billy flashed his headlights before speeding off, muttering to himself, "Good Luck, mate. I've witnessed your loneliness, Graeme, my friend. But, God only knows how this lot is going to end!"

Julie led the way directly to her bedroom. Graeme joined her and kissed her again, gently, lovingly, drinking in the perfume of her.

Julie also knew a feeling of contentment, of just wanting to be close to him.

"You're married, Graeme?" she shyly asked.

"Yes. Her name is Anne. We've been married five years."

"Your career must have really taken off. You have a very senior rank."

He nuzzled her neck, as he said, "It's been hard work, but it has paid dividends. The RAF put me through Cranwell, my degree, a commission, and my flying training. It has helped a little to keep my mind off of you. I finally achieved my secret ambition Julie, my darling, but at a huge cost . . . I lost you. Julie."

She stumbled over her next words, and with a catch in her voice, stammered, "Although I've also realized my secret ambitions, I've wondered many, many times if the heartache of being without you have really been worthwhile . . . Graeme, there's never been anyone like you. You are like my inner being, my soul."

Graeme sighed, "That's exactly how I feel about you, my darling. When I heard about your engagement, I wanted to come and apologise, to tell you how much I loved you. But, shortly following that news, I heard that you were getting married straight away. I guess I was young, naive, actually 'pig headed' is what Billy called me. You had met someone else . . . I didn't know how you felt about me . . . I just couldn't handle it at the time. Maureen knew . . ."

"She was so weepy on my wedding day," Julie recalled. Graeme spoke softly, gently, "I've dreamed of loving you since we were teenagers. I've fantasised about how good we'd be together . . . Julie, I now know I have loved you since the first day I set eyes upon you."

Julie held him close and closed her eyes as he unzipped her dress and let it fall to the floor. When he next unhooked her lacy bra, she heard his indrawn breath of admiration and opened her eyes as he cupped her freed breasts.

"My God, you're beautiful, more beautiful than I had ever imagined," he throatily murmured.

They discarded the rest of their clothing and lay together on the bed. He caressed her breasts as she felt the warmth of her desire for him growing within her. Sensing her arousal, he embraced her and rolled himself on top of her.

Slowly at first, he thrust inside her, deeper and deeper, faster and faster. As she cried out his name, he quickened his pace, keeping up with her urgings. Never in his wildest dreams did he think he would ever find that she would want him so much. She was encompassing his swollen penis with an eroticism he could never have imagined possible.

They both found all of the longing, all of the frustration and denial over the years was about to culminate in a final, mutual, swelling burst. She reached a throbbing orgasm under him as he emptied his seed deep within her. They lay there, sated for the moment, their love for each other consummated at last.

She looked into his dearly loved face and whispered, "I love you, my darling, Graeme. I think I always have."

"Not as much as I you, my precious one," he answered, as he drew her body close and held her.

Taking her breasts in his hands, he began caressing her again, this time taking the time to fully admire her body. She was so sensual, so desirable, even more than he had ever envisaged in every fantasy he had ever had of her.

He remembered the very first time he saw her, as a young girl, twenty years ago. He had known even then she would always be special to him. As he had watched her grow into a vibrant teenager, he found she was always on his mind.

But now, to have her here beside him, responding to his lovemaking with such passion while declaring her love for him, was a fulfilling consummation of all his dreams.

Julie was also admiring his strong and healthy body.

No longer the body of youth but the body of a man, lean, fit and very virile. As his hands explored her body, she found her skin tingling, setting her on fire wherever he touched her. She had known, right from the very beginning, that she had always desired him to be her lover.

Their second coupling was slower, more deliberate. This time he knew that he was even more aroused than the first time but, to his immense joy, her passion matched his own as, in her orgasm, she clutched him with her internal sexual muscles. This gave him such a zenith of erotic pleasure that he felt he would burst. But she gradually released him, allowing him an ejaculation of such exquisite pleasure, deeply within her again.

She whispered, "I have never experienced anything like that before, Graeme, darling. I don't think I have ever felt so completely and wonderfully satisfied."

He kissed her eyes and tenderly smiled at her, "Neither have I, Julie. I think I have been waiting most of my life for this moment."

Sometime later she said, "I can rustle up some supper, the kitchen is well-stocked."

"What a good idea," he agreed. "I'll need to keep my strength up to satisfy my very sexy minx of a lady, won't I?"

As she hung his uniform jacket on a hanger, she tenderly stroked the medal ribbons and the insignia attached to it, before burying her face in his jacket, breathing in the male smell of him.

Watching her doing this small, but so domestic a gesture, he felt that his heart would burst with love for her.

They opened a bottle of white wine and hungrily attacked a pile of sandwiches Julie had rapidly put together. Taking their food out onto the patio, they sat close together facing the sea.

The intervening years had just simply dropped away. They were back to the closeness, the easy mutual understanding of belonging to each other that they had shared in their teens.

A light plane, its strobe light blinking brightly, passed overhead. Graeme automatically looked up and named what type of plane it was.

"Are you a pilot?" Julie asked.

"Yes, I'm an active combat pilot; my rank at present is Squadron Leader. Now . . . that's an idea, how about I take you up tomorrow? Would you like that, sweetheart?"

Julie sighed, "To be with you up there would be just pure magic."

"Well, when I ring in, I'll see if Billy can arrange something."

"Graeme, how come you and Billy are still together?"

"Because, with my rank I get to personally choose my own staff. Billy and I have served together off and on for most of our service."

Julie asked, "I gather you are in charge of the R.A.F. contingent here, but how long are you in the Air Force?"

"I am contracted for virtually the whole of my active working life. I have the topmost security clearance. Hence, I am obliged to regularly check in whenever I am in a private situation, because of the fear of abduction or even assassination."

Julie shivered with horror at his words so he held her close to him, before resuming. "I love what I do and wouldn't want to give it away. Anne, my wife, will never be my soul mate as you are. Her parents left her financially independent and, until now, it has been a convenient marriage for both of us. Neither of us wanted children. How about you? What about your personal and your professional life?"

Julie explained the company structure and added, "The fashion industry is fickle and we have ridden a fine line. The awards we won this week will enhance our reputation one hundred fold, and will probably secure our future." She hesitated for a fraction. "At first I depended upon John more than I ever thought I would. I was alone in a new country; he was virtually the only person I knew."

She took his face between her hands. "I am committed to John, as you are to your Anne. I cannot leave my life without a scandal that could ruin many, many lives. Not yet anyway."

Graeme held her tight against him, kissing her deeply and with passion, before huskily saying, "Then, my darling, we must live for the moments we can share together."

CHAPTER 23

Graeme's personal alarm began a steady, insistent 'beep' at seven o'clock. Attuned to its command, he was instantly awake, but this morning relishing the sweet sensation of Julie's body sprawled beside his.

He gently rolled over to switch the beeper off as she began to stroke him into arousal, murmuring, "More! More!"

"Always willing to oblige, my lady!" he chuckled and proceeded to do so, thoroughly and fully.

Several minutes later, lying there sated and expertly loved, she cried, "Wow! Talk about randy 'flyboys', what a gorgeous way to be woken up." She stretched luxuriously beside him.

Graeme cuddled her to him. "Now, before there is a panic, I'd better make my call." He dialled a number, saying, "McKenzie. Sugar. Lima. Phantom. All AOK, Sergeant. Connect me with Flight Lieutenant Watson, please."

After a few seconds wait, he grinned, "Billy?

Yes, it's a beautiful morning. Yes, she is. I'll tell her you said so. Can you arrange for me to fly with her today? This is the number here." He read the telephone number off, before saying, "Ring us back when it's all set up. Oh! Julie says, will you come back here and join us for lunch . . . Great."

Listening to the one sided conversation, Julie said, in admiration, "You really are 'big brass', being able to organise all of that."

He kissed her again and in a serious tone told her, "God! I'm enjoying this, Julie my darling. I'm so glad we have found each other again."

She looked at him, loving every inch of him so much. "Me too. I love you."

"What shall I wear?" She asked him, standing beside her wardrobe clad only in a lacy bra and bikini panties.

"Trouser suit be okay?"

"Well, it had better be something more substantial than what you have on at the moment! God! How I am supposed to keep my mind on the job, woman!" he groaned.

"I can't help it, I feel like a brazen hussy around you, Graeme McKenzie," she hotly protested.

Taking her in his arms, he softly told her, "Keep on feeling like that. I love it and I love you."

By ten o'clock they were decently attired. Billy took one envious look at the happy pair and ruefully shook his head. He knew he was going to have his work cut out disguising the obvious deep affection between the two of them.

On their arrival at the air base, men everywhere seemed to be saluting Graeme and Billy, which had Julie awestruck. The car pulled into a hangar where several U.S.A.F. personnel were working. Graeme and Billy stood admiring the gleaming Lear jet sitting there. But it was Julie who was greeted by a chorus of wolf whistles, making her blush as pink as her suit.

Billy hooted, "You still blush!"

"Is this the beautiful cookie going with you?" asked a USAF Officer, dripping with gold braid and medals.

Graeme, wearing a wide grin, gallantly answered, giving a wolfish leer, as he remarked, "Rank doth have its privileges!"

Julie asked curiously, "Who owns this plane?"

"The USAF Commander. The one who referred to you as a 'cookie', with all the medals and gold braid that you couldn't take your eyes off, my darling," he answered, with an even wider grin.

Julie was entranced as she watched Graeme competently handling the controls, before he radioed to get clearance for take-off. Suddenly her body was assailed by an enormous push from behind as the aircraft jumped forward. There was a massive acceleration, such as she had never experienced before. The ground flashed by at an amazing speed as they hurtled down the runway. Graeme calmly lifted the plane off the ground, seemingly effortlessly, and they were zooming straight up into the azure heavens.

The joy on his face because he was flying again was completely obvious. He turned to her as she wiped the tears from her eyes. This was his world, his life, his other love.

"You have to see it, have to do it, and have to be up here to know how wonderful it feels, darling. I can see that you understand," he whispered.

Julie nodded, unable to speak. Her heart was so full of loving, tender feelings for him. He took hold of her hand, before he said, "I'd like to share something special with you, my Julie. This is my favourite poem, it was written by another pilot. It describes how I coped during the very lonely times when you were not there . . . It is called 'High Flight' and was written by a Royal Canadian Air Force Pilot Officer, a Gillespie Magee, Junior. He died in 1941.

"Oh! I have slipped the surly bonds of Earth and danced the skies on laughter-silvered wings:

Sunward I've climbed and joined the tumbling mirth Of sun-split clouds—and done a hundred things You have not dreamed of—wheeled and soared and swung High in the sunlit silence, Hov'ring there I've chased the shouting wind along, and flung my eager craft through footless halls of air.

Up, up the long delirious, burning blue, I've topped the windswept heights with easy grace Where never lark or even eagle flew—

And while with silent lifting mind I've trod The high untrespassed sanctity of space, Put out my hand and touched—The face of God . . . ."

Julie's face was wet with tears. In a voice thick with emotion, she whispered, "Graeme. I truly understand, my dearest darling. I'm so happy you let me share this with you."

All too soon it was time to end the idyllic flight. Graeme spoke cryptically to the base Control Tower, giving the plane's call sign, and requesting a landing clearance.

A voice with a broad Australian accent repeated their call sign and asked, "Identify pilot please."

"Sugar. Lima. Phantom," Graeme replied.

With consummate skill, Graeme lined the plane up with the runway and, smooth as silk, brought them down for a perfect, copybook landing.

Taking off his headset, he leaned over and gave Julie a long, loving kiss. "That'll have to hold us, sweetheart, there are too many eyes watching out there."

Julie, overwhelmed with what they had shared together, held his face between her hands. "Thank you, my darling, I'll never forget that poem."

Graeme taxied the plane back to its hangar where a grim faced Billy handed him an official looking paper. Graeme frowned at its contents saying, "I'll go and confirm with them. Right, please take Julie to the car, I'll join you shortly."

"What was that all about?" Julie asked Billy, but could see by the look on his face he was not going tell her.

Trying to make light of the situation, Billy confirmed he had a date for the evening. "Graeme suggested we might attend the Battalion HQ dinner dance. We are expected in full mess kit, so if you have a long dress . . . Crikey! What am I saying! That's your line of business."

Smiling Julie nodded, knowing exactly what gown she would wear that evening, to make Graeme proud of her.

Billy took her hands in his and knew he had to warn her.

"You and Graeme, Julie, be careful. He carries a lot of responsibilities. I can see how much he cares for you and you for him. It's like a searchlight switches on every time you look at each other. But . . . it's not the right time yet for him to do anything about it." His face was sad as he looked into her eyes. "Trust me, Julie. Ahha! 'Ere's his Nibs, looks like we can go. All fixed?" he queried.

"All fixed," Graeme replied. "You were right. Let's face it later. I'm starving! Let's go for lunch, Billyboy!" Graeme sounded cheerful, but Julie saw worry in his eyes.

Remembering Billy's warning, she kept her distance from him until they were free of the base. Once away from there, he laced his fingers through hers and they sat close together.

As Julie gathered up the makings for their lunch, Graeme and Billy sat on the patio enjoying a beer together.

Graeme quietly cautioned Billy, "Don't mention the new orders. I need this time with her, uninterrupted. I have never been so happy in my entire life. I was wrong ten years ago, Billy."

Billy shook his head. "I have to admit it, you definitely belong together, it sticks out a mile. Just be careful though, old friend, our enemies are always close at hand."

"Lunch!" Julie called, as she placed yet another platter of food on the already overloaded table.

"Wow! Not only beautiful, but she can cook as well!" whooped Billy, as he helped himself to the delicious array before him.

The next couple of hours were spent with Julie asking, 'whatever happened to so and so,' or of Billy telling one of his outrageous stories about his and Graeme's exploits. Then, seeing Graeme giving him a pointed look, Billy said, "Well, I'd better get going. I'll pick you up at nineteen hundred hours and arrange for a car to bring my date, Susan Andrews, here?"

As he left, Graeme growled in Julie's ear, "Now we sample the spa bath, my sexy minx." He gave her a lecherous grin. The bubbling water gave an extra sensual, erotic edge to their lovemaking, which quickly reached yet another, very satisfying and highly charged conclusion.

They lingered, their bodies entwined, oblivious to the outside world, exalting in just being together.

CHAPTER 24

Graeme was busy mixing cocktails as Julie stood in the doorway, her heart nearly bursting with love for him, and the handsome, very masculine figure he made in his dress uniform. He caught a glimpse of her in the wall mirror and spun around, staring at the breath-taking vision.

Graeme was standing speechless, so Julie anxiously asked, "Is it okay? It's called 'Blue Heaven', do you like it?"

Clearing his throat, which suddenly seemed to be constricted and dry, in a voice husky with emotion, he managed to say, "Julie, my dearest, you are truly the most beautiful woman I have ever seen. You look sensational!"

"Oh! goodie," she sighed as she clapped her hands in glee. "You do like it. It's the one that won the award last week. By the way, you look good enough to eat."

Putting her arms around his neck, she whispered, "Graeme Stuart McKenzie, I love you, so much."

She pressed closer to him so that could he feel the full, delectable, malleable soft length of her body pressed suggestively against his. They exchanged a long and passionate kiss and he felt a stirring of desire for her begin again, deep in his loins.

"I realise it is a dangerous thing, but I do wish I had a camera," he huskily told her.

"Ah! Wait here, darling." She hurried into one of the other bedrooms and came back with a small camera. "Look, instant pictures, no negatives. That way we can keep them hidden from other prying eyes."

She lined him up against a blank wall and, looking through the lens at the handsome sight, she sighed, "Graeme, I could rush you to the bedroom again! If only there was time!" Catching him with a wicked grin on his face, she snapped the camera. It had captured him perfectly. Her hands were shaking as she looked at it. Now she had proof that it hadn't all been a lovely, lovely dream.

Graeme put his arms around her. "I know what you are thinking, and it isn't a dream. I'm here, darling," he said, as he kissed her again.

He quickly took her photo before he let his emotions get the better of him.

Hearing the sound of a car they hastened to hide the photos. Billy appeared on the patio and stopped dead in his tracks when he saw Julie. His mouth gaped in awe.

"Isn't she something?" Graeme said proudly.

All Billy could say was, "Wow! Wow! Wow! How are we going to get out with our lives when the Yanks see her! They'll lynch us, trying to get near her!"

"Oh! For God's sake, have a cocktail and settle down you two," Julie protested. "You'll have me with such a swollen head."

Graeme grinned as he kissed her on the cheek. "But . . . you do look scrumptious, my darling."

They heard the sound of a car and Billy went out to meet Lieutenant Susan Andrews, his date. She was immaculately groomed in the feminine version of the male dress uniform.

The Battalion H.Q. looked more like a castle than an army headquarters. It sat majestically on the cliff edge, with the open sea pounding on rocks at its base. Huge braziers and torches, giving the impression that they were arriving at Camelot and the court of King Arthur, lighted the entrance.

They were welcomed by a much be-medalled Brigadier, resplendent in his Victorian styled scarlet jacket, and accompanied by his elegantly gowned wife. An obligatory group photo was taken by the army photographer, after Billy discreetly manoeuvred Julie away from Graeme, separating her from him by putting himself one side of her and the Brigadier on the other.

Entering on Graeme's arm, Julie was aware of how glamorous a couple they made. Graeme glanced at her and gave her a conspiratorial wink. Every eye in the large room swivelled towards them as they made their way to their table. In her award-winning gown, she was instantly recognised by many of the women present.

The band struck up a slow fox trot and Billy sucked in a nervous breath as Graeme, with a proprietary gesture, took Julie by the hand and led her onto the dance floor. Their fluid, faultless movements and their immaculate timing drew many eyes.

When the USAF Commander himself came to ask Julie for a dance, Graeme reluctantly reintroduced Colonel Aaron Benedict.

He knew that to allay any suspicions about their relationship, he had to let her go. He sat down grumpily and Billy heard him muttering, "darn that goddam Yank!"

Julie was whisked away by the tall USAF Colonel. She thanked him for the loan of his personal plane that morning. He startled her by gently asking, "You love him very much, don't you? Look, forgive my intrusion; it's my American Indian half talking. You go back a long way?"

"Since we were eight and ten years old," Julie replied.

"Well, what happened, how come you didn't marry?" he queried.

"Oh, it was a stupid misunderstanding, partly pride, stubbornness. We were very young," she attempted to explain. "Is it so obvious how we feel about each other now? If so, it's dangerous for both of us."

"No, be calm, honey, let me explain. There is an aura around you that only my people can read. He still has a very important part to play in his chosen profession. Nothing must interrupt the status quo until he has completed that task. I have only known him for five years, but I know the quality of the man and his work." He paused.

"You were destined to be soul mates, but because of your early split, each of you must now follow your individual star. He is bound to you and you to him. You will find one another again, before long."

They danced in silence for another minute as Julie tried to digest what he had said.

"Well, am I right?" her partner asked.

"Yes, you are right, Aaron. I know I cannot be with him yet. But, it will be a great comfort when he goes away to know that someday . . . I love him enough to let him go, for a while at least. Thank you, Aaron."

Aaron took her back to her table. He kissed her hand and said quietly to Graeme, "Thank you. Take good care of her."

Graeme looked at Julie quizzically, but she mouthed, 'Later'.

The next dance began, and when an RAAF officer came sniffing around, Graeme immediately asked Julie to dance with him, cutting the poor Aussie off mid-sentence!

As he took her into his arms, she whispered into his chest, "Isn't this bliss? I'm so happy."

As the mess dinner progressed, Billy gradually relaxed his guard, nobody seemed to question their unusual grouping. As one officer's wife mentioned, "Perhaps we don't find it so unusual in Australia as so many of us emigrated from the U.K. Most of us still have family and friends back there. Meeting old friends happens all the time in our service lives."

When Billy thought an unwary endearment between Julie and Graeme might cause an eyebrow to lift, he immediately called Julie 'darling' or 'dearest' himself—so that these Antipodeans would think that it was just a 'Pommie' affectation.

The dinner was followed by the inevitable after-dinner speeches. The portly Brigadier gallantly mentioned 'The Ladies' and singled out Julie for special mention, as a 'young and rising star in the fashion world'.

Graeme had been asked to respond to the 'Our Visitors' toast. As he spoke, Julie was once again made aware of how distinguished he looked and his handling of his senior rank with consummate ease. Her throat choked with emotion and unshed tears welled in her eyes. Billy moved his chair closer to her, as he quietly warned, "Hold on, Julie."

When the music began again, with a grin, Graeme whispered, "Do you think we can handle a tango without me making love to you on the floor in front of everyone?"

Trying not to laugh and choking back a lewd response, Julie replied softly, "I think I can wait until we get back to the villa!"

"Jealousy?" he asked, quirking an eyebrow at her.

She nodded. She had waited ten years for this moment.

Graeme spoke to the orchestra conductor. The music from the bandstand swelled and a startled Billy looked at the two of them. "Be careful," he warned.

The opening stanza began as Graeme reached for Julie's hand and they glided onto the floor, in perfect unison to the hypnotic melody. They were oblivious to everyone else as they went through the complicated sensual steps. Other couples gradually stopped and drifted to the edge of the dance floor to watch.

As the music reached its climax, Graeme pressed his pelvis hard into Julie's and bent her into the 'submission' hold before he whipped her upright and claimed the traditional 'victors' kiss. He broke away from her, grinning wickedly, and murmured softly, "Sorry, darling, couldn't resist it."

The whole audience erupted into a wild frenzy of enthusiastic applause, cheering and even whistling their delight.

The band struck up for another tango. This time, as the singer crooned, 'Your eyes are the eyes of a woman in love', they glided effortlessly into the dance again.

Julie was the perfect foil for Graeme's masculine role of the matador as he twisted and bent her, imitating the matador's cape. He threw her away from him one second, and brought her back tight against his body the next. Caught up in the surreal magic of the dance, Julie danced with the suppleness of a Machiavellian rag-doll. It was as though she was held in a hypnotic trance by his deep blue eyes as they penetrated to her very soul.

The dance concluded, this time without the 'victors kiss', but Graeme spun Julie in a final twirl, to imitate the matador's cape. Once again the applause rang out.

With his arm around her waist, Graeme led Julie back to their table asking Billy, "Did we blow our cover?"

Billy shook his head. "Unbelievable! You two dance that tango like it was made for you . . . The Brigadier is departing, so we can leave soon."

CHAPTER 25

Waiting until Billy and Susan were out of sight, Graeme opened the villa door and, gently pulling Julie inside, kissed her with great passion.

"We were terrific, sweetheart!" He discarded his jacket onto the nearest chair. "How about a nightcap? Brandy?"

"I think I'd better get this gown off first." Julie gazed lovingly at him, Aaron Benedict's words echoing in her head. She decided it was time to have a serious talk about a subject that needed to be discussed rather urgently.

Graeme unzipped her gown and butterfly kissed her all the way down her spine. Kicking off her high heels, she stood almost naked in front of him. She turned and kissed him hard, pushing her tongue into his mouth. He clutched her by the buttocks and pulled her against his already stirring loins.

As they parted he looked into her face. There was something troubling her, he could see it hiding there in her eyes.

"What is it, my darling?" he asked gently.

"How do you do that, Graeme McKenzie? How do you read my mind?" she retorted in amazement, as she gathered up her gown and, almost naked, tried to walk with some dignity into her bedroom. "I'll just be a moment."

He made a growling sound at her retreating figure.

"Don't be too long, sweetheart. I have plans . . ." he called as he went off whistling to the kitchen.

Minutes later she came back dressed in a cream silk kimono. Graeme had also changed into his towelling bathrobe and they were both barefooted. As Graeme admired her, he knew she was so womanly, so desirable and for the time being, unquestionably all his. Handing Julie her brandy, they headed for the large, lounge sofa.

He sat as she laid full length upon it, with her head in his lap. "Okay minx, shoot. What's on your mind, darling?"

"I had a very interesting chat with Aaron Benedict. Isn't he a special, intuitive and wise person?"

"One of the best. He is well respected all over the service world. Did he tell you about having Red Indian ancestry?"

"Yes, he did . . ." she broke off. His eyes looked questioningly as he waited expectantly for her to continue.

She decided that there was no need to be diffident about talking to him, she could implicitly trust him and be as frank and as open as she wished.

"Darling, he broached a subject that is getting just a bit urgent regarding you and me . . ." She hesitated, looking at him tremulously.

Softly, she said, "Graeme, he told me, with such conviction that he knows that you and I will be together one day, forever. I want so much to believe that."

He was now holding her so tightly that she was almost in pain. "I've got to believe it, Julie. During the past ten years, my life has been so empty without you to share it with me. Somehow, my dearest love, it has got to happen! What else, sweetheart? There is something else, isn't there?"

She hesitated again and then, taking a deep breath, "I've got to ask, perhaps a painful question. You and Anne have no children, why?"

"My choice, my decision, sweetheart. I didn't want any with her." He kissed her and said softly, "We don't share a bed, haven't done so in years."

"You haven't had a vasectomy?"

"No, darling, I'm still intact. I still live in hope . . ." he broke off and looked deep into her eyes. "Julie, the penny is dropping. We have been making very passionate love. I've not been using a condom. Are you using any birth control?"

Julie shook her head. "I've wanted to tell you all day, but didn't know how to. John is virtually sterile, a rugby injury, just on puberty. I have been on a fertility programme, but it didn't work out. We have been advised to look for a sperm donor. John has told me to go ahead, if that's what I want."

She continued in a whisper. "I have been taking medication to increase my ovulation. "Her voice dropped to an even lower whisper. But . . . I did my sums. This weekend would be the right time in my cycle for me to conceive."

"Julie," he whispered, "darling, Julie, will you have my baby? I don't want to father a child with anyone else but you. Will you allow me to be your 'donor', and give you our child?"

Tears began pouring down her face unheeded as she sobbed, "Oh, yes, my darling. That's what I want, more than anything else in this world."

"Who knows, perhaps we have already done the deed, my darling, but just in case I haven't, how about we spend the next few hours making sure?" He smiled tenderly at her.

He kissed her tears away, as she sobbed, "I thought you'd tell me, no way. You didn't want a child. Darling, Graeme, I love you so much I think I would have gone ahead anyway. If I can't have you by my side daily, at least I'll have a part of you."

He took the brandy glass away. "No more alcohol for you from now on, my darling. Good healthy food only. If I'm to make you a mother . . . Oh, Julie, I love you so much."

"Graeme, I think I've died and gone to heaven, I am so happy."

He kissed her deeply, passionately, gently caressing her breasts and her body through the sensuous silk of her kimono. He picked her up and carried her to the bedroom. "I want to give you my baby, right now," he told her huskily.

They found their lovemaking this time was extra tender, more loving, and each hoping that this would be the time that a new life was created, born of their enduring love for each other.

Afterwards, as they lay close together, Julie was dreamily drowsy, and sated with his love. Graeme, speaking softly, said, "I'll get you my medical history. There's nothing in it, all clear and clean, just records of when and where I have been inoculated, that sort of thing. We need a code signal. Something that will reach me, should you need me at anytime, anywhere. I'll leave you my private, unlisted service telephone numbers. All you'll have to do is leave the code word and I'll contact you."

Julie was silent, thinking for moment, before saying, "Remember the poem today? How about we use the words 'High Flight'? Rather apt, I would say, wouldn't you?"

"Indeed, clever girl!" He rubbed his hands over her abdomen and, in a voice imitating an old movie gangster, he said, "Kid, you gotta smart broad for a mother! Now, how will I contact you, sweetheart?"

"I'll give you my answering service number. They always know where to contact me. Just say 'High Flight' and I'll know it's you."

Just then the phone rang beside them. Julie glanced at the clock, startled, it was after one a.m.! She picked up the phone and said with relief, "It's Billy, for you. He's just got back, there's a message for you."

"Goddamn it, Billy! What d'ya mean, what am I doing?

Well, actually I am trying to make a baby, satisfied?"

Laughing heartily, he held the receiver so that Julie could hear Billy choking, coughing and spluttering, trying to catch his breath.

"Hello Billy, yes, we are rather busy just now, doing just what Graeme said, 'bye." She handed the telephone back to Graeme.

"Okay, I'll be there, goodnight. Yes, I'll tell her and I agree wholeheartedly." He put the phone down. "Billy says you'll make a beautiful mother, darling, and I've got a briefing at eleven hundred hours. Now back to the serious business of making babies. Come here, my darling."

The serious business took a long while as the prospective parents took their time and enjoyed each other for another hour or so, practising.

They lay tightly wrapped around each other as Graeme asked, "How about Lauren?"

Nearly asleep, Julie murmured, "Lovely. She'll be born about February, around my birthday in fact, that makes her born under the star sign of Aquarius."

"Or him . . . maybe . . ." said a drowsy 'paternal' voice.

CHAPTER 26

As his alarm began its morning beeping, Graeme woke in surprise. 'Must be something in this sexual activity that acts as a sleeping pill.'

After doing his check in, he lay beside Julie thinking about becoming a first-time father.

Would John accept the child? Supposing something went wrong? Supposing something happened to him? The longing for her to always be at his side was overpowering. Why don't we just take off somewhere and start a new life together? Perish the thought man, she would never agree to that! What about Anne? Well, be honest, she wouldn't miss him any more than he would her.

Julie felt his kiss giving her, once again, that exquisite sensual arousal. "Ummmmmm, that was delicious," she said, languorously, wantonly, as she lay under him.

"Good morning to you, my sexy darling," he murmured against her ear. "Dear Lord, Julie! I just can't get enough of you—you are definitely good for me. I haven't slept for so long, or felt so well for years."

He kissed her abdomen, saying, "Swim in the right direction fellas. Stay there, darling, give my strike wing a chance to release its missiles on the target."

Giggling like a schoolgirl she mused, not only was he the perfect lover, handsome and intelligent, but he also had such a sense of humour.

"What shall we do today, sweetheart? I have to attend my briefing—which means Billy will be here in a couple of hours. How about I bring him back for a quick lunch and we can borrow the car for the afternoon."

"Oh, wait. I know!" she sighed. "Graeme, there is a very secluded Italian vineyard just up in the hills. It's a magical place, owned by two of the nicest people I know. Their grandchild is being christened in the vineyard Chapel at two o'clock this afternoon. There'll only be family members, we'd be back here by nine o'clock at the latest. It's one of my most favourite places. Would you like that?"

"Yes, dear one, let's do it. Now I had better get ready for Billy." He held her close. "Julie, darling, I'll pack my gear now and Billy can take it back to the base. That way we can forget about tomorrow and enjoy today."

"What time will you be leaving me," she whispered.

"Probably just before midnight tonight, my darling. They secure and lock the base down at least six hours before we take off." He lifted her face between his hands and looked directly into her eyes. "Julie, it's going to be hard saying 'good-bye' for both of us. At least I will have my mind fully occupied getting the detachment airborne. Can you get your friend, Kate, to come back? I would feel happier if I knew that you were not alone, my darling."

As her tears spilled over, he felt an all-consuming sick, leaden, heart-breaking feeling of despair as she cried, "Graeme, how am I going to live without you?"

Holding her close, he let her cry, and when she was quieter, calmer, he said tenderly, "If we really cannot go on, Julie darling, I will come back for you. But, there are other people, other contractual details that must be met. When we do finally come back together, let's do it freely in the knowledge that we have not hurt anyone else."

"That's what my Gran said. She was right, you are right, my darling, but it doesn't make it any easier." She smiled through her tears at him.

Julie went to make them breakfast, 'to keep his strength up' she said, with a giggle. She gently rubbed her abdomen. "Hang in there junior."

When Billy arrived and helped himself to coffee and toast, he enviously studied the pair of them. Graeme was in his shirtsleeves, and Billy had never seen him looking so relaxed, or so happy. Julie was wearing a sundress in primrose yellow, using an equally brilliant gold scarf to tie her hair up in a ponytail. She was barefooted and radiant.

Graeme told him what they had planned, Billy chortled with glee, rubbing his hands together, he exclaimed, "Great, another superb lunch. No wonder you're looking so good, Graeme."

Graeme nearly choked on his coffee as Julie, with a mischievous twinkle in her eye, said, "Gotta keep his strength up."

Billy, not privy to the in-joke between them, said, "I'll arrange some golf with Susan and her father this afternoon." He looked at his watch. "We should be going. I'll put your gear in the car, Graeme."

As Graeme straightened his cap in the mirror, he said quietly, "Ring Kate, please, for me."

She dialled the number. Kate's cheery greeting brought a lump to her throat, making her voice hoarse and croaky. She immediately asked Kate to come back.

"Hey girl! Have you picked up a bug or something? I said you were overworking. Right, I'll be there. Have you rung John?"

Julie was momentarily stunned. John! She hadn't given him a thought since Friday evening! Recovering her wits, she pleaded, "Kate, come as soon as you can, I need you here."

"Yes, of course I will, Jules. Get some rest, Doctor Kate's orders! 'Bye for now, I'll see you tomorrow."

Julie sat with her head in her hands. Ringing John was next. Apart from Graeme, John was the only person who knew her well enough to pick something was wrong. She did not want to alarm him sufficiently so that he would insist on coming instead of Kate.

She dialled her home number. John greeted her, "We are all very excited with the awards. Tried ringing you but got no reply, so guessed you were at the club for dinner. So what's new?"

Clearing her throat, and trying to sound normal, Julie replied, "I wasn't at the Club. I was at a mess dinner at the Army Battalion Headquarters. I wore 'Blue Heaven' and it was a smash with all of the Officer's Ladies. Trouble is John, I think I am coming down with a grotty cold. I've just rung Kate and asked her to come back." she said, trying to sound light hearted. "We have so many orders to follow up. Do you remember Zena from that retail chain in Melbourne? Well, she has more or less promised a big order. Isn't it exciting?" She knew she was prattling, but it was the only way she could cope with her emotions.

John seemed unaware, saying, "Good idea to get Kate back if you are coming down with something. I'll get her on a plane as soon as I can. Stay there as long as it takes, Julie, this is our big opportunity. Anything you need from this end?"

"No, thank you, John, but my mind is running wild with ideas since being at the military dinner . . . Get Kate here quickly."

"Okay, will do. Ring if you need anything else,

'bye for now, take care." John said, before he rung off.

Putting down the receiver, Julie buried her head in her hands. She had got away with it.

She was on the patio putting the finishing touches to the lunch when she heard the car.

Calling, "Out here," the two men joined her. Billy was dressed appropriately for his afternoon game of golf. Julie stood with her hands on her hips, admiring Graeme in 'civvies'. He dropped a soft fawn cashmere sweater on the chair and did an exaggerated twirl, imitating a fashion model.

"Do I pass muster?" he asked, as he put his arms around her and kissed her.

"You look gorgeous. You know you do," she laughed.

Graeme pulled out her chair for her and as she sat down, she found one fresh red rose on her side plate.

He kissed her on the back of her neck, and said, "For my love, with my love."

Billy just grinned goofily at the pair of them, recalling the conversation he and Graeme had before returning to the villa . . .

Graeme had begun, "Okay, what I am about to tell you is extremely confidential. It must never be revealed without either mine or, in the event that I'm no longer able or capable of doing anything about it, without Julie's permission. Savvy?"

Billy butted in. "That baby bit. You guys were joking, weren't you?"

"Should Julie find she is pregnant, the child will be mine," Graeme answered. He briefly described John's problem and of Julie's fertility programme. He continued, "We go on active duty in a few days so just in case something untoward happens in the interim, I am confiding in you Billy. I'm leaving a sealed envelope with my London Solicitor acknowledging paternity, to be opened if I should die, so that my child has a claim upon my estate."

He held his head in his hands, hiding the emotion in his eyes, saying huskily, "She is my lifeblood, Billy. Someday we will be together, forever. We have to go on until all obstacles are removed. We know and accept it could take some time, even years."

Billy stammered brokenly, "If only I had tried harder to persuade you. Neither of you would be going through this agony. You'd be together, happily married, probably with a a whole bunch of kids. Dear God, Graeme! I give you my solemn oath, I'll look after Julie's interests if ever I am called upon, my friend."

"Don't blame yourself, Billy. If I had been stronger or more mature, who knows?" he shrugged. "We were so young, so naive. We thought we had all the time in the world. Don't we all at that age? Come on, let's shuffle it, I can't wait to get back to her. If we pass a florist that's open, please stop."

CHAPTER 27

Billy excused himself and departed for his golfing afternoon. As he strode off, Julie wondered how long it would be before she saw him again. Graeme, sensing her unease, turned her towards him and kissed her.

From her wardrobe, Julie selected a two-piece cream silk suit with a blouson top and a full skirt, and added a bright orange and brown striped scarf.

She grinned cheekily at him, "Well? Will I do?"

"You are definitely safer with your clothes on sweetheart." Crushing her in his arms, he kissed her eyes, her nose and murmured, "I love you so much."

When they reached the sharp hill, Julie told him, "Stop at the summit, my darling."

They got out into a silence so thick it was as though it could be cut with a knife. Suddenly, startlingly, bursting the silence as though pricking a balloon, the air was alive with a cacophony of noisy birdcalls. She led him down the track to a vista that caused him to take in a sharp breath of appreciation.

"Shangri-La, Australian style," Julie informed him, with a sigh. "Isn't it beautiful? I've loved this place ever since I first came here. Maria and

Giovanni Martini, are from Northern Italy, hence the vines. She looks upon me as an adopted daughter and I love her like a mother."

She frowned, "I can't help feeling that something beyond my comprehension is organizing some of my coincidences. Why, at this very special time in my personal calendar have you and I found each other again?"

She paused. "I nearly didn't come to the Country Club Friday. If I hadn't done so, we should have passed like ships in the night." She shuddered.

Graeme put his arms around her, "Thank heavens, something made you, my darling. Even I had almost decided against the Country Club invitation. I still have no idea why I changed my mind. But, sweet Julie, am I glad I did!"

Julie touched his face and murmured, "But that's not all. Add Aaron Benedict's and Maria's words. She told me years ago that John and I would have no children. She said my true love would reclaim me in my fourth decade, and then we'd be together forever. That's twice I've been told that, Graeme darling." She whispered.

Holding her tightly, he said softly, "I've felt since the first day I saw you in your garden twenty years ago that I'd known you far longer. That day I recognised you, I knew you, yet we had only just met. There are some things I never have to ask you, you know already what I'm thinking, and vice versa for you. True?"

She nodded. "Yes, it has always been there between us, a something, an understanding. All I know is that I love you very, very much my darling."

Graeme tenderly kissed her and vowed, "The ending to our story must be a magical life together."

They continued down the hill to the Chateau.

Maria called out, "Si, ma Bambina Julie, she is here!"

"Mama Maria, 'tis me," The women hugged each other, laughing happily. "Oh! I am happy to be here! Giovanni, ma papa." He enfolded her in his huge muscular arms, embracing her, and kissing her on each cheek.

Meanwhile Maria was studying the handsome, tall, fair-haired young man that Julie had brought with her. Her face broke out in a huge smile and she turned and rubbed Julie's abdomen. Speaking in Italian, she said, "Aha, thisa is the real one! You carry his child. Thisa one good enough for my Julie. Thisa one loves her more than himself, or life itself, Capisco, si."

Graeme, to Julie's astonishment, answered Maria in fluent Italian. "Grazie, si. Buon giorno, Signora Maria, Signor Giovanni. Il mio nome e Graeme McKenzie. You are correct this chosen daughter of yours is more than life itself to me. Hopefully, I have sown a good seed and soon she will bring forth, like your best vintage wine, our beautiful creation." Taking Maria's hand he kissed it.

Laughing heartily, Giovanni slapped him on the back. "Come, Graeme McKenzie, you must taste my good red wine, it will strengthen your seed and restore your body. Let our womenfolk talk for few minutes."

Maria looked into Julie's eyes, amongst the glow of love for Graeme she saw pain, as he went off with Giovanni.

"How thisa happened, my child?" Maria asked.

Julie explained Graeme's presence, and added, "I really don't know how I can cope without him."

Maria hugged Julie to her buxom bosom. "I tolda you years ago whata woulda happen. He needs time to come back to you, free. He hasa something important to finish first.

Capisco? You have things to sorta out. It's nota going to be easy for either of you, but you willa nota be alone in your autumn and winter years, he willa be with you. Take heart, my daughter, he willa never stop loving you. Your bambina, she willa be born, Aquarius, si?"

Maria walked Julie into the tiny stone chapel where the rest of the family were assembled waiting for the priest. She was greeted with hugs and kisses befitting a long lost daughter. Like all of the women, she had taken her silk scarf and draped it over her head.

Giovanni and Graeme entered from another door, just as Julie picked up the baby to be christened. Graeme felt a lump catch in his throat and a band of pain clutch at his heart. She looked like a beautiful, eternal Madonna, as she gazed fondly at the tiny bundle in her arms. She looked up at him, tears in her eyes, knowing perhaps he would never see his child this small.

Maria came over, took him by the hand and said softly to him in Italian, "In this life we must have unhappiness to make us appreciate how lucky we are when we are happy. She is yours, she will always be, only yours. Your child will always know how much both her parents love her."

Maria kissed him on both cheeks. "Come, my son, let us celebrate my grandchild's entrance into our Church. The priest is waiting to begin."

Graeme joined Julie and she whispered, "They've asked us to be honorary godparents. How do you feel about that, Graeme?"

"I think it is a great honour, sweetheart. What a caring family they are, and how much they love you, my darling."

Father Francis, Maria and Giovanni's nephew, had flown in specially from the Vatican in Rome to conduct the ceremony. Around the ancient family font, Julie holding the baby, Graeme with his arm around her waist, they gave the chosen names of the child, Rico Milano Vittorio. His parents Bianco and Victor Martini looked on, smiling benignly at their handsome son and his new honorary Godparents.

When the family moved outside at the conclusion of the ceremony, Father Francis touched Julie's arm and said, "Aunt Maria would like me to talk with both of you. Will you stay behind for a few minutes, please?"

"You are both married, but not to each other, although according to Aunt Maria you should be. Well, that's not for me to speak about. Julie, what concerns my aunt is that you feel that you are not strong enough to carry on without Graeme. I can perhaps help you both spiritually."

Graeme answered in Italian for both of them. "Father, it would be an honour for Julie and I to accept your help."

The priest nodded. "Come to the altar, both of you. Join your hands please." He wrapped his sacrament scarf around their joined hands. "Holy Father, bless the earthly love that these innocent children share. Make their love for each other ever stronger so that one day it can be recognised as an everlasting partnership. Bless the unborn fruit of Julie's womb. Make it a strong and true blessing for them both. Give her your support and strength in her time of need. Amen."

He removed the sacrament scarf, saying softly, "A depth of love for each other, such as yours, is rare, and it deserves fulfilment. When both of you are free of encumbrances, and if you are still of a like mind, I would like to be the one to marry you. I am returning to Italy, but my Uncle Giovanni will know where to find me. I'll leave you now to perhaps speak together, make some vows before God. Take heart Julie, you are never alone. In your minds and in the eyes of God you are already joined as one." Smiling gently at them, he quietly left the Chapel.

Graeme gazed with wonder into Julie's eyes. "I feel like I have just been married to you, darling."

"Yes, Father Francis's blessing feels to me like he was as good as saying 'let no man put asunder.' Oh, Graeme my love, I do love you," Julie replied.

Taking her hands in his, Graeme looked deeply into her eyes, as he promised, "Julie, I pledge to you when we are free and able to do so, I want to make you my wife for as long as we both shall live. Here, before the altar of God, I plight thee my troth."

Julie replied, "Graeme, I also pledge to you when we are free, I want you to be my husband for as long as we both shall live. Here, before the altar of God, I plight thee my troth."

Graeme gathered her in his arms and they sealed their pledges with a tender kiss. Maria and Giovanni, hidden in the shadows at the back of the Chapel, left quietly, tears of joy pouring unheeded down Maria's cheeks.

One of the many Martini uncles brought out a piano accordion and couples began dancing. Graeme held Julie close as they danced to all of the old tunes of Italy.

Introducing his niece, Leah, Giovanni announced, "This is for our dearly loved Julie and Graeme. Leah will sing two songs from 'Kismet' especially for them."

A short while later Maria came over, "You two are excused. You needa time alone together. Go in peace my darlings. Don't leta it be too long before we see either of you again."

Stopping at the top of the hill they turned to each other and exchanged a deep, passionate kiss.

Holding her close he softly told her, "In Maria's language, Dio come ti-amo, cara mia . . . Oh God! How I love you, my darling."

CHAPTER 28

As soon as they were safely inside the villa, he reached for her and kissed her tenderly.

In a quiet, calm voice he explained what he had arranged. "Darling, on your dressing-table you'll find my private telephone numbers. We'll use 'High Flight' as our code word. Now that he knows about us, Billy will always know where to find me. This morning I wrote to my London solicitor . . . Well, just in case, darling."

Julie gulped back a sob. "I know I am going to be good for nothing for a while, but Kate will be here. Oh, Graeme, I do love you so."

He knew he must not break down, although his heart felt as heavy as a lead boulder. He stepped out onto the patio to stand gazing up at the stars, trying to come to terms with the reality of leaving her.

Julie came looking for him after changing into her cream kimono. Gathering himself, Graeme followed her into the lounge. She said, with a gentle smile, "Maria implied we would have a daughter, didn't she? Are you happy with the name Lauren? Or how about Bernadine? Hey! But just supposing he's a he, and not a she?" She giggled as she rubbed her abdomen.

Matching her mood, knowing she was trying to make light of the situation, he smiled broadly, "I like all of the names, but if we've made a son, perhaps Stuart, Cameron or Andrew?"

She kissed him gently, saying, "I promise." She took off her kimono. "Now I want you to love me, one more time, Graeme, my darling."

He caressed her naked breasts, feeling her desire for him in her swollen and erect nipples. Her bare skin was tingling both at his touch and with desire for him. Graeme carried her to the bed.

Her eyes were dark with passion, gazing unfocused and wantonly up at this man she desired and loved, more than life itself.

He huskily murmured, "Dear God, Julie you are so beautiful. My darling, I love you so much."

Not giving her time to answer, he slowly thrust himself fully into her, and she held him tightly, deeply within her. He could feel himself swelling inside her, growing larger and longer than he had ever been in his life. At her urgings, he quickened his thrusts. At the point when he felt he was about to burst, she climaxed under him. He plunged deeply one final time and, with an exquisite sensual shudder, he released his seed into her, calling her name as he did so.

He laid his head on the pillow beside hers. "My darling, Julie, I shall never forget this wonderful day for as long as I live . . . Maria, Giovanni, and the gorgeous sight of you holding the baby. That whole wonderful family who love you so much."

They lay wrapped tightly together, hardly daring to move, until they both knew the inevitable time had come for him to leave. After kissing her ardently and deeply, he went into the bathroom to shower.

Graeme came and handed her a small gold brooch. "Give this to our child when you decide the time is right, darling. Let our baby know its father will always deeply love its mother, that it was a very much-wanted baby, and was conceived with undying love. And that one day we shall all fly—together."

The brooch was a solid gold miniature of Graeme's 'wings'. 'G.S.McKenzie' was engraved on its back, together with the R.A.F motto 'Per Ardua ad Astra'.

He clasped her tightly in his arms. "It's time, Julie, sweetheart. Don't come out to the car. I love you, Julie, with my heart, my soul, my very being. One day I will claim you again, truly as all mine."

Their final embrace and kiss was long, lingering, and tenderly loving. He quickly broke away from her arms, and hurried out of the door—unable to look back.

Seconds later she heard the car accelerating away.

Staggering, as though she had drunk too much wine, she fell onto the bed that they had so recently shared. She could still smell the spicy aroma of his aftershave on the pillows, and the musky smell of their sexual love on the sheets.

Sobbing pitifully like a wounded animal, she rolled herself into the foetal position.

The ringing of the telephone startled her awake and she looked with disbelief at the clock beside the bed. It was dawn!

A quiet voice, with an American accent, said, "Julie, it's Aaron Benedict. Would you like to come here to the base and see the R.A.F. squadron fly out? I can send a car in about an hour for you."

"Oh, yes please, Aaron. Thank you."

Running into the bathroom, she looked in the mirror and saw, with a shock, her swollen red eyes.

"I can't let anyone see me like this," she moaned into the mirror. After half an hour of facial 'first aid' and a shower, she felt she was passable once more.

There was a soft knock on the door. To her surprise, Colonel Aaron Benedict himself was standing there. "I thought it would cause less fuss if I came myself," he explained. "We'll get right through all of the security checks without questions if I'm with you."

He smiled warmly at her and helped her into a covered Jeep. "Mind you, I don't know what it'll do to my reputation, being seen with the glamorous friend of the dashing R.A.F. Squadron Leader! It'll certainly earn 'Old Thundersides'—that's my nickname, the one that I'm not supposed to know about—many brownie points with my staff."

In spite of her heartache, Julie smiled, grateful for him showing her such kindness and understanding.

At the base, she saw the security had been really stepped up. There were guards and Military Police everywhere. The sentry gave his senior officer a snappy salute, but his eyes nearly popped out of his head at seeing Julie in the passenger seat.

Laconically Aaron returned the man's salute, before drawling, "Just pass us through, Sergeant, and put 'em back in your head, son."

The guard obviously phoned ahead because at the next checkpoint there was a knot of several uniformed USAF officers watching the progress of the jeep. Aaron chuckled, "Told ya, be all over the base within the hour. Servicemen are notoriously the worst gossips in the world. That's why Graeme asked me to bring you out here. He knew that if he had done so, well, who knows what damage it might have done."

Julie's eyes lit up. "Graeme asked you to bring me?"

"Yep. He's waiting in my office, right this way."

Aaron opened a door in the far corner of the building, and gently pushed her inside. Graeme, already dressed in his flight suit, caught her as she launched herself at him.

His arms closed around her soft, beautiful body and he whispered, "I just had to see you once more, to see if you were okay." Searching her beloved face, he could see the dark smudges and the redness under her eyes.

"We only have a minute, darling," he told her.

"Aaron met me last night when I got back and we had a long talk. It settled my mind. I'm about to be sent to Africa on active duty, there's big trouble looming there. If you need me, send our code, I'll get it within hours. I will come immediately. Promise me, my darling."

"Yes, Graeme, darling," she murmured, "I promise that if ever I have to send you a message, it will be urgent. I will not cry wolf."

There was a discreet knock and Aaron put his head in. "Sorry, folks, time to go."

They kissed and held each other tightly one more time.

Graeme got into a jeep and was driven to a distant hangar. Aaron and Julie headed for the Control Tower.

The place was a hive of bustling activity. Aaron steered her over to a window, where she could see the RAF squadron of fighters lined up.

Aaron explained, "Graeme is in the lead aircraft. His call sign is, Sugar Lima. Flight Lieutenant Watson is the Point Man, front and right. His call sign is Leader One. When a squadron leaves a foreign friendly base they all take off together, in our case left to right. They climb and circle left before flying in a low formation pass over the Control Tower. Graeme, as their senior officer and leader, will fly slightly above his squadron and will dip his right wing in salute as he passes the tower." He turned to an airman beside them. "Patch us into the Squadron Leader, Captain please, and give Mrs Field a headset."

"Ma'am," a young airman grinned and passed Julie a headset. She could hear English accented voices saying, "Roger that, Leader One", and suddenly the whole squadron was moving.

The cryptic talk between aircraft continued and she heard Graeme giving his call sign, "Sugar Lima, clear for take off . . . Affirmative . . . Let's roll, gentlemen."

Led by Graeme, the squadron lifted off just as Aaron had described.

She silently told her unborn baby, 'He loves us both so much, we have to get along without him for a while. We have got each other, he is the one that is so alone.'

The headset crackled as she heard his voice saying,

"High Flight, take care. Fare thee well Australia, Sugar Lima, out." He dipped his right wing in salute and soared up to lead his squadron.

The Control Tower answered, "Godspeed, Phantom."

Julie whispered, "Oh! I have slipped the surly bonds of Earth." Her eyes followed them until they were small dots, rising so high in the clear blue sky . . . and then they were no more.

CHAPTER 29

Aaron led her back to the jeep in silence. He knew she was incapable of talking, and would be desperately trying to hold herself together.

When they arrived at the villa, she smiled weakly at him, expecting him to drive away.

He shook his head, "I'm going to stay with you for a while. When does your friend arrive from New Zealand?"

"About five o'clock."

"Right, go to bed and rest, I am going to mix you a special old American-Indian remedy. It'll help relax you, make you sleep for a while. Give that baby a chance to rest up." Seeing her startled look, he said, "Yes, he told me about that."

"I'll be catching up with some paperwork out here on the patio, and will wake you at four o'clock. I'll leave before she gets here." He took out his wallet. "Julie, honey, here's my card it contains all of my contact numbers, should you need my help at any time."

"Aaron. I cannot thank you enough. It has helped me considerably," she said wearily.

"Honey, it's my pleasure. Go, get into bed and I'll bring my ancient medication to you."

In less than an hour she was sleeping deeply and peacefully. At precisely four o'clock Aaron Benedict gently woke her and quietly took his leave.

Hearing a car door slam, she heard Kate's happy greeting.

"Hello, hello, Julie! 'Tis only I come to rescue you!" Kate's high heels click, clacked in, then she saw Julie's face. "Jules! You look awful! Well, I'm here now, so come on, back to bed, mother hen's orders."

"Katie, Katie, I'm so glad you are here," Julie sobbed. "Oh Kate! I think I'll burst if I don't tell someone soon."

"What on earth has happened to get you into this state? Julie, what is it?" Puzzled, Kate looked closely at the ravaged, red-eyed face.

Julie smiled weakly. "It hasn't all been a disaster; in fact it has been the most wonderful couple of days of my life."

She left Kate speechless, stunned by this contradiction of terms. Julie then told Kate about her unbelievable weekend. Kate was staggered by what she was hearing. On Julie's face was a look of total adoration as she softly spoke his name. Kate told herself, 'I was right! I always knew there was more to that Graeme fella than meets the eye.'

Kate listened, heard the longing in Julie's voice, and said softly, "You obviously love him deeply and have done so for such a long time, Jules. What a brave pair you are to let each other go again. I don't know if I could've found the strength to do that."

"It's just not possible for us to be together at this time, Kate. He has responsibilities to think about way beyond our relationship. I too have lesser responsibilities to John, to you and the Company, but responsibilities nevertheless."

She looked nervously at her friend. "Kate, there is something else I'm going to need some support for . . . Kate, I'm ninety-nine per cent sure I'm pregnant."

"Wow! Jules! Gosh! After what you have told me, it'll truly be a love-child." Kate hugged her friend asking, "Will you still visit Andrea Martin?"

Julie nodded, "I still need to see Dr Martin, need her advice. Wait, I almost forgot, I do have a photo of Graeme. We secretly took one of each other Saturday night."

She extracted the photo of Graeme from the sycamore trinket box.

"Wow! What a peach! He's certainly a handsome dog, Jules." In her own mind, Kate wondered how Julie had managed to live with grumpy old John for so long, when this handsome and distinguished looking man had been hiding in the back of her heart and mind for so many years.

"I wore 'Blue Heaven' that night. He loved it, I shall never part with that dress, it holds too many wonderful memories for me," sighed Julie.

Kate took Julie's hands in hers. "Julie, I'll always be there for you. I'm truly happy for you."

"Oh Katie! I'm so glad you feel that way. I thought you might tell me what an adulterous, wicked person I'd been." She shrugged. "I know John will be difficult and I cannot really see much of a future for us—and who can blame him. I realise I have loved Graeme since the day I first met him, when we were just children. I don't know, I just feel so complete when I'm with him."

Kate didn't answer, she just hugged Julie, she was too choked with emotion to speak.

Later Kate telephoned her husband, Harry. She asked him to pass on the message to John that Julie was a bit 'under the weather', and they would be staying until possibly Friday. She warned her husband, "There is more to it than that, but it'll keep, Harry, dear. Julie really needs me here."

Next morning, Kate rang Andrew Martin and arranged to meet him at his sisters' clinic later that morning.

Julie was nervous and apprehensive when they arrived at the elegant, modern clinic. To her immense relief, Dr Andrea Martin was a caring, female version, of her older brother Andrew. She greeted Julie with a wide, warm smile.

"Please, call me Andrea. What a successful week you have had, Julie m'dear. My congratulations to you. Have you been following the charts I've sent you?"

"Yes, religiously, Andrea. But . . . there has been a rather startling development over the past weekend." Julie blushed, not knowing where to begin.

"Wouldn't have something to do with a rather dishy RAF officer, by any chance?" Andrea Martin asked, with a merry twinkle in her eye. "Oh! Look, I'll put you out of your misery. I was at the Army Mess Dinner Saturday night. I saw and heard your story from an RAAF friend, when you were brilliantly dancing a very sensuous tango with that handsome young pilot. I heard all about you having known each other since you were children and hadn't seen each other for, what was it, ten years?"

Andrea continued, "I didn't come over and introduce myself as it was obvious to me that you two were really enjoying each other's company. I am an inveterate observer of people, Julie."

She paused and gestured with her hands. "Personal matters are safe with me. So . . . would it be presumptuous of me to ask, might you already be pregnant, Julie?"

Staggered by the good doctor's revelations, Julie could only gulp, nod and utter, "Well, there's no use beating around the bush. If the calculation chart is accurate, and the medication you prescribed for me has worked—then yes, definitely."

"Julie, he is obviously very fit and healthy—otherwise he wouldn't be holding the rank that he does. He is also very good-looking, with the mix of his colouring and yours it should make for a very handsome baby. Genetically, observing the pair of you, I couldn't have found a better donor for you."

"I know his blood group and his medical history. I can get the official version from him, if it is needed," Julie said, feeling she must justify herself to this kindly woman. "I love him dearly, Andrea, I always have. It wasn't just a weekend fling. It was something we should have settled between us ten years ago. He is an honourable man and he will legally acknowledge his paternity. I know he wants this child as much as I do. It's not something we wish to hide, but circumstances force us to do so, for the time being."

"Julie, let me examine you. You came here expecting to be impregnated by an unidentifiable sperm donor. Until the pregnancy is confirmed, say nothing. When it is, we'll discuss what to do then."

Dr Andrea Martin ran Julie through the full gamut of tests, taking samples of her blood and other bodily fluids. At the end of a full half hour, she told Julie, "You are as healthy as you can be, Julie. Although it is far too early yet to say one way or the other, I'd say it is very likely that you are pregnant."

Julie's face beamed, "That's just what I wanted to hear, Andrea. Thank you."

"Keep in touch, although I dare say that brother of mine won't be able to keep quiet about you. He really cares for you, in a very nice paternal way. Tell him your story, you'll find you have a staunch ally there. All we can really do now is—wait and see."

Coming out to the waiting room she found both Andrew and Kate looking anxiously at her.

"All's well." Andrea Martin assured them. She patted Julie's shoulder, "Take care."

A happy Julie took Andrew's arm. "Andrew, your sister is an angel and I have something, on her advice, to share with you . . ." As Andrew escorted them to his Club for lunch, Julie explained and added the strange coincidence of his sister also being at the Army mess dinner. Hearing Kate's audible gasp of breath, Julie laughed, "She'd already put two and two together Kate, when she saw me with Graeme. I'm probably already pregnant, which I'm absolutely deliriously happy about."

Andrew took Julie's hand in his. "It goes without saying Julie, m'dear, you have my unequivocal support. I will be there for you, always."

Julie thanked them both. "Your friendship and support will help act as a buffer between the loneliness of not having Graeme at my side, tempered with the absolute joy of having his child growing inside me."

After leaving Andrew, Julie and Kate were gazing absently at the shop windows, when Julie suddenly stopped. Almost hidden at the back of one window display was a very handsome, small dark green leather chest with a curved lid, rather like a pirate's chest. But, what had caught her eye was the tooled, sycamore leaf pattern, carved all over the chest.

Grabbing Kate's arm, she exclaimed, "That's just what I need, something to store memorabilia for my baby, as a reminder of who its father is."

The elderly shop owner informed her the box was over one hundred years old. He showed her two secret hideaway places, a false bottom and a cunning device in the curved lid.

The whole concept enchanted Julie, who immediately fell in love with the unique box, and happily paid the modest purchase price.

CHAPTER 30

For the next two days Kate and Julie answered numerous telephone calls, quoting, pricing and writing up specific orders. They found themselves literally running through the airport concourse to catch their flight home.

Once home, she told John "I saw Dr Martin we'll know in about a month if I'm pregnant."

"Well, that's what you wanted, Julie."

Julie was shocked by his tone of indifference. "John, have you changed your mind?"

He laughed. It was a sneering, unpleasant sound. "Good God! No! I'd be delighted if it'll keep you at home. You must have had your fill of the publicity and hype. You'll be ready enough to settle down and play little mother now, wont you? Oh, by the way, you'll see some differences around here. I've moved my stuff into the blue room so that you, and . . . your child . . . can sleep in peace."

He downed his drink in one gulp. "Right, I'm off to the Club. Don't wait up for me.

"Jules, I've got something to show you," Kate pointed to a magazine. "This is an advance copy which will be on the stands next Monday."

The glossy Australian magazine carried a cover picture of Gloria wearing 'Blue Heaven', with the caption 'Design Winner's Heavenly Choice, see page 11'. On that page was the group photo taken at the Army Mess Dinner. The caption read:

"Seen at the monthly Army H.Q. Mess Dinner. The designer herself, Mrs Julie Field from Auckland, New Zealand, wearing her Fashion Week winning creation 'Blue Heaven'. Julie Field is flanked by (from left) Brigadier J. Harrison, Flight Lieutenant W. Watson, Mrs J. Harrison, Lieutenant Susan Andrews and Squadron Leader G.S. McKenzie."

Julie gently stroked the photograph. "It was a night to remember, Katie. Doesn't he look gorgeous?" She sighed.

Kate peered closer at the magazine photo. "No wonder the dishy Squadron Leader couldn't keep his eyes off of you. You virtually created that dress for him!"

Three weeks later, Kate and Julie were on the stile at the top of the hill when Julie said, with a giggle. "How do you reckon a label reading, 'Growing Flowers of the Field' will go down in the Maternity section?"

"Maternity! Are you . . . are you sure?" Kate took one look at Julie's glowing face and nodded. "Yes! You're sure! Yippee! So when are you due?"

"About my next birthday. So what d'you think?"

"With you designing it, it'll be a certainty." Kate hugged her friend. "Have you told John yet?"

"No, not yet . . . Kate, he's drinking again, and I know his Mum and Dad are worried about him," she said quietly. "He moved himself into the blue room."

Kate and Harry had already observed John's strange behaviour around Julie and mutually decided to keep a close eye on the situation.

For the following two weeks Julie spent much of her spare time working on maternity designs.

John watched all of this new activity with sardonic looks, and with more than his usual cynicism.

Now almost twelve weeks pregnant, Julie was working quietly in her studio, finalising the working patterns for her maternity collection. She looked up startled as she heard John's car roar up to a wheel-skidding stop outside their front door. A glance at the clock showed it was only three o'clock in the afternoon.

The front door swung open and crashed with a splintering crack against the hall table. Then she heard John yelling, "Where are you, you dirty, cheating whore!"

He bullocked his way down the hall to her studio as Julie crouched defensively behind her design easel. Smashing his way through the door, Julie saw his reddened face contorted with rage.

His eyes were bulging, spittle was dribbling down his chin, as he roared at her, "You whore! You're another man's whore! Sperm donor, eh? I bet he enjoyed himself giving you that little implant, you bitch!"

He threw a letter at her. "Read that, my high and mighty, Julie. It was delivered to my office at lunchtime today. You disgust me!" He stumbled from the room, yelling, "I need a drink."

Julie picked the letter and the nausea in her throat rose, she saw that the letter was signed 'Anne McKenzie'.

It began:

"My dear Mr Field, My name is Anne McKenzie and I am married to Squadron Leader Graeme McKenzie.

He and your wife Julie spent an adulterous weekend together in the Villa Rosa, at the Country Club in Sydney.

They were seen on several occasions by a reliable witness in what can only be described as 'compromising situations'. They were observed looking at each other in my witness's words 'as though they were deeply in love and as though they couldn't keep their hands off each other.'

I have confronted my husband with the facts, which he does not deny. I have warned him that if he has anything more to do with your wife, or even attempts to contact her again, I will go public with all of the dirty, degrading and sordid facts I have been given.

I will drag her name as the 'other woman' in a very messy divorce settlement. I will ruin him totally, by ending his career, making sure that at the same time her precious reputation would be in tatters as well.

So Mr Field, I suggest you confront your disgusting wife, and if she is with child, as I understand could be the case, you should perhaps give her an ultimatum. You should demand she have an abortion, and also have absolutely no further contact with my husband.

Should the child be allowed to live and any attempt is made, either by his bastard or your whore of a wife to contact my husband, I will publicly inform the child as soon as it is old enough to understand, that it is the product of an adulterous, dirty weekend between two evil, cheating people.

I await your comments, Anne McKenzie.

"Oh, My God! Oh, My God!" Julie cried out.

Julie was clutching her abdomen when John stormed back into the room. "That's it, protect the little bastard. You're having his child. I thought I could see something more in that Australian magazine photo, but I certainly didn't expect to see him reach such a high rank. It'll kill his precious career if this gets out, won't it?"

He raged blindly as Julie fought for control over her shivering and shaking body.

"One night stand was it? Did he think you were fair game, eh?" John stormed around the room, angrily knocking over furniture in his path. "Alone in a strange country, thought you'd be a tasty bit on the side away from home, did he? Or have you always had the hots for him, eh? You even kept the precious trinket box he gave you. Oh how that has always galled me."

He spun around to face her, his anger turning his face beetroot red. "Was it planned? You disgusting cheat! Sperm donor. Boy! I fell for that one, hook, line and sinker. And I trusted you, Julie, when you wanted to go to Dr Martin's Clinic."

"I cannot kill my child, John. It is still half mine. "Julie pleaded, John, it wasn't like that . . ."

"So, give me one good reason why I don't just throw you and your baggage out the front door," he yelled at her at the top of his voice. "How far do you think you'd get without my support, eh?" He slammed his glass down.

Julie looked at him in alarm. "I don't think you can do that John. I understood you and your parents gave me this house and the land as a wedding present."

He smashed his fist into the door. "So give me a good reason why I shouldn't bugger off and leave you to stew in your own juice, eh?"

"That'll be another of your choices, John," she said in a low, cold voice. "You've already moved yourself into another bedroom, without consulting me first."

More in control of herself now, thinking clearer, she tried to reason with him. "John, I do understand your anger. You have every reason to rant and rage at me, but even if it had been an unknown donor, you still wouldn't have accepted it, would you?"

He laughed; a cruel, sardonic, crowing hoot. "Isn't that ironic? It was me that gave you my permission to go to Dr Martin, remember?"

Julie faced him, her voice icy with anger. "Yes, you did. You gave your permission, but be honest John, you were playing games of your own, weren't you? You wanted me pregnant . . . to keep me at home. Wasn't that your real reason?"

He yelled, sneering into her face, "You have committed adultery. Oh God! I've had enough of this. You are still in my eyes another man's whore!" With that he slammed out of the house.

Julie heard his car skidding and slipping at high speed down the drive.

Julie rang Kate and tried to hide her concern, but Kate knew her too well. She picked up the panic in Julie's voice as she was told about the letter from Anne McKenzie.

"I'll be there in half an hour. Go up the hill until I get there, Jules, in case John returns."

Julie made her way to her favourite place and vowed to the heavens, "I cannot give our baby away, my darling Graeme."

She sat shivering upon the stile, waiting for Kate, her mind in turmoil. Who could have told Anne? It had to be someone at the Army Mess Dinner, but who? In her head she heard again the voice of Aaron Benedict and his words 'servicemen are notoriously the worst gossips in the world'.

Anne's letter was surprisingly venomous. Did Anne really care for Graeme after all? Or was she just feeling socially compromised? Then Julie saw car headlights coming up the drive. Kate had arrived.

CHAPTER 31

Kate clasped her distraught friend to her, assuring her, "Jules, I'm here, my dear friend. You can come home with me if you'd rather, or I can stay here with you."

"Stay with me, Kate. This is my home, it's where I want my baby to grow up." Julie sank wearily onto the sofa.

"What exactly has happened? You weren't very coherent on the phone, Jules."

"John has received a letter from Anne McKenzie. Someone has told her about seeing me with Graeme in Sydney. She's given an ultimatum, demanding I have an abortion and no further contact with Graeme. Otherwise she'll go public and destroy us both. John was very, very angry, he . . . called me names . . . horrible names."

Julie looked down shamefaced, unable to meet Kate's eyes. "I can't have an abortion. I need this baby so much."

Kate wrapped her arms around her distressed friend. "Oh, Julie. I told you at the start I'd always be here for you. From what you have told me, Graeme would want you to keep your baby."

Julie nodded positively, "Yes, Kate, that's exactly what he would want."

Kate mused aloud, "John cannot just walk away, we are all equal partners. I also wonder what Naomi and George would think of it. They've always supported you, Julie. Might be a good idea to talk to them."

"No, first John and I must come to an agreement Kate. I must make sure Anne McKenzie doesn't destroy Graeme. I shall have to agree . . . not to contact Graeme again." Having said the fatal words, forced painfully from her mouth as though speaking through a fiery, red-hot toothache, she gulped, "We're a long way from the U.K. Hopefully, Anne will let sleeping dogs lie."

Kate was anxious to persuade her to rest, and reluctantly Julie agreed. "I'll not be able to sleep, Kate."

Kate grinned and giggled, "Well, I'm no good at singing lullabies, and I'm not going to read you a story, but I'll sit on the bed and talk to you. How about that?"

An hour later they heard John's car racing up the driveway. As he slammed the front door, Julie winced and tensed, waiting for another verbal onslaught.

But John had obviously seen Kate's car in the driveway, and went straight into his own bedroom, slamming the door noisily.

"Well, that settles that. I'm not leaving," Kate said, in a resolute voice. "Move over, I'm sleeping with you tonight."

It was dawn when Julie awoke. Her thoughts were how she must make sure Graeme was protected, and how she must resist any attempt by John to force her to abort her child.

Kate stumbled, still half asleep, out to the kitchen.

"Oh, so you're still here are you? Still blindly supporting the dear, virtuous friend?" sneered John, as he came into the kitchen, unshaven, dressed in clothes he had obviously slept in.

Kate almost felt sorry for him. He looked so beaten and pathetic. "You have got to come to some sort of agreement John. Otherwise you'll destroy what all four of us have worked for over the years."

He snorted, with a cynical laugh, "Pity your pure friend didn't think of that before she committed adultery, eh?"

Kate winced at his harsh words, but soldiered on. "She really cares for Graeme. You know your wife better than that, John."

He did not answer, so Kate pushed on. "What I have heard of this man proves he isn't the type to undertake infidelity lightly. He's a senior officer for God's sake! We all have a lot at stake here. All of us, John. Not just you and Julie. Harry will be home later today. Let's try to thrash out an agreement."

John looked at Kate and she saw the pain in his eyes. "Will she give him up, Kate?"

Kate nodded, "Yes, I'm positive she will. If she can be assured no scandal will affect him."

"She won't abort the baby, will she?"

"No, John. On that she's adamant."

"Will she stay here? Does she want to go, or for me to leave?"

"She wants to stay. We need her talent, John. She's the inspiration that keeps the rest of us afloat."

"Whatever happens, Kate, I'll never forgive her. It goes too deep." He left the kitchen.

Kate breathed a long, deep breath, telling herself, 'Well, it's a start.'

Taking tea into Julie, Kate said, "You are both going to have to compromise. He needs something, some incentive to stay in a house with another man's child."

Julie implored her friend, "I'll do anything he wants in order to protect Graeme and my baby, Kate."

"Yes, Jules. When Harry gets home we'll sit down and work something out."

"I don't want Naomi and George brought into this, Kate. The least number of people that know who's my baby's biological father the better."

Kate rummaged in Julie's extensive wardrobe for some fresh clothes to wear.

"Help yourself, Kate. I can't get into any of them at the moment, anyway," Julie said, with a wry smile.

When she met her husband several hours later at the International Airport, Kate rapidly filled him in on the upsetting news.

He gave a long-suffering sigh, resigned to the part he would have to play in the unpleasant task ahead. "Yes, my love, let's go and try to make some sense of this messy business."

Arriving at Julie and John's home, Kate was startled to see the house was a blaze of lights. Then they heard John's voice yelling for Julie. Flinging open her car door before Harry had fully braked, she ran to the house, crying, "Oh No! Julie! Julie! Where are you?"

"Kate! It's okay!" Harry called. "I just saw her in the headlights. She's coming down the hill. I'll go inside and try to reason with him. Keep Julie out here until I calm him down."

Kate hared up the path towards Julie, who calmly greeted her friend, not looking at all distressed. "Hello, Katie, is Harry with you . . ."

She stopped as she saw all of the house lights were on and could hear John's voice loudly exclaiming, "Where is she? Have you spirited her away? Where is she, Harry?"

Harry answered calmly, "She's here, John. She's coming in with Kate. Calm down old chap."

As Julie and Kate entered the lounge, John almost sobbed at Julie, "I came home, and there wasn't a light on in the place. I thought you'd gone . . . Oh, my God! I thought you'd gone."

Surprised at the pain and the panic in his voice, Julie stared at him, puzzled by his tone.

Harry took charge. "Let's sit down, my friends. John, we must talk this problem through. As I understand it, you have an ultimatum from Mrs Anne McKenzie. Julie, you have no wish to have an abortion, correct?"

Julie nodded, "Absolutely correct. I'll do anything else John wants, but I keep my baby."

Turning to John, Harry asked, "What do you want from Julie, John?"

"No further contact with McKenzie, of course."

Julie responded, "I'll agree to that. I want to notify him when the child is born, just the birth notice from the newspaper will suffice."

Harry looked at John, saying, "Sounds a humane thing to do, John."

Julie looked directly at John. "I want to stay here and raise my child in this house. Do you want to stay or go, John?"

Surprised by her directness, John answered, "I might as well stay here—for the time being at least."

Julie spoke in a soft, calm voice. "No one outside of our immediate family circle and Kate and Harry need ever know you are not the father. John, I promise you, I will not have any further contact with Graeme, except to send him a birth notification."

Harry said, "Well, old chap, sounds sensible to me?"

Julie realised it was time to plead with John. "He really does have a very responsible job, John. There are far more important issues at stake here than whether or not he should be destroyed because we have committed . . ." she hesitated over the distasteful word, " . . . adultery."

Harry looked determinedly at John. "We also need to know what, if anything, you want to do about your partnership with us. Do you want to carry on as per usual, or do you want us to release you?"

John looked in alarm at Harry. The blunt question caught him off guard. He blustered, "Of course I want to stay on. I've put a lot of my own blood, sweat and tears into the business." Then, in a calmer, more controlled tone, "I'd rather be away doing the overseas buying and selling. I'd find that easier to handle, right now."

"I can't argue with that, John," Harry acknowledged. "You have always had the expertise for that side of the business, and to be frank, John, the business needs you. None of us would relish seeing you pull out just now."

Harry looked kindly at both Julie and John. "At the moment both of you are hurting, shocked and very angry, and with good reason. Mrs McKenzie sounds a formidable foe.

"Take a few days, both of you, to think things through.

You two have a unique and enviable working business relationship. It would be disastrous to see such an alliance falter at this time, just when the business we have all fought so hard for is on the crest of a wave."

When they had left, Julie turned to John. "I'm sorry I have caused you so much pain. It was seeing him again, after so many years, that we both became aware of the depth of our feelings for each other. It wasn't planned . . . in fact it almost didn't happen."

When John did not respond, she valiantly tried another tack. "I was very young and naive when we married. I loved you in the only way I knew how. Over the years my feelings for you have never changed. I sincerely promise I will keep my end of the bargain."

Wearily, John replied, "When I came home tonight and found the house empty, it was as though someone had ripped my heart out. I couldn't envisage my life without you in it, Julie. Let's just take it one day at a time, see how it works out, Okay?"

They called a truce and Julie knew, for the moment, her baby was safe. And so was her beloved Graeme.

PART TWO

INTERMEZZO

1989-1995

CHAPTER 32

"Just one more, Julie, dear, then we've finished," called T.P. from behind his camera.

Julie smiled as she posed in the final maternity outfit and the baby inside her gave a kick to remind her it was still there. T.P., seeing her enigmatic 'Mona Lisa' smile, quickly took several shots.

He called, "Take a rest, honeybunch. Check I've got the whole maternity range in the bag. Right, I'm off." He kissed her on both cheeks, "You still look good enough to eat, my pretty one."

Laughing at T.P.'s flattering comment, Julie went into the office and saw Kate looking puzzled.

"What's up?" she asked, rubbing her aching back. "Gee, I got some kicks today that an All Black would envy!"

Kate handed her a slip of paper. "It's from our message service."

Julie paled visibly, "High Flight—desperately asking—is everything AOK?" It was from Graeme McKenzie, using their code word.

Feeling Kate's eyes upon her, Julie said, "I can't reply, Kate. John is only now beginning to treat me like a human being. Our agreement only allows me to send a birth acknowledgement," she added wistfully. "I must adhere to my promise."

That evening, alone in her house and after writing her long weekly letter to her parents, she felt restless unsettled. She knew that a trip to the top of hill was not possible in her condition. Turning off all of the house lights, she went outside where she scanned the Milky Way and spoke in a soft, gentle voice. "Let my dearest Graeme know we are fine. Our baby is healthy and very active. Not long to go now."

Two days later, T.P. brought his proof photos back. Studying them through her magnifying glass, Kate looked up startled.

"She's a natural, isn't she?" he said. "A modern day 'Mona Lisa'. Take a look at this one. I'd like to enter it into this year's London competition. It's the same competition I entered when she was just a teen, with the bolts of silk."

He uncovered a poster-sized print. Julie was gently touching the growing baby, but it was the expression on her face of a tender, maternal love that was so striking and breath taking.

Tears sprung into Kate's eyes. "Wow! T.P. It's wonderful. You must title it something simple like, 'Motherhood' or 'A Secret Love' . . . but . . . I doubt John will agree."

"Why on earth not? I know the man is a bit moronic when it comes to Julie, but surely, even he can see the beauty here? You'd think he'd be proud to acknowledge his beautiful wife and child."

Kate squirmed on her chair thinking, 'that's the nub of the problem pal! One, John is so jealous of her success; and two, it ain't his child!' Of course, she could not confide this to T.P. and for ebullient Kate, forced to hold her tongue, it was a great pain indeed.

"Well, put in a good word for me, Kate. I need your final selection for the maternity layouts ASAP."

Julie arrived groaning, "Doc Matthews says three more weeks at least."

Kate saw Julie looking at T.P.'s poster sized photo in amazement. "Kate, why has T.P. blown this one up?"

Kate explained T.P.'s idea. "I told him not to hold his breath."

"But, my dear Kate, as you pointed out, John is in Hong Kong!" Julie grinned wickedly. "Tell him to go ahead, but keep it quiet. Oh! dear God," she closed her eyes, "Perhaps . . . just perhaps, Graeme might get to see it."

For weeks after that terrible day, Kate worried about Julie's health. She lost weight, instead of gaining any, suffered a few bouts of something very like morning sickness. Then one day, as they worked on the new maternity line, the baby quickened. From that moment on Julie had blossomed.

The maternity photos were published throughout the world in many women's magazines. The designs literally became an overnight success, causing Harry to fondly remark, "Julie is a living Midas. Everything she touches turns to gold!"

With her pregnancy nearing full term, Julie was virtually confined to her home. She had a daily visit from her in-laws, with Naomi Field's 'char', a treasure named Daisy Green, handling the housework. Kate was planning to move in with her for the last few days, at Harry's insistence. Harry was horrified when John casually rang from Hong Kong announcing he would be extending his trip.

When Harry stuttered, "But Julie is almost due, shouldn't you be home?"

John had replied, "She's the one who wants a baby. I'll be home mid-February."

In all of the years she had known Harry, Kate had never seen her placid husband so outraged.

The night was hot and humid and Julie's heavily laden body could find neither a cool nor comfortable place. Kate brought a cold wet facecloth to drape across Julie's forehead.

Julie grimaced. "What's the time, Kate?"

Kate looked at the bedside clock. "It's just turned midnight. Well . . . Happy Birthday, Julie!"

"Something is happening, Kate. I've had rumbly sort of pains. I told you! Right on cue, two birthdays for the price of one! He's a good Scot. Ouch! That was harder."

Julie slept fitfully. When she was awake, Kate taught her some new swear words to ride the pain. Julie stared at her usually ladylike friend, "How d'you know those words?"

"Many brothers, and growing up on a sheep station," Kate replied, with a truly wicked grin. "Don't let Naomi Field hear you, she'll be here soon."

Some weeks before, Julie's in-laws had become appalled at their son's attitude. Julie decided to confide in them. She had frankly and fairly told them why John was acting the way he was. They had listened and then given their son the opportunity to put his side. But had reluctantly given up when John's attitude could not be breached. Since then they had quietly supported Julie.

George Field knocked on the door. "Fancy a cuppa, love?" he asked. "Happy Birthday, Julie, dear. Have your cuppa, and then we'll get you up and walk around for a bit. When you get to the stage of declaring that all men should be castrated at birth, I'll leave."

"Dad, you're priceless!" Julie tried to laugh, but just then another pain caught her breath.

"There's one good thing us males quickly learn about giving birth. Our brave womenfolk forget all about the terrible pains the moment they hold their new born in their arms. If it was left to us males, well, there'd probably never be another child born."

He supported her as she walked around the adjoining room to take a final look at the room he had helped convert to a Nursery.

It had been redecorated in pale lemon with John's refurbished old wicker bassinet standing in pride of place. White painted furniture, numerous soft toys and a nursery rhyme frieze gave the room an airy, loving ambience.

"It's lovely, Julie," said George Field, in admiration. "I have never seen a prettier baby's room."

Naomi watched and timed the labour pains. "It's not time to go yet." She took Julie's hands in hers. "Julie dear, today is your birthday and possibly your child's. George and I have bought you this."

Julie opened the gift-wrapped parcel and discovered a camcorder camera. "Now you can have a permanent record of all the things your child gets up to. A very Happy Birthday, Julie dear."

"I couldn't have wished for anything better, Mum and Dad. Thank you both from the bottom of my heart," Julie replied, her eyes glistening with tears.

After George Field had departed, Naomi took Julie's hands in hers. "I can understand what happened between you and Graeme McKenzie. I had such a love, but before we could do anything about it, a war intervened and took him away.

Sometimes, even now, I still think and wonder . . . what if? We women are strange creatures."

"Mum. I need you to know I sincerely didn't know how deeply I felt about Graeme until I saw him again in Sydney. I didn't marry John under false pretences—I really cared for him. He's been so difficult since he discovered his sterility problem. Mum, I really need this baby . . . Oooh! Here comes another one! God! This had better be worth it!"

Laughing gently, Naomi Field assured her, "It will be really worthwhile. Ah! Kate's back." She left saying, with a twinkle in her eyes, "You can both use Kate's delicious swear words again now."

Julie implored Kate, "Before this gets too much for me to concentrate clearly, I'm not being morbid, but should anything go wrong, open my green leather box. You'll find how to contact Graeme there. Make sure he knows, please, Kate." She paused as another contraction wracked her body. "You'll find that box also contains all of the memorabilia I have collected. Make sure Graeme gets that as well, please, Kate, dear."

"Of course, Julie, honey, but nothing is going to go wrong . . . Another one coming? That's only eight minutes. I'll get Naomi when it passes. Come on! Swear like a trooper. Here we go ****** ****, and ******, and *****!!!!"

"Right, Julie, dear," said Naomi Field, "Time to go."

Julie took one last lingering look around. The next time she saw it she would be a mother, bringing home her precious, much wanted first-born.

CHAPTER 33

Lauren Catherine McKenzie Field arrived at 4 o'clock in the afternoon on the 14th February 1989, her mother's 29th Birthday.

The last six hours of Julie's labour had been hard on Kate. Julie had loudly declared, "Graeme McKenzie, you should have had a vasectomy!" and at the next pain, "Graeme McKenzie why are you so *   *   * virile!" Then, just moments before her daughter was born, "Dad Field was right, all men should be castrated at birth!"

Kate had not known whether to laugh or cry as Julie, with a final push, delivered her daughter declaring, "I'll never feed him again to keep his strength up. He can starve first!"

Julie, feeling tired but happy, gazed down at her daughter. All she wanted in the whole wide world was Graeme to be with her.

Naomi and George Field sat proudly holding their new granddaughter as Kate captured unforgettable moments with the camcorder.

George read out the Birth Notice he had written. "How's this? 'FIELD Julie and John announce the birth of a daughter. 7lbs 4ozs. At 4p.m. on 14th February 1989. All well.'"

"Yes, lovely, Dad," replied Julie. "Kate has offered to take it in on her way back."

Late next day Andrew Martin rang from Sydney. "Julie, my dear, dear girl. Heartiest of congratulations from Andrea and I. Kate tells me Lauren is gorgeous and that you are well. Julie, I have more splendid news for you. Are you ready for this? It's just been announced in New

York, 'Growing Flowers of the Field' has won an American Award! It's for the 'Best New Collection' Julie, as well as a very handsome trophy, it has a cash prize of one hundred thousand U.S. dollars. How about that, little mother?"

Julie exclaimed, "Wow! Andrew, that's absolutely staggering! . . . Andrew, would you ring Maria for me, and tell her about Lauren? Aah! Kate has just walked in, I must tell her the news right away. Good-bye and thank you, my dear friend."

"Tell me what?" queried Kate, as she spilled a handful of cards onto Julie's bed. "More mail for your Highness. How's our baby?" Without waiting for a reply, Kate had bent over Lauren's bassinet smiling down at the sweet, sleeping bundle.

"Katie good news! In fact, outstanding news, literally hot off the wire." she told Kate what Andrew had learned.

Kate stared dumbstruck at Julie. She sank down on a chair as her legs turned to jelly.

"The other day Harry jokingly likened you to King Midas, Jules," she managed to mouth croakily. "He said everything you touch turns to gold. Jules, do you realise what we can achieve in the business with that kind of money?"

"The world's our oyster, Katie girl," but Kate saw a dark shadow pass over her friend's face.

Kate threw her arms around Julie and felt her tears wet against her face. "I know, I know, Jules. All YOU want is for him to be here, I do understand, honey, I really do." Kate held her tight, saying softly, "He has given you a beautiful daughter. Enjoy her, who knows what the future will bring for all three of you."

That night Kate broke down and sobbed in Harry's arms as she told her husband how heart breaking it was to see Julie so sad, so lonely. Comforting her, Harry bitterly angry, told how he tried to locate John. "I can't find him at any of his usual haunts. I just hope he hasn't gone off on a binge."

Two days later, George and Naomi Field collected Julie and Lauren. Not to be left out, Kate raced from her office early, planning to stay overnight with Julie, and to get some 'hands on' experience at baby bathing.

It was just on dark when they heard a car coming up the drive. "That sounds like John's car," Julie said in surprise.

"Well, at last!" Kate replied sarcastically, as John walked into the lounge.

"I got Harry's message three days ago and I've been travelling ever since. I did try to get here sooner. How are you Julie? How's the baby," He looked very tired, embarrassed, and ill at ease.

Julie took pity on him and gently invited him, "Come and see for yourself."

He followed her into the Nursery. "Her name is Lauren Catherine McKenzie Field. She can be my daughter . . . or our daughter. The choice is yours John."

John gently stroked the face of the tiny sleeping baby, feeling how soft, smooth, vulnerable and beautiful . . . but . . . she was not his! He drew away.

"Give me time to get used to the idea, please." He attempted to stifle a yawn. "Sorry, I've been travelling for thirty-six hours. I'm out on my feet. I'm glad you're okay. I'm so sorry I didn't get here in time."

Kate stood up, saying, "Now that John has returned there's no point in me hanging around."

Julie nodded her agreement. "You're right. Thank you, my dear Kate. I really needed you." She fumbled in her pocket. "Kate, there's just one more thing . . . will you post this." She handed Kate an envelope, so thin it appeared to be empty. "It's a copy of Lauren's Birth Notice, for Graeme, as promised."

Kate took it from Julie's fingers; she felt them tremble, as though reluctant to let go. Then, almost as though it burned her skin, Julie pushed it quickly into Kate's hand.

For Julie the next six weeks was a time of wonderment and discovery. Lauren was a placid, stable and happy baby, who fed well and gained the right amount of weight. Julie sent her UK family detailed descriptions of the newest family addition together with the first precious photographs. Her doting NZ grandparents visited almost daily and even John marvelled at how well she progressed. When his parents asked about a christening, he supported Julie's wish for Kate and Harry to be Lauren's Godparents and guardians.

Julie felt a slow change coming over John's attitude towards her and Lauren. With only a handful of people knowing Lauren's parentage, she sensed he was slowly feeling more comfortable when people referred to Lauren as 'your daughter'.

At ten weeks of age, Lauren Catherine McKenzie Field enjoyed her christening. She burbled and blew bubbles at the Vicar throughout the whole service. She wore an exclusive creation designed by Julie from a length of unique handmade lace sent by Maria and Giovanni Martini.

As Julie was still breast-feeding Lauren, she found it easier to stow her daughter into a Moses basket, taking her everywhere she went. It soon became a familiar sight to see any one of the staff carrying her.

The four partners mutually decided to use the maternity award money to buy the commercial building they had been leasing. They threw a big party for all of their staff. To Julie's delight, Andrea and Andrew Martin accepted her invitation to come from Sydney to join them.

Andrea drew Julie to one side. "Andrew told me about the letter. I'm so sorry we didn't have the opportunity to devise a strategy beforehand. It was a vicious thing for her to do. You have a wonderful, healthy daughter, so genetically like her father."

Andrew then chimed in, "I've got some good news, Julie. Do you remember the photos T.P. took of you for the maternity layout? Well, he apparently enlarged one and entered it into the same competition as before . . . the one of you with the flying silk, remember? I saw it in a San Francisco Gallery, two days ago. He's won 1st prize with it. He called it 'A Mother's Secret Love',"

"Wow! Good old T.P." Julie remembered her hopes that one day Graeme would see that photo somewhere, sometime.

A significant day in their lives occurred when Lauren crawled over to the sofa and attempted to stand up.

John, watching, moved in closer to make sure Lauren did not fall. When she somewhat groggily, got fully up on her two feet for the first time, and began to topple, he instinctively put out his hands and caught her, clasping her safely to his chest.

Without thinking, he had broken his self-imposed barrier of not actually touching Lauren. The little girl, finding she was still standing and being held safely by this nice warm, strong body, climbed up over

John's legs, sloppily kissing him on the face, before saying for the very first time, "Papa."

Tears poured from John's eyes as he hugged the little mite to him, before she wriggled down and took her first steps towards her astonished mother.

Julie stood transfixed in the doorway, holding the camera in her hands, understanding the importance and the significance of what had just happened.

John said huskily, "I'd better get those door barriers in place in a hurry. There'll be no stopping her now. Did you get any of that on film? 'Cos here she comes again!"

From that day on, John acted as a normal father around Lauren. He happily fed her, bathed her, talked incessantly to her, changed her clothes, but steadfastly refused to change nappies!

Now that Lauren was mobile, Julie could no longer allow her to roam the factory, as she was a safety risk.

In a wry twist, John now found Julie was content to stay and work from home.

CHAPTER 34

At a company forward planning meeting, Kate suggested they should be more selective with their participation in the world 'Fashion Week' shows.

Kate read aloud the next decade schedule. "My first choice is New York. Our market there is booming, they like Julie's style, and the money's reliable"

The vote was unanimous, New York 1994.

Naomi and George Field offered to have Lauren for two or three days a week, assuring Julie it would be a real pleasure for them. Knowing it would also be good for Lauren, Julie happily accepted.

Lauren had developed her own special co-joined names for everyone. It started with 'Papajon', believed by her family to be her confusion at him being referred as John by adults—yet being taught to call him Papa. Soon Naomi became Nananomi, George-Papageorgie. Kate became TantKate and Harry, NunkHarry, and the names stuck.

For her third birthday, Nananomi and Papageorgie bought their crazy-about-all-animals granddaughter a small brown Shetland pony. Lauren named him Mr Brown.

Lauren sat like a miniature Joan of Arc on Mr Brown, closely followed by her flag bearer, the always-waving tail of Cleo, a Golden Retriever. Next would be her pet lamb, Cuddly, then two nameless fat farm cats, who never let any other human get close to them—ever! Followed by Boy, an orphaned kid goat and last, a guinea pig called Sam.

To Julie and John's utter amazement, the animals never fought or attacked each other, they just seemed happy being part of Lauren's parade.

On one of those days, Julie was in fits of laughter, watching as John filmed Lauren. She had discovered she could scramble upon Mr Brown's back by persuading him to stand alongside the fence. Getting off demanded yet another unique technique. The enterprising three year old somehow managed to persuade Cleo to stand alongside Mr Brown, so that she could use the dog as a buffer cushion against the long drop down.

On this particular day, Julie was almost hysterical with laughter. John, concentrating on getting all of Lauren's antics on film, was standing astride an animal water trough. Suddenly he lost his balance and fell into the water trough. Then, although standing knee deep in water, he continued filming!

At three and three-quarters years of age, Lauren was picked to play a fairy in her kindergarten Christmas Nativity Pageant. Naturally Julie was asked to make the costumes. Julie sat night after night, sewing sequins onto tiny costumes, while John stuck yards of coloured gauze over wire frames, making 'Angel' and 'Fairy' wings.

On the night one of the 'shepherds' spotted his mother, he demanded, in a shrill tearful voice, that he wanted to go home. A familiar female voice, very unfairylike, rang out, "Oh, for goodness sake, Jason, shut up! Don't be such a poofy-booby!"

John and Julie sat stunned, whilst Kate, Harry, Naomi and George and the rest of the audience dissolved into gales of hysterical laughter. But . . . she hadn't finished yet! Taking centre stage, Lauren flicked her 'magic wand' over the poor, hapless shepherd boy, and in a clear voice she ordered him to, "Dry your eyes and come and warship whatshisname."

She searched the audience for John and yelled at him, "I forgot his name again, Papajon, what is it?"

The whole audience was again in an uproar of side splitting laughter, with Harry asking John if he could go and 'warship whatshisname' too. Julie attempted to hide her blushing face behind George Field, but he was bent double, his shoulders shaking with mirth.

Half an hour later, she ruined her whole act by vomiting up her supper, all over the costume that Julie had taken weeks to make!

New Year 1994 started with a summer to end all summers. With her sketchpad on her knees, Julie sat cooling her feet in Lauren's newest present from her grandparents, a large paddling pool.

Lauren was 'swimming' up and down the pool, when Julie heard the phone ringing. Hastily drying her feet, she padded inside to answer its persistent ring, keeping one eye on Lauren in the pool.

In a voice that she hardly recognized at first, John stammered, almost unintelligibly, "Julie, there's been a car accident. I'm at the Public Hospital, Mum and Dad . . . Mum has gone already . . . Dad is not expected to live much longer. He's calling for you, Julie. Harry and Kate are on their way to fetch you and to look after Lauren . . ."

"Oh, No! Oh! No! It can't be, Oh John! . . . I'll be ready for Harry. I'll soon be there, tell Dad I'm coming."

Julie heard Harry's car arrive and Kate's voice calling Lauren. Kate and Harry dressed Lauren and secured the house as Julie emerged, white faced, unable to speak.

Harry, his arm around her, led her to his car, as Kate buckled Lauren into her car seat.

Julie croaked in a whisper, "What happened?"

Harry replied, in a quiet voice so that Lauren could not hear, "A truck hurtled through a STOP sign, hitting Naomi. She didn't make it to the Hospital. Be prepared, Julie love, George is in a bad way."

At the Hospital, Julie ran to the Emergency Room. John was sitting with his head in his hands. His face as white as Julie's, he pointed to the door beside him, "Dad is in there. They're still working on him . . ."

Julie sat trembling beside him, holding his hands in hers. A young, white-coated figure came out of the room.

"It's not good. He knows his wife has died. He wants to speak to Julie . . . is that you Mrs Field? Go right in. There's not much time," the doctor urged.

George Field was a tangled mess. His eyes were open and he tried to focus on Julie's face.

She softly said, "I'm here, Dad."

"Naomi? . . . Is it true?" he murmured.

Julie nodded and kissed his forehead. "Yes, she's gone, Dad. She felt no pain, it was quick."

"Julie, about Lauren, my Will . . . it's for her. Tell her the truth in time . . . don't let anyone sully her father's name, or yours. You have been a good daughter to us . . . Lauren, she's my delight in my old age . . . I love you both. Don't let John destroy himself or you, Julie."

Julie had called John into the room and they stood beside the hospital bed as George Field whispered, "We always loved you, son . . . Treat Julie right, John . . . Lauren is not to blame . . . We love her . . . It's time for me to go . . . Naomi is calling . . . she is alone . . . I mustn't leave her alone . . ."

The machine beside the bed emitted a shrill one flat note whine . . . and he had gone . . . happy to join his beloved Naomi.

Later, Kate explained to Lauren, as simply as she could, what had happened to her beloved grandparents. The little girl sobbed until she fell into an exhausted sleep, wrapped tightly in Kate's arms.

John and Julie both in shock, hardly knowing which way to turn next, formally identified Naomi's body. Harry had already arranged for a funeral director.

John whispered to Julie, "I don't want to be alone tonight."

"Oh, John, I need you near tonight. They were as close to me as my own parents. I just can't believe they're gone."

They had lain side by side on Julie's bed, not undressing, not touching, but together in their grief for two people that they would miss so much.

Kate brought Lauren back to their home two days later. Julie cuddled her daughter as she gently explained, "Now, my darling, Nananomi and Papageorgie have gone to live in Heaven. They were too badly hurt to stay here with us. They needed God's help and have gone to live with him now."

Three days later, their little local church was filled to overflowing for the joint funeral of two people who had always been the backbone of the community.

Afterwards, John and Julie were kept busy accepting the many condolences and words of sympathy. Ever-reliable Kate and Harry bustled around them, feeding and watering all the people that came back to the house.

When the family lawyer read Naomi and George Field's Will a few weeks later, as anticipated, the bulk of the estate had been left in trust for Lauren, and her siblings. John and Julie were left separate, substantial endowments. There was also a sealed letter, in George's handwriting, for Julie.

"To Our Dear Julie, If you are reading this letter it means we both have departed this world.

We fully understood your need to have a child and regret that, in our ignorance, we had possibly denied John the chance to father that child.

Julie, we beg your forgiveness for what we next have to confess. When you told us about your forthcoming pregnancy and who the father was, we approached our lawyer. We asked him to discreetly find out more for us regarding Squadron Leader McKenzie.

The results we received all told us of an honourable and greatly respected RAF Officer. His capabilities as a pilot, a negotiator and strategist are eagerly sought from the highest defence personnel in the world. He is more than worthy to be called Lauren's father. We urge you to tell Lauren about him when she is old enough to understand.

We saw what it cost you personally, to release him, to let him fulfil his destiny, and we respect you for your brave decision. That is why you have always had our full support in everything you did.

Julie, we have been blessed having you as our daughter-in-law. We have seen your excellent qualities as a mother to Lauren, and as a talented woman in the fashion world.

God Bless You.
With our love, Naomi and George Field."

CHAPTER 35

Julie read the letter again. She felt no anger for it only proved how much they had cared for her and Lauren.

She invited John to read it but, to Julie's surprise, he had adamantly refused to do so. Puzzled, it left Julie thinking perhaps George had already told him of its contents.

It was arranged for the Farm Manager, Bob East, and his family to lease 'Greenfields' farm and to oversee the day-to-day working of the farm.

Julie sorrowfully told Kate, "I feel as if a bright warm light in my life has been abruptly switched off. They were my stability, always supportive in showing how much they cared for Lauren and me. Oh! God! Kate, I miss them so very much."

John was despondent, morose and, to Julie's despair, had begun drinking heavily again. At first he had spent several hours a week at his parents' home, sorting through their possessions. Then the hours stretched, until one night he did not return home.

It all came to a head one morning as once again, he had been out all night and had only arrived home to change his clothes before going to his office. Julie, seeing the miserable, hung-over state he was in, gently suggested, "John, you can't go on like this. You are making yourself ill. You need to get some help."

John had whipped around, his face an ugly, diffused red, and angrily burst out at her, "I'm nothing but a homeless, adult orphan! You own this house and land. Lauren owns my parents' home." He stormed out of the house, with the car engine screaming as he hurtled down the driveway and away.

Lauren shyly crept into Julie's workroom during the afternoon and wrapped her chubby baby arms around her mother's neck. "Why is Papajon angry at us, Mama?" she asked. Julie knew then it was time to confront John.

He arrived home earlier than usual, joining Julie and Lauren for a rare dinner together. Later, after Lauren had gone off to bed, he apologised saying, "I'm sorry for what I said this morning. I've decided to convert the top floor apartment of our workshop building. I'd like to spend weekdays there, and be home at the weekends."

Julie reluctantly accepted the arrangement, assuring him, "At least you will be safer, as you will not be drinking and driving. I don't want Lauren growing up seeing her Papajon in an increasingly bad light. This way, at least Lauren will only see you for short periods when, hopefully, you can control your drinking."

Julie realised it was time for her to rearrange her own domestic affairs. As she pondered her choices, Daisy, her mother-in-law's 'daily', and now a regular helper in Julie's home, tentatively made a suggestion.

"Look, Julie, I'm on my own, I have no-one else to worry about. How about I come here on kindergarten mornings, you can go off to your office and I can take Lauren to her kindergarten. I can fetch her, stay here until you get home, and have a meal ready on those days, for you and Miss Shirley Temple. If you have to stay late, or go away overnight, I can always sleep in your guest room."

Julie was overjoyed. Daisy was in her mid-fifties, an energetic, cheerful soul who was a great home organiser, and a good cook. She simply adored Lauren, who jumped around for joy when she knew Daisy was going to be a semi-permanent fixture at their house.

Kate and Harry learned with a modicum of relief about John's arrangements and decided it was time to ask Julie if she still wanted to go ahead and do the 1994 New York Fashion Week.

She quietly asked Julie, "How are you really, Jules?

How are you coping? How are John's arrangements working out?"

Julie sighed. "Daisy has been a Godsend. The house runs like a well-oiled machine. Lauren is enamoured of her. It's always, 'Daisy did this or, Daisy said that.' I don't think I could have coped without that dear lady." She hesitated fractionally.

"John . . . well, John has been home the last two weekends, and it has been great fun for Lauren. Between Bob and him, they take good care of the farm."

"Great, I am pleased for you, my dear friend." Kate had put her arm around Julie's shoulders. "Now, what about you? What about Fashion Week '94? Where do you stand on that?"

After drawing a deep breath, Julie confessed, "I haven't been able to concentrate on working up any designs lately. I'm so far behind . . ."

Kate took hold of Julie's hand. "We miss you so much, me in particular. Nobody else understands my weird sense of humour, or laughs at my jokes like you do. It's wicked not having my soul mate Julie there!"

Julie was working on some sketches in her workroom and playing some CD's as background music. The last CD in the pile was an older one of George Field's, by the pianist Errol Garner. The machine clicked off and Julie heard an unusual sound.

John had previously moved his late parents baby grand piano into the lounge, and what Julie heard was the sound of someone running up and down the scales. Someone carefully picking out the notes of the tune that had just finished playing. Mystified, Julie crept into the lounge and was staggered to find Lauren at the piano, picking out the right notes to emulate the Errol Garner tune.

Not letting Lauren see her, she stood in the shadows, watching. 'Now where did that come from, and right out of the blue? It has to be from Graeme's family—they were always playing the piano in his house.'

Julie encouraged her by playing CD's of piano music each day for Lauren to copy. In less than a month, she was able to put together a string of recognisable tunes, and showed no loss of interest in her newly found ability. Daisy declared she was a child prodigy, a genius in the making, and Julie had to admit she was also pretty impressed!

All too soon Lauren turned five and Julie found herself escorting her 'baby' to her first school day. After saying 'good bye' to her, Julie cried all the way home.

At home time she waited at the school gate and soon saw her daughter dancing towards her with her blonde curls bouncing in the breeze, and looking the spitting image of Graeme.

Spotting her mother, Lauren cried, "Mama, that's the school bit over. Tomorrow I can help Uncle Bob with the drenching."

Taken aback, Julie gently informed her daughter, "School is for every day, darling."

Lauren looked in disbelief at her mother. "Are you sure I have to come back tomorrow, Mama? It's really a waste of time, I can't read, I can't write and they won't let me talk! Oh, well, if I have to, I think I'll join the Brownies with that Sarah girl."

So Brownies became her next passion and within weeks the independent Lauren was made a Pack Leader, although her newly acquired bosom friend, Sarah, reckoned it was because she was the group's biggest 'bossy boots'!

Now that Lauren was at school every day, Julie told John that she intended to return to working full-time. "Fine with me, I can resume my old selling and buying routine. How will you cope with Lauren after school though?" John queried.

"John, if you are not moving back, I'm thinking of asking Daisy to move in with me, as a sort of live-in housekeeper," Julie informed him. "I have been waiting to see what your plans are before making my own. Have you decided want you want to do?"

Thoughtfully John responded, "I'm happy with the present arrangements. In fact, I'd like to buy the apartment outright."

John hesitated before continuing, "Julie, I can't forget, I'll never be able to forget, Lauren's father will always be between us. Even that trinket box of yours reminds me he gave it to you. That's the way I am. I'm happy to be at the farm with you and Lauren some weekends, if I am still welcome. So go ahead, ask Daisy to move in."

"Until Lauren is old enough, I have no wish for a formal separation or a divorce," he continued. "You still have a lot of working life ahead of you, and you have a great talent. I'll be happier travelling overseas, doing the job I love. In our business, we desperately need stability, so I'd like to keep the status quo, how about you?"

This was the longest, the soberest statement Julie had heard from John in a long, long time, almost like the John of old.

Julie smiled, "I agree with every one of your sentiments, John. We do work well together, in spite of everything that has happened. In the meantime, I've got some new designs I'd like to put up for discussion, perhaps we can still do New York, later this year."

John willingly helped Daisy to move in with Julie the following weekend. Julie immediately found she had both the time and the inclination to begin working full-time once again.

Lauren was delighted to have 'no nonsense' Daisy close at hand, and a very glamorous mother to boast about at school. .

CHAPTER 36

After the dramatic changes she and John had made in their domestic lives, it took Julie several weeks to get her mind set into a working regime again.

Trying to explain this to Kate one day, she also hastened to add, "Well, that's not strictly true, I do have six one-off 'Haute Couture' designs I'd like you to look over. Then I had this brainwave . . ." she hesitated before saying, "How about we enter only the 'Exclusive Haute Couture' category. It will be a bit of a surprise for the other houses. They'd be expecting a full range collection; the controversy will keep them all guessing. What d'you think?"

Kate replied by giving Julie a hearty bear hug. "Oh, Jules, you're back! I like your proposal, it's an excellent idea."

Kate gasped in admiration as Julie showed her the preliminary working sketches of the six exclusive designs. She had named them 'The Four Seasons' and 'Two Little Black Dresses'. Kate looked across at Julie's face and saw, to her surprise that her dearest friend was blushing!

The penny dropped—Julie had created these gowns—for herself—to wear for Graeme McKenzie!

Kate said softly, "They're beautiful, Julie. Some of the best you've ever designed. You'd look stunning in them, he couldn't help but fall in love with you all over again."

Julie smiled shyly, wistfully. "Am I so obvious, or do you know me that well, Katie Reynolds?"

Kate giggled, "A bit of both. If I left designs like these around for Harry to find, I know what he'd soon be thinking!"

Soon they were both chuckling together as Kate noticed with pleasure that Julie was happier and more relaxed than she had been for many weeks past.

Julie's proposal was unanimously accepted. She had barely six months to work up the design patterns, choose the fabrics, make the gowns and have them ready for the Fashion Week. Her primary task, as always, was to constantly refine and update the garments that the workshop produced on a day-by-day basis. Their 'bread and butter' goods Harry called them.

Julie consulted with John and Kate on the all-important fabric choices. John analysed the structure and construction of the gowns, assessing which fabric was best suited to which gown. "It says in the rules for the 'Exclusive' selection, each gown has to have an individual name," he mused. "You have named them 'The Four Seasons' collectively, so how about we give each one a name of a season? As an example, the toga styled, cream silk could be 'Summer', or how about, 'La primavera bianco, Roma' . . ."

"Yes!" Kate butted in, "That's perfect! 'Roman White Summer.' The Spanish one screams 'Autumn' at me, 'Rojo encajes el otono', 'the red lace of autumn.' That leaves the jade silk, as 'Spring'. What's French for 'Spring Green Goddess'? It's 'Le printemps vert' something, isn't it? If we do the burgundy one in velvet, we can make it 'Winter'. How about we keep that one in English, 'Winter Dreams', or something. Can we still get authentic lace from Madrid, John?"

"I'll sure try, and I know just where to get the burgundy velvet. Singapore or Thailand will be the place to find the jade . . . Ummm, definitely India for the cream and gold silk. What about the two black numbers?"

Julie explained, "I thought one of them for hot weather, a light crepe, sleeveless, with a sheer georgette floating coat. The other? Well, how about in a wool jersey, for cooler days?"

Kate and Harry persuaded her to make them for her to model them herself. Julie agreed, "But only if Kate does the commentaries."

While they waited for the precious chosen fabrics to arrive, they began working up Kate's commentaries. "Let's start with 'Spring'," she suggested, her auburn curls bouncing and gleaming under Julie's studio lights. "With my colouring it's my favourite. I love wearing that Jade Green shade . . . Maison Chevalier proudly presents Blah, Blah, Blah . . ."

In her usual poetic style she described details of the gown named 'Spring' . . .

"Please note the Victorian styled draped apron which flows around to an almost bustle effect, and the fuller fishtail skirt for dancing . . ."

"That's great, Katie, spot on. I looked up the official schedule today. They only allow fifteen minutes between changes. Let's get another model for the two black dresses; just leave me with the 'Four Seasons'. Otherwise I'm going to be 'smoking' in a rather undignified way down that catwalk; that won't do the gowns justice."

"Whew! You'll be going like a cut cat to get in and out of those gowns in that short time, girl! You're right, let's ask Gloria."

"I'll ring her." Julie settled into her armchair. "Now let's hear your dulcet tones on 'Autumn', Ole!"

"Aha! So this is the tango dress, Si? The one we want to dance in—with him. Si senorita?" Kate clicked her fingers, imitating castanets and batted her eyes at a blushing Julie.

Then once again, in a few descriptive sentences, she succinctly captured the excitement and romance of the Spanish styled, red lace gown.

"That's lovely, Kate. Nothing needs changing. We should soon know what fur trim John has managed to source for 'Winter'. I hope it is the faux fur white ermine, as I had a Northern Hemisphere traditional Christmas in mind when I designed it. You know snow, holly, the whole bit. Something I do miss some years."

Kissing Lauren a loving 'good-bye' as she went off to school that morning, Julie knew her occupation gave Lauren plenty of kudos with her friends. They were especially impressed because Julie was off to New York. Lauren had given a 'morning talk' to her class and her teacher had shown the children where New York was on the world map.

The previous evening she had cuddled Julie before settling down to sleep saying, "New York is a long, long way away from me, Mama. You won't forget me will you? You will remember I'm still here and come back for me?"

Julie had lovingly assured her, "You are the most adored daughter in the whole wide world, and no way would I forget you. Lauren, you are the light of my life."

"Well, that's okay then." Then she pleaded, "You won't forget to bring me back something that I can show Sarah, that's really from New York, America, U.S.A. And, don't forget, bring it in a bag with the shop's name on it, please Mama."

"I'll go to Macy's or Bloomingdales, especially for you, my precious one," Julie promised. "But, you haven't told me yet what you'd especially like for Christmas. We still have time for you to write to Santa."

"Mama, do you think we could order me a baby brother from Santa? Sarah's getting one and I'd like one as well."

Julie looked at her innocent face as she replied, "Ummm, could be a bit difficult darling, I'll have to think about that one. Could you have another think while I'm away, see if there is anything else Santa might manage."

Today Julie was to present her latest designs for approval before an audience of her toughest critics, her team members. In just ten days' time, she would be departing with Kate and Gloria for the prestigious Fashion Week in New York.

Julie and the hairdresser had previously practiced sweeping Julie's long hair up in a chignon for 'Spring' and then putting the hairpiece in place for the Roman toga look of 'Summer'. It was just as quickly removed before covering Julie's hair with the mantilla for 'Autumn'. A hasty comb through, and her hair was down and loose, ready for the romantic look of the cape and hood of 'Winter'. After several attempts, they had perfected the quick-changes and were confident they had it right.

As Julie entered to parade the last gown, 'Winter' and Kate began her descriptive narration, spontaneous applause and cheers broke out from those present.

John at the back of the room had been assessing the gowns from a distance, seeing them as a judge might see them. Watching Julie, looking so beautiful and so desirable in all four of the new gowns, had aroused thoughts of 'what if'? He shook his head; there could never be reconciliation.

Leaving Lauren for the first time caused Julie some mixed feelings. She decided she would take an album filled with photos of her precious daughter and also loaded the camcorder with clips of Lauren growing-up. Finding a message on her dictaphone from Lauren, she decided to take that with her as well. Now she could hear Lauren's voice, and also look at photos of her, whenever she felt the need.

Watching Lauren going off to school on the last morning on which she would see her precious daughter for several weeks, Julie tried to hide the feeling of panic that was threatening. John, standing by her side, saw the unshed tears and the brave face Julie was putting on. He put his arm around her shoulder.

"She'll be in good hands," he assured Julie. "Daisy dotes on her, and Harry thinks the sun shines out of her. Don't worry; you have a big enough task ahead of you. I'll get back from Hong Kong as soon as I can."

Surprised but pleased at John's caring attitude, Julie sighed, "It's the first time I have been separated from her, John. It feels weird. I know Lauren will love having her Papajon to herself for a few days."

John looked awkward and embarrassed as he said, "Julie, I have seen Lauren's Christmas 'wish list'. We know I cannot provide that, but perhaps Dr Andrea Martin can help. Lauren is nearly six, so if you are going to have another child, now is the right time. Anyhow think about it."

Julie looked at John, dumbfounded.

She was beyond words.

CHAPTER 37

Several hours into their flight, Julie walked around the cabin stretching her legs. She was wearing her latest trouser suit tailored in a new, non-crushable material in the colour called Mocha Coffee. She wore it over a striking silk blouse of burnt orange and silver stripes.

"This suit is going to be a hit, Kate," she enthused happily, "I received so many good vibes and smiles on my walkabout just now."

Hearing Kate swallowing hard, Julie turned to see Kate desperately trying to contain herself and not collapse into a fit of giggles. "Take your jacket off, Jules," Kate managed to splutter. "Look at the back."

"What! Oh, No! The little minx!" groaned Julie, as she read the postcard sized notice pinned to her jacket, 'Please, Mama and Santa, bring me a baby brother for Christmas'. "No wonder everyone grinned at me!"

Trying to hide her embarrassment, Julie huddled down in her seat and turned her flushed face towards the cool window. She stared into the blackness beyond as she remembered John's surprising words earlier that day.

Questions flooded her mind. Was he serious? Well, he seemed so. Could Andrea Martin help? The answer was yes, of course. Then, before she could block the thought, her mind was asking the inevitable question, 'I wonder where Graeme is at this moment?'

She abruptly interrupted Kate's reading, asking aloud, "Will Andrew be there before us, Kate?"

Kate dropped her magazine with a perplexed look. "They arrived in New York yesterday . . . I told you that not two hours ago, Jules! What's the matter? Are you still worried about Lauren?"

"Sort of . . . Kate, John told me to think about having another baby this morning . . . I'm a bit confused, that's all."

"Really, John said that? Wow! My old Harry must have second sight or something, he'd noticed John's kinder demeanour towards you . . . Jules? Oh no! Don't tell me! Methinks we are wondering where a certain fair-headed, blue-eyed Adonis is at the moment—are we not? Last I heard a certain lady in some sort of pain was wishing him castrated!"

Julie knew Kate was only joshing, but Kate was so near the truth that it caused her to squirm uncomfortably. Fortunately, Kate soon became entirely engrossed in the menu for the imminent meal.

They'd arrived in hustling, bustling New York, and although it was two o'clock in the morning, the streets were grid locked, jammed by endless streams of yellow taxicabs.

Once they were safely ensconced in their hotel suite, Kate declared, "Well, the world can take care of itself for a few hours. I'm bushed. Anyone who disturbs me in fewer than six hours does so at their peril."

Kate heard Julie's howls of indignation as she opened her suitcase and discovered Lauren had left more 'Wish List' messages pinned to every garment inside it. "The little wretch, what a fiendish minx! She's definitely inherited her father's sense of humour."

A jet-lagged pair lingered over breakfast.

"We'd better get Gloria in here and do a rehearsal with her first thing," yawned Kate. "I'll give Andrew a ring."

Andrew and Gloria arrived together that afternoon. Andrew's first demand was to see Lauren's latest photos. To Julie's feigned disgust, Kate related the story of the 'baby brother' request from Lauren, which made Andrew roar with unbridled laughter.

"Julie, love," he chortled, as Julie threw a cushion at Kate's head, "This daughter of yours is a little, golden headed beauty. I love this one of her here . . . and look at those magnificent deep blue eyes."

The photo that had taken Andrew's eye showed Lauren in close-up and, as Julie knew only too well, she was the spitting image of her father. Julie remembered that Alicia McKenzie, Graeme's mother had kept, in her sitting-room, an almost identical photo of Graeme at the same age.

Julie suggested to Kate, "How about you take Gloria into your room and have her try on the black dresses, and I'll show Andrew 'Four Seasons'."

Inspecting the four gowns closely, Andrew admired the excellent workmanship, and particularly Julie's creative touch on the innovative designs.

"These are made with much love, ma cherie. Perhaps with one certain gentleman in mind, Julie, m'dear?"

Feeling her cheeks turning pink, Julie stated indignantly, "First Kate, now you, Andrew. I must wear my heart on my sleeve!"

Putting his arm around her shoulder, Andrew gently murmured, "No, that's not true. Kate and I, Maria too I suspect, know just how deeply you care for that young man. Deep down in your heart they will only come alive when he sees you wearing them. They have been created for him and for him alone. They are every woman's fantasy dream gowns, worn to make her look at her most desirable."

"Yes, Andrew dear," Julie acquiesced, "you do know me so well, but then I love you for it." She planted a big kiss on his cheek as they went to admire Gloria in the black dresses.

"They fit perfectly!" cried Kate. "No adjustments needed, you've got it spot on, Jules."

"I think she needs her hair swept up, that's the only suggestion I'd make," Andrew said, walking around Gloria.

"It's a classic gown, Julie. Can be worn anywhere and will stay in a woman's wardrobe for many seasons. Well done."

Kate was already working up her commentary. Now she had seen Gloria wearing the gown, she could visualize an aura to describe what she saw.

Julie felt Gloria needed a spot of colour. She went into her room and came back with two silk scarves, one scarlet and the other glistening silver lame, each two yards long.

By artistically draping them around Gloria, she had Andrew shaking his head in astonishment at the mystical transformation she had created. He said admiringly. "That gives the whole outfit a totally different perspective."

He looked at his wristwatch. "T.P. is here, wouldn't be a true Fashion Week without him, would it? I'll be seeing him later, I'll ask him to contact you for some publicity photos."

"Ummm, please Andrew," said Kate, pensively, her mind already thinking ahead. "As we are only doing evening gowns, shots done downstairs in that magnificent foyer would be ideal. It's like 'Le Grande Ballroom' down there, all mirrors and lashings of gorgeous gold, green and maroon draperies. I'm sure the management wouldn't be averse to a bit of free publicity. I'll go and see the manager straight away."

Kate bustled Andrew and Gloria out of the suite, holding her finger to her mouth, signalling to Andrew she wanted to talk to him out of Julie's hearing.

Gloria bid them farewell as Andrew quietly asked, "What is it, Kate? Is it Julie?"

Taking a deep breath, Kate nodded. "Yes, I'm worried about her, Andrew. She's been crying in her sleep again and calling for Graeme. It's tearing her apart being separated from him. She obviously tries so hard to hide it," Kate sighed. "Now John, for whatever his reasons, is suggesting she should think about having another child. Julie is already talking about seeing your sister again when we return home. Andrew, you are one of the few of us who knows about Lauren's father. Do you know, I've even been tempted to try and get in touch with him myself."

"Oh! God! Kate, don't do that! Much as I love and care about Julie, we must not interfere. Help her, yes. Support her, yes, yes. But do not initiate anything whilst Anne McKenzie is alive. That woman would crucify him, Lauren and Julie."

Andrew put his arm around Kate's shoulder and hugged her to him. "We both care a great deal for that talented young woman. Let's just play a watching brief, Kate. Now go get that manager lined up for some spectacular photos."

T.P. looked closely at Julie. He saw, with his photographer's eyes she was more mature, but she was still a strikingly attractive young woman. She was thinner in the face, which gave her bone structure a more haunting plane, something the camera always loved. Hearing from Andrew how photogenic her new collection of gowns would be, he was anxious to capture them with his camera.

Kate assured him the management of the Meridian agreed to him working—preferably during the evening.

"That's great, Kate," T.P. said enthusiastically. "They'll have all of the chandeliers fully on. Tremendous!"

Julie was curious about one thing. "T.P., what happened to the photo of me, 'A Mother's Secret Love', after you won the award?"

"An American bought it, I'm trying to remember why . . . Ah! I know . . . he said it was going to be a wedding present for two wonderful parents. I remembered because I thought his words a little strange, not quite in the right order of things somehow. Still, he was the customer and he paid the right price." He grinned.

Against the resplendent setting of the mirrored foyer of the Meridian Hotel, or 'Le Grande Ballroom' as Kate referred to it, T.P. took shot after shot, as Julie posed in each of the four gowns.

T.P. decided on an angled corner of the room as the background for the 'Winter' gown shots. Lining Julie up against a mirrored backdrop, even he, the true professional was taken aback as he looked through his viewfinder.

Because of the angle of the long floor to ceiling wall mirrors, what he had captured was the figure of Julie, repeated over a dozen times by the reflections, in an ever decreasing perspective.

Inviting Kate to look through the viewfinder to see the stunning effect, T.P. whispered in awe, "I think we have another winner here, Katie girl."

CHAPTER 38

Julie played Barney's music. She closed her eyes, visualised the catwalk and took herself through her routine. She listened for the subtle nuances Barney had inserted. Cues to perform a 360-degree turn, swirl a skirt, or maybe highlight a bodice. There was even a correct moment to slip off the hood of the 'Winter' cloak.

Promptly at seven o'clock, the Concierge advised that the car had arrived. Julie and Kate managed to follow the Bellboy at a dignified, ladylike pace. It was difficult though because, in their exuberant, hyped-up mood, their natural instincts were silently urging him to 'hurry up, mate!'

At the theatre the well-remembered glitz, and paparazzi hype, surrounded them. They were swept up in the unfolding drama by the blare and fanfare of loudspeakers, the flashing of photographer's bulbs, and the yelling crowd waiting for celebrities to make their appearance. Added to the evening 'buzz' was a pure Hollywood touch of many searchlights, raking the buildings.

"Whew! These gigs get noisier and noisier, or I'm getting older," breathed Kate fanning her face with her commentary notes.

A small, dark haired woman waited in the dressing room and introduced herself as Mary, Julie's dresser. A friendly, calming influence, who soon had Julie dressed in the jade 'Spring' gown.

Mary gave a deep sigh. "You look lovely, Mrs Field. We don't need Lucy the hairdresser, your hair is perfect. What a lovely, romantic gown."

Julie waited in the wings until her cue from Kate. As she stepped onto the stage, Julie was momentarily taken aback as wave after wave of applause washed towards her.

When Julie returned to the dressing room, Mary was ecstatic. "Did you hear that, Mrs Field? They loved it!"

For the next gown Kate seductively described the romance and the sensuality of the toga styled 'Summer' gown, and as Julie strolled through her music, it was reminiscent of the young Elizabeth Taylor as Cleopatra, bringing audible sighs all around the audience. Julie exited to perhaps even more enthusiastic applause.

Gloria meanwhile stood ready to take the stage in the first of the black ensembles.

Back in the dressing room, Mary's smile was even wider as Julie entered. "It knocked 'em out, eh? Come on, into this gorgeous 'Autumn' lace affair. Mrs Field, it makes you look . . . I hope you don't mind me saying this . . . sexy! Gee! I wish I could wear something like this, it is exquisite, Mrs Field."

Lucy, whipped out the hairpiece and brushed a few stray hairs up and under the mantilla comb.

Kate restarted the music, now looking towards Julie who now was dressed in the scarlet red, Spanish influenced, 'Autumn.' She could see a certain tell-tale glow on Julie's face, and in her eyes. She knew instinctively Julie was thinking of Graeme.

The audience went crazy as Julie sensuously moved onto the catwalk to the music of the tango, displaying the gown as though dancing the 'love dance'. She clicked the castanets rhythmically in her hands as she executed her turns to perfection. Cheers rang out as she reached the finale with even Kate applauding.

Gloria had a hard act to follow as she showed the second little black dress.

Mary was speechless after helping Julie put on the final outfit, the elegant, burgundy velvet 'Winter' ensemble. Lucy combed Julie's hair, letting it lie loose around her shoulders. Mary then handed Julie the white faux fur ermine muff and bent to fasten the buttons on the Victorian looking bootlets.

She stood back in admiration. "Mrs Field, you look like every Dickens Christmas card I've ever received from the 'old country'. It's a beautiful gown, full of nostalgia, the sort of gown every woman would love to own."

Kate gave Julie the thumbs-up signal and started the 'White Christmas', sleigh bells jingling and reindeer prancing type of music. The spotlights momentarily dazzled her, but Julie could hear cheering and a strange rustling chair moving noise. But, it was not until she executed her 360-degree turn at the end of the catwalk that she saw the whole audience clapping and cheering her, with a standing ovation.

Kate had big tears running down her cheeks, but she was also smiling a wide, wide grin at the same time. "They have never ever seen scenes like this, Jules. We must have won. If we haven't, the audience will lynch the judges!"

Andrew arrived beaming at them as he enfolded Julie in his arms, and murmured, "Little lassie, you were magnificent, particularly in that tango dress. I wonder what you were thinking about, or rather, whom were you thinking about, eh? It dinna take much imagination to work that one out. He would have been so proud of you, lassie."

Turning to include Kate, Andrew enthused, "Kate. You played that audience like a fly fisherman plays a champion trout. Ah! Such finesse." He kissed his fingertips in a truly Italian gesture. "I tell you both, it took my breath away. Congratulations! You'll be the toast of New York after this!"

Julie was still on Cloud Nine as she sipped a cool orange juice drink, trying to keep calm after such a remarkable reception. Kate was bubbling over, she could not sit still, eagerly hoping it would not be too long before the judges announced their decision.

But it was quite a wait before a dramatic voice was heard calling, "All entrants on stage, please."

When Kate and Julie were spotted, the whole audience cheered, whistled and stomped their feet.

It was an unbelievable reception.

The Master of Ceremonies called for silence, but the audience only wanted the answer to one question . . . Who won?

"Well, without further ado, Ladies and Gentlemen, make welcome please, our Senior Judge, Senor Ballesteros."

"Senors, Senoritas, it has been our pleasure to have been fortunate to witness tonight one of the most outstanding displays of 'haute couture' genius. We do not see this young woman often enough, and been the poorer for it. She has been away for far too long. Ladies and Gentlemen, the winner, unanimously voted by all of our Judges is—Julie Field's 'Four Seasons plus Two little Black Dresses'."

Nobody in the theatre heard anything after Julie's name. Julie walked up to Senor Ballesteros in a trance.

As he embraced her, he smilingly whispered in her ear,

"Anytime you want a partner for a tango, senorita . . . You were bueno, si, nos ha gustado, gracias, you were good."

To the enthusiastic cries of, "Julie speech, Julie speech," ringing in her ears, Julie stepped up to the microphone.

"Thank you, a million thanks. I've never felt so welcome. I particularly want to offer many, many special thanks to my co-model Gloria who gave me valuable time, showing me how to walk-the-walk."

Applause acknowledged Gloria's assistance before Julie turned to where Kate was standing. "Without your loving support, my dear Katie, I would never have made it. My heartfelt thanks, Kate."

More loud applause caused the usually unruffled Kate some momentary confusion, making her face redden with a pretty blushing of her cheeks.

Julie took her victory walk around the perimeter of the stage, beaming a smile, 'warm enough to light a fire' wrote a journalist for the next morning's paper.'

Andrew came into the dressing room and announced, with a huge smile, "I'd better warn you clever lassies, they are starting a big party on stage. Well, how does it feel to be the toast of New York, eh?"

"Julie, Harry always said you were a modern day King Midas. I'm off to ring him right now and tell him how right he is."

Julie dialled her home number, longing to hear Lauren's voice. She was a little disappointed when Daisy answered. "John's just rung off," she said. "The weather in Hong Kong is atrocious, a typhoon apparently, lots of flooding. He has rung each day, but he cannot get a flight out. Lauren is out riding. How did you do, Julie, dear?"

Julie explained the excellent results.

"Oh, Julie, my dear, I am so happy for you," exclaimed Daisy. "Send Kate my good wishes, please. Now you had better ring off as John may be trying to ring you. Everything is fine here, no problems, so go and enjoy your success, Julie, dear."

"Thank you. Give Lauren a big kiss and a hug from me."

Kate came rushing into the room. "Harry has had a call from John, he's stuck in Hong Kong. The connection was very poor . . ."

The phone ringing interrupted Kate and Julie was relieved when she heard John's voice, albeit on a very crackly line. "The situation here is volatile, I've never seen it so bad. Roads are flooded, the wind is screaming, buildings are collapsing, it's nigh on impossible to get out. There are just no flights to anywhere. Anyway, what happened at the show?"

As Julie began to tell him, there was a violent crackling noise in the telephone. She reeled back, as the terrible cacophony continued. Eventually it receded and she called, "John? John? Hello . . ." but the line was dead.

Julie asked the hotel telephonist, to try and re-connect her. After a few seconds the woman apologized. "I'm sorry, Ma'am, all lines to Hong Kong have been temporarily cut due to severe weather problems."

Disappointed and slightly uneasy, Julie reluctantly joined Kate at the boisterous party on the theatre stage.

CHAPTER 39

The insistent ringing of the telephone woke Julie from a deep, exhausted sleep. Groggily she reached for the receiver.

"Julie! Wake up! It's Harry! Speak to me, Julie."

"What's up? It's three o'clock a.m. here. I've only been in bed two hours!"

"Julie, I'm sorry, honey, but it's not good news. It's your mother . . . she's had a bad attack. Your sister Carole rung. I said I would ring you. Julie, there's a plane from JFK at five thirty; they're holding a seat for you. Just go."

"Where's John and Lauren?" Julie asked.

"He's stuck in Hong Kong, there's a typhoon. Lauren's okay and getting spoilt rotten by Daisy and me. Don't worry about us, Kate and Gloria can come home as planned. John will ring you at Carole's later. Go!"

But in spite of a frantic race across the Atlantic, her mother died before Julie arrived. Her grief stricken father was in deep shock.

The weather was bitterly cold as the funeral cortège wound its way through grey streets to the church where Julie and John had been married fourteen years before.

As her mother's coffin was lowered into the bare frozen ground, next to her Gran's grave, Julie's heart was breaking. This was the end of an era.

Julie was trying to come to terms with her sorrow as she stood shivering under the bare branches of the sycamore tree. She looked across at what used to be Graeme's house, his parents had long retired to a smaller home.

With the her parents house now possibly passing out of the hands of her family, it was time to retrieve the locket Graeme had given her, so many years ago. There were still a few winged sycamore tree seeds lying on the ground. She scooped up several, thinking, 'Well, it's probably too late, but I'll take you with me.' She stuffed them into her coat pocket.

She was shivering almost uncontrollably now. She turned to go back inside the house just as Don came rushing out of the garden shed.

"Here, Sis, will this do?" He showed her a small trowel. "Can you remember where you buried it? Better hurry though, it's freezing out here."

After much puffing and grunting, he managed to loosen the soil. Suddenly the trowel hit something metallic, and he gingerly extracted an orange-red, rusty tin.

Julie's hands were frozen and she could hardly handle the tin. "Thanks Don. Let's go inside, I'm going to catch pneumonia out here." She turned and took one last, lingering look at Graeme's old home. There were just so many memories of him around this tree.

The lid came away in small rusty pieces, mixed with blackened cotton wool. Hidden amongst the mess, gleaming a dull golden colour was the locket and chain. It looked to be still in perfect order.

Her mind flooded with the memories of the day Graeme gave her the locket. He had said, "I'll leave this part of me with you, for now." Julie sighed, so much sadness, so much water had passed under the bridge since that day.

"Don says you found it," said her younger sister, Carole. "Isn't that the one Graeme McKenzie gave you? There's a bit about him in the local paper just last week . . . He'd been promoted . . . or something."

Lisa chimed in, "Yep, Maureen told us Billy had also been promoted. Boy! They've both done really well for two local lads. Billy married an Italian girl, quite a definite improvement on Graeme's. Marisa is dark and quite lovely, not like Anne McKenzie. What a sourpuss she's turned out to be. Lady La-de-da they call her. She's apparently been like it for about five, six years now."

"Well, you'll be winging your way home, back to the sunshine tomorrow, Sis," said Don, with a rueful smile. "Got any room in your case for me?"

"I'm only going as far as New York tomorrow," Julie laughed, glad to be off the subject of Graeme. "I've got to pick up the rest of my luggage and Lauren wants something special from Bloomingdale's."

"Gee! You lead such an interesting life. It makes us seem such a dull, stodgy old lot," said Lisa grumpily. "It's no wonder you haven't got a tribe of kids . . . look at you . . . you still have a fabulous figure, great clothes, and you look ten years younger than you should."

She stopped as the others howled in protest and threw cushions at her. "Oh! 'Orright take no notice of me. I'm just green with jealousy, and a lousy old grudge." She hugged her older sister. "Julie. I'm so proud of you, but watch out girl, your biological clock is running down."

"Oh, for goodness sake, leave her alone, Lisa!" cried Carole. "Come on, let's lock up and go back to my place. Julie hasn't stopped shivering since we got here."

That evening, Carole casually handed Julie the local newspaper. "Here, thought you'd like to see this."

There, on the front page, was a smiling photograph of the Royal Air Force's newest Group Captain, Graeme Stuart McKenzie, aged thirty-six.

Feigning tiredness, Julie yawned, "I'll take this to bed with me, if that's okay with you, Carole, dear."

Julie sat on the side of the bed and looked longingly into the dear face in the photograph in front of her. She gently stroked the paper and kissed her finger before pressing it to his smiling image. She whispered, "Well done, my beloved darling. I'm so happy for you. Oh, dear God, Graeme, you look so handsome and I miss you so desperately. Our daughter looks so much like you, I can see so much of you in her, my darling."

Tears welled up in her eyes and the old, familiar ache encircled her heart. Carefully tearing the page from the newspaper, she tucked it away in her cabin bag. Another precious memory to be squirreled away in the leather box.

Travelling next morning to Heathrow, Julie knew she looked pale and wan, but thankfully her family put it down to her grief over their mother's death. Her deepest secret stayed safely tucked away, still untold.

"Make sure Lauren comes with you, next time," said her father as he hugged her tightly. "We've never seen her in the flesh. Your mother would've loved to have been able to cuddle her, it was one of her dearest wishes and dreams, y'know."

"It's such a long way, Dad," Julie whispered. "Lauren isn't really old enough to handle such a long flight yet. Perhaps in a few more years when she's older, eh?"

Throughout the flight, Julie's thoughts lingered on her father's words. If her parents, in spite of regular letters and photographs, felt denied from seeing and holding their granddaughter, how much greater was Graeme's pain?

New York's weather was not much better than in London, so Julie decided to make it a quick trip to Bloomingdale's to get Lauren's gift.

She rang the Concierge to order a cab for her. As she walked out of the hotel lobby, she inexplicably stumbled and dropped her room keys onto the sidewalk. As they bounced and slithered towards the kerb, a uniformed figure broke away from a group standing waiting to cross the road. He nimbly grabbed them before they landed in the gutter.

"Well caught, Jeremy!" his friends told him, as he turned to Julie and, with a gallant bow, offered her the rescued keys. The group of young men were dressed in the all too familiar blue RAF uniform, and all of them she noted were Flight Lieutenants.

Gulping, Julie managed to smile, and say, "Thank you, kind sir. Aren't you all a long way from home?"

"We're here at the United Nations." He indicated the building across the street. "You're not an American, Ma'am.?"

Julie laughed. "London born, New Zealander by marriage." Her heart was thundering in her chest as she heard herself ask, "Tell me, are you acquainted with Group Captain Graeme McKenzie, or Bill Watson?"

"I'll say! The Group Captain is our boss. As he speaks several languages, he's hardly needed us around. The Old Man sent us out for some fresh air," the young pilot added proudly. "They are both here, leading the British delegation and, I might add, doing a damned fine job too."

Her heart began racing. He was here, just across the street! Thrusting her trembling hands deep into her coat pockets, Julie forced herself to calmly ask, "when will you be seeing them again? They are old friends from way back . . . when we all lived in London, actually."

"In less than half an hour . . . Once we can get across this road. The traffic is worse than in London," the young man laughingly complained.

The taxi driver impatiently honked his horn. "Hey, Lady! Are you coming—or what? Time is money, my money, you know," he whined in a pure Bronx accent.

"Just a moment, I want to go to Bloomingdales," Julie pleaded. Turning to the young officer, she asked, "Do you think you could give them a message from me? Tell them, 'High Flight—Meridian Hotel'."

"Sure, will-co. 'High Flight—Meridian Hotel'. Here, let me get the cab door for you, Ma'am."

His friends looked admiringly as the cab pulled away.

"Wow! If she's a friend of the Guv'nor and the Old Man, you'd better make sure they get that message—pronto!"

Julie sank back into her seat and rubbed her hands over her face, as she asked herself, 'Dear God! What have I started again?'

She had been unable to get him out of her mind for several days. The longing and the need to see him, or talk with him again, had been growing to an almost overwhelming desire.

CHAPTER 40

Flight Lieutenant Jeremy Jones, at the behest and prodding of his friends, knocked respectfully upon the door marked, 'Senior Officer R.A.F.'.

A voice snapped out, "Enter."

He gulped, pushed open the door and confronted his superiors.

They looked up at him expectantly. The Group Captain asked, "Yes?"

"Sir, Er . . . I have a message. I picked up a key for a lady. She'd dropped it . . . er . . . just across the road. She asked if we knew you, Sir. She's from New Zealand. Well, she asked me to deliver a message that she said you would understand. Er . . . High Flight, Meridian Hotel."

As Jeremy Jones told his story later, regaling his peers with all the details, "The Old Man dropped his coffee cup on to the tray, in fact he almost smashed it. Then he shot out of his seat and went over to the window, staring at the Meridian Hotel. The Guv'nor positively growled at me, 'don't leave anything out'. I told them again, and added that I heard her tell the cab driver she wanted to go to Bloomingdale's. He practically pushed me out of the door."

As soon as the door closed on the hapless young man, Billy joined Graeme at the window. "It must be Julie. No one else knows your code word. How long is it since you had any contact, Graeme?"

Graeme replied, "Not since Sydney, over six years ago. Something must be wrong, Billy." Turning from the window, "I've never told anyone the rest of the story. Come, sit down, I'm feeling a bit shell shocked.

When Anne found out about us, she wrote to Julie's husband John. They gave us an ultimatum, abortion, or no contact whatsoever. Julie, as I hoped she would, chose no contact. Our daughter was born on Saint Valentine's Day, 1989. Julie sent me a newspaper Birth Notice."

Rifling through his wallet, he brought out a much-thumbed two-line notice: 'FIELD, Julie and John, announce the birth of a daughter, 7lbs 4ozs, at 4p.m. on 14th February 1965. All well.'

"I've never told any one else, fearing what Anne would do. I had to protect Julie and . . . my daughter. The letter acknowledging my paternity is tagged 'Highly Confidential' with my solicitor. Even Anne can't touch it."

Graeme murmured, in a sad and reflective voice, "My daughter is nearly six years old. I don't even know her name for sure, or what she looks like. If that's Julie over there, I need to go to her. She said once, she would never 'cry wolf'. If ever she called for me, it would be urgent."

"Okay, let's plan this," answered Billy, trying to conceal his concern at Graeme's revelations, and the agonising, heart breaking decision Julie had been forced to make, alone. "Let's go back to the Officer's Club and change. According to Jones, she's at Bloomingdale's, so we've some time up our sleeves."

Billy pressed the intercom switch, "Jones, get the car out front. We'll be down in ten minutes," Billy suggested. "If asked, I could truthfully say you were out visiting friends. We are sharing a suite so I can cover for you overnight. We'll be free again at fourteen hundred tomorrow, we take off for Washington at twenty-one hundred. You'll need to put in an appearance with me from, say—twenty hundred hours?"

On arrival at the USAF Officers Club, they hurried inside. Only his military bearing and discipline stopped Graeme from running up the stairs. Glancing at Billy, he saw a cheeky smile starting at the corners of Billy's mouth.

"What?" he asked.

"Oh, I was just wondering what Julie would be cooking, 'just to keep your strength up', of course," Billy innocently said, before he dived into the safety of the elevator, to avoid the spectacle of a very senior officer publicly swatting his junior officer with his briefcase.

Shaking his head, but smiling in spite of himself, Graeme replied, "God! I have missed her. I always feel as though part of me is somehow missing. Don't you feel the same when you are away from Marisa and the twins?"

Billy nodded. "Although I ring her every night when we are away, it's not the same. I've watched you through the years and I know how lonely you have been."

"It's been a lot closer call than you know," Graeme replied grimly, with a rueful smile. "There have been times when I've nearly chucked it all away and gone after her. If I hadn't been able to do some flying occasionally, I think I would have done so by now."

Graeme looked at his wristwatch. It had been almost two hours. He grabbed the telephone directory. "Here's the number. Ring them, Billy, please."

Billy dialled. "Hello, Meridian. Mrs Julie Field please. It's ringing . . . Hello, Julie, yes, it's Billy—wait he's here." He handed the receiver over to Graeme with a huge smile. "I'd know that voice anywhere." He left the room, quietly closing the door.

"Julie?" With a catch in his throat, Graeme murmured.

"Darling. I'm here. What's your room number . . . 505? I'll be there very soon, my darling."

Billy handed him an overnight bag. "I've collected up all of your toiletries from the bathroom. Just throw in a change of clothes and go!"

Changing from his uniform, Graeme said, "It's room number 505. Only if its 'do or die'. Otherwise leave me out of your plans, Billy okay? I'll only contact you if it's dire. I'll see you back here just before noon tomorrow."

Fortunately a cab was just disgorging its passengers at the Officers Club door and Graeme was able to claim it.

Arriving at the Meridian Hotel, he took the first elevator and punched in the number five. It whisked him quickly up to the fifth floor where he thankfully saw that the corridor was deserted.

Hearing the soft tap, Julie ran to the door and flung it open. Graeme stepped quickly inside and closed the door. He dropped his overnight bag on the floor and for a second he drank in the vision of the beautiful, highly desirable woman in front of him.

With a sob in her voice as she murmured his name, she came to him, held safely at last, within the circle of his arms. He clasped her tightly against his chest, kissing her eyes, nuzzling her neck, smelling the sweet, remembered perfume of her. The now familiar electrical current sparked and flowed between them, with both their hearts frantically beating a tattoo of wanting and longing. With a groan, he claimed her lips, passionately kissing her before whispering, "Dio come ti-amo, cara mia."

Julie's body strained against his. "You are here, you came. I have missed you so much, my darling. I just had to break my agreement for the chance of seeing you again. It's been so long."

"What are you doing in New York, sweetheart?" Graeme whispered. There was no awkwardness between them. It was as though they had parted only yesterday. I only ever want to be with her, his mind told him. She did not look a day older than the last time he had held her. A woman whom he still loved passionately.

Julie also felt the closeness the simple understanding between them of always seeming to know what the other was thinking and feeling. It was still there, nothing had changed between them.

She answered his question. "I've been here in New York for a fashion show. Just over two weeks ago I got news, while here, that my Mum had suffered a stroke. I've just returned from the U.K." Tears welled up in her eyes. "I didn't make it, Graeme, she was gone before I got there."

Graeme kissed her salty tears away and held her protectively, even more tightly in his arms.

"John was supposed to come from Hong Kong, but he got stuck with a typhoon and flooding."

Holding her close to him, he explained, "I've been in Washington for several weeks. I am at the United Nations until tomorrow evening when we fly back to Washington. Billy is covering for me until noon tomorrow. So we have a few hours to talk and be together, my dearest love."

"Come, sit with me, my legs feel like jelly. Let me look at you." She led him to the big sofa. "I just had to see you, Graeme. I wanted you to know about Lauren. I couldn't abort our child. I just knew that one day you'd get to see her and love her as much as I do. I couldn't give her away."

"Julie, my darling, when we decided to go ahead and have our baby, I prayed that you would give her life. I couldn't tell you face-to-face. Anne and John made very sure of that. I tried every way mentally to let you know that's what I wanted. Thank God! You were brave enough to do it, my darling."

Seeing her relief at his words, he continued, his voice deep with emotion, "I only knew what you had decided when I saw a copy of a Australian woman's magazine. The one showing photos of your maternity collection, I still have a treasured copy of that magazine."

He paused to kiss her, before huskily continuing. "There you were, proudly pregnant, pretty as a picture, and I'd sit there sometimes, alone at night, touching your 'bulge' and telling myself, I did that! That's my baby. Those photos were the nearest I could get to you, Julie. It was one of the lowest and loneliest points of my life."

Then he softly murmured, "Lauren. We have made a daughter called Lauren."

Julie leant over him and kissed his lips. "Come, I've bought some supper bits and pieces from Bloomingdale's. Oh, Graeme, I have such a lot to tell and show you."

"You aren't trying 'to keep my strength up' by any chance, are you?" he said, with a knowing grin.

"You betcha! Oh! I have got designs on you later, my darling, flyboy." Suddenly she turned and, with a worried look on her face, asked, "You are staying the night . . . ?"

CHAPTER 41

Graeme assured her, "Yes, I can stay. Tell me about Lauren, darling."

Wrapped in each other's arms, Julie told him some of the details. "I was in labour eighteen hours; your name was mud—for at least six of them."

"Oh, why was that?" he asked innocently, ducking the playful blow she aimed at his head.

"Your manhood was cursed, the virility of your sperm was cursed . . . I think I also declared at one point that all men should be castrated at birth."

Julie collected up the Lauren things she had brought with her and led him through the album that pictorially depicted Lauren's life. "This was taken the day she was born," she said softly. "You and I had already chosen Lauren. My dear Kate is really Catherine. McKenzie for her father, my truly beloved one. Field, obligatory for birth registration."

Graeme found it difficult to control his emotions as he looked at the photos. Turning the pages, he saw a cherub, growing from a small helpless baby to an independent toddler. The latest one showed a blonde, blue-eyed, curly headed moppet with a huge smile. This caused him to take a sharp intake of breath. There was a very similar male version of that photo, sitting on his parent's sideboard at his home in England!

She threw her arms around him and giggled in his ear, "Just noticed it, eh? She's the spitting image of you, there's no mistaking who's her father. She's placid, stable, and happy, just like you, darling. Ready for another surprise?"

She handed him an official looking certificate. "Here you are, especially for you, my darling. But, I couldn't send it in case it fell into the wrong hands."

It was a copy of Lauren's official registered Birth Certificate. Boldly and clearly typed in the appropriate column he read;

FATHER'S NAME: Graeme Stuart McKenzie.
OCCUPATION: Serving Officer, Royal Air Force
DATE OF BIRTH: 14th day September 1989

"How did you manage this?" he stammered, a look of total amazement on his face.

"A friend in the appropriate department. It's done all of the time for unmarried mothers who want to claim maintenance from the biological father."

"Julie, my darling. At last I have something tangible of her that officially acknowledges her as . . . as mine."

Julie hugged him, delighted at his positive response. "I intend telling her about you as soon as I think the time is right. But, look what I dug up from under the sycamore tree a few days ago."

From the familiar sycamore patterned trinket box she pulled out the golden locket and chain.

"I feel it is rightfully hers now. Given in love from both of her parents, is what I shall tell her."

Graeme sat holding the Birth Certificate with such a look of paternal pride on his face, it had Julie gulping down great emotional lumps in her throat.

She brought her Dictaphone machine over. Before it started, she rested her head on his shoulder. "Listen my darling, this is our daughter."

A very young child's voice rushed breathlessly from the speaker. "Hello, my darling, Mama, I had a lovely day at school today. We made muffins. Mine turned out a bit soggy, but Cleo loved them." A delightful giggle and a sharp bark emanated from the machine. "Ooops! Mama, she has just eaten them all up! Now there won't be any for Nunkharry's tea. Don't forget to get me something from New York, please, pretty please, so that I can show that awful Sarah girl where my lovely Mama has been . . . Mama, I love you very much, and I miss you, come home soon, 'bye."

Julie could feel Graeme's shoulders heaving as tears ran down his face. He pushed the replay button and listened to the tape right through again. She held him tightly as he buried his face against her shoulder.

The sound of his daughter's voice had broken through the iron resolve he had built around his deepest emotions for the past six years. It suddenly hit Julie with a full realisation of how he must have suffered at not being a part of Lauren's early years "They are yours my darling," she whispered. "I also have some film."

Striving to recover his composure, Graeme kissed Julie tenderly. "Dear God, Julie darling, I haven't been moved like that since I left you that night at the Villa Rosa. My darling, I blubbered the whole way back to base. Aaron Benedict found me at the gate. I'd almost turned around to come back to you. He made me see sense and talked me into letting you come to see us do the fly past. Did you hear my message?"

"Yes, my darling, yes, I did. It was wonderful seeing you in your rightful element. Did you know Aaron stayed with me until Kate was due? Where is he now?"

"In Washington, at the Pentagon. I'll see him in a couple of days, and I'll be able to show him the photos of Lauren, my beautiful daughter."

His reactions had more than convinced her it had been the right decision to contact him, and for him to see and hear about Lauren at last.

He realised how much he had missed the mental closeness, the total intimacy and the complete spiritual understanding between Julie and himself.

Looking at him, Julie could only guess at what he was thinking. She had set him free last time, to follow his dream. Could she do it again?

Julie smiled, "When you see her on this film, she will blow you away!" As the film began she explained, "This was the day she was born."

Graeme pressed the PAUSE button as he gazed at the beautiful Madonna on the screen, holding the tiny bundle, their daughter. One of Lauren's tiny hands was locked firmly around her mother's index finger.

Graeme kissed Julie tenderly, then said, "That is one of the most beautiful sights I've ever seen in my life."

He started the film again and Julie continued her commentary. "This is her christening. She burbled right through the ceremony, blowing bubbles at the vicar and cooing at everyone else. Oh look, there's her

Godparents, Kate and Harry, they adore her. They have no children yet, although Kate's biological clock is running down. Funnily enough, my sister just told ME the same thing!"

A small body, with bouncing golden curls, and gurgling gleefully, tottered drunkenly towards the open doorway. "She had made a couple of attempts until I remembered the camera. Typical Lauren, she wouldn't give in . . . It took her two days to master it. Then, of course, we couldn't stop her, she was into everything."

The film rolled on. "She was three years old and was determined to get on that Shetland pony. John fell into the cattle trough that he was standing on. See the camera wobbled just there—I did try not to laugh, but I couldn't stop. He was soaked to the waist—but he kept on filming. Hey! Look at your daughter, she'd mounted the pony, got her ride, and now she can't get off! Watch this! See what she has commanded Cleo, her golden retriever, to do. That's your daughter!"

Graeme was in fits of laughter as the scene changed and the little moppet on the screen was now enchantingly dressed as a fairy. Julie continued, "She's almost four years old here in the Kindergarten Christmas pantomime. She was so sweet—until she sicked up her tea right down the front of that dress. It had taken me weeks to sew all of those sequins on by hand!

"This is her first day at school—Oh, how I cried—in fact I cried all day. When she came home, she told me, that's the school bit done, tomorrow I'll be able to help Uncle Bob, our farm manager. She's joined Brownies, isn't she a cutie in her uniform?"

Pausing, Julie kissed Graeme and gently stroked his face. "Oh! my dearest Graeme, she doesn't just look like you, she also has your sense of humour. This is her four . . . no five weeks ago. Butter wouldn't melt in her mouth, eh? What that little minx had done was pin notes to all my dresses, with her Christmas 'Wish List'."

She shook her head, still in disbelief at what Lauren had done. "On the flight to New York what I didn't know was that on my back was also pinned a note with, 'Please Mama, or Santa, get me a baby brother for Xmas'. But how I love and miss her, the precious, wicked, little wretch."

Graeme was choked with laughter as the film finished.

"What a character! What a delicious package! She calls you, Mama?"

"That's the Martini influence. She speaks Italian fluently. She loves that magical place, almost as much as I do. Lauren and Rico . . . remember our honorary Godson? Well, they have a 'thing' an understanding, which reminds me of us."

Julie said softly, suggestively, "If you'd rather get more comfortable darling, there's a robe for you on my bed."

"What a good idea." He walked into the bedroom chuckling, his jacket already off, he reached for the robe.

But suddenly . . . it was snatched from his hands and Julie stood in front of him, her caftan discarded. She curled her arms around his neck murmuring, "Darling Graeme, I've waited so long for you to love me."

Immediately, they found the mutual rhythm that excited and gave them so much exquisite sensual pleasure. When finally they simultaneously and mutually reached the zenith of their lovemaking, they lay spent, locked together.

As their breathing and heartbeats gradually settled, they were stunned by what had just happened. The intensity, the depth of the desire they still shared for each other, overwhelmed them.

CHAPTER 42

Julie stirred, the room was dark and she wondered what had woken her from a deep sleep. The clock beside the bed showed three a.m. A voice whispered in her head, 'It's your time, Julie.'

Time, what time? She lay musing on the date, puzzled, wondering. She did a rapid, more personal calculation. This confirmed she was at the peak time of her month for conception.

She looked at the dear face so close to her own. 'He's so virile, my ova are probably swimming in baby making sperm,' she thought. Unable to resist a giggle at her own thoughts, she tried to stifle it in the pillow.

Graeme stirred and, such was his training, was instantly awake. "Why are you giggling?" he growled at her. "Didn't I satisfy you enough to make you sleep? Well, I am here to please, my lovely lady.

Without waiting for an answer, he rolled her over and under him. Julie gasped with surprise by the swiftness of his move. He explored her mouth with his tongue and at the same time thrust his hard erect penis deep inside her. She moaned with delight as once again he had her straining against him, taking her with him to a mutual breathless and heart-pounding paroxysm of desire.

He kissed gently. "Ummm, what a delicious Venus of a woman you are, I love you, minx, especially here in bed beside me."

"Graeme Stuart McKenzie, you are one very sexy man and I love you to distraction," she replied, as she languorously stretched her body like a cat down the full length of him . . .

The 'beeping' of the telephone finally woke Graeme again and he picked up the receiver. Julie rapidly rolled over him, putting her hand over his mouth.

He grimaced and mouthed, "Sorry darling," but he could not resist caressing the two beautiful breasts that were now tantalizingly presenting themselves inches from his mouth.

As Julie replied to the room service on the other end of the telephone, he kissed and teased both nipples. Julie was still on top of him, so he gently parted her legs and penetrated her, pulling her down on top of his turgid erection. Her eyes opened wide at this exciting, ravishing invasion of her body. Her breathing became rapid as she valiantly tried to concentrate on what the person on the other end of the telephone was asking of her.

Graeme was enjoying his work on her breasts, but when he put a hand on each of her hips and pulled her even further down on him, at the same time teasing her sensitive nipples, Julie slammed the phone down with a bang.

As he swelled inside of her ready to explosively ejaculate, she lasciviously writhed on top of him, holding him fast, exquisitely punishing him and prolonging his climax until she could not hold her own any longer. He reared up under her and she felt him give one final shuddering thrust deep inside of her. Panting, sighing, breathless and sated, she sank down beside him and looked at him with a wily, womanly, cat-that-got-the-cream look on her face and breathed, "Gotya!"

"Oh, boy, lady—And how!" Still panting hard, he grinned at her. "Hoist by my own petard, in no uncertain way there. Sorry about the phone, good job you stopped me, darling. Mind you, I wish I could be stopped that way every morning."

"Well, I'm not sure what I have ordered for breakfast . . . We shall have to wait and see what they bring."

He kissed her mouth. "What woke you in the night? Mind you, I'm not complaining, I liked giving you that extra sleeping draught. It worked too."

"I slept like a baby after it, my love. What did wake me, though, was weird. I thought I heard a voice calling me. It was saying, 'It's your time, Julie'. But in light of all the other strange coincidences that seem to follow us around. I only came back to collect the rest of my gear. I had nothing else in my hand when I dropped those keys. It was as though someone, something, deliberately pulled them out of my hands, at that very second."

Graeme shook his head, "We seem to be literally in the hands of the Gods. It seems our destinies have criss-crossed all of our lives."

There was a discreet knock on the door and Graeme hastened into the bathroom. Julie donned her caftan and wheeled in the room service trolley. With some trepidation, she lifted the lids.

Thankfully, she saw all of the usual dishes for breakfast. She heard the shower turn off and called out to Graeme that it was all clear.

"I don't know how, but we have got a normal breakfast. Surprising really, for I was under great duress ordering it!"

"Ummm, and how you made me pay for your duress," he said, as he caressed her breasts.

"Down boy! Come, eat some breakfast," they laughed together as they simultaneously repeated their familiar joke, "just to keep your strength up!"

As they ate, Julie looked longingly at him sitting across from her. Sensing her look, he clasped her hand as she said, "I'm supposedly more mature, more able to contain my feelings. But I seem to love you more each time I look at you."

"Same for me, Julie, my sweetheart. I know just what you mean. I just can't get enough of you, not just sexually, although that part is always totally and absolutely fantastic. But, it's just being with you. You're still the one being that gives me a reason to be living, you always will be. As far as I can see, the older I get, the more I need you."

Julie took a deep breath, she was going to wait and see. But, did she have that right? Didn't he have the right to say 'Yea' or 'Nay'?

He sensed her turmoil. "What is it, Julie? Darling?"

"Graeme, my dearest one, I figured something out. It's what woke me in the night, and why the Gods, Fate or whatever, have put us here together again. I think I am about to become pregnant again . . ."

His eyes were bright and twinkling. "Really! Do you mean that I could have hit the target again?"

"It all begins to make sense. I've done my calculations. Since Lauren's birth I haven't been using any birth control, you know the situation with John. Her birth regulated my cycle. With almost 100% certainty . . . I am now pregnant."

She looked into his face, stunned by her own statement.

He saw her confusion, so held her close and said gently, softly, "Julie, if we have made our second child, I am absolutely delighted . . . But, this time I need to definitely have more of a 'hands on' part."

"Yes, I know. I saw it in your face when you looked at the photos of Lauren. You deserve better than that, as their father. How can we do it though?"

"I'll think of a way, I'm determined to do so. We'll find a way. Rest a while; give the 'boys' a chance to meet the 'girls'. I'll shower and meet Billy for my wrap-up meeting, I'll probably be back by fifteen hundred hours. We can have dinner together, before the car picks me up for my flight to Washington."

It was nearly two o'clock when the meeting broke up. During the meeting Billy had been so proud of his friend. Graeme had shown why he was so respected. His negotiating skills and his tactical knowledge were nothing short of brilliant. Billy knew Graeme's light heartedness was entirely due to being around Julie. He too had seen, heard and been the butt of the vitriolic tongue of Anne McKenzie. He knew that, given the slightest chance, she would cruelly destroy Graeme, his career, Julie, and Lauren.

Now there might be a second child.

Graeme had divulged his thoughts over lunch. "Neither one of us is getting any younger, Billy. As Julie pointed out, her biological clock is running down. Someday I know we'll be together, it'll be too late then to wonder why we didn't have children."

Billy saw the look of wonder on Graeme's face as he said, "She makes me feel like a young stallion, Billy. Everything she does makes me love her more. Billy, somehow I'll have to find a way to circumvent Anne and her agenda."

Graeme had proudly shown Billy the photographs Julie had given him. When he saw the most recent picture of Lauren, he had let out a whistle. "Your mother's got a photo of you at that age. Wow! She's certainly your daughter, Graeme, old son!"

"Wait until you see the film, she's a real cutie, my daughter! I've even heard her voice, Billy. That cut me up a bit, I can tell you." He sighed deeply, "I'll be off, will you get my gear stowed? Toss you for who does the flying tonight." He flipped a coin and, with a boyish grin, delightedly found he had won the pilot's seat for their trip to Washington.

CHAPTER 43

"Hello again, my beautiful darling," he greeted her. Her freshly washed hair smelt of rosemary, her skin was glowing, her eyes were full of love for him. When he kissed her it sent sensuous shivers right through his body.

"Come darling, you must be tired," she told him, suggestively. Pushing him gently down on to the bed, she slowly undressed him. Then she kissed him from his Adam's Apple all the way down his chest, where she licked and nipped at his nipples. A sharp, erotic flame of desire shot down to his groin and Graeme knew that this incredible, sensuous woman had aroused him sexually, yet again.

He grabbed her and pulled her onto the bed beside him. She was giggling like a schoolgirl as he pulled her caftan aside and found, as he suspected, she was completely naked under it. With a lustful groan, he discarded the rest of his own clothing as her hands began to stroke and caress him. Not letting go of her, he continued to thrust into her as her orgasm throbbed against his own concupiscence.

They lay sated, wrapped together. Suddenly Julie could feel his chest rumbling with laughter. He explained about Billy's startled reaction to Lauren's photo.

"My sister told me our permanent bachelor lad Billy is now married," Julie said in a lazy, sexually sated voice.

"Yes, to Marisa. Let me think . . . it's their fourth anniversary next Easter. I was Best Man at their wedding."

He stopped speaking. Julie could feel his pain, as he asked, "Julie, there's got to be somewhere in this world where I can see Lauren."

Julie had already been thinking along the same lines.

She knew the one place where their secret would be kept, their privacy respected—Chateau Cornacchia.

She could legitimately be there next Easter. She softly told him her thoughts.

His whole face lit up with a joyful smile. He kissed her lips very tenderly, "I can pull a few strings and get myself seconded as an observer for a few days. Whoa! How far along will you be by then? Will it be safe for you to travel, honey?"

Julie counted, "I'll be twenty weeks, still okay for travelling. Yes! It's possible. Lauren would be on school holidays. John would be in Japan. Perfect!"

"Julie, my dearest, sweetest darling. Let's do it!" He crushed her to him, smothering her with kisses. "Come now, I'd love to see the film of Lauren again before I pack it away."

Cuddling close together, they played the film through.

Graeme softly asked, "How are you planning to explain our new baby, darling?"

"Sperm donor. We'll learn from our mistakes with Lauren and make sure Anne doesn't get to know. I'll not be photographed pregnant this time!" She told him wistfully. "We can eat downstairs to the hotel's smaller restaurant. It's almost empty at this time."

There was a grand piano in their secluded alcove and Graeme wandered over and began tinkling the keys.

Julie's mouth dropped open at the quality and professionalism of his playing. His fingers moved along the keys like a concert pianist. With a suggestive lift of his eyebrows and a lecherous leer towards her, he played the tangos, 'Jealously' and 'Your eyes are the eyes of a woman in love'.

As he finished, there was a loud applause from the waitresses, waiters, bar people and other diners.

Hidden behind the fernery, Julie saw him grin and take a mock bow, before returning to their table.

"You old fraud! You never told me you could do that," she growled at him.

"I knew all your family played the piano so it's no wonder Lauren can play as well as she does, she darn well gets it from you."

"Did you say Lauren plays? Has she had lessons?"

"Nope. One day she opened the piano lid and started running up and down the scales. I had been playing an old Errol Garner CD, and next thing I heard she was picking out the tune. Would you like her to have lessons?"

"Wait until I have heard her play, sweetheart. If she only wants to tinker, fine, but if she has a real talent, then sure, get her taught professionally. Gee, yet something else I can't wait to see and hear her do!" His face beamed at the prospect.

The Maitre d' himself served them their coffee and said to Graeme, sotte voce, in a broad Brooklyn accent, "Any toime yer wanna job, der boss says to tell ya it's yours. Yer play pianer pretty good, son."

Julie spluttered and hid behind her serviette. "Oh God," she giggled, "talk about 'play it again, Sam'. Come 'ere, boy! I'm goin' to make yer a star! Oh, if only they knew what a high ranking Air Force officer they were offering a job to!" She was in peals of laughter with tears running down her cheeks.

"Pity Billy didn't hear that. He would have demanded a contract for me to sign by now," he chortled.

"Speak of the devil!" Julie jumped up from her seat, as a very familiar figure searched the room. "Look who just walked in? Billy, over here."

Graeme looked at his watch, Billy was over an hour early.

Meantime Billy had swung Julie off of her feet. "Golly girl, you get better looking the older you get. No wonder his Nibs can't keep his hands off you, or his zipper shut!"

"Billy Watson, you don't improve!" Julie said, blushing to the roots of her hair, yet again.

"Got her! She still blushes!" He swung her around again.

"What's up, Billy?" Graeme asked.

"Urgent message. They want us A.S.A.P. Sorry Julie, he has to go, stat." Billy looked sorrowfully at the pair of them. "The car's outside, our suits are in it."

"Okay. I'll see Julie back to her room and be with you."

"Billy, it was lovely seeing you again," she told him sadly. "I hope I'll meet your family one day."

Julie was determined not to cry as they clung to each other in the privacy of her room. Graeme was equally stoically trying to keep his composure.

Her arms were tight around his neck, as she whispered, "It's just au revoir, I shall be with you in a just a few weeks. I will bring you your daughter, and perhaps half of our newest addition. Take care of yourself, my most precious love. I need and love you so much."

Graeme looked deeply into her eyes. "This has been another magical time for me," he told her quietly. "You are everything I have ever wanted by my side. Take care of yourself and our children, my lovely." He grinned wickedly at her, saying, "Do let Lauren know that I tried my very best to get her a brother for Christmas. Dio come ti-amo, cara mia."

He hurried out of the door.

Turning on her CD recorder to listen to some relaxing music to settle her nerves, Julie spun around startled, as a very familiar voice said, "This next set of music is dedicated to two very special people in my life."

Piano music began to play 'As Time Goes By.'

She switched it off and extracted the CD to read the label. 'High Flight', 'Music by the Central Band of the Royal Air Force, featuring G.S. McKenzie on piano.'

Now, when had he put that in her machine? From a man who was always surprising her with his caring attitude, and his thoughtfulness.

Taking off her shoes, Julie started the CD again, and danced around the room. It was filled with so much of his presence she could almost feel it. She danced with her eyes half closed, visualizing him holding her.

He played every tune that held a joint, special memory for them.

She whispered, "Thank you, my darling. I will now be able to hear you each time I have a need for you."

Going into the bedroom, she found a gift-wrapped parcel sitting on the bed. Inside, hanging from a very long and slim golden chain, was a beautiful heart shaped, amethyst pendant, her birthstone. The attached note simply read, 'Once again I leave my heart in your keeping.'

The long chain dropped between her breasts, lying immediately over her heart. Smiling, she realised the significance of his intention, two hearts beating as one.

Flying south towards Washington D.C. with every second of the flight taking him further away from her, Graeme piloted the jet fighter, with Billy in the second seat. At first his thoughts were dominated by the military news Billy had just given him.

As the lights of New York City rapidly faded behind them, Billy, aware that all cockpit conversations were recorded, asked cryptically, "Everything AOK?"

Graeme grinned widely at Billy, "Affirmative. We are setting up an Easter meeting in Australia. I'm to meet the junior member at last."

Billy gave a 'thumbs up' gesture of his approval.

As the sleek jet flew ever further south, its pilot had a small smile hovering on his face as he visualized Julie's surprise when she found both the CD and the pendant he had left for her. This memory dulled the ache of parting.

He deliberately turned his attention to the immediate matter at hand, that of showing the U.S.A.F. how a British jet fighter is landed—softly, gently, like a lover's kiss—upon the unyielding runway.

CHAPTER 44

At the airport Kate offered Julie her sincere condolences over the death of her mother before chatterbox Lauren's torrent of 'who-did-what-to-whom' chatter.

When Kate dropped off mother and daughter at their home, she scrutinised Julie's face and saw there an indefinable something, a serenity.

Seeing Kate's penetrating look, Julie blushed and whispered, "Later."

With her eyebrows raised till they were almost under her hairline, Kate managed to stutter mindlessly, "Right."

Lauren chattered on nineteen to the dozen, making Julie constantly reflect, 'she looks so much like her father', or 'that's just how Graeme gestures with his hands', or 'that's what Graeme would say'. The similarities between father and daughter were uncanny.

Eventually Lauren fell asleep and Julie was able to ring Kate. Kate's effervescent voice chortled gleefully down the line and then, almost in mid-sentence, she choked off her excitement. "So what happened to you, Jules? What's put such a glow in your cheeks?"

Julie could almost visualize Kate's eyes popping out of their sockets when she quietly answered, "I'm probably pregnant again. Same wonderful father."

"Wwwhhhaaat!" Kate bellowed down the line. "Say that again!"

"By the way, Group Captain Graeme McKenzie to you, no less," she added with pride.

"What?" retorted the irrepressible Kate again, unable to keep silent any longer. "Jules, I saw how happy you were about the whole thing, but . . . realistically . . . how are you going to explain another baby to John?"

"Honestly, Kate, at this point I don't really care. This a much loved and wanted baby. I'll go and see Doc Matthews, but in my heart of hearts I already know the answer. Be happy for me, Katie."

"That goes without saying, Jules, my friend," Kate Murmured, huskily. "Your best interests are always closest to my heart. Sleep well, we'll talk more tomorrow."

Going to check on Lauren, Julie found tears welling up as she looked upon her sleeping daughter. A pain of such longing for him shot through Julie's heart. She decided there and then to ring Maria and Giovanni.

Maria effusively greeted Julie and asked after Lauren. Then she asked, "Whata has happened, cara? How is the beloved one? You seena him again, eh?"

"How did you know, Maria?" Julie stammered.

A throaty chuckle echoed down the line. "So you have seena him, eh? Maria knows everything! Whena you bringa him again?"

Too surprised to even trade words with the all-knowing-all-seeing Maria, Julie suggested, "How about next Easter, after the usual autumn photo shoot? I'll also bring Lauren and perhaps half of bambina number two."

Hoist by her own petard, Maria recovered well and managed to splutter, "You meana it, cara? You mosta welcome, all quattro, four of you. See, I tolda you I see another bambino, you no believe old Maria, eh? Cara, you are mosta welcome and our lips are sealed. You come, you stay as longa as you canna, mio cara."

Julie thanked her and promised to be in touch as soon as possible.

When John returned home a few days later, Julie saw the strain, as he told her, "There's signs of prostate and possibly testicular cancer, Julie. I've been to specialists in Hong Kong and Bangkok, both confirm the diagnosis. Remember what Doc Matthews said? Well, regrettably, it's here."

A shocked Julie said sincerely, "Oh, John, my dear, I'm so sorry. What can be done? What treatment have they offered?"

"Doc Matthews is setting me up with a local man for some, er, radical or chemotherapy, I think he said; starting next week, anyway. I'm just miserable that it has happened now."

Julie was startled when she heard him say, "Julie, this treatment will possibly make me impotent. The old biological clock has started ticking Julie. If you want to have another child, make it this year, before it becomes general knowledge that any future child couldn't possibly be mine."

Julie sat speechless, unable to answer. He continued, "I'm going to be in Asia for March to May and I'll be trying out alternative treatment whilst I'm there. What d'you think?"

Julie, still in shock, his words so agonisingly close to the truth, managed to utter, "I'll need some time, John. I'm planning on taking Lauren with me to the Martinis for Easter, but my plans are still flexible after that.

"John, would you like to move back here? Daisy would enjoy having you to look after, and Lauren loves your company."

John, with a self-deprecating grimace, said, "Thank you Julie, but I am going to be very cranky, nauseous, possibly lose my hair . . . No, I'll be better on my own, just coming out here at the weekends, as usual."

Julie was feeling a modicum of guilt, but a ton of compassion, while a myriad of other equally mixed emotions tumbled over inside her head as she urged, "If it gets too much, John, the offer is always there. This is still our home."

Christmas arrived and Lauren was over the moon with her presents, especially the one from 'Bloomingdale's, New York, U.S.A.'. Touching the famous name stencilled on the parcel, Julie's thoughts were catapulted backwards in time. She subconsciously touched her abdomen before lovingly caressing the heart shaped, amethyst pendant.

Watching her friend from across the room, Kate knew just what, where and with whom her thoughts were at that moment. Julie had happily whispered, conspiratorially, "I'm a week overdue. Fingers crossed."

In the New Year, John began his treatment. Julie visited him in his apartment every day. She persuaded him to eat his favourite dishes, specially prepared by Daisy. But, she had an uphill battle as his weight dropped dramatically.

Then one evening, John, in a voice which was barely audible, said, "Julie, what about that baby?"

Julie had been wrestling for days of how to broach the subject. How much of the truth to tell him?

Dithering again, she looked compassionately at John. His face was grey, and he was looking old and very tired. "Not now, John, let's wait until you are feeling better."

An opportunity arose shortly afterwards. Daisy had gone with Lauren on a weekend Brownie camp, after being 'volunteered' by Lauren as, 'the best cook in the world'. Not knowing whether to feel 'put upon' or to puff out her chest with pride at the compliment, a bemused Daisy had gone along with the idea, declaring that she 'hadn't been under canvas since World War Two!'

On the pretext of wanting to discuss his upcoming three months sojourn in Asia, Julie made plans for a quiet dinner together.

Over their after-dinner coffee, Julie asked about his latest test results.

A shadow passed over his face as sadly he answered, "Not good long-term, but I still intend to seek alternative treatment in Asia."

"It goes without saying, you have my support in anything you want to try . . ." Julie's words faded as a large lump welled up in her throat. "John, what I have just said still stands, in spite of what I am about to tell you . . ."

John interrupted her, by placing his hand over hers.

"Julie, my illness has made me see a lot of things differently. I have been forced to face my own mortality, and have been sincerely grateful for your support. I know, in the coming months, I'm going to have to rely upon you more and more. We do have a very special business relationship."

Julie gave him a wan smile. "I can't deny that, John."

He smiled back. "I love Lauren more each day, she is a delightful little human being. In my own way, I shall always be extremely grateful to McKenzie, for giving her to us. That you loved him enough to have given her life, yet you stayed here, is something I am beginning to appreciate and accept. There is nothing from now on that would cause me to criticise you, in anything you choose to do."

Julie said softly, "I'm pregnant again, John."

John asked, "When did it happen? While you were in the U.K.? It's his, isn't it?"

She gathered her thoughts for a moment before answering, "Yes. I still love him, John. I can't deny it. I always will. I met him by accident in New York. We realise neither of us is free. I cannot let Anne do what she threatened before, he's now a Group Captain and his job is so vitally important. I am being brutally frank with you, John, because I feel you deserve nothing less."

She pleaded, "It was as though Fate had stepped in and brought us together again, just for it to happen."

John, somewhat wearily, placed his hand over hers. "I told you to go and get pregnant and I am content that it is his and not a stranger's. Who else knows? Kate I presume . . . Well let's keep it that way, shall we?"

To Julie's surprise, John showed no anger. "I'll be happy to play a full part, supporting you as you have supported me during the last horrible weeks."

Two weeks later, Doc Matthews sent Julie for an ultrasound. There, miraculously through a monitor screen, Julie could see her baby moving deep inside her womb.

John showed a genuine interest, "I'm so happy for you, Julie. You know how much I wish it were me that had given you so much pleasure, but now Lauren will have a full brother, or sister to grow up with."

Embracing John, thanking him for his understanding, Julie was appalled to feel how thin and bony his usually muscular body felt.

It was time to send a cryptic message to Graeme, advising him that the Easter visit was on. Julie puzzled over her words of how to also convey to him that they were expecting their second child.

Eventually she settled upon. 'High Flight, target hit, Easter rendezvous cleared, all very AOK'."

CHAPTER 45

For the next few weeks life was idyllic and settled. Kate and Harry agreed with Julie when she suggested that she should work from home as much as possible while Lauren was on school holidays. Even John slowly regained his strength as he joined Lauren swimming. Julie appreciated the real effort he was making to offer Lauren a normal family life.

On her 35th birthday, Julie shared the news with Lauren that her Christmas wish had been granted and that a new baby brother, or sister, was on the way. Lauren ecstatically informed everyone who would listen that this was because she specially ordered it.

Daisy was especially happy that another baby was on the way, and immediately got out her knitting needles to begin making delicate, intricately patterned, tiny soft white garments.

John basked in the reflected glory of purportedly becoming a father again, smiling benignly and accepting all the congratulations coming his way.

Julie decided it was time to update her maternity wardrobe. When Kate saw the newest designs, she suggested that a sample range be made up and for Julie to model them. As she made her suggestion with her usual bubbly enthusiasm, she suddenly saw Julie's look of horror.

"My God, Julie, what is it? What on earth is wrong? Are you in pain? Is it the baby? Julie, sit down."

A horrified Kate assisted Julie to a chair.

"No photos, not of me," Julie managed to splutter through tightly clenched lips. "Anne . . . Anne must not know . . . Kate, Anne must not know!"

Kate realised her mistake and hugged her dearest friend as she apologised profusely. It was a bad moment.

Julie decided to send a second cryptic message to Graeme. Impulsively she picked up the office telephone and dialled his special number.

When an official sounding operator answered, Julie asked for the message, 'High Flight—Easter A.O.K', to be conveyed to Group Captain Graeme McKenzie. She hurriedly rang off. So great had been the temptation to wait for him to answer and to speak with him, her palms were sweating and beads of perspiration had broken out on her forehead. It had taken all of her strength of mind and willpower to cut the connection.

When Kate burst into her office a few minutes later and saw the dreamy look on Julie's face, she asked, "What's up?"

With an impish grin, Julie told Kate what she had just done. Laughingly Kate dived for the cover of the door, before stage whispering, "Well . . . At least this time he can't make you pregnant." She slammed the door shut.

For the next couple of weeks, the happy, euphoric feeling pervaded much of Julie's days and nights then . . .

Daisy had gone on an overnight visit to friends, so John had put himself in charge of the barbecue. Julie became a little concerned at the amount of alcohol he was consuming, and decided to advance the time of the evening meal, hoping it would help slow down and dilute his consumption.

Going inside to the kitchen to bring more food for the barbecue, she was surprised when John followed her and loudly asked, "Why are you staying at Maria's for Easter? Why are you taking Lauren?"

His breath reeked of alcohol, so Julie immediately tried valiantly to fend off his aggressive questions with a friendly smile. "I always do, John. You've known all of this for weeks."

Leering at her, his face only inches from hers, John staggered. Spittle ran unheeded from his mouth as he spat his words out, menacingly,

"There was a very suspicious telephone call made to a U.K. number. I was asked by Accounts to verify it before they passed it for payment. He's going to be there, isn't he?"

His voice was now becoming louder and louder, as he angrily yelled, "All clear for Easter, isn't that the message conveyed?"

Raising his arm, he struck Julie across the face with his open hand. As she staggered back, she was horrified to see Lauren witnessing the whole ugly scene.

Far from being scared, Lauren launched herself at John. She pummelled his legs with an angry tattoo from her small closed fists, as she cried, "You leave my Mama alone. Don't you hurt my baby brother. Get away from her!"

Her frantic message penetrated and pierced right through John's anger barrier. He recoiled in horror at his actions. Sobering up immediately, he put out his hand to Julie, who was holding her stinging face, already showing a bright red weal where he had struck her.

"Oh, my God. Julie forgive me, please forgive me."

He staggered out of the kitchen and into his own room, loudly slamming the door behind him.

"Mama, Mama. Are you all right?" A concerned Lauren pleaded with her mother.

"Yes, Yes. I'm okay, honey." Julie cuddled her daughter close to her. "Papajon has just had a little too much to drink. It's okay. Come into the bathroom while I put a cold facecloth on my face. It'll be okay in a minute or so."

To reassure Lauren that she was all right, Julie made her daughter one of her favourite meals and in the coolness of the early evening, they walked up the hill with the usual menagerie of pets.

Julie checked the fenced off area where she had planted the sycamore seeds she had brought back from London. Sadly, in spite of both mother and daughter carefully scrutinising the spot, nothing was to be seen of any new seedling trees.

Lauren and her faithful entourage raced over the hill, leaving Julie to contemplate her favourite panoramic view, now gloriously bathed in the soft light of the approaching sunset. She whispered, 'Soon, my darling, so very soon.'

After tucking Lauren safely into her bed, Julie softly knocked on John's door. But there was no response. At dawn the next morning, Julie awakened to the sound of his car as he raced away towards the City.

Just as Lauren was about to leave for school, there was a knock on the door. Lauren was first there. "Oooh, look Mama, what beautiful flowers."

Julie picked up the card attached to the box of long stemmed yellow roses, and read, 'Please forgive me, John'.

Ten minutes later the telephone rang. It was John ringing from the Airport.

After thanking him for the beautiful flowers, Julie assured him, "I'm okay, John, and so is Lauren. Please don't leave us in anger."

John was apologetic. "It was the drink. I was warned not to mix alcohol with my new medication. I couldn't face you or Lauren this morning. Then I found I also couldn't leave without talking to you, and trying to make things right . . . I'm going to be away for such a long time . . . I'm going to miss you and Lauren. This summer has been a special time for us, hasn't it?"

Hearing the longing in his voice, Julie responded accordingly, "Go in peace, and yes, please keep in touch, we'll look forward to it."

Julie breathed a sigh of relief that he did not ask again if Graeme would be at the Chateau.

Kate was all concern after Julie, somewhat reluctantly, told her of the nasty incident. Once John was safely on his way to Asia, Kate and Harry too shared mutual sighs of relief.

Julie's morning sickness began two days later, earlier than it had when she was expecting Lauren. Fortunately, by lunch time each day she was free of any discomfort.

Daisy, full of sympathy and comfort, sagely told her, "Must be a boy, eh?"

A son! Could it be? Julie's mind raced ahead—they would have to decide upon names at Easter. Easter! Just a few days to go and they would be together again. In the privacy of her bedroom, Julie looked at her naked reflection in the full-length mirror. Yes, she was 'showing'. Her breasts were fuller, heavier, her stomach definitely rounder. She knew Graeme was going to be over the moon at the prospect of becoming a father for the second time.

The morning sickness stopped as abruptly as it began and Julie also experienced the first, satisfying, fluttering movement inside her womb.

Lauren was practising daily on the piano, having become an avid listener to Graeme's CD. She was obviously valiantly attempting to copy his style. It had been hard for her mother to keep the identity of the pianist a secret.

Lauren had declared, 'I want to play well for Mama Maria and Papa Giovanni. These are 'oldies' tunes, and they will like them a lot.'

"And so will someone else I know," Julie murmured under her breath.

At last it was the morning of their departure. Lauren's excitement knew no bounds as she found everything fascinating. Once seated inside the plane, she seemed to be soaking up all of the pre-take off drills and flight information with the absorbency of a huge sponge. Looking across at her, Julie could see the same happy glow on her daughter's face that she last saw on Graeme's. 'It's in her blood, just like his'.

CHAPTER 46

Maria rushed to embrace Julie to her ample bosom. Her words of joy, uttered in a rapid flow of Italian, were spoken emotionally and too quickly for Julie to understand.

Maria gently stroked Julie's abdomen. "Aaaah, si, the new one."

Rico had not taken his eyes off Lauren. Now she turned towards him and seemed mesmerised by the tall, olive skinned boy, who shyly offered, "Si, come. I show you the way."

Giovanni gave Maria a knowing smile. Maria murmured, "Tolda you it wasa in the stars, didn't I?"

"Those two are destined for each other, that's what she predicts," said Giovanni, with a loud guffaw.

Maria softly murmured, "No-one willa trouble you here. Julie, cara, we are verra happy you are here. The new bambino, he is due when?"

Julie embraced Maria, saying, "I'm due mid September. Oh, Maria, I miss him so much and he needs to meet Lauren."

"How soona he arrive?"

"I'm not sure." For the first time, Julie looked troubled. "I sent him a message and I know he couldn't reply . . . I do hope he makes it."

"Pouf!" admonished Maria, "Wild horses willa not keepa that one away if knows you and his daughter are here! So husha up and take a siesta. Lauren canna stay with us until you are rested. I'll unpack the little one for you in the other bedroom. Whata you going to tella Lauren? Giovanni and me, we thinka you shoulda just act natural."

She looked wistfully at Maria. "I'm anxious to see Lauren's reaction."

"Pouf! They willa luva each other on sight, me predict. Now, rest. Ciao cara."

Later that evening Julie confided to Maria. "Lauren's already told me she loves Rico . . . Aah! That's how I felt about her father, the first time I saw him, but was too stiff upper-lip British to tell him in time . . ." Her voice tailed off as she smothered a yawn.

Giovanni smiled, "The little one is fast asleep. Now do the same, my child. If the telephone goes for you, we will switch it through, Ciao cara."

To Julie's amazement, the next thing she knew it was eight in the morning and Maria was bringing her breakfast in bed! Maria had a big grin on her face as she put the tray down. "You hadda better put on your best bib 'n tucker, 'cos guess who will be flying in, in his helicopter, at eleven o'clock, eh?"

"What! Has he rung?" Julie asked in astonishment.

"He ringa at halfa pasta seven thisa morning. Giovanni tella him you still asleep. He forbid us to wake you, but to say he be here at eleven o'clock. Giovanni tella him we prepare the helipad for him. Lauren is having her breakfast with Giovanni and me." Maria left the room with a wide smile on her face.

Julie lay back on the pillows, 'He is here, he has come!'

She dressed her little daughter in a simple, candyfloss pink 'Daddy's little girl look' dress. As she gazed into innocent baby eyes, as deep a blue as Graeme's, Julie explained, "A very special person will be arriving very shortly. Someone Mama loves very much and I know he's going to love you. His name is Graeme McKenzie."

Lauren exclaimed, "Ooh Mama, that's my name too. What shall I call him, Mama? Mr McKenzie? No. If he's really special, why don't I call him NunkyGraeme, or Papagraeme?"

Julie swallowed the hard lump that had risen in her throat. She knew that Graeme would be over the moon with delight if Lauren called him 'Papa' anything!

"Papagraeme would be lovely darling. I'm sure he'd like that. Listen . . . can you hear that?"

The distinctive 'thunk, thunk, thunk' noise of a military helicopter's rotors could be heard in the distance.

Leaving Lauren in Maria and Giovanni's capable hands, Julie, trembling with anticipation, headed towards the helipad.

A helicopter with the RAAF insignia painted on its sides swooped over the Chateau and landed as gently as though delivering a parcel of newly laid eggs. The young pilot was obviously keenly aware of the valuable package of 'top brass' he was delivering.

Graeme alighted athletically from the helicopter, carrying his weekend bag, and gave the pilot the 'thumbs up' signal. Once the down draft had settled, Graeme looked expectantly towards the Chateau. Standing behind the safety fence of the helipad, Julie was momentarily spellbound. Then, with a sob, she ran to him.

Clasped in his arms at last, she whispered, "Oh, my precious, dearest love, you are here!"

His words came out in a very hoarse, emotional murmur, as he held her close to him and kissed her passionately, "Julie, my darling. Dio come ti-amo, cara mia. How I have missed you. You look terrific!" He grinned as he felt the roundness of her abdomen. "Our baby suits you, my darling. So . . . we've done it again?"

"I couldn't wait to get here, I hitched a ride straight from Canberra. I didn't want to waste a minute." He kissed her again, deeply, lovingly.

"My darling gorgeous, flyboy, Lauren is going to love you in your uniform," chuckled Julie, against his shoulder.

Julie gently stroked his cheek. "Come my love, our daughter will be bursting with curiosity. She'll have a million questions."

Lauren broke away from Maria's restraining hand and hurtled gleefully towards them, shouting, "Mama! Mama! You didn't tell me he was a pilot!"

Graeme stood stock-still, gazing dumfounded at the small figure at his feet. A sweet, rosebud mouth smiled brilliantly at him, saying, "You ARE a pilot! I can see the wings up there on your jacket!" Two identical pairs of startlingly deep blue eyes solemnly gazed at each other. Graeme experienced the feeling of almost seeing into a reflection of his own soul.

"Hello, I am Lauren-Catherine-McKenzie-Field," she said, rather shyly. "My Mama says you are very special to her."

Graeme took off his cap and the breeze ruffled his hair. Lauren gasped, "You and me are the only ones with the same hair. Do we belong to the same family or something? And, oh," she hesitated for a brief moment, "Can I please call you Papagraeme?"

Startled, Graeme looked up sharply and caught Julie trying to hide a smile behind her hands. "I did try to warn you, Papagraeme," she said pointedly. "Lauren, honey, it's okay to give Papagraeme a big hug."

Crouched down on his haunches, Graeme tried to contain his emotions, as Lauren wrapped her baby arms tightly around his neck. This beautiful child was his! Lauren kissed him on the cheek. "Ummm, you smell nice, Papagraeme. I think I love you."

Graeme found his voice and huskily told her, "I loved you, my sweet Lauren, before you were even born. You and your Mama are very precious, very special to me."

Graeme was totally engrossed listening to Lauren, who had her arms wrapped around his neck as she fired non-stop questions at him. He carried her in his arms, doing his best to answer her, but feeling somehow he was losing the battle to keep up.

Giovanni relieved Graeme of his bag. "It's so good to have you here. Welcome, my friend." He patted Graeme's shoulder.

"Giovanni, it is my pleasure to be here again," replied Graeme, in Italian. "A million thanks, my friend, for all of your help in arranging it."

Graeme spoke to Maria, still wiping her eyes. Speaking in Italian again, "Thank you, Maria, a thousand thanks for allowing us to come here to your wonderful home, to be finally together. It is truly a privilege."

Maria answered in Italian, "You maka my Julie verra happy, thata isa thanks enough."

Lauren, still clinging to Graeme, said in a surprised voice, "Capisco. Parla l'italiano? I understand. You speak Italian?"

Smiling Graeme answered, "Si, mi bambina."

"Mama! Papagraeme also speaks Italian!" she cried in a voice full of awe and admiration.

Leading the way to the guest villa, Julie could hear Lauren behind her, bombarding Graeme with questions about his rank, his job and could he fly? Graeme, for his part, patiently and gently explained what he did.

Julie smiled as she saw Lauren wearing her father's gold braided uniform hat.

Lauren said, with a dazzling smile, "We are staying here, isn't it beautiful? I have a bedroom down the hall." She looked at her father's tall figure, "But it only has one small bed. Where are you going to sleep, Papagraeme?"

Without any embarrassment or hesitation, Graeme answered, "With Mama, of course. Is that okay with you, sweetheart?"

"Oh yes, dear Papagraeme! She needs someone to look after her and my new baby brother. Did you know I ordered him from Santa last Christmas? He's growing inside of Mama's tummy. Are you staying here as long as us? We don't go home until Tuesday morning."

"I'm here until oh eleven hundred hours next Tuesday, that's eleven o'clock in the morning to you, honey. Then the helicopter will come and pick me up again."

Julie looked at the pair of them open mouthed! Graeme had handled a sensitive problem frankly, and more importantly, Lauren had accepted it, without question.

Catching Julie's expression, Graeme gave her a grin as he unzipped his bag. "Now we cannot have you sleeping alone, honey, can we?" he told Lauren. "Well, a very beautiful ladybird told me that you like things from famous shops. Well, here is something I have brought for you from the shop that Her Majesty the Queen herself shops at, in London." Extracting the famous green and gold carry-bag of Harrod's of London, Graeme handed it to Lauren.

With a very feminine squeal of delight, Lauren brought out a large and very English teddy bear.

"Now you have something to cuddle and keep you company at night, when I'm not there, my precious honeybunch," Graeme solemnly told her, as she threw herself at him.

With a shout of happy laughter, he lifted her high in the air and hugged her, as she smothered his face with kisses. Lauren squealed with delight as she told him, "I love my Mr Bear, thank you, thank you, thank you, my dear Papagraeme."

Giving Julie a cheeky grin, he asked Lauren, "Now what has Mama prepared for lunch, 'just to keep my strength up' of course."

CHAPTER 47

As Lauren raced off to fetch a book she wanted Graeme to see, he followed Julie into the bedroom. He closed the door and tenderly took her in his arms. "My dearest, darling Julie, I think I must be the luckiest man alive at this moment. Our daughter is delightful. Did I handle her sleeping arrangement question okay?"

With her arms draped around his neck, Julie answered, "Perfectly, my beloved."

"Well, if you had taught as many young, naive chaps as I have . . . Well . . . I guess some of it rubs off with one's own child . . . Did you hear that? 'one's own child', isn't that just a marvellous phrase?"

They kissed again, before he huskily told her, "Dear heaven, I have missed you so much." Rubbing his hands around her rounded abdomen, he grinned, "Didn't I do that well?"

There was a timid knock on the door. Julie raised her eyebrows in total surprise. Lauren never knocked. She always entered a room like a whirling dervish.

Graeme tapped the side of his nose and whispered in her ear, "She asked—I explained—when the door is shut it means the 'boss', wants privacy. One should always knock before entering." Still holding a stunned Julie in his arms, he called, "Come in honey."

Lauren bounced into the room; her face broke into a knowing happy smile as she saw them in an embrace. "I've found it, Papagraeme."

Minutes later, Graeme and Lauren sprawled side by side on the bed discussing the book. Julie smiled, what a marvellous picture. She went into the kitchenette to prepare lunch.

After a few minutes, Lauren followed and, to Julie's astonishment, began to set the table for lunch. Seeing the surprised look, Lauren smiled coyly, "Papagraeme will be a few minutes, and he's just changing from his uniform. He said I should help you. Mama . . . he's really very, very extra special isn't he?"

She danced around the table happily performing her tasks. "Mama, he's going to listen to me play the piano, after he has had a siesta with you."

Julie nearly dropped a plate at Lauren's matter-of-fact summation of her conversation with her father.

In a faint voice, she stammered, "Siesta, me and him?"

"Yes, he's been up . . . 'since before the cock crowed at dawn', and he says he needs a siesta as well. I'm going to swim with Rico, and then Papagraeme will come and play the piano with me."

To Julie's astonishment, she realised Lauren seemed only too willing to follow his orders to the letter! Something she had never done, for anybody!

'It's uncanny,' she told herself, 'they act as though they have known each other all of their lives. They have the same gestures, the same mannerisms and seem to understand each other's thoughts . . .'

Wait! But that was how it had always been between herself and Graeme. So, was it any wonder he had immediately melded with his daughter so naturally and so fully?

Hearing him coming, Lauren's face lit up, "Oh goodie, here he comes."

Lauren gave a cheeky wolf whistle, learned recently from one of Kate's brothers, which stopped Graeme in his tracks, as his daughter yelled, "Wow! You look so handsome, Papagraeme!"

Graeme pirouetted with flamboyant gestures, parodying a male model. Lauren collapsed on her chair with peals of laughter. Picking up his still giggling daughter, he placed her upright again with a bear-like growl and a hug.

Relishing the luncheon feast before him, Graeme kissed Julie's palm. "Darling, as usual you have made a meal fit for a King."

Lauren gazed intently at him. "You love my Mama very much, don't you, Papagraeme? You call her 'darling' and my Mama kisses you all of the time. That shows you do love her."

Without turning a hair, Graeme nodded and picked up a peach from the bowl on the table. He put one on Lauren's plate. "Yes, my honey, quite right. I love your Mama more than anyone else in this world." He sliced her peach for her. "And my second love is a lovely peach called Lauren Catherine McKenzie Field. That's why your Mama gave you my name."

Beaming at him, Lauren giggled, "I was right! We are the only two people here with blonde hair. All the rest have dark hair."

She paused, before shyly asking, "Papagraeme, we do look alike, don't we? Can I pretend to be your daughter while you are here? 'Cos I need a Daddy for the three-legged and the sack races at the Sports Day on Saturday."

Dumbfounded, Julie looked across the table at him. His face was a mirror of many emotions, which he was valiantly trying to control.

Calmly, Graeme picked up Lauren's hand and, bowing from the waist, he answered, "I'd be proud and delighted to be your Daddy and have you as my daughter anytime, anywhere, honey. Count me in."

Julie looked at him, tears threatening to fall. Although he seemed to be answering coolly, calmly and collectedly, she recognised his superhuman effort by the small tremor in his hand as he cut the peach. Sensing her look, he met her eyes as they exchanged a secret, loving smile.

The telephone interrupted her thoughts. At Maria and Giovanni's insistence, to ensure their security and total privacy, all incoming calls were monitored. Therefore, confident that it was safe to answer, Graeme reached for the receiver, answering in Italian, "Si, Maria . . . per favore . . . grazie, ciao."

He turned to Lauren. "Mama Maria says that Rico is waiting at the pool. If it's okay with your Mama, you can go. I will be down at the music room about four o'clock, and you can show me what you can do on the piano."

Julie nodded, "Fine with me, honey, do what your f . . ." she corrected herself with a blush, "Papagraeme suggests. We'll see you later, have fun."

Lauren bounced down from the table, planted a wet sloppy kiss upon her mother's cheek before throwing herself into Graeme's open arms and giving him the same treatment.

Julie pleaded, "I don't think of you as anything other than her father. I'm going to slip up sooner or later. That child of ours is too quick on the uptake not to notice!"

Graeme grinned, "Let it happen, darling. I'm almost sure she's guessed already, but hasn't yet worked out how to put it into words. Now my precious darling, 'Siesta time'.

In the privacy of their bedroom, Graeme took Julie in his arms, finding the amethyst pendant hung between her breasts. "I left you my heart in safekeeping in New York, my lovely sweetheart."

"I've never taken it off since the day you left it for me. As you intended, two hearts beating as one. Your CD gets played whenever I need to feel you close to me, it gives me such comfort."

He gently ran his hands over her bare breasts, now fuller, heavier with her pregnancy. He traced the swell of her abdomen with his two hands, marvelling that inside, his second child was steadily growing. He lovingly kissed his child.

Julie pointed towards the bedside table. "I have something special to show you. It's in that envelope."

Graeme picked up the envelope and slid out the photographic print inside, exclaiming, with a big grin on his face, "Is this what I think it is?"

Julie nodded happily, "Yes, darling, I saw and heard such a healthy and strong heartbeat. I didn't want to know its sex, I wanted it to be a surprise. That's the father's copy, Graeme."

"Wow! Isn't this fantastic." He lay with a wondrous look on his face, as he studied the photographic evidence of his paternity. "Julie, I've got to ask . . . . How has John taken the news?"

Julie hesitated. She did not want to tell him of John striking her. So she explained about John's illness and his present state of health. "In fact, he really seems pleased that Lauren will have a full brother or sister to grow up with. I haven't done any maternity publicity this time, so Anne shouldn't find out."

Graeme sensed there was something else. He was enchanted by the ultrasound print and not wanting to spoil such a special moment, he let his disquiet pass.

Kissing her passionately, he asked, "What does your Obstetrician say about a very sexy lady being made love to by the randy father of her child? Actually, I borrowed a book from our base Library, and read up on a few do's and don'ts."

Already slightly breathless at becoming so aroused so quickly by his caresses, Julie answered, in a surprised voice, "You did? Boy, I bet that raised a few eyebrows around the place! Well, he says it's okay to go ahead. Gently at first, but Graeme, my darling, I have longed for you so much, I need you."

Julie smiled as she said, "At least, as Kate told me with great relish, this is one time you can't make me pregnant."

Chuckling, he kissed her once again, informing her, "My precious love, pregnancy just makes you so much more of a desirable woman." He stroked her hair and the outline of her face, his voice heavy with emotion. "Dear God, I have missed you. You are the light of my life. Our beautiful daughter is everything a man could wish for. This new baby will be the icing on the cake. You are my family, something I can anchor my life upon. I am more than ever convinced that soon, very soon, you and I must be together. I need you, and my children, with me always."

Julie replied, equally ardently, "Maria has also convinced me that it cannot be long. Giovanni is adamant that she is always right. Do you know she predicted Lauren and Rico will one day marry each other."

Julie felt his rumble of laughter against her chest. "Wow! What a handful he'll be taking on!"

CHAPTER 48

Promptly at four o'clock, Graeme quietly re-entered the bedroom. He grinned as, without opening her eyes, she giggled, "I know you are there, Graeme McKenzie. It's a motherly instinct."

Chuckling happily, he lay beside her. "Actually, Billy did warn me about that and suggested that I'd better pack some Pj's to cover my modesty."

A yell from outside the closed door of "Mama, Papagraeme, are you awake yet?" sent Graeme into gales of laughter.

Julie groaned, "If we weren't, we sure are now."

He kissed Julie tenderly, saying, "I'll go and be entertained by my daughter. Dear heaven, how sweet those two words roll off my tongue . . . my daughter. She totally fascinates me, and can twist me around her little finger . . . See you shortly, don't be long, otherwise I'll miss you."

Julie arrived, freshly dressed in a candy striped, ice blue and white cotton dress. He gave her a "Wow!" and a low, appreciative whistle, signalling his approval.

"Giovanni is sending Rico to unlock the door for us. So, my two beauties, let's go and make music!" Graeme led the way as Lauren skipped along beside him.

Rico stared intently, first at Graeme, and then quickly switched his glance to Lauren, and back again to Graeme. Seeing this, Graeme quirked his left eyebrow at Julie and mimed '2 + 2 = 5?'

As soon as they entered the room, Lauren sat at the piano and started playing all the tunes on Graeme's CD, note perfectly, faithfully copying his style. Julie, knowing how much Lauren had looked forward to this moment, hid a smile behind her hand when Graeme's utter surprise showed on his face.

Julie laughed at him, "You look like a stunned mullet!"

Although the tunes were played with a heavy juvenile hand, the talent was obviously there. As Graeme sat beside her, Lauren said, matter of factly, "Your turn, dear Papagraeme."

Graeme kissed her cheek. "You have a real talent, young lady. I'm so proud of you, well done. Let's show Mama what we can do together, shall we?"

He played an intricate introduction, his hands lightly tickling the notes in a true concert pianist's style. Rico stood beside Julie with a look of amazement on his face as Lauren played the melody as Graeme played the accompaniment.

"Aunt Julie, when did Lauren learn to play?"

"She just listened and picked out the tunes, learning to play by ear," Julie replied.

Lauren threw her arms around Graeme's neck and kissed him, her face beamed. "Oh! My Papagraeme, you are the best piano player I have ever heard."

They embraced each other in sheer delight. Julie and Rico applauded enthusiastically, as did Maria and Giovanni who had just arrived at the ballroom.

"Magnifico! Bravo! We heard the lovely music and just had to come and see who was making it," a surprised Giovanni told Julie. "I didn't know you had such a wonderful talent, Graeme. You play very well . . . and the little bambina, eh?"

"Stay, eata witha us, cara. Victor, Bianco, Leah and the other families are coming, and afterwards we playa the real Italiano music, on the mandolins. You and the beloved one can dance. Perhaps he'll also play for us, eh?"

Graeme was accepted as 'family' by all of them as he easily alternated between speaking in Italian and English. Although Maria saw his eyes rarely left Julie, it was as though he still could not believe she was there with him. Noting this, Maria also saw that Julie softly and tenderly watched him all of the time.

When everyone was replete, Victor brought out his mandolin and began to play the haunting melodies of the 'old country', as Maria called it. His two cousins on violins soon joined him and they began to play the waltz Fascination. Graeme raised his eyebrows quizzically to Julie and proffered her his hand. She melted into his arms as they danced to the lovely old tune.

Lauren was sitting on Giovanni's lap, watching them closely. After a few minutes, she asked softly, "Papagraeme loves my Mama very much, and my Mama loves him too, doesn't she?"

Giovanni explained, "Yes child, they have known each other since they were about your age. That's a whole quarter of century in years, four times your age at least. They grew up living next door to each other."

Lauren whispered to Giovanni, "If he loves my Mama and she loves him too, why aren't they married then, 'cos then he could be my Papa all of the time?"

Giovanni glanced across her head towards Maria. Lauren was obviously fishing for an explanation. That very afternoon Rico had asked his Grandfather how come Lauren and Uncle Graeme look so much alike? Giovanni had also ducked that one. Too much of a hot potato for him!

Overhearing Lauren's question, Maria gave Giovanni an almost imperceptible shake of her head, warning him to be careful in his answer.

Fortunately for Giovanni, the music ended.

"Well, Lauren, my poppet, are we ready to show everyone how we make music?" Graeme asked.

Needing no second bidding, Lauren immediately slid off Giovanni's lap. Taking Graeme's hand, she skipped beside him to the piano. Accompanying her through her repertoire, Graeme with masterly musical skill, kept her in tempo and in tune, while expertly covering any mistakes.

Victor and his brothers joined them, adding yet another dimension to the music. Graeme started the introduction to As Time Goes By, one of Julie's favourite songs, and then, leaving Lauren to continue playing while Victor and his brothers accompanied her, Graeme took Julie in his arms and they danced to the music. They completed a circuit twice around the piano then, gently settling Julie back in her seat, Graeme returned to the piano and resumed playing the tune with his daughter.

Lauren shyly asked, "I love you, Papagraeme. Will you marry me?"

Graeme looked at her earnest face. "When you are old enough, sweetheart, I'll be too old. But I promise I will love you till the day I die."

Julie came to add her congratulations and heard, to her horror, Lauren say, "But you love my Mama, and I look like you. You wouldn't hit her like Papajon did, would you?"

"Oh, No! No, Lauren!" Julie wailed, before she hurried from the room. For a few seconds, Graeme sat at the piano, stunned. Was this what Julie had tried to hide when he had asked earlier about John's reaction to the new baby?

Maria, sensing something was wrong came to the piano. "What is it? Where is Julie?"

"Mama Maria, keep Lauren with you, please," Graeme urged. "I need to talk with Julie."

As Graeme hurried after Julie, Maria saw that Lauren was close to tears. "Now come, little bambina, it canna be that terrible, eh?"

"Oh, Mama Maria, I told Papagraeme that Papajohn hit Mama. I wasn't supposed to tell, it was a secret." Lauren hid her face in Maria's ample bosom.

Cuddling the upset child in her arms, Maria turned to Giovanni. Speaking rapidly in Italian, Maria told him what had happened. "Out of the mouths of babes, eh? He will kill John for harming her. He will not readily let her go back now." Maria gently prised Lauren away from her. "Come cara, we geta you a drink, while we leta your very wise Papagraeme talka with your Mama. Don'ta worry, they willa stilla love you just as much, cara."

Graeme caught up with Julie in front of the little stone chapel. She was trembling as he took her gently in his arms, asking her, "What happened? How dare he strike you!"

Calming down a little, Julie sighed, "It wasn't that bad. It was only a slapped face. Unfortunately, Lauren witnessed it."

"My darling Julie, in my book there is no excuse on this earth for any man to hit a woman. How dare he, especially as you are pregnant!"

Julie's eyes implored him, "Graeme, he'd been taking a new medication and shouldn't have mixed it with alcohol. When he did, he got a bad reaction. He profusely apologized the next day. It had never happened before, or since. I suppose the worst part was that Lauren saw it. That hurt him more than he hurt me. She went for him like a tigress defending her cubs! I thought I had convinced her it was a mistake, an accident.

"But you have made such an impression upon her, my darling, she trusts you with every one of her deepest thoughts and feelings."

Holding her close, Graeme said, "I'm convinced she's guessed about me, but this changes everything doesn't it? She's just not old enough to handle it. She could confront John, he may have another aberration. We cannot take that risk, darling. If he should harm you, I'd probably do him an irreparable mischief. No, regrettably I don't think Lauren can be told the truth, just yet."

He kissed her passionately and then huskily said, "Julie, we'll talk more about this later but, for now, let's go and find Lauren."

From the shelter of Maria's arms, Lauren saw them coming. Graeme was holding Julie close to his side; then he let go of Julie and held out his arms to Lauren. She gulped back her tears and flew into his welcoming embrace.

He said softly, "It's okay, honey, no harm done. We still love you, so very much. Come, let's go and hear some more music."

CHAPTER 49

Lauren, with her new Mr Bear tucked in alongside her, told Graeme she loved him very much, closed her eyes, and to Julie's amazement, was instantly asleep.

Sitting on the patio he asked. "Are you ready to elaborate on what caused John to strike you, darling?"

She confessed, "I impulsively sent you the last 'High Flight' message using the office 'phone. Our accounts people asked John to confirm whether or not to pay it. He put two and two together."

She shuddered, remembering. "Combined with the alcohol and his medication, it caused him to blow a fuse. He did only slap my face, though a bit hard. When Lauren challenged him and defended me, he understood immediately what he had done. We settled it amicably enough before he went off to Asia."

Graeme nodded. "What's wrong with him?"

"He's sick, Graeme, he has prostate and possibly testicular cancer."

Graeme winced, and let out a low whistle, "Whew! Poor devil, it's the one cancer men dread. What treatment is he having?"

"He's been taking medication, and has had some chemotherapy. He looks so thin." Her voice faded to a whisper. "I owe him and his family a lot, Graeme. His parents really looked after Lauren and me. I know he gets a lot of pleasure from having Lauren around and he really is anxious to see the new baby born."

She tenderly stroked Graeme's face. "I want to yell to the world how much I love you and want only to be with you. How I dearly want Lauren and our new baby to know who their wonderful father is . . . and yet . . . I can't do it. John is going to be so sick, so ill."

She paused. As Graeme remained silent, she continued, "I don't love him with my body and soul. But . . . I can't turn my back on him."

"My dear, sweet, gentle, Julie, you wouldn't be the woman I deeply love if you didn't feel that way. Poor man, what's the prognosis?"

"We won't know for sure until he comes back from Asia. He's seeking alternative treatment."

Graeme softly said, "However much you love me, our love is shared. Nothing in this world will ever change that, my darling one."

As he held her close, he felt a movement against his body, as though something had given him a nudge. A huge grin creased his face. "Was that what I think it was?"

"Here, put your hand just here." She placed it against her skin, just as their baby moved again.

Graeme had an incredulous look on his face as he sat hardly daring to move. When, after a minute of great activity, he kissed Julie's abdomen saying softly. "Grow in peace, my little one."

They went hand in hand to Lauren's room and Graeme gently straightened the blanket around her, still finding it hard to believe that this delightful child was his.

In the privacy of their bedroom, he took Julie in his arms and gently caressed her. Julie felt again the familiar excitement she experienced each time he touched her. As he butterfly kissed every part of her body she became sexually aware, wanting more and more of his erotic touches.

When eventually their mutual arousal demanded a more complete satisfaction, he still disciplined himself to approach her slowly, gently. He discovered he got as much satisfaction himself from this self-enforced control.

Julie felt the full length of his masculine tumescence inside her. Her body responding with paroxysms of erotic passion at having him bring her to another mighty orgasm.

Julie stretched, allowing her womb to relax after such a delicious, lovemaking session. She felt so loved, so wanted and so, so cherished.

Julie heard his chest rumble with laughter. "Mustn't fall asleep before I put my pj's on. Got to cover my 'modesty' before I do."

Julie pulled a filmy nightgown from under her pillow. "Lauren has never seen me in bed with anyone, let alone a male someone!"

Grinning from ear to ear, Graeme responded, "We have never slept together so well covered, sweetheart!"

Chuckling, Graeme kissed her a final time and then said, in an emotional sober voice, "One day, I promise . . . when we are both free . . . we will never ever spend a night apart again."

. . . The room was lighter, must be after seven Graeme's brain reasoned, Julie's body was still wrapped close to his own—in front of him. But, something was breathing on the back of his neck! Slowly turning his head, he looked into the sleeping face of Lauren. She had her arms around his neck and her head cuddled up against him, her warm breath rustling the hair on the back of his neck. She smelled of clean, warm, baby talcum powder.

He chuckled, silently thanking Billy for his modesty' advice.

Julie stirred; Graeme kissed her and said in a whisper, "We have company."

"I did try to warn you," Julie giggled.

"I never knew fatherhood could be so fascinating. It's a unique experience," Graeme whispered in her ear.

Julie laughed quietly, and stroked his dear, dear face. "Well, another side issue of pregnancy is that your baby lies annoyingly close to the bladder. I'll be a minute and then I'll go and make some tea. You and Miss Shirley Temple can have a lie-in together."

Lauren stirred and saw a pair of dark blue eyes inches from her own. "Hello, my Papa, are you awake now? You were still asleep when I came to look for you."

Graeme tried valiantly not to evince any surprise at being called just 'Papa'. He wrapped his arms around her. "It was very nice to wake up and find you here. Mama has gone to spoil us, and make some tea. It's Good Friday."

"We're going to Church this morning, and then Rico and me are going to swim. Will you come with us today?"

"Indeed. I shall be reading the Lesson in Church this morning. Yes! I might join you in a swim, after siesta. Ah ha, here is your lovely Mama with the welcome brew."

"Good morning, Mama. Papa and I were just working out what we are going to do today."

Julie looked questioningly at Graeme and mouthed,

'Papa'? she raised her eyebrows as he shrugged in an 'I don't know' gesture.

As Julie set out the breakfast tray, Graeme exclaimed, "Wow! I haven't had breakfast in bed since I was a boy."

Lauren insisted on watching Graeme shave as she chattered away, standing on the bathroom stool beside him. All at once she paused mid-sentence . . . studying him intently in the bathroom mirror . . . she touched her own blonde hair and whispered, "I do look like you, Papa."

Julie emerged from the shower and heard the words. Her eyes locked with Graeme's, she shook her head and mouthed, "No . . . don't."

Graeme, with a barely discernible nod of his head, grinned at Lauren. "Well, if a beautiful little lady like you thinks she looks like me, that must make me the handsomest man on the block!" He picked the giggling Lauren up and swung her around above his head. The moment had passed. Only Julie sensed how his quick-witted humour had disguised a huge ache in his heart.

Back in Lauren's room, a discussion was taking place on her choice of outfit. "'cos Papagraeme is going to be in his pilot's uniform, I must look really, extra good too."

"Darling, Papagraeme is much more than a pilot. He's a very, very senior and important officer in the British Royal Air Force," Julie gently admonished her daughter.

"Well then, if he's that important, I'd better be super-dooper dressed today, Mama," said an unabashed Lauren.

Julie selected her latest maternity outfit in Cambridge blue to complement his uniform. An Empire style dress with a matching edge-to-edge, three quarter length coat. Pulling the amethyst pendant out so that it lay on top of the dress, she clipped on a pair of matching amethyst earrings. She could see in the mirror that her pregnancy was discreetly camouflaged.

When Graeme came back into the room, still chuckling at something Lauren had told him, he stared at her, "My God! You get more beautiful every time I look at you. Darling, I thought Lauren looked good enough to eat, just like a sweet bundle of candyfloss. Now look at you! I'll be the proudest man in the Church today."

Julie kissed him. "You've brushed up pretty good yourself, Group Captain, my darling, Sir."

Later, Julie nearly burst with pride when Graeme, so handsome in his uniform, read the lesson in his clear modulated voice, meaningfully and with passion, and absolutely word perfectly.

Lauren could not take her eyes off of Graeme as he spoke. Julie had to discreetly stop her applauding him at the end of the reading.

Kneeling in silent prayer, Julie pleaded, 'Please let me be with him soon. I love him so much, and I need him with me.'

Rico approached them and Lauren dissolved into a fit of the giggles when Graeme gave her a cheeky wink and said, in a stage whisper, "Here comes your boyfriend."

"Are you all coming to lunch with us, Lauren?" Rico shyly asked in Italian. "Will you swim with us today, sir?"

"Rico. I told you, in English, only ask one question at a time," admonished Lauren. "Yes, we're coming to lunch and Papagraeme will probably come for a swim after he has a siesta with Mama. Come on, where's lunch, I'm starving."

Graeme was almost doubled with laughter, as Julie looked aghast at her daughter, "Oh God! I give up!"

Graeme, still highly amused, told her, "She is delightful. You have taught her to be so self-confident and independent, my darling. She might physically look like me but there is from you, a great personality. Dear heaven, you both make me feel so proud."

CHAPTER 50

They sat together for the family lunch at long tables, under the shady loggia. The lively, animated conversation ebbed and flowed, alternating easily between English and Italian.

Several womenfolk insisted on trying out their own 'old wives tales,' to define the sex of Julie's new baby. With much hilarity, after trying a variety of these old adages, anecdotes and legends, it was agreed, she was definitely carrying a son.

Whilst all of this feminine frolicking was taking place, Graeme was assisting in the cellar with the decanting of the luncheon table wine. He was amongst the various male kith and kin of the family, for this was considered exclusively a 'men only' task.

Many of the males good-naturedly ribbed him at becoming a father-to-be for the second time. Incredulous though he was at their assumptions, he decided that discretion was definitely the better part of valour. Instead, he happily accepted their slightly risqué and ribald comments.

After lunch, Lauren skipped between Julie and Graeme, trying to coerce Graeme into going swimming with her later in the afternoon.

Finally he pretended to give in. "Okay you win, my honeybunch, after four o'clock. But . . . for now, Mama and I need a siesta after such a large lunch. Agreed? Capisco, mio bambina?"

Cheekily, she saluted him. "Si, Papa, Sir!"

Growling at her like a bear, he chased her into the villa.

Several minutes later, Graeme joined Julie in their bedroom. "Whew! I didn't know little girls had so many buttons! She's eventually undressed and in her swim gear, reading . . . would you believe this, one of my 'Flight' magazines!"

"Darling, Graeme, I had a hard job in church restraining her from applauding every sentence you uttered this morning. Of course you already know that her mother dotes on you."

Graeme gazed tenderly at the lovely woman now dressed in a silky satin caftan, and with her hair loose around her shoulders. He sighed, she never seemed to age. He took her in his arms and passionately kissed her.

Linking her arms around his neck Julie told him, "While you were in the cellar with the men folk, the ladies performed all of the 'what-sex-are-you-going-to-have' old wives tales upon me. Their consensus was that we are going to have a son this time. We must choose some names, dearest. Stuart is my real favourite; it has such a good ring to it. And it's also your second name darling, what do you like?"

"I also like Stuart, there's been a Stuart in our family for generations. Yes, let's keep up the tradition, darling. My son . . . my son Stuart . . . it's a bit mind boggling, isn't it?" He sighed in pure contentment. "But I'm still puzzled, why did all of the men assume this was my child? Why do all of the womenfolk also accept that it is?

"I suppose Lauren is a dead giveaway, she and I couldn't be anything but father and daughter. By the way, when we are alone, I've significantly become just 'Papa'. Well, what if we have another little lass, eh? What have you in mind, my dearest?"

"Gabriella, Angelique," Julie spoke the names almost dreamily. "Something Italian sounding, I think. I love the language, it always has such romance in its words."

"I can't disagree there, it's my favourite as well." He kissed the top of her head. "So, that's the family sorted. Any chance that, as their father, I can now get some exclusive, private attention from their adorable mother?"

She opened her caftan and let it drop to the floor. Standing naked in front of him, she murmured, "Ummm . . . I'm all yours, my beloved one."

"An invitation I'll never be able to resist," he answered huskily . . .

. . . Graeme was dozing lightly, pleasantly sexually sated once again, with Julie wrapped tightly in his arms. He stirred as he heard a soft knock on the bedroom door. Grabbing a sheet, he rapidly pulled it over both their naked bodies, muttering, "Modesty, hurry lad, remember modesty!"

There was another soft knock as he carefully extricated himself and donned his bathrobe. He opened the door a crack and saw his swimsuit-clad daughter waiting impatiently outside.

He whispered, "Five minutes, Lauren, honey. I'll be there."

He turned and saw Julie with a wide smile. "Great being a parent isn't it? Your private time is very, very limited." She stretched languorously. "Mind you, even limited time is always perfect with you, my adored one."

Graeme dropped down on the bed beside her. "I enjoyed our 'limited time' very much, thank you. Now I must go as I have promised the other beautiful lady in my life." He grinned happily as he confessed, "I've never been so organised by 'petticoat rule' before—but boy, am I enjoying it!"

By the time Julie arrived at the pool, Graeme, swimming with a powerful freestyle stroke, had just reached the further end of the pool. Lauren and Rico were sitting on the low diving board using Graeme's wristwatch to time his effort. They were both looking in awe at the watch, as Rico uttered an admiring, "Wow".

Lauren, with a smug look on her face, turned to him, saying, "See I told you, he's as good as any Olympic swimmer. Oh, hello Mama, look at how fast Papagraeme can swim," she said, showing Julie the wristwatch. As Graeme swum at a more leisurely pace towards them, Julie silently mouthed, "Show off!" at him.

He just grinned as he emerged dripping water and picked her up in his arms, pretending to throw her into the pool. Screaming at him, "Graeme McKenzie, don't you dare! Remember the baby!"

"It's only the baby that is saving you, minx," he chuckled, as he kissed her, causing her to squeal as he let his cold, wet hair drip all over her face. Putting her back on her feet, he wolf whistled her, exclaiming, "My, my! Pregnant or not, honey, you look good in that Hawaiian sarong outfit."

Julie, a little flustered by all of this public skylarking, blushed under his admiring gaze. This only caused him to guffaw with laughter, as he dodged her playful swipe at him by diving cleanly back into the pool.

Not to be outdone, Lauren and Rico plunged in after him and soon a three-person race was on between them. Julie carefully lowered herself into the calming waters.

As soon as she was fully in the pool with her feet firmly on the bottom, Graeme swum over to her under water. He began kissing first her feet then all the way up her legs, and finally her abdomen before surfacing beside her, with a happy smile. "Hello, my beautiful mermaid."

Accepting a wet but passionate kiss from him, Julie managed to splutter, "You swim very well, Graeme. Was that another aspect of your pilot's training?"

Soberly he replied, "An essential part. Survival in the water and being able to swim proficiently could mean the thin line between life and death, if one had to 'ditch,' particularly so in a war situation. I see Lauren has been taught correctly, she handles herself very competently. Who taught her?"

"Most New Zealand kids can swim almost as soon as they can walk." she explained. "She had an ex-Olympian as her tutor. He was very strict, but it has paid off."

"How about her sexy Mama, does she swim?" He playfully asked, as he turned her on her back and began to tow her through the water. She skilfully rolled over on to her front and dived under the water. She surfaced beside him as he gasped for air.

"Yes, her sexy Mama can swim, the same ex-Olympian taught me." She swam off to the other end of the pool, leaving him chuckling in her wake. This feisty, beautiful, sensuous package of pure womanhood never ceased to surprise and delight him.

They lay sunbathing a few minutes later when Julie, trying to sound casual, asked, "What is Anne doing these days, Graeme?"

He grimaced at her. "What a way to mar a perfect day! Well, she's still on the cocktail circuit, all fluff and no substantial, intelligent output." The disgust in his voice showed. "I think she's in the Caribbean at the moment, with a group of her equally useless friends."

His face cleared and lit up with a warm, loving smile as Lauren came rushing up. "Can we go and play some piano later, Papagraeme?"

"Of course, I'm looking forward to it, honey," he answered.

True to his word, half an hour later he had changed and led an excited Lauren to play the piano. Julie followed at a more comfortable pace as she heard him playing the beautiful 'Dream of Olwyn'.

Julie and Graeme took their daughter to the solemn and moving Evensong Service and, as was the custom, the family dispersed straight after the service.

Pausing on the front steps of the guest villa, Graeme gazed up at the clear starlit sky and recited the opening words of his favourite poem, 'High Flight.' It was the first time Lauren had heard it, so Graeme read her the complete text in his own well-thumbed book.

Her reaction pleasantly surprised him as she declared solemnly, "It's beautiful, Papa. Will you take me flying so that I can see it for myself?"

His voice was thick with emotion, as he told her, "One day, Lauren, my dearest, I hope to be able to take both Mama and you flying with me."

CHAPTER 51

Waking from an undisturbed night's sleep, Julie rolled over to look lovingly at the handsome male specimen lying beside her.

Graeme leant upon one elbow and tenderly stroked her hair. "Our relationship gets deeper, closer, Julie. Every moment is very precious to me."

He took her in his arms, "Julie, I'm going to be involved in a somewhat risky deployment when I go back. Should anything untoward happen to me, I'd like to know that the children are protected, and have an incontestable legal entitlement to my estate. We should each arrange to have total legal guardianship, in the event of either one of us dying prematurely. Would you think about it, cara?"

"Yes, of course, darling. Rico's father, Victor, is the family lawyer, we could ask him. I own my home and the surrounding land and Naomi and George left 'Greenfields' in trust for Lauren and her siblings."

She paused, before continuing. "They were very special people, Graeme. When they found out you were Lauren's father, they checked up on you."

A surprised look registered on his face. "Really?"

"I didn't find out about it until after they died. It was shortly after that John's attitude to Lauren changed."

She sighed, remembering the generosity and love of Naomi and George Field. "They left everything to Lauren and her siblings. It's another reason why I cannot leave John. I must help him, I owe them that much, Graeme, darling."

"I wouldn't expect anything less . . ."

She interrupted him, "Graeme! What risky deployment are you going on?" His casually spoken words were only now registering upon her brain.

"It'll be somewhere in the Middle East, darling. Could be a bit hairy and dicey there for a while."

Julie stammered, "I never like to ask you about your job. I'm always too scared to know if you're in any danger."

"My dearest, darling Julie, it's what I am trained to do. Believe me, self-preservation is always there to the forefront, especially when I think about you. Nothing is going to stop me living to a grand old age and chasing you all over the house."

Graeme kissed her tenderly. "Anyway, this is far too serious a conversation. Today I'm going to be the 'Daddy' of the most fabulous daughter a man could wish for. Wonder where she is this morning?"

Julie chuckled, "I'm off to the bathroom. I'll send her in."

Opening Lauren's bedroom door slowly, Julie peeked in. Lauren roused, Mr Bear clutched in her arms, plus with Graeme's 'Flight' magazine under her pillow.

"Good morning, sleepyhead. Papagraeme is waiting, if you want to go and get a cuddle."

Lauren nodded sleepily and wandered towards Graeme.

She heard him say softly, "Hello, my Princess. You'd better tell me what I'm to do today, as your Daddy."

After breakfast, Julie sat on the front steps in hysterics, watching their frantic three-legged efforts. Graeme's tall figure and Lauren's little body did not make for an easy partnership.

Julie advised, between bursts of laughter, "Lift Lauren off the ground, Graeme. Just let her toes touch the ground."

Arriving at the village green, their ears and noses were assailed by the smell of hot dogs, fried onions, candyfloss and the sickly sweet smell of caramel popcorn. The air was alive with the raucous noise of music from a variety of Merry-Go-Rounds, Carousels and of crackling loudspeakers barking out the various attributes of the 'not to be missed' attractions.

Giovanni parked the car under a large Jacaranda tree and, with Graeme's assistance, set up the folding table and chairs ready for their lunch later on.

They found the rest of the family already there. Rico greeted Lauren shyly, yet still managed to sneak in a curious sidelong, questioning glance at Graeme. Julie stifled a giggle, seeing that Graeme had noted Rico's look. Lauren was extolling to Rico their prowess that morning in practicing for the races, and that Graeme was to be her 'Daddy' for the day. Once again the young boy looked knowingly at Graeme.

Lauren and Graeme had drawn the third heat of the under ten's. Sizing up her opposition, Lauren confidently told him, "We'll beat them easily, Papa."

"I only wish I had half of your confidence in my ability, honey," Graeme said, ruefully eyeing the giant sized young countrymen around him. "This lot look as though they'd eat us alive!"

He gave Julie a look of 'what have I got myself into?' Julie smiled wickedly back at him, saying with a giggle, "Do your best 'Daddy', remember the bigger they are the harder they fall—or something like that."

Before he could retort, the Umpire blew his whistle, and called, "Heat three."

Lining up on the outside of the ten couples in the field, Graeme tucked his arm around his daughter, and she smiled encouragingly up at him. Then the whistle blew. They were off!

Remembering Julie's advice to lift Lauren, he ran with very short steps down to the winning post, with Lauren clinging to him and shouting, "We're winning, Papa! Hooray, we've won!"

Pulling up, Graeme looked behind to see the unbelievable sight of the rest of the field wallowing in their wake. Julie threw her arms around them as the whole Martini family cheered and hollered!

Lauren cried in jubilation, "We're in the final, Papa," jumping excitedly up and down in her joy.

Graeme reckoned the finalists were younger, fitter and more of a human size. Lauren ran her eyes over their competition and, with youthful optimism, told Graeme, "We can do it, Papa."

The competitors milled around nervously. Some snapped crossly at each other, while others had their cameras clicking to get those all-important family album pictures for posterity. At least one couple had the child whining that it didn't want to race!

Graeme and Lauren grinned encouragement to each other, when, with a big, heart melting smile, Lauren said, "I love you, Papa."

"And I you, honeybunch." He cuddled her to him as the Umpire called them into line.

With the wings of Pegasus beneath his feet, Graeme held Lauren close to his body. They won by a very comfortable margin.

"You were brilliant!" Julie cried, as she embraced them together. "I love you both."

Grinning widely from ear to ear, Graeme murmured, "That's what did it, you see. I got the magic words that she loved me, just before the start. God! I feel good, my darling."

"Have something to drink before the egg and spoon," Julie advised, "We won't eat until after the races, then you can gorge yourself silly on the gorgeous spread Mama Maria has prepared."

The local Vicar instructed them in the rules. "Children run the first length, parents the second. If you drop your egg, you must stand still, replace the egg and begin again. Is that clear, everyone?"

Leaving Lauren with Julie at the start, Graeme walked with Victor to the other end of the field with the other parents. Victor said, "Julie tells me you'd like to have a chat later, Graeme. How about I come at six o'clock, before we all go for dinner?"

"Great Victor, thank you," and added with a grin, "Right, now we are competitors, no holds barred."

Victor grinned back boyishly saying, "I love this Fete. It's the one time of the year I get to be a big kid again, let my hair down and act like a real idiot. How about you, Graeme, it must be quite a relaxation for you also, eh?"

Graeme grinned roguishly, "You said it, Victor. Oh ho, look out, here they come!"

The screams of encouragement coming from the womenfolk on the side lines alerted them. Two had already fallen by the wayside, their eggs smashed to smithereens, leaving their owners in floods of tears. Graeme saw, to his delight, that Lauren was racing neck and neck out front with . . . Rico!

With a huge grin, Graeme called, "It's going to be down to you and me, pardner!

The two children arrived simultaneously. The noise from the side lines hit an all-time high as Graeme and Victor hurtled to the finish line. The contrast between Victor's Italian dark locks and Graeme's blonde hair was stark, as they concentrated on safely holding the pesky oval skittish eggs upon their wooden spoons.

At the finish line nothing separated them! It was declared a dead-heat! Collapsing beside each other, gasping for air, they gave each other a satisfied grin, and clasped hands.

Lauren mopped Graeme's brow with a towel, saying, "Oh, you did so well, my Papa, darling." She plonked wet kisses upon his cheeks.

A metallic voice whistled raucously though the loud speaker, announcing that the prize giving for the morning races would take place immediately.

"We'll have two of them," Lauren told him.

"Well, honeybunch, we shall treasure them forever, won't we?" He hoisted her onto his shoulders so that she could see better. He slipped an arm around Julie's shoulders. "We look just like a regular, normal family, my darling. Isn't it marvellous?"

Julie could not answer; her throat was too tight with emotion. He had just put her exact thoughts into words.

CHAPTER 52

"Ladies and Gentlemen . . . and . . . er . . . children," the voice of the Vicar alternately squeaked, and then boomed out from the microphone. The local radio shop salesman, sweating profusely, dashed around the stage, trying valiantly to do adjustments. "Er . . . We come to the pleasurable task of the prize-giving for the morning races. At the conclusion . . . er . . . there will be a break of one hour for lunch."

His voice boomed out deafeningly, accompanied by another loud rustling of papers. "To start proceedings we have the three-legged race winners."

Graeme hoisted Lauren on to the stage side steps. Here she danced from one foot to the other, fidgeting and squirming until Graeme put his hand on her shoulder and she immediately quietened.

The Vicar sorted through his untidy bundle of papers, "Er . . . 'Under ten years old' . . . the winners Mr Graeme McKenzie and Miss Lauren Field."

Graeme proudly escorted his daughter to receive a small silver cup, engraved with the words 'Winner of the Under 10 year old three-legged race 1995'. Lauren was presented with a life-sized rabbit soft toy.

The Vicar was shuffling his notes again as he nervously announced, "Er . . . . . er . . . egg and spoon, we have . . . Yes indeed! A dead heat! Between Victor and Rico Martini and Graeme and Lauren McKenzie . . . er . . . no, that's Field . . . Lauren Field."

Julie and Graeme exchanged grins as Lauren sadly whispered, "I wish it was McKenzie."

To the cheers, whistles and derisive hoots from the entire Martini family, the four winners mounted the stage.

The two men received a rampant silver spoon holding a small silver egg on a polished wooden plinth. The two children were each awarded a silver eggcup with a matching spoon.

The extended Martini family slowly made their way back to the shade of the jacaranda tree. Bringing up the rear, Graeme was admiring his trophies.

"Who's a clever boy then?" Julie teased him.

"Aah, sweetheart," he said with a deep sigh of satisfaction, "These will take pride of place in the cabinet in my office." Seeing her worried frown, he murmured, "No. She never comes near."

After their picnic lunch, he ruefully rubbed his overfull stomach; he confessed to Julie, "I'm glad the sprint races are over! All I want now is a siesta." He leered, raising his eyebrows questioningly.

Julie blushed, knowing only too well what he was thinking. She murmured, "Your presence will soon be required for the sack races."

Lauren, ignoring his protestations that he had over-eaten, climbed up on his lap, wrapped her arms around his neck and snuggled her head onto his chest. She whispered, "I love you, Papa."

"And I you, honey," he answered softly, as he kissed the top of her golden curls.

Maria patted Julie's arm, "See, whata I tella you, no worry, he love her verra, verra much, and she him."

Bianco, Victor's beautiful, raven-haired wife, was sitting on Maria's other side, and shyly added, "You make the right decision to come here, Julie."

The words troubled Julie. "I know you have all guessed about him . . ." Her voice conveyed her concern. "Mama Maria, nobody must talk about us both being here!" She shuddered at the thought.

Maria assured her, "We are a . . . how you say, Bianco? . . ." She broke off, and spoke rapidly in Italian. "Ahha.. thata it . . . a closed shop . . . and we have verra, verra closed mouths as well, mio cara. Giovanni woulda notta leta anyone speaka of whata goes on in our family. You are safe, cara. Trust us, eh?"

"Yes, my dear Mama Maria, but I must protect him at all times."

A clarion bugle call, usually used to call the hounds to the hunt, boomed over the loudspeakers.

"Ladies and Gentlemen . . . the afternoon races will begin in fifteen minutes," announced the squeaky voice of the Vicar.

Lauren clapped her hands in glee, sliding off Graeme's knee and pulling him to his feet. "C'mon, Papa, let's go."

Julie hid her amusement behind her hand musing, 'there he goes, a very senior officer in Her Majesty's Royal Air Force, docilely following his daughter everywhere, carrying out her every wish, as meekly as a lamb.'

Graeme helped Lauren into her sack. "Now don't try to move too fast, or take big hops, honey. Just small bunny hops."

Doing as Graeme had advised, she managed to stay upright, while most of the field fell over in a variety of tangled untidy heaps. Halfway there and only two bodies remained upright, the other was Rico.

Victor was running along the side line, extolling his son, "Go son! Go son!"

Graeme, on the opposite side, his voice calmer, softer, "Small hops. Small hops, Lauren honey."

But Rico's extra few months in age, held sway. He beat Lauren by several yards. When Rico saw who he had beaten he was immediately downcast.

Lauren cheerfully threw him a morsel of comfort as she told him, in a patronising, haughty feminine voice, "It's okay, Rico. My Papagraeme beat my Mama, ages and ages ago and she still loves him."

Graeme saw the face of the boy brightened at her words, but immediately turn to a typical male expression of puzzlement, not knowing if he had been forgiven, or chastised!

Graeme patted him on the shoulder in a show of masculine camaraderie, "In other words, sport, we men might have won the race, but we haven't won the war! They learn the art, Rico, old son, in the cradle!"

Listening to this exchange, Victor nodded and added, "But, aah, what would we do without them? As the French say, so succinctly—'Vive la Difference' eh Graeme?"

Victor and Graeme exchanged guffaws of laughter.

For several races to follow, Lauren was to be partnered by Rico, so Graeme decided to return to Julie. He was alarmed to see her looking pale.

"I think I've had too much sun and noise. I am just a wee bit tired," she told him.

"I'll take you back, straight away, my sweetheart." Without waiting for her reply, he went to Giovanni. Giovanni glanced over to where Julie was seated, and without hesitation handed Graeme the car keys.

He told her gently, "Come on, my darling, Victor will bring everybody back later. A cool rest for you, Doctor Graeme's orders."

Julie sank thankfully on the bed in the cool room. He drew the window blind and gently placed a pillow under her ankles. "Now rest, my dearest Julie. I'll be right here beside you."

"No, go back and enjoy the rest of the races with Lauren. I'll be fine here, honestly."

He stroked her hair, "Julie, I choose to be here, with the love of my life. Victor's coming at six o'clock to have that talk."

Some time later, Julie roused. "Hello, my darling, feeling better?" Graeme enquired as he came and lay beside her.

Julie stretched her body the full length of his. "It's so good waking up and seeing you here, Graeme. I never got this tired with Lauren, so perhaps all of the experts and pundits out there are right . . . we are expecting a son."

A small human tornado hurtled through the French doors, crying, "Mama, Papa, I'm back! Okay if I go for a swim with Rico? TantBianco will be there to watch us."

Lauren gave Julie a bear hug before flying into Graeme's open arms. He whisked her up, and twirled her around.

"Hello, lovely child. Have you had a good afternoon?"

"Yes, Papa, gotta go, Rico's waiting." She wriggled out of his hold and ran to her bedroom.

Keeping his word to his daughter, Graeme briefly left Julie while he joined the children in the pool. The idyllic afternoon was, for him, complete.

When he later arrived on time as arranged, Victor asked, "Well folks, how can I be of help?"

Graeme answered, "As you may already be aware, Victor, Julie and I cannot marry for the time being. While I have already taken legal steps to acknowledge my paternity for both of my children, I must also face the situation that I am still in a high-risk occupation. And . . . God forbid . . . should anything happen to Julie, I could lose custody of them. We feel vulnerable, we need a legal guardianship. In a nutshell, that's what we want . . . to protect us and our children, Victor."

Victor broached the delicate subject. "Graeme, why don't you and Julie simply divorce your respective partners?"

Graeme painfully explained Anne's vehement threats, made when she discovered Lauren's existence. Graeme sighed, "She hasn't learned Julie is pregnant again, thank goodness. Julie has also discovered John is very ill, with a poor prognosis. Rightly so, she feels she cannot desert him just now."

Having heard of Anne's previous actions, Victor snorted his disgust. "Your wife is the type of vicious emotional blackmailer I hate to deal with. They are unpredictable, and are a fearsome adversary. How did you, a man of much integrity, marry such a viper?"

"I'd lost Julie and was devastated for a long, long time. Anne came along and we drifted into a marriage of convenience. She enjoys my rank, and the social status it gives her. I allowed it to happen and got on with my life. When I met Julie again in Sydney, I knew then she was all I ever really wanted. We discussed John's infertility problems and made a mutual decision for her to conceive Lauren."

He gave Victor a rueful smile. "Adhering to an agreement Julie made, mainly to protect me, I might add, we didn't make contact again until last December. Another strangely coincidental meeting . . . call it what you will . . . our paths crossed again, hence the new baby."

Julie smiled, "One day, Victor, we shall both be free to be together. It may be by then biologically too late for me to have our children. John accepts the situation of me having another, and we discussed using a sperm donor. But, Graeme and I still greatly fear Anne."

Victor replied, "No one who has seen you two together could ever doubt your commitment to each other. It will be my pleasure to draw up some suitable guardianship papers."

CHAPTER 53

Graeme, to his delight, slept undisturbed until he felt a pair of small chubby arms sneak around his neck. It was seven o'clock on Easter Sunday morning.

"Hello, my honey," he whispered. She giggled as she ran her hand over his cheek, feeling his early morning bristles.

"Papa . . . are we going to Church today and will you be wearing your uniform and reading from the Bible book?"

"Ummhumm, yes indeed, to all of your questions, honey. Today is a very important day in our Christian calendar. But first we have the Great Easter Egg Hunt."

Two intensely blue eyes looked into his. "I've never done it before, but Rico says its good fun."

"Well, NunkVictor explained it to me yesterday,"

he told her. "Apparently it's a Martini family custom. On Easter Sunday morning, after breakfast, all the children hunt through the garden for the specially decorated Easter Eggs."

Beckoning for her to bring her ear close to his mouth, he whispered, "I thought I saw a certain Mama out in the garden when I was playing the piano last evening. Guess what she was doing, eh?" He tapped the side of his nose and winked at Lauren.

"What are you two whispering about?" asked a sleepy voice, tucked up close to the other side of Graeme.

He kissed her forehead. "Good morning, my darling. You slept well."

Julie, still with her eyes closed, smiled, "I feel so good!"

Graeme gazed at the enchanting body, the lace of her nightgown revealing a sensational cleavage and the inviting swell of her full breasts underneath. He breathed in deeply; it was only Lauren's presence that stopped him from taking her to him once again. She was very aware of his thoughts as she opened her eyes, stroked his 'modesty' under the cover of the sheet, and wickedly 'glad eyed' him.

He breathed in quickly, and murmured, "You Minx. You'll keep m'lady!"

She chuckled and rolled over, removing the temptation.

"I'll bring in breakfast. Stay there, both of you."

Shortly after breakfast, they heard the church bells ringing, calling all of the children together for the great Easter Egg Hunt.

Lauren dashed off to seek and search for her share of the booty, carrying a little straw lined, hand-decorated basket, specially made for her by Maria. Showered and then rapidly dressing in shorts and shirt, Graeme followed her.

"Oh, look Mama! We found ten eggs!" Lauren shouted out in glee.

"Lauren what beautiful eggs you have, they look too good to eat," Julie replied.

Graeme whistled admiringly as he closely inspected the hand-decorated eggs. "Who does this exquisite work?"

"That talent belongs to Bianco," Julie replied, "I plan to use some of her costume jewellery in our spring collection."

Once again, the small, picturesque family church was filled to overflowing for this very special service. Graeme, so distinguished in his uniform and his upright military bearing, made an imposing figure as he rose to read the Lesson.

Maria grasped Giovanni's hand tightly as she silently prayed, 'Please, my Lord, I implore you, my Julie loves this man so much, give them a sign, please.'

Graeme came over, waving a bunch of car keys in the air. "Darling, look what Giovanni has suggested. He wondered if we would like to leave Lauren with them at the pool for a couple of hours, and go off on our own for a drive. What d'you think?"

"What a lovely idea," Julie responded immediately. "You really haven't had a chance to see the vineyard, or the surrounding countryside."

"I'll just check with Her Highness, shall I? See if it's okay with her." Julie watched him crouch down on his haunches and saw Lauren immediately put her arms around his neck. Seconds later Lauren kissed him and happily nodded.

Graeme returned to Julie. "All settled . . . actually she seemed relieved to be shot of us for a couple of hours." He wrinkled his brow into a frown. "Mind you . . . I think I may have promised to play Ludo, or something, with her this evening in exchange."

Julie grinned, "Come on, I know just the place for a lazy, late lunch."

They threaded their way through acre upon acre of grape vines. Following Julie's instructions, Graeme easily found the country inn she had been anxious for him to see. It was a low slung, typically early Australian building, with red-bricked walls and a green iron roof. Flocks of lorikeets, galahs and cockatoos screeched from the surrounding bush and eucalyptus trees. The fresh air was fragrant and sharp with the distinctive smell of the trees, mixed with frangipani and other aromatic exotic plants.

Graeme breathed deeply, filling his lungs with the invigorating air. Julie insisted on doing the ordering, so Graeme sat back, enjoying the experience of having her take charge. She ordered a typical Australian bushman's lunch for them, fries, pies 'n mushy peas, with an ice-cold Australian beer for him, and a fresh pineapple juice for herself.

Graeme gazed admiringly at the view. "It's so peaceful here, when and how did you find it?"

"We did a photo shoot here, several seasons ago, and I've always wanted to come back—I never thought I'd have the pleasure of showing it to you though, my darling."

"Julie, tell me more about your work, after all, I only get to see the marvellous end results when you wear your gorgeous outfits. I know nothing of their background."

For the next hour, as they ate, Julie told him in detail of her life and her work. She realised he was hungry for an insight into the lifestyle she and Lauren shared and, in an equally sudden realisation, she understood what a lonely domestic life he led.

She emphasised to him, "Lauren and I are the lucky ones, aren't we? At least we have each other, whilst you, my darling, are very much on your own."

Graeme gave a rueful nod. She told him of her own trials and tribulations of selecting fabrics, designing clothing, pattern making, and also some of the 'insider' information surrounding her everyday life.

She continued, "Breaking into the fashion business was so difficult for a newcomer, but once we gained our first awards, all the doors started to open up for us. Financially I'm independent and reasonably well off. I own the house and the land. I have my dear little Scarlet O'Hara—my superb MG sports car, although I must confess, with two bairns to cart around later this year, I may, for convenience sake, treat us to a station wagon model. I owe John's parents such a huge debt, they virtually set me up for life."

She paused reflectively until, with a sob in her voice, she implored him, "Though I love you very dearly, I must stay with John right now with the serious state of his health."

Graeme held her hands in his as he softly said, "I know, I know, my dearest, I do understand, I truly do . . ."

He hesitated for a while but knew he had to impress upon her his own situation. "Julie, I have a task I'm contracted to do later that's risky. I don't want some unscrupulous person using devious means to uncover a link between us. I want the luxury of knowing that you are safe, far away from me, not a part of anything I'm involved in."

Her face paled and she stumbled over her words. "Will you be in danger, Graeme?"

He reluctantly nodded. "It's a tricky deployment, sweetheart. There are radicals on both sides. Yes, I will not lie to you, my darling, it could be dangerous, even life threatening. That's why I think it's imperative we get Victor to finalise something for us this weekend."

He had deliberately skimmed across the danger he could face on his next assignment, not willing to alarm Julie. Deep in his heart, he knew that this time he would be in as great a danger as he had ever been. Kidnapping and the holding to ransom of important dignitaries was a way of life in the area. And, he ruefully reminded himself, so was the murder of the hostages, if their captors did not get their demands fulfilled.

They lingered over their coffee, occasionally touching or holding hands, speaking openly, frankly and seriously, still amazed at how deep were the feelings they shared for each other. Yet, they both felt the winds of change filtering into their relationship as it entered a new, deeper, more mature phase.

They were no longer just two young, carefree lovers, mindful only of the intensity of their love for each other.

They now bore a joint responsibility for bringing two children into the world. Never before had they talked in such depth.

Julie was not surprised to learn that, through judicious investments, he was also a wealthy man in his own right. He explained, "I also own a serviced apartment, close to the base. Anne has the house in town."

With an infectious grin he said, "Right. Come on, we've been serious enough, let's go and do some more exploring, my sweetheart."

CHAPTER 54

Moments later they were driving through a small town that seemed to be virtually in the middle of nowhere. The only moving thing was a sign, gently swaying against a ramshackle building, which read, 'Collectables'.

Graeme stopped the car. "C'mon, darling, let's see if we can find a souvenir, or something, for Lauren in here."

A bell tinkled softly as they pushed open the front door. Inside was the smallest shop either had ever seen. It was piled high, from floor to ceiling, with bric a brac. Piece after piece appeared to be tumbling over its neighbour, as though haphazardly rescued, caught just in time from being dumped in the nearest rubbish bin.

Wandering around this Aladdin's cave, Julie and Graeme admired the treasures from the past—they wondered aloud, if only the pieces could talk, what stories they could tell. Some items were so typically Australasian and new to Graeme's eyes that Julie had to explain their use or their origin.

A small, dark skinned, wrinkled figure of a woman, of uncertain age, emerged from an obscure and indistinct direction at the back of the shop. Her face lit up with a huge, smile when she spotted Julie and Graeme.

"Gidday," she beamed a toothless grin at them. "I knew you were coming."

"You did?" stammered Julie, while Graeme quirked his left eyebrow quizzically.

"Yep, saw your car coming down the hill. Knew you'd stop. Want a memento for the new bairn, eh? Got just the thing. Here, take a look at this. It's over a hundred years old."

She held up an exquisite silver moneybox. Even in the murky light it gleamed with a sheen that shouted, 'I'm solid silver'. Measuring about six inches square, its sides were intricately worked in a vine leafed pattern and it sat upon four clawed legs. Its lid was engraved:-

"First—we had each other.

Then—we had you.

Now—we have everything."

Julie and Graeme looked at each other in astonishment.

"Wow!" Julie breathed, "That's so apt and so beautiful."

"It's perfect," exclaimed Graeme. "We'll take it Ma'am."

The elderly crone of a woman cackled, with a knowing smile, "I knew you would. That'll be—let me see—for you two lovers—how's about a tenner?"

"But . . ." protested Julie, "That's too little. It must be worth a great deal more—its solid silver."

"Umph. It probably is, lass, but I can see you are just the right couple to give it a good, loving and caring home, and that's what it needs. Si . . . a tenner it is. Do we have a deal?"

"You surely do, Ma'am," Graeme replied, with a grin, and handed over the money.

"We'll treasure it, I can assure you—thank you," Julie said gratefully, as she picked up the beautiful little box.

"Take care of yourself, lass. Your son will be a strong healthy lad, and will give his father much to be proud of."

Julie blushed and muttered, "thank you", as Graeme grinned disarmingly and put his arm around her shoulders.

As he steered her out into the warm, sunlit street, Graeme said, "See, even that 'oldie' thinks we are going to have a son."

Julie howled in protest, "They're all convinced of it. How do they know?"

Graeme helped her into the car, before answering, "I don't know or care, my darling, I'm just happy to go along with their magic, or whatever it is. Boy-oh-boy! Am I enjoying all this new father attention? What a little beauty of a present we have picked up for Lauren."

"She'll love it," Julie replied, as she unwrapped the box for another, almost disbelieving, look at their stroke of good fortune.

At five o'clock they reached the boundaries of the vast Martini estate. Graeme was again staggered at the extent of the area planted. "It just seems to go on and on, from one horizon to the other," he marvelled. "It's bigger than anything I've seen in Europe."

"It's all on such a vast scale here. Access to water is the biggest problem though. It costs big bucks to irrigate this lot," she informed him.

Parking the car in front of their villa, they were immediately assailed by an excited voice, calling, "Mama!

Papa! Here I am!" With her blonde curls bouncing and Mr Bear tightly clutched in her arms, their daughter came hurtling down the path from the direction of the pool.

She launched herself into Graeme's open arms and he clasped her to him in a mighty bear hug. "Oh! I've missed you, my Papa," she cried in ecstasy, and wrapped her arms around his neck.

"Hey, little princess, we have something really special for you," declared Graeme as Julie handed Lauren the silver moneybox. Graeme read out the inscription, slowly and distinctly, so Lauren could follow the lovely message engraved upon the pretty patterned lid.

As Lauren gazed deeply into Graeme's eyes, so identical to her own, something in her innermost mind shifted a gear. With a startling flash of insight, she realised this wonderful man was so much more to her. But . . . she also realised, in that momentous mere tick in time, that her newly found juvenile insight must not be put into words. It must be kept as a deep but happy secret.

As their eyes held, Graeme saw the flash of understanding flicker across Lauren's gaze and he knew then his daughter had confirmed the biological connection between them.

The infinitesimal moment passed.

Almost in a whisper, and with an enigmatic smile, she told Graeme, "Thank you, my Papa."

Julie sensed what had happened. Her hand, clasped in Graeme's, trembled and he gently stroked it, neither one wanting to break the spell and the magic of the moment.

Julie turned the silver box over and gasped as she noted the date inscribed upon its underside, February 14 1889. Exactly one hundred years before Lauren was born!

Graeme smiled as he murmured, "It seems Fate, Destiny, call it what you may, is taking a hand in our lives again, my darling."

Lauren placed the moneybox in pride of place upon her chest of drawers and Graeme insisted upon being the first contributor. With great ceremony, he deposited several English and Australian coins inside the slit in the side of the box, declaring it to be suitably 'Christened'.

Later, lying beside Graeme's sleeping form, Julie gently rubbed her abdomen, trying to encourage the restless baby, deep inside her womb, to go back to sleep. She lay remembering when the three of them had played an uproarious game of Ludo. The shouts of laughter and the happy faces of father and daughter as the game progressed, would stay in her memory for a very long time.

She smiled as earlier scenes of the Evensong Service flashed through her mind when, to Lauren's delight and surprise, Rico had read one of the Psalms. The affinity between the two children had brought back pleasant, cherished memories to Julie and Graeme of their own early years as next-door neighbours.

Before finally giving in and settling down for the night, Lauren had done her best to coerce her father into agreeing to accompany her on several of the Fun Fair rides the next day. Bouncing up and down like a rubber ball on her bed, she had pleaded with him, "Please, Papa. Pretty please! Take me on the 'Dodge 'ems' and the 'Big Bertha'."

Graeme had looked appealingly at Julie and had mouthed, "Help!" Aloud he had confessed, "I know what 'Dodge 'ems' are, but 'Big Bertha' is a new one on me."

Julie teased him and exaggerated the disadvantages of the huge, swinging, boat-like structure of 'Big Bertha'. With a straight face, she had described, in gory details, the stomach churning motion of the 'Big Bertha', the great height it reached on every swing, before gravity pulled it down, down, down and then how it swung sharply back up to the zenith of its pitch, high into the air above.

She had let him stew in horror at the idea of his responsibility of protecting Lauren on such a dangerous ride. She waited, prolonging his discomfort, until they had settled Lauren down to sleep and were about to leave her room. She had then let him off the hook casually throwing over her shoulder, "Anyway, Lauren isn't old enough for the 'Big Bertha'. Children have to be over twelve years old to ride it!" With a mischievous giggle, she had run out of the room before he could react.

She had heard his deep sigh of relief, as he murmured under his breath, "You'll keep, you wicked minx!"

"What did you say, Papa?" Lauren had sleepily asked.

"Er . . . Nothing important. Just something I have to settle with your Mama . . . sooner, rather than later."

When he found her collapsed in a heap upon their bed, laughing fit to burst, he had made her pay deliciously, sensuously, pleasurably and satisfyingly for teasing him.

CHAPTER 55

The telephone rang at breakfast time. Julie and Graeme glanced apprehensively at each other as Julie reached for the receiver.

She smiled, "Hello, Victor. Yes, lovely, we'll be here, Ciao."

"Victor has the papers ready, Graeme. He'll be here within a few minutes, darling."

Fifteen minutes later, Victor arrived and produced an official looking document and explained, "I've kept it in simple terms, that way no one can misconstrue your intentions."

After carefully reading the prepared document and finding Victor had expertly covered all the points, Graeme said, "That's perfect Victor." He extracted a business card from his wallet. "Here's the detail of my London man, this added document will come as no surprise to him."

Julie provided Victor with similar details of the late Naomi and George Field's solicitors, who now acted for her.

Victor advised, "Re-read the document and we'll get them officially notarised later today."

Shortly they were on their way to the Easter Monday, Annual Village Fun Fair Carnival.

The day became a riot of brilliant colours and a variety of smells and aromas. Twirling, twisting, spinning rides of every description were accompanied by raucous, tinny sounding loud music.

Graeme was a willing participant as he was enticed onto every ride that took Lauren's fancy. The 'Dodge 'ems' was their favourite and they had a great time banging and crashing into Martini family members.

At the lunch break, the entire extended family sat down to an absolute feast prepared by Maria and her girls. The prowess and exploits of those who went on certain rides were noisily challenged to much laughter. Exchanging frequent happy smiles, Julie and Graeme enjoyed a jovial, carefree family atmosphere into which they were happily absorbed.

Julie told Maria of their encounter with the elderly shopkeeper and of their extraordinary purchase from her. She also told her of the old woman's prediction that she would have a son.

Maria chuckled at Julie's puzzled expression. "We countrywomen always knowa. We canna tell almost from conception. You'll see, cara, it's a son for you!"

After lunch the whole family set off to explore the various colourful produce and craft market sections of the fête.

Much to Julie's delight, Graeme bought a minute, hand knitted, blue baby helmet and booties set. Marvelling at their smallness, he asked the woman, in an awed voice, "Are you sure they're big enough?"

Julie saw a sad cloud pass over his face and knew he was thinking that probably he would never see his child so small. To cheer him up at the next stall, she bought him four exquisite, hand-tooled leather bookmarks, each with an old proverb theme worked into them. "Small enough and lightweight enough for you to pack into your kit, just a reminder of today, my love."

They were strolling past another stall piled high with nick-knacks when, with a gasp of surprise, Julie spotted a silver photo frame depicting the exact same pattern as Lauren's new silver moneybox. Graeme picked it up and they stood speechless at the date stamped on the back. February 14th 1889—exactly the same date as on the moneybox!

Clearing his throat and recovering his voice, Graeme asked the young saleswoman, "How much for this, please?"

She grinned, "My Gran donated that. How about a tenner?"

"Done!" Graeme and Julie looked at each other in puzzlement.

They were still trying to make some sense of it all when they arrived at 'Madame Alice—Fortune Teller'. Bianco and Leah were just leaving, both trying to hide giggles behind their hands. They urged Julie to 'give her a try' before dissolving into gales of laughter, and running off to the next attraction.

"You wait out here, Graeme McKenzie, so that I can thump you if she tells me I'm having quads or something."

As she entered the darkness of the tent, Julie was urged by a hoarse, croaky voice, "Come in m'dear, and sit down. Cross my palm with silver and we'll see what the future holds for you."

When her eyes adjusted to the gloom, Julie could just see the outline of a small figure sitting behind a table. The inevitable crystal ball sat in the centre of the table.

Sitting down opposite the woman, she held out her hand holding several silver coins. She was surprised at the softness of the hand that gently took hold of her own.

"'Tis a love child. Fathered by your spiritual love. This will be a son, you already have a daughter and I see perhaps one more child, much later. You'll live a long, loving life with this man. He is your guiding light. You'll never part. Even in death, you are time immemorial partners. Your Gran . . ." here Julie had a rapid intake of breath . . . "She is saying . . . asking me to tell you, 'Not long, not long now.'"

Julie strained her eyes in the dimly lit tent, trying to see 'Madame Alice'. Her words, her predictions, were too close to the truth.

Sensing this, 'Madame Alice' stroked Julie's palm, soothingly whispering, "It's all here, m'dear. You'll marry your man within five years."

Just then a gust of wind raised the tent flap, letting in a momentary flash of light. Julie gasped as she recognised the elderly owner of the 'Collectables' shop. With a whisper, the old lady croaked, "Go in peace, child. Soon your life will be an enchanted love story."

Stumbling out, temporarily blinded by the sudden brightness, Julie was grateful when she felt Graeme's strong arms around her. "Whoa there, darling. Get your balance. Well, is it quads or the tall dark stranger?"

"Neither. She's predicting a third child—much later

—and we'll be married within five years. This baby will be a son, as we already have a daughter." Julie tumbled the words out in a breathless rush. "How about that little lot for starters?"

Graeme, irrepressible as ever, grinned at her, "Well, I like the five year bit and number three child. Don't you, darling? Aah, c'mon sweetheart, she's obviously a friend of Maria's, and knows all about us."

Julie looked at him aghast. "Graeme, nobody knows about us outside of the Martini family!"

"Well," he conceded, "Let's just accept it's either a great coincidence, or good guesswork. C'mon darling, it isn't bad news. So cheer up, let's find Lauren and do some more rides."

Shaking off her disquiet, Julie agreed, as she laughingly 'glad eyed' him, and said, "Another child, eh?"

He whispered, "Be fun trying, won't it?" With his arm around her waist holding her close to him, they went in search of their daughter.

Behind them the old woman peered out of the tent flap, as she quietly said, "'Tis okay, Gran, she's fine, he's taking good care of her. Rest in Peace, my friend, all's well."

Again Lauren led her father a merry dance, flitting from one fun fair ride to another. At one stage he groaned to Julie, "Thank God my P.E. Sergeant Major isn't here, he'd love to wallow in the glory of seeing his masochistic fitness regime paying off! Where does that child get all of her energy from?"

Five o'clock came and Graeme and Victor collapsed side by side on the grassy bank. "That's it," declared Victor, "I'm done! Let's go home for a beer. What d'ya say, Graeme, my friend?"

"Oh, gladly Victor! Even an Aussie ice cold beer sounds like the nectar of the Gods to me at this moment. C'mon girls, round up your tyrannical offspring—promise them anything, if they'll just let us leave!"

Later, beside the Chateau pool, the adults thankfully relaxed. They had a supply of cold, frosty drinks at their elbows as they watched the children romp, seemingly tirelessly, in the pool.

Victor suggested if Graeme and Julie were happy with the documents he had prepared he would ask Maria and Giovanni to witness them after dinner.

The four copies of the agreement, so vitally important to Julie, Graeme and their children, were lined up upon the large mahogany desk

in Giovanni's study. Julie and Graeme signed, with Giovanni and Maria, officially witnessing their respective signatures.

The business completed, Giovanni decided to mark the occasion by opening some of his award winning wine. He tapped the table. "We hava been privileged to share this Easter together witha our dearly loved Julie, a very special man, Graeme, and little Lauren. Maria and I giva all of you our love and hope you will be able to come back to us often. I give you, Julie, Graeme and Lauren!

Replying to the toast, Graeme said in Italian, "Thank you, Giovanni, and indeed, all of you for making this Easter a very special time for us. Thank you to you all for allowing us to share so generously in your lives."

Outside the open French doors, Victor and his brothers began to play the waltz "Fascination" on their mandolins and violins. Graeme took Julie into his arms and they led the dancers through the doors and out onto the flagged courtyard of the loggia.

Rico, to Lauren's utter surprise, shyly asked, "Will you please dance with me, Lauren?"

She answered, formally, in a very grown up voice, "Thankyou, Rico. Yes, I'd be delighted."

Maria and Giovanni exchanged a secret knowing smile.

CHAPTER 56

The final evening of Easter passed all too quickly. Carrying his sleepy, adorable daughter to her bed, Graeme was struck by the depressing thought of how long it would be before he could perform this paternal privilege again. He pulled Julie close as they stood looking at the beautiful child their love had created. "I thank you again, my dearest, for giving her life, and for bringing her here. In case you hadn't noticed, she enchants me."

They exchanged a tender embrace. Graeme grinned, "Hasn't it been a great Easter, I haven't enjoyed myself this much since we were children, sweetheart. It has made me feel so young, so vital again. I find I want to live each moment to its fullest."

Julie smiled, "It has been fun, hasn't it? It's hard to put into words, to describe adequately how I have felt at seeing you and Lauren together. The way you have bonded is breath taking. It's been a magical time, something so, so special, my beloved one."

He clasped Julie closer to him and she could feel his heart rate had increased. He felt her alarm, and he hugged her tighter. Softly, gently, he advised, "You must melt back to the safety of your own home and deliver our precious junior in your safe and secure environment. Nobody must get wind of our involvement with each other. To avoid any suspicion, the best path is for you to act naturally and carry on as normal with your own life." His voice was husky with emotion, as he added, "When it's all over and I am in the clear, I'll send you a message, my darling."

She tenderly touched his face. "Graeme, I understand what you are saying is wise and sensible advice, but it wont stop me worrying and wondering if you are safe and well."

Julie fitted a photo of herself and Lauren in the silver photo frame, ready for Graeme to give to Lauren as a surprise present next morning. Graeme chuckled at some of the more amusing snapshots she had brought with her and, at Julie's urging, he selected his favourites. He knew they would soon become well-thumbed as he gazed upon them several times a day. Julie knew that, apart from these few snapshots and the bookmarks she had purchased, there was very little else she could give him. Anything more might be found by Anne McKenzie. He reached for her, feeling the small swell of her abdomen and her firm, full breasts as he pulled her close to his body. Later they lay contented and sated beside each other, her head on his chest, his arm wrapped around her, neither wanting to contemplate that tomorrow they must part again . . .

. . . But, next morning came as surely as day follows night. Lauren crept into their bed before dawn and cuddled up behind her father. He smiled, drew Julie's body closer to his, and drifted back into a restful, dreamless sleep. They were eventually awakened by the softly ringing telephone beside the bed.

Graeme answered, sleepily, "Yes Giovanni, grazie, put him through, my friend." There was a short pause. "McKenzie here. Good morning, General." He listened for a few seconds. Julie put her finger to her lips, signalling to Lauren to keep quiet. Graeme looked a little surprised. "Is that so? Well, yes, but not before, if you please. I'll be ready. Good-bye General."

He replaced the telephone and looked straight into Julie's worried eyes. It's okay darling. Just a slight change of plans. I'm going straight to Washington, instead of back to Canberra. My batman will collect the rest of my gear and stow it on the chopper."

Hearing that a helicopter was coming again, Lauren bounded up and down on the bed in jubilation. "Oh goodie, goodie, gumdrops, Papa. I'll get to see it again!"

Julie took hold of Graeme's hands as her own trembled. The bubble of her fairytale dream world had burst. It was over.

The outside world had just cruelly broken into their private oasis. It was time to face reality again. Graeme hugged her to him but she could not stop the tears welling up in her eyes. "Hush, hush, my darling," Graeme tried to comfort and console her. "Remember what we discussed last night. It's not a good time for us to be together, it's not our time just yet, my darling."

Julie whispered, "I love you, Graeme. You are my reason for being, my true love."

At breakfast, which Julie found hard to cope with, Lauren was over the moon at receiving the photo frame to match her silver money box. She thanked them with profuse kisses before she sought Graeme's approval to ring Rico to tell him the helicopter was coming back.

Maria packed Lauren's bags and then discreetly took Lauren with her, offering Julie and Graeme a few minutes of privacy.

The sight of Graeme impeccably dressed in his uniform only served to remind Julie of the imminent danger to which that uniform was about to take him.

He spoke softly as he held her close to his heart. "We've said it all; we have made our peace with each other, darling. It has been a fabulous few days, full of such special memories. Take care, my dearest sweetheart, I'll be waiting anxiously for the good news."

He bent to kiss Julie just one more time. She was dressed in a soft pink travelling trouser suit that almost hid her pregnancy. But as he touched her, his child in her abdomen gave him a hefty kick to remind him. He smiled benignly and stroked the place, saying softly, "You behave yourself for your Mama. Grow in peace, my child."

Julie flung her arms around his neck and kissed him ardently. As he returned her embrace, Graeme could hear the faint noise of the helicopter approaching. Arms around each other, they strolled to the helipad where their daughter was regaling Rico with the importance of her Papagraeme having his own helicopter and of it coming especially to pick him up. Something in the helicopter noise made Graeme look up and squint sharply towards it. His face broke into a huge grin. "Well, well, I'll be darned! You'll never guess who is about to land here, Julie, darling!"

Julie shielded her eyes from the sun and looked towards the approaching craft. There were no familiar red, white and blue roundels on the side of the chopper, but a huge white star. A USAF machine!

Graeme shook his head in amusement. "Seems he couldn't resist an opportunity, darling. That's Aaron Benedict's personal chopper. Looks like I'm flying to Washington with the Major General himself!" he huge machine landed, having sent up clouds of dust before settling down on the helipad.

A tall figure, clad in a flight suit, jumped down and marched towards where they were standing behind the safety barrier. Lauren squealed excitedly, "A real pilot! Look Papa, a real pilot!"

Taking off his flight helmet, the grinning face of Aaron Benedict emerged. Holding out his hand to Graeme, he greeted him cheerily, "Well, Hiya, Group Captain, sir, heard you needed a lift, old buddy. Hello, Julie, honey, it's great to see you again." He bear hugged a delighted Julie, before holding her at arm's length, noting her pregnancy, and saying softly, admiringly, "Who's been a busy boy again, eh?"

Then, with a whistle of surprise, he spotted Lauren and noted her obvious likeness to Graeme. He muttered softly, "Wow! This one is definitely all your own work, Graeme, m'lad." Picking Lauren up in his arms, Graeme said softly, Lauren, honey, I'd like you to meet a very dear friend of your Mama's and mine. This is Major General Aaron Benedict. He is going to fly me to his base. Then we are going to get on a larger aircraft and fly all the way to Washington D.C., in the U.S.A."

Clinging almost shyly to Graeme, her arms around his neck, Lauren said, with a breathless rush, "Hello, I'm Lauren-Catherine-McKenzie-Field, and one day I'm going to be a pilot, just like my Papagraeme."

"Well, little gal, you sure are a pretty one, and we sure could use some help up there. Say, how would you like to sit with your dad . . . er . . . your Papagraeme.. in my cockpit for a second or so. I'm sure we've got time, whatd'ya say er . . . Papagraeme?"

Shrugging at Julie, who was grinning like a Cheshire cat, Graeme carried Lauren in his arms and into the helicopter. He sat Lauren in the co-pilot's seat and slipped into the pilot's seat beside her. Lauren was awestruck! She gazed around, waving excitedly to Julie outside and, with her eyes almost popping out of her head, she listened as Graeme patiently explained the multitude of complex controls in front of her.

"Can you fly this helicopter, Papa?" she eventually asked.

"Umhumm, sure can, honeybunch. One day, if you still want to fly, I promise I will teach you."

"Papa, when will I see you again?"

"Soon, honey. Wherever, and whenever it is, Lauren darling, I will never stop loving you." Graeme tilted her chin and looked deeply into the pair of blue eyes that were a reflection of his own soul. Lauren looked solemnly back at him, as he said softly, "I think you know how precious you are to me, don't you?"

Her eyes never left his, as the recognised, unspoken understanding between them was acknowledged. She nodded, "Yes, Papa, I think I do. I love you too, Papa."

"Come then, sweetheart, it's time for me to go." He lifted her down, the loving rapport between them cemented forever.

Julie watched them coming toward her and sensed something important had occurred between father and daughter. She could see it written in their faces.

Aaron Benedict, standing beside her, his arm around her shoulder, murmured, "You two are as much in love as the first time I met you, and that pretty little gal will forever be his pride and joy. They have something special between them, which nothing will ever put asunder. Julie honey, but . . . he still has a big and important job ahead. Has he confided in you?"

"Yes, as much as he is able, Aaron. He has warned me of the dangers, and I accept his advice," she sighed. "But I need him, Aaron . . . more than ever, we must be together soon, he is my life."

"It's there in your future, Julie," Aaron told her, as he looked at her troubled face. "It will be so, don't worry. When is the new baby due?"

"September, about his birthday, all being well . . . before he finally goes away on his next deployment." She smiled wanly at the kind and gentle man. "Thank you, Aaron, I hope one day we will meet under happier circumstances, and not always as we sadly say 'good-bye' to each other."

Graeme held his chatterbox daughter in his arms as he approached them. "Mama! Mama, did you see me in the co-pilot's seat? Did you know my clever Papagraeme could fly the helicopter?"

"Yes, darling, I did," Julie, replied, with a happy laugh. Turning to Graeme, she saw the glow of love in his eyes for both herself and for Lauren. She also saw Aaron raise his eyebrow and tilt his head towards Graeme, and Graeme gave an almost imperceptible nod in return, indicating he was ready.

Taking Lauren from him, she said, with a sob in her voice, "Come darling, it's time for Papagraeme to go. We must say 'good-bye' for a while."

Graeme shook hands with Giovanni and hugged Maria, thanking them sincerely in Italian for all of their hospitality. He took Lauren in his arms, kissed her, and whispered, "Good-bye, my precious one. Remember, how much I love you, Lauren."

He reluctantly handed her to Giovanni before turning to Julie, who was standing a few feet away. She walked into his arms as Maria and Giovanni took Lauren behind the safety fence. Aaron Benedict headed towards the helicopter, leaving Julie and Graeme alone for a few seconds of privacy.

"It's here, darling. Time for us to part for a while. We both have important tasks ahead of us." He kissed her quivering lips. "Be brave, my darling, don't cry. Please leave me with a picture of your wonderful smiling face to remember."

Julie knew how important this was to him, so forced a smile to her face, as she stroked his face, saying, "Good-bye, Godspeed, my own true love. I love you, Graeme darling, my beloved one."

He whispered, "Dio come ti-amo, cara mia." He turned and hurried to the waiting helicopter.

Julie walked behind the safety barrier as Aaron fired up the rotors and, within a very few moments, lifted the helicopter off the landing pad and into the air.

Lauren walked quietly up to her mother and, seeing the tears coursing down her face, took her hand. Julie wrapped her arms around her daughter. The two of them stood, silently watching the sky, until the helicopter and the sound of its rotors could no longer be seen or heard . . .

Julie whispered, "Godspeed, my beloved, until we meet again."

PART THREE

INTERLUDE

1995-1998

CHAPTER 57

Julie and Lauren emerged from the arrival concourse at Auckland International airport relieved to see the smiling Kate. But Kate was surprised and a little shocked to see the sad and glum looks on the faces of both mother and daughter.

She tried valiantly to introduce some humour into the conversation, but got a flat response. "Hey! Was it a rough flight?"

Wearily, Julie shook her head. "We're just missing a certain person, very, very much."

"Both of you?" echoed Kate. "Wow! He made that great an impact?"

"Tantkate, my Papagraeme has gone to Washington," lamented Lauren, clutching her precious Mr Bear. "I miss him, Tantkate, and . . . I love him!"

Kate stared, staggered by seeing differing aspects of the same pain on both long, sad faces. "You okay, Jules? Everything okay with the baby?" Kate asked softly anxiously.

"Yes all AOK there, Kate. He was very active the whole weekend," Julie answered.

Smiling, Kate put the car into gear. "So . . . it's a 'HE' is it? I wonder who decided that?"

In spite of her misery, Julie could not help but join her friend in a smile. "Sorry to disappoint you, Katie, but it was the entire female side of the Martini family," she added with a mischievous smile. "And Madame Alice. A gipsy fortune teller—at the Carnival Fun Fair."

"My Papagraeme is a real pilot, Tantkate," Lauren butted in. "We won some races at the Carnival Sports Day, when he was my Daddy for the day."

Kate raised her eyebrows.

Julie put her finger to her lips, "Tell you later."

"Youbetcha kid! I can't wait to hear more," whispered the ever-ebullient Kate.

Stepping from the car, Lauren and Julie gazed around at the tranquil green setting of their beautiful home. Simultaneously they declared, "Oh, if only he could see this!"

Once more Kate stared open-mouthed. "Wow! You've both got it—really bad!"

"Mama, let's go up the hill to see if any sycamore seeds have started growing," Lauren pleaded.

Kate saw the longing in Julie's eyes. "Go, I'll unpack the car and put the soup on. Go on, shoo!"

The sun was just on setting as Julie spotted Venus, the evening star. She explained to her daughter how she and Papagraeme were going to use this star. "When I want to talk to him, I'll look at this star called Venus, and he will do the same . . ." Her voice faded her throat constricted as she choked back a sob.

Seeing her mother's distress, Lauren looked at the star and whispered, "Hello, my Papagraeme. We're home again. We wish you were here. We both love you."

Julie hugged her daughter. "We had a special Easter, didn't we? It's something we can only talk about to certain people. Others may be hurt by us talking about it all of the time. Do you understand, darling?"

"Yes, Mama, but I do love him, Mama. Can I still think about him? My Papagraeme is so special."

Julie sighed, "He's certainly that, Lauren, honey."

Later, as Kate and Julie sat companionably together, Kate ventured to ask quietly, "So how was it, Jules?"

"It was fantastic! Right from the first Lauren and Graeme were inseparable. It was the right decision, Kate. He'd missed so much of her growing-up. He even imposed a couple of small, disciplinary things upon her, and she accepted them—without question! Something I've never seen her do before. Oh, Kate, to see and hear them play the piano together was pure magic. Physically, she's the image of him. But, they also have the same mannerisms, they talk and think alike."

Julie paused, remembering. Kate howled with laughter when Julie told her about having to hold Lauren's hands to stop her applauding Graeme in church. Julie fetched the silver moneybox and the photo-frame and related the strange story behind their purchase.

Kate asked enquiringly, "And . . . And? How was it for Julie?"

"It was everything I'd dreamed of, Kate. He made me feel so special, so cherished. I know I love him even more than I did before, but Kate . . . I'm so afraid for him." As she whispered the last words her voice faded away.

Alarmed, Kate jerked herself upright in her chair,

"Afraid for him, why Jules?"

Julie put her hand nervously up to her mouth, trying to stop her lips quivering, as she answered hoarsely, "From about October he's going on active duty in some Godforsaken place in the Middle East, and he's going to be in grave danger. So great a danger that, from now, any contact with him is strictly off-limits as far as Lauren and I are concerned. No one must discover the connection between us, otherwise . . ." She shuddered, cleared her throat and continued. "He could be in danger . . . being taken hostage . . . or worse . . . certain devious people threatening to harm Lauren or me, to . . . to make . . . to make him talk . . . It could also put Lauren and me in grave danger."

Julie stumbled over the horror she was uttering. She paused, looked at Kate, her eyes revealing her terror.

Kate shivered, as though someone had walked over her grave. "Ugh, Jules. No wonder he wants you two well out of harm's way. What about getting a message to him when the baby arrives?"

"I'll possibly have to go through a third party, but for now, we have to cut all communication between us." She stifled a yawn.

Kate noted that the desperately lonely look was back upon Julie's face. The last occasion she had seen it was in Sydney, when she had flown to be with Julie. Kate knew she was helpless to do anything except to offer as much support and understanding as she could.

Julie saw how Mr Bear was never far from Lauren's side, especially when she played the piano. Lauren returned to school, regaling all of her friends with her bag, 'From the shop where Her Majesty the Queen shops,' and introduced her constant companion, her much loved Mr Bear.

Once or twice, as they wished each other, 'G'night, sleep tight,' Lauren whispered, "I wonder where Papagraeme is tonight. I miss him so much."

On another occasion, Julie heard her talking to the evening star, Venus. "Hello, it's me, Lauren. I haven't forgotten you, Papagraeme." The longing in her voice twisted the knife in Julie's heart.

The house again ran on well-oiled wheels, allowing Julie time to visit the factory workroom and her office.

Julie calculated John was due home at any time.

Arriving at the office after dropping Lauren off at school during the third week in May, Julie was greeted by the wan, sickly, indeed almost green face of Kate coming out of their private bathroom.

"Oh, Katie love, are you unwell," Julie cried and, in spite of her own bulkiness, hurried to assist her friend. To her surprise, Kate burst into tears, but at the same time had a big grin on her face. Harry came into the office carrying a steaming cup of coffee.

"Here you are, my love, and here are a couple of biscuits, they might help." Harry greeted Julie with a silly, bemused look on his gentle face. "Oh, hello, Julie. Has she told you yet?"

Sipping her coffee, Kate shook her vibrant auburn curls vigorously. "No, not yet. Go on, Harry, darling, you do the honours."

Harry looked sheepishly at Julie, before blurting out,

"We are going to have a baby! Well . . . Kate is going to have a baby. She's just had her first bout of 'morning sickness', poor darling."

Julie gleefully asked, "When? Oh, Katie! Oh, Harry! After all this time! I am so happy for you both. Congratulations, my dear, dear friends."

"I'm due in January, so we'll be two large barrels, rocking 'n rolling around here, before your number two arrives, Jules. Isn't it amazing and incredible? We only had it confirmed last night. I didn't want to believe what was going on. We've had several disappointments before. After eighteen years of marriage we couldn't believe that this time we might have made it. Oh, Jules, we are over the moon."

"Me too, Katie, love. Look, once John comes home, we need to have a strategy meeting."

Harry quietly added, "I couldn't agree more, Julie love. There's also the question of John's illness to consider. You're right, Kate and I have waited so long for this child, I want to enjoy my fatherhood to its fullest."

"Oh my goodness!" Kate's voice almost squeaked with surprise.

They saw the tall figure of John heading towards them. But it was his face that had them all looking in shock at him. His skin had a greyish-white pallor, his eyes seemed to be bulging out like two fiery balls on the end of stalks, and his lips were so pale they were almost indistinguishable from the rest of his features.

Julie levered her bulky body up and clasped John in her arms as he staggered into the office. In spite of his heavy clothing, she could feel that his body was just a bag of bones. His breath was rank and he was panting with the effort of climbing the few stairs to the office. There were beads of perspiration on his forehead and his hands were shaking as though with an ague. Julie stared in horror at him as Harry hastened to help take John's weight.

In a weak, feeble voice, John managed to croak, "Hello, Julie. Sorry, I'm not feeling so good." His eyes rolled upwards as he collapsed backward into Harry's arms.

"Get an ambulance, please Kate," Harry calmly urged, as he laid the inert body of John down on the floor. He loosened John's collar and tie, and listened to his heart. "I think he's only fainted, but he needs urgent medical treatment, Julie, love."

CHAPTER 58

An hour later, John was hospitalised in the same Cottage Hospital where Lauren was born. Doc Matthews arranged for him to undergo a raft of tests then hastened to attend to a shaken Julie.

After satisfying himself that Julie's condition was not an immediate cause for concern, he said, "M'dear, we'll not know exactly what's wrong with him until we have the test results. For now we'll sedate him, but I do suggest we keep Lauren away until we're sure what we're dealing with." He smiled at her. "Anyway, I don't think he's capable of dealing with that bundle of energy, just yet."

Julie smiled wanly back at him. Lauren had always been one of Doc Matthews special favourites. He had always known the truth of her parentage, and was equally privy to that of the new baby.

John weakly raised his hand, "Hello, Julie, my dear. Not exactly the way I had planned my return. How are you and the baby? How's Lauren? Did it go well at Easter?"

Julie sat beside him. "We are both fine, John, so's the baby."

His pale face lit up and he wearily forced a smile between his bloodless lips. There was a discreet tap on the door and a nurse entered carrying a covered tray.

Julie kissed his forehead, "I'll be back when you wake up, John dear."

For several days John lay in a semi-conscious stupor. Julie's heart was full of compassion for her sick husband, but she was also experiencing huge pangs of guilt.

Her nights were spent restlessly twisting and turning, beset with her old nightmare. Each night it became more intense, more horrifying as the spectre with Graeme's voice faded, disappearing further and further from her reach. Every morning she was awake before dawn, soaked in perspiration, with the bedclothes a jumbled, tangled mess around her body.

After one particularly bad night, she awoke to find Lauren beside her, crying in a frightened, distressed voice, "Mama! Mama! Are you sick?"

At that moment the baby inside of her womb decided to wake as well, and gave its mother a mighty kick. She embraced Lauren, "It's okay, Lauren honey, Mama was only having a bad dream."

Lauren did not look convinced. "You were calling out for Papagraeme, Mama. You were asking him to wait for you and you were crying."

"Yes, I know, darling. It's because I am worried about Papajohn, it happens like that in dreams. Everything and everyone gets all mixed up." She smiled reassuringly at her daughter.

Later, confiding in Kate, Julie admitted, "But . . . I'm not okay, Katie. I'm feeling so terribly guilty. I almost feel it's my fault John is so ill. I've been enjoying myself with Graeme, while John has been seeking alternative cures for his illness. God, I'm such a fraud!"

Kate listened in alarm at the despondency in Julie's voice. "Hey! Stop beating up on yourself. John knew about this baby and that he had this illness. It was his choice to seek the alternative treatment." Kate took Julie's hands in hers and said gently, "In fact, in my opinion, you have done something completely endearing and unselfish in bringing Graeme and Lauren together. Remind yourself of that whenever you feel a guilty tweak, Jules."

"Thank you, Katie. What would I do without you? Here I am bemoaning my problems, completely overlooking how overjoyed you and Harry must be."

"Jules, I'm fine. We are making so many wonderful plans." Happy, bubbly, ebullient Kate still could not quite believe that her own miracle was happening at last.

That afternoon at the hospital, Doc Matthews asked, "Are you having trouble sleeping, Julie?"

Julie nodded, "My old nemesis of a nightmare is back—in spades! I even woke Lauren this morning. The baby is okay though, still kicking the living daylights out of me."

Doc Matthews picked up John's medical notes. "John has been experimenting with a special herbal diet and a rigorous exercise regime. He is physically exhausted and even with the best care in the world; he is not going to snap out of it quickly." He paused and looked directly at Julie. "Regrettably . . . the cancer is still there."

Julie shuddered, a despairing twinge of pain shot throughout her body, momentarily curdling her stomach.

Doc Matthews sensed her distress, softly adding, "We'll probably operate as soon as John is strong enough. But there's no guarantee. We don't know how long it's been lying dormant within him, waiting to emerge. He's still a young man and, up until now, reasonably healthy. The prognosis is . . . well . . . the best way of putting it is . . . the jury is still out."

With a heavy heart, Julie went to John's room. She stood studying the sleeping man she had married. He had loved her in the beginning, and he still did in his own way. She had been received into his family with open arms and they had given her a beautiful home. His parents had totally accepted Lauren and had secured their grandchildren's future by deeding their farm into a trust for them.

Miserably, she asked herself, 'And how have I repaid them?' She had loved Graeme McKenzie, and conceived two children by him. She also had to honestly admit that in her heart, at this very moment, given half a chance, she would run to Graeme again. There was no way to turn back the clock. She could never love John as she did Graeme.

Julie sat beside John's bed, her thoughts in turmoil. She solemnly resolved that the only way in which she could repay John and his family was to make his life as tolerable as was possible. Aloud she murmured, "I owe them that much."

At the sound of her voice, John opened his eyes. His face lit up with pleasure as he weakly croaked, "Hello, Julie, my dear. I'm back with the living again, it seems."

That night Julie was woken in the early hours, not by the nightmare, but by the feeling of a presence beside her bed. The filmy net curtains were swaying softly in the light air coming through the half-open window.

She seemed to hear a familiar voice whisper, "Sleep, my dear child. All's well with him."

The breeze ruffled her hair with a "Sssssshh" sound, and the curtains dropped back into place, hanging still and limp. Julie lay down and was instantly and dreamlessly asleep.

John remained calm, almost resigned to his enforced stay in hospital. He treated Lauren lovingly, even when she had indiscreetly blurted out who had given her Mr Bear.

The following afternoon, Julie asked Daisy to look after Lauren while she visited John. She was genuinely delighted to find him sitting in an armchair looking much more like his old self.

She kissed him before asking if he felt well enough for a chat on a more serious subject.

John answered kindly, "If it's about Graeme McKenzie being at the Chateau with you for Easter, don't worry, I'd already guessed as much, Julie."

"Yes, I'm really sorry Lauren blurted it out," Julie apologised, with a rueful grimace. "I wanted to wait until I thought you were feeling better, John."

He took her hand in his as he said gently, "Lauren has been very circumspect up until now in not talking about him." He smiled, "So tell me, how did they take to each other?"

"I can truthfully answer . . ." she paused, and then smiled, "with a total and instant rapport. They look so alike and they're so in tune mentally. It was good for both of them . . . we didn't tell Lauren what their relationship was . . . we decided she wasn't old enough yet to fully understand . . . but I'm still convinced it was the right thing to do."

"Good, then so am I." He moved himself into a more comfortable position. "My operation is in ten days' time."

Julie held his hand. "John, come back home. Daisy is longing to cook for you, and our home is nearer to the hospital than your apartment."

John's eyes took in the healthy glow her pregnancy gave her, thinking, 'it's no wonder McKenzie adores her.' Aloud he replied softly, "I'd like that Julie, thank you."

"John, I also wanted to discuss our immediate future. Kate and Harry have asked for a Board Meeting as soon as you feel able."

"Yes, of course, Julie, my dear. We should get reorganised before the new spring and summer production begins and . . ." he smiled at her, "before you and Kate get tied down with your new babies!"

The next day John was brought home by Harry and Julie reminded Harry of the strategy meeting.

Harry responded enthusiastically, "Kate has come up with a scheme that I'm sure you're going to go for in a big way . . . but, I'll not steal her thunder."

CHAPTER 59

A few days later John felt well enough to take his place for their business meeting.

Harry began by saying, "Okay, how about we just throw our ideas into the pot, and see what mutual things we agree upon?"

"Good idea," agreed Kate. "For a start I'm not available after what, mid-November? Julie will be out from early September. To be honest . . . I'm not so sure that I actually want to come back and work full time."

Harry nodded. "I agree. I intend to be a full-time father and be at home during the evenings."

Julie chewed her pencil as she digested their comments and turned towards John. "I'll have two bairns to care for but I've got Daisy. She's definitely a big plus in my life and I can work and design, right here in this room."

John replied, pensively, "I'm not sure how my health is going to hold up but I guess overseas trips for me are going to be out of the question for a while." He glanced at Julie. "Now I'd also like to be a full-time father to our children."

Julie reacted with a startled, surprised look in his direction. Kate saw Julie's puzzlement and jumped in with, "Look, I have a suggestion . . . No, it's more than that, it is a definite proposal." She looked nervously around the table at her fellow partners, licked her lips and launched into her radical solution. "I propose we appoint both a Workroom Manager, or Manageress, and an Office Manager." She beamed at them and asked, "What do you think?"

John rubbed his chin, saying dubiously, "Can we afford it?"

Harry answered, "Yes, I've done all the projections. Checked and double checked my figures. We're in a very stable monetary position. We owe nothing, and we own the factory and all the stock . . ." He smiled as he continued, "We currently have all the orders we can handle right through next spring and summer. Our staff is well paid, there are no union troubles or disputes." Harry shrugged his shoulders and gestured with his hands palms up. "In fact, even working on the very lowest profit side, we're in a good financial position. Actually, Kate has someone in mind for the workroom supervisor. Tell them, Kate."

With a toss of her auburn curls, Kate giggled, "You'll never guess who 'tis in a month-of-Sundays! Whom do we know who knows more about the workings of the fashion business than any of us?"

But without hesitation Julie answered, "Gloria!"

Kate's face broke into a huge smile, "Got it in one!"

Julie exclaimed, "Oh yes, I couldn't agree more! She has wanted to retire from the modelling side for a while. Yes, indeed Katie, you have my vote!"

"Gloria is the obvious choice" John agreed. "Yes, she is the ultimate master, or should it be mistress, of the iron hand in the velvet glove. Yes, let's offer her the job, very soon."

Kate grinned happily, "That makes it unanimous, folks.

Harry would like to 'head-hunt' a young man from our local bank, Roger Peters, as Office Manager. Roger's looking for a more personal, hands-on position. I propose Harry be given the go-ahead to approach him and sound him out."

"I'll second that, Kate," John responded, as Julie also nodded her assent.

John had begun leafing through Julie's latest autumn and winter design sketches for the upcoming 1996 seasons. He added sample fabric swatches and spread them on the coffee table. "Take a look at these, Kate, Harry. The bulk of the fabrics I bought in Asia are due here any day, and will be ideal for this new design portfolio of Julie's."

Kate sighed, "John, you have done a great job. Those new fabrics are fantastic. They're so different, so innovative. You must have been reading Julie's mind to get such beautiful matches for her designs."

John looked at Julie, his pleasure at their positive response to his buyer's choice showing on his face. "We've always had that sort of rapport haven't we, Julie dear."

"We sure have, John," Julie smiled back at him. "We were only talking about that a few days ago, weren't we?"

By ten o'clock John was looking very tired and his concentration was fading, so Harry kindly offered to assist him to his bedroom.

Left together in the lounge, Kate chuckled as she asked Julie, "How d'you feel now about John wanting to be around as a father figure, Jules? It looked like it came right out of the blue, judging by the look on your face."

Julie admitted, "It sure did. He'd vaguely hinted at the idea, but it was the first time he'd come out and said it. I'd actually resolved that I'd be around for him, at least until he gets over his operation and we know what the future holds. I dare not have any contact with Graeme, so it will look as though we really are behaving as a normal family, won't it? It could help the situation in the long run," she added with a sheepish giggle. "Still, it did come as a bit of a shock to actually hear him put it into plain words."

John put his plans into practice straight away. The next morning he was the John of old, helping Julie categorise and coordinate the fabrics, something he had not done for a very long time.

Julie realised, for the first time since coming back from the Chateau Cornacchia, thoughts of Graeme had not invaded her mind that busy morning. By concentrating diligently on the task in hand, she had managed to keep the longing for him at bay. She conjured up the image of his dearly loved face and tenderly whispered, 'this is how it must be, my darling, for my peace of mind, and for our baby's health. I must go on. Cara mia ti-amo.'

Julie and John found their lives slipped into a pleasant pattern. They worked together in the mornings, and, if it were a fine day, took a short walk around the garden before lunch. They took separate afternoon siestas before Lauren catapulted into their serenity like a whirlwind.

All too soon it was the day before John's operation. That evening, as she put Lauren to bed, Julie was stunned when Lauren asked, "Mama, is Papajohn going to die? If he does, will you marry my Papagraeme?"

Horrified as she was by the seemingly brutal bluntness of her daughter's queries, Julie realised, to a little girl of Lauren's tender years, all things were either black or white.

Julie decided a simple answer would be enough to satisfy Lauren's curiosity, so she replied, "No, honey. Papajohn is not going to die. We shall be able to see him tomorrow, or the next day."

Next day Julie found it hard to concentrate yet, when eventually the call came from the hospital, she was actually deep in thought. She jumped like the proverbial scalded cat as the strident bell rang.

Nervously clearing her throat, she lifted the receiver. It was not the expected surgeon's voice but the familiar one of Doc Matthews. "Well, my dear, the exploratory operation is over and John is in the recovery room. They've removed several samples for a biopsy. The main one has already come back from Pathology. Regrettably, as we suspected, it's positive."

He hesitated as he heard Julie's intake of breath.

"Julie, my dear. I'm afraid it doesn't look good. We suspect the cancer has spread, how far is still to be determined. We're scheduling him for further surgery almost immediately. Julie, I'm truly sorry it isn't better news." Julie stammered her thanks and, as she rang off, Daisy hurried into the room. "I heard the phone . . ." She took one look at Julie's face and knew the news was bad. She immediately clasped the tearful Julie to her and rocked her as though she were a baby, whispering, "Ssshhh, Ssshh, there, there, my lass. Cry it out."

Later, Daisy suggested that she should call Kate. "I'll collect Lauren from school and take her on to her Brownies meeting."

When Kate arrived she took one look at Julie's red swollen eyes and knew she had received yet another of life's low body blows. Putting her arms around her friend, she gently asked, "How bad is it, Jules?"

Julie explained what Doc Matthews had told her and added, "Oh, Kate, I feel so sad for John, who knows what he has to face from now on."

"Kate, you understand how I cannot love him like I do Graeme, but I do care what happens to him. Oh Kate, I feel like I am being torn in two between them."

She told Kate the question Lauren had posed the previous evening. Kate pursed her lips and winced, "Ouch! Out of the mouths of babes, eh?"

"Oh, dear God, I feel so confused. Am I going crazy, Kate?"

Kate grinned at her friend, "Crazy? You? You are the most sensible person I know, apart from Harry, of course. No, it's just at present everything seems to be coming from all directions all at once. You always had the ability to think things through. You've solved problems that others put in the 'too hard' basket. There's no earthly reason why you can't conquer this one." Kate hugged her dearest friend. "I'm always here for you, Jules, you know that."

CHAPTER 60

The next afternoon, as she gazed at the sleeping figure of her husband in the narrow hospital bed, Julie was shocked to see how white and lined his face had become in just a few short weeks. Even his once black hair was now flecked with grey, while his body, outlined under the sheet, seemed to have shrunk to just a bony skeleton.

Doc Matthews had telephoned her that morning and had invited her to be there when he told John the results of his operation. Looking at her wristwatch, Julie saw that, thankfully, Doc was due at any moment. She sat on an easy chair in the far corner of the room. Emotions still in turmoil, she waited as quietly as she was able.

"Julie? Julie, are you there?" John's voice, weak and hoarse, asked. "I thought I could smell your perfume. Are you there somewhere?"

Julie rose awkwardly from the low easy chair and approached the bed. "Here I am, John. How are you feeling?"

"I'm still a bit groggy and not too with it, I'm afraid, but I'm glad you are here, Julie, my dear."

Before Julie could reply, the familiar figure of Doc Matthews entered, and Julie breathed a silent prayer, thankful that he had arrived before John could ask any awkward questions.

After satisfying himself that John's chart was as normal as could be expected, Doc Matthews pulled the chair close to John's bed for Julie, and sat himself on the end of the bed.

With a serious face, he began, "Well John, the result came back positive as anticipated, old son. Look . . . There's no easy way to tell you both, so I'll keep it simple. The cancer is in one testicle, John, and is probably slowly and insidiously spreading further."

A low moan escaped from John's lips, and he whispered,

"Oh no!" and grasped Julie's hand tightly. She let out a sob she could no longer contain, as Doc Matthews continued, in his usual calm, professional manner.

"We'd like to operate and remove both the prostate gland and the infected testicle as soon as possible. After that we'll probably suggest a course of radical therapy, which will be followed by a vigilant monitoring programme."

"I'll be impotent won't I? How quickly will it spread, Doc?" John asked in a weak croak.

"Sorry, that I cannot predict, old chap. If you undergo the operation, and the subsequent follow up treatment, there could be months and months with nothing new happening. Then just as suddenly it may show itself again and we'll assess what to offer you."

"When would you want to do the next operation, Doc?" Julie asked hesitantly.

"Right away, Julie, my dear. That way John will be home within two weeks. Well convalesced before the baby is due." He smiled reassuringly at her. "Strong enough to withstand any broken nights of sleep a new born can bring you."

John lay with his eyes closed, breathing rapidly, obviously attempting to come to terms with the devastating news. He opened his eyes and looked directly at Julie, "Should I go ahead?"

Before Julie could answer, Doc Matthews brusquely said, "There's no choice here, John! If you do not have the operation you look forward to a very early, and probably painful death, denying your family the benefit of a husband and father!"

John sneered at the Doctor in an almost vehement tone, and retorted, "Oh! Come on, Doc! You know the situation there only too well!"

Julie visibly paled as she heard John's words and his angry tone. John was silent for a few moments as he reflected on how satisfying it had been during the past days as they had put together another probable successful business line for their company to produce.

He looked shamefaced at her, offering, "Sorry, my dear. My anger and self-pity got the better of me there. You're quite right. Okay Doc, let's do it."

As she bade John farewell, he said, "Bring Lauren, next time, Julie. I miss her."

With a heavy heart, Julie drove home to appraise Daisy, Kate and Harry of the situation. Lauren saw her mother's sad face and for once refrained from bombarding her with a million and one questions.

Just on dusk she put on her gardening shoes and waterproof jacket. Hearing her, Lauren came racing out, "Wait for me, Mama, I'll come too."

Taking Lauren gently by the shoulders, Julie looked into her daughter's face. "No, not this time, Lauren. I need to go alone. Stay here with Daisy, please."

"But . . . Mama!" Lauren protested.

Daisy came up behind her, with an understanding smile, she nodded to Julie, "Go, lass." She told Lauren, "You stay with me, young lady. Your Mama needs some time alone. Come, we'll get some hot chocolate ready for your Mama when she comes back."

Slowly wending her way up to her favourite spot on top of the hill, Julie finally reached the stile and sank wearily down upon it with a deep sigh. Venus was shining brightly in her usual place as, in a quiet voice, Julie said, "Hello, my darling. I needed to talk with you alone, without Lauren around. John is very sick, Graeme darling. I feel so responsible, even though I know I'm not."

The air was cool and made her shiver. "Oh, my darling, it's almost getting to the time when I'll not be able to come up here to you, it's becoming too risky for me to attempt the climb. I shall be fully tied to the house, looking after John for the next few weeks—so tonight I've just got to shout it to the world, one more time."

She stretched her arms straight out and at the top of her voice, yelled, "GRAEME STUART MCKENZIE, I LOVE YOU, VERY, VERY MUCH!"

She grinned to herself in total satisfaction.

John came through his operation surprisingly well. Julie visited him daily, sometimes taking Lauren which always cheered him. But he also had morose days, despondent about his future. Julie soon became aware that the tension of not knowing what mood to expect John to be in when she arrived was putting a strain upon her own health.

It came to a head on one of those afternoon visits.

The weather had taken a turn for the worse with a gale force wind blowing; it was cold and lashing with rain. Not a day for a heavily pregnant woman to be out and about.

With a sharp indrawn breath, Doc Matthews watched with concern as he saw Julie struggling up the front steps of the Cottage Hospital. He noted that her face was pale and drawn.

He went to meet her and, taking her arm, and led her into his own warm office. He gave her a stern warning. "Take better care of yourself, young woman, otherwise your baby will suffer! John will still live if you miss a day visiting him. Get a visiting roster going."

That evening Julie told Kate about Doc's warning. An alarmed Kate immediately set about arranging a roster.

Looking at herself critically in the mirror, Julie knew she was looking haggard, but was also definitely a lot larger around the girth than she ever was with Lauren. She grinned at her image, 'you've sown a big one here, Graeme Stuart McKenzie! Guess your name will be mud again if this one causes me big pain getting itself born! So be warned, Papa, darling!'

❧ ✦✦✦ ✧

John had been home for nearly a month, relishing being looked after by Julie and being fed all sorts of delicacies by Daisy. He was a lot quieter than he used to be, never complaining, although Julie knew he suffered pain that he tried to hide. He had a male nurse, Adam, who visited him daily to shave and bathe him, as Julie's advanced pregnancy prevented her from being much use in that department.

Helpfully, Bob East, the Farm Manager had taken it upon himself to drive John around the farm on fine days.

On her latest visit to Doc Matthews, he had assured her, "The second week in September, that's what my calculations tell me. It will only be an average sized baby in spite of your added size. We shall have to watch your blood pressure though, so get plenty of rest, Julie. Let Daisy look after John."

The days passed in a period of peaceful repose as John regained some of his strength and became more active. He even talked about buying some exercise equipment to re-build some of his muscles.

John had been going into the office on two mornings a week, taking their new office manager, Roger Peters, through the buying system. Harry spent the other three days explaining the selling side of the business. Everyone was more than happy with the affable new young manager.

In the factory, the selection of Gloria James as the Supervisory Manageress had proved to be a personal triumph for Kate. Gloria could hold her own with the stroppiest of van drivers, yet could wrap unsuspecting deliverymen around her little finger when she wanted something delivered urgently. She could also wield her 'iron hand in the velvet glove' whenever some luckless carrier was late.

CHAPTER 61

Just a few nights later, Julie experienced a few minor twinges. She knew her baby was making its first moves on its arduous birth route.

That afternoon, when Doc Matthews had completed his examination, Julie saw some concern in his face.

"Your blood pressure is too high, Julie. I'm going to send you home to rest—and I mean full bed rest, young woman. If nothing happens in the meantime, I want you in the hospital on Monday afternoon and we'll induce you the next day. Let me see that'll be . . ."

"September 14th, Graeme's 37th Birthday!" Julie interrupted him with a broad smile. "He got both Lauren and I on the one birthday, now he'll get number two child on his own! That's called getting my own back! Whoopee!" She chuckled with delight.

"Well! What a coincidence, I had no idea," Doc Matthews laughed heartily.

"Coincidence, Fate, Kismet," Julie sighed. "That about sums up our entire relationship, Doc. Everything that has happened between Graeme and I seems to have a sort of pre-ordained destiny. It gets real weird at times."

By midday Monday she was packed and ready to go to the hospital. Lauren stood beside her, her young arms wrapped as far around her mother as she could reach.

John joined Julie and Lauren beside the empty bassinet and said softly, "In a day or so it will be filled with an innocent, precious life. A most welcome and wanted special child." He lifted Julie's hand to his mouth and kissed her palm, "Good Luck, Julie dear."

At the Cottage Hospital, Julie was welcomed as an old friend by the Maternity Staff. Doc's face was all smiles. "I don't think we will be inducing you, Julie. You are more than ready and will probably start your labour very soon. Do you want to stay, John?"

Julie knew what John's answer would be. He had previously gently and sensitively explained, "I just can't face seeing you in pain, delivering another man's child. Forgive me, Julie."

So Julie responded, "I'll be O.K. Kate will be here soon, Doc. She'll 'phone them as soon as there is any news."

Julie's labour began precisely at one minute past midnight. Alone in her comfortable hospital room, Julie chuckled to herself, "Right on time, flyboy!"

As the first light of dawn broke, Julie was experiencing her strongest contractions. A noisy helicopter passed close to the Julie's window and landed on the hospital helipad. The midwife glanced upwards as she rubbed Julie's aching back. "Ahha. Someone in a hurry."

At seven o'clock Julie knew it would not be too long before her child would be born. Kate, all bounce and smiles, arrived ready to help Julie 'do battle', as she put it.

Julie confided in Kate about it being Graeme's 37th Birthday. "He's got it right on the button again, Kate. Wow! Here we go again . . . Oh God! I'll give you a Birthday gift, Graeme Stuart McKenzie, which you'll never forget!!"

"Do you want him castrated again, Julie?" Kate asked, with a fiendishly mischievous grin. "You did with Lauren."

The midwife examined Julie yet again, saying, "Time to go to the delivery suite, Mrs Field."

Kate wiped Julie's forehead with a cool cloth as she whispered, "Go get 'em, Jules. I'll be right here."

Julie was wheeled into the sparkling white delivery suite and a masked midwife came over to her. "Dr McKenzie from England is here."

Startled, Julie asked, "Where's Doc Matthews?"

A tall, gowned figure stood beside her. His face was masked, a surgical hat was pulled down upon his head, but nothing could disguise the deep blue eyes that were shining with love for her. He leaned down, "I couldn't warn you beforehand, my darling."

Julie breathed a deep sigh. "The helicopter this morning, that was you?"

Graeme lifted his surgical mask and kissed her lips. "Guilty as charged, ma'am. Tell you more later. Let's get our baby born, my darling."

Graeme stood by her, whispering, so only she could hear, how much he loved her. His voice and his presence calmed Julie, helping her with her effort. Knowing he would actually see his baby born was a miracle, a priceless, unique moment.

"Doctor McKenzie?" Julie managed to gasp between pains.

"Honorary Doctorate, Cambridge University," Graeme murmured.

"One last push, Julie. Aaaah, here he is!" Doc Matthews gently slapped the baby on the rump and the wail of the new born penetrated the room.

Graeme kissed Julie's face, damp with perspiration with her valiant effort. "Well done my darling, we have our son!"

The midwife weighed him. "A very healthy eight pounder, or if you prefer, 3624 grams," she announced, swaddling the baby in a small, soft blue blanket, before laying him on his mother's chest.

Julie looked up into Graeme's eyes and saw they were wet with tears as he tentatively put out a finger and touched the dark hair on his son's head. He whispered, "Julie, my darling, this has got to be one of the finest moments of my life. Thank you, my dearest sweetheart. I am so proud of you."

Doc Matthews came over and murmured, "We'll be taking you back to your room shortly, Julie. Er . . . Kate will still be there. Get her to go and telephone everyone, once she has seen you, it will give you two a few minutes of privacy alone. I'll take 'Dr' McKenzie into my office until Kate leaves."

Julie nodded, "Okay Doc, I'll ask Kate to go and get Lauren." She clasped Graeme's hand, "Our daughter should be here with us."

After an excited Kate had congratulated Julie, she was ready to hurry off when Julie stopped her mid-stride. "Kate, please wait! I need your help, you're not going to believe this, in fact I'm still having trouble believing it myself. Kate, Graeme is here! He was in the delivery room with me, he saw his son being born! He's in Doc Matthews room at the moment." Julie's eyes glowed with love. "He's here Katie! I don't know how, or for how long, but oh! Kate, he's here! Kate, can you get Lauren here as quickly as possible, without John."

Kate sat down heavily on the chair beside the bed, her mouth gaping in astonishment. "How? Why? When? Oh, heck I don't know. Wait! John will have gone into the office by now. I'll whip home and collect Lauren from school. I'll ring Daisy and tell her. Right, leave it with me; I'll have Lauren here by . . ." She looked at her wristwatch. "Eleven o'clock at the latest. Jules, I could tell by your face something wonderful—apart from your new son that is—had obviously happened. Jules, I'm so happy for you, my dear friend. Right, I'd better ring John straight away suggest he leaves it to lunchtime to come here. Leave it with me, Jules."

Julie hugged her dearest friend. "Katie, you are a treasure."

Doc Matthews led the way to Julie's room, he cautiously opened the door, "All clear, Julie?"

Julie beamed at him. With Kate's help she had freshened herself up, and now only wanted Graeme beside her.

Doc Matthews opened the door wider, "Mrs Field, here is Doctor McKenzie."

Graeme, still gowned to disguise himself, strode over to the bed and took Julie in his arms. "Dio come ti-amo, cara mia. My darling, sweetheart, a million thanks."

"Happy 37th Birthday, Flyboy! You made it a special day for us. Look at him, Graeme, darling, he's perfect!" She looked down tenderly, maternally at the small bundle beside her. "Graeme, my beloved, we have a son and in about half an hour Lauren will be here. Kate has gone to fetch her." Julie looked at him anxiously. "How long can you be here, my darling?"

"The chopper will be back for me after noon, sweetheart. I'm on a flying visit, to appraise the R.N.Z.A.F. of the deployment the Commonwealth is to undertake, the one I told you about. I leave Hobsonville for Canberra at fifteen hundred hours. Rank doth have its' privileges, you see. I was determined to see you and our children."

Holding both of her hands in his, he said emotionally, "I am still stunned, Julie, my darling, at actually being here this morning and seeing him born." He shook his head, almost in disbelief.

He kissed her lips and then gently lifted his tiny son out of his bassinet. They gazed at their child in mutual admiration. Unfolding the blanket, they inspected his tiny feet, toes, fingers and hands, finding them all present and correct, in perfect miniature.

The baby moved and stretched out one hand, clasping one of Graeme's fingers. Julie could see the tender look upon Graeme's face.

"Hello, my son, welcome to the world. What shall we name him, Julie, darling?"

"Stuart Cameron McKenzie Field, has a good strong ring about it, don't you think, darling?" Julie answered, leaning close to Graeme's side as he cuddled their son in his arms.

"Then, Stuart Cameron it is, darling." He looked up as he heard a loud knock on the door. A huge smile lit up his face as he heard a familiar voice.

"Mama, I'm here, can I come in? Tantkate! Hurry up it's this room."

Poor Kate, at five months pregnant, could not keep up with the ball of energy, which only wanted to run everywhere. She saw Lauren safely to the door, and gave her a note to hand to her mother. But, in spite of her curiosity at wanting to see the 'boy wonder' she resisted the temptation. She did not want to intrude upon the special, short time Graeme and Julie had together.

CHAPTER 62

Graeme covered his face with the surgical mask before laying his son back in the bassinet. He nodded to Julie and she called, "Come in Lauren, honey."

Lauren slowly opened the door, saw her mother and hurled herself across the floor and cuddled her tightly. "Oh Mama, I did miss you. Is it the baby brother I ordered from Santa?"

Lauren looked intently at the tall figure standing beside the bassinet. She sniffed the air, "Hello doctor. You've the same after-shave as my Papagraeme."

Then her eyes lit up and her face was wreathed in smiles, as she saw the tiny swaddled baby, "A blue blanket, I've got a baby brother, just as I ordered. Oh, Mama!"

Graeme lifted the tiny bundle, "Here you are big sister, Lauren. Here's your special brother, as ordered, Stuart Cameron McKenzie Field."

Lauren carefully took the baby in her arms her face a picture of absolute joy. She kissed the baby on the forehead and stroked his mop of black hair. "Now you have one that looks like you, Mama."

She frowned and sniffed the air and looked directly into Graeme's face. A pair of identical blue eyes atop the surgical mask twinkled back at her. Lauren stared, finally, she whispered, "Papa? Oh, my Papa."

Graeme dropped the mask so that it lay around his neck, "Hello, my honeybunch."

Julie hastily took their son into her own arms as Lauren cried, "Oh, my Papa, I have missed you so much."

Graeme clasped his daughter and told her, in a voice husky with emotion, "And I you, my precious princess. What perfect timing your new brother has, the best birthday present I could have ever asked for!"

She kissed her father enthusiastically and rubbed her face against his. "You always smell nice, Papa. Happy Birthday, my darling Papa!"

There was a soft knock on the door and Doc Matthews called, "It's only me." He came in waving a camera, exclaiming, "I've got this, if you'd like some photos on this somewhat auspicious and momentous occasion."

"Doc, that's a brilliant idea," Graeme eagerly replied. "I haven't had the chance to tell Julie yet how I arrived on your doorstep just after dawn." He turned to Julie. "This good man invited me in, believed me when I said who I was, fed me coffee, and managed to sneak me into the delivery suite just before you came in, darling."

Doc Matthews laughed. "Well there's the R.A.F. uniform, plus a certain family likeness," he inclined his head towards Lauren.

Locking the door so that Graeme could temporarily shed his surgical gown disguise, Doc snapped off several photographs of the young family together.

He waited for Graeme to don his disguising surgical gown again before he opened the door to leave.

Graeme shook Doc's hand and thanked him profusely, "from the bottom of my heart, Doc," before adding, "I'll be along to collect the rest of my gear when I hear the helicopter returning."

Graeme sat beside Julie on the bed, holding her in his arms as they grinned happily at each other, admiring their handiwork in the form of the two children they had brought into the world with so much love.

Lauren suddenly remembered the note Kate had handed her to give to Julie to read. As soon as she saw its contents, Julie showed it Graeme. In the note Kate had scribbled about John coming to the hospital after midday.

"How is he?" Graeme quietly asked, thankful John had chosen not to accompany Julie that morning. Even so, it had been Doc's good idea to have him dress in surgical gear as a practical disguise.

Julie sadly explained, "The cancer has spread. He has been very ill since Easter. He is only a shadow of his former self." There was genuine compassion in her voice.

She touched Graeme's face. "He'll be delighted with Stuart, and he'll be a good father figure for him." She added in a whisper, "Until you can be there, my darling."

Graeme nodded, "I'll be forever grateful for that."

Graeme paused, he had just heard the sound of a distant helicopter. "Remember a 'High Flight' message will always reach me but, darling, wait until after you hear it is safe to do so. We must ensure there is no connection made between us, especially now that I have two precious children to protect, and most of all you, the light of my life, my sweet darling." He dropped a kiss on her forehead.

Graeme picked up his son, gently kissed him and stroked the wee, defenceless face. "Good-bye, Stuart Cameron. Grow strong, until we meet again."

Lauren clung to him, "Oh, my Papa, I do love you so much."

Huskily Graeme held her close to his face. "You and I will see each other as soon as it is possible, honey. Look after your beautiful brother and mother."

He turned to Julie, saying softly, "Arrivederci cara. Remember, my darling, you are my reason for living. Thank you for such a wonderful birthday gift, there is nothing finer I could have wished for. Dio ti-amo, cara mia."

Julie stroked his beloved face, "You take care of yourself, my darling. We need you so very much."

They kissed passionately. He ran his fingers softly down her face, "I'll be back, as soon as I possibly can, I promise you."

Lauren stood at the window weeping as she watched the helicopter take off and then crawled onto the bed beside Julie, and lay cradled in her mother's arms.

Julie broached a sensitive subject. "Papajohn will be here shortly, Lauren darling. Let me tell him that Papagraeme was here, okay?"

John arrived few minutes later, carrying a huge bouquet of blue Dutch Irises. Lauren ran over to him and drew him excitedly over to the bed. "Come and see, Papajohn. I've got the brother I ordered from Santa, last Christmas. His name is Stuart Cameron McKenzie Field, and he has black hair, just like Mama's."

John laid the bouquet across Julie's knees and, rather shyly, said, "All okay, Julie dear?"

"Yes, John, all very okay," Julie replied as a nurse took Lauren with her, after asking if she would also like some lunch. Julie knew she must take the opportunity to tell him about Graeme's unexpected arrival. "John . . . I had a very pleasant surprise this morning. Graeme arrived, just in time to see Stuart being born."

John's eyes opened wide in surprise, "What!"

Julie gestured with her hand. "I had no previous knowledge that he would be here, he's only in New Zealand for a few hours. It was pure co-incidence that Stuart decided to make his entrance when he did. There wasn't time to consult with you, John. I'm sorry I couldn't let you know." She added softly, "It was such a special time for him and me."

John gently looked down at the tiny body in his arms. "He's a lovely child and he has dark hair like you and I. Julie, I'm glad McKenzie got to see his son being born, he had every right to do so. Thank you, my dear, for telling me."

He looked directly at Julie as he pledged sincerely,

"I'll not hold back like I foolishly did with Lauren. Julie, I want this son as much as you."

He was still nursing Stuart when the nurse brought Lauren back. Lauren looked questioningly at her mother, "Yes, Papajohn knows who was here."

John replied warmly, "He's a very special little man, Lauren, we must take good care of him. But for now, I'll take you back to school and you can tell all of your friends about your new brother. Okay?"

John told Julie, "Daisy sends her love, and she'll be up after dinner."

"That'll be lovely, John." She tried to smother a yawn. "Sorry, but wow! It's been a busy sort of a day, and I am running out of energy, fast."

Shortly after they had left, there was a knock on the door, and a uniformed courier asked, "Mrs Julie Field?" and handed her a small package.

She opened the small sealed gift card attached to the package. It was in Italian and read, "Congratulations, cara mia. A million thanks, my precious jewel. Dio come ti-amo, cara mia. Yours as always, Graeme."

She gasped as she saw an exquisite pair of sparkling amethyst earrings; an identical match for the pendant Graeme had given her in New York.

Julie whispered, "Your father loves us so much, Stuart Cameron McKenzie Field. You are such a special little boy and I love you, very much."

Shortly afterwards, Kate blew in like the proverbial breath of fresh air. She told the sleeping baby he was gorgeous, approved his names, admired all of Julie's flowers, and tipped a handful of cards and gifts from workshop members into Julie's lap.

Julie handed her the jewellers' box and saw the look of admiration on Kate's face when Julie showed her the pendant around her neck. "Perfect match, just like me and him. Oh Katie, having him here this morning was indescribable. Oh God! I love him so much." She hugged herself in delight, before continuing, "Thank you for bringing Lauren, Katie. It was just magical all of us being together."

She saw the questions forming in Kate's mind. "Yes, I told John about Graeme being here, we don't have secrets these days. He may have been surprised, but he accepted what happened. John even held Stuart right away."

Kate hardly took her eyes of the sleeping infant. "My turn soon, Jules."

Julie's final visitor that memorable day was Daisy. She brought with her a complete layette of intricately knitted and exquisitely made baby garments, all trimmed with the traditional 'blue for a boy'. "Oh, thank you again, Daisy. I don't know what I would do without you."

"Well, you could trust me a little more, Julie," Daisy responded. "You could tell me about a certain RAF officer, I think 'Papagraeme' is what Lauren calls him when she whispers 'goodnight' to him every night, and sometimes weeps because she misses him so much. I could be of more assistance if I knew more about him, and perhaps help her handle her sadness."

Julie looked at the kindly woman sitting beside her, a woman who had virtually become a mother to her and a grandmother to Lauren. Handing Daisy her son to cuddle, Julie related the story of herself and Graeme . . .

CHAPTER 63

The household was almost back to a normal routine after the dramatics of Stuart's birth, although his needs were always paramount. Julie, encouraged by Daisy, was about to take her first stroll up the hill since Stuart's birth.

Thousands of feet above her head, high in the atmosphere, a white vapour trail billowed out behind an aircraft that was too high to see with her naked eye. She quoted the opening line from Graeme's favourite poem, "Oh, I have slipped the surly bonds of Earth . . ."

Her thoughts inevitably turned to him. He would have embarked upon his dangerous and delicate mission by now. She prayed aloud, "Dear God, please keep him safe and send him back to us soon. We love and need him so much."

She could see Daisy at the clothesline behind the house. Daisy had accepted the somewhat unusual parentage of Lauren and Stuart and would proudly guard their secret.

Julie thoughts were also of Kate, whose pregnancy had been causing concern, even suffering a real fright with a threatened miscarriage.

Later that evening Julie began sketching a design that had been rattling around inside of her brain for several days. She had been deeply concentrating on the detailed and intricate design she was drawing, when she heard Stuart stirring through the baby monitor. John's voice came through the speaker, "Stay there, Julie, dear. I'll change him and bring him in to you."

John had become Stuart's devoted Papajohn. He had sheepishly confessed to Julie that, in Lauren's case, to be changing a little girls nappy was, to him, not quite right, but a boy baby—well that was different. "A man understands another man, doesn't he, young fella?" he had staunchly told Stuart.

Julie settled with Stuart in the nursing chair. John walked over to her easel and picked up the designs she had been working on. With a low whistle of approval, he turned to her. "Hey! These are great, Julie. You've never designed wedding dresses before. Wow! This one's a knock-out!" He held up the one design that had been bugging her for several days.

Trying to hide her reddening cheeks from John's gaze she knew only too well what THAT particular wedding gown design was all about. It was her special 'daydream' one, the one she saw herself wearing.

John studied the other illustrations scattered over Julie's worktable. "What actually have you in mind, Julie?" John asked a curious interested note in his voice. "I can see a certain maturity of style in all of these designs."

Julie explained, "I was recently reading a very telling article in our trade magazine. It quoted a group of statistics that made me re-read the article, just to see if I had got the facts right."

"It clearly proved that women were getting married at a later age—between 30 and 40 years of age, and usually after establishing themselves in their career choice. Many women it seems do not subscribe to the view of marrying in their early twenties, having their family and then returning to the workplace—in many cases, losing their seniority. Yet, even marrying at the later age, they still want the white wedding gown and all the trimmings. It occurred to me that there could be a niche market out there that warranted a more mature style of gown. A 'modular' interchangeable concept with the ability to change skirt length, fullness of skirt, neckline etc., Still a white gown, but perhaps a more sophisticated gown, without the bows, flounces and fripperies that a younger bride looks for. Most women still want their day in the sun, dressed in full bridal finery. Society still expects a bride to be in white, as it still denotes first time marriage, or whathaveyou, even if the bride is in her 30's and a career woman.

"Anyway, it got me thinking seriously along those lines and . . . Well, you are looking at the results."

John exclaimed, enthusiastically, "Julie, it's a brilliant concept! Show Kate these designs and explain your modular concept. I know she'll be just as excited."

Kate was indeed enthralled with the whole range of more modular bridal gowns. She telephoned Harry, asking him to come and see what she believed to be a whole new direction for their company.

Kate counted the designs and found that there were eleven in all. Thinking that was an odd number, she counted them again, "Where's number twelve, Jules?"

Kate smiled at the blushing cheeks of her friend and teased, "You're not hiding one—created for 'his eyes only', are you, Jules?"

Kate's enthusiasm was infectious and soon had Harry reaching for his calculator. Papers full of figures flew from one to the other, as they worked out details of what, where and when.

John stated, "We must aim for the best of the best in our fabric choice. After all, these are for women who are used to flying first class in a man's world," making a very valid point.

Harry conjured up another page of figures and projections. "Let's aim for, what, next spring or summer? First we should make the sample range and test the market." Harry looked at Julie and Kate. "Both of you 'Mums' happy with that?"

Grinning happily Julie and Kate agreed.

Daisy smiled to herself as she served dinner and told her reflection in the kitchen mirror, "Been sober and quiet for far too long around here. They've missed the cut and thrust and the excitement of a new line, plus all of the chaotic, frenetic planning that went with it."

Over the next month the ideas gelled, samples of fabrics were ordered, scrutinised, accepted or discarded.

Gloria James and Roger Peters became enthusiastic supporters, with Roger working up a simple, practical financial plan for the new promotion. Gloria complained that she felt more like a pincushion on some days, rather than a Supervisor, as the different designs were draped around her still sylphlike, model's figure.

Julie refined her designs made up in a plain cream calico material. They were cut and re-sewn several times, until she was completely satisfied with the end result. She still had to finalise the name for the new line. She wanted it to be romantically bridal, mature in concept, appealing to the career woman. Her favourite was 'Bellamissio Brides'.

Each day Julie scoured the world news in the newspapers and the TV News programme, but could not relate any item to a project that Graeme may be involved in. To allay her fears, she concentrated harder on the bridal gowns. But at times she still stared at Venus on clear evenings, sending him a silent prayer and her everlasting love. Julie knew a certain word, a certain tune, or the sight of a blue uniform would trigger agonising thoughts of him.

When three months old Stuart was due for his routine check-up visit to Doc Matthews, Kate also went along for her regular ante-natal appointment.

Doc, softly asked, "Any news?"

Julie shook her head, "No, we should have heard something by now."

"From what I briefly saw of that young man, he will move heaven and earth to reach you, Julie, when he can," Doc said. "Get my nurse to weigh young Tarzan here. Come in Kate, let's see how you are doing today."

Doc emerged from his surgery and called to Julie. "Can you get Harry to meet us at the Cottage Hospital, Julie? I'm going to admit Kate, straight away. Her blood pressure is way too high . . . Keep Harry calm, don't alarm him. Is it okay for you to drive Kate there and to stay with her until Harry arrives?"

"Yes of course, Doc. I'll ring Daisy she can come and pick Stuart up from here."

Arrangements completed Julie and Kate departed for the Cottage Hospital. Kate was sweating profusely, Julie was glad that Stuart was safe and warm, back at the surgery, as Kate needed all of the windows in the car fully opened to keep her cool.

Since Doc had called ahead, Kate was expected and was soon whisked up to a hastily prepared room. Julie kept a lookout for Harry, whilst the resident obstetrician was hurriedly summoned to examine Kate.

Julie was relieved to see Harry and John hurrying down the hall. Hugging Harry, Julie urged him to go straight into Kate's room. Julie turned to John and he put his arm around her as she whispered. "Oh dear God, don't let them lose their baby. They've waited so long."

John held her close to him as he quietly said,

"She's in the best place. Daisy says wait as long as it takes and send Kate and Harry her very best wishes."

They had been waiting for almost an hour when a grey faced Harry emerged from Kate's room. He staggered, his gait unsteady, his face showing unbelievable shock. "She's got pregnancy toxaemia. The baby is in trouble. They're going to do an immediate Caesarean Section. They say it's a month early but, to save both of their lives . . ."

He sank down on the chair and held his head in his hands. After a short time Kate was wheeled out, robed in a white surgical gown and with her bright auburn curls hidden under a large white mobcap.

Julie, bending over her dearest friend, saw terror in her eyes. Squeezing Julie's hand, Kate murmured, in an almost inaudible whisper, "Oh, Jules, I want my baby, so much."

CHAPTER 64

Aimee Louise Reynolds entered the world five weeks premature and weighed just 2500 grams. Although she was just a minute scrap of a human being with a fuzz of ginger red hair, right from the start she fought desperately for her right to live. As Harry so proudly put it to Julie, "She has her mother's indomitable spirit."

Kate didn't see her daughter for four days as the medical staff fought to control Kate's ever-rising blood pressure and other complications.

Julie devoted all of her spare time to Harry and Aimee that first week, thanking her lucky stars that Daisy was there for her own children. John proved to be a tower of strength as he more than coped with Stuart cutting his first tooth, and with Lauren's normal, bountiful high spirits.

Despite of all the odds, after a week of touch and go, Aimee Louise began to thrive. Kate was now being taken twice a day in a wheelchair to visit her daughter and, though in an uncomfortable state, she never missed her chance to be at her daughter's side.

When Julie arrived at the premature baby nursery on Christmas Eve she saw, at last, the special sight they had all been waiting for. Kate was being allowed to hold her daughter in her arms. Tears of joy poured down Kate's face as she tentatively touched the bare skin of her tiny daughter for the first time. Her gentle husband, Harry, knelt at her side, the muscles in his face working frantically as he sought to control the outflow of his own emotions.

Not wishing to intrude upon this poignant and tender private moment, Julie moved quietly away, going into Kate's room and weeping a bucket of grateful, thankful tears.

On Christmas Day, Kate was allowed to spend a couple of hours to enjoy Christmas dinner with the Field family, Harry and Daisy. It was a happy, boisterous occasion, with Lauren in great spirits, excitedly opening all of her presents with cries of delight. Propping Stuart up on the sofa, surrounded by a pile of supporting cushions, Julie gazed tenderly at her precious son, wondering where his father might be at that very moment.

Having had Kate and Aimee to worry over, it had all but driven thoughts of Graeme from her mind. Now, with the extra time to enjoy a family Christmas, she began, uneasily, to question why Graeme had not sent her the promised message.

Looking across to where John had Lauren draped around his neck, she saw he was explaining the instructions on one of her new toys. Julie brooded on how much he had aged during the past year. He had lost so much weight that his once muscular body was now a frail, mere shadow of its former self. His hair was entirely grey, although it had re-grown after the effects of the course of radical treatment.

Kate studied her friend Julie. She saw that her attention was drawn to Stuart, who was blissfully blowing bubbles as Harry squeezed a soft toy, making it 'Miaow' like a cat. A soft, loving, maternal expression lit Julie's face. But, as she turned, for a split second, Kate saw the lonely, desperate look Julie only got in her eyes when she was thinking and wondering about Graeme McKenzie. Kate squeezed Julie's hand and said softly, sympathetically, "Any news?"

Julie was startled that Kate had almost read her thoughts. Then she shook her head, replying, somewhat wistfully, "Nothing. It's been four months now, Katie. I would have expected something by now, if he was back and okay . . ." Her voice faded away. She struggled to get the words out coherently as she hugged herself. "I still feel he is alive and well, somewhere . . ." She shrugged her shoulders and turned her hands palms up. "But where?"

In the New Year, two much loved infants were welcomed into the body of their respective religions. Four and a half months old, bonny

Stuart Cameron McKenzie Field was christened as such at the local church, during the morning Family Service. One hour later, the tiny, four week old, delicate, feminine smidgen that was to be known as Aimee Louise Reynolds, was duly recognised as such at the local Synagogue.

All four parents shared the honours of becoming Godparents to each other's child.

Stuart Cameron, resplendent in a white satin jump-suit christening outfit, lovingly made by his mother, cooed and blew bubbles all through the service. For Aimee's outfit, Kate had requested the loan of the exquisite lace gown Julie had made for Lauren's christening. The two children were each wrapped identically in white, light as a feather, hand knitted mohair shawls, lovingly crafted by Daisy.

Not to be outdone or outshone, Lauren, as the 'big' sister to both children, had asked her mother for a dress or kilt in the McKenzie tartan. Julie happily acceded to her daughter's request, designing and making her a truly feminine dress, with a Scottish influence. The outfit was completed with a frothy, white lacy jabot, and a matching, McKenzie tartan Tam O'Shanter hat.

Completely out of the blue that morning, as she looked critically at herself in the mirror, Lauren had asked, "Does Papagraeme ever wear a kilt?"

Startled, and wondering what had brought the question on, Julie replied, "Not that I know of, Lauren, honey. I've never seen him in one in all the years that I have known him."

Lauren cuddled her mother, imploringly asking, "Where is he, Mama? Why hasn't he come to see us?"

Julie replied sadly, "I honestly don't now, Lauren. I wish I did."

"Is he still on that secret mission, Mama?"

"I just don't know, Lauren, darling, and there's no way I can find out," Julie said sadly.

Stuart's first birthday was fast approaching. One day, Julie and Kate were working in Julie's workroom on the new bridal collection. Kate murmured, "A penny for them?"

Julie wryly smiled, "Same old problem, I'm afraid, Katie, love. Nothing new—just why, where and how is he. Stuart will be one year

old next week, that's one whole year and nothing, nix, zilch from him."
She frowned. "It's just not like him, Kate."

"It's not only me; Lauren feels so let down. She is forever asking me
why he hasn't been in touch." Julie shrugged her shoulders in a hopeless
gesture, "What can I tell her? Honestly, if it wasn't for this collection, I
think I'd be climbing the walls."

Lauren informed Julie and John that Stuart's first birthday should be
celebrated with an afternoon tea-party, with 'the works and a cake with
one big candle.' Julie countered the independent Miss by suggesting that
Lauren should take charge of the arrangements. To nobody's surprise,
'Big Sister' Lauren coped beautifully with the challenge.

Encouraged by Lauren, the sturdy little boy, with the glossy, dark
brown wavy hair of his mother, and the deep twinkling blue eyes of his
father, took his first steps as an upright 'homo sapient'.

John had delayed his departure to the office, so that he could watch
as Stuart opening his many birthday presents. When he did arrive at
his office, he was greeted by Roger Peters, who handed him a pale blue
envelope marked 'personal', addressed to Julie. Roger asked John if he
would pass it on to her. Concentrating on reading another letter in his
hand, John absentmindedly nodded 'okay' as he took the envelope and
dropped it on his desk.

Several minutes later he picked up the letter addressed to Julie.
Without looking at it, still thinking about the contents of his previous
letter, he slit it open. The pale blue paper contained just a few words,
"High Flight—injured in bomb blast, unable to contact, convalescing,
all now well."

John's hands began to tremble uncontrollably and the single piece of
paper slipped from his fingers. His knees felt weak—unable to support
him. He collapsed with a thump upon his desk chair.

It had to be from McKenzie!

John picked up the flimsy, pale blue envelope, saw it was addressed
to Julie and marked 'personal', and he knew, without question, his
assumption was correct. He put his head in his hands. Just as life was
beginning to settle down, and with Stuart becoming more like his own
son in every way, and Lauren accepting him as her father figure, news
from McKenzie turns up again.

John knew Julie had been worried when she hadn't heard from
Graeme McKenzie, but he had thought that, of late, she was now
beginning to accept he was no longer in her life.

Now this . . . Today of all days!

John made a decision—he would not pass on the note—he would ignore its presence. Picking up the slip of paper, he rose shakily from his desk. He was about to tear it into shreds and flush it down the nearest toilet, when his conscience suddenly got the better of him.

Dropping the slip of paper as though it was a red hot coal, he buried it in the bottom drawer of his desk.

Julie acknowledged that this special day was a deliciously delightful and happy one for her infant son, but it was also his father's thirty-eighth birthday. The longing for Graeme's presence had been overwhelming.

That night the nightmare returned. Once more, Julie found herself caught up in the ghostly horror, as she found herself running on leaden legs, trying to reach Graeme as his voice and his image faded further and further away. The faceless and nameless bodies all around grabbed frantically at her, their thin bony hands and fingers reached out, clutching at her. Black voids of vacuous, toothless mouths screamed at her to stay.

Daisy, hearing her sobs, entered Julie's bedroom and, in a soothing voice, coaxed Julie back to a more natural sleep.

The nightmares had become more frequent since Stuart's birth. Daisy knew only too well what a stressful and debilitating effect they always had on Julie's generally stable and serene demeanour.

Two days later, Lauren fractured her left arm.

CHAPTER 65

Lauren had joined the crowd of pupils who were bemoaning the fate of a baby bird caught under the mesh on the bike shed roof. Chirping desperately, its mother was beating herself against the mesh in an attempt to release her young. Sarah told her the caretaker was on his way with a ladder, but Lauren decided she couldn't wait.

Lauren, using an old gnarled tree branch overhanging the roof, crawled to the mesh. Prizing a corner of it upward, she released the small, panic-stricken bird. A groan, followed by an ominous, loud drawn-out, CRAAAACK came from deep within the tree.

The teacher rounded the corner just in time to see a small, curly headed, blonde moppet fly off the branch and land heavily on her left arm.

After a speedy journey to the Cottage Hospital, to be met by her worried parents, Lauren cried, "Oh Mama! I fell and my arm hurts. But Mama, the baby bird is okay."

Julie hugged her precious daughter, "Doc Matthews will soon have you feeling more comfortable. We'll talk later about how wise it was of you to be climbing up so high."

When Lauren emerged with a plaster cast on her left arm, she was smiling and none the worse for wear. She was somewhat brought back to earth when John and Julie admonished her for her impetuous behaviour.

That night, as Julie tucked Lauren into bed, her daughter asked wistfully, "How will Papagraeme know I'm hurt, Mama?"

Julie winced as she answered Lauren with more confidence than she felt, "Oh, he'll know, sweetheart, and he'll be sending you tons and tons of wishes to get well soon."

Julie sat at her work easel, her thoughts filled with an image of a laughing, loving Graeme, tossing a giggling Lauren high in the air above his head. With a sob, she buried her head in her hands as she relaxed her guard, succumbing to the extreme heartache of her loneliness.

For weeks Lauren's school friends treated her as their heroine. When Daisy remarked on how contrite Lauren was, Julie retorted, "And pigs might fly! Just you wait until the next time. She'll just do the first thing that pops into her head, without giving a fig for the consequences. I have brought forth an ill disciplined monster!"

Daisy grinned; in spite of her protestations, she knew Julie was proud of Lauren's feisty spirit. She sighed and cuddled the warm, chubby body of Stuart. "At least you haven't tried to copy that sister of yours. You are quite content to be cuddled and loved by all and everyone."

Stuart called Daisy 'Nanny', and when Lauren very shyly asked if she could call Daisy 'Nanny' as well Julie had happily agreed.

Once more, Christmas was just around the corner. Lauren had prepared her own list giving it to her mother to 'post' to the North Pole. It caused a sharp band of pain to grip Julie's heart, as she read the simple requests at the top of the painstakingly written list.

'Number One. Please, please, please, send my Papagraeme to see me and Stuart.'

Julie had shown the list to Kate.

"Whew! She hasn't forgotten him then. It's been how long now, Jules?"

"Stuart's birth. Fifteen months ago. I can't believe he's deliberately not contacting us, Kate. I just know something, or someone, is preventing him from doing so. I have tried to physically eliminate him from our lives." She closed her eyes with a weary gesture. "If only it were that simple to shut him out of my mind."

Kate said sympathetically, "It's the only thing you can do, Jules. You have two wonderful children, and now this new collection to launch. Which incidentally . . ." She paused while she clapped her hands and did an impromptu jig and a twirl around the office, continuing, "Harry and I predict will 'Wow' them everywhere!"

At the Christmas morning Family Service, Julie prayed for him to be safe, well, and able, someday, to come to her again. She lovingly caressed the amethyst pendant around her neck as she prayed.

Lauren cast a sidelong glance at her mother and saw the movement. She lowered her head, and prayed, "Thank you, Lord Jesus. I know now my Mama hasn't forgotten him. I know I shall see you again, my darling Papa, one day" . . .

. . . In a tiny chapel outside of the Italian village of D'Arezzo, where the locals had olive skins, raven hair and eyes as black as coal, the stranger in their midst was a tall, blonde, blue eyed man. A pair of crutches rested against the pew seats.

When the priest gave the signal for the congregation to rise, the lone man struggled awkwardly to his feet, and leant heavily on the crutches. His foot was encased in a plaster cast, while his face and hands showed the scars of recent injury. An expression of intense pain creased his brow as he clumsily attempted to stand.

Billy whispered, "You okay, Graeme?"

"I'm fine, Billy, got a bit stiff sitting for so long." With a grin at his friend, Graeme McKenzie turned his attention to the beautiful stained glass windows of the little chapel. But his thoughts had winged their way out of the church and were far, far away. Would she be in a church somewhere with the children? Would she think of him?

He had puzzled as to why she had not responded after he had sent her a coded message regarding his 'near miss' in the catastrophic suicide bombing. As a consequence of the incident, he had suffered numerous cuts and bruises, a broken leg and ankle, and had ruptured his Achilles tendon. The latter was proving extremely difficult to mend, in spite of the weeks he had spent in a military hospital.

He was loathe to send her another message, in case it was intercepted and so causing her unnecessary anguish. Not a day passed when he did not think of Julie and their children.

He was desperately lonely for her.

Anne's input into his life was now non-existent. She was always jet-setting off with her 'cronies', making no attempt at a marriage with him. She had visited him just the once after his accident, brought there as a courtesy by his C.O. She never came again, claiming hospitals depressed her. Her only comment, when he had been recommended for a bravery recognition, was to ask when he would be going to 'Buck House' to get his gong!

Her binge drinking was becoming an embarrassment. He had urged her to seek treatment, her 'in' crowd just pooh poohed the idea. Now painfully standing and leaning heavily upon his crutches, Graeme McKenzie longed to be thousands of miles away. To be holding in his arms the one woman in the world he truly loved, his beautiful Julie.

He yearned to hear again the happy laughter of his daughter, Lauren, and to see for himself, how the tiny son they had named Stuart had grown.

Christmas was a family time, but his family were denied him. 'How much longer, Lord?' he silently prayed. 'How much longer are we going to have to suffer being apart?'

He heard, as from a dim distance, Billy's voice, and the concern in it. "Graeme, you okay? The service is over."

Sighing, Graeme nodded at his lifetime friend and colleague, and murmured, so that only Billy could hear him, "Yes, Billy, I'm just dreaming. You know the usual, what if? Where is she? How is she? How are my children? . . . and lastly, why the hell do I put up with Anne's nonsense! It's the family Christmas bit, Billy, always gets me."

He smiled ruefully at his friend, "Come on, I'll try to be better company once we are away from this very nostalgic chapel. It's too much like the one at the Chateau Cornacchia."

On New Year's Eve, two couples stood on the Field patio and happily toasted each other.

"Will it be fame and fortune?" Harry asked expectantly.

"Definitely!" replied Kate, self-assuredly. "This new bridal concept for the business woman will be a runaway winner—I'm convinced of it!"

Four crystal glasses touched, as the lounge clock struck midnight, heralding the New Year.

John echoed Kate's words in a final toast, "Success to 'Bellamissio Brides'!"

By mid-January, the factory floor hummed with excitement. The specially chosen seamstresses were eager to begin. Gloria was in her seventh heaven. She ran 'her' workroom with her usual smooth efficiency-plus.

As each completed bridal gown came off the finishing line, she paraded in it.

The total collection was proudly mounted on mannequins in the temperature-controlled showroom. Julie consulted with a never-ending stream of shoemakers, jewellers, florists, headdress and veil-makers. She had carefully co-coordinated her special creations, ensuring that each bridal ensemble was totally unique and exquisite.

Kate and Harry had impressed upon the printers that the invitations to the launch must be ultra-elegant, to attract the most fastidious of businesswomen. Roger Peters had taken charge of the task of sending out the impressive, heavy cream vellum invitations, richly embellished with their ornate golden printed words. He had assembled a veritable 'Who's Who' of all the fashion buyers. To everyone's delight there had been no refusals.

Harry and John were busily organising the finishing touches to the magnificent hotel venue and Kate had been rehearsing her commentaries with the parade models.

So it came as a totally unexpected shock to Julie when John announced one morning that he would be moving back into his penthouse apartment before the launch.

He could not overcome the profound, deep feeling of guilt he had experienced over hiding Graeme McKenzie's message for Julie.

There was also another secret he was keeping to himself. Doc Matthews had confirmed the dreaded cancer was back, about to rear its ugly, invasive head once more.

CHAPTER 66

It was launch day for 'Bellamissio Brides.'

Julie gazed critically at the outfit she had designed for this important day. The dusky pink, pearl silk ensemble had a straight ankle length skirt, split to the knee, topped by a heavily self-embroidered, matching tunic jacket with a stiff mandarin collar. Her high-heeled, pink pearlised, satin shoes stood waiting with her exotic cocktail hat made especially for Julie by Bianco Martini, Victor's wife. It was a confection—a frothy wisp of pink milliner's net, holding captive a huge costume jewellery brooch in the form of a magnificent, multi-coloured butterfly—the perfect finishing touch to Julie's Asian influenced ensemble.

Kate's vibrant auburn-red curls would be topped by another Bianco creation in the form of a saucy, peacock feathered, cocktail hat. She would be wearing a similar outfit to Julie, but in a dark, peacock blue colour.

Arriving with Kate and Harry at the venue, Julie saw John waiting under the hotel glassed roof atrium, the Garden Gallery.

Julie was shocked at his physical appearance. His face was drawn and pale. His eyes were sunken, and there were dark bruises of shadows under them. Without being told Julie knew, without doubt, the dreaded cancer was back.

"How are you, John?" Julie asked him, in a soft voice. "Do you have something to tell me?"

"Not now, Julie," John pleaded, holding up and spreading his hands as a physical barrier between them.

"Enjoy your day, and the success I'm sure it's going to bring, Julie dear. We can talk later."

Julie winced at the hidden tones and meanings in his words. She saw the pain in his eyes and she knew her intuition was correct. She opened her mouth to say . . . but John put his fingers to her lips, "Ssssh, later. Come on, this is your day. It can wait."

Gripping her elbow firmly, he steered her inside. Julie's reaction was one of delight when she saw the whole gallery was bright with sunshine from the surrounding glass roof and walls. John, Harry and their team had created a stylised fantasy church setting, decorated for a truly romantic wedding.

The centre catwalk resembled a church aisle. The sides representing pew ends had brass poles, linked with garlands of green leaves, and topped with white posies of flowers tied with huge, white satin ribbon bows. The stage where the girls made their entrance had been cleverly constructed as a stained glass window.

John smiled at Julie's obvious pleasure at the setting for her gowns. "John, it's absolutely wonderful! You've hit just the right touch, this atrium idea is so perfect. We get the indoor-outdoor feeling with the plants and the conservatory decor, yet the catwalk is pure church. It's beautiful, John. Congratulations to you and Harry."

By noon the audience was in place, everyone arriving uncharacteristically early. Gloria wryly remarked, "Don't they know there is no such thing as a 'free lunch! We'll get'ya all in your pockets later, ladies."

Sharp on one o'clock, the resonant, slightly cracked, bell sound of a church clock striking the hour echoed throughout the auditorium. Immediately the noise level dropped away and an expectant, anticipatory hush settled over the audience. All eyes turned eagerly toward the stained glass window end of the catwalk as, over the loudspeakers, a musical peal of church bells rang out.

Harry gently faded down the volume as Kate, resplendent in her peacock blue outfit, mounted the stylised church lectern.

Her voice strong and clear, Kate began her commentary. "Good afternoon, Ladies and Gentlemen. Today we introduce to you to an entirely new and different concept from our company. We feel our partner and chief designer, Julie Field, has more than ably filled what has been, up to now, a gaping void in our fashion world." Kate paused and swept a glance around her audience. They were hanging onto her every word.

"Statistics have recently proved that women are marrying at a later age, many after establishing themselves in their chosen careers. These women are more mature, more sophisticated, more fashion conscious, and most definitely more fashion aware. They also have much more discretionary money to spend, usually on themselves and their own well-being."

Kate heard, by the soft undertones and murmurs, her audience were in complete agreement with her words. She smiled engagingly, as she surveyed the room.

"When it does become the time for them to marry, although a white wedding is still in demand, our older, more sophisticated bride is usually not wanting the frills, the bows and other frivolous furbelows on their gowns as, say, brides who are a few years younger." Once again a soft murmur greeted her words.

"To this end, Julie Field has created 'Bellamissio Brides.' It is a collection, presented to you this afternoon, of fourteen modular gowns, together with their appropriate accessories. Gowns specifically for the bride who either knows where she is going, or indeed has already reached her desired life-time career goals. From these fourteen basic modular gowns, we are able, at 'Maison Chevalier', to adapt a gown to suit individual, personal preferences. Be it for either a different fabric selection, skirt length, sleeve length, neckline, or, if you prefer, even a different colour."

Kate paused and signalled that she was ready for the first visual display. "Let me explain further the concept of the 'modular' pattern gown."

A colourful animated visual appeared on several TV monitors scattered around the walls, showing a gown in several pieces. As Kate continued her explanation, the animated pieces flew together, rapidly interchanging, so that each part of an original gown created and formed an entirely different looking gown.

A concerted gasp of amazement erupted from the whole audience. Kate smiled at their reaction.

"Each order will be treated individually, at no extra cost to the client. This will ensure that each gown will be subtly different from its neighbour. No two gowns will ever be entirely identical. They will be assembled and sewn by a team of speciality seamstresses in our home factory, here in Auckland."

At this point John pressed a button and a new visual display projection flashed on the screens, showing the seamstresses at work. This brought forth another appreciative murmur from the captivated audience.

John's next visual display showed the new salon, with Gloria in front of a bevy of full-length mirrors, being 'fitted' for her gown. Kate paused yet again, as a ripple of gasps and applause rang around the auditorium. "On this display you will see how we have fitted out a suitable suite of rooms as our Bridal Salon. After her initial selection, each bride will be entitled to three private and personal fitting sessions, per gown. Free of charge."

Relaxed and smiling, Kate knew she had them. She chuckled, "I thought that would make you sit up! I did warn you at the start, this is a VERY different and VERY new concept we are beginning here. We freely and unashamedly admit all the bridal gowns are expensive. Those that you are about to see here today are no exception, but they have one huge difference." She paused for effect. "These gowns are individually fitted and hand finished for the mature bride. They remain hers for all time, they are not hired gowns."

A roar of applause greeted the end of Kate's introduction. She stood grinning happily, acknowledging the accolade, before signalling to Harry, with an almost imperceptible inclination of her head, to start the age-old music of Mendelssohn 'Wedding March'.

As the organ music swelled and built, Kate thought about the one design of Julie's she knew they would NOT be seeing. The one Kate knew was secreted away, possibly sadly, destined never ever to become a reality.

Right on cue Gloria appeared, her floor length bridal veil demurely down over her face. It took three and half hours to parade all fourteen gowns, such was the audience interest. There were unprecedented scenes around the catwalk as senior buyers from all of the retail houses asked the models to pause frequently, so that they, the buyers, could observe the way a skirt was cut, a bodice draped, or to query a type of fabric.

It soon became apparent that Julie's input was required to help answer all of the many technical questions being fired at Kate. John hastily fixed a hand-held microphone for Julie and, as she entered and was recognised, a rolling wave of applause resounded around the room.

Looking as beautiful as he had ever seen his wife, John watched as she smiled with an equally friendly, pleasant manner. She answered their many questions frankly and without hesitation.

When Harry noticed several leading media representatives headed for the door in a bunch at five o'clock, he knew they were hurrying to catch deadlines. Judging by their happy faces, he knew their reports were going to be very favourable.

Bemused, Harry shook his head in wonder. "I've said it before—that woman is a talented genius—everything she touches turns to gold!"

The newspaper fashion columns the next day were dominated by photos and commentary on the new concept. All heaped praise on 'Maison Chevalier' and on Julie in particular. The telephone rang non-stop with invitations for Julie to be the guest speaker at women's clubs, for TV and radio interviews and for her to do in depth articles for all of the women's magazines.

At the end of the working day, Kate murmured, with a sigh, "I have just done a rough calculation. Would you believe we have taken nearly a million dollars in orders today! Whew! I'm going home."

After everybody had left, Julie glanced at John lying full length on the office sofa. He looked ill and exhausted. She softly said, "Let's get you up to your apartment. You're all in. I've checked with Daisy. The children will be okay for a while. We need to talk."

CHAPTER 67

Since confiding in Julie on the day of the successful launch of the 'Bellamissio Brides', John had undergone extensive and exhaustive tests that had left him feeling unwell and very fatigued.

Realising that he could no longer handle the strenuous overseas travel, he had spent many hours alone in his penthouse apartment. Here he collated a major revision of all of his contacts in the fabric buying and selling field, compiling an expansive index register to pass on to his eventual successor.

Julie made a point of visiting him when he was unable, through sheer physical tiredness, to attend the office. He had to admit it was still the highlight of his day.

He frowned, "She's never this late. Wonder what's keeping her?"

He felt an almost imperceptible feeling of sheer loneliness creep into his being. Suppose I never got to see Julie or the children again? How would I manage the increasing pain as the cancer progressively took over?

Aloud he murmured, "I don't want to die alone, unwanted, yeah, even unloved. I'll ask her if it's okay for me to move back."

Just as he was about to feel really uncomfortable about her lateness, he heard the sound of the elevator. "Here I am," she grinned at him. "Better late than never! Sorry I'm late but I have just had a call from the U.K., from my sister Carole. She is coming for a visit later in the year. Just think, after all these years, I'll have family to show around our beautiful home and my adopted country."

In a quiet, persuasive voice, she suggested, "John, why don't you come home? Lauren's at school all day and Stuart's not so boisterous when she isn't around. We'll still have plenty of room when Carole comes, and Daisy is dying to 'feed you up'."

He nodded, "Julie, I accept with deep gratitude. Doc Matthews reckons I'll rot away here. I'm very lonely without all of you."

Julie clapped her hands, "Oh goodie! I've hated leaving you here alone. It'd never seemed right, our home is just that . . . our home. You can be safely installed by the time Lauren comes home from school. She'll be delighted to have you back . . . and it'll be a relief to have someone else answer her constant and endless questions."

When she had gone, he sank down on the sofa, the relief of Julie accepting him back to the family home was immense.

Shortly after moving back, he underwent a further course of treatment which left him nauseated and fatigued. Adam, his male nurse, visited daily to keep him comfortable.

The weeks flew past until one cold and stormy night in mid-July. That night a violent gale force wind, accompanied by a thunderstorm, blew up from nowhere, hurling itself around the house like an enraged bull.

Julie, woken by the thunderous noise, hurried to check on the children. Miraculously, they were still sleeping right through the mayhem ranting outside of their bedroom windows. Seeing John's lamp on, she hurried in to see how he was faring.

One look at his face and she knew the pain had become unbearable. Reaching for the phial of painkiller on his bedside table, she prepared a syringe and said softly, "There, that should soon take effect. It's a terrible night, just listen to that wind!"

They watched the havoc the storm was trying to wreak on their garden. Soon the painkiller kicked in and John was able to speak once more. "Thank you, Julie. Somehow the pain always seems worse at this time of night."

Daisy put her head around the door, "Anybody fancy a cuppa?"

John nodded his head, "Yes, please Daisy, but make Julie go back to bed afterwards—she needs to rest."

"Of course, my dear, now that I'm awake I'll stay and play you a hand or two of cards." Daisy smiled and motioned for Julie to follow her.

Outside, Julie told Daisy how much painkiller she had administered to John, and they noted it on a chart Doc Matthews had asked them to keep. The amount and frequency of the dosage line was following a steady upward trend.

Discussing his state and what they were noting, they agreed the medication was no longer keeping him going through the night like before. They had both seen his efforts to avoid showing how much pain he was now suffering. It was time to let Doc know the situation.

Just then there was an ear splitting crack of thunder which seemed to be almost immediately overhead, making Daisy and Julie jump in fright. "By Golly! Hark at that! If that doesn't wake the bairns, nothing will! I'll take the tea in to John. You check on the children and then go back to bed."

But, to Julie's surprise, both children were still sound asleep, so she gratefully slipped back into her own warm bed.

At daybreak, the garden looked as though a truck load of rubbish had been dumped upon it! Bob East came up to check on them, shook his head and promised to send up his 'boys', to clear up the mess.

In answer to Julie's anxious questioning, he assured her, "The farm didn't suffer too greatly, lass, but a few of your olive trees have sizeable splits in them. That last lightning flash hit something high on the hill, might pay you to go up and check later. I'll just go and see if John wants any masculine help this morning.

"Right, now is my chance, I'll ring Doc Matthews," Julie told Daisy.

Doc came immediately. After examining John, he took Julie to one side. "The pain he's experiencing is far too great, much more than I had anticipated. I'll have him admitted to the Cottage Hospital. Mr Burt will see him today."

Julie went back to John's room, put her arms around his gaunt frame and held him gently. "The ambulance will be here shortly." She looked into the sad eyes of her husband, "Oh, my dear John, I hate to see you looking so ill. You don't deserve to be feeling so wretched, my dear. You are a good husband and father, and we all want you to come back to us as soon as you can."

He was unable to speak as another pain gripped him, and a sudden, blinding headache made him gasp. Doc Matthews, hurried to his side as John whispered, "My head, Doc, it feels as though it is splitting open."

After an emergency operation on John, Doc Matthews re-joined Julie in John's hospital room. The grim look on his face did nothing to relieve her anxiety.

She tremulously asked, "How bad is it, Doc?"

"About as bad as it can be, Julie. Mr Burt has removed as much of the cancer as he was able, but it has spread. I'm afraid he is in for more operations, m'dear, and the prognosis is poor. This means the end of his normal working-life, Julie. He will virtually be an invalid from now on, and totally dependent upon you, lass."

Julie's face had lost its colour, even her lips were blanched white, as she realised what Doc was gently, but firmly, explaining. She closed her eyes and buried her face in her hands as she strove to control her emotions. Compassionate as ever, Doc patted her shoulder and quietly left the room.

When John was wheeled back into his room, still only semi-conscious after the anaesthetic, Julie was feeling calmer, having forced herself to come to terms with Doc's prognosis.

Julie drove home, her thoughts in turmoil. Assuming Daisy had probably taken Stuart to collect Lauren from school, she headed up to the stile on top of the hill. She knew she needed time alone to digest the devastating news.

Reaching her favourite place, she uttered a cry of distress while tears poured down her face as she cried in anguish, 'John's going to die, Graeme!'

She knew in her innermost heart that morally she must now devote the whole of her effort, with no half measures, to the care of John. The last few months of his life must be made as comfortable, and as caring as she was able to make them.

She lifted her tear stained face to look upwards to the clear blue sky above. It was his domain, the man who loved to fly. She whispered in a broken voice, "Perhaps one day, when we are both free, then, and only then shall I be able to think of you again."

Stumbling unhappily back down the hill, Julie went straight to her bedroom and took off the amethyst pendant. She kissed it one last time, before gently laying it inside the leather box.

Searching for anything else that might remind her of Graeme, she found the matching amethyst earrings, the CD of his music, and a few other odds and ends that could evoke memories of him. Finally, firmly, she locked the box and put it on the highest shelf in her wardrobe.

Graeme Stuart McKenzie was no longer part of her life.

CHAPTER 68

It was sometime before John showed some stability. Daisy attempted to serve him small, appetising meals. Adam visited daily. Lauren and Stuart learned to be quiet around John.

But, it was Julie's company John sought and enjoyed most. On his good days he chose to be beside her as she sketched new ideas, or updated her present lines. Those days were precious, golden ones.

One day Kate rang, asking breathlessly, "Would John be up to a short drive tomorrow? Harry and I have a surprise we want to share."

The drive took them through quiet, pleasant countryside before arriving at a beach on the Coromandel Peninsula. Harry turned into a driveway and drove up to a log cabin styled house.

Kate jumped out of the car almost as soon as it stopped. "Welcome to 'Chez Maison Reynolds'—a la Beach!"

"What! It's yours?" gasped Julie.

Harry answered modestly, as he helped John out of the car, "We bought it last week. Look at the colour of that water and the golden sand. This is just Paradise for us. Come on inside, it's so . . . ." he shrugged, unable to find the words to express his delight.

The seascape panorama showed a golden beach, stretching for many kilometres, unspoiled, tranquil. Three small children bounded out of the car like jack-in-the-boxes and headed for the sand.

Harry settled John in a comfortable easy chair by the open bi-fold window, as Kate urged Julie to follow her for a house tour.

"It's wonderful, Kate," Julie enthused. "It's near enough to your townhouse, yet far enough away to be a real retreat. Oh, Katie it's just perfect."

Kate's eyes sparkled with pleasure then, in a more sober tone, took Julie's hands in hers and said very seriously, "If it hadn't been for your unique talents, none of this would have been financially possible."

Harry sighed, "Isn't this just brilliant? We plan to come here whenever we can." He glanced at Kate and reached into his pocket and handed Julie two keys. "These are for you. An open invitation to use the place whenever you want. Kate and I want you to consider this beach-house partly yours."

"Julie, we have another idea we'd like to run past you," Kate exclaimed. "When your sister Carole visits, how about she and Peter 'house-sit' the townhouse for us? We'd like to spend most of our summer here."

"I think it's perfect, and I know Carole will approve.

"Thank you, Katie," Julie beamed.

"Well, there's more . . . How about we all spend Christmas Day and Boxing Day here? AND . . . there's even more! Once Lauren has finished her school year, why don't both Stuart and Lauren join Aimee here?"

Julie looked at her perceptive friend and knew she had noted how John winced at the children's noise.

"Once again, Kate, brilliant!" Julie responded enthusiastically. "Why don't you invite Daisy as well? She loves Christmas cooking, but John and I don't do justice to her efforts right now."

They had both been concerned at the obvious toll John's illness was having on Julie. Kate had also noticed the absence of the amethyst pendant. She realised what Julie had so drastically done. Such an exorcism, Kate knew, would have surely broken Julie's heart in the process.

One month later, Julie was at the airport to meet her youngest sister Carole and her brother-in-law Peter.

After a very emotional welcome, as they hugged and lovingly kissed, Carole saw Julie's usually bright, sparkling eyes seemed to be mirroring a huge amount of pain.

As the two sisters walked arm-in-arm back to the car, Julie softly told Carole and Peter what the prognosis was for John. She smiled wanly, as she said, "He loves it at Kate and Harry's beach house—so we spend as much time there as we can."

She continued. "I'll drive you to the townhouse, once you have seen John and met your niece and nephew. They can hardly wait to see their first real Aunt and Uncle."

Approaching Julie's home, seeing the impressive homestead unfolding before them, Carole breathed, "Oh, Julie, you don't know how lucky you are to be living in such a paradise."

"Well, believe me, luck had nothing to do with it," Julie gently chided her sister. "It was blooming hard work that got us where we are today. Still . . ." she looked at the patio and saw the emaciated figure of John. She murmured in a whisper, "I'd give it all away for John's health to be restored. You're about to see big changes . . . don't be alarmed and please . . . don't gush over him—he hates that."

She heard Carole's sharp intake of breath, before her sister noticed two youngsters candidly observing her.

"Hello, Aunty Carole and Uncle Peter. I'm Lauren, and this is my little brother, Stuart."

Julie and John exchanged relieved glances. Thankfully they had broken Lauren's habit of using all four of her given names.

Over a lively dinner, Carole and Peter were bombarded with questions, mostly from Lauren as to what their relationship was with their mother.

At one stage Carole stared at Lauren and touched her niece's blonde curls with a slightly puzzled look. Stuart presented no such enigma as he had both Julie and John's dark colouring. But the identical, deep penetrating blue eyes of both children caused Carole to frown. She knew there was something she could not quite put her finger on. There was a similarity . . . Carole's thoughts were interrupted by Julie asking, "If you'd like, I'll drive you to Kate and Harry's townhouse now. You must be jet lagged. Your three day trip to our thermal city of Rotorua starts at one o'clock tomorrow."

Peter grinned, "Thanks Julie. I can hardly keep my eyes open."

Julie showed them around the townhouse, explaining where everything was kept. She left after arranging to take them for a tour around the showroom the next morning.

Julie and Kate began by showing them the bridal 'Bellamissio' range. Kate selected the 'Regale et Royale' gown, and described its uncanny similarity to the gown recently worn by a European princess.

Carole made a snorting sound, before saying disdainfully, "Humph, we unfortunately have our own lasting memory of that occasion, don't we Peter?"

Peter pursed his lips. "Oh yeah! That's the night that silly, self-indulgent woman got drunk, drove her car into a tree and killed herself. Twice over the legal limit, or something."

Kate raised her eyebrows at Julie, trying not to giggle. The two friends turned away, to hide their amusement, by going to bring out another gown. Carole's raised voice could be clearly heard through the open door, bemoaning the antics of the 'upper class'. But it was Carole's next words that almost caused Julie to collapse in a heap at Kate's feet.

"Mind you, Anne McKenzie was always going to end up in a nasty way. She drank like a fish. How poor Graeme put up with her, especially after he got so badly injured in that suicide bomber thing last year, we'll never know."

Kate caught her staggering friend and saw the distraught, shocked look on Julie's face. Assisting Julie to a chair, Kate hastily closed the door between them and the showroom. "Sit here, don't move. I'll get Gloria up here and get her to take them around. Don't move, Julie."

Julie sat as though frozen, her body trembled, her hands were like ice, her mind silently screaming, 'Graeme had been injured! Anne was dead! Graeme had been injured!' Kate hurried out to Carole and Peter. "Sorry, Julie's on the 'phone, a bit of an emergency, could be quite a while. I'll get our Manageress, Gloria, to take you around."

Before they could answer or protest, Kate picked up the intercom and spoke softly to Gloria. "Come up to the showroom stat, big emergency."

Kate steeled herself to ask, "Sorry about that . . . Now what were you saying, Carole?"

"Oh, it's just someone Julie knew, way back, Anne McKenzie. She was married to such a nice man, Graeme McKenzie, used to be a neighbour of ours. He's just been promoted to an Air Commodore in the R.A.F. One of those crazy, suicide bomber people blew up the Hotel he was staying in. He got injured, broken leg or ankle, or something, but he saved his 'buddy'—another one of our local lads, Billy Watson, a Wing Commander, or something . . ."

Peter chimed in, "Pulled him and several other American chaps out of the rubble. Saved their lives they reckon. He got a gong for it. Anyway, his wife, Anne, a right bitchy Madame that one, got herself drunk again at a party after the Royal wedding. Smashed her car into a tree, a messy end."

"How dreadful," Kate commiserated. Her heart was pounding at an abnormally fast rate as she tried to discreetly elicit information. "Where's the husband now?"

"Probably still at RAF Mildenhall, I suppose. He was in hospital for quite some time, I believe. Anyway, he's definitely better off without that wife of his. A nasty piece of work."

Carole sniffed her disapproval. "Don't suppose he'll mourn her for long."

To Kate's relief, at that point Gloria arrived and after a hurried snatch of conversation with Kate, she graciously took Carole and Peter with her.

Kate rang Harry's office, "Come quick as you can, honey. I need some very urgent help."

Kate ran back to tend to Julie. The shock of the unexpected news still was showing upon Julie's face. She was shivering uncontrollably, her eyes unfocused, her hands two blocks of ice. She clutched at Kate and pleaded in a small, almost hysterical voice, "Is he okay, Katie? Oh, Katie, is he okay?"

Putting her own jacket around Julie's shoulders, Kate embraced her and explained what Carole had told her. Julie nodded she understood.

When Harry arrived, and Kate told him what had happened, he suggested, "Take Julie upstairs to John's apartment. Stay with her Kate. I'll ring Daisy, she knows about this McKenzie chap, doesn't she?"

Kate nodded, "Right, she can cover for Julie. Julie needs peace and quiet. She's had a bad shock. I'll see the relatives off to Rotorua. Thank goodness, it'll give Julie some breathing space."

Kate whispered to her husband, "God help her. I know she has valiantly tried to put him out of her life for John's sake." Kate kissed him, "Thank you, my dear, sweet, husband."

CHAPTER 69

In John's penthouse, Kate rustled up a duvet and wrapped Julie in it on the lounge sofa. "Talk to me, Julie dear, or just rest there for a while. I'll be here."

Half an hour of silence elapsed before Kate thankfully noted Julie's colour was slowly returning. Julie murmured weakly, "Thank you, Katie."

Several more minutes passed, before Julie whispered, "I tried to shut him out of my life, Katie, for John's sake. I believed if I gave Graeme up and devoted my life to John, somehow John wouldn't suffer any further."

Her face was paper white, her mouth pinched and bloodless, her deeply sunken eyes held a haunted, almost maniacal look.

Kate knew she had a case of intense shock on her hands and must tread carefully. She recalled Harry's murmured words to her, "Ring me if you are at all concerned, honey." Julie began speaking again. Almost inaudibly, she stammered, "When I didn't hear from Graeme, I doubted him. Now I hear this . . ." She wailed, "Oh, Katie, how could I've been so wrong, so stupid to believe he would desert us."

Kate made no attempt to stop the flood of tears that followed Julie's heartbroken words. She just rocked and comforted Julie in her arms, allowing the grief stricken woman to sob her heart out.

Eventually Julie fell into a nervous, fitful, twitching sleep.

Going into the kitchen, Kate picked up the telephone and rang Harry. "She's sleeping. How's things your end? Did they get away, okay?"

Kate heard an exasperated note in Harry's voice. "They were very 'huffy' about Julie not being there. Gloria procured her favourite limo for them. Daisy says you're not to worry, stay with Julie, she'll cope. If there's no improvement in Julie, say by six, I'll take all three children and Daisy back to the beach house tonight. But Katie love, if that does happen, we'll have to bring John into the picture."

At four o'clock Julie yawned sleepily. "Hello, Katie," she said, "Oh heck! What's happened to Carole and Peter?"

"Harry got them off to Rotorua, after telling them you had an emergency. They were a bit put out but, very 'chuffed' arriving at the tourist bus, chauffeur driven, in our friendly limo, courtesy of Gloria, bless her heart."

Julie could not resist a grin, "I bet!"

"Well, my dear girl, how do you feel now? Do you need more time, or do you want to go home?"

Julie shook her head. "I can't hide away, Katie. I always find unpleasant things easier if I carry on as normal. Kate, I'm so pleased I have you as my friend. Thank you, from the bottom of my heart."

Hesitantly at first, she told her, "I must go to the top of the hill tonight . . . Thank God, he's still alive . . . Oh, Katie . . . I can't stop loving him but . . . John needs me now . . . perhaps more than ever. When he knows Graeme is free he'll be so afraid that I'll go off and leave him."

When Harry arrived to pick them up, Julie hugged him, thanking him. Harry reddened, as he stuttered, "Julie, honey, we care deeply for you. You'll find Daisy has handled things superbly. It's up to you how much you tell John."

The children were safely tucked up in bed and the male nurse, Adam, was attending to John's final night-time ablutions. Julie asked Daisy to join her in her workroom.

Closing the door, Julie explained what her sister, in her ignorance of certain matters, had unwittingly blurted out.

Daisy hugged Julie close to her ample bosom. "Oh, you poor, wee lass. What a way to find out such tragic news. But, the young RAF man, Graeme, he's okay now?"

"As far as I know, Daisy. I'd like to go for a walk up the hill would you mind keeping an ear out for the children? Once Adam has left, I'll go in to John, he'll guess, for sure, that something dramatic has happened . . . I won't be long."

It had been many weeks since she last climbed to her favourite place. Julie saw Venus had already risen and was quite a bright spot in the early evening galaxy. Choking back a sob, she sat on the stile. For several minutes she sent loving thoughts to him, hoping he had now recovered and condolences over Anne's death. Her voice thick with emotion, she whispered, "I'm here, my beloved. Oh, my darling, I love you so much, Graeme. Please forgive me for ever thinking you had deserted us."

Returning home, Julie took a deep breath and went into John's room. Without any preamble, he greeted her, "What went wrong today? Everyone was kind, trying to keep calm, but something untoward happened, didn't it?"

Without exaggerating or over-dramatizing the facts, Julie related what had occurred. Her reaction and how Kate and Harry had taken over and handled everything.

When she finished, John grimaced in pain. An ache deeper, more cutting and painful than any cancer could bring on, gripped his body.

"Are you leaving me, Julie?" He asked "Are you going to McKenzie?"

Startled by his words, Julie saw the pain he was experiencing. A total and enveloping feeling of compassion filled her being. She reassured him, "No, no, John, I wouldn't and couldn't do that to you. I cannot deny how I feel about Graeme, but I am here for you, for as long as you want me to be."

John's face visibly relaxed and his head sank lower on his pillow. "Julie, although I'm hard to get along with some days, I have enjoyed your company immensely. Seeing you each day is still the highlight of my life. But, McKenzie has a huge claim on you. I know that . . . so . . . whatever you choose to do will be okay with me . . ."

Before Julie could reply, she saw that his medication had taken hold and he had drifted into sleep.

John's conscience was troubling him. He woke drenched in perspiration in the middle of the night, as he remembered his deceit over the message from Graeme McKenzie. He knew deep in his own subconscious what extreme pain and heartache he had caused Julie through his selfish, blindly foolish and jealous act. In spite of his caring words to Julie, he knew he could never summon the courage to confess or reveal to her what he had done.

It was nearly dawn before he slept again, only to be rudely awakened one hour later by a repetitive, amateurish cacophony of sound. Someone was thumping loudly on the grand piano keyboard.

Julie was also jolted awake, but it was by the sound of angry raised voices, shortly followed by a harsh slapping sound and a loud crash.

She hurried to the lounge. The ugly scene that greeted her seemed to be frozen in time. John was doubled up in pain, groaning beside the grand piano, its lid tightly closed.

Lauren was seated at the grand piano, her face pale, her eyes wide and terrified. One of her cheeks was glowing with a rapidly spreading, angry red welt.

Daisy, glowering like a caged mother tiger, stood between the children and John. She had an arm around Stuart, who had his head buried in the skirt of her housecoat, sobbing piteously.

"What on earth is going on?" Julie demanded.

Lauren tearfully stammered, "I was only teaching Stuart to play 'Jingle Bells', Mama."

John slumped down on a chair. "They've been playing the same notes repeatedly for over half an hour now! My nerves couldn't take it any longer. Yes, I slapped Lauren,.. and yes, I slammed the piano lid down and frightened Stuart. It's my piano and it stays locked from now on. Is that clear?" With that he staggered off to his room.

Daisy soothed Stuart, saying, "Your Papajohn is very sick and not feeling well, my dear. We must forgive him."

Julie took Lauren into the bathroom and put a cold, wet face flannel cloth over her reddened cheek. "I'm sorry Papajohn has hurt you Lauren. I'll talk with him later, see if we can find a time when you can play."

Lauren was crestfallen, then said, "I don't think Papagraeme can hear us, I don't think he's listening any more."

Julie hugged her daughter, "Oh yes, Lauren, he'll be listening, darling, I promise you. He loves you dearly, Lauren, never EVER forget that."

The tension in the house worsened. John was hardly seen, and when he did make an appearance, he was grumpy and hard to please. Julie was thankful when her sister Carole returned. It gave her a reason to be out and about, as she took Carole and Peter sightseeing and for a barbecue at the beach house.

At the beach, telling Kate about the awful morning, Julie admitted she was worried. "He's so morose, depressed, and acting rather unkindly to all and everyone. I've spoken to Doc Matthews and he'll visit John today. He says it could be John's medication. God, I hope it is only that. He really is a monster at the moment—ill or not!"

"Could it have been the news of Graeme?" Kate asked, with a worried frown. "Look, if he gets too difficult, pack the children up and come here, Jules."

"Carole and Peter fly off to Sydney for the New Year with Peter's relatives. They are going to Paihia for a couple of days this weekend. I'll see how John is first."

Kate suggested, "For now, let's just walk for a bit along the beach, on our own, minus children, husbands and peculiar relatives. Just us, communing with Nature. I do this every day we are here and I find it blows the cobwebs away and refreshes my spirit."

"You're getting quite poetic, Katie Reynolds!" Julie cried, "I think you must be turning into a 'beach bum'."

CHAPTER 70

Julie took Carole up the hill for one last look around. Carole asked, with some reticence, "What's the prognosis for John? Will this be the last time we see him?"

"John's cancer has spread, Carole. Doc Matthews told me his life expectancy is less than a year if they don't get it all this time . . . It's hard for the children though."

Carole laughed nervously. "Talking about the children. How come, Lauren is so blonde? I mean Stuart looks so much like both of you. They do have beautiful blue eyes . . . Y'know, I'd swear I've seen eyes like those before."

Although Julie had seen Carole giving Lauren several questioning looks she was not prepared to confide in her sister. She ducked the question suggesting a family throwback.

Julie and John had opted to leave the children at the beach, when they returned home to prepare for John's next operation. Waking during the night, she heard John moan and call her name. But she realised he was dreaming. The dream had actually woken John, but he had lain still, feigning sleep, a prisoner of his own deceit. Even when Doc Matthews had closely questioned him, he couldn't bring himself to confess. Now, most nights, his culpability came back to haunt him.

The new operation was more complicated than expected, and John seemed to be making slow progress. Until one morning when, to his consternation, he found he was unable to read the newspaper. His vision became increasingly blurred and he could not distinguish which way he was headed.

"Julie, where are you? I can't see very well." His voice was weak, as he staggered around the room. Julie and Daisy hurried to his side. "We're here, John, dear. Adam will be here in a moment, he'll know what to do."

It was a grim faced Adam who emerged from John's room half an hour later, saying, "I've rung Doc Matthews."

Doc Matthews hospitalised John immediately. Later that day, with great reluctance, he told Julie, "I suspect John has a brain tumour, Julie, my dear. He can see a little better now, but he has a blinding headache, and is not in the sweetest of tempers. You can go and see him but, I'm afraid he's not handling this latest news too well."

As Julie entered John's room he bellowed, "For God's sake! What do you want now! Leave me alone!"

Closing the door quickly behind her, Julie said softly, "It's only me, John."

A somewhat quieter, more subdued John replied, "Julie. You are the only one I need. Come closer to the bed where I can see your beautiful face, my darling wife."

Surprised by his endearment, Julie picked up his hand. His skin felt hot and dry and so pathetically thin. He told her, "I'm in dreadful pain, Julie. I can hardly see you. What are wearing? Is it one of the newest designs? What perfume are you using?"

With a smile Julie answered. "No, it's something I've had for a while, John. My perfume is the one I always use, the one you bought me for Christmas."

A guttural, bestial sound emitted from John's throat, as he snarled, "Not like the good stuff you'd wear for McKenzie then? No new gowns need be worn for your sick husband, eh? The 'cuckold'—that's the term for me, isn't it, you filthy whore. Oh, go away; I can't deal with your virginal sweetness tonight."

Doc Matthews, entering the room, heard the last sentences. Julie shook like a leaf as Doc took her unresisting arm and led her into the hallway.

"He'll not remember saying any of that next time you see him."

The next afternoon, after what seemed such a long time, Julie was relieved to see the familiar figure of Doc Matthews coming from the operating theatre. His face was weary and, for the first time since she had known him, he was looking his age.

He smiled wanly. "It's not good news, Julie lass.

The tumour was huge, and very difficult to get at. Mr Burt has done as fine a job as I have ever seen. We can only wait and see."

John was immediately subjected to more radiation and chemotherapy treatment. Again he was unable to keep any quantity of food down and became ever thinner. With his consequent hair loss, he was now sporting a shiny, bald pate. Stuart was really taken with this new look. One day he fetched John's electric razor and asked John to shave off his hair, so that he could look more like his Papajohn. John, being in the emotional state that he was, found it hard to control his tears.

Julie hugged him, "See, it doesn't matter what you look like. To me and the children you are just our much loved Papajohn!"

As Doc Matthews said later to Julie, "It was such a simple thing on Stuart's part but, believe me, for John it was the best pick-me-up medicine he could have had. He couldn't stop telling me about it!"

Spring came with its usual promise of new life, and John took his first walk outdoors after being confined for weeks indoors. Julie saw on his pale, pain ravaged face, the pleasure it gave him. He now weighed only half of his normal weight. Previously always proud of his sartorial elegance, his once superbly tailored clothes now hung shapelessly around his body. He wore a woollen beanie hat on his head during the day to keep him warm, and also to hide the disfiguring operation scars. When he attempted to walk, it was the shuffle of an old and infirm man, no longer the purposeful stride of a healthy young man-about-town.

For a few weeks John enjoyed sitting on the patio, even staying around for the whole day on Stuart's third birthday. The little boy had nominated himself as John's personal 'gopher', bringing him the newspaper, a book or whatever John wanted.

Julie had been on the verge of enrolling Stuart at the local Kindergarten, but when she saw the rapport building between them, she had let that decision wait.

Bob East had again accepted the role of John's chauffeur, driving him around the farm for an hour or so. But those outings became fewer and further between, John simply had not the strength or the stamina left to handle it any more.

It was decided that Lauren and Stuart would once again stay at the beach house, once Lauren finished school for the year.

Julie suggested, "Let Daisy come and prepare Christmas dinner for you, Katie. She cannot do it here, lingering food smells just make John feel so nauseated."

While Kate gratefully agreed with this, she gazed intently into Julie's eyes. "You are looking old and grey, Julie Field, and so, so tired."

Julie brushed her hair wearily from her face. "I'm all he's got, Katie. I'm the only one he tolerates around him. Doc Matthews warned me he is deteriorating rapidly." Julie's eyes filled with tears. "Once the cancer hits his brain it will be over quickly. I cannot leave him alone to face that; I must be there for him."

Kate embraced her friend tightly, "You do whatever you feel comfortable with. We love you, Julie."

Several nights later, John cried out in pain, "Julie, help me put an end to it! Help me to die, Julie. It's really bad tonight." John twisted and turned as Julie administered his pain relief. "My headache is a real doozie, it feels like I'm splitting in two."

Soon the pain relief helped him to be calmer and she changed his sweat soaked pyjamas once more.

John roused again and tenderly touched her face. "I don't think I can last much longer, Julie, my darling. The pain is bad. There are a couple of things I must tell you before the morphine takes over, and perhaps I can't speak lucidly . . ." Then he drifted off again into a drug induced half-sleep.

Adam let himself into the house to find Julie with her head on the bed beside John, both asleep. Gently touching Julie's shoulder, Adam whispered, "I thought I'd come back to see if he needed anything further tonight."

Adam noticed that Julie looked exhausted. "Go and have a rest, Julie. I'll stay and call you if he wakes."

Preparing to write down John's vital signs on the chart, Adam frowned at his instruments. "Julie, has he complained of anything unusual?"

Wearily, Julie nodded, "Yes, he said the pain in his head was almost unbearable."

"There has been a change. I think I'll get Doc to come out. I'll go and give him a ring."

John opened his eyes. "Julie? Are you there, sweetheart? . . . Ah, there you are . . . Julie, please listen to me carefully. Take the children back to McKenzie; give him back his children, Julie . . . and you too. Promise me?"

Julie, her eyes full of tears, nodded, "Yes, I promise you, John."

"Julie, I can hardly see you, hold my hand please, so that I know you are there. Julie, I have something terrible to confess, it's been bothering me for so long."

A spasm of pain wracked his body, but he struggled to continue. His voice was weaker and Julie had to bend close to his mouth, as he murmured, in staccato phrases, "He sent you a message . . . I hid it . . . It's in the 'odds and sods' drawer of my desk . . . Please forgive me, my love . . . for all the unnecessary pain . . . and heartache I have put you through . . . Oh, my darling, Julie, please, please say you forgive me."

Julie was now crying openly. "Oh, Dear God! He did send me a message! Oh, John, my dear, of course I forgive you."

Julie softly and compassionately told him, "John, you are at peace now, no more hidden secrets, no more pain. You are free, John."

John's face lost all of its tension, the worried, pain-induced frown melted away. He suddenly looked ten years younger, serene, and at last at peace with himself. A gentle smile played around his bloodless lips.

"Aaah, thank goodness . . . good-bye, my darling . . . you are still the best thing that ever happened to me . . . Dad and Mum are waiting for me . . . Julie, it's my time . . ."

Later signing the Death Certificate, Doc Matthews noted John Field died at exactly ten o'clock that night, December 17th 1998, aged 42 years . . .

CHAPTER 71

The next morning, Julie sat on the stile at the top of the hill as the local undertaker and his staff carried out what they had to do. Kate and Harry fielded the numerous calls of sympathy from those who had heard the sad news.

In a firm, kindly way, Harry had advised Julie, "The children are fine at the beach with Daisy. When what has to be done is done, we'll take you there. Kate has drafted a newspaper notice, you can vet it and she'll telephone it in. I'll inform the Vicar and he can confer with you tomorrow. Now, off you go, take at least half an hour."

With that, Harry had hung her coat on her back before shepherding her out the door. Numbly, she had taken her familiar route to her special spot. She sat there for over ten minutes before the tears came. Her thoughts tumbled over and over, a veritable kaleidoscope of memories of her life with John.

As she sat holding her head in her hands, she felt a gentle, warm, comforting breeze encircle her, making a soft 'Huussshhh, Huussshhh' sound, until it completely surrounded the grieving woman in a cocoon, suspending her in a vacuum. She could almost feel the spirit of her much loved Grandmother, so overpowering, so real, so close, she half expected to see her standing there in person.

That afternoon Julie took Lauren and Stuart out along the deserted beach and explained what had happened.

Stuart sat in stunned silence, but Lauren said quietly, "He was very sick, wasn't he Mama?"

"Yes, my darling, he was really hurting most of the time. Now he isn't any more, my dears."

Stuart sat not uttering a word, suddenly he buried his head in his mother's chest, and sobbed, "But I love him, Mama. Why did Papajohn get so sick?"

Julie simply answered, "It wasn't anything we could stop, Stuart, dear."

Sitting talking on the beautiful isolated beach, so beloved by John in his last months, Julie made no attempt to hurry them back. She was prepared to talk with them for as long as it took.

Kate saw how wisely Julie had handled the situation when Stuart exclaimed, "TantKate! My Papajohn has gone to live with Jesus."

Lauren informed her, "He has gone to look after Nananaomi and Papageorgie in Heaven, TantKate. They needed him up there."

Three days later, the local family church was overflowing with mourners. Floral tributes of vibrant coloured tropical plants, mingled easily with native New Zealand flowers. A simple sheaf of blooms from the part of their garden that had become John's favourite, decorated his mahogany coffin. The simple, but moving service, contained music of which John was particularly fond.

Finally, Lauren read a short poem that John had taught her.

"You can shed tears that he is gone, or you can smile because he has lived.

"You can cry and close your mind, be empty and turn your back,

"Or, you can do what he'd want: smile, open your eyes, love and go on."

Watching Lauren, Julie could not stop the thought of how, every year she grew physically more like her biological father. As she moved her hands in a descriptive gesture, or, in the tilt of her head as she expressed a phrase—it was pure Graeme.

Finally, a lone piper played a soulful lament as John was laid to rest beside his parents. Julie felt numbed by all of the condolences, the sympathetic noises and the numerous handshakes. Flanked by Andrew Martin, Kate and Harry, she began to feel the sad day would never end.

Daisy had taken all three children back to the beach right after the funeral service. Kate and Harry were proposing to leave as soon as the house cleared of people. Julie had invited Andrew Martin to stay the night with her.

Kate hugged Julie, saying, "Jules. I'm so proud of you. We'll see you in four days' time. Golly! That'll be Christmas Eve and Daisy will be cooking up a storm! Promise me you'll be okay?"

Julie's voice trembled and she nervously rubbed her chin. "Kate, I have an appointment with the solicitors, before they close down for Christmas. Andrew is coming with me, before I drive him to the airport. I need to go into John's office. After that, the way I'm feeling, I'll probably sleep the clock around!"

As she and Andrew sat in companionable silence a couple of hours later, drinking a nightcap, Andrew quietly asked, "Where to from here, Julie?"

Julie smiled. "You already know, Andrew dear, but that could be the impossible dream. Things change, people change, time takes its toll. I'll have to give it some serious thought before I do anything."

After a few pensive moments, she continued, "Thank goodness, money is no problem. I own this house and land outright, and the farm is held in trust for the children. The business is thriving. 'Bellamissio' has gone through the roof! The orders are flowing in, literally in torrents. We've planned another speciality line, just to keep up with the demand. So you could say I'm sitting pretty."

She wandered out onto the patio. "But am I? I haven't done any real designing for nearly six months. My life this past year has been solely devoted to John. I'm burnt out, Andrew. I need time alone, not being at anyone's beck and call, recuperating my spirit. Am I making sense?"

"Oh yes, Julie, my dear, perfect sense. I went through the same process after my wife, Ellen, died. Although I loved her dearly and was completely bereft when she died, I felt as though my head was stuffed with cotton wool. I didn't feel I was my own person, but rather a puppet with everyone else pulling my strings. Is that what you mean?"

Julie sighed, "That's it exactly, Andrew. Oh, what a relief! I thought it was just me!"

There were no surprises in John's Will as it was an identical one to Julie's. The formalities were virtually over in minutes.

At the airport, Andrew embraced Julie and sagely advised, "Julie, now that you are both free, give him a chance. Remember Maria's words of wisdom—she is rarely wrong about these things."

Julie took the private elevator directly to John's office. Unlocking the door, she had a moment of panic. A shiver ran down her spine and she had to force herself to go forward into the room. 'Odds and Sods' drawer,' she intoned as she pulled it out. She rummaged through and found a single sheet of pale blue paper. There it was the message that would have saved her years of heartache.

"High Flight, injured in bomb blast, unable to contact, convalescing. All now well"

A simple thirteen word sentence, words that would have given her the comfort of knowing he was alive.

That night, completely alone in her house for the first time, Julie found she did not feel lonely at all.

With a happy smile, she went into her workroom and pulled out, from their various hiding places, all of the presents she had been accumulating for the children's Christmas. It would be a healing time, a time to recoup and recharge her batteries.

Harry regularly collected the large bundles of mail that accumulated. Amongst the various Sympathy cards had been one from her Maureen Barker (nee: Watson), Billy's sister. The caring, sincere message brought many pleasant childhood memories flooding back. A feeling of homesickness was followed by an overwhelming desire to see Graeme again.

Going on one of her daily walks, this time with Kate, Julie broached the subject. "Kate, a card came from the sister of Graeme's best friend, Billy Watson. Well, Katie, it made up my mind for me. I'm going to the U.K. to find Graeme, see if there is still a ghost of a chance for us."

Kate whooped with glee, "Great Jumping Jodhpurs'!! Thank goodness! Harry and I hoped, with time, you'd come to that conclusion." Kate hugged Julie in delight. "So? When? How soon?"

"I'll talk with Daisy first; see if she has any plans of her own. I'd like to see Lauren settled in school and get Stuart started at Kindergarten. We've got the new Bellamissio' factory line up and running . . . so, I'll see if I can get away, about March/April. What d'ya think?"

"Yep, brilliant idea! That should silence those 'gossipy old harpies'. According to the older generation, wealthy, beautiful young widows are expected to wear their 'weeds' for at least a year."

Julie looked at Kate aghast, "Do you think I should wait a YEAR, Kate?"

"Heavens, woman! No, I don't, I wish you'd go next week. But, I can see your reasoning in getting the children settled first. Besides, it's perfectly natural to want to visit your family over there."

But Kate was right. Julie met with anger, resentment and downright rudeness. Julie was so upset when one of their regular buyers was overheard to say, "A 'Merry Widow' already, eh?" that she had lifted the telephone to cancel her flight. She was only stopped when Kate knocked the receiver out of her hand.

Kate had yelled at her, "What are you doing? This is YOUR life. You gave up the chance to be with him twice before, are you prepared to do it again? Jules, you owe it to your children, to him, and to yourself."

At the beginning of March, with Daisy's full support, Julie began to quietly prepare herself and her children for her upcoming trip. No one but Kate, Harry and Daisy knew the true nature of her intentions. She had purposely not informed her siblings of her arrival. She wanted to travel quietly, and without any fanfare, to RAF Mildenhall.

If it didn't work out, she planned to slip out of the country again, after spending a couple of weeks with her family.

Daisy suggested, "You are leaving on Saturday, I'll take the bairns down to the beach after school on Friday. You can then sort yourself out quietly, lass, without any weepy farewells. Go! Bring him back, my love."

Julie hung the amethyst pendant back in its rightful place. She smiled. "That's better, now I feel whole again. My darling Graeme, I do so hope you still want me."

CHAPTER 72

Julie felt fortunate because the jet was lightly loaded so she had the luxury of an empty seat beside her. This negated the need to make polite small talk with a complete stranger. Smiling, she recalled how Kate had done everything in her power to smooth her way. Yet, underneath her apparent outward calm, she knew Kate would have been striving to contain her own undercurrent of excitement.

Kate was so sure Julie was about to undertake her rightful destiny. Dynamic red-headed, green-eyed Kate would have had a red-hot lava flow, a bubbling internal volcano burning inside her.

Julie chuckled to herself, 'I bet she's having a very stiff drink now that I'm safely on my way.'

"Mrs Field? Hello, Mrs Field?"

Opening her eyes, Julie saw the smiling face of the stewardess. "Hello again, Mrs Field, we're about to serve breakfast."

Estimating they should be landing in Los Angeles in about four hours, Julie rose and walked down the plane's aisle, stretching her legs and swinging her arms.

As was returning to her seat, she saw the cabin crew coming from the galley with the heavy metal food cart and was about to slide across to her window seat. Suddenly, the aircraft lurched violently, in a vertical downwards movement.

Her feet flew from under her and she was flung off-balance against the arm of the outer seat, with her head jutting out into the aisle. From her awkward, almost prone position, she saw the trolley careening out of control, at breakneck speed, along the aisle toward her.

Before she could move out of its way, the sharp corner struck the side of her head with a bone crunching, bruising bump.

"Wind shear!" yelled a knowledgeable voice. Julie lay sprawled like a broken doll. She heard yelling, screams of pain, hysterical noises of fear and sounds of utter chaos . . . then . . . blissfully . . . nothing . . .

Panic reigned in the jet's cabin.

Cabin staff and the man who uttered "wind shear" raced towards Julie.

A male passenger pushed through, calling loudly, "I'm a Doctor, let me pass!" Bent over Julie's inert body, he quickly examined her. "She's out cold. Help me get her into a more comfortable position, and get a blanket please."

He left her in the immediate care of a woman passenger who had volunteered that she had limited nursing experience. He then checked on other passengers who had suffered a range of injuries.

Once the cabin staff had restored a comparative calm as the aircraft resumed level flight, Dr Steven Lambert returned to Julie. The woman passenger shook her head when he asked if she had moved. He listened to her breathing and checked her vital signs discovering, to his consternation she was deeply unconscious.

A worried looking Co-pilot appeared from the cockpit and was directed by the Purser to Dr Lambert.

"What happened?" the Doctor asked. "Was it wind shear?"

The Co-pilot nodded. "We dropped about 300 feet. It came out of the blue, no warning, nothing. What's the extent of the injuries out here, the Captain's anxious to know."

"Well, I've managed to get around them all," the Doctor grimly reported. "Several minor cuts and bruises. One of the cabin staff has a broken wrist. Two severe scalds from hot drinks, a suspected broken collarbone and one young woman knocked out. She's the most urgent, and is in need of more medical attention, pronto."

The Co-pilot quietly told him, "The Captain would like to see you, sir, A.S.A.P."

Dr Steven Lambert nodded and, giving Julie one last concerned look, he asked his temporary nurse to please stay with her.

The Captain was talking on the radio, advising Ground Control they would need medical assistance. He turned to the Doctor. "Thank you for your assistance Doctor, its most appreciated. How bad is it?"

Dr Steven Lambert read the list he had compiled. "The one that has the worst scenario is . . . ?" he looked at the Purser as she studied her passenger list.

"She's Mrs Julie Field, from Auckland, en route to London."

"She'll need urgent attention. We need to assess how severe her head wound is." Sounding worried, Dr Lambert asked, "What's our E.T.A. at Los Angeles, Captain?"

"In about three hours, Doctor. I'll get a special clearance, have medics waiting for us."

Ambulances were waiting as the big jet landed and soon the lesser injured were off-loaded, leaving the aisle clear for Julie's inert body to be strapped onto a stretcher.

The Purser checked she had Julie's entire cabin luggage, advising Dr Lambert, "Mrs Field's Passport and her other details are all here. I am Chief Purser, Vicky Chan. I have been designated by the airline to accompany you, and to contact Mrs Field's next-of-kin."

Dr Lambert acknowledged, "Right. Initially we'll be going to Cedars-Sinai Medical Centre for an assessment. I'm attached to the Saint Francis Medical Centre, Santa Barbara, but I did my internship at C.S. so I'm known there."

On arrival at the hospital, Julie was soon hooked up to monitoring devices to record her condition.

"She's well out to it, Steven," the Registrar said, pursing his lips. "She could come out of it anytime, or it could take a while. It's safe to move her if you want to transfer her to St. Francis. But, you'll have to get permission from her next-of-kin, and the airline, before doing so."

"That's going to take time," mused Dr Lambert. "How about we admit her until I can get the paperwork sorted?"

They advised Vicky Chan of their decision. She assured them the airline would agree to act on whatever medical advice they gave. She left to contact Julie's next-of-kin.

Going through Julie's papers, Vicky Chan soon found Kate was named as Julie's first contact. Ringing Kate's number in Auckland, mindful of the time zone difference, Vicky Chan knew she must handle her call delicately and gently.

When a sleepy voice answered, she identified herself.

Instantly awake, Kate could not conceal her alarm.

Shaking Harry awake beside her, she asked, "What is it? Is it Julie?"

Vicky Chan slowly explained the wind shear problem and where Julie was now, and who was caring for her, before she discreetly asked, "Is there a Mr Field?"

"No, Julie is widowed. My husband and I have Julie's Power of Attorney while she's overseas. What do you want us to do, Miss Chan?" Kate, the practical businesswoman, had taken over.

"The present medical opinion is that Mrs Field should initially be admitted to Cedars-Sinai, where they can fully monitor her condition. Then, Dr Steven Lambert intends to take her to Saint Francis Medical Centre in Santa Barbara, where he is the Medical Superintendent. It is run by the Franciscan nuns, the Saint Francis Sisters, their reputations as skilled and efficient nurses are well known."

"You have my verbal permission to do whatever is necessary, Miss Chan," Kate assured her. "Please ask Doctor Lambert to ring me as soon as he can. I am able to fly there at short notice, here is my number, you can contact me at any time."

Vicky Chan assured Kate, "I'll stay with Mrs Field until you, or someone in her family arrives."

They waited anxiously until Dr Lambert introduced himself and impressed Kate with his calm, professional manner.

"We understand Mrs Field had been recently widowed. She's deeply unconscious, but we believe she's able to hear speech, although she's not capable of answering at present. What I'd like is an audio tape relating her life-story, which we shall play repetitively to her. Can you do that for us, Mrs Reynolds?"

Quickly Kate replied, "Yes, of course. We have known each other for many years. We are as close as two sisters."

"That's fine . . . ideal! Start at the earliest point in time and come forward to the present day," the doctor advised. "Go into as much detail as you can, particularly of significant events that have happened to her. Mrs Reynolds, are people expecting her?"

"No, she had no exact plans," replied Kate. "She's booked into a Hotel in London. I can contact them."

Steven Lambert reassured her, "At least we now know we do not have anxious relatives at Heathrow. Let's get you started on the tape, see what reactions we get before we do anything more drastic. I'll have Mrs Field moved to Saint Francis's and I'll ring you within the next twenty-four hours. Will that give you enough time?"

"Yes, certainly," replied Kate, "I'll start immediately. Could you ask Vicky Chan to book me a seat whenever you are ready for me? Dr Lambert, Julie is a very precious person to all of us here. Take good care of her."

Hanging up the phone, Kate dissolved into tears in Harry's arms.

"Come on, Katie. You have an important job to do for Julie. Go to her house with the recorder—start at the beginning and just keep talking. I'll take care of things here, my love."

Kate sat in Julie's favourite place on her patio, with the recorder beside her. Gathering her thoughts she began, "You were a new bride, just arrived from the U.K. You were twenty years old . . .

. . . Julie had been brought from Cedars-Sinai to Saint Francis Medical Centre. She lay on her back, eyes closed, in a stark white room, covered by an equally snowy white, stiffly starched sheet. Dr Steven Lambert crossed to the bed and stood observing the dials on the machines.

Sister Theresa murmured, "There's been no change, Doctor."

"Just keep her comfortable, Sister," he replied in a soft voice. "I'm about to play the first tape from her friend in New Zealand. Will you assign a novitiate to sit with her all of the time and report to me immediately if they notice any difference, however minor."

"Be assured, Doctor, you'll be the first to know," replied the elderly Nun, in a soft, lilting, Irish accent.

"We have prepared the adjoining room for Mrs Reynolds. The Chief Purser said she'll stay until Mrs Reynolds arrives."

She paused and gently stroked Julie's face. "She is a beautiful young woman. We are all saying special prayers for her."

Julie slumbered in an unnatural sleep, deep inside a dark world of her own. Headphones had been placed on her head. The tape played for an hour, before it rewound itself back to the beginning, and started again, repeating Kate's dialogue, over and over.

CHAPTER 73

Her flight from Auckland to Los Angeles had seemed to Kate to be interminable. Harry had been his usual supportive self, telling Kate not to worry about a thing at home, as he gave her a final farewell at Auckland Airport.

He added, "Just get Julie safe and well to where she wants to be, my love."

Running into the cell-like bare room, Kate had trouble holding back her tears. Julie looked so still, small and white upon the narrow bed.

Sister Theresa soon summoned Dr Lambert. He watched the red-headed, willowy slim figure as she leaned over the bed. Kate put her arms around as much of Julie as she could, "I'm here, come back, Jules, we need you."

After a while Kate turned to the doctor, her mind full of questions, "How is she? Is there any improvement? Any reaction to the tape that I sent? I've another here, following on from the first one. Well?"

Dr Steven Lambert ruefully shook his head as he responded, "Dear lady, you are so very welcome here, no doubt your help to us will be very valuable. To answer your question, No, there's no improvement, but I hasten to add, that's not entirely unusual. I have her in a medically induced coma. She caught a bad knock from a very heavy food trolley. Her brain needs to rest as much as anything."

He took Kate's hand, "Can I call you Kate? My name is Steven."

"Please do, Steven." Kate squirmed uneasily, "Julie is a widow, she was on her way to see Graeme McKenzie. There are some extraordinary circumstances as to why Julie was undertaking this trip and all highly confidential."

She swallowed hard. "She is a well-known and very successful 'Haute Couture' dress designer. We must make sure her identity is kept out of the media. Can you do that? My husband Harry and I have already had to duck and dive to avoid the story reaching the media." Kate paused and, with tears in her eyes, told Steven, "God help me! I pressured her into making this wretched trip."

Steven Lambert handed her several large tissues. "It was a very unfortunate accident, Kate. It couldn't have been predicted," he consoled her. "Chief Purser Vicky Chan has already spoken to me about the media interest. I have forbidden any release of any her personal details, her privacy is assured . . . Now do you know how to get hold of this Graeme McKenzie chap?"

"Yes, but only by going through some private papers Julie carries with her. I'd rather not do that, Steven, unless it becomes dire, and only then as a last resort."

Kate felt most uncomfortable. "Except for my husband and me, nobody really knows her plans. Julie didn't want him to know she was coming. If it had not worked out, she was just going to get back on a plane and return to New Zealand."

Steven Lambert nodded his head. "I can understand that and, I'll respect your confidence. You are virtually as close to Julie as a blood relative. In that case, you and I together, will make any decisions regarding Julie's well-being. In the meantime, do you have another tape for me? The first one was excellent; you covered those years so well. No wonder you won a Gold Medal for 'Best Descriptive Commentary'. I'm impressed! The pair of you, have accomplished so much in such a short time."

Rummaging in her travel bag, Kate said, "This tape starts when Julie was pregnant. It was a happy but traumatic time in her life . . ." She paused and Steven saw a shadow full of sorrow pass across her face. "Julie and I became even closer . . . It wasn't easy . . . anyway, listen then you'll understand, Steven."

⟨⟨⟨≈≈≈⟩⟩⟩

. . . The new tape began and although it did not register upon Julie's outward countenance, inwardly she secretly smiled. Several ghostly faces floated above her inert body.

Each whispered urgently, "Please darling, stay with us . . . Come back, Mama . . . Mama, come back . . . come back."

Sister Theresa listened closely to Julie's breathing and, using her many years of experience, detected a slight change in the rhythm. It did not register on any of the instruments, as yet, but . . . Ah! There it was again, a much deeper than usual breath.

Was she coming out of it, or was she sinking deeper? 'Time to alert young Dr Lambert, methinks,' Sister Theresa told herself.

Steven Lambert was busy quizzing a colleague, a trauma consultant in Boston about a new coma technique recently introduced by another colleague. Sister Theresa waited anxiously for him.

"Nothing is showing on the monitors, but I can detect a slight difference that wasn't there yesterday. To my observations she is more relaxed, but, I can't be sure."

"Set up every monitor we have, please, Sister. Ask Kate Reynolds to join us and then we must eliminate every extraneous noise we can. We'll need total silence for a technique I want to try."

Hurrying into the room, wearing a worried frown, Kate asked, "What is it? What's wrong?"

Steven Lambert said, reassuringly, "Something need further investigation. I have reached the point, a colleague tells me, when I must make a serious decision."

He took Kate's hands in his. "Our choices are these. We gradually withdraw her medication over the next twenty-four hours, and hope she will resurface naturally or, we put her medically into a deeper coma for several more days. As her spokeswoman, Kate, are you happy with any decisions I may make?"

Kate whispered, "Yes, of course, Steven. Please, do what you think is best. What do you want me to do?"

Steven Lambert gestured around the room. "Once we have darkened the room and made it as soundproof as we are able, I want you both to watch the monitors extra closely as I ask each question. Try not to react, sigh, or make any extra sound. We'll pool our observations once I've asked my questions."

The two women from opposite sides of the world, and equally diverse lives, intently watched the earnest young doctor.

In a soft, but distinctive, clear voice, he asked,

"Julie, are you listening?" The monitors did not change, but continued their regular, normal beep, click and hiss sounds.

Unperturbed, he asked, "Have you seen Lauren today?" One of the monitors gave a double 'Click, Click', a slight, but significant change.

Steven Lambert, using a small penlight torch, made a small notation on the clipboard on his knee. "What about Stuart?" Another double 'Click, Click' echoed loudly in the darkened room.

"Kate? . . . Harry? . . . Daisy?" He paused, but there was no obvious reaction, or significant change.

"Can you hear me, Julie?"

The only response was just the monotonous beep, click, and hiss from the machinery.

Waiting for a few seconds, Steven Lambert then asked,

"Did Graeme come by?"

Before their astonished eyes, every single needle on every dial on the various monitors dramatically swung wildly to and fro.

Wide-eyed and startled, Kate stared into the darkness towards Steven Lambert's voice.

After a minute or so, the dials had settled back to their monotonous rhythm. He continued his questioning, in his soft, persuasive voice. "Will Graeme be coming back?"

More wild activity from the machines caused Dr Lambert to switch on his penlight, making further notes.

He cast a glance towards Kate before his next question. Speaking slowly and very deliberately, he asked, "Do you want to see him, Julie?"

Julie's breathing increased rapidly, the dials on the machines registered intense activity, but her body did not move. She remained motionless on the narrow white bed.

Steven Lambert paused, patiently allowing the machinery to return to normal. Glancing at the luminous dial on her wristwatch, Kate noted it took a full five minutes. She stared into the darkness as she wondered what interpretation, or analysis, Steven Lambert would put upon such a violent reaction.

Deep in her own reverie, she jumped at the sound of his voice, as he softly asked, "Do you want him here, Julie?"

Again the needles on the various dials flew around agitatedly, demonstrating Julie's brain had registered the question, and had given an emphatic answer.

Steven Lambert silently waited until all of the dials settled back. He signalled for Sister Theresa to open the windows. He turned to the two women. "Let's go next door into Kate's room." Once there he stated, "There is no point in continuing with any further questioning which will only agitate and disturb Julie's state of mind.

Even before I analyse this data, I'm convinced that we must get Graeme McKenzie here. His name is the catalyst that stimulates her, and activates her brain."

Tremulously, Kate pleaded, "Will that be enough to pull her out of this coma?"

He scratched his chin, shook his head. "I don't know, Kate, but it's a chance we must take. I propose to gradually withdraw all of her medication over the next twenty-four hours, see if she resurfaces naturally. If not, our only alternative is to get him here. That's what she obviously wants."

Sister Theresa sagely nodded, saying, "Julie seems to have such a depth of feeling for that man. To my lay knowledge, and judging by what we have just witnessed, she needs and wants him close by."

"Yes, I agree," Kate said with a heartfelt sigh.

"I suppose I've known all along I should have contacted him right at the beginning." She rubbed her eyes wearily.

"Well, I'll leave the latest tape that I have made. It brings Julie's life story almost up to date."

"Kate, I know you have been sworn to secrecy over Graeme's whereabouts," Steven said, "I wouldn't ask you to break such a sacred promise if I didn't feel it was imperative to restore her life to some sort of normality. We must try everything available to us."

Kate gulped and forced back a lump in her throat. Sister Theresa smiled encouragingly and said softly, "I'll support you, Kate. I'll testify that you've broken your sacred promise in order to help give Julie back her life. Go along with what Dr Lambert is asking you to do, child."

Kate's eyes were welling with unshed tears as Steven Lambert softly asked, "Kate, how confident are you that you know how to contact Graeme?"

Kate said, "Yes . . . I know."

. . . A lone vapour trail marked the path of a high-flying military aircraft. Inside were a complement of high-ranking, international defence service personnel, on their way to yet more negotiations in the search for world peace.

"Something wrong?" the junior ranked officer asked as the Air Commodore's arm suddenly jerked, breaking his pencil in two on his note pad.

A look of consternation crossed his seniors face. "Got the darndest feeling, Billy. It was as though someone was trying to attract my attention, calling my name." Unsettled for moment, he raised one eyebrow in a question mark. "Most peculiar tha . . ."

CHAPTER 74

The solitary figure of a slim, tallish woman, walked beside the pounding ocean. She left a jagged line of fresh wet footprints momentarily defacing the otherwise pristine sandy beach. A flock of sea birds wheeled and screeched in protest at her unwelcome intrusion.

Kate Reynolds faced a moral predicament. She was about to break a solemn vow.

She shivered, "I must try and get him here, Jules. Whatever it takes—we need you so much."

Julie's luggage was moved into Kate's room. Half an hour later, she stared perplexed at the sycamore trinket box—it contained only jewellery.

Turning the box over Kate heard a 'chink, chink' sound. There, in an almost invisible pocket on the inside, were two small golden keys. They belonged to Julie's green leather box! Too heavy to carry with her—it would still be back at the house.

She went to Julie's room and found Dr Lambert and Sister Theresa, wearing ominously concerned looks.

Sighing wearily, Kate asked in a broken voice, "Will getting Graeme McKenzie here do any good at all, Steven?"

He held out his hands in supplication, "I honestly don't know Kate. I thought . . ."

Sister Theresa uncharacteristically interrupted him. "I did. So did you, Kate. Julie's reaction certainly gave the impression that's what she wanted. Have you had any success, Kate?"

Kate twisted her wedding ring, and wrung her hands, "No. I realise the box Julie would've kept such personal data would've been too heavy to carry with her . . ."

"Well, where is it, Kate? Can we send someone to open it, collect it, and bring it here? What?" Steven Lambert ran his hand through his hair as he said, in an exasperated voice, "Time is of the essence, Kate. We must hurry."

Kate stared and stuttered over her next words, "It's that urgent?"

Steven Lambert bowed his head, and in a barely audible voice, uttered one word, "Yes."

Kate sobbed through her tears, "I'll ring my husband. ..have him go and get the box . . . There's no point in just breaking it open I've got the keys." She held them up. "I'll contact Vicky Chan, have it picked up and brought here. But, however much we hurry, it's all going to take until tomorrow, then goodness knows how long for Graeme to get here."

A much puzzled Harry asked, "Kate? What's up darling?

This is not your usual time. Lord, is it Julie? What's up?"

Kate tried to calm herself. "She's sinking Harry; the only hope is to find Graeme McKenzie. They . . . me included, think he's her only hope. Julie must keep all of his private contacts in a green leather box. You'll find it on the top shelf of Julie's wardrobe. There'll be someone from the airline to meet you and fly it here. I've found the keys in Julie's luggage. Harry, I'm still uncomfortable about prying . . . ."

"Right, consider it done." He paused and Kate could hear concern in his voice. "Kate, you are doing this to save Julie's life. She'll be happy she had the good sense to share with you where to look. Take care, my darling."

Kate next rang Vicky Chan's emergency contact number. After a minute or so, and sounding as though she was in an echo chamber, a sharp, business-like voice said, "Vicky Chan."

Kate rapidly conveyed what was needed and Vicky Chan grasped the urgency straight away. "I'm actually on a flight to Auckland. They've patched you straight through to the cockpit. We land in just over an hour. I'll have a car go and collect the box."

Kate hurried to tell Steven Lambert. "The box is on its way. How's Julie doing?"

"No change, Kate." He ran a worried hand through his hair. We're fast running out of options."

Kate stared at him before aghast said, "You're saying she's dying!"

Steven Lambert saw her shocked face. "I just don't know Kate. She only has a 50/50 chance of coming out of this wholly as you knew her before the accident."

Kate slumped in her chair and whispered, in a strained, shocked voice, "That's dreadful, Steven. She has so much to live for." She turned to where her friend lay comatose beside her. "Julie, fight—I'll find Graeme—I promise you. Just keep fighting my dear, dear friend."

Kate sat beside the open window of Julie's room for most of the next day. The only sounds were the machines as they kept up their relentless, mechanical movements.

A Police Patrol car with blue and red flashing lights entered the driveway. A man alighted and hurried into the building holding a bulky security bag.

"Must be the box!" Kate whispered and rushed out of the room.

She was met halfway along the cloister by Sister Theresa. The elderly nun breathlessly thrust the bag into Kate's hands. "Here you are, Kate, good luck!"

Opening the beautifully tooled box and not wanting to intrude upon the very personal and poignant collection of memorabilia, she carefully sorted the contents.

Amongst the many photographs and newspaper clippings, was a large envelope stating: "TO BE OPENED IN THE EVENT I CANNOT ANSWER FOR MYSELF," signed by Julie.

But, there was NOTHING on how to contact Graeme!

As Steven Lambert entered the room she put her trembling hands to her mouth, to stop a hysterical cry of panic escaping from her throat. "It's not there! Steven, I can't find it!"

"What! Think, girl! If it's a secret . . . Wait. Try the lid, Kate. My Grandfather had a similar box to this. The lid had a false top or something."

Kate closely inspected every millimetre until she found a small, almost invisible keyhole. Turning the second key and with a small, sharp 'click', the lid opened. A small slip of paper fluttered onto the bed. Written upon it were the words, 'GRAEME—password HIGH FLIGHT', and an English telephone number.

"I've got it!" Kate cried triumphantly.

"Good-oh! Ring it now," Steven Lambert grinned.

Kate had already dialled half of the number.

"R.A.F. Mildenhall, Special Operations, can I help you?" asked a very English voice.

"Yes, please. An emergency message for Air Commodore Graeme McKenzie, please. The message is: High Flight, most urgent you ring, Kate Reynolds, at St. Francis Medical Centre, Santa Barbara, California, U.S.A. Julie needs urgent help. Please ring this number . . ." Kate read from the piece of paper Steven Lambert held in front of her.

Kate queried, "How soon will he get the message?"

"I'm sorry Ma'am, I'm not authorised to give out such classified information. All of our senior personnel's movements are strictly confidential."

Wearily Kate put down the receiver. "Well, Steven. Now we wait and hope he's not off fighting a war some place."

"Air Commodore, eh? He's 'Big Brass' all right. Will he respond?"

"Oh yes. I'm certain he will." Kate still felt guilty, as though she was intruding into something that was not any of her business.

Studying her, Dr Steven Lambert asked, "Are you the guardian for Julie's children, Kate?"

"Yes, both my husband Harry and I are joint guardians well, that is, after their natural father . . ." She broke off in confusion.

He softly said, "I respect your reluctance to talk without Julie's consent, but patient/doctor confidentiality does apply here . . . I have heard your tapes. I know who he is."

Three hours later, Sister Angelique signalled Kate was wanted on the telephone.

Kate prayed as she ran down the short corridor, "Oh, please God . . . let it be him."

Breathlessly she said, "Hello, Kate Reynolds here."

A well-modulated male voice with a clipped English accent, replied, "This is Graeme McKenzie, Mrs Reynolds."

"Oh, thank goodness it's you! Please, call me Kate."

"What's wrong, Kate? Is it Julie, or the children? Where exactly are you?"

"The children are at home in New Zealand with Harry and Daisy. They're fine, Graeme. It's Julie." She paused to catch her breath. "Graeme, I'm at St. Francis Medical Centre, Santa Barbara, California. Julie is here, ten days ago she was on her way to the U.K. when the plane . . . Well, you're a professional pilot; you'll understand the technicalities better than me . . . the plane had a 'wind shear' and fell or dived nearly 300ft. Julie received a blow to her head from the food trolley. She's been in a coma ever since. Fortunately the Medical Superintendent of St. Francis was also on the plane and he had Julie brought here."

Kate looked up as Steven Lambert hurried in. He raised his eyebrows questioningly.

Kate nodded. "Yes, explain what you want from him."

Steven Lambert introduced himself. "Sir, Julie Field is not responding to our treatment. We have tried audio stimulation and word association with no response." He paused as he heard a soft groan in his ear. "Sir, the only stimulus we get is when we mention your name. It's the only positive response we get. By analysing our data we have reached the conclusion that you are the only person, Sir, that can bring Julie out of her comatose state."

Graeme asked in a soft but firm voice, "Do you want me to come there?"

"Yes, yes. Sir, I don't want to sound alarmist, but Julie is sinking fast. We need you here very quickly."

"Hmmmmmm, put Kate Reynolds back on, please, Doctor."

"Yes, I'm here, Graeme."

"Where was Julie going, Kate?"

"To find you, Graeme." she stammered. "After John died, let me see, four months ago now. God help me! I persuaded her to make the trip to the U.K. and make contact with you. You are all she wants, Graeme. Please come, don't let her die."

Kate had to strain to hear his next words as he whispered, "She's free! Did you say John had died, Kate?"

"Yes, John passed away last December . . ."

Kate heard the emotional change and the elation in his voice, "Dear God, at last! Kate, I'll get there as soon as is earthly possible. Tell her I'm coming Kate, and tell her . . . I still love her dearly. Tell her, Kate, Dio come ti-amo, cara mia, she'll understand."

She shakily put down the telephone, and sobbed tears of sheer relief and joy. "He's coming! He's coming!"

Taking a moment or two to recover her equilibrium, she resolutely dried her eyes and ran to Julie's bedside. Her voice husky with emotion, she exclaimed, "Julie, listen, Graeme is on his way. Julie, he says to tell you he loves you and to tell you, I hope I get it right, Dio come ti-amo, cara mia." She held Julie's hands. "Julie, he's coming, Graeme is coming. Fight it, Julie. Please, my dear friend, fight back!"

CHAPTER 75

Air Commodore Graeme Stuart McKenzie, OBE MVO MA B.Sc., put down his private telephone with a hand that trembled, trying to contain his overwhelming emotions.

When he first read the High Flight message, he had sat immobile, unable to move. Now, after speaking with Kate, he planned a feasible strategy to follow.

Rapidly putting Billy in the picture, he stated, "I'll get Aaron Benedict on the blower, tell him my problem. See if I can hitch a lift. I'll see the Old Man and organise myself some urgent leave."

Air Vice Marshall Brown, without hesitation, granted him, "As long as it takes, m'boy. Go, I'll handle the paperwork. Ask Watson to keep me in the picture."

Aaron Benedict answered Graeme's call within minutes. When Graeme explained why he needed to get to Julie, A.S.A.P., Aaron offered amazingly prompt assistance.

Exactly an hour later, Graeme was a passenger in a USAF fighter, winging his way across the Atlantic.

Landing at San Diego, he found, to his surprise, it would be Aaron Benedict in his personal helicopter taking Graeme to Santa Barbara.

Aaron told him, "Couldn't resist the opportunity, I'm supposed to be in Washington, but your little lady needs me more, Graeme, my friend."

They soon reached the St. Francis Hospital, which sat majestically upon its high parapet. But, there was an unexpected problem—it was not equipped with a helipad.

Graeme eyed the neatly sculptured gardens below. "Put me on the strop, Aaron. Drop me. Send my bag back by road. Come on, let's do it. I've done this a hundred times or more."

Aaron shrugged and nodded to his crew, "Okay. At least if you get hurt, you'll already be at a hospital!"

Graeme tucked his uniform cap inside his flight suit as the crew fastened the strop harness around him. Without preamble, he began the downward drop. In seconds he was safely down and Aaron breathed a sigh of relief. It could have been just a trifle awkward if he had suffered any mishap.

Graeme grinned disarmingly at several black robed Nuns staring wide-eyed at him. They were clutching at their wimples as the downdraught of the helicopter threatened to blow them away. Their gardening tools lay in a tumbled heap where, in their shock, the good Sisters had dropped them.

Graeme bowed gallantly to them as he removed his flying suit, straightened his cap and jacket saying, "Good Morning, Sisters. Lovely weather," and strode rapidly through the cloister door.

When Sister Theresa saw a very senior military officer in front of her, she gasped, "Goodness me! Where did you spring from?"

Graeme smiled charmingly, "Please, Sister, where do I find Kate Reynolds?"

"Just wait here." Sister Theresa hurried off to Julie's room.

Gasping breathlessly, her hands fluttering around her head, Sister Theresa stammered, "There's an officer in reception. I think he flew in—from somewhere—I don't know how—but he's here! He's got a lot of medal ribbons here." She gestured to the left side of her chest and then flapped her hands around her head, "And gold braid around his hat."

Steven Lambert, monitoring Julie, looked up with a startled, incredulous expression. "What! Good Grief! It must be the Air Commodore! Would you get somebody to find Kate Reynolds, please Sister?"

Hurrying back down the cloister, Steven Lambert was met by Graeme, who was following the route he had seen Sister Theresa take.

"Sir, you must be Air Commodore McKenzie, I'm Steven Lambert. Am I glad to see you, sir?" He clasped Graeme's outstretched hand. "How did you get here? You have mystified our Sisters!"

Graeme grinned, "You don't have a landing pad for a helicopter, Doctor, so I had the U.S.A.F drop me on the winch. Yes, the good Sisters in the garden did seem a little surprised. Not exactly your usual 'manna from heaven' am I?"

Steven Lambert chuckled. He knew just what the talking point after Mass would be. "Well, sir, you are certainly my 'manna from heaven'. I'm overjoyed you are here."

Graeme's face became serious. "Where is she, Doctor?"

"Come into my office, sir," Steven Lambert requested quietly, "I'll be as brief as I can."

"Shoot, what do you need?"

"Kate Reynolds is here, but which of you can legally speak for Julie if there is any dissension?"

"He can," said Kate entering the room. "He has every legal right, it's all here in this letter." She held out an official looking envelope. "You'll find all of Julie's wishes in here." Kate looked admiringly at the tall, uniformed figure thinking, 'Julie was right, he sure is a handsome one!'

She held out her hand. "Hello, Graeme, we meet at last. I'm Kate Reynolds, I'm so glad you're here."

Graeme swept his uniform hat off and Kate gasped, "Oh heavens, Lauren is so like you!"

Graeme grinned, "Hello, Kate, I'd know you anywhere. Julie has accurately described you. It's good to meet you at last, although I wish it were under different circumstances."

Steven Lambert said, "Well honestly, I'd swear she knew you were coming, or that you were already here! I was monitoring her when Sister Theresa came in with the staggering news of your surprising arrival." He grinned at Kate, "Very unorthodox, Kate, you'll hear all about it from the Sisters! Anyway, the monitors were jumping around a bit . . ."

"Doctor Lambert," Graeme interrupted, saying almost impatiently, "please, just let me get close to her, we can talk later."

The ache in Graeme's heart threatened to overwhelm him as he leaned over his beloved Julie, and kissed her lips. Steven Lambert and Kate, watching the monitors, saw the needles jump as Graeme tenderly whispered, "Dio come ti-amo, cara mia. I'm here, my darling."

Steven Lambert signalled to a joyously weeping Kate, "We'll leave you to talk to her, sir."

"We'll just be next door, Graeme," Kate said in choked voice.

Once they left, Graeme put his head close to Julie's. Warmly and tenderly, he whispered, "Oh, Julie, my beloved, I have missed you so much. You are free at last, so am I. We can be married. Will you marry me, Julie, my darling?"

Julie did not move, but Graeme sensed that she had taken a couple of deeper breaths, almost as though she was recognising something familiar.

"Yes, it really is me. Julie come back, we have a whole new life together. I can't wait to see our beautiful Lauren again, I have missed her so much, and I've yet to meet our son, Stuart. We are both free, Julie darling. We can be married, at last."

As he looked around the spotlessly clean, yet sparsely furnished room, an idea formed in his head. Yes, it was large enough, but would the good Doctor agree? Would it shock the good Sisters?

Muttering to himself, "Oh, to heck with it," he reasoned that if it worked and brought his beloved Julie back to him, so what!

He called Steven Lambert, "Come in, Doctor, I have an idea."

Steven Lambert automatically scanned the many machines. "There's been a significant change here! Look, this machine is almost normal—and here, look! Things are happening!"

He beamed jubilantly at Graeme, "Your presence here, sir, is doing the trick! What's your idea?"

"Look, first of all, please call me Graeme." He paused, and had the grace to look slightly uncomfortable, running his finger around his shirt collar before continuing. "Well, could you possibly get a double bed in here and move Julie on to it?"

"You're going to get into bed with her—is that it?"

Kate said in an amused voice.

"Well . . . Yes . . . I can't hold her properly . . . I believe she has already sensed I'm here . . ." His voice faded.

"Great idea! Come on Steven, there's got to be a double bed around here somewhere. If not, we'll buy one," said Kate triumphantly.

Sister Angelique came in; her hands fluttering like the wings on a small bird. "Dr Lambert, there's another one . . . Er . . . I believe he's one of ours. I think it's our Chief of Defence Staff."

"Oh, that'll be Aaron Benedict," Graeme answered casually. "He must have found somewhere to land his helicopter. He's probably dropping off my bag."

"THE Aaron Benedict!" breathed Steven Lambert.

"Yessir. The one and only," replied the large, uniformed figure of an American Indian. Kate's mouth dropped open—this was the USAF officer Julie talked about in Sydney.

"Well done, Graeme, old son. You haven't lost any of your skills. Scared the pants off those Nuns out there though . . . Ooops, sorry, Sisters," he gallantly apologised to Sisters Theresa and Angelique, who stood gaping at two extremely senior and much be-medalled military officers in their midst.

Aaron Benedict turned towards Kate. "And you, with the gorgeous red hair, must be Kate."

Kate warmly greeted this huge man, "I've heard much about you too . . . and all of it good."

Grinning, Aaron Benedict turned back to Graeme. "Right, what's the score, Graeme?"

"We are about to organise a double bed. I can't get hold of her in this single contraption. If I'm to bring her out of this, I need to talk and talk plenty, and I need her in my arms to do it."

"Okay Doc, where do we get this bed from?" Aaron asked. "I've got a helicopter crew out front. All healthy, strapping guys their mothers are rightly proud of, they can shift a Sherman tank if I give the order. Okay, where's the nearest hotel? We'll go and commandeer one. See ya soon, old buddy." He bent down and kissed Julie on the forehead. "Come back, sweet lady, we have a wedding to go to."

"Wedding?" Kate said weakly, as the big man left the room.

"Ummm, perhaps," Graeme chuckled. "I'm not letting her out of my sight from now on. So I guess she'll just have to make an honest man of me."

Kate gave Graeme the leather box and explained how she had invaded Julie's privacy to find him.

Graeme said sincerely, "Kate, we'll be forever grateful to you and Harry, for having the initiative to do what you did for us. And 'us' it is going to be from now on. I need her with me, Kate."

"Kate, one more thing." He looked sheepishly at her, "Where are Julie's clothes? Can you get me a lacy nightgown? The one she's in is more like a rough Nun's habit; I think it's made of calico!"

The commotion outside reached a crescendo before the biggest bed Graeme had ever seen was manhandled into Julie's room.

CHAPTER 76

As Sisters Theresa and Angelique made up the bed, they marvelled at the softness of the bed linen 'purloined' by Aaron from the nearby Hilton Hotel.

When Graeme, completely unfazed by their presence, had opened Julie's case and extracted a lace nightgown, the sisters blushed at its skimpy nature.

Kate invited Graeme to dine with her. She grinned before wickedly saying, "Julie tells me she feeds you 'to keep your strength up', for some reason."

Graeme dissolved into laughter. "You girls sure know each other very well for her to tell you something so intimate." He looked admiringly at the vibrant woman. "You two are very close; I share a similar relationship with Billy Watson."

Kate nodded, thinking, no wonder Julie absolutely adores this man, he really is unique. Obviously sensitive and sensible, he had a great sense of humour, and rather good looking to boot. Aloud she said, "Dear God! We must get her through this so that you two can finally find the happiness you so richly deserve."

After showering and shaving, Graeme donned an RAF tracksuit and lay beside Julie. He softly played a CD of his piano music and heeded Steven Lambert's advice by talking quietly to Julie.

He opened the leather box and found Doc's photographs, taken the day of Stuart's birth. He spread the entire collection over the bed, together with photos of Julie dressed in the 'Four Seasons' gowns. He softly told her, "You are my sex goddess, my darling. I hope I get to see these in the flesh, real soon, my cara."

There was a soft knock on the door and Sister Angelique entered. "Please excuse me, sir; I need to check Julie's blood pressure." She gasped as she saw the photographs on the bed. "Are these Julie's children? Er . . . but . . . isn't that you, sir?"

"Yes, Sister. I am their father." Graeme said proudly.

Sister Angelique smiled shyly, "The little girl certainly looks like you, sir."

Sister Angelique stared in amazement at her instruments. "I don't believe it! Everything reads normal! Whatever you have done, sir, it has worked! I'll ring Dr Lambert. He's got to see this."

Steven Lambert hurried into the room and did his own checks. His face beamed, "She's coming out of it, Graeme! She's no longer beyond our reach. Thank goodness we got you here in time!"

Kate, hearing the added movements ran in and saw the happy faces. She kissed Graeme's cheek, whispering, "Are you okay, Graeme?"

In a husky voice, Graeme croaked, "I'm over the moon, Kate. She's going to make it."

Steven Lambert advising caution, said, "Graeme, Julie will need to resurface in a quiet, restful atmosphere. She'll likely be confused. When you notice her moving, speak at once in a soft voice. Press the call button straight away. It will possibly be a few hours yet, so try and get some sleep yourself, Doctor's orders."

Taking Steven's advice, Graeme put on pyjamas and got into bed beside Julie. Smiling, he whispered, "I didn't forget my 'modesty' clothes, my darling. I love you so very much, cara mia. Tonight I am in the only place in the whole wide world that I want to be."

Before long he was lulled into deep, contented slumber.

The nightmare sequence began . . .

Her body tensed, waiting to see faceless, ghostly bodies, and to feel the horrible, bony fingers clutching at her clothing . . .

But, something was different . . . That face was SMILING at her . . . Is that you Lauren? Who was that one? It's Stuart! . . . Who was that over there, grinning at her? Katie! . . . Is that a crow? No, it's a Nun in a black habit, but she has Gran's smiling face . . . I want to be with Graeme . . . Ah, there he is . . . . Go to him, hurry, run, run faster, faster! . . . Come on! You must reach him this time, no more chances, Julie . . . Let's go, run! . . . Graeme! Oh please, my darling Graeme, please wait for me . . . I'm coming Graeme! . . . Oh, please wait, my beloved, I'm nearly there . . . Graeme!!!

Julie's eyes flew open and she felt Graeme's arms around her. Her brain registered the immediate situation. 'Safe! I'm safe. He's here! Where are we? Oh, well, I'll find out in the morning. He's here, that's all that matters, and he's wearing pyjamas. That means the children are around, somewhere. Don't disturb him. It's still dark, go back to sleep for a while. I love you to bits, Graeme Stuart McKenzie.'

The next morning, Sister Theresa, on her way to early Matins, decided to check all was well with Julie and Graeme. She quickly swallowed a gasp of astonishment as she saw the positions of the two bodies in the huge bed.

She hurried as fast as her elderly legs would carry her, and rang Dr Lambert's doorbell.

Yawning, Steven Lambert looked bleary eyed at the agitated Sister Theresa. Short of breath after her hurried walk, Sister Theresa waved her hands signalling everything was okay. She panted, "Come to Julie's room, quickly. I think she's out of the coma."

"What! Great! Let's go, Sister." Grabbing his robe, Steven Lambert ran to Julie's room.

"Hush now, Doctor. They're still asleep, don't startle them," the elderly Nun cautioned, as she tried to keep up with the younger and more fleet of foot doctor.

Dr Lambert put his head around the door and saw Graeme still sleeping, his arms around Julie. She was sprawled half on top of him.

Cautiously approaching the bed, Steven Lambert lightly touched Graeme's shoulder, and placed his finger over Graeme's lips. Graeme woke instantly, but lay stock still when he saw Steven Lambert. In the same instant he felt the weight of Julie's body. A huge smile lit his face.

Steven Lambert whispered, "Move slowly. See what happens. Careful now."

Graeme turned his face towards Julie and kissed her forehead, "Good morning, my darling one."

Julie stretched her body and Graeme tried not to look too startled as her hand covered his 'modesty' and began to stroke him suggestively. Julie, with her eyes closed, murmured, "Hello, flyboy."

Steven Lambert and Sister Theresa still beamed benignly as Graeme gently, and he hoped surreptitiously, removed Julie's prying fingers, and murmured huskily, "Hello, darling?"

Julie gazed upon the one face she wanted to see beside her every morning, but why was he crying? "Graeme?" she queried, and started to sit up.

Steven Lambert, anticipating this, helped Graeme to hold her gently down, so that she did not pull out the monitoring equipment.

Graeme swallowed hard to clear the lump in his throat.

"Lie still, my darling, don't be frightened, but there is something I must explain to you. Look around, darling."

Julie's eyes darted around what she could see of the room from her prone position on the bed.

"Julie, you're in a hospital in California in America. You have been here for over two weeks after being taken off your flight to London. You were on the way to find me, darling . . ."

. . . He explained what had happened to her and continued in a soft, tender voice. "So, when despite all of their valiant efforts, including Kate's tremendous input, you stayed critically ill, they decided I was the only one who could help. Kate found out how to send me a 'High Flight' message and, my sweetheart, here I am."

Julie ran her hand over his face. "You are really here then, it isn't all just part of a wonderful dream? Oh, Graeme, I have missed you so much."

"And I you, sweetheart. Dear Lord, you'll never know how much. Now turn over slowly and meet Dr Steven Lambert, and Sister Theresa."

Julie rolled slowly over onto her back, trying not to blush as she saw two smiling faces and remembered what she was doing to a certain part of Graeme's anatomy when she first awoke. She looked into the concerned face of the Doctor she vaguely remembered speaking with on the flight.

"We meet again, Julie," he said, with a wide grin on his face. "Welcome to St. Francis Hospital."

Sister Theresa put her soft hand on Julie's arm. "Welcome back, m'dear."

Julie clutched Graeme's hand, not willing to let go of him, in case he turned out to be a mirage! She could recall the flight and why she was on it, but all else ????

"Try to sit up, Julie," Steven Lambert instructed. "Support her, Graeme. She could feel a bit nauseous at first. Right, slowly does it. Slip some pillows behind her, Sister."

"Ummm, you're right, I do feel light-headed." Julie suddenly spotted a dear, familiar figure standing in the doorway. "Kate? Oh, is that you, Katie?"

With auburn curls vigorously shaking, Kate ran across the room and hugged her. With relief in her voice, she cried, "I heard the noises . . . Oh, my dear, dear friend, you are back." With tears of joy running down her face, Kate kissed Graeme's cheek. "Well done, Graeme. Don't let anybody EVER tell you the power of love doesn't exist!"

"I gather you two have already met," Julie said in a happy, weak voice. "The children . . . ?"

Graeme shook his head, "No darling, I'll take you home to them."

Julie almost unbelievingly asked, "You'd come to New Zealand with me? Oh, Graeme that would be so special. Have you got leave or something?"

"Or something. We have a lot to sort out. I am still waiting for an answer to my very, very special question, sweetheart."

Kate took the hint. "I'll go and ring Harry and Daisy if you'd like, Graeme."

"And I'll go and organise you both some breakfast,"
Sister Theresa offered.

"Well, I guess that just leaves me playing gooseberry, so I'd better leave as well," laughed a happy Steven Lambert. "I'll look in after breakfast and we can chat about what happens next. Okay, Graeme?"

Julie noted how they all deferred to Graeme for any decisions to be made. He was acting like a husband . . . wait . . . she stared at him . . . a husband, that's it!

Taking his face between her hands, she looked deeply into his incredible blue eyes and whispered, "The answer is YES. Yes, please, Oh, my darling . . . YES!"

His voice was just a deep, emotional croak, "You heard? Julie, my darling, you heard me?"

"I kept hearing you say 'we're free, we are going to be married, will you marry me?' I couldn't get back quickly enough to say YES. You saved my life, didn't you, darling?"

Gathering her in his arms, Graeme kissed her long and passionately.

CHAPTER 77

Sister Angelique brought Julie welcome news. "Dr Lambert has given permission for you to have a shower and wash your hair. I'll put a stool in the shower and get a wheelchair." She looked pointedly at Graeme. "Perhaps you'd like to use the one in the men's bathroom, sir."

Graeme obediently gathered up his gear and, with a wink at Julie, departed.

Julie let the hot refreshing water wash over her, while Sister Angelique waited discreetly behind the door. As Sister Angelique helped her to dress in a clean nightgown, Julie saw the young Nun stroke the flimsy silk of the negligee longingly.

Julie got an appreciative wolf whistle from Graeme and she chided him, "Look at yourself, you handsome dog, you look good enough to eat."

Young Sister Angelique reddened at their repartee, but secretly thought to herself the RAF officer did look like a Greek God with his blonde hair, blue eyes, tanned skin and a shirt that showed off his muscular body.

Steven Lambert arrived, pushing a large armchair and said he'd like Julie to sit on the outside balcony for an hour, to absorb some fresh air and sunshine.

In answer to Julie's questions Graeme, explained what happened in the suicide bomb blast and the injuries he had sustained. He soberly related how Billy and their staff nearly died under the rubble. "I did send you a message, darling."

Julie softly answered, "John found it by accident and stupidly hid it. It was a silly, jealous reaction and his guilt severely affected his health. He had a painful last few months."

Speaking in a whisper, she told him how she had learned of his injuries and of Anne's death. She clasped his hand even tighter. "It was an awful, awful time, my darling. But now I just want to be with you, Graeme. Where shall we live?"

He gently told her, "I couldn't live in Australasia, sweetheart, my base is Europe. Ideally, we need a home that is strictly yours and mine, a new beginning."

Julie nodded, "I can sell my house and land, but legally the farm belongs to Lauren and Stuart. I love my house, but Graeme, I've been far too lonely without you. When do you think they'll discharge me?"

"Tomorrow, all being well, sweetheart. Soon we'll be a real family at last," he said with a gleam in his eyes. "I'd like to show you a small village where I have dreamed many times of living with you and our children. It's close enough for me to travel to the base daily, and has an excellent country village school. It's rather an exclusive little area, with most of the inhabitants being academics from Cambridge University. An exclusive fashion boutique wouldn't go amiss there either, the locals could certainly afford to patronise one," he concluded, with a cheeky smile.

Julie studied him, amused and surprised at seeing an almost guilty look on his face as he mentioned the boutique. "Graeme Stuart McKenzie, you have already cased the place!"

He chuckled, and confessed, "Yes, I have. Guilty as charged, Ma'am. I regularly drive through the village. I know quite a few of the men there, we play golf and squash and they frequently 'dine in' when we have a Mess Dinner. It's a typically spacious, rural environment, Lauren could have a veritable zoo of animals . . . What does Stuart favour?"

"Aircraft! Particularly noisy ones. Now I wonder where he gets that from?"

"Does he now," Graeme rubbed his chin thoughtfully. "Chip off the old block, eh? Anyway there's a particular house that has rather taken my fancy. I've even had a builder friend check it out. After Anne's death, I knew I wanted to have a proper home. I didn't wish John any harm, but somehow I knew you and I couldn't stay apart for much longer. I was getting so lonely without you, Julie."

He paused and smiled. "The house has everything, modern kitchen, dining room, large sitting room, 3 bathrooms, five huge bedrooms, and a sort of library-cum-study, plus a huge conservatory with a magnificent indoor pool. Julie, upstairs there's a suite of rooms . . . I mentally named 'our place' I had such marvellous visionary plans . . ."

Julie, interrupted him, "Graeme, buy it! Go with your instincts!" she urged excitedly. "If it's only half as good as you have described, I'd love it. Graeme, I want to be married to you as quickly as possible, I don't want to wait a second longer than we have to. I too have been so lonely without you, my darling."

Spotting Kate in the doorway, Julie beckoned to her, "Come on in, Kate. We are deciding where we are going to live after we are married."

Kate fidgeted with her wedding ring. "Look . . . I have a proposal for you to think about. Harry and I had hoped and anticipated that you two would soon marry, and with Graeme's position, you would probably choose to move back to the U.K. I hope you don't think we are jumping the gun but . . . Look, you know I've always loved your house, Julie, and well, Harry wants to retire and become a Queen Street farmer . . . Anyway, the bottom line is . . . if it's for sale, we'd like to buy it."

The relief on Julie's face was evident to see. "Kate, I couldn't wish for a nicer family to pass my beautiful home on to. Oh, Katie, I'm so pleased."

Kate grinned sheepishly. "There's something else. When Harry floated the idea of retiring the other week, Roger Peters and Gloria, well . . . they told him they'd like to buy the franchise."

Seeing Julie's raised eyebrows, she giggled, "Yes, surprise, surprise, they've become a 'hot' item those two. How's that for news?"

"How marvellous!" Julie exclaimed, "I can't think of anybody I'd rather see following us. They've worked so hard with us."

"Well, you'd end up with a fair sized bank balance out of that deal, Jules." Kate suggested with a wide smile. "Enough to make all of those exclusive little gowns you are so clever at designing, my friend."

Coming into the room, Steven Lambert smiled as heard the happy laughter. "Kate, your car is here. I sincerely thank you. You were Julie's stalwart in getting Graeme here—opening those doors I'd never have known existed. Thankfully, we can see the excellent results," he said as he gestured towards Julie.

Already some colour had returned to her face and there was no way those two were ever going to be parted again.

Kate said cheerfully, "Thanks also go to you Steven. Now, you two, I'll not tell the children, let that be your own special surprise. I'll let Daisy know when to expect you." Bubbling over with excitement, she embraced Graeme. "Thank goodness you came!"

Graeme hugged the vibrant woman and said sincerely, "Kate, I'll always be deeply in your debt. I am so looking forward to meeting Aimee and Harry."

Julie looked appealingly at Steven Lambert. "How soon will I be able to go home, Steven?"

"I'd like to keep you here for another day, Julie. It's a long flight to Auckland and I'd want to be sure your body can cope."

While Julie had a siesta, Graeme rang Billy. His closest buddy could hardly stop himself from cheering when Graeme suggested he had better dust off his best uniform in order to perform the duties of 'best man'.

Graeme explained, "We'll probably be married at the Chateau Cornacchia, possibly mid-June. We both have a deep, spiritual feeling about that chapel."

Then, hardly drawing breath, Graeme said, "There's one more thing you could do for me, Billy. Get hold of that real estate chap and tell him I'll be buying that house for sure." Hearing Billy's gasp of surprise, he chuckled, "Yes, Julie agrees, we'll settle in the U.K. for now. Here's Julie's home number. ..Contact us there . . . Thanks, Billy boy. Cheers."

Ringing his legal adviser, he quickly explained where he was, then gave a brief summation of what had happened to Julie. He added that they were to be married very promptly and would he kindly get the house finance under way.

After heartily congratulating Graeme and giving him the usual 'couldn't happen to a nicer chap' routine, his friend issued a cautionary note. "Graeme, regarding the two children. Even though you are their biological father, you still have to legally adopt them to enable them to take your name. I can draw up the papers for you if you'd like. Good Luck, Graeme, I'm sincerely happy for you."

That evening Julie took her first walk. She reacted with peals of laughter when Graeme pointed out where he had been winched down from Aaron's helicopter. Imagining the scene and the shocked faces of the Nuns really tickled her fancy.

After they had exchanged a deep, passionate kiss, he said huskily, "I was determined to reach you, my beloved darling, as quickly as I could . . . Julie, do you still want to be married in the chapel at Chateau Cornacchia?"

"Oh, yes, my beloved. We always thought Father . . . no he's Monsignor Francis now, actually married us that special, memorable day."

"Then let's ring Maria and Giovanni from New Zealand. Apart from Billy, I'd like to invite my parents and Aaron. What about your siblings?"

"Well, I'll invite them," she replied thoughtfully, "but it's a long way for them to come. We can have a special second celebration when we arrive in the U.K."

"I spoke with Billy this afternoon and asked him to be my 'best man'," Graeme told her. "Their new baby is due, so Marisa will not be able to travel. I also spoke to my lawyer and arranged for my Will to be changed to include my new next-of-kin, my darling wife, and to start proceedings for me to legally adopt Lauren and Stuart. Silly though it sounds, that's how it's got to be done to give them my name."

He could not resist a grin as he deliberately added his choicest morsel. "Oh, by the way, I've asked him to buy the house for us."

Julie threw her arms around his neck, assuring him that anything he did was just fine with her. As he clasped her close to his body, Julie felt the stirring within her own. "I can't wait for you to make love to me. I want you so much, my darling."

Huskily he murmured against her lips, "Just another day, my dearest one, then you'll be in the clear. I need and want you too, my darling.

He kissed her and seemed to look deep within her soul as he vowed, "And I, my darling, promise I will make all of your dreams come true."

CHAPTER 78

Once Julie had been cleared to fly, Vicky Chan had expertly arranged their travel. While Julie had dutifully rested after lunch, Graeme, at her urging, had gone shopping for 'Thank You' gifts. A cashmere sweater for Steven, the biggest boxes of assorted lavender lotions and talcum for Sister Theresa and Novitiate Mary Magdalene and finally a flimsy, silk nightgown for Sister Angelique.

When he had raised his eyebrows quizzically at the latter, Julie remonstrated, "She'll find a way."

Graeme didn't divulge he'd never bought anything like that before. He mused, 'Well I'd better get clued up, pronto! I am now a man with two ladies.'

His last stop was to purchase an amethyst engagement ring.

At Auckland they were met by Kate and Harry. With a grin as wide as the ocean, Harry strode toward Julie and hugged her as she buried her face in his shoulder. He said with a break in his voice, "Thank God, you're back safe, Julie. Hello, Graeme, I'm Harry Reynolds. It's a real pleasure and honour to meet you at last."

Kate explained, "We thought we'd give you a couple of hours alone. Daisy plans to drop Aimee off on her way from the beach before bringing Lauren and Stuart home."

As Kate admired Julie's engagement ring, Harry marvelled at the uncanny likeness between Graeme and Lauren, and how Stuart had the distinctive 'pilot's eyes' of his father.

Once home, Kate and Harry quickly excused themselves, knowing their two lovebird friends would want some time alone.

Julie proudly showed Graeme her home. But, it was in the children's rooms, Lauren's frilly and lacy, and Stuart's with its space theme and aircraft, that he lingered. Here he suddenly found his hand trembled and his throat became tight and constricted as he touched a toy, or looked at a photograph.

Finally tearing him away from the children's rooms, Julie led him to her bedroom and shyly told him, "Everything in here is new."

He opened his arms to her, "It's just perfect, my darling. Come here, let me hold you. Dio come ti-amo, cara mia."

Their bodies strained against each other as the kiss became deeper, more passionate. Huskily he told her, "It's been four long years since I've been able to hold you like this, my darling."

"I don't think I want to wait any longer, my dearest, darling Graeme," Julie whispered. "Love me now, please."

It was a coupling made in heaven, swift, deep and passionate. She urged him to even greater heights, as she enjoyed the erotic sensation of him right inside the core of her being.

Together they reached a tumultuous, soaring and heart pounding climax that seemed to go on and on as they both sought sexual release from four years of loneliness and separation.

Graeme stroked her face, whispering, "We have over half of our lives left to enjoy being together. I aim to fully satisfy you every time you let me near your fantastic body. That's my promise!"

Later, as hand in hand they climbed the hill, he said, "I am humbled by the sheer beauty of the whole place. I feel I'm cheating you by being selfish in asking you to give it all away . . ."

"No! Don't," Julie cried, "All I want is you, Graeme. Yes, it is a very special place, but my heart is with you. Where you are, that's my home. Far too many times on this hill I've cried buckets of tears, yearning for you. Up here I have shouted your name to the Heavens."

Clinging to him with tears in her eyes, she implored, "Believe me, I have been so dreadfully lonely without you.

No, I repeat, with all honesty, all I want is to be with you, my darling, everything else is of no significance to me, at all."

He was so moved by her words, he could not speak. He just held her tightly in his arms.

As they strolled back to the house, Julie saw Graeme glance at his watch, so she rang Kate's number.

She wrapped her arms around his waist. "They've left Kate's. Come out the front, you'll see the car turn into the drive."

He kissed her lovingly and held her close for a brief moment. "Julie, my precious darling, I'm so looking forward to us being a family. Hey! Is that a car I can hear?"

"Yes, my love, they're here!" Julie cried.

Julie ran down the steps as Lauren opened the car door and flung herself into her mother's arms, closely followed by Stuart. They both cried, "Mama, Oh, Mama, I missed you so much."

Graeme watched from the top of the steps with a lump, as big as a tennis ball, forming in his throat. There she was, she was much taller but she was still his golden, curly top princess, his first-born, his Lauren.

His face softened even further when he saw the sturdy, handsome, dark haired small boy, who hugged his mother as though he never wanted to let her go. That's my son . . . my heir . . . Graeme's mind whispered. Yes, but, they are ALL mine, my family, the proud voice in his head was telling him—ALL MINE! ALL MINE, NOW AND FOREVER MORE!

With tears threatening to fall, Julie held her children close to her, "Oh, I too have missed you both, so much, my darlings, but, I have such a wonderful surprise for you. Lauren honey, look up, there is someone very special waiting for you."

Lauren saw the tall figure standing there with his arms outstretched. She whispered, with an almost unbelieving cry, "Papa? Papa? Is that you? It's my Papa!" With a cry of joy, she bounded up the steps and threw herself into Graeme's open arms. "Papa, Oh my Papa, you're here at last. I have missed you so much, and I love you so much, Papa."

Graeme tried to control his emotions as he embraced the precious bundle to him, and answered with a catch in his throat, "Hello, my princess, I too have missed you terribly. Look how tall you have grown and how beautiful you are. I love you so much, my precious, precious child."

Taking Stuart's hand, Julie led him up the steps and softly, but simply said, "Darling, here is our son."

With Lauren clinging tightly to one side of him, Graeme crouched down on his haunches and gazed into the candid blue eyes of his son. He held out his free arm and Stuart, without hesitation, walked towards him, threw his arms around Graeme's neck and kissed him on the cheek. Then, quite matter-of-factly, said, "Hello, Papa. Lauren told me you would come back for us and Mama."

The look on Graeme's face as he embraced the two small bodies of his children was a mixture of wonderment, joy, pride, fulfilment and, above all else, sheer, unadulterated love.

Lauren whispered, "You are my real Papa, aren't you?" Graeme looked across at Julie. Tears still flowed freely from both her and Daisy, as he nodded, "Yes, Lauren, my sweet, I can state most proudly—I am your real father and, young man, I am also your real father as well."

In a breathless rush, Lauren cried, "I knew you were! You look like me, and Stuart has got the same colour eyes as us. Rico told me ages ago you were. That time in the helicopter I almost knew, but it wasn't right, was it, to tell me the secret until after Papajohn died. I knew you were, 'cos you love Mama so much. See, I told you Stuart! I told you he would come back for us and Mama!"

Graeme was astounded and nonplussed by the logical and forthright way she had worked it all out. He darted a glance at Julie in amazement, as she tried to hide her laughter at his reaction. "Thank goodness, you are here at last, darling. Now you can help to raise her!"

She brought Daisy forward as she said, "Graeme, darling, this is my 'treasure', my dear friend, Daisy. This is my truly beloved, Graeme. The 'young RAF man' you called him once. We are together at last."

Graeme smiled, "Daisy, I have heard so much about you and your cooking. I'm looking forward to getting much better acquainted with both you, and your culinary skills."

Daisy had tears streaming down her wrinkled face as she studied this blessed, handsome man, of whom Lauren was the spitting image. A distinguished and honourable man whose incredible blue eyes Stuart had inherited, and whom Julie absolutely worshipped and adored.

Graeme kissed her on the forehead. "Daisy it is so good to be here at last. By the way, what's for dinner, I'm starving!"

His honest, down to earth remark broke the emotional tension. Daisy's face split into a broad grin. She patted his arm, "You're a good 'tooth man', Julie tells me. You'll do me, Graeme McKenzie, my love. I've got some choice steaks in the car."

The two children dragged a very willing Graeme inside to show him their treasures, but he was back within a couple of minutes. He hugged Julie and proceeded to thoroughly kiss her, "Thank you, my darling, for two of the best children." Then he disappeared again.

Julie sighed, "He's always doing things like that. Look at my gorgeous engagement ring, Daisy,—and I got the full proposal treatment. He even went down on one knee . . . God help me, but I love him so much."

Julie's next words took Daisy completely by surprise.

"Daisy, we'll be married as soon as possible. We'll be going to live in the U.K. Graeme's base is there, and where he is, is where I want to be. We'd love you to come with us, or, if you'd prefer, you can stay with Kate. Would you like to think it over and give us your answer, when you're ready?"

A few minutes later, the house rang with superb music as Graeme and Lauren discovered the piano. As Julie waltzed around the room with Stuart in her arms, father and daughter played, in perfect harmony.

CHAPTER 79

They had retired to bed as soon as the children were settled for the night, finding jet-lag weariness catching up with them.

Waking up beside her in the morning, Graeme made sure the door was locked before pleasuring her and himself again. Having showered after leaving a sexually sated Julie, Graeme went to find Daisy busily preparing breakfast.

Lauren ran to him and smothered him in kisses. "Good morning, my Papa. Do you have your pilot's uniform? Can you come down to my school in it, so I can show all my friends my Papa?"

Graeme sat to digest this wonderful conversation, but Stuart climbed into his lap, "I love you too, Papa. Can you come to Kindy with me too, please?"

Daisy laughed, "I think you have been 'organised', Graeme! How about I take you two rascals and your Papa can come along later, say at morning play time?"

"Fine with me," Graeme replied happily. "Now finish your breakfast. Then you can come quietly and say 'Good Morning' to Mama, we'll tell her what we are planning."

In unison they replied, "Yes, Papa."

Two small words, but to Graeme, priceless as he gazed at two innocent young faces beaming up at HIM—their Papa. He exchanged grins with Daisy as he accepted a tea tray set for two.

After Daisy returned from dropping the children off, Graeme re-joined her in the kitchen. "Julie will need you, Daisy. It's going to be new country for her, a new way of life, plus new schools for the children. Please say you'll come with us."

Daisy replied, "We have been through a lot together and I know only too well how much she has missed you, Graeme. I look upon Lauren and Stuart as 'adopted' grandchildren. Yes, I'd love to come with you."

Spontaneously he embraced the older woman, "Wow! That's marvellous Daisy. Gee! I feel great!"

Dressing, Julie reflected on what Graeme had told her about the social side his senior rank offered. How he had avoided taking part because of Anne's bizarre behaviour. He had confessed he had missed out on so much 'Esprit de Corps'. He had fired Julie's imagination with talk of Mess Dinners, of 'Dining In', Military Parades, Ambassadorial receptions, Charity Balls, and Gala dinners. Even Royal occasions, he had assured her, all came within his realm.

Julie recalled how much she had enjoyed the Army Mess Dinner in Sydney. What better places to show off her designing talents, and to wear her exclusive gowns.

She had also broached the idea of another child. Enthusiastically he had breathed, "Oh, yes, my darling. That would put the icing on the cake. We'd better make it soon, while you are young enough for it not to be a risk to your health."

Julie promised to pay an early visit to Doc Matthews and to update the children's 'shots'.

⌒≁⑂⑂⑁⌒

Nervously, Air Commodore, Graeme Stuart McKenzie, brushed his uniform jacket and adjusted his cap. He had confessed earlier that he would rather be going into combat than face Lauren's classmates. "Children can be so frank. They're NEVER diplomatic!"

Coming to see if he was ready, Julie felt herself go weak at the knees, "Dear God, Graeme, you look so handsome! Lauren's friends are going to think you're Prince Charming! Come here; let me show you what the sight of you does to me!"

Grinning at him, she took his hands and placed them against her breasts. Graeme felt, through the silk of her dress, the shapely firmness and her erect nipples. He growled appreciatively at her, "Later, my sexy wench, I'll fix thy needs with pleasure."

At the Kindergarten he heard, "Papa! I'm over here."

Graeme saw Stuart sitting in the cockpit of a wooden model RAF Spitfire. He was wearing a very ancient flying helmet and goggles several sizes too big.

With a boyish grin, Graeme murmured, "So, another pilot, eh?"

Julie laughed, "So, where else would you expect to find your son, darling? The other children refer to it as 'Stuart's plane'."

As Graeme lifted Stuart down, other children followed, them, as though Graeme was the Pied Piper. Stuart called out proudly, "Mrs Morgan, my Papa is here. Look Mrs Morgan, this is my Papa. He's a REAL pilot."

Stuart impatiently pulled at Graeme's jacket, "Papa, come and see what I've made you."

Graeme grinned disarmingly at Wendy Morgan, as he told her, "It is a pleasure to meet you, Mrs Morgan. I'll leave Julie to speak with you whilst I go and satisfy this young man."

Wendy Morgan took Julie into her office and closed the door. "Wowee! What a dish! He's gorgeous! Okay, come on! I'm dying of curiosity and . . . Oh, by the way, I'm delighted to see you back and in good health, after your accident."

Julie laughed as she thought, 'Graeme attired in his uniform, seems to have this effect on most women.' "Well," she said, "he's actually my childhood sweetheart, literally the boy next door. He's recently widowed and you know about John. Well, Graeme and I met again in America, and we're to be married just as soon as we can. We feel at our age there's no point prolonging the inevitable. Graeme's due back in the U.K., and we'll move there with the children after our wedding. Daisy will be coming with us, end of story."

"Stuart calls him, Papa?" Wendy queried.

"Convenience, and to stop confusion. It didn't make sense to be calling him 'Graeme' and then 'Papa' after we were married. Anyway, Graeme will be legally adopting both children. Now let's go and rescue my gorgeous man, he's probably being hassled to death!"

But, they found all of the children sitting totally absorbed on the floor in front of Graeme. He was drawing simplified fighting aircraft 'dog fights' on the blackboard and telling an exciting story.

As they left, Stuart looked up at Graeme, and said simply, "I love you, Papa."

During the ride to Lauren's school, Graeme sighed with pure pleasure, "This father business, it's so great!"

Lauren was waiting at the classroom entrance to escort her parents. She greeted her father shyly, as she gazed lovingly up at his tall figure. "You look so nice, Papa."

Graeme bravely swallowed the lump in his throat as he hugged his daughter. In the classroom, all of her classmates sprung to attention and Miss Read shook hands with Graeme with a broad, welcoming smile on her face.

Miss Read invited Lauren to introduce Graeme. Word perfectly she announced his full rank and then, to everyone's surprise, "My Mama is going to marry Air Commodore McKenzie, and then he will be MY Papa, forever and forever!"

The children cheered wildly, and then the questions began! For nearly an hour Graeme patiently answered a wide range of queries. He had their full attention when he demonstrated aviation tactics and manoeuvres by drawing clear, concise illustrations on the blackboard.

At the gate, Graeme swung Lauren up into his arms and planted his hat on her head to the cheers of her classmates.

Back at the house, they had a discussion regarding some practical issues in arranging their wedding. Graeme felt he should go back to the U.K. to oversee the house purchase and arrange all of the domestic details. "I should really get my immediate service duties re-assigned to Billy."

Julie reluctantly agreed she would need at least three weeks to get her wedding gown and bridal party ensembles arranged, and to pack up her house and possessions.

Julie rang Maria and immediately told her all the good news. After a few minutes alternately laughing and crying, Maria could not resist a few, 'I told you so's.'

"Cara, I willa ring my nephew, Francis. Letta us make a date for the twenty first of June for your wedding day. You come witha Daisy and the bambinos a few days early, and Graeme canna come with his family, eh? Giovanni and me verra happy for you both. Daisy and the bambinos, they staya here, while you anda Graeme go for a little honeymoon alone somewhere, eh? What d'ya say, cara?"

Julie immediately replied by thanking Maria enthusiastically for her suggestions and saying, "I'll check the timing with Graeme. Ciao, my dear Maria, I'll ring again, very soon."

Julie's next call, to Andrew Martin, was just as emotional. She asked her dear friend to give her away and to bring Andrea with him. Andrew happily agreed, saying, "Julie, my dear, you deserve to find much happiness."

By the time the Reynolds family arrived for dinner, plans were well in hand.

Stuart came to collect Aimee, "C'mon, Gingernut," he said disparagingly, and Aimee followed him like a doting puppy. It was a simple scene, but Graeme somehow knew it would be indelibly printed on his mind forever.

After dinner, Graeme made their first call to the U.K.—to his parents. He succinctly told them of what had come to pass and his tearful mother murmured, "At last, you will be really happy, my son."

"There is more, my dear Mother, but I'll tell you, when I'm home next week."

Kate held Julie's hand after she had nervously dialled her sister's number. When Carole answered, Julie carefully explained what had happened. But, when she mentioned who she was to marry, she heard a hiss down the telephone line, "I knew it! Of course! Their eyes! They're his kids, aren't they?"

Taking a deep breath, Julie clutched Kate's hand and said, "Yes, but please Carole, give Graeme a chance to explain to his parents first, next week."

Her sister appeared to have gone into a state of shock, and it took several repeated explanations before Carole fully understood. Eventually Julie elicited a promise from her to pass on just the wedding news to Don and Lisa.

Graeme then telephoned Billy, asking him to inform the Air Vice Marshall of his plans. After Graeme had solicitously asked after Marisa, Billy made a comment that brought a grin from Graeme. "Everything is just fine in that department, nosy parker!"

Julie blushed as a laughing Kate asked, "Does Billy want to know if Julie is keeping your strength up?"

After the phone calls were completed, Harry made Julie a firm cash offer for her house, which she accepted, unconditionally, and they drank a toast to seal the deal.

Harry proposed, "Look, why don't you come in tomorrow with Julie, Graeme, and I'll take you on the grand tour? The girls will be quite a while making plans with Gloria."

CHAPTER 80

Julie and Graeme arrived at the factory the next day to a tumultuous welcome. The staff embraced Julie and others shook Graeme's hand, thanking him for returning their 'boss lady' to them.

The irrepressible Gloria was introduced to Graeme and, much to his amusement, after eyeing him up and down, she put forefinger and thumb into the recognized 'thumbs up' sign. She told Julie, "Weeow! He's one sexy dish, a real bit of all right. Yep, he'll do."

Julie blushed, but Graeme chuckled with laughter. When told why Julie was there, Gloria said, "I'm truly and sincerely happy for you, Julie. Did Kate get a chance to tell you of our proposal?"

"Yes, indeed," Julie replied, as she linked arms with Gloria and asked, "Aren't congrats also due for you?"

Gloria shyly answered, "Yes, they are. Roger and I would like to buy the penthouse as part of the deal, and move in as soon as we can."

"In that case let's get organised. We're all here, so after lunch let's hear from you."

Seating Graeme on one of the loveseats in the 'Bellamissio' showroom, Julie heard his appreciative whistle when she slid the mirrored doors apart to reveal the gowns stored behind them. Selecting one gown in the elegant style she knew Graeme preferred, she held it against herself. "Are you sure you want me to wear a white gown, veil, the whole bit, Graeme? After all, it isn't my first wedding and I'm hardly a virgin bride!"

Speaking softly, he stated emphatically, "Julie, my darling, I want you to be my bride, to the fullest extent of the word. Let's pretend you ARE my virgin bride and we are marrying, as we should have done back then."

He took her in his arms as she said quietly, "Graeme Stuart McKenzie, that's exactly how I feel, but I wanted to make sure that was how you saw it."

Graeme was staggered by the beauty of the gowns Julie selected for his inspection. She judged his reactions well and it came as no surprise that the one design she had long secreted away, her own dream gown, matched all of his criteria.

Kissing him ardently, she told him he was not actually going to see her in it until the day of their wedding, just like any other bride. "Now, Kate and I have to consult with Gloria for a while and get things moving. I'll take you to Harry and he'll show you around. We'll meet up for lunch, once we have the female side sorted, darling."

Harry saw, by the incredulous look on Graeme's face, he had been blown away by the bridal concept. "Our Julie is a little genius, Graeme. 'Bellamissio' hit a niche market that no one else had ever thought about," he declared, in an admiring tone. "I have said several times, she is literally a Madame Midas, all of her ideas simply turn to gold. Her designs are innovative, practical, elegant yet affordable; don't ever let her stop designing. She has put this franchise at the top of our profession."

He paused before continuing, "When she lay in that coma, the whole factory, en masse, prayed daily for her. She will be sorely missed when you marry. But, Kate and I know how much she has missed being without you. We don't begrudge her one moment of happiness, Graeme. But, take good care of her, old chap. She's one in a million."

This was the longest speech Graeme had heard from quiet, gentle Harry, which gave it an even greater depth of sincerity.

Graeme soberly replied, "I'm only just beginning to realise how very, very talented she actually is. But, I really do need her at my side, and I believe she equally needs me. Without her and my children, life for me just wouldn't be worth living."

Harry grinned ruefully, "Forgive me but I get a bit carried away when it comes to Julie. She won't tell you this, but John became difficult. He was brilliant at his job, but he had a darker side, when he wasn't sober and obsessive of Julie. You really are the man Julie needs. You'll keep her on the right path, by encouraging her, without being jealous of how she got there."

Graeme was stopped by various people and was not surprised when they repeatedly told him what a lucky man he really was. His own charming personality was not lost on the womenfolk, and more than one very married lady was heard to remark lewdly on his very obvious, masculine attributes!

Meanwhile, Julie and Kate had selected the materials for their gowns. Julie's choice was a heavy ivory silk, which she guiltily produced from its hiding place. She had also been saving a length of exquisite handmade lace for this very gown. On learning her secret, Kate dissolved into fits of laughter at her friend's 'deceit'!

Julie chose a waist length veil and an elegant, pearl and orange blossom stylised wreath headdress.

Kate and Aimee, with their auburn curls and green eyes, were naturals for a peacock blue/jade green, shot silk fabric. Kate's sophisticated long gown, and Aimee's short, bouncy, flower girl style, more than complemented the delicate sea-green blue of Lauren's waltz length dress. Julie had decided Stuart would be attired entirely in McKenzie tartan. Long trews, a military styled jacket and lacy jabot.

"Couldn't be better!" Kate enthused. "With the McKenzie tartan being predominantly blue and green, and with Graeme's uniform also blue, it's nigh on perfect."

Gloria popped in, saying, "Ready for me to run the tape over you, ladies? Our top seamstress, Madeline, will fit you in private, which will keep your gowns totally secret. By the way, half the female staff are head over heels in love with your gorgeous man! He's wowed them out there!"

Julie giggled, thinking how she'd tease him and make him pay dearly for that little compliment—privately—later!

After a convivial lunch, Roger and Gloria were ready to present their proposal. Graeme rose to excuse himself, whilst they conducted their business, but was vociferously urged by them all to stay.

"This is your business, as much as mine, darling," Julie told him, as she held his hands in hers.

Roger laid a dossier of paper in front of the three partners, outlining what he and Gloria proposed.

Harry summarized the proposal. "Basically, Roger and Gloria want to purchase the franchise as a 'going concern', plus the penthouse and our townhouse for their private accommodation."

Julie did a few sums on a piece of paper and was flabbergasted to find she is now a multi-millionairess. The overall price the two offered had staggered Graeme.

Shortly he afterwards, commented quietly to Julie, "Guess I'll be a kept man now, in the manner to which I have not yet become accustomed! Well done, my darling. Now you can make all of your wishes and dreams come true."

Julie gently admonished him, "Graeme Stuart McKenzie, I only have one dream, one wish—and it's standing right here in front of me."

Kate brought glasses of champagne over. "Come on you two, let's celebrate!"

The company's legal representatives notarised the deal, with the date of June 15th designated as takeover day. As Kate had already booked air tickets to Australia for June 16th, it was all beginning to dovetail neatly.

The following weekend, celebrated as Queen's Birthday Weekend in New Zealand, they departed, en masse, for the beach house.

Graeme's flight back to the U.K. was confirmed for the following Wednesday, but he had mixed feelings about leaving, albeit for just a few days.

Julie knew her time was going to be more than fully occupied, with wedding arrangements and packing up her possessions. As they walked together arm in arm along the pristine beach, as they had done so many times before, Julie said, "A penny for them, Katie?"

Kate gave a wry laugh. "Caught me out. We have had such a special friendship, Julie. I'll need to see you a lot more than once a year. We'll have to find somewhere half way between us, so that we can spend a mad few days, every so often, shopping, lazing in the sun, and just talking."

Julie squeezed Kate's arm. "I've been thinking along the same lines. We'll work it out, Katie, you are too special to me for us to drift apart, my friend."

After a sizzling barbecue dinner outside on the deck, Graeme proudly vowed and declared he had mastered the Australasian art of barbecue cooking. Three small children, who had been rolling about on the sand in hysterics, watching him incinerate yet another sausage, had reached a far different conclusion to this bold claim.

Once the children were settled for the night, the four friends sprawled comfortably on the deck. The radio was playing softly in the background and, recognizing the sweet voice singing an old song of their youth, Julie remarked, "Oh listen, darling, that's 'Ssshh'."

Kate looked around at her friend, startled, "Ssshh?"

Graeme was rumbling with laughter, as he explained, "It seems that all of the males in 'Our Gang' were madly in love with this particular lady vocalist. We were what . . . ? twelve, fourteen, darling? . . . When she was singing, we 'boys' would all sit around, mooning and sighing for our lovely romantic lady, but the girls would start yapping like a bunch of puppies! So they got told, rather brusquely, to 'ssshh'. Henceforth, from that day forward, to the girls of 'Our Gang' she's known simply as 'ssshh'!"

Harry wiped laughter tears from his eyes, saying, "You two have such a wealth of amusing anecdotes of your youth to tell to your children."

Graeme kissed Julie's forehead, "Aye that we have: what's more, thank God, we have the rest of our lives in which to tell them."

CHAPTER 81

The following Wednesday, Julie, Lauren and Stuart drove Graeme to RNZAF Hobsonville.

A Sergeant opened Julie's door. "Good evening, Ma'am. The C.O. extends his compliments and invites you to join him. We are ready for take-off as soon as you give the order, Sir."

Clinging to Graeme's hand, Lauren whispered, "You are a very important man, Papa. Everybody salutes you."

Graeme winked at her, "As long as I am your very important man, Lauren honey, that's all that matters."

Spotting a whole cabinet of scale model planes, Stuart broke away from Julie's restraining hand and stood with his nose pressed against the glass. The Sergeant grinned at Julie, "Don't worry, Ma'am, I've got one just like him at home. Chip off the old block, eh, Sir?"

"Looks like it, Sergeant," Graeme acknowledged. He was still getting used to this wonderful brotherhood of 'fatherhood'.

After Graeme had hugged Lauren and Stuart for the final time, the C.O. took them to watch proceedings, discreetly leaving Graeme and Julie alone in his office.

They exchanged a final kiss, as Graeme murmured, "Dio come ti-amo, cara mia."

As he walked across the tarmac to the waiting aircraft, Graeme looked to the window where his family stood waving farewell. As he mounted the steps he overheard a whisper, in a very New Zealand accent, remark, "Wow, the Old Man sure has got a looker for a missus!"

Graeme grinned happily. Julie was going to be a 'knock out' in the Mildenhall mess! . . .

The following Monday, he was in the office of his superior officer, relating all that had happened to him since last they met. He ended by saying, "Julie and I will never hide the fact that the children are mine. It will probably be a five day wonder around the base, but after that I'm hoping people are mature enough to let us get on with our lives."

After listening to Graeme's touching story, Air Vice Marshall Brown looked kindly at his junior. "Graeme, you'll have the total support of both my wife and I. We've missed your presence, and your excellent piano playing skills. As far as the service goes, you are, and always will be, a hero." He chuckled, before adding, "In fact, I'd be surprised if it doesn't enhance the mystique surrounding yourself even further. Keep Watson in the picture. Good Luck, and very best wishes from my wife and I."

Graeme's next appointment was with Richard Fraser, Q.C. The house purchase was just a formality and soon finalised. The lawyer advised him that the adoption papers were ready and only waiting for Julie's signature.

Graeme drove to his new property. He wandered slowly through the empty rooms and immediately felt a comfortable and warm ambience enfold him.

The rooms were as spacious, light and airy, as he had remembered, and as Julie would have come to expect.

He picked up the telephone and dialled her New Zealand number. Checking his watch, he noted that as it was their breakfast time, all of his family should be there.

"Good morning, this is Lauren speaking." Her voice was as clear as though she was standing beside him.

"Hello, honeybunch, how is everyone?" he asked, in a voice thick with emotion.

"Papa! Oh, Mama, it's my darling Papa! Papa we are nearly all packed, and my bridesmaid dress looks real neat, and so does Stuart's suit. But,

Papa, Mama looks like a Princess. Oh, Papa we miss you. Here's my brother, 'bye my Papa, darling."

"Papa, I'm here, it's me, Stuart. Papa, we're going on the big plane. Papa, I love you and I miss you, here's Mama, 'bye Papa."

After they had exchanged loving greetings and he told where he was ringing from, Julie suggested, "Graeme, darling, show your parents the house, ask them what they think of it."

"Okay, my darling, will do. I'm on my way to them now. I've rung Carole. None of them can come, but she was warm enough, and congratulated me, so that's something."

He hesitated, reluctant to break the connection between them. "Look, I'll ring you tomorrow. Take extra care of yourselves, my precious trio. I am one lonely man without you all. Good-bye, my darling. I love you so much, cara mia."

Alicia and Grant McKenzie listened intently and looked delighted as Graeme gently and lovingly told them his and Julie's story. When he reached the part where Lauren entered the picture, he handed the photographs to his Mother.

Alicia McKenzie gasped as she recognised the obvious likeness. She stared in astonishment at her son. "You have a daughter!"

"Yes, a beautiful, intelligent little girl. She is called Lauren Catherine. You'll love her Mum. Look," he picked up the photo of himself at Lauren's age.

"That's not all, this is our son, Stuart Cameron. I was actually at his birth." Graeme handed his parents the photos Doc Matthews had taken. "You have two beautiful grandchildren, and after Julie and I are married they'll legally become McKenzies."

His mother clutched at her husband's hands. "I want to go and see them, Grant. I want to be at your wedding, Graeme. Julie's so beautiful and ..our grandchildren look so wonderful. Oh, I can't wait to hold them, Graeme. Thank God, son, at last Julie and you are able to be together."

As Alicia McKenzie embraced her son, he grinned happily as he took from his pocket two First Class return air tickets, London to Sydney. "With love from Julie and I. Tomorrow I'd like to drive you to our new home. I only signed the deeds today, so you will see it before even Julie does, but that's what she wants."

He was still hugging his mother when he added, with a mischievous grin, "Oh! Just one more thing, Mum. I have strict instructions from Julie to escort you to 'Maison Chevalier', and have you select a Mother-of-the-Groom ensemble."

He reached inside his jacket pocket. "Here are the colours the other ladies in the bridal party are wearing, so that you can colour coordinate with the rest of the girls."

Alicia urged him to tell her more about Julie's career. His father sat enthralled, studying the photos. At one point, as he looked at the panoramic shots of Julie's house and land, he asked, "Is she giving all this away to marry you, son?"

Graeme pointed out various landmarks on the photograph, including Julie's stile. "Yes, it's already sold to her partners, Harry and Kate Reynolds. It's one of the most beautiful places I have ever seen, Dad. But, I still have years of my contract to go, and my job is here in the U.K. So my precious darling has opted to be here with me. We have been so lonely apart; I need her by my side. It's humbling, isn't it, that she can love me that much?"

Grant McKenzie shook his head. "There always was a special bonding between you two. It was only stupid pride on both sides that parted you back then, wasn't it?"

Graeme grinned ruefully at his father. "Absolutely correct, Dad. So I aim to spend the rest of my life making it up to her. Look, I'll take you to our new home tomorrow and ring them at my usual time. You can speak to all three of them, and of course there's Daisy. She is one of the world's treasures, and will also be coming to live in with us."

Julie visited Doc Matthews, who was delighted to learn she and Graeme McKenzie were to be married.

Julie asked, somewhat nervously, "Graeme and I would like to have another child. Do you think I am too old, Doc? What are the risks? He's adamant he won't let me conceive if there were any."

Fifteen minutes later, after an extensive examination, Doc beamed at her, "You are physically fine in all departments, Julie, my dear. Good Luck."

Julie had one more appointment that day, the final fitting of her wedding gown. The bodice, with its bejewelled shoulder straps, was moulded around her breasts, while the full skirt flowed gracefully to the ground. The satin toes of her shoes were just peeping out from the hem. The hip length over-jacket, of exquisite handmade lace, with its wrist length sleeves, was soft and alluring.

After placing the fine veil and pearl headdress on Julie's head, Madeline stepped back to admire her work.

Julie smiled; it was perfect, exactly as Graeme wanted her to look. "Thank you, so much, Madeline, it's just lovely. It can now be packed with the other outfits."

Julie checked the other hangers. The vibrant peacock blue/jade green shot silk of Kate's sophisticated gown shimmered under the showroom lights. Its balloon sleeves and Victorian stylised, flounced skirt back, almost a bustle, was topped by a headpiece consisting of a peacock feather amongst a swirl of net.

Aimee's was in the same colour, perfectly complementing her mother's gown. A short, full skirt supported by many stiffened petticoats, and short puffed sleeves, perfectly imitating the balloon sleeves of Kate's gown.

In a similar style, Lauren's very feminine, waltz length dress was in a lighter colour of sea-green to highlight her blonde colouring.

Both girls were to wear Juliet cap headdresses, made in the matching fabric of their dresses, and entwined with pearls. Two pairs of frilly white, Victorian styled pantaloons for Lauren and Aimee, plus three pairs of silver strap sandals in three heel heights lay in their respective boxes.

Julie smiled tenderly as she lifted Stuart's McKenzie tartan suit down. It was a little masterpiece of which she was extremely proud. The slim fitting trews were topped by a tartan cutaway jacket with tails at the back, and adorned with silver buttons and shoulder epaulettes. The shirt had visible lace cuffs and a lace jabot at the neck. Around his waist Stuart would wear a miniature sporran to carry his parents' wedding rings. On his head, a McKenzie tartan Tam O'Shanter, and black patent shoes adorned with large silver buckles. When they had tried it on him, he had marched up and down in front of the mirrors. It had taken all of Gloria's persuasive powers to get him to take it off again!

Julie breathed a sigh of relief; every item was ready and perfect!

CHAPTER 82

Organised chaos reigned as the professional packers moved in gathering up what was to be sent to the U.K.

When the telephone rang, Lauren picked it up, saying, "Hello, this Lauren speaking."

A hesitant woman's voice said, "Hello, Lauren, my dear. Oh, I'm so happy to hear your voice. My name is Alicia McKenzie, I am your Papa's mother and that makes me . . ." a sob came down the telephone line. "It makes me your grandmother, my dear . . . next to me is your Papa, and his father, Grant McKenzie, who is your . . . grandfather . . . Is your Mama and your brother Stuart there with you?"

Lauren whispered to Julie, "It's a nice lady who says she is Papa's mother, my grandmother . . . and there's a man, Papa's father."

Julie wiped away the tears that had welled up in her eyes, as she told her, "They want to hear your voice, darling. Yes, they're your paternal grandparents, Papa will be there listening."

"Hello, grandmother, this is Lauren. Mama says it's okay for me to talk to you. Are you coming to my Papa's wedding? Stuart is here, but he's only little and he's not very good on the telephone yet. He usually yells too loud. 'bye for now."

Stuart bellowed loudly, "Hello, this is Stuart. I'm going to be a pageboy thingy. Where's my Papa?"

Graeme came on the line, "Hello, my son. Are you looking after your Mama for me?"

"Papa, we're moving! We're going on a big plane. Papa, when are you coming home? I miss you and I love you heaps."

Julie smiled, "Hello, darling. What a lovely surprise. Are you at your parent's home?"

"Hello, sweetheart, it's so good to hear your voice again. I'm actually in our new home . . . Julie, my mother is bawling, she was so overcome at hearing their voices. Can you ask the children what they would like to call their paternal grandparents who, by the way, have accepted our invitation. Darling, Mum and Dad would like to have a word."

"Julie, this is Alicia McKenzie. We are delighted with the news, my dear, and can hardly wait to we see you all. It was such a lovely surprise to learn of their existence. Thank you, my dear, for the outfit offer. Graeme will be taking me within the next couple of days. I thought perhaps a pale lavender colour would suit me."

"That sounds perfect, in fact just right, Mrs McKenzie. Lauren and Stuart are so like Graeme, you are going to love having them around."

"Julie, my dear, I would have welcomed you with open arms years ago, had it been on the cards. We are so looking forward to seeing you again, 'bye for now, here's Grant."

A voice, with the same timbre as his son, echoed down the line. "Hello, Julie, m'dear. We're absolutely delighted with Graeme's news. He's also told us what you are so unselfishly giving up for him. Julie, your new house is marvellous, an excellent choice."

Julie was also finding it hard to speak, but hesitantly replied, "Where he is, is where my life is. I can't wait to be married to him. I'm so pleased you agree with his choice of house for us, it does sound truly delightful."

"Well, I'll not keep him from having a quiet word alone with you, Julie," Grant McKenzie told her. "We send you all much love, from two very proud grandparents. Good-bye, Julie, my dear."

Graeme's beloved voice was next on the line. "Hello, Sweetheart. I'm off to pick up our wedding rings today. Just a simple band of gold, but it will tell the world, Julie McKenzie is all mine—at last—and I'm certainly all hers! Been an emotional call today, hasn't it, my darling. But, Oh boy, have we got two people here who can't wait to get to Australia!"

"Darling, Graeme, I'm overwhelmed, so I know how they must feel. Well, darling, everything's ready. Will you take your mother into Michael and Denise, what day should I tell Maria to expect them?"

Graeme shuffled the documents, "Ah, here it is, they arrive in Sydney, seven thirty a.m. on the 19th June."

"Oh, Graeme, everything is planning out so perfectly. Maria's adamant, you are not to stay with me the night before our wedding; according to Maria it's bad luck! So Williamtown will have to cope with you and Billy."

Graeme chuckled, "So you'll be my virgin bride after all then, won't you, minx?"

Julie was glad he could not see her blushes as she pretended to scold him, "Graeme McKenzie, you behave! Oh yes, before I forget, what's our new address!"

He was still chuckling, "Here, my sweetheart, is your new address, I've been keeping it a surprise for as long as I could. Are you ready for this? "MacCoinnich House, Sycamore Lane, Hockwold-cum-Wilton, Norfolk, England."

Julie whispered, "Graeme, MacCoinnich is Gaelic for McKenzie—and Sycamore Lane! It must have been Fate, it was meant to be, my darling."

"I know it hit me when I first saw it," Graeme admitted. "The previous owners are ageing, and it's too big for them now. They could hardly believe it when I told them my surname. It's in immaculate condition, my darling, the garden is over an acre. I just know we're going to be so happy there."

When they had said their emotional and loving farewells, Julie took the address to show Daisy.

"A house with our name already on it, and the street named Sycamore. Oh Daisy, it's magic! I must go and ring Kate. Do you realise something? I no longer own any part of 'Maison Chevalier'—or this house!"

Julie gave Kate her new address, adding, "Wow! Kate! What an uncanny coincidence. I'm so happy Graeme's parents will be there. They have taken the unexpected news very well. A lot better than my lot, I'm afraid."

Kate asked, "Jules, come in, have a last look around with me tomorrow, for old time's sake?"

"Yes, why not, Katie. I'm taking the children to the Field's grave site after school today. Give them a chance to say, 'good-bye'."

Julie was determined to make the visit to the Field graves a celebration and not a sombre, grief filled occasion. She brought along happy family photos and beautiful flowers from their garden. She encouraged Lauren and Stuart to talk about Papajohn, Nananaomi and Papageorgie.

Stuart asked, "Mama, have I got another Grandmamma and a Grandpapa still to come?"

"Yes, darling, your Papa's Mama and Papa. We have to decide what to call them. Lauren, have you any ideas?"

"Sarah calls her grandparents Nanny and Gramps. I like Gramps, but we already have Nananaomi."

"I agree, I like Gramps. 'Nanny' sounds a bit like a goat." Here both children howled with laughter. "Somehow 'Gran' sounds too old, so does 'Grandma' and 'Grannie'. I think you should call her 'Nana'."

The next day, Julie was about to leave to meet Kate for lunch. Daisy came in with a big smile on her face. "Er . . . you'd better come and see this yourself!"

Gathering up her keys and handbag with a mystified look, Julie followed Daisy to the front door. There in the driveway was the longest, whitest limousine she had ever seen. Kate popped her head out from the depths of the back seat, holding a glass of champagne. "Didn't think we'd let you go off and get married without a traditional New Zealand Bridal Shower."

Daisy whipped off her overall and grabbed the high heeled shoes she had hidden on the front steps. "Come on, honey. Let's celebrate! Bob East and his wife are collecting the little ones. Lauren wants to settle her pets, so let's go!"

Laughing gaily, Julie said, "You have ganged up on me. What deviousness!"

The luxury car purred its way—to the factory! As a totally surprised Julie alighted, she heard church bells pealing over the loudspeakers and saw white ribbons and balloons festooning the cafeteria. All of her staff was there, cheering and clapping. She was led by Gloria to a long table decorated with bridal flowers and piled high with gaily wrapped parcels. There was even a two-tiered wedding cake in the centre of the table, and bottles of champagne now being opened by Harry and Roger.

Harry tapped the table. "My Friends. She came here to New Zealand as a young bride, still an apprentice. But, she had vision! And what vision! Along the way we have all benefited from her talent and her foresight. She has had tragedy aplenty in her life, and has come through with courage. She has come back from a near death coma. Kate and I are convinced, brought back by the power of love. We have all recently met the distinguished Air Commodore, and we couldn't wish for a finer man for our Julie to marry."

"Ladies and Gentlemen, I give you a toast to one helluva lady, who has made what we do here possible. Julie Field, soon to be, Mrs Julie McKenzie." He raised his glass in salute, "To Julie!"

Julie stood smiling through emotional tears, as they raised their glasses. The notes of, "For She's a Jolly Good Fellow" rang around the cafeteria.

To the cries of, "Speech, Speech," she walked to the centre of the room. "Thank you all for such a lovely, and total surprise 'Shower'. This place has always been a most happy workplace. We have had our share of stresses and strains. In particular that first award we ever entered for. The little place from 'down under' that cheekily won all of their big prizes. Oh, victory was never so sweet! Most of you who were there then are still here now, so we must have been doing something right."

The whole room erupted in applause at that statement. She continued, "We have shared our successes, either monetary, or for better working conditions, and we have all reaped the benefits."

There were murmurs of, "Hear, Hear" around the room. "On a personal note, my time spent in New Zealand has been a precious period in my life. My life with John was also very, very special. Graeme and I have both recently endured the sadness of being widowed. Now it is time for us to join our lives together. I thank you all, most sincerely."

CHAPTER 83

This morning Daisy watched Julie closely. Julie sighed, "It's okay, I'm fine. I'm naturally a little sad. But, no mere bricks and mortar could ever compensate for my desire to be with him."

Julie knew her children were too young to comprehend the significance of this day. Possibly their last day for several years in the land of their birth.

She heard a loud "Wow!" from Lauren as Stuart came hurtling into the house. "Mama! It's as big as three cars!"

'It' was the white limousine again! This time resplendent with fluttering white ribbons on its bonnet, and a pair of dolls, appropriately dressed as a bride and groom, decorating the back window.

The smiling chauffeur saluted and handed Julie a be-ribboned, cream vellum scroll. It read:

"All brides usually arrive at the church in a wedding car. You, my darling, will miss this tradition. Enjoy my compensatory gesture, and these words from W.B. Yeats:

'I have spread my dreams under your feet, Tread softly because you tread on my dreams.'

Hurry to me, cara mia. Dio come ti-amo. Graeme."

Julie wept tears of joy reading the loving, cherishing gesture from Graeme. Blowing her own nose loudly, Daisy ushered herself and the children into the car while Julie took one last lingering look around the house.

The hustle and bustle at the Airport had somewhat subdued Stuart, Lauren and Daisy so Julie was relieved when the Reynolds joined them and she had Harry's assistance.

She showed Kate Graeme's romantic words. Kate marvelled, "He seems to have an incredible ability to think and plan so far ahead. No wonder he holds the high rank he does!"

When they later landed at Sydney Airport, Julie was delighted to see Victor's smiling face waiting for them. As they embraced, Victor told them, "Mama Maria seems to go around telling everyone how clever she was at predicting this would happen!"

As the Chateau came into view, Julie sighed, "At last, I am here to complete my dearest dream."

Maria clasped Julie tightly in her arms. "Cara, I tolda you so, didn't I? Giovanni and me, we so happy you coma here to be forever joined to the beloved one. Come here bambino, Stuart, leta me see you. Yes, this is his handsome son. Si, Lauren you are stilla the image of your Papa."

Julie introduced Daisy, and the two older women struck an instant rapport. "We botha love her and the bambinos, eh? You also likea the beloved one? He quite a dish, eh?" Maria gave a truly Gaelic eye gesture, Daisy laughingly agreed.

When Rico arrived, Julie saw her daughter gaze at the tall, handsome boy as though mesmerised. Julie had an instant flashback of her own experience when she first met Graeme. So, was this another of Maria's famous predictions?

After they were alone, Maria held Julie and studied her face, "You are verra happy, I thinka, my cara. You give hima the third child soon? To put, now howa you say, puta the glue between the bricks, eh?"

"Who knows? Oh Maria, pinch me, I can't believe my years of loneliness and heartache are nearly over."

"Come to the Chapel witha me. We thanka God together. Francis willa be here. He comes all the way from Rome to marry you, justa as he promised."

Entering the chapel with Maria, Julie found it decorated with a mass of exotic, tropical white flowers, bows and ribbons. She gasped at the magnificent sight and hugged Maria, whose face was beaming fit to burst. "Oh, it's beautiful! A thousand thanks, my dear Maria."

"You likea a daughter to me, cara, and the beloved one, he also verra special. We enjoy doing it for botha you. Now come, sit witha me, we thank God together."

As they were leaving the chapel, Julie saw Kate gesturing for her to come and see. The ballroom had been transformed into a banquet hall, with tables set with white linen napery, and white and silver decorations. Overhead, the many chandeliers sparkled and gleamed, adding a magic of their own.

In the middle there was a beautifully burnished dance floor. On a raised dais sat the grand piano upon which Graeme's previous virtuoso playing had delighted everyone.

Julie identified the artistic handiwork of Victor's wife, Bianco, and was not surprised when, together with several of her female cousins, they stepped out from behind the doorway where they had been hiding. Bianco hugged Julie, "We wanted you to see it before we covered them to keep them fresh for your big day."

Julie exclaimed, "It's magnificent, Bianco. A thousand thanks, we are going to have such a fairy tale wedding day."

Julie felt somewhat restless and was unable to be still, so she was relieved when Graeme's call did eventually came through. "Oh, my darling, you've arrived safely. I couldn't settle all day," she told him. "We have come so close I couldn't bear it if anything upset our wonderful plans now."

Even though he was tired after his long and uncomfortable military flight, he reassured her, "I am here, my sweetheart, I would've swum it if I had to. Nothing, and I mean nothing is going to stop me marrying you, Julie, cara."

Just to hear his voice and his loving words calmed Julie. "Hey, that was a very romantic car ride to the airport, darling. Your words on that beautiful scroll had me bawling into one of Daisy's half sheets that she calls hankies! I need you, Graeme. I need to feel you close by."

Graeme chuckled happily, "Not long now, my darling, and nothing will ever come between us again. Now my best man is dying to say hello."

"Hello, Julie. We are both just about out on our feet; Australia is one helluva long flight!"

Julie replied, "It's so good to hear your voice again. Look after him, Billy, we need him so much and love him to bits."

"I'll do my very best. G'night, sweet lady, see you tomorrow. I'll put my man back on."

For a few precious minutes the two lovers talked before reluctantly wishing each other a loving goodnight.

Graeme called her the next morning at nine o'clock from Sydney Airport to tell her they were about to leave for the Chateau.

Daisy grinned at her, "Okay, go titivate what is already perfect anyway, and I'll round up the bairns."

Julie heard Stuart yelling, "Papa is coming! Mama, Nanny Daisy says my Papa is coming!"

"Your Papa will be bringing Gramps and Nana McKenzie here very soon, my darlings. They have just left the airport, so not long now."

Lauren held her mother's hand. "You and Papa have known each other for such a long time, Mama. Tell us again about the day you first met each other."

Julie retold her children of her first meeting with their father when they were children, about the sycamore tree and how their new Gramps and Nana lived next door to her family. A story she had told many times recently.

Lauren was the first to spot the car coming down the hill. Alicia and Grant McKenzie stared in amazement at Lauren, and her likeness to Graeme. Alicia McKenzie was already wiping emotional tears from her eyes as she witnessed the incredible reception her son was getting from his family.

Grant McKenzie cleared the lump in his throat and quietly said, "Give them a minute, Alicia. What a beautiful place this is, Billy. Have you ever been here before?"

"No, Mr McKenzie, but Graeme described it to me. It's a special place for both of them . . . Aah, we have been noticed. Hello, Julie, my love, great to be here at last."

Julie hugged Billy, telling him, "You are still as handsome as ever, I see. Please forgive our rudeness, we do love him so much and we've missed him heaps."

Graeme was holding Stuart in his arms. "Mum, Dad, meet my beloved Julie and your grandchildren Lauren and Stuart."

Julie looked at the slim woman of medium height that she had not seen for twenty years. Her once blonde hair was now delicate silver, and she had the deep blue eyes that her son and grandchildren had inherited.

Grant McKenzie was an older, greyer version of his son, a fact not lost on Lauren. She asked, "Gramps, my Papa looks like you and I look like my Papa, don't I? Were you a pilot before you retired, Gramps?"

Graeme still holding Stuart grinned at his father, who was trying to recover his composure after being called 'Gramps' by this gorgeous child. "She's very self-confident and independent, Dad, you two are going to get along famously. They tell me Stuart must be a chip off the old block as he is crazy about aircraft."

Alicia held out her arms to Stuart, "Can you give me a hug, Stuart. Now what are you going to call me?"

Stuart informed her, "You are my Papa's Mama, so you are my Nana."

"Darling, show your parents to the guest wing," Julie suggested to Graeme. "Let them freshen up and then perhaps you'd care to join us for morning tea which our dear Daisy is preparing. She's also made your favourite muffins, Graeme. She's spoiling you again!"

Lauren was holding her grandfather's hand and in deep conversation with him as she led the way. Stuart was busy regaling his new Nana with details of their flight.

When Stuart finally ran out of words, Julie asked, "Did you get an outfit from Michael, Mum?"

"Julie, they were splendid. I could tell he and his lovely wife Denise were overjoyed that you two had found each other again. He was most enthusiastic about 'Bellamissio Brides', Graeme had explained the concept to me. What a brilliant idea, Julie. Are you going to give it all up for my son?"

"If I need to, then so be it. Graeme is all I want and I think he needs us almost as much as we need him."

"Absolutely, I have never seen him so happy or looking so well. Julie, my ensemble is delightful. They went to so much trouble to select an outfit that would complement your colour scheme. I think his exact words were, 'nothing is too good for our young Julie'."

Graeme suggested, "Go on in, meet Daisy, Billy, the children will show you the way. I just want to have a quick word with my bride."

Graeme steered Julie into her bedroom. "So how much did you say you needed me?" he asked, as he pulled her close and kissed her passionately.

CHAPTER 84

The next morning Julie took an unexpected call from an old friend, photographer Tony Prentice, T.P. He explained that Michael and Denise Armstrong, discovering he would be in Sydney, had contracted him to come and photograph the wedding as their wedding present.

The bridal florist duly arrived and Julie was delighted by Graeme's romantic choice. He had chosen for her a trail of exotic miniature white and green orchids, delicately entwined with pearls and white satin ribbons. In the centre sat one exquisite white orchid. There were also orchid sprays for all the bridal party ladies, while Aimee had a small basket of pink and white rose petals to scatter before Julie. For every male guest there was a single orchid buttonhole.

Graeme had called before he and Billy had gone for an early morning jog. He confessed it was to fend off the slight hangover from the carousing at his stag party the night before. He was adamant though that he had kept his own consumption down, not wanting to miss a moment of this special day. He had told Julie, in an incredulous voice, "Gee, these Aussies sure can put away the beer, and darling, they drink it ice cold!"

"Anyway, I just wanted to hear your voice and to tell you I came through all the ribald jokes with flying colours. Plus to say how much I love you, my darling. I'll be ready and waiting, in eager anticipation, for you at the altar at three thirty."

Julie's next visitor was Monsignor Francis Ignacious Martini. He wanted to spend a few minutes with Julie. Taking one look at the glow on her cheeks and the happiness beaming in her eyes, he knew he need have no qualms there.

Andrew and Andrea Martin arrived before noon with, as a special surprise, hairdresser Lois and make-up artiste Diana in tow.

At Daisy's insistence Julie swallowed some fruit juice and fresh fruit for her lunch, before relaxing and letting the hairdresser and make-up team work their magic. Kate and Daisy then took charge of Aimee and Lauren and began the formal dressing of the two little girls. Harry had already captured Stuart with Victor's assistance, and they took over the little villa as their dressing rooms.

Graeme and Billy were to join them and Billy would place the two precious wedding rings in Stuart's sporran.

Julie asked Alicia and Grant McKenzie to join her once they were dressed, so that T.P. could photograph them with their grandchildren.

Suddenly the time seemed to be flying past on golden wings. Julie sat in her bedroom, her hair shining and slicked into a sleek chignon, her nails polished and her facial make-up professionally applied. Now, with Andrea Martin's help, she was about to don her fabulous gown.

Andrea picked up the beautifully crafted silk gown and lowered it carefully over Julie. It fitted as smoothly as a glove. The strapless boned bodice, with its bejewelled shoulder straps, emphasised her bust line and small waist in a very alluring way, exactly as Graeme had ordered.

Next came the exquisite and delicately hand-made lace over-jacket, with its deep cleavage, which again moulded perfectly to Julie's body.

Finally, Andrea picked up the intricately woven wreath headdress and waist length veil and placed them upon Julie's head. Andrea gasped, "You look stunning Julie, like a delicate, Dresden figurine, and a princess. My dear girl, you'll blow him away! Now, have you got the usual 'something old, something new'?"

Julie ticked them off on her fingers. "Something old, my amethyst ear studs, something new, my gown, something borrowed, Kate's lace hanky down my bra, and something blue, the lace garter from Graeme."

"I'll just go and get Andrew to get a male's perspective," Andrea told her as she left the room. Even she was mopping at her eyes, the beautiful sight of Julie making even a medical professional like herself emotional.

Knocking discreetly on the door, Andrew entered and stood mesmerised. "Julie, I have seen you in many gowns . . . But this one . . . Well my love, what has gone into this creation shows and glows. My dear, sweet lady, you are every man's vision of how his bride should look. Congratulations, my dear."

Alicia called out, "If you are ready, my dear, the photographer chappie is here. Can I come in?"

Julie replied, "Please do, I'm dying to see your outfit."

Alicia wore a three quarter silk coat over a matching ankle length, sheath dress, in pastel lavender. She was wearing satin shoes in a darker shade, and a cocktail hat consisting of a frothy confection of net held together with a matching lavender coloured rose. She stood stunned in the doorway as she gazed upon the young woman soon to be her new daughter-in-law.

"My dear child, you are looking like something out of a fairy tale story. Graeme told me he had some input into what he wanted you to wear. All I can say is . . . His every dream has come true!"

"Thank you, Mum. You look lovely. Michael and Denise have done us proud. The colour and style are just perfect for you. What did Dad say? Was he pleased with it?"

Alicia chuckled, "Oh yes! It put quite a twinkle into his old eye! Anyway, the photographer man is waiting, time is passing."

There was a collective gasp of appreciation as Julie walked majestically into the lounge. Kate whooped with delight, "Wowee! What a knock out!"

Lauren stared at her mother, before shyly saying, "Mama, you look so beautiful."

"So do you, my darling." She whispered, "Just wait 'til Rico sees you!"

Lauren reddened, but she looked mightily pleased with herself for all that. They were joined by Harry, resplendent in his tuxedo, and Stuart in the McKenzie tartan, which once again brought tears to Alicia eyes.

T.P. was snapping off shots from every angle.

Julie started to ask Harry, "Is . . . ?" but he interrupted her, with a cheeky grin, "Yep, he's here, all gold braid and rows of medals, 'he looka lika Prince Charming', according to Maria. That uniform surely does something for a man, but when he gets an eyeful of you, Julie, he'll forget everything else!"

Just then the chapel bells began to peal welcoming chimes and everyone with a watch looked at it. Where had the time gone? It was three fifteen, time for them all to be making their way, in procession, to the chapel.

Kate and Harry assembled their young charges, as Daisy, elegant in a navy and white silk ensemble, kissed Julie gently on the cheek, and whispered, "Next time I do that, you'll be Mrs Julie McKenzie. Lass, I'm so proud of you."

The bells continued their happy pealing as Kate and Harry escorted their special charges. T.P still danced around, photographing the children as they made their way to the front door of the chapel.

Julie removed her amethyst engagement ring and put it in her handbag. Her hand looked strangely bare, for she had taken her previous wedding and engagement rings off after John's death. She smiled happily. The next ring to adorn her hand would be evidence for all to see that she was legally Mrs Julie McKenzie.

Gently taking her veil, Andrew kissed her on both cheeks, before dropping the gossamer fine fabric over her face. He linked her hand through his arm, handed her the exquisite bridal spray, and said softly, "Ready?"

Julie beamed at him, "Oh, yes, Andrew dear."

As she reached the chapel front door on Andrew's arm, the bells stopped pealing and Graeme, standing anxiously at the altar, knew she had arrived. He turned to face the direction in which she would enter. The organist began to play the age-old, traditional, triumphant march from Lohengrin, by Richard Wagner, 'Here Comes the Bride.'

First in the bridal procession were Aimee and Stuart.

Aimee, a small, Titian beauty in her full skirted dress and frilly white pantaloons, was scattering the rose petals from her basket with great aplomb. Graeme wrestled with an emotional lump in his throat as he saw his small tartan clad son and heir walking so proudly beside his little friend. When Stuart spotted his father at the altar, he gave him a beaming, loving smile, which Graeme acknowledged by giving Stuart a wink and a discreet 'thumbs up' sign.

Closely following them was his beloved first-born child, Lauren. She was looking so elegant and grown up in her sea-green, bridesmaid's dress, reminding him of a beautiful flower about to blossom. She smiled shyly at her handsome father as he blew her a kiss.

Kate and Harry followed, resplendent in their respective ways. Harry was in a royal blue tuxedo and Kate in a breath-taking gown of peacock blue and jade green. Kate 'glad eyed' and mouthed 'Wow' at Graeme as she saw him for the first time in his best dress uniform. Graeme grinned cheekily back at her, before turning to catch the first glimpse of his bride on Andrew's arm, as she slowly made her way down the aisle towards him.

He could hear the sighs of appreciation as she passed the members of the congregation and knew, before she reached him, she was causing emotional tears of joy because she looked so fantastic.

As Graeme gazed in awe at the beautiful angel seeming to float towards him, he murmured, "Pinch me, Billy, and tell me I'm not dreaming. Is this for real?"

Billy grinned and whispered back, "Youbetcha mate! Gee's, have you ever seen anything so gorgeous?"

Julie, for her part, could now see the tall blonde uniformed figure in front of her. Her heart melted as she thought, 'Oh he is so, so handsome. Dear God, I love him so much.'

The sun shone through and caught his blonde hair and the golden lanyard over his shoulder glistened. With his many ribbons and awards adorning his left breast and wearing his officer's ceremonial sword, he really looked as though he was her knight in shining armour.

Graeme's face was a picture to behold, as his eyes took in the gown he had chosen and the special, bewitching, tantalizing body it encompassed.

As Julie stepped up beside him, he murmured, "You aren't a dream, are you? You look so beautiful, my angel. Dear God, I love you so much."

As the last notes of the bride's entrance music died away, Julie whispered, "What about you, then? My handsome flyboy. I love you too, my darling."

CHAPTER 85

Monsignor Francis began the ceremony with the familiar words, "Dearly beloved, we are gathered here today to join together this man and this woman in Holy Matrimony . . ."

Julie gazed through her bridal veil into the deep blue eyes of the man she had loved for so long. Graeme feasted his eyes upon the beautiful, talented woman standing beside him, as he heard the age-old words being uttered over them.

In a sepulchral, sombre tone of voice, the Monsignor began the charges to Graeme. "Graeme Stuart, do you take Julie Eve, to be your lawful wedded wife . . ."

Julie and Graeme answered the Monsignor in clear, audible voices. Their eyes fixed upon each other, each living their most dearest of dreams.

When the Monsignor requested the wedding rings for him to bless, Stuart, walked proudly up to the Monsignor. He carefully opened his sporran and placed the two rings on the Monsignor's purple velvet cushion.

Billy and Harry exchanged a special proud smile. The little boy had only one rehearsal with them to get his most important task right. Graeme took Julie's left hand and kissed her palm. He repeated the Monsignor's words, "With this ring I thee wed . . ." Julie glanced at the ring she had not seen until this moment, and gasped when she saw the intricate sycamore leaf design upon it.

Julie picked up the other identical ring. She kissed his palm and, in a voice husky with emotion, repeated the vow, "With this ring I thee wed . . ."

Once Julie had plighted her troth to Graeme, Monsignor Francis raised his voice slightly and announced to the gathered congregation, "I now pronounce you husband and wife . . . Graeme, you may now kiss your bride!"

Graeme carefully lifted the veil from Julie's face and back over her beautiful headdress. He gazed, as though bewitched for a second or two, into the beautiful face of . . . his wife! Leaning down, he gathered her in his arms and kissed her fully and thoroughly in front of the whole congregation.

Monsignor Francis then invited the newly-weds and their witnesses to sign the marriage register.

This done, the organist struck up 'The Wedding March' by Mendelssohn and, grinning broadly, Graeme offered his arm to his Julie, his beautiful new wife, and they made their celebratory walk down the aisle.

Julie had a fleeting, déjà vu flashback of a scene she had witnessed so many years ago. With a sudden realisation that the happy couple she had seen that day had actually been Graeme and herself!

The bells began pealing out again, broadcasting the good tidings of their union. Julie and Graeme McKenzie posed in the chapel doorway for T.P.

Graeme had just collected his hat from Billy when a contingent of RAAF Officers marched from the side of the chapel and formed up as an honour guard, with swords crossed high above the bridal couple.

Graeme grinned at her, "Welcome to the Air Force, my darling wife, Mrs Julie McKenzie!"

Julie clutched his arm tightly. "We are married, Graeme, officially married. I still feel like I should pinch myself, to see if it is real!"

Daisy brought their children forward. As he flung his arms around his mother, Stuart produced a silver be-ribboned horseshoe and said, "For Luck, Mama, from me and Lauren."

Lauren hugged her father. "Oh, Papa, you do look handsome in your uniform, and I do love you and Mama, so much."

Graeme said softly, "We are a real family now honeybunch. No more separations. Mama is now Mrs Julie McKenzie, and very soon, you and Stuart will be McKenzies as well."

Kate came forward holding the arm of Aaron Benedict. "Look who I found at the back of the chapel!"

Julie hugged the big American Indian and Graeme vigorously shook his hand. "I'm so glad you made it, Aaron. I knew it was going to be a close call for you."

"Man, look at your gorgeous bride! Did you think I wouldn't come? It was worth the trip, just to get an eyeful of this gal again! Congratulations ole buddy, you nailed yourself a reee..al beauty!"

Leading the way to the ballroom for their wedding breakfast reception, Graeme felt as though his heart would burst with happiness. He murmured, so that only she could hear, "Hello, Mrs McKenzie. Do you know how much your husband wants you?"

Julie replied, teasing him, with a simpering Southern Belle accent and fluttering her eyelashes, "Why, Mr McKenzie, Sir, your wife has got to behave herself for at least a few more hours. Then she'll show you, kind sir, what it's like to be a married to a very lovin' lady."

The ballroom was a picture to behold, but it was the huge pile of wedding presents that were stacked on a table next to the grand piano which staggered Julie and Graeme. Set up next to the heavily laden table were four mysterious artists' easels, with white cloths covering whatever was underneath. Seeing Graeme's puzzled look, Giovanni assured him, "All will be revealed in good time, my dear friends. By the way, I hid your car Graeme, so that your RAAF friends cannot doctor it. Here are the keys."

"Thank you, Giovanni, that was very kind and thoughtful of you, my friend," Graeme said. "Now where are our children? I think it's an appropriate time to give them their special presents, don't you, Mrs McKenzie?"

Graeme extracted the wash-leather pouches from the piano stool seat where he had secreted them earlier that morning.

Graeme crouched down in front of Stuart. "What happens, my son, when an airman becomes a pilot and is allowed to fly a plane on his own?"

Stuart pointed to the wings on Graeme's chest. "He gets those, Papa. It means he is a real pilot, like you, Papa."

"So, when a man gets his 'wings' and later has a son who also wants to fly, he gives his son a very special pair of 'wings'. These are my special 'wings', I am now passing them on to you, until you win your own set."

He pinned the miniature golden wings onto Stuart's jacket and hugged his son close. "Fly as high as you can and as high as you want, Stuart, my son."

Stuart looked down in awe at the shining brooch on his jacket. Then, standing to attention, he saluted his father with a very snappy salute. Graeme proudly returned his son's salute.

"Now, it's your turn, Lauren, my darling." Julie took the golden locket from the pouch. "Papa gave me this on my sixteenth birthday. It was the very first gift he ever gave me."

Julie fastened the locket around Lauren's neck. "Now we'd like you to have it, as a memento of our wedding day."

As mother and daughter embraced, Lauren said, "I'll treasure it forever. Thank you, Mama and Papa."

Graeme reached across and pulled out a scroll of paper, tied with a red ribbon. "Here you are my darling, wife. My wedding gift to you. Given with my eternal love."

Julie, a puzzled smile on her face, untied the red ribbon. The legal looking document stated: "This is the deed and title to the property known as MacCoinnich House', Sycamore Lane, Hockwold-cum-Wilton, duly registered in the name of Julie Anne McKenzie"

Graeme had given her the new house as his wedding present! Holding him in her arms, Julie whispered, "I love you, thank you, my darling."

Holding her tightly, Graeme whispered back, "By the way, while I've got you captive here for a moment, how come my secretary kindly reminded me when I checked in, that my brand new joint bank account, needed my specimen signature, before I could draw upon it?"

"That's my wedding present to you, my darling. We're married now, what's mine is yours. I never intend to let you go again, Graeme McKenzie. You are mine!"

Graeme kissed her, "I'll second that Mrs McKenzie, Ma'am."

The wedding breakfast meal ended with the traditional toasts. Billy, as best man, finished his toast, "I have known Graeme and Julie most of our lives. Today, I saw my greatest wish come true, a joining of two people who truly love and cherish each other. Now, without more ado, I give you our happy bridegroom, Graeme McKenzie."

Graeme, without any notes, began, "Julie and I welcome you all, and thank you for being present here today. Every bridegroom, at every wedding I have been privileged to be a part of, always begins his speech, 'on behalf of my wife and I', and today I know why. Today, at last, Julie is 'my wife', my very beloved wife, and I find I cannot stop saying the magic word 'wife'."

A ripple of laughter and applause echoed around the room. "All of you who are privy to our story know our marriage has been a long time in coming but, at last she is Julie Eve McKenzie, my very beautiful—wife! We deliberately chose to be married here at the Chateau Cornacchia, because the chapel has always had a very spiritual significance for us both."

Here Graeme spoke in Italian. "We give a million thanks, Maria and Giovanni, Monsignor Francis and to your extended family, for always giving both of us a warm welcome. You know how you have made certain things possible for Julie and I in the past, and because of this you will always have a very special place in both of our hearts. We thank you, most sincerely, our dear friends."

Reverting back to English, Graeme continued, "In a few days time, I shall be taking my family back to the Northern Hemisphere, there to begin a new era in our lives. But I can assure you that Julie and I will be forever thankful that we had the chance to be part of the 'down under' scene. A sincere thank you to you all," he grinned before he added, "on behalf of my wife and I." He sat down to thunderous applause.

It was time to cut the wedding cake. Billy handed Graeme his ceremonial sword. Graeme placed his hands over Julie's and, amidst the blinding and constant flashes of cameras, they cut the cake in the traditional way.

Kate, as Matron of Honour had, until now, taken charge of their Marriage Certificate. Beaming at the obviously happy couple, Kate laid the document in front of them. "Here you go, here it is, in black and white, all legal and official, folks. Mr and Mrs—at last!"

CHAPTER 86

After the final toast and the symbolic cutting of the wedding cake, Victor introduced Aaron Benedict who strode over with T.P. to the four covered easels.

Aaron explained, "I bought my wedding gift some time ago because I knew that this happy day would eventually have to take place. T.P asked me why I'd bought it. He didn't understand at the time, but today, when we met again, the penny dropped. Julie and Graeme, I present to you, at last, something that belongs to you alone. It's only been held in my safekeeping until now. Now I give it back to the two people to whom it rightfully belongs."

Pulling down the white cloth, he revealed the large framed original photo that T.P had taken of Julie, which had won him such fame, entitled 'A Mother's Secret Love.'

Julie gasped in surprise. On Graeme's face was a soft, tender expression. The master photographer had immortalised his wife, pregnant with his first born child.

Lauren whispered, "Is that me, Mama?"

Julie nodded, "Yes, darling. It won a big award for T.P. and it's worth a lot of money."

Graeme leant across and kissed his wife on her quivering lips. "Dear Lord, you looked like the beautiful Madonna herself, my darling one."

T.P stepped up to the other easel as the applause for Aaron's gesture died away. "Well, Julie and Graeme, my wedding gift goes back even further. Graeme, I know from Billy that this particular shot has a really deep meaning for you personally, so here it is."

With a dramatic showman's flourish, he pulled the cloth away to reveal the original photo of Julie with the bolts of silk that he had taken when she was just seventeen years old. But, T.P. had not finished his surprises yet. He announced, ruefully, "I didn't take the next two photos, but I wished I had, they're masterpieces. Julie and Graeme, my final offerings."

There, on the last two easels, were enlargements of the photos Doc Matthews had taken the day Stuart was born. The tender loving shot of the four of them earned loud, applause. But the one of Graeme and Lauren, with the newly born Stuart lying over Graeme's shoulder, brought many sighs and emotional tears.

Graeme thanked them profusely, assuring them all four photos would be prominently and proudly displayed in their new home.

Victor stood and made an announcement. "Ladies and Gentlemen, our bride and groom, and the Bridal Waltz."

Graeme took Julie in his arms. A circle formed around the dance floor, applauding them as they danced by. As the music ended, Billy smiled a secret, cunning smile as he conferred with Victor and a familiar upbeat tune resounded around the ballroom.

Startled out of their absorption in each other, Graeme grinned at Julie, "Shall we, Mrs McKenzie?"

Julie spiritedly retorted, "Of course. Mr McKenzie. Let's show 'em how it's done!"

Graeme swung Julie into the tango Jealousy. They danced the intricate steps as their wedding guests gasped in awe, shouting cries of "Ole". When the dance reached the ultimate conclusion, Graeme bent Julie backwards from the waist, before he swung her up for his 'victors kiss'.

The place went wild!

Lauren and Stuart stood open mouthed beside their Grandparents. Stuart asked, "Where did Mama and Papa learn to dance like that, Gramps?"

Grant McKenzie wiped a tear from his eyes, as he replied, wistfully, "A long, long time ago, but now, at last, they are making their own music, together."

Julie led Graeme to the grand piano, as she commanded,

"Come on, husband, play something with Lauren, while I get my breath back."

Reaching the grand piano, Graeme launched into a concerto styled arrangement of Lloyd Webber's, 'All I Ask of You'. Julie knew he had never played better, his happiness and his love for her showed in his every note. The applause and cries of 'Bravo, Maestro' echoed around the room, and Julie heard Maria whisper, "My goodness, he mucha one happy fella."

Graeme gestured for Lauren join him and was delighted when his young daughter upstaged him by playing many of the 'twiddly' bits. Father and daughter took a bow together to enthusiastic applause and cries of 'encore'. But Graeme held up his hand indicating he wanted to be with Julie.

As the music started again, he put his arm around Julie's waist, "Will you dance with me, Mrs McKenzie?"

He murmured in her ear, "Go and change, darling, it's time to go."

Graeme caught Kate's eye and bobbed his head toward Julie. Kate nodded back that she understood. They waltzed over to a door and swung out into the fresh air. He delivered her into Kate's capable hands, before rushing off to change from his uniform.

The two friends giggled like schoolgirls as Kate helped Julie out of her lovely gown and spotted the blue lace garter still in place, high on Julie's shapely thigh.

"That's going to be coming off, very shortly, methinks, Jules," Kate leered.

As Julie brushed her hair from its confining chignon, her new sycamore patterned wedding ring caught the light. Kate leaned over her shoulder, "The sycamore again, eh?"

Julie responded, "It brought us together in the first place, and now we are one, just as Graeme predicted."

Kate hugged her friend, "Have a really romantic honeymoon, my dear Julie. What am I saying? With him, what else would you have? Go make a run for it."

Graeme cruised to the ballroom doors and then hit the car horn, blasting it until he knew everybody inside had heard it. He gunned the motor and they both waved and laughed at the astonished but happy faces, before they drove away in a cloud of dust.

At the Country Club, Julie collected the keys to the Villa Rosa but Graeme insisted on first taking her back to the tree where they had exchanged their very first kiss.

Breathlessly, Julie murmured, "It hasn't changed, Graeme. I still tingle all over each time you kiss me, and I still go weak at the knees!"

With her head on his shoulder, they retraced their steps back to the Villa Rosa, just as they had done that first time. Unlocking the door and without putting on the lights, Graeme swooped Julie up in his arms and carried her directly into the bedroom. Graeme laid her on the bed and slowly, erotically undressed his bride.

Lying beside her, he murmured, "Julie, you are my heart's desire. I have dreamt of this moment, our wedding night, for so long. Your body sexually excites me to heights I never knew existed. I adore every part of you."

Julie felt her desire for him grow as though a flame was flaring inside of her. As she kissed his bare chest, he caressed her full breasts with their nipples already hard and erect.

She called his name as he thrust as deep inside her as he had ever done before. The erotic movements she was making under him excited him further. Then, with a final thrust, he spilt his seed inside of her as she trembled under him in her own mighty orgasm.

They lay together for a long while, gently kissing whichever part of the other's body came into contact, letting their heartbeats and breathing slowly return to normal. Julie looked at him silhouetted in the moonlight beside her, and softly whispered, "Mr McKenzie, you are one helluva satisfying lover. Mrs McKenzie enjoyed that."

Graeme chuckled, as he answered, "It never ceases to amaze me how each time it's as new as it was the first time with us. I just love making love to you, my adorable wife. What's more, I can now do it over and over again, whenever you want me. Now we belong to each other for always. No one can come between us, any more."

By mid-morning, feeling a little peckish, Graeme wandered into the kitchen in search of food. On opening the fridge, he found it well stocked with a variety of superb delicacies. A large note was pinned to the milk, 'Got to keep your strength up!' Laughing heartily, he took the note to show Julie, who was lying sunbathing on their private patio, with just a towel covering her nakedness.

"That's Kate's writing," she told him, with a giggle.

"Graeme, I want to fly with you again. Is it possible to arrange something?"

Graeme's face lit with pleasure at her suggestion. "Would you really like that, my darling? I'll ring a chap I know. Won't be a tick." He hurried off with a spring in his step, tunelessly whistling.

When he returned fifteen minutes later, with a full tray of delicious food and the aroma of fresh coffee wafting from the percolator, she sleepily said, "I think I'll keep you on, flyboy. Not only are you a satisfying lover, you can also find the necessary food when required."

He told her, "I have found us a doozy of a plane to take up at two o'clock this afternoon, darling."

At the base they met one of Graeme's brother RAAF Officers with his own private executive jet plane, who said, "There you go, mate. She's all fuelled and ready to go."

Graeme boosted Julie up the steep side of the jet, fastened her harness, and talked to her through the intercom, making sure she understood him clearly. Julie just sat back, relaxed, ready to enjoy being up in the blue heavens again with this man who just loved to fly.

Graeme broke into her reverie, "How are you, darling?"

"Oh, I'm just fine, my beloved. Say the words of the poem for me, Graeme."

Graeme quoted the words of the 'High Flight' poem as Julie reflected again on how important those two words had become to them. She gazed out of the window and under her breath said, 'I'm fine, Gran. He's with me, at last. I'm safe in his care. Thank you for guiding me back to him. My wildest dreams have come true at last. Rest in Peace, my Gran.'

Julie smiled as, out of nowhere, a vibrant coloured rainbow appeared in the western sky, and a voice in her head seemed to whisper, "Goodbye for now, Julie, my love."

Graeme's voice interrupted her reverie, saying, "Wow!

Look to the left Julie, darling. Can you see that rainbow!

What a beauty!"

Julie smiled, "Yes, I see it, darling," under her breath she murmured, 'Thank you, Gran.'

ADDITUM—JUNE 1999

The young fickle, flirtatious, warm westerly wind whispered regretfully to her Mediterranean mistral lover that she could not stay. She had to travel on northwards—somewhat urgently. He huffed a passion filled hot breath over her main body, causing a minor heat wave upon the Italian beaches, before he relented and released his lascivious friend.

She departed swiftly for she had news of much importance to pass on to the matriarch sycamore tree. News she knew took precedence over a mere fling, however passionate, with the mistral. Seductive and satisfying lover that he always was . . .

Sighing over the French coastline and swishing close to the large yachts beating up the English Channel, she headed for the greyer skies over London.

Zooming in once she had spied her destination, she caused dust to rise in small grey will 'o the wisps along the roadside, and freshly laundered washing to flap noisily on a thousand and one clotheslines.

Then . . . Aaah, there she was! Straight in front of her rose the tall, majestic, mature matriarch sycamore tree. The warm wind hastily smoothed her tattered edges and gently calmed her forward thrust. As though kneeling at the feet of a Royal Queen, she dropped softly beside the magnificent tree to deliver her news.

Waking from a pleasant daydream, the old tree sensed a messenger had arrived. Straightening her many boughs she gently shook herself upright, ready to receive and to hear what this young hoyden of a wind had to tell her.

In a breathless rush, divulged too speedily for the old tree to comprehend at first, the warm visitor imparted her news. So, there had been a wedding . . . a union of the two special people from her youth . . . they were returning . . . would be living close by . . . they were still speaking her of fondly . . . Yes, they would possibly pay her a visit . . .

Then the capricious siren wind was off again, swooshing briskly on her way to an Irish jig and a meeting with yet another of her full-o'-the-blarney friends.

The old mother tree smoothed her skirts and began to look forward to renewing her acquaintance with the giver of her life, the young, dark-haired woman and the tall blonde man . . .

Aaah, she sighed, they were together at last!

PART FOUR

FINALE

1999-2000

CHAPTER 87

The sleek Boeing 707, resplendent in its USAF executive livery, had been stranded at RAAF Williamtown for almost a week, the result of a bird strike. Now fully repaired, it resumed its return flight to RAF Mildenhall and, courtesy of Aaron Benedict, contained some very special passengers.

Julie found it hard to believe that only three months ago that she had begun her quest to contact Graeme. Now having had to say 'good bye' to Kate Reynolds had been devastating.

Graeme explained to his parents, with Daisy's help, how close Julie and Kate had been. "Indeed, had it not been for Kate's determination in contacting me, Julie could have died in that coma."

Throughout the long night, they lay together on a narrow single bunk. Graeme promised, "Once we land, we'll go straight to the house . . ."

A small voice, from the bunk over their heads, asked sleepily, "Will there be room for pets, Papa?"

With a mischievous grin Graeme answered, "Yes, honey, there'll be as much room as you need, but . . . your pony? Well, he'll have to be stabled further down the road . . ."

Before he could finish, a small, pyjama clad body landed on his midriff. The now fully awake young face was looking wide-eyed at him.

"Did you say MY pony, Papa?"

"Well, only if he likes you, of course," Graeme teased, as Lauren squealed and smothered his face with kisses. "Now sleep, little angel, so that you're nice and alert, and the pony will adore you as much as your old Papa does," he said as he boosted her back onto the top bunk.

Before re-joining Julie, he checked the opposite lower bunk and gently pulled the blanket over Stuart. He was still coming to terms with the glorious, almost unbelievable feelings of protective paternal love his children invoked in him. Feelings that, until a few weeks ago, he had thought had been denied him by a cruel act of Fate.

At Mildenhall they fondly farewelled Graeme's parents, and Billy left them in a hurry to get back to Italy, to the impending birth, promising, "I'll ring as soon it happens."

Graeme's personal batman, Sergeant Morris Wyberg, was unable to stop grinning. "Cor, it's great to have you back! Sir, you look ten years younger. Mrs McKenzie, Ma'am, it's a great pleasure to meet you. Don't turn round Ma'am, but . . . there are about a thousand eyes watching us. Listen, Sir!"

A wave of applause began to emanate from all around them. Bodies of service personnel hung out of open windows, cheering and clapping. Suddenly someone yelled, "Three cheers for the Air Commodore and his family!"

Graeme grinned roguishly and took an exaggerated bow before coming to attention as his C.O. appeared. Air Vice Marshall Brown shook his junior officer's hand, "Great to see you back, Graeme."

The senior officer heard the tenderness and pride in Graeme's voice as he introduced his family. The Air Vice Marshall responded, "Mrs McKenzie, it is with the greatest pleasure that I meet you. I am delighted to see you restored to perfect health. You are a most welcome addition to our Air Force family."

With a gentle smile, Julie responded, "Sir, I thank you most sincerely for the help you gave to Graeme, allowing him to join me when I needed him most."

The Air Vice Marshall came face to face with the smiling Lauren. "My goodness, Graeme, this little beauty is definitely all your own work. Welcome, young lady. You are going to break many hearts around here in a few years' time."

Graeme grinned and winked at Lauren behind the Air Vice Marshall's back.

Turning to greet Stuart, the older man was pleasantly surprised to receive a very snappy salute from the little chap wearing his father's miniature 'wings' on his jacket.

"This handsome chap I see already has his 'wings'. Officer Cadet material in about fifteen years' time, methinks."

Finally, with great courtesy, he said, "Mrs Green, a warm welcome to you."

"So, Graeme, what are your immediate plans?" he asked.

"Sir, we are off to visit the house we have just purchased in Hockwold-cum-Wilton, and work out our immediate furniture needs. We'll all squeeze into my apartment for a few days."

Lauren tugged at his hand and whispered, "And go to see my pony, Papa."

Graeme smiled at her, "Yes, honeybunch, of course."

Stuart piped up beside him, "And my tree house, Papa."

"Of course, my son, can't forget a man's hideaway, can we?" Graeme tussled Stuart's hair and grinned at his son.

The Air Vice Marshall watched the loving interplay, more proof of Graeme's capabilities in communication—as the spontaneous reception he had just received had borne witness.

Turning to Julie, a thoughtful Air Vice Marshal asked,

"Would it be too soon to invite you to our Mess Dinner in two weeks' time Julie? I'm sure my wife and a few more of the ladies are just dying to meet you."

Julie looked enquiringly at Graeme, "Is that okay with you, darling?"

Graeme could not contain a cheeky grin, "Do you know what you're letting yourself in for?" Turning to his superior, he added, "Yes, of course, it'll be fun. Thank you, Sir, we accept."

"Right then, Hockwold eh? Nice little spot, very suitable area for a man of your rank, Graeme. Ideal place to bring children up, Julie. See you at the weekend."

Bundling everyone into the car, Graeme ordered, "Okay, Sergeant, onward to Hockwold."

He directed Sergeant Wyberg down a sycamore tree lined avenue, causing Julie to gasp in delight. Halfway down the lane, Graeme pointed to a head-height, red brick wall, and the Sergeant turned into the driveway between two imposing, black wrought iron gates. An elaborate plaque upon them announced, 'MacCoinnich House.'

Graeme pressed an electronic remote gadget and the impressive gates swung open. The stately, two storey, red brick house, with its mullioned windows and black slate roof, was surrounded by rose bushes of every hue, together with a stretch of immaculate lawn and a mass of other flowering shrubs and trees.

Graeme helped Julie out of the car as her eyes feasted on the beautiful, glorious sight of their new home.

The Sergeant gallantly opened the door for Daisy, but was too late to help the children, who bounded out of the car, whooping with glee.

"Well, darling, what do you think?" Graeme asked anxiously.

Julie threw her arms around his neck and exclaimed, "Darling, it's absolutely gorgeous! Let's explore!"

Graeme unlocked the front door and, before she could take a step, whisked a laughing Julie up in his arms and carried her over the threshold, in true romantic tradition.

They held hands and admired the sunny dining room, the large airy lounge and the conservatory atrium containing an indoor full-length pool. Julie gasped as she and Daisy marvelled at the pristine, modern, state-of-the-art fitted kitchen, the walk-in pantry and the separate utility room.

Cries of, "Mama, Papa, come and see our rooms," brought them to two large bedrooms, separated by a bathroom, on the sunniest side of the house. Each room had floor to ceiling French doors and extra-large, built-in wardrobes.

Graeme, seeing Daisy was reluctantly holding back, gently took her arm and led her to the other end of the hallway. They entered a spacious room with its own en suite bathroom and private access to the garden. He gently asked, "Will this be okay for you, Daisy?"

"Oh, Graeme, its lovely, look at the size of it. I can get a three-piece suite in here, besides my bed! It's perfectly lovely, thank you, Graeme."

The three final rooms downstairs included two guest rooms with en suites.

The other room Graeme had selected for his study. It was an airy room with enough space for his desk, easy chairs and walls lined with bookshelves. A man's room.

"Now both of you rascals stay down here while I show Mama the upstairs, which I warn you, is going to be our own private space. Peace and quiet away from the hordes of children we expect you will bring home with you. Go and explore the garden. Stuart, my son, your tree house is in the large oak tree, outside your bedroom. Daisy, if you and the Sergeant would like a cuppa, the makings are in the kitchen."

Taking Julie's hand, he led her upstairs to what he had called, 'our place.' As he guided her into the bedroom, she sighed as she gazed at their special room. It had a large bay window, and a walk-in wardrobe the size of a single bedroom. The palatial bathroom had all the ambience of a luxury Roman bathhouse.

Opening a connecting door from the bedroom, Julie saw a room with its own covered balcony over-looking the garden. It was the one Graeme had described as a private sitting room, or perhaps, hopefully, a nursery?

Julie threw her arms around his neck and kissed him in a passionate embrace. "Graeme, my darling, it's perfect! I love every inch of it. I love you, my wonderful husband."

Daisy had made tea and also had explored the kitchen from top to toe. It more than met with her approval.

Back downstairs now, Graeme said, "Come on, this way." He opened a door almost hidden by purple wisteria growing rampant over the red brick wall. It opened onto a large field where a grey dappled pony was contentedly grazing, until he spotted the human invasion and trotted towards them.

Lauren was overwhelmed. "Oh Papa, he's so beautiful."

She ran her hands over his head, telling him, "You are a handsome boy. He is called . . . Oh! It says, 'Pegasus—The property of Lauren Catherine McKenzie'. Papa, he's mine!"

"Ummmm, if you are said young lady, my dearest daughter. Now over there," Graeme pointed to the end of the field, "those buildings are the stables where this fine young fella is looked after. He has a very appropriate name for our family. 'Pegasus' is the Flying Horse!"

Graeme hugged his first-born. "Now we must go, but we'll be back tomorrow. Say your own 'good-bye' to Pegasus, we'll wait for you in the car."

Putting his arm around his wife, Graeme said huskily, "I just love being their father. It gives me such a great feeling of belonging. I've got negotiations in hand to purchase that field for Lauren. Now, I must make sure Stuart doesn't feel left out. Where is he?"

Julie hugged him, "Guess? He's inside his tree house. He's over the moon with it, darling. He doesn't feel left out at all. You are a wonderful father figure, Graeme McKenzie."

CHAPTER 88

Somehow they had all fitted into Graeme's small apartment that night. They had dined on takeaways and had all fallen asleep early.

Next morning, Graeme rang Richard Fraser QC who agreed to an appointment that very morning. Daisy begged off saying she would rather stay put and let her body catch up with itself.

After an emotional hour spent with Richard Fraser, they started upon their mammoth furniture buying list.

It came as no surprise when Stuart opted for an aerospace theme and, with his father's eager and enthusiastic help, selected everything aeronautical in the shop. Lauren, not unexpectedly, chose animals for her décor.

Their last stop was at the local car dealers, where Julie found just the station wagon she had in mind.

"A station wagon?" Graeme had queried.

"For the dog, Papa," Stuart seriously informed him.

"What dog? We haven't got a dog," his father protested with a puzzled expression on his face.

Julie sighed, he still had a lot to learn. "If we don't acquire one for ourselves, Graeme, one will acquire us," Julie informed him. "They follow Lauren home from school, or turn up on our doorstep with the biggest, saddest, brownest velvet eyes, begging to be let in. Or, they simply smell us out from a hundred miles away, as the greatest, softest touch put on this earth for canine enjoyment."

She said, resignedly, "Graeme, my love, as you will soon discover, we shall own a dog within weeks of moving into the house. Usually the largest, scruffiest, mangiest, bag of fleas you have ever seen in your life. So we might as well be prepared, darling."

Graeme chuckled with laughter. "Lauren, what is it with you? You are a regular, female version of Dr Doolittle."

For the next few days, the house just buzzed with trades people from morning to night. But all work stopped when a crate arrived from Australia. There was no mystery to the wedding presents inside. But, again, the range of gifts and generosity of the people staggered them. Daisy reckoned there were enough gadgets for her to set up the best kitchen anyone could ever hope or wish for.

Further crates also arrived from New Zealand. For the two children it was Christmas all over again, as they unpacked all of their favourite toys and games. With the help of their father and his batman Sergeant, everything was soon hung or placed, just as they had envisaged.

With her first Mess Dinner looming, Julie had carefully planned what she would wear. She settled upon the hot weather 'little black dress' from the 'Four Seasons' collection. She added a long scarf in R.A.F. colours and her amethyst jewellery. Finally her hair was arranged in a classic chignon. Julie relished the admiring look on Graeme's face, knowing she looked classically elegant.

Entering the base dining room on his arm, after being announced for the first time in an official capacity as 'Air Commodore McKenzie and Mrs Julie McKenzie', Julie felt every eye in the room swing toward them.

When the ladies retired, leaving the men to partake of the traditional port, Julie felt a pleasant warmth building between her and the other women.

As one wife stated, "He's one of the most popular officers here. It's great to see him so happy."

The next morning, Billy rang to say Marisa had been safely delivered of a son. "He's just a smidgen, but has a good pair of lungs on him."

Julie was anxious for her family to meet Graeme and her children, so telephoned her brother Don. He arranged for the rest of the family to be at his home.

As they arrived at Don's house, they heard angry voices coming from inside.

Graeme calmly said, "Daisy, love, be a dear, stay in the car with the children. Julie and I will spy out the land first."

Graeme murmured, "Remember, we are legally married—with no encumbrances, my darling. Nothing can hurt, or separate us, ever."

Graeme rung the house bell and for a few moments there was an ominous silence. Then Don opened the door with his wife Stella at his side. Evidently she had been crying.

Julie said quietly and calmly, "Hello Don, good to see you again."

"Yes, yes, Julie," Don said in a harassed voice. "Come in both of you. We are all here, even Dad. Where are your children?"

Graeme answered, "They're in the car with their Nanny, Don. We heard raised voices. If there's to be any dissension, I'll not bring them in, if you don't mind."

Stella looked close to tears again. "It's Lisa and Carole . . . Carole has said some terrible things . . . Lisa has slapped her face . . . telling her to grow up."

Don grudgingly said, "Well, you had better come in, our little place is just modest. Not what you are used to as an officer's wife, Julie, I suppose."

Graeme squeezed her arm and shook his head in a 'let it go' gesture. They followed Don to where Julie's sisters and their families were sitting on opposite sides of the room . . . like adversaries lined up for battle, thought Graeme. Nobody spoke. Julie spotted her father.

"He'll not recognise you," Carole called after her.

Julie was shocked to see how shrunken her father had become. She softly said, "Hello Dad. It's Julie."

Her father said in a weak voice, "Ah, Julie. Did that Graeme fella come back for you?"

Julie beckoned to Graeme. "Here he is, Dad. We're married now."

Julie's father studied Graeme and in a clear, strong voice said, "Thank goodness you came to your senses, lad. She's loved you since the first moment she set eyes upon you. Take good care of her, son. She's the best one of the whole, motley lot."

With that, he fell instantly asleep.

Carole, in a voice full of vindictive malice, said, "You always were his favourite, Julie. Dad will not realise you've married your lover, before your first husband was hardly cold in his grave!"

Julie's face paled as she staggered against Graeme. He put his arm around her waist. This was going to be far worse than he had anticipated!

Furious that Carole should malign Julie so dreadfully, Graeme turned to face them all. "Do you all feel the same way as Carole?"

Lisa stood up and hugged Julie. "No, we do not! She's been this way since she came back from New Zealand, green with envy."

But Carole was not done with her older sister yet. She launched herself towards Julie, but Graeme stepped swiftly between them, holding Carole at arm's length.

Softly, in a voice as cold as ice, he said, "Don't touch her, Carole. I heard from Kate Reynolds how you handled the news of Anne's death. Julie and I both became widowed at an adult age and we decided there was no good reason to prolong, or delay the inevitable. If that offends your sensibilities, then so be it. We are legally married in every sense of the word, and nothing you say, or can do, will ever alter that fact."

Carole struggled out his grip, but he stood protectively in front of his wife.

Carole spat out, "What about your love-children, eh?

You weren't widowed when you fathered them, Graeme McKenzie. Got a bit on the side away from home eh, did you? You caught him twice, Julie girl. Two pregnancies! A nice investment with his high rank. Done all right for yourself there, haven't you? No wonder his poor wife drank herself to death!"

This time Graeme's face was like thunder as he replied, in a voice full of anger, "That's enough, Carole. You go too far!"

"I'll say she does!" Lisa stood up. "I slapped your silly face once before, Carole. Now I think, Don, it's time she was asked to leave."

Don joined Lisa as he said, "Carole, go home.

Think about what you've done to someone who has never hurt you, who has always been kind and considerate towards you. Get real, Carole."

Carole turned on her heel and slammed out of the house.

Graeme saw how shaken Julie was, her face white and strained. He took her in his arms, asking softly, "Do you want to leave, darling?"

It was Stella who answered, "No, please, don't go yet. Please, we want to apologise and I'd love to see your children, Julie. Please stay."

Graeme, with his arms still around Julie, looked around at the others. "We came to invite you all to a family wedding breakfast. We know you were unable to come to Australia to our wedding. We deliberately chose to be married at that chapel; it was neutral country for both of us. We didn't want to bring any excess baggage with us from our previous marriages. We wanted a fresh new start, and we hoped you'd understand the reasons for us doing that."

He smiled lovingly down at Julie. "As to Carole's assumption, that I'm a good catch for Julie, I'm afraid she got it around the wrong way. Julie is the 'good catch' for me. I don't think any of you realize what a successful businesswoman your sister has become. She is a very, very wealthy woman, by anybody's standards, and got that way by sheer talent and hard work. Don't think of my rank as anything more than a job promotion, compared with what she has achieved world-wide."

He paused, letting his words sink in, before he continued, "Think about it, folks. Come and admire the material things her efforts have brought to our marriage, but also listen to what people have to say about your sister as a person. She is loved and respected everywhere she goes. I am just the lucky man she happens to love, and to whom she brings even greater happiness every day I am with her." He smiled tenderly at Julie before he continued.

"Our children adore her and so do I. Now, if there is anything else sticking in your craws, spit it out. Let us clear the air, once and for all. She is my dearly loved wife, and we have two wonderful children."

There were sheepish looks as one by one they came and hugged Julie and shook Graeme's hand.

Stella asked, pleadingly, "Bring your children in, please, Julie. I'll make us all some tea."

Graeme inclined his head towards Julie, "Okay?"

Lisa came and sat beside Julie, as she quietly told her, "That man worships you, Julie. He's quite a dish."

Julie smiled at her sister, saying, "He's a rather special human being, Lisa. In spite of his deprecating words about his rank, he's one helluva man, in every sense. I adore him, I always have. It just took me a few more years than usual to realise it."

Graeme re-entered the room holding Stuart's hand, closely followed by Lauren and Daisy. "Now children, these good people are Mama's sister and brother. Everyone, this is our son, Stuart, our daughter Lauren and our good friend and the children's Nanny, Mrs Daisy Green."

Everyone was minding their 'P's and Q's' after Carole's outburst, although they were taken aback as everyone always was by Lauren's likeness to Graeme.

After an awkward hour, Graeme raised an eyebrow at Julie. "Sorry everybody," she said quietly, "we must go now, we're due at Graeme's parents for dinner. The family wedding breakfast will be in about a month's time. You're all very welcome, so please come. When we settle on the date, I'll ring you all."

Settling his family into the station-wagon, Graeme silently uttered, 'Whew! That was tricky!'

CHAPTER 89

The new purchases had been arriving daily and Julie had supervised her sometimes-bemused husband into placing items exactly where she wanted them. Graeme's athleticism was somewhat tested to its extremes as he hung Stuart's model airplane collection from the high ceiling. Then, yet again, when he mounted Lauren's frilly four-poster bed canopy.

An enthusiastic group of young RAF cadets had been rounded up as 'volunteers' on moving day by the indomitable Sergeant Wyberg. Their promised reward: 'the best muffins you have ever tasted since leaving your mother's knee'.

Graeme grinned disarmingly at her as he said, "Thank you, Daisy. My popularity and reputation has risen by hundreds of points, because of your culinary skills. The only trouble is—we'll never get rid of them. You have no idea what healthy, lusty appetites these young 'Erks' have!"

Daisy knew, in spite of his jovial protestations, he was walking on air. By mid-afternoon it was done. The children were busy sorting through their own possessions. Daisy had been shooed away by Julie, with strict instructions to rest until at least six o'clock, when Graeme had promised to take them to the local pub for dinner. Graeme whisked Julie off her feet and carried her to admire their own special domain. A delicate creamy pale green, self-patterned wallpaper adorned the walls. Cream tulle sun filter curtains billowed in the gentle breeze wafting through the large doors of the open bay window. To add a contrast, there were heavy, damask silk, side drapes and padded pelmets in Julie's favourite colour, soft avocado green. On the specially made king-sized bed was a matched quilted bedspread and cushions.

The cream and green theme was echoed in the loveseat, on the shades of the bedside lamps and also the ladies chair beside Julie's dressing table. Julie's crystal and perfume bottles, struck by the sun, sent prisms of colour dancing around the walls.

Opening the mirrored doors to the huge walk-in wardrobe-cum-dressing-room, Julie showed Graeme how she and Sergeant Wyberg had hung all of his uniforms and regalia together, separate from his more casual civilian clothing. Graeme also discovered two large chests of drawers had been assigned to him. He nodded his approval at the way his wife had organised him. Turning to her side of the massive room, he admired how all of her clothes were similarly hung, with the appropriate shoes and accessories set out on shelves under the garments.

Looking admiringly at the shared room, he knew the satisfaction of being a fully committed married man—and it felt great!

They sauntered in to inspect their palatial, peach marbled bathroom. Again Graeme admired Julie's tasteful touches in the subtle lighting and mirrored walls. Definitely a room in which to indulge one's hedonistic fantasies.

Laughing happily, they investigated the small sitting-room, presently furnished with a natural cane suite and coffee table, covered in bright, terracotta coloured cushions.

He took Julie in his arms as he told her, "I sincerely hope this becomes a nursery, before very long, Julie, my darling."

The Westminster chiming of the front door bell interrupted them. Lauren called, "Papa, there's a letter for you to sign for." They perched around the room on the unopened boxes, in his brand new study, as Graeme slit open the impressive looking package. As he had anticipated, when he saw the name of his Queen's Counsel on the envelope, it was the completed adoption papers! He looked at Julie, a slightly stunned look on his face. Then he announced, in a voice husky and cracking with emotion, "We're all McKenzies!"

Julie flew into his arms and he hugged her tightly. "Oh, my dearest, my darling, at last!"

Lauren, perched on the corner of his desk, whispered, "I'm now officially your daughter, Papa?"

Graeme unable to speak just nodded. Stuart, precariously standing on top of a wooden crate, beamed at him, "And me too. Am I now Stuart Cameron McKenzie, Papa?"

Graeme managed, with difficulty, to get the words out, "Yes, Yes! At last! My darling, beautiful wife and my gorgeous, delightful children, we are ONE—we are all McKenzies!

On hearing the commotion, Daisy had hurried quietly to the kitchen. She picked out the bottle of champagne Graeme had specially put there to await this momentous occasion. Gathering up a silver tray and crystal champagne flutes, she marched triumphantly back to Graeme's study with her spoils. "Thought this might be the right moment, Graeme."

With just one word, "Brilliant", Graeme opened the bottle. He poured three full glasses and two smidgens of the bubbling brew, announcing, "No man could be happier than I at this moment. To Us—The McKenzies!" Clinking their glasses together, they responded in unison, "To Us—The McKenzies!"

Lauren said excitedly, "Let's ring Nana and Gramps." Graeme looked at Julie, his face working to control his emotions at Lauren's spontaneous response. Julie smiled lovingly at him, knowing how touched he would be by Lauren's suggestion. "Yes, let's," she agreed.

When Grant McKenzie answered, Lauren enthusiastically shouted, "Gramps, I'm a McKenzie, just like you—and so is Stuart . . . Gramps? Gramps, why are you crying?"

Graeme gently took the receiver, "Hi Dad. Yes, it's true the official papers just came. We're just a little bit excited . . . Yes, we've had the toast . . . fortunately Daisy remembered the champagne . . . Yes, we are going down to the pub shortly . . . We moved in today. What a great day it has been, eh? Yes, she's here." He handed Julie the receiver. "Hello, Mum. Isn't it exciting? I don't know who was the more stunned, Graeme, or the children . . . Yes, thank you . . . No, it was Lauren's first reaction . . . The feeling is truly reciprocated, Mum. They both adore you and Dad."

Alicia McKenzie was sobbing happily, as she said, "I'm so happy, Julie, my dear. At last you and Graeme are a whole family. You've waited so long for this day. Thank you Julie for making him and us so happy."

The local pseudo Tudor pub, 'The New Inn', had a warm, mellow ambience. The ex-Metropolitan Policeman publican had already noted the presence on his 'patch' of his newest neighbours. Now he found he had the pleasure of serving them or the first time.

He introduced himself. "Sir, it is a pleasure to see you and your family. We know you have just bought the MacCoinnich House, and have been moving in. I am William Read and I run this place with my wife, Kitty."

Graeme shook the hand proffered to him. "Well, thank you, Mr Read, for your welcome. I'm Graeme McKenzie and this is my wife, Julie, my daughter, Lauren, my son, Stuart, and our dear friend Daisy Green."

William Read's face broke into a wide smile. "McKenzie eh? Well, you've certainly bought the right house!"

A middle-aged man approached their table. He was dressed in a countryman's tweed suit, and a thick shock of white hair topped his outdoor healthy appearance. "Hello, I am Jack Daniel, the local vet." He shook hands with Graeme and turned to Lauren. "You, young lady, must be the proud owner of Pegasus. I've seen you from my surgery window."

Lauren's face was wreathed in smiles as she answered, "Yes, I'm Lauren . . ." she hesitated slightly before giving a truly wide smile, and added, "McKenzie." "He's a great pony and so intelligent, I love him."

"Well, lass, if you need me, I'm only next door." He ruffled Stuart's hair, "If you need a dog to walk, come and see me, young man." Julie rolled her eyes and groaned at Daisy, "Better start saving up the scraps again, Daisy, we'll have a dog soon! See, I told you, Graeme, it happens every time."

The next visitor to their table introduced himself as, "I'm the grocer-sort-of-cum-butcher, Alec Dale." He was a man in his mid-sixties, medium height and with twinkling brown eyes. Graeme did the introductory honours again, bringing Daisy forward as the main foodstuff buyer for their household.

They received a further visitor. This time it was a woman in her late forties, dressed in a well-cut navy business suit and flat walking shoes. "Hello, I'm Susan Blake, the local G.P. Unless you are extraordinarily and abnormally fit and healthy, no doubt our paths will cross, sooner rather than later. Although you, sir, will no doubt be covered by the base medical staff."

Graeme nodded in agreement with her last assumption. Susan Blake turned her attention to Julie. "I hear you are from New Zealand. Well, my surgery is on the right side of the village green. If you would like to register with me, I'd be only too happy to add you all to my list."

There were no further interruptions, although they could feel others of the pub clientèle were watching, sizing them up. As they left, there was a chorus of 'goodnights' from all around the room and a host of smiling faces.

Graeme had set the outside lights timer and now the house was basking in the soft, welcoming lights of the many lanterns hanging around its walls and gardens. "Oh, Graeme," Julie sighed, "It's so beautiful."

"It's just as though it's saying, 'Welcome Home, and come on in," breathed Lauren, enchanted by the sight.

"Papa, it's a fairyland house," Stuart exclaimed, as he took hold of Graeme's hand.

"Yes, my son, that it is. It's going to be a house with much love and happiness inside it. Mama and I make that promise to you both." Graeme gazed at Julie and saw the radiance upon her face.

Daisy whispered, "Thank you, to whoever guided me here. I'll be in your debt for the rest of my life."

Inside the house, several table lamps with large, cream silk shades lit the lounge. These highlighted the leather settees and easy chairs, upholstered in a deep peach. Cream silk curtains complimented the pale apricot walls and the magnificent Persian hand-knotted rug with its peach, white and chocolate brown tones pulled the whole room together. Julie had left the large space in the bay window empty, pretending she still had yet to decide what she wanted there. But, unbeknown to her husband, a big surprise would be arriving the next day.

Daisy excused herself saying she was 'pooped'. The children were soon curled up in their respective beds, and Graeme and Julie found themselves alone in the beautiful lounge.

Graeme said, "It has really been such a special day, my darling. I love you so much." Julie whispered, "Your wife adores and desires you. Take me to bed, please, flyboy."

CHAPTER 90

The next morning they awakened to the 'Dawn Chorus' echoing all around their garden, sounds Graeme had not heard for many years. He sighed with deep satisfaction. Julie had made their special room a sanctuary, a cocoon, a love-nest.

"Penny for 'em, sexy flyboy?" Julie murmured suggestively, running her hands over his 'modesty'.

He growled, "Careful minx, you're on mighty dangerous ground," his body acknowledging she had fanned the embers of a fire always ready and willing for ignition. A fire only she could ignite into a white-hot heat and then satisfactorily extinguish, until it was required again. She groaned with pleasure as he rolled on top of her, fully aroused and erect in seconds. She arched her body beneath him as he plunged deeply inside of her, pleasuring them to a mutual, shuddering climax.

"Oh, sweet heaven, what a marvellous way to start the day," Julie murmured. "Mr McKenzie, you are one very satisfying lover."

As if reading his thoughts, Julie said, "Finding this home was an inspired piece of work on your part, Graeme. I love every inch of it, my darling husband."

Graeme gazed at her, knowing that, as usual, with the uncanny instinct they seemed to jointly possess, she had anticipated his thoughts. Later they joined their children for a noisy, pre-breakfast swim in the sunny conservatory pool—just enjoying being together.

A special delivery was due and Daisy and Julie connived to get Graeme out of the house. Julie suggested he take Lauren and Stuart to introduce them to their new school. Daisy urged, "You could perhaps pick up some fresh bread and milk for lunch."

Graeme hid a smile; he had never done such a domestic task before. He wondered what Sergeant Wyberg would make of it. Graeme chuckled, imagining the look of horror on his Sergeant's face. Confessing quietly to Daisy, she took pity on him and gave him explicit instructions on what he had to buy. They watched him walking proudly with an excited child on either side, trying to keep up with their father's long strides.

Daisy hastened to retrieve an identical rug to the one in the lounge and unrolled it in the bay window space.

A delivery truck arrived and a beautiful, burred walnut grand piano was unloaded and set up adjacent to the bay window. The professional installer checked the tuning and declared it ready to play. They just had time to close the lounge door and make a hasty retreat back to the kitchen, as they heard Graeme and the children returning.

Graeme displayed his purchases as proudly as a primitive cave man bringing home the 'kill' for his womenfolk. Lauren and Stuart fell about laughing as Lauren said, "Mr Dale asked Papa if we wanted sliced or un-sliced bread. Papa didn't know. He thought all bread came sliced!"

Seeing the funny side himself, Graeme grinned, shrugged and protested, "Well, it always does in the Officer's Mess. Anyway, both of these brats are duly enrolled and can start tomorrow. It was great handing over their birth certificates and being asked if I was their father." He squeezed Julie tight in his arms as he murmured, "I did enjoy that part, Julie, darling."

Julie held his face in hers. "Well, my darling, I have a surprise for you. Close your eyes."

She led him to the lounge as Daisy signalled to the children to keep quiet. Julie said, "Happy housewarming, my dearly beloved husband."

Graeme feasted his eyes upon the elegant grand piano. "Wow! Julie sweetheart, it's magnificent!" He ran his fingers reverently over the highly polished surface before lifting the lid. He sat on the stool and tinkled the keys, stretched his fingers and began to play, 'I Can't Stop Loving You.' A smile of pure pleasure lit his face, as he said, "Couldn't think what to put in this space, eh? My wife, the devious minx! It's perfect, a million thanks, sweetheart."

Julie kissed him and motioned to Lauren to come and play a duet with him. They grinned at each other, before happily launching into a complicated concerto, two pairs of hands flying in unison. Graeme nodded toward Lauren and mouthed to Julie, "Not bad!"

Daisy had quietly taken Stuart back to the kitchen; a smiling Julie also crept out. The melodious notes rang around the house, filling it with a sound so sweet that it brought tears to Julie's eyes. This was something she had dreamed about for so, so long. She stood leaning against the wall in the hall and did not hear Graeme coming until his arms went around her and his mouth covered hers. "Thank you, once again, my precious, precious darling. My cup runneth over, I have really missed my music."

Giving Julie yet another deep and passionate kiss, he grinned boyishly at her before hurrying back to the piano.

Eventually, Graeme and Lauren dragged themselves away from the piano to join the others for lunch. They both advanced upon Julie and smothered her with kisses. Recovering her composure, Julie proposed, "It's time to sort your study, Graeme, darling? Your haven away from all Your annoying domestic distractions." In this special masculine domain, Julie had added floor to ceiling bookcases, a bar, and an antique desk with a comfortable executive chair. There was also a pair of leather easy chairs, each with its own wine table and floor standing reading lamp.

Hidden in a corner cupboard sat a TV so that Graeme could keep up with world affairs. In accord with his wishes, she had kept the colour scheme to a deep maroon and gold, with brass fittings. Shaking out the heavy wine coloured velvet curtains with gold tie back tasselled cords, she sighed proudly, "It's all yours, my darling husband, and it suits you. Masculine, comfortable, practical and I hope, well loved."

From halfway up a stepladder, hanging T.P.'s picture of Julie, Graeme looked down upon his own personal domain. "Darling, it's every man's dream room."

For the next hour they assiduously opened the many boxes and stacked the shelves. He passed to Stuart many of his airplane models, but had kept a selection that he had personally flown throughout his service career.

In one dust-covered box, Julie found many framed testimonials and photographs from prominent people. Many thanked him for his assistance and all were personally signed. "Where have these been hidden, Graeme?" Julie asked curiously.

"Anne stored them in the attic, darling, when she found out about Lauren. She called me a hypocrite, amongst other choice names."

"Well, Mrs Julie McKenzie wants them on the walls! Get a hammer, Graeme. We'll put them up here, beside the desk. Darling, I am so proud of you and what you have achieved!"

They had finished and were admiring their joint achievements when Daisy knocked discreetly upon the door. "Excuse me, but the Air Vice Marshall is here to see you, Graeme." Graeme raised his eyebrow at Julie. "Must be important."

Julie and Graeme came to the door of the study. Julie said warmly, "Welcome to our home, sir."

Martin Brown whisked off his hat. "My goodness, Julie, from what I have seen it's truly magnificent. But I'm afraid I am not here socially, my dear. I need to speak with Graeme, urgently."

Still smiling, but trying to calm her lurching heart, Julie suggested, "I'll rustle up some coffee."

She tried to control the fluttering in her stomach. This was the first time they'd had a military incursion into their idyllic space. She admonished herself, "Get a grip lady, he's a high-ranking officer. He has an important role to play—grow up, Julie!" She shook herself and hurried to get the promised coffee.

Relaxing in an easy chair and munching upon a cookie that melted in his mouth, the C.O. sighed, "God, I hate to take you away from this heaven on earth you have created for yourselves. But . . . there's trouble brewing and the powers-that-be in Whitehall have requested your presence, Graeme. You sorted out their last mess, and they want you again. Aaron Benedict specially requested you."

At the mention of Aaron's name, Graeme automatically raised his eyes to gaze at the picture 'A Mother's Secret Love', Aaron's wedding present to him and Julie. It had been hanging on the wall for less than an hour.

Following his gaze, Martin Brown drew in an appreciative breath, asking, "Is that your son or daughter she is carrying?"

"My daughter, Lauren, sir," Graeme replied and explained the history of the portrait. "If Aaron Benedict wants me, I know it must be serious. When?"

"Three days' time, five at the most, I'm afraid."

Graeme looked pensive, "The children start school tomorrow . . . it's a new country for them, strange ways and customs to adjust to. I'll need a couple of days with them, sir. After that, well I'm all yours."

The C.O. rose from his chair wearily. "You shall have your two days. I'll get Sergeant Wyberg to get your gear together and have the arrangements made. Now, my boy, how about a quick 'reccy' of the manor? My wife will be full of questions when she knows I've been here. She was mightily taken with Julie, and I am under strict instructions to make sure you both take a full part in all the social events from now on. On a personal note, I can see, for myself, the improvements marriage to Julie has already made to you, m'boy."

Graeme chuckled out loud, agreeing with his boss but, silently under his breath, 'And how! You don't know the half of it!'

Graeme relished showing off his wonderful home with its unique and elegant décor created by Julie. Finally, the two men strolled around the garden, admiring yet more of Julie's handiwork. Reaching the wisteria covered gate, they leaned upon it companionably, watching as Lauren schooled Pegasus over some small jumps, with Julie and Stuart giving vocal encouragement from the side lines.

Martin Brown sighed, "Yes indeed, Graeme, heaven on earth."

CHAPTER 91

After his C.O. had departed, Graeme telephoned Aaron Benedict in Washington. After warm greetings, Aaron said, "We need you here, old son. I wouldn't pull you away from the delectable Julie for nothing, but it's getting 'hairy' out there. We need to put an end to it quickly. Our so-called friend is throwing his weight around again and needs putting in his place," he chuckled down the telephone line. "I cannot think of anyone else who can do that so precisely, so succinctly, than you, my friend, We need your special magic again. How soon can you get here?"

Graeme answered, "I've got two days grace before I'm required to report for duty, so expect me, say, in four days' time, Aaron." He heard a gasp and twirled around to see that Julie had heard his last statement. Hastily making his farewells, he gathered a white faced Julie into his arms. "It's okay, darling. I'm only going to Washington for talks. I'm not going on active duty, nor will I be in any danger whatsoever."

Julie clung to him. "I know I shouldn't react so stupidly. I'm sorry, darling. Please forgive me. I'm so proud of you and the work you do, Graeme. I guess I'm just a bit vulnerable at the moment . . ."

He kissed her tenderly, "I love knowing you care so much what happens to me, Julie, my darling. It's something I haven't been used to and I'm wallowing in it."

Graeme explained what had been arranged. It would only be after those special, precious days that he needed to fly to Washington. That night, their lovemaking was especially tender. They both realised that the first stage of their marriage, the honeymoon, had come to an end, for the time being. The world and its on-going troubles had once more forced its way into their lives.

Next morning, amongst the usual organised chaos that the first day back at school and kindergarten always brings, Graeme did his best to bring some sort of military order to the way things were moving, but to no avail. Later, it came as a surprise to him when both children were ready on time.

A girl hailed Lauren, who excitedly told her parents, "Mama, Papa, this is Christine, she has a pony named 'Polly'. Her mother is the Doctor."

The two girls walked on ahead, animatedly talking about their respective ponies. Julie squeezed Graeme's arm, "Yes! A new friend on her very first day. Brilliant, just what she needs!"

Julie let Graeme have the pleasure of signing in as her principal guardian and next-of-kin. He swallowed hard as he came to that part; Julie gave him a knowing smile as she saw him hesitate. Graeme rubbed his chin as Lauren disappeared to her classroom. "I've always heard that most mothers have a good howl. Now I know how they must feel. It's as though I'm giving her away to a host of strangers!"

Julie softly laughed, "Come on, you old softie, time to divest ourselves of the other one."

Graeme groaned as he took Stuart's hand in his. "Oh God, I'm losing two of them in one morning. How am I going to survive this?"

At the kindergarten, Graeme proudly signed similar next-of-kin forms. They went to wish their little son 'good-bye', only to find he was busily hoisting up a flag, under the 'bossy' instructions of a chubby pair of female twins. Graeme crouched down on his haunches, "We're off now, Stuart. Have a happy morning, son." Stuart gave him a blindingly happy smile, "Bye Papa, I've got to get the flag up, 'cos the Captain says so."

Julie chided him, "You've been usurped, my darling Air Commodore, by the Navy!"

Daisy and Julie had pre-planned the family wedding menu and had settled upon the 21st August as a suitable date. At the large supermarket in the adjoining City of Cambridge, Julie, with consummate ease, filled the supermarket trolley, ticking off the items that she and Daisy had previously decided were needed. Graeme expressed his amazement at how easy she make it seem.

Julie replied, "I guess we've done it so many times for the fashion crowd. We'll need a few willing hands to help out as waiters or waitresses, can Sergeant Wyberg arrange that for me? There must be a few likely lads or lasses that need a free feed."

He looked at her quizzically, "Do you miss that glamorous life, darling?"

She retorted, "Miss it! I haven't had either the time or the inclination to miss it, Graeme. I adore 'entertaining' you my darling, and never want to do anything else."

As Graeme drove them around the district for a bit of familiarisation sightseeing, he pondered how she would respond to a suggestion Aaron Benedict had posed that morning. He stopped the car on top of a hill and they got out to enjoy the panoramic view. Julie knew he was anxious to either tell, or ask her something. She wrapped her arms around his waist as they stood admiring the view. "What is it, Graeme? What's troubling you, my darling husband?"

Graeme grinned as he held her close. "You know me too well, Mrs McKenzie. How do you feel about coming to Washington with me? I'll be busy during the day, but we'll have the evenings and the nights together. Aaron asked me this morning if you would consider coming."

"Graeme!" Julie flung her arms around his neck and kissed him fully, "Oh, yes please. I'd love to come with you, my precious one!"

Graeme chuckled with delight at her response, adding, "I had better warn you to pack some of your delightful sexy gowns. There's a White House visit on my agenda, and a very special International Ambassadorial Reception."

Julie squealed with delight, "Oh yes, being married to you, my sexy flyboy, does have its advantages—apart from the obvious attributes of course. Oh Graeme, how exciting, I'll be so proud, my darling husband."

"And I will be equally as proud to have you by my side, my beautiful minx. We leave in two days' time and we shall be away for five, perhaps six days."

She held his face in her hands and looked directly into his brilliant blue eyes. "Let's get one thing straight, my sexy flyboy. I'll come with you any time, anywhere. You need never have to ask."

Later, Julie, ecstatic with delight told Daisy of the exciting news, asking, "Will you be okay here, on your own?"

Daisy gently took Julie by the shoulders as she admonished her, "You and I made a pact, long before I agreed to come with you to the U.K. Julie dear, I'll always be there to look after the children. Nothing has changed. His needs are paramount now. If he wants you with him then that's how it's got to be. You two belong to each other now. He's had a lonely life, lass, up to now. He already looks younger, healthier and happier with you around. Anyway, I've always got his parents to call upon. They'd be here like a shot. Go; wow them in Washington, Julie, my love."

That evening, Graeme and Julie sat together at his desk, writing out invitations to their family wedding breakfast. Stretching her back after an hour of writing, Julie looked across the desk at her husband; a blonde lock was drifting across his forehead. As he brushed it back into place, his eyes met hers and his face broke into a smile. It was the same heart-melting smile he had given her all those years ago, when he had seen her for the first time in her very first grown-up dress.

He softly asked, "What are you thinking about, darling?"

Dreamily she replied, "Oh, a certain social, when we first danced together . . ."

He softly interrupted, "You wore a dusky pink dress and I couldn't take my eyes off of you. I'd never seen anything so beautiful in my whole life. You're still the centre of my world, but now you are my beautiful wife and woe betides anyone who tries to put us asunder!"

The next day, after getting the children fed, watered and on their way out of the house, Graeme retired to his study to make the final arrangements for the Washington trip. Daisy shooed Julie away, telling her to go and pack her case.

Julie enjoyed once again picking the clothes she knew Graeme most admired her wearing. He had advised a delighted Aaron earlier that morning that Julie had accepted the invitation to accompany him and he had secured a tentative list of the social events he and Julie could be attending.

Julie had gasped in astonishment when she read through the programme exclaiming, "Wow! Do you have to be at every one of these, darling?"

Graeme had looked sheepishly at her. "Actually, no. If I had been on my own I wouldn't have gone to a quarter of them, but now, with you coming with me . . . well . . . it's like this . . . Look, I want to show you off. I am so proud of you and how you look in those fabulous designs of yours . . . I just want to be seen with you. I want to boast 'eat your hearts out fellas, she's all mine' . . . I've never been able to do that before. Do you mind, darling?"

Julie had collapsed with laughter upon their bed, tears running down her cheeks as he had stood looking down at her in astonishment at her reaction. She had spluttered, "You looked so much like Stuart then, just like a little boy caught out in something he shouldn't be doing."

Growling at her, Graeme had fallen onto the bed beside her, and had proceeded to show her that he was no 'little' boy, but a grown-up man with great desires and designs on his wife. At the completion of their sensuous, passionate union, Julie had whispered, "I'm so proud you want to show me off, Graeme, my darling. I'll do my very best to come up to your expectations. I adore you, Graeme Stuart McKenzie."

CHAPTER 92

The USAF V.I.P. jet carrying Julie, Graeme and a whole raft of senior officers, from every branch of the defence forces of the U.S.A. and the U.K., swiftly flew across the Atlantic. Julie, elegant in a cream silk, non-crushable trouser suit, and an orange and chocolate striped shirt, chatted animatedly to the equally fashionably dressed Liz Connors. Liz was the fashion editor of one of New York's leading magazines, their paths having crossed at several fashion shows.

Until now, Julie was unaware that Liz was also happily married to a U.S. Army Colonel. Julie was eagerly catching up on all the latest gossip and Liz was anxious to learn what had caused Julie to 'drop out' of the current fashion scene.

When the tall figure of Graeme came looking for his wife, Liz gasped in surprise. "Now I see the reason I haven't seen you all year, you have remarried! No wonder I didn't recognise your name on the passenger manifesto. It's McKenzie now, not Field!"

She gave Julie an exaggerated 'glad eye' look, as she exclaimed further, "Hey girl, you snared yourself a heartbreaker here! He's caused many a young and not-so-young heart to flutter on the Washington scene. But no one could get near him! How did you manage it?"

Julie and Graeme's eyes locked in a secret smile. Graeme answered in a light tone, "Well, she 'snared' me, Mrs Connors, at the ripe old age of . . . what was it? You were ten years old, weren't you, darling?"

Julie joined in his light-hearted banter, "Ummmm, we go way, way back, Liz. We have known each other for most of our lives, we were next door neighbours. We were married just last month, after we had both become recently widowed."

Seeing that Julie was happy and enjoying her talk with Colonel Connors' wife, Graeme excused himself and returned to his favourite place, in the cockpit. Liz Connors watched him, "Gee, that man is a legend himself. I'd like to look you up later and do an article on both of you."

Before Julie could open her mouth to reply, Liz resumed, "Are you still designing, Julie? Have I missed the latest output? Just a mo, weren't you ill or something earlier this year?"

Julie laughed, "Liz, so many questions! Yes, I was ill, and no, I haven't had time this year. I've sold my interest in 'Maison Chevalier'. Graeme and I were married in Australia last month, and we've just moved to England. We live near Mildenhall, and our children go to the local school."

Liz Connors noted the 'our children', but let it lie, intending to dig deeper later. Her encyclopaedic memory activated itself, doing an immediate recall of Julie's fashion successes and of Graeme's prowess and testimonials. They certainly made a glamorous couple.

She tuned herself back in as Julie asked, "Are you going to the State Reception, Liz?"

"You betcha! Wouldn't miss that one, Julie. It really is such a glittering, glamorous night. Better even than the Oscars—believe me! Everyone who is anyone will be there. Wear your most snazzy gown and 'the lot' as far as jewellery is concerned. For the White House affair, black tie and all that, black is also the most preferred colour for us girls. We aren't expected to outdo the First Lady, not the done thing. What else are you down for?"

"Everything, I think, judging by the list Graeme gave me, Liz," Julie admitted rather ruefully. "Thank goodness, I've a rather wide range to choose from. All he has to do is change from one uniform to the next."

"Indeed, yes," Liz agreed. "Sometimes all mine has to do is change is his shoes, while I have to start from being buck naked and work outwards. I don't know how the lesser ranks wives cope sometimes, poor darlings. There's an idea, Julie, design an economic line that those gals can afford."

When Liz went off in search of her own husband, Julie idly expanded upon Liz's suggestion. Before long, she was busily sketching ideas on her note pad. When Graeme returned and spoke, she looked up at him, slightly unfocused, "Ugh? What did you say, darling?"

Graeme's own eyes twinkled, "Would you like some lunch, sweetheart? What are you designing?"

Julie blushed, "Sorry, darling. It was something Liz suggested about the wives of lower ranks, trying to ring the changes on a limited budget. It gave me an idea."

He took her hand, "Come, lunch with your old man." "Old man, indeed!" Julie scoffed. "From what I have been hearing you are the 'Don Juan' of the Washington set!" Graeme guffawed with laughter. "I really hadn't noticed. What a hoot! You had better stick close to me when Liz Connors tells them all I was 'cradle-snatched'. He pulled her to her feet and kissed her cheek. "But, I wedded and bedded the sexiest minx a man could wish for!" Still chuckling, he led her to the buffet in the rear of the plane. He introduced her right along the line, "Everybody, please meet my wife, Julie." Julie smiled acknowledging the many 'hellos' and 'welcome Mrs McKenzie'. Graeme was obviously a very respected member of this international group.

She heard a voice at her elbow say, "Hello, Mrs McKenzie, Ma'am. Have you dropped any keys of late?" Julie's eyes opened wide as she recognised the face of the gallant young officer from that fateful, yet wonderful day in New York.

"Hello again, Ma'am. I'm on the C.O's staff, although he speaks most of the languages anyway. That's why they always want him as the negotiator. He understands their language and therefore their culture. I've rather a soft number really. The C.O. is looking so well, since your marriage." He shuffled, somewhat shyly. "Oh, please excuse me, Mrs McKenzie, I'm out of line."

"No, not at all, Jeremy Jones," she responded, "see I remembered your name! I am delighted that you were on hand in New York to retrieve my keys. Yes, you're quite correct, he's much happier with his life now."

Graeme came back to her side saying, with a wide grin, Well Jeremy, judging by the huge smile on your face, Mrs McKenzie hadn't wished you'd been more of a 'butterfingers' in New York then?"

"No Sir! Rather the opposite!" his interpreter replied enthusiastically. He looked from one to the other of this happy, devoted pair. "No Sir! Definitely not a butterfingers."

Graeme pointed out the many memorials as they hummed along the wide streets of the nation's capital, while Julie marvelled at the many buildings she had previously only seen in pictures. They arrived at their hotel to be greeted in the foyer by the tall, smiling figure of Aaron Benedict.

Protocol was blown to the wind as he twirled Julie off her feet, "God, girl, it's good to see you again!"

Julie grinned widely at him, "The feeling is reciprocated, Aaron my dear, dear friend. Now I'd kill for a nice cuppa, will you join us?"

"No way am I going to be 'gooseberry' tonight. You love-birds settle in, I'll send a car for you tomorrow Graeme, my friend, at nine o'clock. Then the driver can come back, Julie, say at ten? You can direct him to take you wherever you want to go."

They were shown to an enormous suite overlooking the White House gardens, which were floodlit and looking so elegant. Though the White House appeared to be a lot smaller than Julie had envisaged.

Later, stretched out on the soft king-sized bed, they relaxed after being cooped up in the plane all day. Graeme held her naked softness, a gentle pillow against his hard muscular torso, relishing the closeness of each other, knowing the other was going to be there, always and always and forever . . .

. . . To their joint astonishment, a musical alarm clock playing 'Yankee Doodle Dandy', informed them it was half past six—in the morning! They had slept for eight hours, solid.

Graeme grinned at Julie's slightly shocked face. "Good morning, sweet lady. Boy, I feel good. What a sleep! Ummm, you feel good enough to eat, Mrs McKenzie, especially around this part . . ." He nuzzled her nipples as she writhed erotically under his firm hold, but this only seemed to urge him to a greater ardour and eventually he flipped her over onto her stomach and mounted her from behind. Julie moaned in rapture as he thrust his now enormous erection inside of her.

A sensational, erotic feeling overwhelmed his every sense, as he felt an insatiable, primitive sexual lust of male power. His swollen penis ecstatically responded to her sexual invitation, to invade her body with his own concupiscence. He quickened and deepened his thrusts, plunging into her until he felt he was about to burst. Then in a moment of pure joy, he released and spilt his seed deep inside her. She called his name as she reached her own quivering orgasm. For several minutes they lay joined, letting both of their racing heartbeats return to normal.

Graeme, still lying half on top of Julie, murmured, "Dear God! Wasn't that something else again, my darling?"

Julie smiled her secret cat-that-got-the-cream smile. "Oh yes, if I'm not pregnant now, after all of that, well! It felt as though you were in the very central core of my being. Graeme, my darling, I seem to have an insatiable sexual appetite, as far as you are concerned!"

Graeme rolled her over and tenderly said, "I love you so much, my ravishing, cara mia. It's a sensational feeling to know you are enjoying it as much as I am, sweetheart. If we have made another baby I'll be over the moon, but don't let's leave it to chance. I'm going to be taking you to bed every chance I get during the next few days, my own darling."

"Graeme, I adore you more each day, if that is at all possible," she said, as she passionately turned to kiss him again.

"Well, my dearest wife, you rest there for a few more minutes while I shave, shower and order breakfast. Do you have enough U.S dollars to do whatever you want today? I'll be back by five, we are due at the reception by seven."

"Please don't worry about me, just concentrate on your mission," she urged him. "It's so important, much more important than anything else at the present time. I am so proud of you, my darling husband."

This support from the one person in the world he loved, more than life itself, was still new to him. For far too long his life had been a lonely, empty shell.

CHAPTER 93

Emerging from the lift into the massive foyer of the hotel, Julie knew she looked elegant in a trimly tailored, two-piece coffee coloured linen suit, worn over a vanilla cream silk camisole. As one bellboy was heard to murmur to his colleague, "If only my cuppa of Cappuccino looked half as delectable."

A Marine Sergeant held the car door open and asked respectfully, "What is your pleasure, Ma'am?"

"I'd like to drive past some of the famous buildings, and then onto the main shopping area, please."

Once over his reserve at having such a V.I.P. passenger to squire around, the Sergeant proved an entertaining and amusing guide. Before they both realized it, it was lunch time.

Julie apologised for taking up so much time, saying, "Just drop me at a large department store. I have a long list to fill for my son and daughter. Many thanks; I'll get a cab back."

She wandered around, selecting items that Lauren and Stuart had asked her to bring home. Finally, she could not resist visiting the Ladies Fashion Wear. With the old thrill she always experienced at seeing her own creations displayed, she noted the store's latest range of 'Flowers of the Field' clothing was attracting a fair number of customers.

But her fingers itched to just change the display arrangement around to the way she had designed. As she stood contemplating, an assistant approached, noting Julie was wearing the latest 'Flower of the Field" suit.

She did a double-take as she recognized the customer. "Mrs Field! . . . I was with you in New York when you swept the board, winning all the awards."

Julie cried, "Mary! Yes, of course. You were such a calming influence and helped me so much. I'm Julie McKenzie now. I remarried after my husband John died last year."

"Please excuse my crassness. What are you doing in Washington?"

Julie explained, "My new husband is an R.A.F. officer here on an assignment. I'm fortunate enough to be able to accompany him." Julie hesitated. "Mary, who's in charge of the 'Flowers of the Field' display?"

Mary indicated a smartly dressed young woman, "Our Section Supervisor, Miss Topski. Why, is something wrong?"

Julie bit her lip, "Look, the ensembles are put together wrongly." She edged closer and touched the offending ones. "They would look so much better if that top and that skirt were reversed. That one has the incorrect colour combination, it should be . . ."

"Is there something wrong?" a haughty voice asked.

Mary turned, "Miss Topski, this is Mrs Julie McKenzie, the creator of the 'Flowers of the Field' label. Mrs McKenzie was just pointing out that we have mistakenly put the display together wrongly."

Julie could feel the frost emanating from the young Supervisor and hastily said, "Please forgive my interference, it's just that, as you'll see by the directive that came with your order . . ."

To her surprise, the young woman blushed and said, in a low voice, "Would you please show me how it should be done, Mrs McKenzie?"

Within five minutes the alterations were done. Mary sighed, "She's young and ambitious, but she's willing to learn. Will you be attending the Ambassadorial Reception tonight, Julie? We've had several customers looking for a suitable gown."

"Yes, I'm really looking forward to it, and to a very grand White House function tomorrow night. There's also an officers mess dinner, a 'dining in' Graeme, my husband, called it. The following evening, an official night at the Metropolitan Opera in New York. Whew, it's going to be hectic, but wonderful!"

Mary queried, "What are you wearing? You don't need a 'dresser', do you? I could come to your hotel after work and help you—as I did in New York."

"Would you really, Mary? I'd love your help. I must confess I'm more than a little nervous. It's my first official outing as Graeme's wife. I do so want to make a good impression."

Mary asked, "Where are you staying, dear?"

Julie pulled out her room key and read off the hotel address.

"I can be there by just after five, it isn't far. It will be my pleasure to help you, honey."

Later, Julie struggled from a taxicab under a prodigious stack of brightly wrapped packages. She was happy to see the staff car pull in and Graeme alight.

He greeted her with a look of mock horror on his face as he relieved her of some of the load, exclaiming, "Good grief woman, have you bought up the whole of Washington in one go?"

As they ascended in the lift, Graeme leaned against his wife. Tilting her face to his, he covered her lips with a passionate kiss.

As usual, when he kissed her all other thoughts flew out of Julie's head. She stood pressed in the corner of the lift, completely at his mercy. They were still locked in a close embrace when the doors opened.

A U.S. Colonel, whistled his appreciation at the scene, asking, "Would you like me to press the UP or the DOWN button to give you more time, buddy?"

Graeme pushed himself away from Julie's body and grinned at his fellow officer. "Nope, it's okay Al. I'll continue this in the privacy of my suite. See you later at the Reception, 'buddy'."

Julie swung her carry bags at Graeme's retreating figure, "I'd almost accuse you of doing that on purpose, Graeme McKenzie!" She stalked to their suite saying in mock rage, "Boys will be boys—must show their peers how sexy they are, how macho. Ugh!"

Graeme chuckled at her mock feistiness. He also had to admit to a feeling of smug satisfaction. With Al seeing him in the lift kissing a beautiful female, he knew his reputation rating was sure to soar. Speculation would be rife! Rumour and gossip spread like wildfire when the officers met together. He could not wait to see their faces when he introduced them to—his wife!

Julie had stomped into their suite pretending an affront. She kicked off her shoes, quickly took off her jacket and camisole and unzipped her skirt, letting it fall on the floor. She flung herself into his arms, and gave him back as good a kiss as he had given her in the lift.

She relieved him of his cap, sending it sailing onto an armchair, undid his jacket and slid it off his arms, unzipped his trousers, letting them fall around his ankles and began to massage his already hardening maleness. With that he scooped her up in his arms and laid her on the bed, entering her with one swift thrust, plunging into her again and again, roughly, passionately, with his huge erection filling her completely.

It was a coupling of pure lust, erotic and animalistic. Their mutual climax was a long, shuddering, mind-bending release that left both of them gasping for breath.

Julie looked at his face on the pillow beside her and whispered, "Oh boy! That'll teach me to try and tease you, flyboy. But I can be a slow learner."

Graeme quirked an eyebrow and declared, "Well, that sure beats a G & T with the boys!" He pulled her towards him, "Ummm, I do like this married lark, sweetheart?"

Julie clung to him, "I love you so much, Graeme, it's almost indecent how much I enjoy our sex life!"

"Indecent? Woman, never think that! I hope we'll always enjoy an uninhibited sexual relationship." He chuckled at the thought, "Me and my 'modesty' will always be ready and willing to oblige."

Julie giggled, then was shocked to hear the clock beside the bed tinkle. "Graeme! It's five o'clock, Mary will be here soon. Come on sexy flyboy, into the shower, double quick time, m'lad."

"It's okay, the car will not be here until eighteen-thirty . . . Who's Mary?"

Julie divested herself of her jewellery, calling out Mary's details.

Julie emerged through a cloud of perfumed steam, looking ten years younger than her age, and absolutely delectable. Graeme gently kissed her lips. She fully responded to him before running into the bedroom, calling over her shoulder, "Later!"

"Promises! Promises!" came a loud masculine howl from the depths of the bathroom.

Julie quickly donned a pair of black lace briefs and black, lace-topped stockings. She lifted the 'Green Goddess' gown off its hangar. With its strapless boned bodice, no bra was needed. The dress still fitted her like a second skin, even though she had not worn it since New York, before Stuart was born.

She heard the knock at the door and let Mary in. Mary sighed, "It's still a marvellous gown, Julie. You never put them on the open market?"

"No, I designed them for one man, the man I married." She smiled reflectively, "Graeme darling, Mary is here."

The silk gown, in Jade Green, was a strapless, semi-sheath dress with a unique 'fishtail' skirt and semi-bustle back. It had a richly embroidered bodice of white opals and beryl semi-precious stones. The matching full-length, floating coat had three quarter length sleeves and a stiffened mandarin collar. The coat's collar, cuffs and full-length borders were decorated to match the bodice.

Graeme came out fastening his cufflinks, and stopped as he saw Julie—his own 'Green Goddess'—looking stunning.

Mary and Julie gaped at HIM.

Julie stammered, "WOW! Move over Prince Charming! Darling, you look gorgeous! Oh, sorry Mary, this hunk is my husband, Graeme McKenzie. Graeme this is Mary O'Brien."

Graeme graciously took Mary's hand as she struggled to find words, "Hello, Graeme. My goodness what a glamorous pair you are!"

Julie put on her amethyst earrings and pendant and high heeled, jade green sandals. Mary quickly brushed Julie's hair up into a chignon. She then critically looked Julie over before declaring, "There, you look absolutely lovely. You'll be the Belle of the Ball." She grinned at Graeme. "You, sir, will have all the ladies swooning. Look, here's my number, call tomorrow if you'd like my help again. It would be a pleasure, my dears."

A few moments after Mary had gone, Graeme gave Julie a jewellers' box. "Look what I found at lunchtime." He fastened a bracelet of amethyst set in a gold filigree sycamore leaf pattern around her wrist. She gasped in delight at the exquisite item.

"Sycamore leaves and amethyst", she exclaimed, "they'll always be special to us, thank you, my adorable husband."

"Are you ready, my JEM, i.e. Mrs Julie Eve McKenzie?"

"As ready as I'll ever be, my darling," she replied, gathering up her evening purse. As she swished past him, he was made aware of a cloud of provocative French perfume assailing his nostrils, and the sensuous rustle of silk.

CHAPTER 94

The magnificent floodlit Foreign Embassy building had Julie uttering an awestruck 'Wow'. A long line of limousines mingled with military cars of every description.

Handing their official invitation to the U.S. Marine usher, Graeme took Julie's arm and threaded it through his own. They followed what looked like an Arabian Sheik and his bejewelled, veiled consort. As the line moved slowly forward, Julie let her eyes roam around the beautiful room, determined to drink in every morsel of this superb occasion.

The ballroom was long and elegant. A hundred or more crystal chandeliers sparkled above their heads, reflecting the glittering scene below many times in the surrounding mirrored walls. The rich maroon velvet, floor to ceiling draperies added warm colour, while the central gleaming floor issued a tantalizing welcome to any would-be dancers. A breath-taking scene that Julie would later describe as coming straight from a 'Gone with the Wind' movie set.

The women were gowned in a dazzling array of silks and satins and were adorned with more jewellery than Julie had ever seen. Their throats, hairdo's, ears, together with many other places, sparkled with jewels.

The men were resplendent either in evening suits or in a more varied and colourful array of military uniforms than Julie had ever seen. Add to this with their many lanyards and gold coloured braid, they seemed to be trying to outdo their womenfolk by wearing every colour of military uniform imaginable. Added to this 'colour' there were so many medals in evidence that they could not possibly have been won in two lifetimes, let alone one.

Sneaking a glance at Graeme, with his upright military bearing and his stylishly tailored, dignified mess dress uniform, Julie's heart melted. He looked so distinguished, so handsome and so masculine, compared with some of the dandified men around her.

She stopped herself ogling like 'a country hick from the sticks', as Daisy was fond of saying, as Graeme murmured, "We are next, sweetheart."

The uniformed aide announced, "Air Commodore Graeme McKenzie, and Mrs Julie McKenzie."

Graeme advanced forward with Julie on his arm and shook hands with the Ambassador and his matronly wife. With a kindly smile of welcome, she held Julie's hand for a second or two longer than was usual. "My congratulations, Graeme, you have a very beautiful consort. And to you, Julie McKenzie, on your recent marriage to this very pleasant young man. My daughters are great fans of your clothing range, my dear. They have at last become stylish young women. I'd despaired of them ever giving up the Bohemian 'op shop' look. I'd like the opportunity to chat with you further. Enjoy your evening, my dears."

Julie, mesmerised and absolutely floored by the Ambassador's wife's warm words, asked, "Do you know them that intimately, Graeme?"

Graeme did not answer straight away, as he escorted her into the dining room. His hand was on her elbow, acknowledging greetings with a wave of his hand, a subtle nod of his head, or a raising of his eyebrows. Julie was conscious of many stares and heard more than one gasp of surprise at seeing Graeme.

Graeme seemed oblivious to the reaction he was getting, "Ummmm, what was that, darling? Oh yes, I dine with them and Aaron most times when I'm in Washington. Ah, here is our table. Good they have seated you next to Aaron."

Julie was swept up in a powerful hug as Aaron Benedict spotted her. "Wow! Perfect as usual, Julie. That is one helluva gown, Mrs McKenzie, and you look truly great in it. Come, don't let that husband of yours keep you all to himself."

"Ladies and Gents, this glamorous woman is Julie McKenzie, Graeme's beautiful wife. Julie, meet Colonel Alan and Mrs Lyn Beaumont, USAF, Monsieur Yves and Madame Caron Roget, from the French Embassy,

Count Luigi and Countess Maria Mendoza, from Rome, and my partner for tonight, my niece, Ellie Benedict."

Julie acknowledged her fellow dinner guests, who seemed rather exotic and aristocratic looking, except for Aaron's niece. She smiled warmly as Julie asked, "Do you live in Washington, Ellie?"

"No, I'm a teacher and I live in Hawaii. As I am here on a research scholarship, Uncle Aaron roped me in."

She looked admiringly at Julie. "He has a great deal of time for your husband and has told me a little of your joint backgrounds. I must say I find your love story fascinating, and you are finally together, at last."

Julie smiled, warming to this bubbly, chatty young woman, who now edged closer. "You must have felt some surprise as you made your way here. Well, to put you in the picture, it appears your husband has been rather a lone wolf for many years. Now, out of the blue, he turns up with you! Not only are you exquisitely dressed, but you are beautiful. Wait until they find out what your background is—they'll be falling over themselves to talk with you."

She giggled conspiratorially, "Your presence with him here tonight will have really rocked the boat in some quarters!"

Aaron then seated himself between them, picked up her hand and kissed the back of it. "You coping okay, honey? You'll get used to us; we don't actually bite, well not in mixed company, anyway."

With an almost paternal look on his face, he looked across Julie toward Graeme. "He's looking great, Julie. He did a great job today, actually managing to make some progress by getting the main protagonists talking. They had steadfastly refused to do so, until he threatened to bang their heads together. He told them his two young children had more acumen in their juvenile heads than all of them put together."

"Some of them looked very surprised at his down-to-earth and very un-diplomatic approach. As one startled leader exclaimed, they didn't know he was married let alone had two children. By the time they had all seen his 'brag book' of you, the children and your wedding photos, the air around the table was extremely convivial, with everyone wanting to talk at once."

"You're a miracle worker, Julie, my lovely. He always was the best at his job, but you have 'humanised' him."

Julie blushed at his compliment and turned to look at the man in question as he conversed animatedly in Italian to the Countess on his left.

Graeme happily saw how well Julie coped with all of those around her. She had a sparkling wit, matching all the repartee from Aaron, or Yves Roget. She fended off Colonel Al Beaumont's lurid comment about passion in the hotel lifts, with an innocent, "But we ARE married, Al."

Julie answered the questions about her fashion successes amusingly and honestly, admitting, with candour, "Yes, it was hard work, but very rewarding, both financially and in a personally satisfying way. No, I have no plans at the present time to return to it. I am more than content just being Mrs Graeme McKenzie."

After the dinner, as an orchestra began to play and people started dancing, Graeme murmured, "Shall we?"

Julie smiled at him, "Yes, please."

They excused themselves from the table and he opened his arms to her and she glided into them, enfolded in his warm, safe and secure embrace.

He murmured, "At last, I get to hold you close to me and tell you how much I love you."

He twirled her around, noting once again how he was getting envious looks. "I've never enjoyed myself at these functions until tonight. Now I see it all with a different perspective, because I have you at my side. Before, it was such a lonely, almost boring chore for me."

Softly, he added, "Proud of you doesn't cover half of how I really feel. Julie, cara mia, I feel as though my real life is just beginning."

As they danced, tongues were wagging, questions were being asked, "Who is she?" Those in the know smugly answered, "She's his new wife, his childhood sweetheart."

Many who had tried to snare Graeme in the past had to grudgingly admit he looked very happy, a lot younger and very much in love with his wife. Others admired Julie's gown and passed on the information of her fashion prowess.

As the dance finished, Graeme took Julie to meet some of his fellow officers in the international brotherhood of those who love to fly. Julie was greeted warmly by this very cosmopolitan group, whose current topic of discussion was the merits of buying or leasing a plane to further their flying pleasure.

Their voices were mostly European, but Julie also detected an Australian twang, and a distinctive American drawl. All of them vociferously and emphatically agreed that to lease an airplane was the only way to go. The conversation ebbed and flowed as Julie suddenly realised she had solved the problem of what to get Graeme for his next birthday.

Seeking out the man who seemed to have his finger on the pulse, she quietly asked, "How much would it cost to lease a four to six seater executive jet in England?"

"If you had landing and hangar rights, say at an R.A.F. base, it would be even cheaper. I would say that probably half to a million English pounds would buy a five year lease. At that price, still a bit of a dream, eh?"

Julie looked at her watch and saw it was almost midnight. The time had flown past and she had to admit that she really had enjoyed herself. Graeme quirked an eyebrow at her, asking the silent question, "Ready?"

When they made their farewells, the Ambassador's wife gave Julie her home telephone number. "Come and take tea with me, before you return home, my dear."

Alone in their hotel suite an hour later, Graeme leaned over Julie's naked body as she lay beside him after they had pleasured each other into magical heights of passion he had never known existed, or were possible.

Kissing her lips gently, he declared, "My darling, precious wife, tonight was how I had always envisaged my service life should be. I was truly bursting with pride every time I looked at you. I love and adore you, so much."

Julie curled languorously around his body, and whispered, sleepily, "Goodnight, Prince Charming, your wife worships you."

CHAPTER 95

In the cool, air-conditioned luxurious suite in the elegant Washington Hotel, an alarm clock beeped discreetly. But Graeme was already stirring; years of being awake by a certain time meant his body was automatically attuned.

Last evening was so perfect. Julie, in her 'Green Goddess' gown, had looked a million dollars. The flame of his male ego had been fanned as never before, and he had drawn great satisfaction from the openly envious stares.

She slumbered on, only waking when he had showered, dressed and was offering her a morning cup of tea.

Seeing he was already dressed in his uniform, she looked anxiously at the alarm clock, but relaxed when she saw they had not overslept. "Someone gave me one heck of a sleeping pill last night!" She stretched her body, suggestively. "I feel so good, Graeme, you are just a wonderfully satisfying lover."

He chuckled as he bent down to kiss her, saying, "Funny that, they were the self-same words I was thinking about you earlier, my delicious, sexy minx . . ." He checked his wristwatch.

She gently stroked his face. "Graeme, Aaron told me what you accomplished yesterday and remarked it was nothing short of a miracle. I just wanted you to know I am really proud of you, my darling husband. I'll be thinking of you all day and I love you heaps."

The same Marine Sergeant was holding the door for him and eagerly asked, "Good morning, Sah. Will Madam require me later?"

"No, not today, thank you Sergeant." Graeme hid a smile when the Sergeant's face visibly dropped in disappointment. Graeme mused, yet another conquest for the delicious Mrs McKenzie.

Julie lay in bed pondering, perhaps go shopping? Perhaps work on the designs that were buzzing around in her head? She shrugged and procrastinated. She was about to step into the shower when the telephone rang.

Thinking it might be Graeme, she hurried to answer it. It was not Graeme but a woman's soft voice telling her, "Theresa Romanski here, Julie. I wondered if you had time to lunch with me today, my dear. My daughters are so anxious to meet you."

"Mrs Romanski, I'd love to, thank you. What time would you like me to arrive?"

"Julie honey, don't dress up, come casual and would you bring your portfolio? The girls would love to see something straight from the horse's mouth, so to speak. I'll send a car for you, say at twelve noon, my dear?"

Julie hugged herself in glee as she skipped to her waiting shower. Wait until His Nibs hears about this little outing!

Julie opted for what she called her 'Scottish Countrywoman look', a McKenzie tartan kilt and matching sleeveless jerkin. Underneath she wore a long-sleeved, white silk blouse with a frilly jabot, and mid-heeled, black patent leather shoes. Looking at herself in the full-length mirror, she approved her casual outfit. She added a large antique Scottish Thistle brooch and matching earrings Alicia McKenzie had given her from the family collection.

The chauffeur-driven Cadillac purred its way along streets lined with truly expensive looking real estate. Large leafy trees, high brick walls and intricately worked iron gates. All had security cameras mounted above their impressive entrances, and most also had a security guard on duty. Julie sat in the back of the enormous car, telling herself that she and Graeme had just as big a house, complete with stately trees and electronic gates. Theirs was also in a beautiful part of the English countryside, and no security guards or cameras were needed. She smugly acknowledged, "We also have our own name on our gates."

On arriving at one of the more homely looking of the houses, Julie was met by a pair of excited American spaniels. Their mistress, Theresa

Romanski, came to the door, a warm, welcoming smile on her face. "Hello, Julie, my dear. Do excuse the dogs, they'll settle down. Nina, Pinta! Now you behave yourselves! Come my dear, my daughters will be here in a few minutes."

She took Julie's arm and led her through an open door into a glass covered, inner courtyard. It was tastefully furnished with comfortable white wicker furniture and several birdcages that contained exotic birds with bright, multi-coloured plumage. Placed in the far corner was an old fashioned Jukebox and an upright piano. In the middle, a white marbled, Italian styled fountain splashed and tinkled a constant stream of cool water. A table to one side contained many dishes of food and fruit.

Julie immediately felt the relaxed ambience. A charming, restful and obviously a well-loved family meeting place. Julie's face had now relaxed into a wide smile, as she said. "What a gorgeous room, Mrs Romanski. Oh! I could live in a room like this."

"Please, Julie, call me Tessa, that's what Graeme calls me. That's exactly his reaction to the room. He once told me that he knew someone special in his life that would love this room. Somehow he felt the presence of that special person here. He never mentioned a name but I think, my dear, he meant you."

"Yes, Tessa if Fate hadn't stepped in . . . Still, we are now, and we're deliriously happy."

"That, my dear, is an understatement, judging by what I observed last night! I've never seen Graeme so happy. He's become like a favourite son to Anton and I, we always enjoy it when he visits. We're delighted he's found the happiness he richly deserves. You, Julie honey, are the sole cause of it."

The barking of the two dogs interrupted them momentarily, as a voice yelled out, "Hello Ma! Oh, for God's sake, Nina, leave my shoes alone. Pinta bring that back! Oh, you wretched dog!"

Tessa Romanski shrugged, "Deborah has arrived. Her sister, Caroline, will be parking the car." She smiled a motherly, how-did-I-manage-to-get-such-a-daughter smile. "Prepare for your peace to be shattered, Julie."

Julie, expecting a hoydenish, gauche teenager, opened her eyes wide when a tall, slim girl, in her mid-twenties entered carrying the spaniel Nina. She had all of her mother's dark colourings and, with her face splitting into a broad grin, showed as white a set of teeth as Julie had ever seen.

"Great to meet you, Mrs McKenzie. I am Deborah Romanski. Go Nina, find Caroline." The little dog went into raptures of ecstasy before bounding out of the room.

Julie studied the young woman, full of vitality and energy, dressed in the latest 'Flowers of the Field' clothing, and wearing it with such panache. Seeing Julie's look and obvious appreciation, she giggled, "Well, do I pass? Your clothes, as my dear mother has already probably imparted to you, were the saving grace for my sister and I. Until your affordable and stylish range came onto the market, we lived out of the Op shops and Oxfam stores, much to the disgust of our dear parents. You have a lot to answer for, Mrs McKenzie, you made us grow up—I rather enjoyed my 'Peter Pan' existence."

Softening her words, she laughed, the healthy sound of a young woman who knew who she was and where she was going. Julie was impressed.

The dogs returned closely followed by a softer, quieter version of Deborah, in the form of—to Julie's surprise—her twin, Caroline.

The young woman went over and kissed her mother, before introducing herself to Julie. Once again she was wearing Julie's designs and, as she remarked, "Has Deb told you how we became converts to your label, Mrs McKenzie?"

"Look, please call me Julie. Yes, indeed she has. It completely justifies why I designed them. I strongly believe in the concept that we are women, and should look feminine, and enjoy doing so. I know how much pleasure I get when my husband notices what I'm wearing, and enjoys seeing me dressed as his sweetheart, not as some bag lady or a pseudo male."

"Yes, well Graeme is a bit of a hunk, I think I'd enjoy him noticing me too! I must admit my social life definitely looked up when I started wearing your label. How about you, Carlie?"

"Yeah Deb, even down at the Vet Club I get a few compliments. Come on, let's eat, I'm starving, Ma."

Over a lively lunch, Julie learned that Caroline was in her final year before qualifying as a Veterinary Surgeon. Julie related how Lauren seemed to be a magnet for every waif and stray in the district. She described Graeme's reaction when buying a 'stodgy station-wagon', and how she was resigned to the fact that a homeless dog would soon find them.

Deborah, the more outgoing of the twins, was a qualified doctor about to start her internship. At one point, when her sister and mother were away from the table, she softly told Julie, "One night, a couple of years ago, Graeme offered me a lift home as he was coming to dine with my parents. I found him staring through the glass wall of the new born nursery, looking at the babies. His eyes were wet with tears and he looked absolutely shattered. I thought someone close to him had lost a baby, or something. So I crept away and came back, making a loud noise so that he had time to regain his composure. He never enlightened me and I've always wondered. Then I heard of his marriage to you and know that you have a son who is now, what four, five? Could he have been thinking of him, d'you think?"

Julie nodded and gulped down a lump in her throat. "Yes, Stuart. We also have Lauren, she's almost eleven. Graeme has legally adopted both of them."

Julie could see Deborah was waiting for a further explanation, but felt she should wisely keep her counsel. Inside, her heart wept as she heard how lonely and bereft Graeme must have felt, being separated from his children.

To cover her heartache, Julie hastily produced her design portfolio. Both young women bombarded her with questions regarding styles, suitable colours, and whether she had a new line in mind.

Shaking her head, Julie laughed, "No, I'm too busy being Mrs McKenzie at the moment, perhaps later."

At two thirty, the young women declared they must be going. They hugged and thanked their mother for their lunch, then they bid Julie a cheery 'good-bye and thanks'.

Tessa Romanski fare-welled Julie saying gently, "We are delighted to see Graeme so happy, we owe him so much after he saved the life of our son in that terrible suicide bomber fiasco."

CHAPTER 96

When Julie heard Graeme come in, she walked into his open arms. "Hey! You look tired, my darling, come, relax, while I tell you about my day. I had an unexpected call from Theresa Romanski. She invited me to lunch at their home, with her two daughters. So she sent over a huge American car—and I purred on over."

She cuddled close to him on the couch. He slipped his arm around her shoulders, saying, "Now that's what I call a very nice surprise."

She decided to tease him. "Well, you are classed as a favourite son, a hunk and a new age man—in the opinion of the Romanski women."

He pulled her closer, his feeling of tiredness had already begun melting away now he was near her again. "Okay, explain, wife."

"Well, Tessa told me how you saved their son's life." Julie stroked his face. "A lot of people owe you so much, my darling, in the aftermath of that horrid day."

"Well, tell me more about the hunk bit. Boost my flagging morale, wife," he teased.

"That was Caroline. I quote, you're 'a bit of a hunk anyway.'"

Graeme chuckled as he nuzzled her neck. Julie took his face in her hands, while she reminded him of the incident when Deborah had found him at the nursery window.

His eyes held hers, "Yes, it was one of many occasions when the loneliness and yearning to be with you was getting too much to bear. Seeing all of those scraps of humanity, no bigger than when I had last seen Stuart, just completely overwhelmed me. Thank God, Julie, those days are over."

Julie urged him, "Tell me about your day, darling." Graeme stared at her in brief surprise. To actually have someone to confide in, someone that was interested in his work and what he did for a living was still a very new experience. He outlined the progress they had made, making her giggle as he described one amusing incident and then had her clucking her tongue at the childishness of another delegate.

Julie was fascinated to hear him talk with such authority, but also with a straight forward fairness and impartiality. When she heard a knock on their door, Julie shooed him to shower and change. By the time Mary had again swept Julie's hair up into the chignon and then helped her put on 'Night Sky', they could hear Graeme coming into the room.

"Hello Mary. Wow! Julie, darling, you look sensational! That sure is one helluva gown."

Julie looked admiringly at the tall, immaculately dressed man, asking, "What about you, Graeme McKenzie! Isn't he a 'hunk', Mary?" She teased. He seemed oblivious as to how the mess dress uniform just made him look even sexier than usual.

After Mary left, Graeme embraced Julie, "Thank you for being such a wonderful, considerate wife. I've never had all of my clothes laid out by a woman before, you didn't forget a thing. I think I rather like having a wife around. Dear Lord, you look even more stunning than last night, my darling."

The fine, black silk georgette of 'Night Sky' shimmered alluringly around her body. The silver threads in the material glistened and twinkled as they descended and entwined, emulating the appearance of the celestial 'Milky Way' in the heavens high above.

Julie picked up the three-metre long, matching georgette scarf. She draped this loosely around her head in a snood, throwing the two long ends over her shoulders. This made them so that they became floating panels drifting behind her.

Yet again Graeme was aware of the admiring glances they received as they crossed the hotel foyer. The Marine Sergeant driver whistled softly in appreciation. Opening the door for Julie, he smiled and said, "You look beautiful, Ma'am."

As she gracefully thanked him, Graeme saw her blush and chuckled at his delightfully feminine wife. Julie gripped his hand as the car swept around the drive of the White House. She was struck by the overall smallness of the building—it had always seemed much bigger on TV.

She was absorbing as much as she could of this historic building, so that she could give their children an accurate account of it all.

Graeme presented their invitation to a uniformed Marine. Then suddenly she was face-to-face with the most famous and well-known faces in the world, the President of the United States of America and the First Lady. They were warmly greeted with a courteous, "So happy to see you here, do enjoy your evening."

As Graeme led her into the room, Julie was still recovering from having just received two gentle handshakes. She burbled excitedly to Graeme, "I don't think I'll wash this hand again. Wait until I tell Lauren and Stuart. Well, Lauren anyway. At least she's old enough to understand what her Mama is getting at!"

Graeme found that in enjoying her reactions, he was also having fun himself, on the delightful voyage of discovery that marriage to Julie was taking him.

The long dining tables were set up in a U formation, with the President and the First Lady sitting at the head of the table. Glittering gold plates and cutlery and an individual array of fine crystal glassware marked each place setting.

Gold and white flower arrangements vied for their place amongst antique gold candelabra, tall white candles and golden cruet condiment sets of equal vintage.

Julie gazed around, her face slightly flushed, her eyes shining as she observed her fellow diners. All of the ladies were dressed in black, as the protocol demanded, but once again the men were bedecked in their dandified, peacock finery. She secretly preferred Graeme's distinguished, tailored, masculine appearance to the more fanciful 'costumes'.

Graeme broke into her reverie, "Darling, let me introduce you to your neighbour. Julie, this is Luc de Latour, the French Ambassador to Washington. Luc, may I present my wife, Julie."

"Aaaah, Madame, it is my pleasure to be seated next to you. We have mutual friends in Monsieur Alexandre and Madame Bouvier. As a true Frenchman, I admire your gown.

"It's exquisite, it suits you verrrry well."

At that point the Master of Ceremonies rapped his ceremonial gavel on the top table and announced, "Ladies and Gentlemen, please be upstanding for the President of the United States, and the First Lady." A hidden band struck up 'Hail to the Chief', the traditional tune played to herald the entrance of the President.

The official party took their places and a buzz of conversation ran around the room as neighbour greeted neighbour. The various courses of the meal came and went in a blur for Julie, who felt as though she wanted to pinch herself! Here she was dining, not only in the same room, but also at the same table as the President of the United States of America and his First Lady! Several times between courses Graeme caught a startled look on her face as she recognised yet another guest, stammering to him, "Isn't that . . . ?"

He whispered, "Look who is sitting next to Aaron."

Julie gulped, "Oh my! I paid nearly a week's wages to hear him sing in Auckland."

"Well, he's probably going to sing for his supper tonight and you, my darling, will get to hear him for zilch."

As the meal drew to a close, the Master of Ceremonies announced, "Ladies and Gentlemen, The President and the First Lady invite you to join them in the Music Room."

Graeme whispered, "Told you. Come on, I'll get you a seat as close to him as I can."

A grand piano sat in the centre of the room as the famous singer accompanied the President and First Lady to their seats. Aaron Benedict was also with the singer and there appeared to be a discussion going on before Aaron scanned the room.

Then, with a relieved smile, he walked towards Graeme. "Graeme, we've a slight hiccup, we've a singer but no pianist. He's been delayed. Can you accompany him?"

Julie's mouth, very unladylike, fell open as she gaped in total astonishment, "You want Graeme to play for HIM?"

Graeme did not hesitate, "Well sure, Aaron. I know most of his repertoire anyway, play them all the time. It will be my pleasure." He got up casually, as though he did this sort of thing every day, as Julie looked on astounded. "You'll be okay, darling?"

Julie could not make her mouth work properly, so she just nodded numbly.

As other guests recognized Graeme's tall figure, a ripple of applause rang around the room, led by the President and the First Lady. Graeme shook the singer's hand and they conferred as Graeme played a few chords on the keyboard, relaxing his fingers.

The singer smiled and addressed his audience. "Well, this is a first for me, Ladies and Gentlemen, a pianist, dressed more sartorially elegant than moi."

Amid the laughter that followed, Graeme played an introduction. Thereby began for Julie one of the most magical hours she had ever spent. Graeme led into the songs, but gave the performer room to move with his unobtrusive, delicately subtle accompaniment.

At the end, after the tumultuous applause had died down, the singer turned to Graeme and said into the microphone, "That was just great, my friend. If the Royal Air Force ever runs out of airplanes, and you want a job, call me! Ladies and Gentlemen, this man is a musical genius. I give you, Graeme McKenzie!"

Graeme grinned, as he shook the singer's hand. He was immediately surrounded and it was several minutes before he could return to Julie. She had tears of joy in her eyes as she hugged him. "Oh my, Graeme, that was just wonderful, my darling. I have never heard you play better, or heard him sing sweeter."

Suddenly a serious looking Aaron approached them. He quietly said, "The President wants to see you, Graeme. We have a problem with 'our friend' I'm afraid."

Luc de Latour immediately offered, "I will see Julie safely back to your hotel, Graeme, my friend. Go, I'll look after your precious young wife, have no fear."

Graeme picked up Julie's hands, "Is that okay with you, darling? I shouldn't be too long."

Julie nodded, "Yes, of course. I'll be fine. Go on, go, and don't keep the President waiting, darling."

CHAPTER 97

Julie could not sleep. She switched the TV on, then immediately turned it off again. Going over to the balcony, she stood watching the lights from high up in her eagles' eyrie of a room. The White House was still a blaze of lights. The red tail-lights of several cars going in and out of its gates shone mockingly at her.

She checked the time—two o'clock. She chastised herself, "Oh, come on, Julie, and stop being a wimp. Go to bed, woman, relax, give him one less thing to worry about."

Determinedly, she threw herself onto the bed. But it was still not right, gathering up all of the pillows, she hugged them, pretending it was his warm body close to hers . . . .

. . . Graeme crept in as quietly as possible one hour later, to find her smothered in pillows, and with the bed cover wrapped tightly around her sleeping body. He discarded his clothes and pondered how he was going to get into the bed. Julie solved the problem by turning over.

Grabbing his chance, he sank his weary body down beside hers. She automatically wrapped herself around him, as he relaxed, allowing deep sleep to mercifully overtake his exhausted mind and body . . .

Four hours later, the telephone rang. Julie's first reaction was one of relief to find him lying beside her. She whispered into the receiver, "Yes?"

"Good Morning, Julie. It's Aaron Benedict. If Graeme is still sleeping wake him, get some food into him, and have him ready to be picked up by nine o'clock, please." Julie realized Aaron must be in a public room and could be overheard, hence his impersonal call.

She replied, softly, "Leave it to me, Aaron. I'll organise that. 'Bye."

Graeme stirred, "Hello, my darling."

Julie threw her arms around him, as she explained what Aaron wanted and asked what time he got to bed. Graeme was reluctant to move from his special soft pillow and buried his face deeper into her breasts.

With a muffled, "Four o'clock, I think," followed by, "Oh, I could stay here all day." Then he groaned and came up for air.

After kissing him thoroughly, she told him, "Come on, my darling, the car will be here at nine. Go, have a long shower, I'll order some breakfast."

She rubbed her face against his, "I love you so much, Graeme Stuart McKenzie, and I missed you last night."

Graeme chuckled as he related how he found the state of the bed, and how he had guessed what she had used the pillows for. Julie dropped to lie spread-eagled on top of him, pinning him to the bed, as she huskily told him, "No pillow is a substitute for your fabulous body, my darling."

As they ate breakfast, Graeme told her what had occurred during the long hours of the night. How there had been numerous telephone calls and international link-ups and how 'our friend' had gone away to think seriously, and sensibly about the compromise he and Aaron had put to him.

Graeme concluded by sighing, "Now it'll be back to the Pentagon for us this morning." He added, ruefully, "Don't bank on tonight's mess dinner, sweetheart."

"Graeme, no worry, we could probably both do with an early night. What time do we leave for New York, tomorrow, darling?"

"It's also in the lap of the Gods, sweetheart. I'll get in touch as soon as I can. I suspect it's going to be another long, slow day." He held her close for a few seconds after kissing her with passion. "Hold this thought, Mrs McKenzie. Dio come ti-amo cara mia. I'll be back as soon as I can."

When he had gone, Julie felt momentarily deflated. Picking up the 'The Washington Post' she scanned through it to see what entertainment was on offer.

She found she could board a sightseeing bus, or could spend the whole day at the Smithsonian, or a third option, which sounded the most intriguing, attend the 'Art and Fashion Exhibition, 1890-1990'.

Julie opted for the latter.

One hour later, dressed in a lightweight, two-piece suit in a deep, dusky pink shade, silver grey shoes and handbag, she rang the Concierge to call her a cab.

She was soon being whisked through the impressive streets of modern Washington and then back, almost a century in time, to a wonderfully preserved and restored neighbourhood of the early colonial America.

The cab dropped her in front of a three-storied, white stone building that was entirely draped with a multitude of American flags. They ranged in size from a massive pennant fluttering proudly at the pinnacle, to more normally dimensioned flags hanging from each window. Smaller versions were strung on lines down the roof and walls, making the whole building resemble a mighty circus tent. To complete the picture, small, lapel-sized flags were arranged in conical tree shapes, planted in tricoloured flower pots and lined up along the windowsills.

As she entered the foyer, Julie smiled appreciatively at the eye-catching and impressive patriotic display that was so, so American.

A woman stepped forward, dressed in traditional Quaker dress. She handed Julie a glossy catalogue and smiled, "Have a nice day."

Julie wended her way through displays depicting the latter years of the nineteenth century and on to the present day. Every ten years was shown as a complete walled room. Mannequins were dressed in the fashion of the era, while around the walls were hung the appropriate art and craft work of that specific decade.

Julie was deeply concentrating when she heard a gasp of surprise. Turning around, she came face to face with Liz Connors, "Julie! Well, I'll be darned! Care for some lunch? There's a superb restaurant upstairs."

Julie happily agreed to join forces, saying, "I'm having a great time. I must admit some of the fashions are stirring the creative juices and giving me the urge to make some notes."

Liz Connors looked at her enquiringly. "You'd never really stop designing, would you, Julie? We women need you to keep fighting for us."

Julie laughed and shook her head. "I must confess to getting 'itchy' fingers sometimes, Liz. But Graeme is my life's number one priority just now, with our children's upbringing running a close second."

Liz remarked, "Your recent marriage to Graeme McKenzie has obviously worked wonders, not just for you, but for him as well. I've overheard several comments as to how calm and relaxed he is. How well and happy he looks and how extremely competently he is handling the very delicate situation they're all involved in. So, what's your secret, Julie? Is there a story for me here?"

Julie looked down as she twisted her shiny new wedding ring, "Yes, Liz, there is a love-story. It's one of a true and binding love that goes back to the 1970's. But it also involves two precious, innocent children. They are too young to cope with, or understand adverse comments and could be seriously damaged by cruel gossip and innuendo. It also concerns Graeme's career, his credibility and reputation. I'll tell you the bare bones of our 'secret', but it would have to be strictly 'off the record'. You couldn't write it—not yet anyway. Not until our children are old enough to understand how and why their parents made a decision to do what they did. It's still, in the eyes of many people, completely adulterous, and very, very wrong."

Liz's eyes nearly popped out of her head, "I'm intrigued. My nosey journalistic dander is up. I give you my word and solemn promise it will be strictly 'off the record'. I give you that total assurance."

Julie knew of Liz's reputation as an investigative journalist, after all, she didn't gain the nickname 'The Terrier" for nothing! Julie was also aware that if she delayed, Liz would probably delve into her own research sources. She would find the controversial facts of their lives, without hearing the human side of how and why it happened.

Julie started, with a deal of reluctance, relating their story; she finished with their marriage and a new life together—at last. Liz listened without interrupting, noting that not once did Julie over-dramatise events, or attempt to excuse or justify their infidelity.

Liz breathed a heartfelt sigh. "That's so romantic and yet it tugs at my heart strings." She sighed again, "It will stay locked in my heart until the day comes that perhaps it can be told, without rancour. World opinion, society, morality, is changing so rapidly."

Julie returned to the hotel and, as she unlocked the door, she saw the heavy bedroom curtains were drawn shut.

Creeping quietly in, she found Graeme fast asleep. A note propped up by the telephone read. "Darling, dinner cancelled. We have evening to ourselves. I love you, G."

She quickly undressed and lay beside him and was soon asleep herself. They stirred around eight o'clock and happily lay locked in each other's arms.

Graeme told her how the meeting had eventually broken up with 'our friend' flying home for talks with his ministers. He explained it had been decided to cancel the mess dinner when most of them had been put on alert, in case 'our friend' decided to return to the negotiating table.

Julie told him of meeting Liz Connors and of entrusting her with their life-story, and why. Graeme agreed it was the best way, "With her own husband's senior Army rank to protect, she'll more than understand your reluctance. Telling her gives her added information to stave off, or deny, any rumours she might hear or encounter."

Graeme said that he would have to stay within reach of a telephone, and added, "let's just lie here, I feel so peaceful holding you close to my heart."

When Julie asked about the planned visit to New York, Graeme told her that at that stage their attendance at the 'Samson and Delilah' Opera in New York was still happening for them."

Julie ran her fingers through his hair, as she said, "Delilah cut off his hair and Samson lost all of his strength. The music always makes me cry, it's so poignant."

Graeme pulled her down to him and kissed her lips before caressing her full, shapely breasts. "This Samson hasn't lost any of his strength, my Delilah. Let's delay our dinner order for a while, my sexy minx, whilst I satisfy my other hunger."

CHAPTER 98

The stand down telephone call came in after midnight, so they delayed ringing their children until the morning.

After Graeme had left the next morning for the Pentagon, Julie basked in the sunshine on their balcony as she began working, surely and swiftly, pencilling in several silhouettes. She made numerous notes on skirt lengths, fabric choices and other intricate details. Ideas on a fashion range Liz Connors had suggested.

Concentrating, she was startled when Graeme appeared on the balcony. "Hello, darling, I'm all finished. We can go now."

Julie stared at him with suspicion. "You haven't come down on a strop again, have you Graeme McKenzie? I heard a helicopter a few minutes ago, was that you?"

Graeme grinned mischievously at her, "Yep that was me, sweetheart."

Julie continued to look at him in amazement. With a horrified look on her face, she asked, "Graeme! I haven't got to be winched up have I? I've never even been in a helicopter!"

He could not resist the opportunity to tease her—just a little more. So he said airily, "Oh, it's perfectly safe, my darling. After all, I'll be there beside you. Come on, I've got the cases."

Julie stumbled after him, her mind in turmoil. He punched the lift button 'UP'. The doors slid open and Julie saw a large USAF helicopter sitting on the helipad. Its side door was gaping open, but, it had a set of steps leading up to it.

Graeme laughed at her look of pure relief. He slipped his arm around her, "Do forgive me, my darling, it was just too good a chance to miss."

Within seconds they were high in the air with the ground looking like a toy town. Julie gripped his hand tightly at first, until she got used to the different movement and the sound of the rotors. Then she relaxed and found she was enjoying being once again in his chosen element.

Casting a surreptitious look at his face, she saw the twinkle in his eyes that he always got when flying. Then and there she decided she must get an aircraft of his own and to heck with the expense!

It seemed to Julie that, within minutes of the familiar New York skyline coming into view, they were landing. A bellboy smiled a welcome. Graeme said, "Take Mrs McKenzie to our suite. I'm going on to the U.N. building, darling. I'll just be a couple of hours." He kissed her on both cheeks and returned to the helicopter with a cheery wave.

When he returned, he asked, "What shall we do for lunch and this afternoon, Julie, darling?"

"Let's just be tourists," she suggested. "We can pick up lunch on the way, wherever takes our fancy."

"By the way, Mrs McKenzie, you look delicious." He admired her tailored McKenzie tartan trouser suit, saying, "I think your idea is perfect, my lovely."

He shrugged his arms into a brown leather, flyer's bomber jacket. "Right, let's go be tourists, sweetheart."

They boarded one of the 'Hop on—Hop off' tourist bus tours and spent an enjoyable afternoon 'discovering' New York. Lunch, bought from a street vendor on the foreshore of the Staten Island Ferry, consisted of a 'Genuine-New-York-Hot-Dog', dripping with bright yellow mustard and blood red ketchup. They washed it down with the inevitable can of Coke, followed by the largest ice-cream cone Julie had ever seen.

They had returned to their hotel at five o'clock and a while later, while Graeme was taking a shower, she heard a knock on the door. Opening the door, she found a bellboy holding a corsage! Obvious Graeme must have ordered it before they went out. She read the card attached to it with amusement.

"For my own Queen Delilah, from her Samson."

Though she had earlier been in the shower, Julie now hurriedly dropped her bathrobe and walked straight back into the bathroom. She walked into the shower and curled her arms around Graeme's neck. As the warm water spray coursed over their entwined naked bodies, she kissed him passionately, before saying, "Thank you. I want more from my Samson later, please."

Before he could react, she slipped out of the shower, and danced away with a teasing twinkle in her eyes. Graeme continued his shower happily whistling.

Julie commenced to dress for the evening and dropped the 'Four Seasons' gown 'Summer—La primavera bianco Roma' over her head. The toga styled, pure silk gown, in a vanilla cream shade was interwoven with a real gold thread. It flowed silkily shimmering around her body, draped from only one shoulder, leaving the other bare.

Picking up Graeme's corsage, she pinned it with a large Roman styled, scarab brooch. Whisking her hair up in a classic ponytail, she entwined and braided it with ribbons of the gown fabric, and teased a few strands of hair into a wispy fringe over her forehead. She then added an Egyptian styled jewelled headband. Slipping on a pair of bejewelled high-heeled sandals, she finally applied brown kohl to her eyelids.

Graeme, coming out from the dressing room, stood open mouthed at the regal vision. He stammered, "My God, Julie. You are a Queen Cleopatra, Nefertiti and Delilah, all rolled into one delectable royal package. That gown . . . that hairstyle! My darling wife, you look fantastic!"

Her cheeks colouring shyly under the undisguised admiration, she murmured softly, "It's the first time I've seen you in a tuxedo. You look so handsome, absolutely, devastatingly scrumptious. I love you so much, Graeme, my darling husband. Look how well your beautiful flower suits this colour scheme?"

He clasped her hands in his, quietly saying in an awe struck voice, "I've never seen you look more beautiful than you do tonight, my own special Queen."

Julie slipped the gold-fringed stole around her shoulders, pulled on her vanilla cream elbow length gloves and picked up her gold lame evening purse. Taking Graeme's proffered arm, she walked proudly beside her handsome husband.

There were gasps of admiration as they walked into the hotel foyer. But, it was their turn to be overawed when they arrived at the Metropolitan Opera House.

Located in the massive Lincoln Centre, the ten storied high building was aglow with many lights, with the six-storey high glass entranceway floodlit. They walked into the impressive foyer entrance, adorned with many works of art and dominated by the famous Marc Chagall murals.

Graeme saw with pride that Julie was also attracting attention from the assembled opera goers—both male and female. Her exquisite gown and her feminine, yet proudly held carriage so in keeping with the theme of the opera they were about to see.

They were hailed by the huge, resplendently tuxedoed figure of Aaron Benedict. But as he and Graeme shook hands, Aaron could not take his eyes off Julie. Aaron let out the breath he had sucked in at the sight of her with a whoosh, asking, "How does she do it, Graeme? Every time I see this little lady, now a mother of two, I might add, she looks even younger, and more beautiful."

Julie laughed, accepting his compliments with a small curtsey, but Aaron intercepted a private loving look between the husband and wife. He offered up a silent prayer of thanks, for being able to do his part in making sure these two made it back together.

Graeme replied in a quiet voice, "I still have to pinch myself every now and again, Aaron, to ensure I'm not dreaming it all."

The bell rang, urging the audience to take their places. Julie's eyes, bright with anticipation, observed the glittering glamorous audience below them. Graeme could see several pairs of opera glasses trained on Julie as they sat in their V.I.P. box.

Julie was totally absorbed by the famous Saint-Saens opera. Written in the classical French tradition, with its elegant, precise detail and form, the music washed over and around her. It totally filled her sight, hearing and mind. Tears of joy overflowed and ran down her cheeks when Delilah sang the truly lyrical, and very romantic, 'Mon Coeur s'ouvre a ta voix'(Softly Awakes My Heart). Graeme handed her his handkerchief as she clutched his hand, overcome with the emotion of the music.

At the finale, the audience gave the performers rapturous applause, bringing them back, again and again for many curtain calls. For a couple of minutes Julie sat speechless, as Graeme and Aaron exchanged comments on how much they enjoyed the performance. Graeme gently touched her arm, "Ready, darling?" She looked at him as though coming out of a trance. She sighed, "Wasn't that divine, Graeme, darling? Thank you so much, Aaron, for inviting us."

As they stood in the foyer, there were several flashes from photographers. Feeling a touch on her arm, Julie swung around to find Liz Connors smiling at her.

"Hello, Julie, would you mind if we took a photo of you and your two distinguished escorts?"

Graeme smiled at his wife, "Why not. I'll need something in print to remind me this was real."

Aaron then wished them 'goodnight' as his car arrived, closely followed by an empty cab. Graeme signalled to it and held the door for Julie, who suggestively and mischievously whispered, so that only he could hear, "Hurry up, Samson, don't keep Delilah waiting!"

CHAPTER 99

They were halfway across the Atlantic en route to Mildenhall when Graeme chuckled and handed Julie the New York morning newspaper. His eyes twinkling with merriment, he pointed to a half page photograph, saying "Look 'Delilah', darling, you are the toast of New York!"

Julie blushed as she remembered how wantonly she had performed for him. The wicked grin on Graeme's face revealed, with much pleasure, the sensuous, erotic ending to their memorable day. Under his amused gaze, Julie read the caption with Liz Connors' by-line.

"Glamorous International Trio enjoys a 'Night at the Opera'. Pictured are: Chief of Defence Staff, Aaron Benedict and his guests, Air Commodore Graeme McKenzie RAF and Mrs Julie McKenzie. Mrs McKenzie is the creator of the 'Flowers of the Field' fashion label. The elegant figure of Julie McKenzie was a stand out in her beautifully crafted and biblically inspired toga-styled gown. Mrs McKenzie was a fashionable and refreshing sight last night at the Metropolitan Opera House. We of her era and peer group hope she hasn't gone into permanent retirement with her recent love-match marriage to the dashing Air Commodore. We 'who only stand and wait' also need you, Mrs McKenzie. Don't desert us!"

Julie was covered in confusion but Graeme proudly said, "You, my darling, looked wonderful and you deserve every compliment paid to you. I must get a copy of that photograph, it's a beauty. Do you think you'd like to answer the call Mrs Connors has made?"

Julie shook her head vigorously. "Not a chance! I'm more than busy, just now, trying to get pregnant—any way I can!"

He raised an eyebrow at her and asked, with a wicked gleam in his eyes, "Really? Any way? Er . . . Have you heard of the famous 'Mile High club', Mrs McKenzie—I'm ready to oblige."

When they landed back at Mildenhall, they found Daisy and two excited children waiting in the Reception area. Stuart headed for his father and was soon whisked high in the air. The little boy ecstatically wrapped his arms around his father's neck, crying, "Hello, my Papa."

Lauren was folded in Julie's arms as she said, "Oh, Mama, we missed you and Papa."

They were oblivious to all of the envious looks they were getting from the rest of the contingent disembarking from the USAF aircraft. Even the wily Sergeant Wyberg had to swallow hard, at seeing his important and distinguished 'Guvnor' just being a loving father.

Graeme, with Stuart held in his arms, saw Daisy close by. He said, with a smile, "Daisy, it's so good to see you."

Saluting Graeme, and with a broad smile on his face, Sergeant Wyberg said, "Glad to have you back, Sir."

Graeme was now flanked by a child on each side, both firing rapid questions at him. One from Lauren stumped him, and it had him casting an urgent 'Help! look, towards Julie.

Lauren had asked, "Did you order a new baby sister or brother while you were in America, Papa? 'Cos that's where Mama got Stuart for me."

Compromising, he answered, "Lauren, honey, we'll need to talk about that question privately at home, okay?"

She nodded, giving him a smile that could light a thousand lamps, or melt the hardest of hearts.

Within minutes they were home! Julie hugged Graeme, telling him, "It's so good to be back here, darling. I love our home so much . . ." Her voice trailed off as a black and white shape came hurtling around the side of the house, its tail wagging furiously. With a resigned note in her voice, she stammered, "Don't tell me—we have a dog."

Daisy shrugged her shoulders, "He arrived two days ago, Mr Daniel brought him. His owners are going overseas and can't take him. He's a Border collie, fifteen months old, with a pedigree as long as your arm. I hate to admit it, but he's the best we've ever had. He's obedient, a real gentleman, in fact. He's clean, not unusually noisy, except when he hears a car in the driveway. Which isn't a bad thing; we'll know when someone is here." She shrugged.

"What's his name?" Julie asked resignedly.

"Beau Brummel of Cairn brae," Lauren answered, in a rush. "But we call him 'Beau'—is it okay, Mama, Papa?"

Julie looked over at Graeme who was trying to be serious, but he looked as though he would break into laughter at any second. "Fine by me, darling. Come Beau. Let's have a look at you, m'boy."

The dog got up and walked over to Graeme, sat down and held up his left paw. Graeme crouched on his haunches, shook the proffered paw and then ran his hands over the glossy black coat and wet, pink and white nose. Two intelligent, huge pools of brown velvet eyes looked back at him. Graeme spoke softly, "You certainly are a beauty. I've always wanted one of this breed. As far as I'm concerned he can stay."

Julie hugged Beau's warm body, "Yes, welcome, Beau McKenzie."

The two children whooped with delight and raced off.

Daisy smiled at the Sergeant as he passed by with the luggage and he gave her a wink. They had both supervised the bathing of the dog earlier, so that he would make a good impression.

Graeme was closeted in his study for the next hour or so, reading papers delivered by a military motorcyclist. The children could be heard playing with Beau and teaching him to climb the steps up into Stuart's tree house. When Julie offered Graeme coffee, they stood, arms entwined around each other, watching their children.

Graeme told Julie of Lauren's question.

Julie giggled, "Yes, I caught the 'you had better ask your mother look', darling. Well, let's hope she doesn't ask again, until we know for sure whether all that Samson and Delilah action has worked. If not . . ."

"We'll have every excuse to try a bit harder. Glorious thought. Come wife, kiss me properly and then scat, so that I can get through this in time for dinner."

"Darling, when is Billy due back? I'm dying to meet Marisa and their children."

"Probably by the end of the week. I'll check when I ring the base later."

Julie had decided to seek Billy's help in arranging a lease of a suitable aircraft for Graeme.

She had also taken Daisy into her confidence about a birthday party. She thoughtfully replied, "It's a lot of money, lass, but . . . We must have a proper party this year, 'cos it'll be their first joint birthday. Stuart will be four and Graeme will be what—forty-one? I think we'll do a birthday cake in an aircraft shape. What d'you think, lass?'

Julie agreed—a brilliant idea, but first—the family Wedding Breakfast! Julie sorted through the pile of return envelopes, ticking them off from her master list.

One was going to delight Graeme—from his older sister, Beth Brent and her family, now living in Spain. Their acceptance was warm and welcoming, and expressing their joy that Julie was at last part of the McKenzie clan.

Sadly, there was one glaring and noticeable absence, her sister Carole. She sighed, 'Who knows, perhaps she'll change her mind.'

Billy first reaction when Julie approached him to put out feelers for a suitable aircraft for Graeme, was to ask, "Julie, have you any idea what big bucks you are talking here?"

When she told him exactly how much she thought it would cost, he had whistled appreciatively, "I'm gobsmacked! Wow! Leave it with me. I know just who to contact."

Unfortunately, Marisa and the children had not yet arrived from Italy, as their new baby son, Winston, small at birth, was taking a while to develop and thrive.

The children already doted on their newly discovered, fun loving Uncle Billy. As Julie remarked to Graeme, "He's never changed, has he? He's rather like an adult Peter Pan."

Graeme roared with laughter at this description, "Peter Pan, eh? Well, he might be so off duty, but at work he's all efficiency, loyal, popular and jolly good at his job, darling."

Julie had the feeling the world was her oyster as the long summer days drifted along. But a niggling, uneasy and uncharacteristic feeling descended upon her. It was the knowledge that something was not quite right deep within her body.

Two days later, she was standing on the top of the stepladder in the kitchen. Suddenly, a ripping pain shot through her abdomen, and she felt a hot rush of sticky fluid.

With a cry of, "Oh no, it can't be," Julie hurried to the downstairs bathroom and confirmed her period had started. She had been so certain she would be pregnant by now.

After walking the children to kindergarten and school, she met Dr Susan Blake. Julie asked, "Susan, can you spare me a minute?"

They strolled the short distance to her surgery and, once inside, Susan asked, "Well, what's wrong, how can I help?"

Julie explained the shock she had had that morning. "I was so sure I'd be pregnant, Susan. After all, I fell pretty damn quickly with the other two. Why not this time?"

"How long have you been on the birth control programme? Wait, let me see . . . Umm, four years. When did you stop, two-three months ago? Well, this is not uncommon, Julie. The uterus is probably having a good clean out, so that it is healthy and ready for a new life to begin within."

She smiled encouragingly, "Take it easy over the next few days. Also, you may be feeling weepy as your hormones will be jumping all over the place, so just warn your husband. If anything more untoward happens, call me."

Julie felt devastated all day. She so much needed to feel the comfort of Graeme's arms.

As soon as Graeme arrived home, he entered their bedroom and saw Julie, eyes swollen and reddened from weeping. She flew into his arms and sobbed, "Oh Graeme, we never made a Washington baby."

He wiped her tears away, then lifted her face, and urged, "Look at me, Julie. My darling, I do understand your grief. But, we can try again. If it is to be—so be it. If not—then so be it also." Gently he held her close to him.

CHAPTER 100

Within a couple of days, Julie had adjusted to her disappointment. Graeme breathed a sigh of relief when he heard her throaty laughter again during a very welcome visit from Billy and his family.

With his usual touch of humour, Billy explained they had named their new son Winston, because he was so small and the complete opposite to the old, British bulldog Sir Winston Churchill.

The hectic week passed quickly as they, Daisy and Sergeant Wyberg prepared for the wedding breakfast.

The day dawned fine and Julie and Graeme were in their bedroom, watching the scene below as Alicia and Grant McKenzie received guests on their behalf. Lauren and Stuart peered through the window alongside their parents, occasionally asking, "Who's that, Mama?" or "Look, there's another pilot, Papa!"

Julie watched her brother Don wheel their father's wheelchair towards the senior McKenzies, and saw Alicia bend to kiss her former neighbour.

Then, with a gasp, she saw who was getting out of the next car. "Graeme! It's Carole!"

He grinned, "Yes, I know, I went there last week. She said she'd think about it."

Julie beamed and kissed him.

"Here comes the mushy bit again," Stuart told his sister, as he rolled his eyes.

"Yep, they're allowed, 'cos they love each other," Lauren admonished her brother. "One day, we'll be doing that with someone we love."

"Me, kiss a girl! Yuk!" replied her brother, with a shudder and made a disgusting noise, pretending to vomit.

The flow of arrivals had stopped and Grant McKenzie raised his arm, the signal that everyone was assembled.

Graeme smiled, "Right, McKenzies. We're on! Lauren, honey, you and Stuart lead the way, on and into the marquee, and take your seats beside Nana and Gramps."

Julie held the bridal horseshoe her children had given her on her original wedding day, carrying it in lieu of a bridal bouquet.

Graeme fastened his ceremonial sword in place and, with a roguish smile, held out his arm to his bride.

Graeme murmured, "Dio come ti-amo, cara mia."

Julie replied, "I adore you, Graeme Stuart McKenzie."

As they walked towards the marquee, they could hear the Bridal March music, then Billy announcing, "Ladies and Gentlemen, please be upstanding to welcome our bridal couple—Graeme and Julie."

With their two children in front of them, Julie and Graeme entered to the applause and happy smiling faces of their families and friends. There was an audible and appreciative sigh as, at last, the handsome, glamorous couple could be seen in all of their bridal finery. Cameras flashed as they posed under the specially prepared floral archway.

Julie saw her father gazing at her, tears running down his cheeks. They headed towards the elderly man and Julie greeted him, "Hello, Dad. We are so glad you are here."

In a clear, lucid voice, he said, "You look just like your mother. So you've married that Graeme fella at last.

Good Luck to you both, Julie." Julie stooped to kiss his wrinkled cheek as his head drooped and he seemed to fall instantly asleep. Julie straightened up with a gentle smile on her face, and looked straight into the eyes of her younger sister, Carole.

"I'm glad Graeme persuaded you to come, Carole. We'll have time later to talk."

"You look beautiful, Julie. Yes, we must talk later,"

Carole replied quietly.

"She not only looks beautiful, but has a ton of brains to go with it!" Julie gasped as she was hugged by her old boss, Michael Armstrong and Denise, his wife. "My God! I always knew you were something special, girl."

With tears in her eyes, Julie introduced Graeme. Michael exclaimed, "We knew all about you, old man, years ago. We knew even then where her heart lay. Still all's well that ends well. Happily ever after, and all that, eh?"

Julie urged, "Michael, Denise, I'd like to run something past you both later. So see you then."

Walking around to the other side of the table to where Maureen and her husband Ron were seated, Julie hugged an emotional Maureen.

"You two are something else again," Maureen cried. "That gown, Julie, I heard you more or less designed it, Graeme. You must have dreamt of seeing her in it for such a long time. And look at you, Graeme McKenzie, you handsome dog. I'm so happy you two have found each other, at last."

Billy inclined his head towards Graeme, asking, "Ready?"

Graeme helped Julie with her chair and nodded.

Billy rapped the table, "Ladies and Gentleman, our illustrious bridegroom, Graeme McKenzie."

Graeme, in a natural conversational tone and with a warm, friendly smile, welcomed their guests. He paused, before continuing, "Julie and I have now been happily married for exactly two months. We felt it was important that our marriage should be in a place that had a spiritual significance for both of us. That place was in the chapel of the Chateau Cornacchia, in Australia. We knew that many of you present here today would not be able to make it 'down under', so evolved the idea of having a second family wedding breakfast." He paused again.

"Julie, Lauren, Stuart and I are delighted that everyone we invited is here with us today. We are especially proud that Julie's father and my parents—the elders in our family group—are with us to witness what has been the successful union of two families.

"To all of our siblings and their families, we look forward to enjoying our ever-growing family circle with you all. To our friends and colleagues, we welcome you to our newly amalgamated family group."

Sergeant Wyberg's volunteers began serving the specially chosen meal Julie and Daisy had spent weeks planning.

Julie and Graeme cut the second tier of their original wedding cake, using Graeme's ceremonial sword.

While everybody's attention was drawn to this traditional ceremony, the volunteers re-entered, pushing several large easels, draped in white sheets, into the marquee. Graeme looked questioningly at Julie who nodded to Billy.

Rapping a spoon against his glass, Billy announced,

"Ladies and Gentlemen, we can now show you what the original wedding was like. Courtesy of T.P.—Tony Prentice, the world famous photographer. We present—June 21st 1999, the wedding day of Julie and Graeme McKenzie."

The volunteers swept the white sheeting off of the easels to reveal the magnificent photos recording the magical moments of the wedding day in Australia.

It was as much a surprise to Graeme. "T.P.'s done it again," he murmured, "He seems to capture something special in you, Julie darling."

"You certainly had a marvellous day, Julie," said a quiet voice.

Julie turned to see Carole beside her. She said, "Graeme didn't tell me he had come to see you, but I'm so very happy that he did. You are always welcome in our home."

Julie wheeled her father closer to the easels as her family group admired the images before them.

Julie was tapped on the shoulder by a younger version of Alicia McKenzie. "Hey, new sister-in-law, remember me? I was once Beth McKenzie, now I'm a Brent, for my sins, this is my husband, Carlos. We only flew in from Alicante this morning, so haven't had time to catch up, as yet. Well, Julie, I don't know what you have fed that brother of mine, but it's as though he's got a new lease on life."

Graeme hugged his sister as he caught her last words. "I sure have, Sis. Billy calls her Wonder Woman. I just call her my darling wife."

Blowing Julie a kiss, Graeme wandered over to his parents with his sister, as Michael and Denise Armstrong joined Julie. Michael chortled with glee as he studied T.P's photography. "You haven't actually stopped designing have you, Julie?"

"Well, that's what I wanted to run past you both," Julie explained. "Look, I have this idea for a range of evening wear for the women of the junior officer ranks in the services. They are expected to attend quite a few formal social functions and are always expected to look like they have just jumped from the cover of 'Vogue', YSL or something. Most of them have young families to raise, so there may be little left in the budget for such luxuries as evening wear.

Reaching the photograph of a happily smiling Julie and Graeme walking under the honour guard of RAAF Officers, Julie continued, "Look at this photograph, all the men know each other well. Let's face it, they literally put their lives into each other's hands, in time of conflict. If a man is to keep that camaraderie, the esprit de corps, the trust of his fellow officers, he needs to be taking part in the social side. If his wife doesn't come along and join in, then he either stops going, or worse still, goes alone. That may eventually spell big marriage trouble."

"Whew! Well said, Mrs McKenzie, Ma'am." Julie found Graeme behind her, wearing an admiring expression. "I have never heard you talk on that subject before. I'm enlightened and couldn't agree more with your sentiments, darling. So this was the germ of an idea you have been working on? Well, it'll have my full on backing."

"You shall have ours as well, my dear Julie," Michael answered, as he and Denise looked appreciatively at her. "Come and see us, the door is always wide open for you. Now, keep her up to it Graeme, old son."

Graeme winked at his wife, "Come, Mrs McKenzie, enough Women's Lib today, I want to dance with you."

"Women's Lib, indeed!" Julie retorted, but one look at the twinkle in his eyes and she relented. He told her, "I think you have hit the nail on the head with the social problems, my love. It can't be for lack of babysitters, there are always plenty of those around any service base. The mess dinners and suchlike are usually fairly inexpensive, or subsidised . . . No, I think you're right. The clothing factor may well be an issue. Much too often I have seen a man alone, drinking too much, coming on to another man's wife. Often it can be for the lack of someone to talk to."

When just their immediate families were left, they grouped around the piano and Graeme played for them as they sang every song they knew. Daisy, helped by the indefatigable Sergeant Wyberg, served a supper in Grant McKenzie's words, 'fit for a king'.

Eventually, after two o'clock in the morning, Julie and Graeme made their way, tired but happy, to their inner sanctum.

CHAPTER 101

Earlier that morning, Billy had telephoned Julie, telling her, "I think we're in business! One of the 'good ole boys' is going home to get hitched. It's virtually brand-new, low hours and with four years lease still to run. They'll fall over themselves to transfer it into Graeme's care! Julie, there's a ton of hangar space here. The C.O. will co-operate, I'm sure."

Julie had told Billy, "If it's what Graeme would want, do it Billy."

Billy had cautioned her, "It's a lot of shekels, Julie. You aren't selling off the family silver, or anything, are you?"

Julie laughed, "No, Billy, nothing like that. All my own hard earned. Just to be with him and to see the look on his face when he's flying . . . You know how the old saying goes, 'if you can't beat 'em, join 'em.' So go . . . get it for us, please, Billy!"

Julie waited anxiously.

"Well, I've done it!" Billy boomed down the line a few hours later. Julie heard him chortling with glee as he said, "Once I had sworn them to secrecy and explained it was his surprise birthday gift, the flood doors literally opened." He paused.

"Dream up some shenanigans to get him to the Aero Club, Julie. He has to personally sign for everything," He told her.

Julie smiled, "Oh that's the easy part, Billy. We'll pretend we are booking a surprise flight for Stuart. That should do it. Thank you so much, Billy, my dear friend, for all your help."

Julie heard Billy's heartfelt sigh, "Believe me, it was pure pleasure, Julie love. He's going to be over the moon, I'm just going to make sure I'm there to see his face, 'bye."

Daisy firmly declared, "I really don't like flying that much. So, Julie lass, I'll stay and look after Beau. How about we plan a birthday party dinner, say at six or seven in the evening, complete with the aircraft cake and all the trimmings?"

Julie exclaimed, "Golly! I don't know how I'm going to keep the secret, Daisy." She mused, "I'll have to find something else to give him in the morning, and I'll take the children shopping tomorrow. I'll give his Dad a ring for suggestions of where to go for this first flight of ours."

When a flabbergasted Grant McKenzie had recovered his voice at hearing what Julie had organised for Graeme's birthday, he suggested, without any hesitation, "Go to Pitlochry in Scotland, it's the ancestral home of the McKenzies. Oh, to be a fly on the wall when you present our son with his Birthday present!" He rang off still chuckling.

Stuart was still in the quantity not quality range, but hidden behind the lounge settee, Graeme and Julie had secreted a special gift. A sit-in wooden model in the shape of a Spitfire, complete with a propeller that spun, whirring very realistically as it was pedalled around. It was specially made for Stuart by an elderly craftsman Graeme had met at an RAF reunion.

Julie pre-warned Graeme that it was the New Zealand custom for fathers to be brought their birthday presents in bed by their children.

He had sighed, "I promise faithfully to lie here and be waited on, hand and foot, by my handmaiden wife and my children, like an Eastern Potentate."

Giggling, Julie threw his pyjamas at him. "Right genius, then don't forget your 'modesty'."

Julie was first up and anxiously scanned the sky. Not a cloud in sight. She kissed a very excited Stuart, "A very Happy Birthday, darling. Come on, I'll carry the tea and croissants for Papa—you two bring his presents. There might be a few surprises for you as well, Stuart."

The two children rushed into the bedroom crying, "Surprise! Surprise! Happy Birthday, Papa!"

Graeme pretended to yawn, "What? Oh, my birthday, already? What a lovely surprise, breakfast in bed! Wow! I am being a spoilt Papa. What's this, presents too. Hello, my son. Happy Birthday to you, this is a very special day for your Papa, you know."

"I've never had so many presents in my life," Graeme declared, grinning like a schoolboy after the ceremony had finished. "This married man and father bit suits me very well. Thank you one and all for your lovely and most welcome gifts."

"Well, darling, have we forgotten anything?" Julie said with a exaggerated wink.

Lauren recognised this ploy, it meant hidden presents. She grabbed Stuart's hand, urging him to hurry downstairs.

Graeme pulled Julie to him and kissed her long and hard. "Thank you for giving my life meaning, my darling."

"Mama, Papa! Come on!" Lauren yelled up the stairs.

Stuart let out a yell as he discovered what was hidden behind the lounge settee. Graeme assisted him onto the lawn, as Julie grabbed the camera. Stuart raced his aircraft around the garden with Beau circling him, his tail wagging in all the excitement.

"Graeme, please persuade him to come inside, so that we can tell him about his other surprise," Julie urged. Time was passing she knew.

Carrying Stuart high on his shoulders, Graeme dumped him at the table, "If there was anything we could wish for, on our birthday, what would you wish for, Stuart, my son?"

Stuart screwed up his face as he thought about this, "Go flying, Papa, with you, in a real plane."

"Okay then, let's do that," Graeme casually replied.

Stuart's eyes widened, and his mouth dropped slackly open as he stared at his father. "You mean it, Papa? You really mean it? Whoopee, we are going flying, Mama!"

Daisy hustled the children for their shower and dressed them in warm tracksuits.

Julie drove them, playing up her hand maiden role for the 'Birthday Boys'. When they arrived at the base, Graeme was surprised when the Aero Club Manager himself came to meet them. "Good morning, Air Commodore, I understand it's your birthday. Best Wishes and Many Happy Returns, Sir."

"Er . . . Yes, thank you," Graeme said politely. "We've come for my son's birthday flight, actually."

"Come through to the hangar, Sir, if you will."

Julie could hardly contain her excitement as they walked through and saw a gleaming white executive jet aircraft, bedecked with red, white and blue bows, ribbons and balloons. A white banner, stretched across the fuselage, read, "Happy Birthday Graeme McKenzie—I'm all yours."

Graeme stopped dead in his tracks, before slowly turning to face a smiling Julie. Her hands were clasped so tightly together her knuckles were shining white and tears filled her eyes. She whispered, "Oh, heavens, I hope you like her. She's really all yours, darling. You just have to sign the necessary lease papers and show the man your credentials, or something. Happy Birthday, Graeme, my darling, from me."

He took her hand and, like a man in a dream, walked towards the beautiful plane. Stuart and Lauren were 'oohing' and 'aahing', as shocked as their father.

Climbing into the aircraft, Graeme sat Julie beside him in the cockpit. Deliberately closing the door to the outside world, he emotionally said, "How did I ever get to deserve someone like you, Julie McKenzie . . . ?"

Julie interrupted him by placing her fingers over his lips. "Well, it's yours for four years, my darling husband. Graeme, I'd give you the moon, if I thought that was what you wanted. It has been my absolute pleasure to get it for us, for both of us. I so want to be part of your world, Graeme. I love you so much."

A shout came from outside the plane and Billy's voice saying, "Hey, you up there! Happy Birthday, old chum. Come down and talk with us mere mortals, will you?"

Graeme helped Julie down and swung her around in his arms, asking Billy, "Did you have a part in this, as well? You are as sneaky as this minx of a wife of mine!"

Billy grinned, as Graeme playfully punched him.

"So did we do well?" Billy asked. "Isn't she a beauty? Look at her low flying hours and her mint condition. I tell you what, me old mate, you've got yourself one helluva good businesswoman as a missus. She knows what she wants and goes and gets it."

The two children were still staring awestruck at the beautiful flying machine, after their Uncle Billy had just assured them, "Yes, that's right, it's your Papa's."

The Aero Club Manager stood smiling broadly at the happy scene being played out in front of him. Julie handed him a cheque and pushed

Graeme into the office to do the paperwork. "Come on darling. You CAN fly this?"

Graeme almost reverently replied, "Oh yes, my darling, I can fly her."

"Well, shoo, hurry up then, we're all waiting. There is a flight plan lodged already. Billy prepared it—we are going to fly to Scotland and back. Now, there is a parking lot or something, in the hangar closest to your office. The C.O. has Okayed it, Billy tells me, on the condition that you take him up at least once a week for a spin."

"Good God, woman! You think of everything!" Graeme stammered in utter amazement.

Within minutes, all was in order. Billy removed the fancy decorations and stood looking on with admiration, as Graeme taxied the gleaming white aircraft out of the hangar and on to the runway. He saw the smiling faces waving to him and watched as Graeme leaned over and kissed his wife, before giving him a pilot's salute.

After familiarizing himself with the controls and running up the engines as they stood at the end of the runway, Graeme got a clearance from the control tower.

Stuart did not know which way to look first, as he tried to take it all in. He glanced sideways out of the window, as the ground fell away below them, making him cry out, "Papa. We're really flying."

Julie softly repeated the words of 'High Flight', as the children gazed around in awe at entering the special world of their father. Julie looked lovingly at the man in the pilot's seat. "You promised us that one day we'd all fly together, my darling. Well, here we are—our dreams and our promises have come true."

Graeme's face was a picture of pure joy as he said, huskily, "This has got to be my day of days. Up here with the three people that are my whole world. I thank God for all three of you."

CHAPTER 102

Graeme had been in raptures on the flight, declaring 'she's a little beauty' and 'she handles like a dream'.

Stuart and Lauren were enthralled as Graeme pointed out Air Force bases where he had either been stationed, or where he had done flight training.

When he heard their call sign on the radio, he had spoken to Billy who asked if all was well. Graeme had replied 'as sweet as'. Billy informed him twenty of his peers watched the take-off, all 'drooling buckets of saliva, enough to sink a battleship' as Billy had so succinctly put it. Many also asked if Julie would consider divorcing Graeme, and marrying them instead!

With a wide grin he retorted 'Not a chance!' and he added a rude raspberry.

They had landed on a tiny airstrip outside of the Scottish town of Pitlochry. Graeme taxied his newest pride and joy towards the Aero Club. Julie's first task was to find the man she had spoken to previously when arranging to park the aircraft. She would also ask him how to get a taxi.

A wiry man, dressed in a kilt and tweed jacket, with a very broad Scots, accent greeted her, "Och, wee lassie, you're McKenzie from down

London way. I'm Jock Fraser, Part-time Manager and general dogsbody around here. We have been expecting thee and thine. Come, my car is here, it'll be my pleasure to take the distinguished McKenzie into town meself."

"Er . . . Well thank you very much. Er . . . Why the distinguished McKenzie?"

The man laughed and beckoned Julie to a large room adjacent to his office. This room contained memorabilia of RAF origin, but Julie was totally surprised to see a whole partition devoted to—Graeme! There was a large photograph when he was promoted to Air Commodore and a wall depicting a montage of his exploits, including him receiving his most recent honour from the Queen—the award for bravery from the suicide bomb incident.

Jock Fraser said, very dryly, "Now d'ya unnerstand, lassie? He's one of our favourite sons. There's several people who're dying to meet our man."

Julie responded, "We'd only planned to stay for a picnic lunch. We are due home again at six o'clock . . . How many people Mr Fraser?"

"Och, only a dozen at most, lassie. Sadly, we old RAF 'Brylcreem' boys are a dying breed. They just want to see him in the flesh, so to speak."

"Let me go and talk to him, Mr Fraser."

Julie hurried out as Graeme asked, "All set, darling. Taxi coming?"

"Well, not exactly. Er . . . Graeme, it seems you're a local hero. There are several 'oldies' who want to shake your hand, that sort of thing. You'd better come and see their lovely Museum, especially as you are the centrepiece exhibit! Mr Fraser will take us in for you to meet the ex-RAF members."

Graeme arched an eyebrow at her, thinking she was pulling his leg. He realized she was in deadly earnest when he recognized the man. His face broke into a huge smile, "Jack Fraser, is it really you?"

"Aye, lad 'tis, your Dad's old mate! Come inside and see, we are mighty proud of you up here. Come lassie, bring the bairns in."

Lauren and Stuart were suitably impressed that they had such a famous father, famous even in this pretty, but remote part of Scotland.

After that there was no question, Graeme simply had an obligation to be taken out to the Veteran's Home. On the way, Julie rapidly repaired her own make-up, ran a comb through Stuart's curly mop and did her best to straighten Lauren's long locks. Thankful they were casually, but smartly dressed in decent leisure tracksuits.

"Och, don't fash yerself, lassie," said Jock Fraser, as he eyed her in the rear vision mirror. "Ye look fine and bonny. Mind you, all the McKenzies pick good-looking women. Look at who your father snared. Alicia MacDonald was the belle of the ball. She broke many hearts, mine included, when she married your father,—an ARMY man!"

Graeme caught Julie trying to smother her giggles. "I can't wait to confront my wicked mother-in-law tonight," Julie stammered to her equally amused husband.

The Veteran's home was a pleasant rambling old Manor House, with an old Spitfire mounted on the front lawn, much to Stuart's delight.

Jock Fraser strode down a long hallway, dotted everywhere with reprints of Churchill's speeches, flags of every Allied nation and photographs of war heroes. Suddenly Lauren gasped as she saw a large photograph of her father, taken the day he had graduated from RAF Cranwell.

Their sprightly guide entered a large drawing room and clapped his hands. About a dozen elderly men were seated in large comfortable club leather chairs, reading newspapers, dozing, or playing chess.

Jock Fraser declared, "I've found him! Here he is lads, Air Commodore Graeme McKenzie, with his wife, Julie McKenzie and their two bairns, Lauren and Stuart. It's both of the lads' birthdays today, Mrs McKenzie informs me. They've flown in today in the Air Commodore's new airplane. A real little 'popsy'."

Graeme's tall figure was soon bent over a gnarled old hand, or bending low to speak more slowly and distinctly to a hearing impaired elderly gentleman.

A Nursing Sister, immaculate in a white starched uniform and scarlet cape asked Julie, "Would you and your daughter care to freshen-up?"

Outside she smiled, "Sorry about the subterfuge, but Jock has told us about the two birthdays, and we'd like to bring in a cake with candles. It would give the old boys a real thrill; we even have a ceremonial sword to cut it."

Julie replied, "What a lovely, thoughtful gesture. Look, we've brought a picnic lunch with us and could eat with you. That'll give Graeme more time with them. Perhaps have the cake at the end?"

"Perfect, Mrs McKenzie. On fine days, we normally eat lunch under the trees."

'Under the trees' proved to be picnic tables, comfortable chairs and large, brightly coloured sun umbrellas. It was obviously a favourite eating spot.

At the end of the al fresco meal, during which Graeme spent much of the time chatting to one elderly man after another, a large cake, topped with five candles, was brought in. The Sister explained, four for Stuart, and four plus one, representing Graeme's forty-one years.

After they had blown out the candles, Graeme was handed a ceremonial sword, and he and Stuart cut the cake as the whole body of residents, staff, visitors and families sang 'Happy Birthday'.

To the cries of 'speech, speech', a smiling Graeme rose to the task. "Well, what can a man say . . . Thank you, from the bottom of my heart, to all of you on behalf of my son and I. This has been quite a memorable day already for young Stuart here—and likewise for me."

Graeme looked directly at Julie, as he continued, "I have received a Birthday gift today from my wife that a pilot's dreams are made of—my own personal aircraft. Those of you who are pilots will understand the emotions I have gone through today. The marvellous feeling deep inside your being—of an unsurpassed freedom of spirit—which you only experience when you fly, almost to the face of God and back again."

Several of the elderly ex-servicemen nodded their wise old heads, "Aye, 'tis so."

Graeme's voice softened, "Stuart is a mad keen aviator in the making. Where you gallant and intrepid gentlemen learned to fly bi-planes, tiger moths and spitfires and I, turbo-jets, pure jets, jump jets, helicopters, and the like of today's modern Royal Air Force, he will be an aviator of the next generation. Who knows? He might even be an astronaut, a spaceman, flying to the Moon and the stars beyond. Stuff fantasies and dreams were once made of, but not, I suspect, for much longer in this very fast moving world of ours.

"This has been a wonderful experience for my family and I, to meet in the place where once some of my ancestors fought and won the freedom of this special piece of land. I wish you well, our very sincere thanks for your most welcome hospitality, thank you."

He sat down to hearty applause as Julie gazed at him in amazement. He had put together an impromptu, charming speech and delivered it with such aplomb and sincerity. As he quirked an eyebrow at her, asking how did he do, she murmured, "That was just beautiful, darling."

They took their leave, Jock, as promised, made a detour to the old Presbyterian Kirk, which proved to be an historic eye-opener. The McKenzie headstones soon had Graeme and Julie proudly reading to their children of a brave heritage in peace and war of their paternal ancestors.

A short while later they smoothly took off, and returned to Mildenhall right on time. Graeme taxied to his place in the hangar and lovingly patted the console in front of him, "Well done, baby, you and I are going to become real close, bosom pals in the future . . . Come on, let's go party!"

Soon the house was full of happy laughter as Stuart and Graeme opened even more presents.

Graeme grabbed his mother by the waist and growled at her, "What's this I hear about you being the 'Belle of the Ball' in Pitlochry, and then adding insult to injury by snaffling an Army man? We heard today how you broke many hearts, Miss Alicia MacDonald!"

Alicia gazed at her handsome son, "Ne'er you mind, Graeme McKenzie. Just think, you might never have been born if I hadn't snaffled your father, so there!"

Grant McKenzie said, with a twinkle in his eye "We must compare notes later, when sanity once again prevails around this house. But, there's at least twenty youngsters out there, all with voices loud enough to make an RSM shudder, baying like zoo animals, demanding food. Are we ready for the onslaught, yet, Julie dear?"

Julie grinned, "Okay Dad, open the cage, let 'em in!"

Amidst colourful streamers, balloons that burst loudly for no apparent reason, party hats askew on little heads, crackers being pulled with ear piercing 'bangs' and dishes of food that disappeared as though a cloud of locusts had descended upon the table, the party got under way.

Daisy brought in the aircraft cake masterpiece she and Julie had crafted between them. Once it had been much admired and photographed, Graeme and Stuart did the cutting honours, for the second time that memorable day.

CHAPTER 103

The idyllic 'Indian Summer' month of September passed quickly. The air developed that peculiar autumnal smell, a mixture of smoke and damp foliage. Mr Lu Wong, the inscrutable gardener Julie and Graeme had inherited, solemnly issued his prophecy, "Snow coming, hollible cold—good for garden, kill bugs."

He had turned up shortly after they had moved in, emphatically telling Julie, "My day to do garden, Missus, you pay me at end". He had similarly arrived, rain or shine, every week since. As Julie told Graeme, "There was no argument, he was here 'to do garden'," she smiled ruefully.

One evening in mid-October, Julie saw Graeme with a pile of sheet music stamped, 'Pre-Christmas Charity Concert.' She asked "What's that, darling?"

Graeme explained, "We hold a charity concert annually on base and raise heaps of cash. It always has a theme, this year 'The Big Band Era.' I play pieces that have been requested."

Graeme told her that the base orchestra was involved, with Major Davis, its conductor. He said that there was always a sell-out crowd and it was amazing where all the talent came from each time.

"What about some fashion models darling? I could set it up with Denise Armstrong."

Graeme leered at her suggestively, "With all the raw testosterone jumping around the young 'erks', I think that would go down very, very well, my darling. I'll put Hugh Davis in the picture. Make them really feminine and sexy, and I'll arrange music to suit."

"What about Lauren playing something? Is she good enough?"

"Darling, she's superb, but as she's under twelve, I'll have to check with Hugh."

The next morning, Julie quickly sketched a design burning her imagination since Graeme had mentioned the Charity Concert. Playing Graeme's recorded music, she eliminated them until only 'You Made Me Love You', remained.

Satisfied, she sighed, 'Yes! Now to the costume . . . what did he want . . . really sexy and feminine wasn't it?'

The female figure she had drawn was clothed from head to feet in a figure hugging, very sexy cat costume. Calling Daisy in, Julie went through her proposed routine.

Daisy reacted with tears of laughter and spluttered, "Oh, I must be there, I wouldn't miss this for quids, lass!"

"Great! Now all I have to do is convince Hugh Davis."

His reaction turned out to be very positive when he responded, "Yes, Ma'am, the Air Commodore said you had an idea to 'liven up his stodgy playing' . . . Stodgy playing indeed! The man could have become a legend in his own right . . . I think your idea will go down a treat. We'd need a rehearsal. I see no problem with young Lauren. From what the Air Commodore has told me, she is headed the same way as her talented father."

Julie gulped. "Er . . . There's one number I'd like to do . . . I'd like it to be a full-on surprise to Graeme."

Intrigued, the Musical Director suggested Julie bring sketches of the gowns to show him, as her pretext for being there.

Her next call was to Denise Armstrong. Within minutes she agreed to supply the models, offering to drive them to the air base and act as dresser.

Julie arrived at Major Hugh Davis' next day, confirming the model parade was all go; she rather nervously put her own 'act' to him. She explained that, to get the full impact, it must be a total secret from Graeme, with only those that really needed to know, actually knowing.

Hugh Davis was delighted, as he saw it, Julie's contribution would only enhance the most popular officer's standing with his men.

Lauren had chosen for her musical item a trio of Glen Miller's tunes.

As Hugh Davis remarked, "She plays with the aplomb of one much older." He added. "She has the ability to be even greater than her father, and that's no Welsh bull dust!"

Major Davis had a secret rehearsal with Julie to discuss timing. He had applauded appreciatively, "You are going to 'Wow' them, Mrs McKenzie. If you were my wife I'd be so damn proud of you! You're going to blow our Air Commodore away."

The theatre was filled to capacity. Every act was generously applauded by the enthusiastic audience.

Soon it was Lauren's turn. There was a hush as the tiny figure, dwarfed by the grand piano, swung into a spirited arrangement of, 'In The Mood'. It soon had the audience stomping in unison with the music. Faultlessly and effortlessly she played 'American Patrol', to the whistling and shouts from the 'erks in the balcony, which had Lauren smiling cheekily. For her final selection Lauren had chosen 'Moonlight Serenade'.

As she struck the opening notes, there was a collective sigh from around the auditorium. The mellow notes hovered around the walls, floated up to the very top of the ceiling and glided back again. There, like a gentle musical cloak, they wrapped themselves around the heads of those in the audience old enough to have heard the original sound. The melody brought back happy memories of their youth. Hugh Davis cued in the orchestra, to back Lauren to a soaring climax in the renowned Glen Miller style.

As the last notes faded away, there came a swelling wave of applause, and shouts of 'bravo' and 'encore'. Lauren was given a prolonged ovation. By this time, Julie had quietly slipped away and, with Daisy's help, put on her cat suit.

Billy announced, "Now it is the maestro himself, with his virtuoso fingers on the ebony and ivories. He will be accompanied by gorgeous models displaying a range of stunning gowns, brought to you courtesy of Mrs Julie McKenzie. Ladies and Gentlemen, please welcome your very own, Graeme McKenzie!"

Graeme walked on to the darkened stage to enthusiastic applause. He began with 'I'm In the Mood for Love'. Dramatically, on the otherwise completely blacked out stage, a blinding spotlight picked up the first model, wearing the romantic, toga styled 'Summer'. The beam of light followed her as she sashayed around the stage, 'glad eyeing' the audience. The 'erks' in the balcony howled and wolf-whistled her as Graeme played the tune, very suggestively.

Following the same format, the second model appeared to 'I Can't Stop Loving You'. This time, with a large cushion under her skirt to simulate a pregnancy, she wore one of Julie's maternity evening outfits. This girl was quickly followed by a truly concerto styled rendering of 'Stardust', as Graeme played the tumbling, descending glissando's and two models paraded the magnificent 'Night Sky' and 'Blue Heaven' gowns.

Graeme slid effortlessly into 'As Time Goes By'. There were gasps aplenty as the brilliant, burgundy coloured velvet and white fur trim of the Dickens Christmas card outfit 'Winter' could be seen in all its glory. Once again the applause was deafening.

Graeme played, 'I Can't Give You Anything But Love' for the next model, dressed in Julie's full bridal outfit. This brought forth a multitude of sighs from every woman present.

Julie listened carefully, hidden with Daisy at the edge of the stage.

The lone spotlight was on Graeme as he played the opening bars 'You Made Me Love You', the cue for the next model to come on stage. Julie took a deep breath and began to sing huskily, in a sexy, torch singer voice. The spotlight picked her up as Graeme looked up in surprise, to see a sexy black 'kitten' advancing towards the piano. She began bussing up against him, rubbing herself against his legs and his arms, as she sang the suggestive words. She ran her long soft tail under his nose and pulled it to its full length around his head and over and across his eyes. All the time, Graeme manfully kept playing, shaking his head and smiling, while the 'kitten' kept singing. She playfully ran her fingers through his hair, and flirted with him by batting her long, false eyelashes coyly at him. She felt his muscles and then mimed with an exaggerated movement to the audience, what lovely large biceps he had under his tuxedo.

The audience loved it, laughing hilariously at her antics and lapping up what this anonymous, surprise 'kitten' was doing to one of their most senior and popular officers. Graeme went along with the gag, continuing to play the main melody, but adjusting his accompaniment by slowing for her husky high notes, and making the piano 'talk' with a wolf whistle when the kitten put a shapely leg up on the piano stool beside him. He vamped a simulation of a rapid heartbeat as, at one stage, she leaned over and kissed his forehead. He ran up and down the scales in a waterfall of notes, a sighing, soaring sound of romantic strings, as she curled up kittenishly beside him on the piano stool, purring against his shoulder.

The melody came to its climax with the final long, slow, drawn-out phrase, "You . . . know . . . you . . . made . . . me . . . love . . . YOU!" On the last note, the spotlight on the kitten was abruptly switched off. Julie was supposed to scamper off stage before the stage lights were put on, but Graeme was quicker.

As the audience erupted into thunderous applause, his voice was heard over her microphone, saying, "I'd know that perfume and those sensational legs anywhere. Put the lights up Billy, please."

Billy was not privy to this surprise act. As the lights went up, they saw Graeme holding the wriggling body of the 'kitten' tightly in his arms. As the audience cheered him on, and the 'erks did their stomping and whistling act even more loudly, he gently pulled the cat's mask and hood off and gave the sexy 'kitten' a long, long kiss on the lips.

He immediately said into the microphone, "Believe me when I tell you I had no idea . . . This, is my beautiful, but very devious wife, Julie McKenzie!"

As Hugh Morris had predicted, it brought the house down. People were stomping, clapping and cheering as they saw Julie's laughing face and saw her hug him as they kissed once again.

The audience did not want this magic moment to end. The ovation was continued for another minute or so as Graeme and Julie stood, hand in hand, bowing and acknowledging the accolades.

CHAPTER 104

Julie had seen the dangerous glint in Graeme's eyes and knew she was in big, delicious trouble when he finally had her alone! They stood together, getting hugs and words of amusement as to how well Julie had kept her secret from Graeme and what a masterly response from him.

Each generous compliment Julie knew was only adding fuel to Graeme's fire, as he impatiently whispered in her ear, "Out of here, now! I have a rather urgent bone to pick with you that cannot wait, Mrs Julie McKenzie!"

He pushed her out of the nearest Fire Exit door and with his arm around her waist, marched her towards their station wagon. Julie panted breathlessly, trying to keep up with him, "Graeme wait! Not so fast. Graeme it's freezing out here!"

"Hush woman!" He growled in retort.

The Fire Exit door opened behind them and three heads poked around it, all trying hard to control their amusement. "Methinks, a certain naughty lady is about to get her comeuppance," Grant McKenzie chuckled. "Come on Daisy, Graeme had already asked me to take you and the children home."

Meanwhile, Graeme had pushed Julie into the front seat before driving off at high speed. He brought the car to stop with a skidding spray of gravel at a local area, known as 'Lover's Lane'.

Julie looked at him, a wild, wicked gleam in his eyes as he discarded his tuxedo jacket and wrapped it around her shoulders, before crushing her lips under his with such force and passion that it took her breath away.

His voice husky, he held her close, whispering, "So, you thought you could flaunt that desirable body, you minx! You devilish, wicked sexy woman! I couldn't wait to vent my passion upon you. Do you know how sensational you looked this evening? How I could have made love to you right there and then? Have you any idea what you do to me, you wanton hussy?"

Julie touched his lips, quieting him as she gazed at him. "Graeme, my beloved husband, I adore you and love you so very much. Wasn't it fun, darling? You played along with me so expertly, so brilliantly. Tell me, when did you realise it was me?"

Graeme chuckled, "Actually, it was when you put your foot up on the piano-stool. You hadn't come that close to me until then. Didn't quite trust me not make a grab for you, did you? I saw the scratch you got from the rose bush."

Julie playfully punched him, "So it wasn't my sexy legs, you cad!" He stilled her protests with another long passionate kiss.

Julie stroked his face and said, with a catch in her throat, "I have something so very special to tell you, my sexy flyboy."

Julie held his dear face between her hands. "Graeme, my dearest, darling husband, we have made our third baby. Susan confirmed it this morning."

Graeme sighed a deep sigh of total contentment and held her close to him. "Sweetheart, that's just about the greatest news you could have given me! So when?"

"A June baby, a summer baby. Oh, Graeme, my love, we've done it again."

"The most welcome news to end such a special day. Wow! I feel great, but don't think you are off the hook minx, you are not going to escape that easily. You have been very promiscuous, taunting me, my desirable, wanton, sexy minx. So, I'll take you to the comfort of our marital bed, where I can enjoy you even more."

Julie looked at him in pretended horror, and giggled, "Graeme McKenzie, you weren't? . . . In the car? . . . Were you?"

He grinned at her, "As I am feeling very raunchy, very amorous, I think I might have!" Julie stroked his modesty suggestively, "Let's hurry home, my darling."

After doing a rapid check on their children, Graeme proceeded to extract from her 'payment as promised', in a wild, prolonged, passionate and very satisfying copulation. Soberly the next morning they came down to breakfast, hand in hand, to cheers and applause from both of their children and Daisy.

"Wasn't it fun, Mama, Papa?" Lauren said excitedly. "Did I play okay, Papa?"

"Lauren, you were magnificent!"

"Mama, you played tricks on Papa!" Stuart waggled his finger accusingly at Julie. "Papa, did you know it was Mama?" Graeme tapped the side of his nose and winked at his son. "Oh, yes, my son, a man always knows his own woman!"

A grinning Julie threw a tea towel at him, "Cad!"

Unperturbed, Graeme said, in a gentler voice, "We have rather an important piece of news this morning. Mama and I are going to present you with a new brother or sister next June."

Daisy gasped, "Oh my! Congratulations to you both! A baby in the house again! Oh my!" She dabbed tears from her yes.

That afternoon, the children bounded out of the car, both wanting to be the first to tell their Grandparents about the new baby. Alicia McKenzie ran towards Julie and hugged her, tears of joy running down her cheeks as Grant McKenzie shook his son's hand vigorously.

As they raised their glasses, Grant McKenzie proposed a heartfelt toast, "Julie and Graeme, we are so proud of both of you. Congratulations! We look forward to being able to share with you a new life, a new grandchild."

Putting his arm around Lauren's shoulders, Grant told her, "Young lady, you are a credit to us all, and we love you so much, little granddaughter."

He ruffled his grandson's dark curly hair. "Stuart, having you as a grandson has given me a new lease on life. Your Gramps is your biggest fan, my little man, believe me."

Grant raised his glass again, "Julie and Graeme, your mother and I have been overwhelmed watching the love you two share for each other. Yours is truly a marriage made in heaven. But . . . that act you two performed last night tops it all! My sides were still aching this morning.

I don't think the audience could quite believe what they were seeing, especially when you unmasked Julie and told them who she was. My goodness, that brought the house down!"

Stuart had been listening intently. Looking directly into his grandfather's face, he said, with all seriousness, "Gramps, you know, a man always knows his own woman. Doesn't he, Papa?"

Graeme nearly choked on his drink. As Alicia tried to hide her smile behind her hands, his father looked stunned and flabbergasted at his grandson.

Julie burst out laughing, saying delightedly, "Hoist by your own petard, Graeme, my love!"

When they had all managed to regain their composure, Alicia asked, "When are Kate and Harry due?"

"They'll be here 18th December, Mum. Katie saw me through quite a few hard years." Julie looked lovingly at Graeme. "If it wasn't for her, none of this would be taking place."

Alicia smiled at them, "I'm so excited and can't wait to get out the knitting patterns again." Then, more seriously, she took Graeme's and Julie's hands in hers, saying, "I never thought I would get the chance to make something for a baby of yours, Graeme, my dear son. Your father and I thought that pleasure had passed us by. You two have made this old couple so happy. As Dad has told you already, your 'love-match' of a marriage has blown a breath of fresh air into our lives."

Alicia's eyes filled with tears, "Words fail me, I cannot express adequately how much I welcome you as a daughter, Julie. You alone have been totally responsible for Graeme's complete transformation. Thank you, my dear, from the bottom of my heart."

Graeme stared at his mother, astounded, this was the longest speech he had heard from her in his entire life. Julie embraced her mother-in-law, whispering her thanks, as she saw how touched Graeme had been by his mother's words. Lauren said, wistfully, "Do you think we will get a white Christmas, Papa? I've never seen snow and would really like to play snowballs, just like you and Papa used to as children."

Graeme answered, "Snow means cold, princess. Still, it'll be fun while it lasts and we'll certainly be able to have some winter games. They tell me the lake up the road always freezes, so we might even get in some skating."

"Can you ice-skate, Papa?" his daughter asked in awe.

"Well, we'll have to see if it is the same as riding a bike. The theory being that once you learn, you never forget."

Julie added, "You tried to teach me once when we were what? About eleven or twelve, wasn't it?"

Julie's mind slipped back, etched in her memory, to when the local ice-rink had opened. Maureen had asked Julie and Graeme to come with her and Billy. Julie could still see Billy scampering ahead. He couldn't skate and he just pulled on the hired skates and had launched himself on to the cold, grey ice. He ignored Graeme's shouts of staying close to the side and went sailing right to the middle of the rink. Julie and Maureen had watched in horror at Billy doing a good imitation of comedian Charlie Chaplin's tramp walk, before falling flat on his back. Graeme had shaken his head and had skated out and rescued him.

Graeme had offered to skate with Julie and she let him tow her out onto the ice. Bur her feet acted as though they belonged to someone else. Graeme had eventually taken pity on her and left her to her own devices and humiliation. He had gone swishing around and around the rink at top speed, looking even then like a young Greek God.

"Darling, time to go," Graeme's voice broke into her reverie. "Where were you?"

"Back in time, recalling the one and only time I went ice-skating with you. I never did conquer that ice, I still can't skate."

Lauren stared at her parents. It had suddenly dawned upon her that they were talking about something that happened between them when they were her age! Alicia murmured, "You two go back such a long way." She sighed, "It was almost as though you were destined for each other, even then."

Julie and Graeme exchanged their secret smile as Graeme replied, "Yep, Mum, even back then we knew there was something special between us, but we were too young to know that it was the beginning of a lifetime commitment."

CHAPTER 105

The snow began in the middle of the night. Julie tiptoed over to the window and gasped at the ethereal, picture postcard scene in front of her. Lauren's wish for a white Christmas had been granted!

Hearing her gasp, Graeme could also see the awestruck look on her face. Feeling the warmth of his arms as he encircled her waist, Julie whispered, "Just look, Graeme, it's a Winter Wonderland out there."

"It looks darned cold to me," was his first unromantic reaction, earning him a dig in the ribs from her elbow.

He nuzzled her neck, drinking in the wonderful fragrance of her soft pliant skin as he cupped her full breasts. Last evening he had informed her that she was now a third of the way through her pregnancy. "How soon do you think you will be wearing maternity clothes? So that everyone can see what a clever Old Man they've got."

Julie teased him, saying, "Oh yeah! You know what the young are like, you aren't expected to indulge once you are over forty. So it'll be more like a 'dirty old man', for someone as ancient as you, my darling!"

The playful remark had earned her a beautiful 'punishment', a long, languorous, but gentle lovemaking session. He reminded her how careful he had to be with her in her condition.

Now wrapped together in Graeme's robe, they continued to gaze down at the peaceful scene below them. Their few minutes of peaceful contemplation were abruptly shattered by Lauren's voice, yelling with excitement, "Mama, Papa, come and see! "It's been snowing! Stuart, look, that's snow, real snow!"

Graeme kissed Julie's neck, saying, "See you later, pretty Mama. Time to make sure those two dress sensibly. You spoilt Antipodeans don't realise how cold snow can be!"

He pulled on a track suit and with a boyish grin blew her a kiss and hurried downstairs. "Big Kid," Julie yelled after him. She knew he was going to enjoy educating his children to the wonders of snow, as much as they were going to enjoy having such a vitally alive father to teach them.

Catching sight of herself in the full-length mirror, she grinned. "So he wants me in maternity clothes already!"

There were shouts and squeals of delight coming from the garden as the snowball fight began. Next it was all hands on deck for making a snowman. The sheer cold drove them inside by eleven o'clock, to where Daisy was waiting, with fresh cheese scones and home-made vegetable soup.

Graeme's face was glowing from the cold and his eyes were twinkling. "I feel about ten again!" He said as he gave her a peck on the cheek, making Julie shiver—his lips were icy cold. Graeme filled his mouth with scone, "Daisy, the Ambrosia of the Gods. Anything I can do to help inside?"

Julie assured him, "Nope, darling, all done." Stuart complained to his father, "I wanted Aimee with me, but Mama said it was best for her to be in Lauren's room."

Graeme teased his son, "But, she's a girl!" Stuart said staunchly, "No, she's not. She's Aimee!" Graeme chuckled, "Oh, I see."

Kate, Harry and Aimee were driving from London and were due to arrive mid-afternoon, but Julie was getting concerned.

"What's up, darling?" Graeme asked, circling Julie's waist. "Are you getting fidgety?"

"Ummm, just a bit," she replied, leaning back against him, "I won't be happy until they are here. They're not used to snow covered roads."

Julie admired the beautiful and colourful Christmas decorations Graeme had put up a couple of days ago. He had also ordered a Christmas tree to be brought to the house for the children to decorate. The room looked warm, welcoming and so traditionally festive. Graeme, with Sergeant Wyberg's help, had rigged dozens of small twinkling Christmas lights all around the front porch and the eaves of the house.

Graeme had proudly explained to Daisy and Julie that this Christmas custom of decorating a family home of his own was yet another first for him.

With her hands linked around his neck, Julie made him a promise, "My dearest husband, this year we will follow every single Christmas custom and tradition in the book."

Just at that moment, car headlights shone through the electronic front gates, sending Beau into a paroxysm of barking. Julie flung the door open wide, as the dearly familiar, exuberant figure of Kate rushed up the front steps, her red curly hair bouncing around her smiling face. They met and tightly hugged each other, as their tears of joy ran down their faces.

Harry and Graeme vigorously shook hands and playfully punched each other on the shoulders. The children hailed Aimee as a long lost sister with Stuart grabbing her by the hand and dragging her inside. Kate sighed, "Julie, Graeme, your home is just beautiful and look, you've turned on the snow for us! My goodness, you all look so disgustingly healthy." In a softer voice, she added, "And so happy. It's just so wonderful to see you together, a real family at last."

Stuart tugged at his Godmother's sleeve. As she anticipated what was coming, Julie held Graeme's hand in hers, while they exchanged smiles. Stuart said, with a totally straight and serious look, "Auntie Kate, I have something very important to tell you. We are getting a new baby next year."

Kate's bouncy red curls flew around towards Julie and Graeme, "Wowee!" she cried, "That's real news, and I'm delighted for both of you. Congratulations, my very dear friends."

Harry's face beamed as he kissed Julie and patted Graeme's shoulder, "Heartiest congratulations. When?"

"Should be a first Wedding Anniversary present for us," Graeme replied, with a grin. "I'm very well organised, as previous occasions will testify. You always get two for the price of one with me."

Kate laughed and retorted, "Oh yes, I can sure remember a certain time when your timing was being cursed to the high heaven!"

Graeme helped Harry put his car away in the garage. Leaning on the bonnet of the car, Harry asked quietly, "It doesn't take much to see you are deliriously happy. Has everything worked out?"

"Absolutely, Harry. I have legally adopted the children, they are now all mine. Julie and I are over the moon about the new baby. The house, as you've seen, is a real home. Daisy is a gem and a true friend. My parents and sister are really chuffed, they absolutely idolise the children."

Harry was listening closely as Graeme continued, "One or two of Julie's family were a bit more difficult, but they are beginning to realise that I'm here for the duration. Julie told you in her letters what she bought me for my last birthday; it's my pride and joy. Just the stuff dreams are made of, eh?

Graeme confessed, "I think I must be living a dream." He ticked off on his fingers as he said, "a wife who is my true soul-mate, whom I love more than life itself, and we have two really healthy children. Even though I'm a newcomer to this fatherhood role, I enjoy every minute of it. And now we've the new baby, a baby we both want so very, very much.

Harry grinned at his enthusiasm, saying, "I've never seen Julie so happy. She seems to have blossomed. How's your work going, now you have your family around you at long last?"

Graeme responded that it had made him even more satisfied with his profession of choice, which still offered him great stimulation and satisfaction. Harry noted that, like the rest of his family, Graeme looked a picture of health.

Graeme replied that his job responsibilities demanded that he maintain a high fitness level, providing him with the justification to go to the gym most days, or to enjoy playing squash and golf when time allowed.

When Harry mentioned Julie's change of lifestyle, Graeme told him, "I know Julie is just as contented with her own life, plus she has recently begun designing again. We do so much together as a family, especially having my own plane to fly, whenever and wherever we want. But most importantly, we are more than financially secure, and that's a comforting thought."

Graeme paused in thought before commenting, "At last, Harry, the lonely years for Julie and I are well behind us."

Harry mused, "I know what you mean about the fatherhood bit—it's so satisfying isn't it? I'm still staggered to find that, when Aimee seeks my opinion or advice, she treats me as though I'm God himself giving her an answer. It's a bit frightening sometimes, to have someone trust your judgement so implicitly. It's magical being loved so completely by a child."

Graeme patted Harry's shoulder, "I know exactly what you mean, Harry. It isn't something we big brave men talk about very much, is it? Lauren to me, is so special, she's our first-born and, oh how we surely wanted her. I look at Stuart and think; he's my son, my boy, my heir, someone to follow in my footsteps, to carry on the family name."

Graeme continued, "Our new baby is yet one more unique event for me. It's important to me that this will really be the first time I will have been around for a new precious life, right from conception until he, or indeed she, is born.

"Then afterwards, for those first few magical, growing months. I missed out on so much with the other two. This baby will be our 'swan-song' and is wanted so much by both of us."

They returned inside to find the children had disappeared and Kate and Julie were closeted in the upstairs sitting room. Of much interest to Kate were Julie's newest designs for the 'budget evening wear'.

She explained to Kate, "It's meant for a young wife and mother to dress stylishly, but without breaking the family bank."

"Brilliant concept, Jules! Did you say Michael and Denise showed interest? Before you get too tied up with junior number three, pull finger, and make it happen!"

Graeme called up the stairs, "We'll be in the study, darling. Come and join us for a 'snifter', girls."

Kate hugged Julie, telling her, "By the way—your sycamore tree is thriving. It's taller than Harry now. I put the flowers on all three graves, like you asked. Do you miss it at all?"

Julie shook her head, "Just people sometimes, Katie, especially the Reynolds family! My life is here, with Graeme, I know that without him there would only be a half-life. I need and love him so much, I couldn't envisage life without him, ever again, Katie."

CHAPTER 106

Grant McKenzie arrived with the refurbished snow sled and for hours on end they slid down the gentle slope of Pegasus's field. Pegasus stayed in his warm stable, content with a daily visit from Lauren and Kate.

Beau was a different kettle of fish. He was in his element with three small lively human companions to chase—endlessly.

Graeme invited Kate and Harry for a spin in his beloved plane. As the plane only seated six, Julie said, "Look, I have a pre-Christmas check-up with Susan Blake. Go and enjoy, I insist."

Graeme was reluctant, "I said I wanted to share in everything to do with this baby, and now I'm ducking out at the very first hurdle."

Julie teased him, "Oh, you aren't missing out at all, my darling. There's plenty more to come yet! You can't be at EVERY appointment."

Julie's check-up by midwife, Sister Rose Collins, progressed well, until her face creased in a frown as she listened to one instrument.

Susan Blake came in cheerily saying, "Hello Julie, my dear, don't panic. Rose just wants me to clarify something."

The doctor listened to the monitor and then looked at Julie with a big smile on her face. "Hey, lady, we can hear two heartbeats inside there! Here, listen for yourself."

Julie listened, her mouth gaped open, "Twins! Oh no, he was only boasting the other day, he always gets two for the price of one! Dear God! There'll be no holding him now."

Susan Blake joined in the merriment, "What a bonus Christmas present for that handsome husband of yours, Julie. I'll arrange for an ultrasound within the next few days, just to confirm. Bring him with you, let him see for himself how clever he's been."

Julie returned home in a daze. The snow crunched under her feet, the sun shone on her head and her heart sang with joy. She decided to do something she rarely did.

Entering the house, she called out to Daisy, "All's well, everything is fine, I'll be upstairs."

Dialling Graeme's direct line, her hands trembled with excitement as she stroked her abdomen—two babies!

"Hello, darling. This is a nice surprise, are you wondering where everybody is? They've hied off into Cambridge, for some shopping. We flew over the house, but you would have been at the Doc's by then . . . Julie? . . . Darling, you don't usually ring me here . . ."

"Everything's fine, Graeme. I just wanted to know when you would be home . . ."

He butted in, "I can tell by your voice, some thing's up. I was about to wrap things up here. Whatever it is, I'll be there in half an hour, sweetheart. I'll be there soon, my darling."

Julie slammed down the phone, exasperated. "He can read me like a book! Just you wait, McKenzie, two for the price of one, Hah!" But her face softened to a maternal smile, as she glanced at her reflection in the mirror. Twins, eh?

A few minutes later his sports car hurtled through the gate, at more than his usual high speed, causing Beau to scatter out of the way. Graeme patted the dog's head in apology, "Sorry old chap, in a bit of hurry," and he ran inside, calling for Julie as he bounded up the stairs, two at time.

Julie met him at the door to the Nursery. He gathered her in his arms, one eyebrow arched in a question mark and with his eyes mirroring his concern.

"Well . . . What is it, darling?" he asked, searching her face for tears or signs of distress. Instead, the corners of her mouth turned up into a smile, as her eyes twinkled up at his.

"What were you boasting about the other day? Something about two for the price of one, wasn't it? Well, my darling, gorgeous, sexy flyboy, Mr McKenzie, Sir, that's what we've got. We're going to have twins, Graeme Stuart McKenzie! Twins!"

Graeme's face broke into a wide, wide smile as her words sank in. Twins! His voice husky and hoarse with emotion, he stammered, "My darling, sweet wife, who's the clever one? No wonder you couldn't wait to contact me. You must have been staggered by the news. Wowee!" He twirled her around and kissed her lips. "Dear heaven, how I love you! Or perhaps you have already got the proof of that pudding inside of you."

"And it's going to be a whopping big pudding!" Julie assured him. "Seriously though, Susan is arranging an ultrasound promptly. She says to ask you to be there." Julie gazed at his happy face.

"I wouldn't miss the chance for quids. Julie, my darling wife, I was ecstatic at fathering just one more child. But now . . . there are two. Words cannot express how I feel at this moment."

Julie hugged him to her, as she quietly added, "Yes, you are right, we are blessed, Graeme darling. It's as though someone, somewhere, is trying to make up for all the years we've missed."

He embraced her tenderly, murmuring, "Whomsoever or whatever it is, I'm right behind everything that comes our way, my beautiful wife."

Hearing Daisy's call, "Tea. Where would you like it?" They went downstairs and Graeme twirled Daisy around, before saying, "Er . . . . My lovely wife has just told me that we are expecting twins!"

Daisy's face was a sight to behold. "Oh my! Twins, two babies! Oh just wait until the bairns hear that. Well, it couldn't have happened to nicer parents, I'm delighted for both of you. Now we'll have to get cracking and get a second set of everything prepared, lass."

Julie laughed, "Practical Daisy. But what fun it will be!"

"You, young woman, are going to have to rest a lot more," Daisy cautioned. "But, I've no doubt Graeme will keep you strictly in check this time."

"Youbetcha Daisy, this beautiful woman is my most precious asset. I intend to be there every step of the way, this time."

Julie nestled against Graeme and they grinned idiotically at each other, still coming to terms with such a wonderful, yet mind-blowing turn of events. Graeme could not stop smiling as he gently caressed Julie's abdomen. "Two of them, eh?"

An hour later they heard a car entering the driveway. Daisy anticipated they would want to tell everyone as soon as possible, so took the three children and organised them out of their coats and shoes. Kate and Harry, surreptitiously trying to squirrel several mysterious parcels away into their bedroom, were grateful for what they thought was Daisy's understanding.

Stuart piped up to Graeme, "When I asked Santa for a baby brother, Papa, he told me to go and ask you! What kind of Santa is that?" He gave a junior sized snort of disgust. "When I told him that Aimee was here from New Zealand, just so he would know where to come, he said he already knew that too. How did he know, Papa?"

Graeme listened sympathetically and murmured, "We'll have a talk about it later, shall we?"

Kate smiled as she overheard the gentle promise Graeme had made to his little son, before saying, "Julie, this lad of yours is one helluva pilot. We did enjoy ourselves up there, so thank you for letting us share your world for a while."

Graeme stood up and executed a mock low bow. "Thank you, for your kind words, I enjoyed your company. Well, as I now have your attention, come here, my darling." He grinned roguishly at Julie, saying, "Mama went to see Dr Blake today, to make sure our baby was growing properly. When Doctor Blake listened to the baby through a special instrument, she heard not one heartbeat—but two! Mama has two babies growing inside of her—we are going to have twins!"

Kate watched with tears in her eyes as Julie and Graeme embraced their son and daughter saying, "Yes, yes. Two babies."

Stuart confronted his father. "Well, Papa, can you make sure one of them is a boy baby for me."

Ebullient, bubbling Kate hugged them, saying exuberantly, "What a surprise. What wonderful news, my dear, dear friends. Oh, I am so, so happy for you."

Quieter Harry shook Graeme's hand vigorously, saying, "Just what we were talking about the other night, eh? The special state of fatherhood—and all that goes with it, eh? Congratulations, my friend."

Stuart asked, in his serious way, "Let's ring Gramps and Nana, Papa?" Getting the nod from Graeme, he grabbed Aimee by the hand, "Come on, Gingernut, you can help me dial their number."

Harry smiled at Graeme, "They really love your parents," and received Graeme's reassuring, "Yes, and it's reciprocated, one hundred per cent. Come, I'll put them on the speakerphone in the study."

Stuart dialled and Graeme switched on the speakerphone as his mother answered, "Hello, Alicia McKenzie."

Stuart replied, "Hello, Nana, this is Stuart McKenzie here." They heard a chuckle down the line as Alicia replied, "Now would that be THE Stuart Cameron McKenzie, himself?"

"Yes, Nana. You're on Papa's speaker, so we can all hear you. Is Gramps there?"

They heard Grant McKenzie say, "Yes, my grandson. Are you being good for Santa? Only two more sleeps and he'll be here, little man."

"Yes, Gramps. We've something important to tell you. Mama went to the Doctor lady today and guess what? She has got two babies growing . . . What's it called, Papa? . . . Twins, she is going to get twins for us . . . Nana, why are you crying?"

Grant McKenzie cleared his throat, "Your Nana is very, very happy Stuart. Ladies always cry when they are happy. We men sometimes try to be brave, but we cry with happiness as well, now don't we? Graeme?"

Graeme answered, "I'm here, Dad. Isn't it wonderful news? We're still in a bit of a stunned state. All is well, we're going for an ultrasound soon, to see the evidence for ourselves . . . believe me we can't wait."

Alicia had recovered her voice. "Julie and Graeme, we are delighted."

Julie added her piece, "Get out the knitting needles, Mum, we're going to need plenty more of your handiwork, for sure!" Graeme signed off the call by saying, "Well, cheers for now, folks, we'll see you here, bright and early Christmas Day. 'Bye for now."

After dinner, they decided to end this momentous day by a carol singing session around the grand piano. Graeme sang along with the words of 'And Unto Us A Child Is Born', but he held up two fingers to Julie, mischievously mouthing 'two for the price of one'.

CHAPTER 107

There was a staff Children's Christmas party at the base. The noisiest reception reserved, as ever, for the rotund gentleman, resplendent in a red suit and fluffy white whiskers. He arrived in the cockpit of a jet fighter, towed by a Jeep.

As each child's name was called, the eager, the more than reluctant, the tearful, the bashful, or the grinning self-consciously, all made their way to receive their gifts from the magical Santa.

As they watched, Graeme squeezed Julie's hand, signalling another 'first' for him. Stuart ripped his wrapping paper off to find a lifelike scale model aircraft of the latest RAF jet fighter. "Look Papa, it's the same one Santa came in," he excitedly told Graeme.

Lauren was more circumspect as she carefully undid the wrapping without ripping even one small piece, to discover, 'The A-Z of caring for your pets.' She gasped in total surprise and looked at her parents with an unbelieving look on her face. She had been extolling the virtues of this very book to her father, after she had seen it in Jack Daniel's Veterinary Surgery!

Aimee was looking as though she could not believe her eyes. "Daddy, Mummy, it's the doll I saw in the window! The one I wished I could have. Oh, what a clever Santa!"

Kate looked across at Graeme, as she said, "He sure is, honey. Quite a guy!" Graeme grinned back, winking at Kate, pronouncing, "He aims to please—all of his ladies."

After the traditional Christmas Eve hanging up of the stockings, and the very important task of leaving Santa a drink and a fruit mince pie, Graeme led them on the piano in singing the quieter carols of 'Silent Night', 'Holy Night' and 'Away In A Manger'.

At eleven o'clock, there was silence at last from the bedrooms. The stocking fillers were produced and stuffed until they could not hold another single item.

Graeme and Harry downed Santa's nightcaps, Kate and Daisy the mince pies, before Julie placed a note, "Many Thanks from Santa. See you all again next year!" Graeme, relishing all of this tradition, grinned boyishly, asking, "So, what do we do next?"

"We go to bed!" echo Kate, Julie and Harry in unison.

"They'll be up at dawn, laddie," Daisy grinned at him.

Graeme turned off the lights. Taking a piece of mistletoe, he held it over their heads, and kissed his wife with passion. "Aaaah, my darling, today has been one out of the box for me."

Julie knew this had been a sensational, emotional day for him. So many 'firsts'. So much happiness. "I have loved it, sharing Christmas with you, at last, my beloved husband."

* * *

. . . The "Wow's!" and the squeals of delight from the two girls, as predicted, began at dawn, shortly followed by Stuart's enthusiastic whoops of joy.

Lauren called up the stairs, "Mama, Papa! He's been!"

With a boyish grin on his face, Graeme grabbed his robe, leaned over and kissed Julie's lips. "Good morning, my darling. Merry Christmas, my own special angel. Time to go."

He literally bounded out of the door and Julie smiled as she heard him saying to the excited children, "Here we come. Have we got presents? My goodness, what a pile!"

Graeme sat at Julie's feet on the floor, surrounded by children, paper and gifts, his face a picture of happiness. Kate and Harry, watched the scene unfold before them, noting how Graeme touched Julie every now and again.

After a hectic hour of present giving, Graeme softly said, "I do have something else for you, my darling". He brought out a very elegant, oblong shaped parcel, wrapped in gold paper. He kissed her, "Merry Christmas, my darling."

Julie gasped as she saw the name of a very prominent furrier on the lid. She lifted out an exquisite imitation, silver fox fur, a hip length cape. She felt quite stunned as Graeme draped it around her shoulders. "This is for the times when I can't put my arms around you to keep you warm, my darling. I also thought a cape would be more comfortable as maternity wear."

Kate said, "That is one beautiful accessory, Jules. Oh my, you look so pretty."

Julie put her arms around her husband's neck, and in front of them all, kissed him ardently. "Thank you, my darling," she said, "once again you have made me feel so cherished. Oh, Graeme it's so lovely, so soft and so feminine."

He whispered, "Just like the beautiful woman inside it."

Graeme had a pretended surprised look on his face as he pulled out the settee beside him. "Oh Ho! What have we here?"

The object was a large wicker basket and, as the children opened the lid, two pairs of deep blue eyes opened and two small furry faces yawned, showing two very pink mouths. Both uttered a plaintive "Miaow", which immediately had Beau's ears pricked!

"Oh, Mama, Papa, they are so beautiful," Lauren sighed and picked up one of the fluffy, cream coated kittens with dark brown ears, faces, feet and tails. "They're Birman cats."

Julie stroked the beautiful kitten. "Yes, they are Birman and what's more, they're twins. Stuart, darling, you'll be pleased to know that they are both boy cats. Now you've your own set of twins to look after. Here are their pedigrees and their official names, but you can choose what names you'd like."

Beau came to investigate, and promptly got a sharp pat, from a tiny paw on his inquisitive nose. He backed off with a plaintive yelp and Graeme stroked his head, "Give 'em time, old lad. They'll come around."

All too soon it was time for them to dress for Church, as Graeme told them, soberly, "We need to go and give thanks this morning for so very, very much."

Julie stroked the cape as she looked at herself in the bedroom mirror. Dressed in the burgundy velvet 'Winter' outfit, she knew she was glowing with health and looking her very best.

Graeme said tenderly, "You look terrific, my darling. I knew that cape was just you, as soon as I saw it in London. I'm so proud of you, Julie. Come, let me show you off to the world."

He was dressed in full uniform, including his RAF greatcoat, and was completely unaware of how handsome he looked. Julie proceeded to tell him by embracing him and whispering, "By God! You are one very sexy flyboy. Hope we have some time soon for me to show you."

"Grrrrr . . . Very soon, minx! You're on, it's a date!" . . .

At the St. Peter's church, they caused quite a stir. The Vicar greeted them with a serene, smiling face, saying, "Welcome, to you, Air Commodore McKenzie, and to your family. Aah! This must be Mr and Mrs Reynolds and their daughter, Aimee, from New Zealand."

As they led the way up the aisle to their designated front pews, they passed several familiar faces. Included amongst them was Midwife Rose Collins, who quirked an eyebrow and inclined her head towards Graeme. Julie grinned happily, as she whispered back, "Overjoyed".

Several of the children's school friends looked wide-eyed when they saw Lauren and Stuart's father in his RAF uniform. Those with parents and other relatives in the RAF recognised his senior rank and whispered it to the others.

The Vicar announced, "I welcome you all here this morning as we come together to celebrate the birth of Jesus Christ. It is with great pleasure that I call upon a very new member of this parish, Air Commodore Graeme McKenzie, who will read this morning's lesson."

Graeme walked to the lectern, his blonde hair gleaming in the winter sunlight streaming through a stained glass window that appropriately depicted a tribute to the RAF and the Battle of Britain pilots of World War Two. He read with sincerity and meaning.

Julie knew that Lauren had learned not to applaud her father but, to be on the safe side, she held Stuart's hands. She had forgotten Aimee!

It was Aimee that led the applause and, to Graeme's surprise, the rest of the children in the congregation joined in! He solemnly acknowledged their acclamation with a discreet nod, sitting down beside Julie, not daring to look at Kate's mortified face, or at Harry trying to hide his amusement. They overheard a loud stage whisper from the pew behind say, with a deep sigh, "Ooh, he sounds like Sean Connery and Colin Firth all rolled into one."

Julie pulled her cape collar up, till only her eyes could be seen twinkling at him. A muffled, choked back throaty chuckle was all he heard, but knew his wife's devious, wicked sense of humour was working overtime to extract a suitable payment from him later.

They were soon standing among their neighbours, exchanging Christmas good wishes. The Vicar approached and thanked Graeme and saying, "Well, I mustn't keep Mrs McKenzie out in the cold for too long. Perhaps we may see a christening, here before long—I do hope so. Thank you, once again, Air Commodore."

Julie took Graeme's arm, "How did he know we were expecting?" Coming up beside them, Dr Blake overheard Julie's question. "Good morning, to the McKenzies. Julie, the whole village knows everything. This place has a 'grapevine' all its own, but it's a benign one, especially towards your family. You, my good sir, are already a legend around here! Anyway, your ultrasound will be done on the 27th. They are fairly quiet over Christmas and I prevailed upon them to get you in as soon as they could. So, 27th it is, at eleven o'clock. Okay with you?"

Graeme answered, grinning from ear to ear, "Thank you, Susan, we can't wait. I might add that we shall be delighted if what you suspect turns out to be a reality."

Susan chortled, "Yes, Julie told me about the theory of 'two for the price of one' you subscribe to."

She walked off, leaving Graeme, for once, at a loss for words. Julie chuckled, "Come on, 007, your 'fan club' is waiting."

Later that day, Julie exchanged telephone greetings calls with Carole and Lisa and Don, who also invited them for a New Year 'drink and a family get together'. Julie happily accepted, it would be a great opportunity to pass on the news of the babies.

CHAPTER 108

A very special Christmas Day was nearly over as Julie and Graeme lay in bed, recalling the excitement. Graeme chuckled, "I can still see Beau, his ears pricked, watching the two kittens. He really seemed to accept their presence."

Julie, tucked in closely beside him, giggled, "What about when he had lain down and they found his warm underbelly. And then, they simply curled up against him and went fast asleep. Wasn't it priceless! Poor Beau looked scared stiff, as though he dare not move a muscle in case he hurt them."

She rolled over on her back, to allow her rather swollen abdomen to settle. "I often wonder why people accept it as the norm that cats and dogs are always enemies. Ours have always seemed to live quite amicably together."

Graeme gently massaged her abdomen almost absent-mindedly, as he chuckled, "Yep, but Beau drew the line when one of them tried to suckle from him! Wasn't his face a picture? It most indignantly stated—back off! I hope I got that on film."

He cuddled Julie even closer to him. "They haven't agreed on the names, yet?"

"Nope, still a toss up between Oliver, Henry, Charlie and Sam. Stuart's favourite is Sam."

Boxing Day—The kittens had finally been given the names of Oliver-Charlie and Henry-Sam. It was left to the youngest, Aimee, to find the perfect solution.

As they sat together on the floor of Stuart's room, setting up his new car-racing set, Stuart stoutly told his father, "See, Papa, I told you she wasn't just a girl."

Graeme replied with equal seriousness, nodding sagely, "Yes, my son, I see what you mean."

Graeme remembered back some thirty years when he had thought the same way about a certain 'girl'. They had also shared a closeness, an indubitable understanding. 'Yes,' he mused silently, 'even then.'

Billy rang, saying that the local lake had frozen over sufficiently for skating. Julie replied, "I'm sure I'll get some 'takers', Billy. Come back here for a meal afterwards and join the general mayhem."

There was a scramble to don suitable warm and waterproof clothing. Graeme happily found his own skates and a spare pair for Harry. Daisy hastened to fill all available Thermos flasks with hot chocolate drinks.

An enterprising local man, who hired out skates, was doing a roaring trade and soon had all five children kitted out. Graeme and Harry found a pair for Billy, but the four women declined to join them.

Julie was firmly warned off by Graeme. "Don't you even think of setting one foot on the ice, Julie McKenzie."

Marisa declined, as she was nursing baby Winston, and Daisy declared, "I'm just too old. I'll enjoy watching."

Kate shook her auburn curls adamantly stating, "Snow and ice is strictly for looking at, or sitting upon in something comfortable, such as a fur-lined sled. Not on one's unprotected derriere, which all too soon would be my ultimate position."

The total adult female contingent sat huddled close to the warm, glowing brazier set up next to the kiosk. The air was so cold that every exhaled human breath produced a cloud of steam. Julie had a long, warm, soft scarf entwined around her neck, two pairs of woollen gloves on her hands, and she also had two pairs of Graeme's uniform issue socks under her winter boots. Yet, she could still feel the chill slowly seeping through her extremities.

On the ice, Graeme was leading the way. Julie saw that Billy had vastly improved his technique since she had seen his last débâcle on ice, so many years ago. She watched Harry and Aimee and saw them moving competently, gracefully, to the middle of the lake.

Expressing her surprise to Kate, her friend laughed, "Harry was born in Southland, New Zealand, he has skated all his life. He taught Aimee almost as soon as she could walk. I just couldn't get the hang of it."

After nearly an hour, the three fathers brought their offspring to shore and Daisy fed them all a most welcome mug of hot chocolate.

This led to an immediate male challenge to a race around the lake perimeter. Freed of the restrictions of caring for small children, they were off!

Harry led, with Graeme a close second. Billy was not able to match the speed of the two more experienced skaters.

Agreeing that perhaps there was just enough time for one more foray, the intrepid young fathers towed their delighted children back onto the ice.

Julie, Kate, Marisa and Daisy decided they had been cold for long enough, so packed up their belongings and retired to the warmth of the station wagon.

Next morning, as Julie gazed at her reflection in the dressing-table mirror, her thoughts drifted . . . 'It had been such an eventful year . . . This time last year I was alone and so lonely without him. I also nearly died trying to reach him. Now here I am married to him, and on my way to have our new twin babies confirmed . . . Such a wonderful, miraculous year.'

At the hospital they met Sister Rose Collins and Julie introduced Graeme. He grinned disarmingly at Rose Collins, assuring her, "Sister, I sincerely hope you are right."

"Well, I'm delighted you were able to come, Sir. This ultrasound is something so special. I always feel, if the baby's father misses it, he misses something he helped produce which can never ever be recaptured. Well, let's go in. Julie, there's a gown for you. Sir, there's a theatre gown for you, to protect your uniform. Come through when you are ready."

Graeme hesitated, not knowing the protocol regarding him being with Julie while she changed. But she grabbed his sleeve, "In here buster, your education regarding the rigmarole of having babies is about to begin!"

Grinning, he helped her don the very skimpy short gown, saying, in a slightly shocked tone, "Is that all there is? It's a bit on the 'mini' side. It hardly covers you, darling."

"Welcome to the world of pregnant Mums, my dearly beloved. Come on; put your theatre gown on. Not that way, darling, back to front, arms in, tied at the back."

In the next room, Julie lay back on the clinical couch and Sister Collins covered her with a muslin blanket. The Sister pumped the bed up until it was level with Graeme's waist and then painted Julie's exposed abdomen with a jelly like substance.

"There you are, all ready. I'll call in the operator." Rose whispered, "Its Angela. She's the best. This is going to be a very special, very emotional time for you . . . even fathers, Sir. Enjoy, my dears."

There was a discreet knock and a cheerful round faced woman entered, "Hello, I'm Angela."

She placed a small instrument on Julie's abdomen. A picture appeared on the screen and a gurgling noise. Adjusting her controls, Angela refined the noise and it became a regular beat. Graeme, who was more used to monitoring a radar screen than Julie, could see two images beating in time from within.

Angela moved the instrument around, "There they are, folks. Two babies and two very strong heartbeats. You definitely have twins. Because it's a multi-birth, I have to record the sex of each baby, but you do not have to know. I'll give you a moment or two to think about that one, while I monitor your blood pressure and other vital statistics, Mrs McKenzie."

Julie looked at Graeme and he kissed her, before resuming his study of his two babies. He said in an awed voice, "Darling, will you look at that! Hey! Look! I can see an arm thrashing around and there's one head and look, there's the other!"

Julie was too overcome to speak. She gazed awestruck at the two babies that their love for each other had created.

Graeme kissed her tears and then gently wiped her eyes, as he bent over her. "Dear God, Julie. Dio come ti-amo, cara mia." He kept his head close to hers, trying to clear the lump in his throat, not trusting himself to speak.

The two infant heartbeats were resounding around the small room as Julie huskily asked, "Well, what do you think, darling. Do we want to know? One half of me wants to know, the other half not so sure."

Graeme replied, "My feelings are the same as yours, my sweetheart, I'm not sure either. In that case, let's wait until we are, or we need to know. How does that sound?"

"Yes! That's the best idea, you wise, wise man. Oh Graeme, isn't it just a fabulous sight?"

Angela returned and Graeme said, "We'd rather not know the sexes for now, Angela. If the time comes when we need to know, so be it."

Angela called Rose Collins in and advised her of their decision. "That's fine with me, folks," she said cheerily. "It's funny, older parents never want to know, but the very young always do. Anyway, let me see how our babies are doing."

She told Graeme, "Sir, your wife will need to rest a lot more in her last months. At forty years of age, you are nearing the end of your biological breeding years, Julie. But, reading your previous maternity notes, I see no real problems. We will do all the usual and necessary tests though, to be on the safe side."

Graeme chuckled, "Now, will you wear maternity clothes?"

Julie in front of a beaming Rose Collins, kissed her husband, "Yes, you can do your show off bit. We used to call someone like you a 'skite' in New Zealand."

Watching her scamper out, Graeme admired the view he got of her naked rear end and her still shapely legs. He gave her a low wolf whistle making her blush when she saw Angela and Rose Collins watching with amused interest.

Later, Graeme stopped the car high on a hill. His face wreathed in smiles, "Hey! Lovely lady, I just wanted a moment alone with you, to tell you how much I adore you. My dearest wife, this morning I have experienced something so special in my life that I cannot find the words to describe adequately how I feel."

Julie leaned against his shoulder and sighed contentedly, "Just having you there to share it with me was so wonderful, Graeme. I love you so much, Graeme Stuart McKenzie."

CHAPTER 109

All flying had been cancelled at the base, but the Search and Rescue unit were on 'full emergency alert'. This necessitated Graeme and Billy as part of the team, being on a round the clock roster.

Graeme advised Julie against driving herself, until the weather improved. He emphatically stated, "You're not used to these treacherous conditions, sweetheart. No, my darling, I want you to stay safely at home, or at least let me drive you, if you need to go anywhere."

Julie meekly nodded, accepting his earnest request. But, it did not stop her from ducking out from his embrace and teasing him, by retorting, in mock anger, "That's it, Graeme McKenzie! All you want is to keep me barefoot and pregnant, and tied to the bed!"

Laughing at her supposed anger, he recaptured her, saying, "What an absolutely delicious thought, you bare, buck naked and tied up, unable to resist me. And permanently pregnant, a state which you tell me always makes you feel extra raunchy!"

Manoeuvring her over to the bed, he proceeded to strip her naked as he butterfly kissed her in what he knew were her erogenous zones.

She writhed under him, demanding huskily, "More, more, my sexy flyboy."

Much later, as he took her face in his hands, he declared, tenderly, "You are one tantalizing and adorable minx. But Julie, my precious darling, promise me you will heed my words?"

Julie answered softly, "Yes, of course I will, Graeme. I never meant to do anything else. But, you also take extra care, I need you as much as you need me."

During the next day, the winds eased, but it was still bitterly cold, grey and bleak. Graeme was due home to change, before Sergeant Wyberg drove them, with Kate and Harry, back to the Mess for a New Year's Night dinner.

Julie had decided to wear her loose fitting maternity clothes, so that Graeme could 'skite' in front of his peers. She selected a softly draped dress, in his favourite dusky pink shade. It clung just enough to show her changed figure, but fell comfortably and elegantly to just above her still trim ankles. The scooped neckline was low enough to take a pair of sparkling drop earrings.

Completing her ensemble, she admired herself in the cheval mirror. 'Umm, not bad, for a mother of nearly four children. Four of them! It's a sobering thought, Julie girl.'

She heard Graeme drive into the garage, his cheery voice greeting the children as they went through their usual evening ritual of throwing themselves into his open arms.

She heard him bound up the stairs, two at a time, calling for her. Tonight though, for a few seconds, he stopped, stood leaning laconically against the door jamb, pushed his uniform cap to the back of his head and blew a low wolf whistle of admiration.

"Wow! Julie darling, you look sensational in that colour, and so beautifully pregnant! Tally Ho! Wait until the lads get an eyeful of you tonight!"

Julie blushed under his scrutiny, she said, "Umm, I thought I didn't look too bad, for a mother of almost four. Did you get that—four, Graeme Stuart McKenzie? If you haven't proved your virility by now, God help us when you finally admit you have!"

"Julie, you don't look a day older than when you were expecting Lauren." He held her tightly against him, as he said suggestively, "As you can probably feel, my virility is very much to the fore, just now. Mind you it is never far away whenever you are around, Mrs McKenzie."

Julie laughed gently and kissed him long and hard. "Hurry up, you gorgeous hunk. So, go, shoo, make yourself even more handsome than you are right now."

An hour later, as she walked into the Officers Mess on his arm, Julie could see his chest bursting with pride as her pregnancy was noted. She exchanged a surreptitious glance with Kate, seeing, by the dangerous twinkle in Kate's eyes and the twitching of her mouth, she was about to burst into a giggle. Kate had also noted the rustle of whispered conversations, the head turning and the downright, open-mouthed gaping of the assembled Officers and their wives and partners.

Leading them towards their hosts, his C.O., Air Vice Marshall Martin Brown and his wife, Dulcie, Graeme knew they had made the entrance impact he had anticipated.

Dulcie Brown, greeted them with an enthusiastic, "So, the rumour I overheard is true, you are expecting again! Julie, my dear, you look so elegant and that pretty colour certainly suits you. Aah, so these are your friends from New Zealand. How lovely to meet you. Now tell me when is the new baby due? We haven't had any babies since Wing Commander Watson's little one was born earlier this year. Goodness, it is hard to believe there are only a few hours left in this year. It has been one you will not forget in a hurry, m'dear, I'm sure."

Before Julie could answer, Graeme proudly said, "Well, Ma'am, actually it will be babies, plural. It seems we are having twins this time, a double blessing indeed. They are due at the beginning of June, all being well."

"Twins!" both Martin and Dulcie Brown echoed in unison, with his C.O. adding, "Well I never. Well done Graeme and Julie. Heartiest and sincere congratulations!"

After the dinner, when the ladies retired, Julie and Kate found that they were bombarded with questions regarding their gowns, Julie's multiple pregnancy, life in New Zealand and what's hot in the fashion world.

Kate studied the gowns of the other wives, commenting to Julie, "I see why you want to help these women. They're all highly intelligent and really fashion-wise young women. Your designs are just what they're waiting for, Jules. Get that '2BE1' line into production, as soon as you can, girl. There's definitely a niche market here, just falling over itself to buy what you have in mind."

Julie nodded. "Yes, you're right, Katie, these women do wonders on their limited budgets and deserve someone championing them. I will certainly take up the cudgels for them again. It will help pass those interminable long months of waiting we women have to endure in our pregnancies . . ."

Her face broke into a smile as a waft of a familiar aftershave tickled her nose and Graeme whisked a proprietary arm around her. Encircling her waist he nuzzled her neck and whispered, "What cudgels are those, sweet thing? Come, dance with the man voted the most virile in this room."

He swung her onto the dance floor and chuckled, "Oh, my darling, you should have been a fly upon the wall in there as we passed the port. I had to endure quite a 'roasting' over my 'veteran age' of becoming a father again. They made me the butt of many a ribald joke about my ability at making two babies, with just the one shot at the target. Now what was that about cudgels, I overheard?"

As they danced, Julie briefly explained what she and Kate had been discussing. He listened, hearing her out, before quietly saying, "Julie, there can be no long days, or late evenings. You must promise to rest as much as is needed."

He swung her gently to the side of the dance floor.

"I once promised Andrew that I would never stop you designing, because I'd been privileged to see your unique genius close up. With this particular line you are proposing, I'll be right behind you, you know that. But your health, my darling one, will always be to the forefront."

Julie giggled at his slightly Victorian words, but he was very new to this father-to-be, hands-on situation. She put her arms around his neck. "Graeme, I adore you and want our babies too much to risk any harm coming to them. Thank you for your understanding and your support, my dearest husband. Now, let's dance this old year out, because at the moment, I am in the only place I want to be, here in your arms."

The resonant sound of Big Ben playing on the radio boomed out the magical twelve chimes, and the room erupted with rousing cheers and cries of 'Happy New Year'.

Graeme tenderly kissed Julie, saying, "Happy New Millennium, my adorable wife. This new century and New Year, Julie, Dio come ti-amo, cara mia."

Julie clung to him, as she replied, "To you, my dearly beloved husband, a Happy New Year and one we shall treasure the most."

As usual, their superb dancing skills drew more than a few sighs. Dulcie Martin watched them and remarked to her husband, "What a difference Julie has made to young Graeme's private life, my dear. You have always admired and backed him professionally I know, but now, well . . ."

The Air Vice Marshall confided to his wife, "Umm, quite right m'dear. I see further promotion for him in the not too distant future, if he'll take it, that is."

Tired but happy, Julie snuggled up to Graeme's strong shoulder in the back seat of the car as Sergeant Wyberg drove them home. Julie smiled, saying, almost under her breath, "I'm Mrs Julie McKenzie." Graeme heard her whispered words and he murmured, "Forever and ever, 'til death us do part, darling one."

On arriving at the front door of the house, Graeme picked up a small parcel and handed it to Harry with a grin. "It's a piece of coal and, as you are the darkest haired male, it's traditional, you enter first. It's called 'first footing'. Will you do the honours, please Harry."

On New Year's Day, they all piled into the station wagon for the trip to Don and Stella's home and the family get-together. Don, smiling broadly, asked, "I believe you have something to tell us?"

Graeme grinned at him, saying, "The McKenzie clan is expanding. Julie and I are delighted to announce that we are expecting twins, early in June."

The small room erupted in chaos as everyone tried to congratulate Graeme and Julie at once.

CHAPTER 110

With the snow finally disappearing, essential services quickly returned to normal. Graeme could now safely take a few days off. It was decided they would have a two day sightseeing visit to London.

Lauren, acting as scribe for the younger pair, had written down the places they would like to see. Knowing only too well the way to her father's heart, Lauren wound her arms around his neck and leaned her golden head on his shoulder.

Graeme whistled in amazement. "Whew! What a prodigious list."

"We have been saving them up, so that you can take us, please, Papa darling."

Kate looked over his shoulder. "Well, Julie can't do some of them, she'll get much too tired." She tapped an elegant scarlet finger at the list. "Look, Jules wants to see Michael and Denise and so do I. How about you two nice fit and healthy Daddies do the Zoo, while we two ladies sit nicely snug in Michael's plush centrally heated office?"

"Katie Reynolds, I think you are as cunning and devious as your friend Julie!" Graeme retorted.

Harry protested, "Katie love, it's mid-winter out there!"

"You didn't seem to notice the cold when ice-skating!" Kate flung back, "Come on, guys, where's your true British grit and stiff upper lips?"

"Went the same way as the snow, Katie Reynolds. It disappeared, Pouf!" Graeme winked at Lauren as he tinkled a few notes of, 'But Baby, it's cold outside!'

A well-aimed cushion, thrown by Julie, landed in the middle of Graeme's back. He responded with a wicked grin at her and by playing the opening notes to the tango, 'Jealousy'.

Julie chuckled at him, "Oh No! Not in my condition!"

Graeme settled Lauren on one side of him, Stuart on the other and put Aimee on his knee. Leading them, he indicated on the piano, which note they should each strike as they played and sung together 'Twinkle, Twinkle Little Star' and a host of other children's songs.

Kate whispered to Harry, "How does he do it? He always gets them eating out of his hand, without even trying."

Harry answered, "He listens. That's the secret of his success. He's openly honest, and people everywhere respect that, knowing they can trust him."

Harry paused, as his own daughter laughed loudly at something Graeme had said.

He went on, "I've heard he's like the 'Pied Piper' where the new recruits are concerned, they'll follow him anywhere. His superb record makes him their hero." Harry paused in reflection on this man who had quickly become his close friend.

"I was told he's an excellent flying instructor, but holds too high a senior rank for him to be risked in that category. Did you hear him say he has plans to teach Julie to fly? He's really quite a remarkable man, honey, and I think they're a very special charismatic couple."

Kate murmured softly, "Have you noticed how they both watch the other?"

Harry nodded, "I'd noticed, honey. To me it seems as though they still can't believe their luck at finding each other again."

Julie called across, "Hey, Katie girl, come and take a decko at this. See what you think."

Kate noting the clean, elegant and stylish lines of the long evening skirt and blouse design, exclaimed, "Hey! That's great, Jules. It'll work perfectly. All that's needed is one or two good quality, long black, or dark coloured skirts and several different coloured tops. The skirt can be manufactured in a classic crepe type fabric, home washable and inexpensive."

She studied the design again. "The top can be made in any material. As inexpensive, or, as rich as the budget will stand, makes an ideal and easy present for a young husband to buy for his wife's birthday, or whatever. Yep! It's the modular 'Bellamissio' concept, all over again, Jules. I like it, Julie. I like it very much."

Next day, Graeme helped Julie out of the station wagon, in front of the imposing Maison Chevalier building—where it had all begun. He kissed her warmly, saying, "Go get 'em, darling."

Michael and Denise greeted them with such enthusiasm that it had the rest of the staff wondering. One of the junior members frowned as she looked closely at T.P.'s enlargement photographs hung in the office foyer. She nudged her office mate, "Look! That's the same woman. She must have been very young in that wind and silks photo. And look, that's definitely her in the other, 'Mother's Secret Love'."

The young girl studied the photographs. "Those are of Julie Field, you know, the 'Flowers of the Field' label. I thought Mr and Mrs Armstrong were expecting a Mrs McKenzie?"

"That's the name she gave me! Mrs Julie McKenzie."

Michael had his arm around Julie's shoulders as he said, "Twins eh? Its great news, Julie, send Graeme my good wishes."

While Julie explained her design concept and why she felt there was a need for it, Kate and Denise pinned up Julie's sketches on the design easels around the room.

They scrutinized the designs closely, occasionally raising an appreciative eyebrow at Julie's intricate and professional detail.

For several minutes nobody spoke as Michael rattled away on a calculator, fingers flying over the keys, a frown of concentration upon his brow. Denise got up, walked around the room, studying the individual designs, and making some notes. Gradually the tension in the room mounted while Michael and Denise conferred.

At long last, with a big smile, Michael uttered the magical words, "We think the whole idea is a brilliant concept. Julie, my dear, your working title using your initials 'JEM' should really appeal to the young women. It's catchy and has great marketing prospects. Well done, my girl, we think you might just hit the jackpot again with this one!"

Denise's comments were equally supportive, as she added,

"It's a line that can be launched any season. It doesn't need to be exclusively for any set time of the year . . . Now to brass tacks. What input do you want, Julie? Do you want a full hands on, or do you want a franchise basis? We don't mind either way, name your poison, honey?"

Julie sat speechless. It did not matter how many times, or how often it happened, every time a new line was accepted, she experienced this same humbling feeling. This time though, Graeme would be there, beside her, all of the way.

She took a deep breath, and then lightly touched her bulging waist. "I am going to be too busy with these two to want too big an input. The franchise idea sounds fine to me. I'd like to oversee the initial designs, and see them as finished garments, then . . ." she sighed, "It's all yours."

Kate's exuberant whoop of joy brought smiles all round. "Now I can go home, knowing all is AOK here. I can go back to the peace of my olive plantation, in my own piece of paradise."

As they left, Julie looked at herself immortalised in T.P.'s photos. "You know we have the originals of these.

Graeme has them on the wall in his study. We are unbelievably happy, but these new babies are the icing on the cake, for both of us. I shall be forty next month. Golly, that makes the first photo twenty-three years old! Frightening, isn't it, where time vanishes to."

Graeme was standing beside the waiting station wagon, a huge welcoming grin on his face, when he saw them coming through the revolving door. He took a few steps towards them and tucked Julie's arm through his. "Well, darling, are you in business?"

Julie smiled, as she answered, "Yes, they liked them. I've agreed to a franchise and a commission. Is that okay?"

"Darling, I'm relieved, I must admit." His blue eyes twinkled, "I wouldn't have stopped you going the full hog but I'm glad you haven't done so. I need you around me, Mrs McKenzie. It's as simple and selfish as that."

Julie knew later, in private, she must tell Graeme how she had felt, knowing he was downstairs waiting. The delicious feeling of having him, for the first time in her professional career, to share in the euphoria of having a new line accepted. Also the knowing that this time it would be accepted completely unselfishly and without jealousy.

After lunch, they strolled through St. James's Park and up the Mall to Buckingham Palace. The massive palace impressed Stuart and Aimee by its sheer size, and Lauren informed the two younger children, "This is where the Queen sometimes lives, and she's at home now."

"How do you know that?" scoffed Stuart.

Lauren pointed to the roof of the Palace. "Look up there, see, that's the Queen's own flag, flying from the flagpole, and it's only flying up there when the Queen is in her home."

Graeme added, "It's called the Queen's Standard. Hello, well I'll be . . . What have we here? Look, see who is in the large black car in the middle of the road."

Graeme automatically stood straight and to attention, as the royal car drove past them and swept through the gate. All three children had a front row view of the smiling, familiar face that adorned their paper money and their postage stamps.

Stuart cried, "Papa, it really was the Queen Lady. I saw her!"

Kate was making weird, soft squealing noises, "He's right, he's right! It really was the Queen and the Duke! It's the first time I've seen them, 'live'! Oh boy! Wait until I tell them at home! Harry did you see?"

Harry smiled fondly at his excited wife, "Yes, honey, I sure did. We were in the right place at just the right time."

Graeme was holding Julie's arm through his and felt her tug at his sleeve. "You've actually met Her Majesty, haven't you, my darling? After she had decorated you following the dreadful suicide bomber incident."

Lauren's sharp ears heard her mother's query, asking, "You have met the Queen, Papa? Oh please, tell us about it."

"Later, honey. Suffice it say, she is one charming and sincere lady. It was a pleasure to be in her company. Now, I think we'll whistle up a taxi to take us back to the hotel, it's beginning to get too chilly out here for Mama."

CHAPTER 111

At their hotel, Graeme kept his promise, retelling his awestruck audience how he had received a Palace summons and was decorated for his bravery by the Queen. After satisfyingly answering their many questions, the awestruck children were eventually tucked up in bed. Kate and Harry also pleaded they were 'pooped' and made for their room.

Graeme kissed Julie tenderly. "Now, my darling, put on your very sexy negligee, and then come lie with me. I want to hear, every detail of your visit to Maison Chevalier."

She began, "I know it probably sounds unusual, but I want to start at the end, after Michael and Denise had accepted the new line." She paused, searching his face. "Graeme, my darling, it was such a precious sensation, knowing I had only to go outside and you would be there to share my success."

He tenderly kissed her, saying huskily, "Since our marriage I have also found I cannot get back quickly enough to share something with you."

She lay with her head on his chest, retelling what occurred with Michael and Denise. Graeme massaged her abdomen and then kissed 'them'. Julie gently stroked his face, as she said wistfully "I wonder what they look like?"

Graeme replied, with feeling, "As long as they are as strong and as healthy as those other two beautiful children of ours, I don't care. To you and I, my darling, they will be the most gorgeous twins on this planet."

The next morning they headed for their final destination, the Tower of London. Stuart relished the slightly eerie, ancient atmosphere, while the two girls giggled nervously, and emitted feminine squeals at some of the more gory scenes.

The unique Beefeater uniforms had Julie and Kate quipping and exchanging outrageous fashion ideas, while Graeme and Harry found the military weaponry fascinating.

Once home, Lauren wrapped her arms around Graeme's neck, as she sighed, "We saw everything on our list, dear Papa. Thank you for taking us."

All too soon it was time for the Reynolds family to return to New Zealand. Watching them disappear through the departure lounge, Julie felt the pang of separation, and Graeme put his arm around her shoulder to comfort her. She turned to him, her eyes brimmed with tears, but she wore a loving smile on her face as she told him, "Have no fear, my darling, I'm right where I want to be."

The cold grey January of 2000 passed.

Though Graeme's duties frequently took him to various European capitals, he always telephoned on those nights that he had to be away. To Julie these were the most tiresome months of her pregnancy, the waiting months. She amused Graeme by describing herself as being as big as a galleon under full sail.

Whenever Graeme was away on his short duty hops, she filled her time consulting by telephone with the staff of Maison Chevalier. They regularly sent samples of the new line for her scrutiny and approval. Michael and Denise themselves were also frequent visitors, as Julie added the finishing touches to her new JEM line. Michael asked Julie if she would be interested in one off special commissions, such as designing gowns for participants in the BAFTA awards. At first she was dumbfounded, but then, on collecting her thoughts, enthusiastically said, 'Yes, Yes please!"

Her JEM ideas included large, sparkling, bejewelled flowers or tropical birds that buttoned onto the bodices of the evening tops. The buttons were frequently the eyes of the animals, or the centres of flowers.

In a market research trial conducted around several service married quarters, they were staggered by the overwhelming approval the garments received. Michael planned the full launch after Julie had her babies.

On their joint birthdays, Julie's fortieth and Lauren's eleventh, Graeme planned a matinee visit to see a West End musical, to be followed by a special dinner at an exclusive restaurant.

Following the colourful show, Graeme retrieved their coats from the cloakroom. As he made his way back to Julie and the children, he paused to look appreciatively at his family. Stuart was looking up at his mother as she bent to hear him better against the babble of noise coming from the exiting audience. His strong, sturdy little figure was dressed in the latest style for a boy of his age, and Graeme reflected he certainly was a handsome little chap.

Beside his son, his beautiful wife was dressed in a pale blue silk maternity pants suit, her amethyst jewellery sparkling and glistening as she moved. In Graeme's eyes, her pregnancy gave her an added femininity and an even more delicate vulnerability and desirability. He felt a really great desire to protect her.

Graeme shifted his gaze to look proudly as his first born, demurely dressed in a new dress. He smiled ruefully, recalling how that morning she had used all the wiles of her eleven years in an effort to 'have him on'.

Lauren had been given a birthday cheque by her grandparents to buy herself a new dress for this family outing. An hour before they were due to leave home, she had appeared in Graeme's study. Reading a memo he only half heard Lauren's question. Looking up he saw, to his horror, Lauren's new outfit was opaque. He could see her underwear through it!

He had stuttered, "No way, Lauren. You are not going out dressed like that! I can see right through it. Go and change, please."

"Papa! This is my new dress! You just said, Okay," she protested.

"No, Lauren, I must have misheard you. Go and change please," he had repeated firmly, as he headed for the door, yelling, "Julie! Julie! Have you seen what Lauren is wearing?"

Before Lauren could argue or protest any further, he retreated back into his study and firmly closed the door on his daughter. Sitting at his desk, he realised he had just played the heavy father for the first time.

After a while there was a discreet knock and Julie, trying to hide her amusement, asked, "Would you kindly agree to see your daughter, Papa dear, and see if you approve of her clothing?"

Lauren marched defiantly into the study in the same dress, but this time wearing a discreet, full-length petticoat under it. Graeme bade her twirl around in a full circle, before saying, softly and tenderly, "Much better, much more ladylike and suitable for my beautiful daughter." So saying, he held out his arms to her.

Lauren let out a small sob and rushed into his embrace.

Alone, Julie and Graeme clung to each other, their laughter muffled, as Julie stammered, "Lesson for number one daughter. Papa might be a pushover pussycat most of the time, but woe betide growing up daughter if she crosses the line! Well done, darling, you earned many 'brownie points' today."

Coming out of his reverie in the theatre foyer, he saw Julie beckoning, urging him to hurry. With a disarming grin, he hurried over and distributed their outer garments. Wrapping Julie's cape around her shoulders, he dropped a discreet kiss upon the back of her neck and bear growled appreciatively into her ear. She playfully smacked his arm, but gave him a searchlight beam of a smile.

To Lauren's total delight, Graeme confirmed he had purchased the field for Pegasus. So between riding him and her weekly visits to her new piano tutor, life had become an ideal existence.

Stuart had no such demands upon him. With Beau and the two fast growing kittens, Oliver-Charlie and Henry-Sam, he spent much of his spare time conjuring up adventures and exploits. These often included visiting kindergarten friends who joined him, either up in his tree-house, or sprawled over his bedroom floor racing his car-racing set. For car racing he really preferred it when Graeme or Billy, and sometimes both of them enthusiastically joined him in friendly competitive races.

Julie was the only one who found the pace of life limiting as she gradually gained weight and bulk. Came the last weekend in May, Julie had laid down to have a siesta one afternoon. Graeme was seated on a chair beside her as they were tossing possible names around.

"Let's include one each of our parent's names," Julie suggested. "That's Grant Iain and Alicia Gabriella for yours, and Edward Nicholas and Victoria Angelique for mine."

As Graeme readily agreed, Julie sighed, as she felt the last few weeks had been endless, surely by now the end was in sight . . .

CHAPTER 112

Julie lay awake and looked at the clock beside her, five o'clock, June sixth. Her mind registered—the anniversary of World War Two 'D Day'. Could this be her own personal 'D Day'? She had been warned to expect her babies a couple of weeks earlier than previously calculated.

Restless, uncomfortable, she was not able to get her ungainly body into a settled position. She felt her brow, which was dry and hot, as were her feet and legs. The very air around her seemed to be extraordinarily hot and oppressive.

Graeme heard her stirring. Clasping his hand, Julie whispered, "Darling, I'm not sure yet, but this is how I started with Stuart. I'm hot and uncomfortable, no pains yet, but I just know things are about to begin. I thought I'd better let you know, just in case."

Graeme snapped on a small reading light beside him, glancing instinctively at the clock. He stroked Julie's brow, telling her, "Darling, you are very warm! How are your feet? Wow! They are just as hot!"

He quickly went into the bathroom, returning with a cool, wet towel for her head and one each for her feet.

Julie had a déjà vu feeling as she remembered Kate doing the same for her. She had remarked then to Kate that it would be just the sort of thing Graeme would do. Now, here he was, actually doing it for her, in real life!

For another hour, Graeme calmly talked to her, soothing her nerves, encouraging her to relax. Every now and then Julie walked around, trying to get comfortable. Then, during one of these moments, Julie staggered against him as a sharp twinge shot through her body. Smiling a crooked, one-sided grin at him, she whispered, "That's it, flyboy, I'm sure now. I guess we are in the baby birthing business again."

He hugged her close to his body. "Well, my wonderful darling, settle in the armchair while I tackle the list of who, what and where we have to contact. I'll be right here, all of the way. I'll not leave you for a moment."

His first call was to the Maternity Annex, informing them they would probably be needed later in the day. The Duty Sister cheerily informed him that she would contact Sister Collins and have her come to their home and she would also alert Doctor Susan Blake.

Graeme rang Billy, advising him he would be 'out of the loop', for however long it took, to which Billy responded with his and Marisa's good wishes.

As Julie had another twinge, he gently stroked her hair, assuring her, "I'm right here, my darling one. I'll give Daisy a call."

Julie smiled, "Graeme, darling, it's wonderful having you here with me. Ouch! That was a harder one!"

Daisy knocked on the door, "Hello, lass. I hear we are on the way again. Anything different from the other two?" Julie shook her head, "No, Daisy, everything seems to be following the same pattern as Lauren and Stuart."

They heard Lauren call out from downstairs, "Papa, Mama, Sister Collins is in the drive . . ." Realisation suddenly dawned and she called, in a softer tone, "Oh Mama! Are our babies coming?"

Daisy smiled, "Leave it to me, I'll make you something to eat, Graeme, love. You'll need it, even if Julie doesn't fancy anything, just now."

A few seconds later a soft knock upon their bedroom door heralded the friendly, smiling figure of Sister Rose Collins. "Well, good morning, folks. Help her onto the bed please, Graeme, so that I can examine her. Go and have that cuppa, Daddyoh, whilst I get organised."

When he came back, Graeme found Sister Collins was on the phone to the Hospital, saying, "Yes, we are in business . . . Twins, full term . . . Mrs Julie McKenzie, Sycamore Lane . . . Right, send the ambulance . . . it will be more comfortable for her than a private car . . . Yes, me and Mr Graeme McKenzie, accompanying his wife . . . Okay, get it in the pipeline, pronto! Ciao."

Daisy knocked discreetly and handed Graeme a breakfast tray. "We'll be just downstairs, Julie love."

Sister Collins suggested to Julie, "How about a shower? It will cool you down a little and give your good man a chance to eat some of this delicious food Mrs Green has brought him. Come on, little mother, in we go."

Julie was grateful for Rose's soothing, calm professional manner as she stood under the cool water cascading down her body. Stepping out of the shower, she was instantly wrapped in a big soft towel and the strong muscular arms of her husband. Graeme held her close to him as he murmured endearments and gently dried her. He dropped a fresh cotton nightgown over her head, and kissed her lips, before brushing her hair into a ponytail and tying it back with a ribbon. It was something he had discovered Julie always found very soothing, during the latter months of her pregnancy, Holding her in his arms, he gazed down at the woman he loved so much. With her face bare of any make-up, she did not look a day older than when he had found her again in Sydney, over a decade ago. Huskily, Graeme told Julie so.

She whispered in reply, "And you look as handsome to me as you did that wonderful, wonderful day, my beloved one."

There was a sharp knock on the door, and Lauren asked, tremulously, "Can we see our Mama, please, Sister Collins?"

Both children ran to their mother who held her arms wide open. "Now, my darlings, just follow what we have planned with Daisy for this special time. Papa will be staying with me, as we get our babies born. When there's some news, he will come and tell you."

"Remember, I shall be in the hospital for a couple of days or so, and then we'll have them home with us to cuddle and spoil. Look after Papa for me, won't you? Don't forget that I love you both very much."

They reluctantly left with Daisy as Julie experienced her strongest contraction yet and clutched at Graeme's hand for support. Sister Collins checked her watch.

Graeme assisted Julie out onto the bedroom balcony, so that she could wave to the children as they left with Daisy for school and kindergarten. Beau and the two kittens followed in a single file, behind them, which had Rose Collins laughing with delight as she watched the charming tableau below.

When the electronic gates closed, the two kittens sat with their heads through the gate railings, stretching their necks as far as they were able to watch the children, Daisy and Beau, disappear down the road.

Once they were out of sight, the two kittens danced and pranced around each other, playing 'scaredy cats', as Stuart called it, before scampering back through their cat flap in the back door.

Sister Collins mused. 'This is such a magical home, so full of love and mutual caring.' She watched, with obvious pleasure, as Julie walked around her bedroom with Graeme's arm around her waist, supporting her physically and mentally, as he tenderly murmured encouraging endearments.

Julie clutched at her abdomen at another contraction and she quickly did her deep breathing exercises. Rose Collins checked her watch again—the ambulance she had requested would not be here any too soon. She quietly checked Julie's pre-packed case and put it on the bed, alongside Julie's handbag and quilted housecoat.

Daisy and the ambulance arrived simultaneously. Daisy hugged and assured Julie, through happy tear-filled eyes, "I'll be here, waiting for the welcome news, Graeme. I'll ring your parents and Julie's family as planned. Go my lass, with all my love."

It seemed to her that in no time she was lying, as comfortably as she was able, upon the special bed in her hospital room, and was expertly being linked up to various monitoring machines. This gave Graeme a momentary, sickening feeling of déjà vu of when she lay in the coma. But, this time for a very happy reason, as he heard the monitor speaker relaying two strong heartbeats.

The theatre-gowned Dr Susan Blake breezed cheerfully in and conferred with Rose Collins. They examined Julie before Susan announced, "Babies before lunch time today folks. So hold onto your hat, Daddyoh, it's all about to happen very soon!"

Graeme grinned self-consciously as he deftly caught the bundle of theatre greens she threw at him. Julie's contractions continued ever closer, more and more frequently. At eleven o'clock, Rose Collins decided she was ready to be moved into the clinical white Delivery Suite.

Clutching Graeme's hand, Julie could just see his blue eyes over the mask, as he bent down and whispered, "Dio come ti-amo, cara mia. I'm here my darling."

Through the confused mists of pain, she knew very soon she would give him the greatest gifts she could give her beloved husband.

With her labour moving into its final stage, she heard herself cry out in pain. But, close beside her ear, she heard his soothing, calm voice encouraging her, telling her how much he loved her. After one particularly agonizing, long drawn out contraction, she also heard the agony in his voice as he lamented, "Dear God! If this job were left to men, there would be no more babies! How much longer does she have to suffer, like this, Rose?"

Rose Collins calmly went on with her examination of Julie, before answering, "A head is crowning. Right, next contraction, give me one big push, Honeykins. Ready! Here we go!"

The newly born infant slipped into this world and was quickly caught by Rose. The umbilical cord was cut and the baby expertly wrapped in a warm blanket, all in one fluid movement.

She smiled at Julie and Graeme, "You have a dear little, healthy lad here." The tiny baby opened his mouth and gave voice to his first cry. "Oh yes! A good pair of lungs as well. Here Daddy, hold your son while we get the other 'smidgen' born."

Julie smiled weakly as she whispered, "We welcome you, Nicholas Grant McKenzie. He's all yours, darling. You'll have to look after him for a moment . . . I'm a bit busy . . . just now."

Graeme stood awestruck beside Julie's head, gazing down at the tiny bundle almost lost in his strong, muscular arms. He was speechless. He, who always found the right words, was momentarily stunned and silent. His hands trembled and a large lump formed in his throat as he held the precious baby, conveying everything by his silence. His son!

CHAPTER 113

Sister Collins was still urging, anxiously, "Come on, Julie, m'dear, one more push, we still have another baby to go."

Julie's head was wet with perspiration. Her whole body seemed to be one mound of raw nerves. As though from a distance and working as though on autopilot, she felt her second baby slip from her body. Rose's voice came back into focus as she laid a tiny body on Julie's chest. "She's a perfect little girl, Julie. You've got a 'pidgin pair', one of each. And hey! They're a good size as well."

Julie looked into the eyes of the one and only person she needed at this moment in time, and heard him saying, in a husky, emotional voice, "Well done, my darling. They are just beautiful. Nicholas Grant McKenzie, eh?" He grinned at her. "And, how about—Gabriella Angelique McKenzie? You are one clever lady, my sweetheart. From the bottom of my heart, their very proud father thanks you."

He bent down and kissed Julie's parched lips, as her features relaxed into an exhausted but happy smile for him.

Dr Susan Blake carried the 'McKenzie twins' over to the scales to be weighed, while Julie was euphemistically speaking, 'tidied up'. She sank gratefully against Graeme's chest as he sat beside her pillow. He cradled her close to him, as though he never wanted to let her go.

Susan Blake called out from across the room, "Wow! What a pair of whoppers, Julie! You have done really well, my friend. The little lad weighs 5lbs 4ozs, and the dear wee lass, just on 5lbs. Both have all their fingers and toes in the correct numbers . . . and all seems in order with his masculine bits, before you ask, Graeme," she grinned at them.

"So heartiest congratulations to you both. We'll take you back to your room shortly, Julie, for a rest and Graeme can go and inform the world of your good fortune. From me, on a personal note, I'm delighted. I know what these two mites mean to you both."

Alone a while later in Julie's room, Graeme held her once more, saying, "Thank you, my dearest, darling wife. I think I'm floating in a Paradise, a Garden of Eden, on Cloud Nine, I am ecstatic!"

"Graeme, they're so perfect! Lauren and Stuart were bigger of course, and these two seem like little miniatures in comparison. But they are yours and mine to share, my darling husband. A dark haired daughter, and a blonde headed son. We are truly blessed, Graeme."

He smiled at her, his heart bursting with pride. "We sure are, my angel. Now, you need to rest. I'm about to be shooed away for a while to let you do so."

He started to leave but turned to her again, saying, "I have just witnessed something all men should have the chance to experience—the birth of my own children. In case you need to be told once again, I do love you so very much you, clever, clever darling. I now have the pleasant job of tackling the list of who needs to know. My parents should have arrived by now, so no doubt they'll be up to see you later." His face was still wreathed in a wide, wide, proud smile, as he tenderly said, "Darling, I can't adequately tell you how great I am feeling right now. Dio come ti-amo, cara mia."

Julie's eyes were drooping as he gave her a final kiss and quietly slipped out of the room. His feet hardly touched the floor and his mouth seemed to be stuck in a permanent happy smile, as he made his way to Dr Susan Blake's room to ring Sergeant Wyberg, requesting him to pick him up. After making his call, he stood at the New Born Nursery window, gazing in awe at the two bassinets which stood side by side, proudly displaying their name tags, "Male, McKenzie, Nicholas Grant" and "Female, McKenzie, Gabriella Angelique" D.O.B. 6/6/2000, Twins."

Dr Susan Blake came out of the Nursery to stand beside him. "Well done, Graeme. You helped Julie through what could have been quite an ordeal."

She chuckled as she walked away, leaving this sensitive military man still gazing in wonder at his new-born twins. As she told Rose Collins later, 'With a look as soft as butter on his face.'

Sergeant Wyberg's boots could be heard clumping down the corridor, but it was several seconds before Graeme could pull his eyes away from the window. The Sergeant joined him at the window, saying, "Blimey, sir! One of each! How did you arrange that? Mrs McKenzie, is she okay?" When a still dazed Graeme nodded, he went on, cheerily, "Well, Sir, the news is probably already halfway around the base, they'll have the stork up on your office roof by now, with both blue and pink bows. I've no doubt they'll all be waiting for you to dish out the cigars later, Sir."

"Right, Sergeant, seems as though I'll have a busy day, so let's not disappoint them. Home first to see my parents and to change. Mrs Green will, hopefully, have some sustenance for us, so let's make haste, my man."

He made one last, but very important stop before reaching the car. At the Hospital florist he ordered two dozen red roses to be sent up to his precious wife, writing on the card, 'Dio come ti-amo, cara mia, forever and always, Graeme'.

On his arrival home, the front door was thrown open as soon as the car stopped. His parents and Daisy stood there asking as one, "Well?"

Laughing merrily, Graeme almost danced up the front steps and clasped his mother in his arms. "All VERY well, folks. That clever girl has given us one of each, a perfect pair . . . no, belay that . . . a beautiful perfect pair. I have just had one of the most awe inspiring experiences of my life, better even than the day I flew solo, Dad, and that's saying something, isn't it? You are all invited to come and see what a clever pair we have been, later today, after Lauren and Stuart have met their new brother and sister." He twirled his laughing mother around once more, before saying, "Now I must change and go to the base for a couple of hours. Daisy, dear, what's for lunch—I'm starving!"

An hour later Sergeant Wyberg drove his boss extra slowly through the base gates. He had made a secret call to Billy, informing him of the imminent arrival of the new father.

The USAF military band was lined up at the Main Gate, playing congratulatory music and the RAF theme tune in Graeme's honour, as Sergeant Wyberg drove the car slowly to Graeme's office. A huge, white plastic stork stood on the building roof with pink and blue ribbons streaming from its neck. At the entrance to his office, Graeme found all of his staff lined up, smiling and clapping enthusiastically.

A voice called out, "Three cheers for the Air Commodore and Mrs McKenzie," and the rousing cry echoed around the immediate buildings. Billy came with an enormous box of cigars. "Here you go, Daddy, courtesy of the USAF boys, especially the Texan ones."

Graeme's face seemed to be permanently split into a grin as wide as Texas, as he handed out cigars to all and sundry. Coming upon his C.O., he stood smartly to attention but was soon put at ease by Martin Brown, who shook his hand vigorously, saying, "Well done, Graeme. Dulcie and I wholeheartedly congratulate you and Julie. As you can hear and see, your news has been a popular morale booster around this place today." He tapped the side of his nose. "It isn't only the Yanks that can get sentimental, is it, lad?"

Entering his office with Billy close on his heels, Graeme was staggered to find his usual masculine domain had been decorated with pink and blue streamers and balloons.

On his desk sat a pile of parcels sporting baby wrapping paper, and there were several large bouquets of flowers scattered around his office.

Turning in bewilderment to Billy, he stammered, "How did they all get to know, so quickly?"

Billy grinned mischievously at his life-time friend. "The base radio station has a link to the Hospital. The news was on an hour ago, and the messages and presents have simply been coming in ever since. You and Julie are popular people around here, sport. People care what happens to you guys. By the way, Marisa and I offer you our sincere congrats, as well. You have shown your human side, once again, and the troops like what they see. I'll get Sergeant Wyberg to load all of these into the car for you, so that you can take them up to Julie later."

Graeme mused on his Commanding Officer's words regarding the birth of the two small babies being a huge morale booster. The people stationed at the vast air base were basically mostly young men and their equally young wives and families. To witness a senior officer bringing new life, that of his own children, into an uncertain world, would be sending a solid message to them. It was a declaration of faith for the future on this active military base. For the many that daily faced testing and sometimes warlike conditions as part of their everyday working lives, the event today would be seen as something to follow and believe in.

He grinned to himself as he thought, 'Well, once before a single child brought so much comfort to our troubled old world, now Julie and I have given them two!'

CHAPTER 114

News of the successful twin births spread like wildfire around the air base, the village and amongst family and friends. Alicia and Grant McKenzie escorted an excited Lauren, Stuart and Daisy up to the hospital early on the first evening. Both children were in awe of the two tiny bundles of their siblings, swathed respectively in a pink and a blue blanket, as they lay in side-by-side bassinets next to their smiling mother's bed.

Graeme lifted Stuart onto the bed so that he could hug his mother but, after hurriedly doing so, anxiously eyed the two bassinets. Graeme motioned for Lauren to sit in the chair beside Julie and asked, "Which one would you like to hold, poppet?"

"My . . . my sister please, Papa," Lauren smiled, almost shyly at her father.

Graeme lifted the tiny form of the dark headed Gabriella out of her bassinet and carefully placed her in Lauren's arms, murmuring, in a proud, paternal voice, "Here you are sister, Lauren, meet your new sister, Gabriella Angelique."

Lauren's face was a picture to behold as she whispered, "She's so tiny, so small, but so beautiful, Mama and Papa." As if on cue, the tiny baby opened her eyes and clasped Lauren's little finger in her own minute hand.

Meanwhile, Stuart, who was still being cradled by Julie, broke away from his mother's arms and asked his father, "Okay, then, can I cuddle the boy one, Papa?"

Graeme gently picked up his second son and placed him in Stuart's arms. Stuart scrutinised the sleeping baby before saying, in a voice much older than his years, "He's very small, Papa. He hasn't got much hair, but it's the same colour as yours, Papa." Bending down, he sighed and said, with relief in his voice, "Hello, you are my brother Nicholas. I'm glad we have another boy at last!"

A doubtful frown then formed on Stuart's chubby face as he turned to Julie, asking, "Mama, do you think he will get big enough to play with me?"

Julie stroked the hair of her older son, saying, with a tender smile, "Of course he will, darling. You were once that small, you know. Haven't Papa and I been clever in getting two babies, and especially in getting one of each?"

Alicia and Grant McKenzie marvelled at the unique miniature bodies, before Grant McKenzie turned to his son and daughter-in-law, saying, "Thank you, Julie and Graeme, well done. This is great! Now we each have one to spoil, and I no longer have to wait my turn like a good mannered, gentlemanly Gramps, while your mother 'coos' and 'gooes' her heart out. Now I'll be able to have one of my own, straight away, to cuddle!"

Daisy, who had been hovering in the background, was brought forward by Graeme. "Here you are Nanny, Daisy, two more to spoil and to feed up."

Alicia handed Daisy the tiny bundle that was Nicholas Grant McKenzie.

For Julie and Graeme, the following couple of days were a constant happy blur of receiving congratulations, baby gifts, flowers and telephone calls. One of the first calls Julie received at the hospital was from Kate and Harry in New Zealand. They told her that they were determined to visit their newest Godchildren-to-be, as soon as poss.

The second was a very special and emotional call from Maria and Giovanni, from the Château Cornacchia. Maria could hardly contain her excitement, as she cried, "Oh my cara, Julie! All of the family, we are so verra happy for you and the beloved one. Senda me photos, quickly."

During the twins first full day of life, who should walk into Julie's room but T.P. He declared, emphatically, "It wouldn't feel right if I

were not to complete my 'full house' collection of the McKenzie clan!"
Offering his own warmest congratulations, he quickly proceeded, in his
own inimitable way, to snap the usual, as well as the unusual, getting the
sort of photographs that had made him world famous.

The two babies cooperated magnificently by yawning delightfully
at him with their pink rosebud mouths, or by sucking their minuscule
hands with tiny, screwed up faces. When he included Lauren and Stuart
to complete family poses of all four children, he saw through his camera
lens their loving, radiant smiles beaming back at him of their pride in
their new brother and sister.

At one time, he captured Graeme with a baby over each shoulder,
yawning simultaneously. A laughing Graeme gave him the ideal caption,
"That's the so-called generation gap, they're bored by their father's words,
already!"

Yet another occurred when Julie was cradling the babies, for once
with their eyes wide open and gazing up at their mother. It embraced the
very essence of the tenderness of a mother's love.

Shortly after this, an unexpected incident happened as T.P. was
about to press the button on a traditional family pose. The two babies
were lying 'box and cox' upon a sheepskin rug on a side-table, with
just the heads and shoulders of their parents and older siblings visible,
as they crouched down and surrounded the babies. A single sunbeam
suddenly spilt through the hospital window. It slanted across the room,
striking the bodies of the babies, as though someone had just switched
on a spotlight.

It illuminated both of the babies, giving them an ethereal, almost
unreal, even mystical appearance, and causing even an old hand like
T.P. to release a gasp of astonishment as he quickly clicked the shutter.
He knew if he had caught the fantastic lighting effect in time, that shot
would most certainly be his masterpiece of the whole session.

It was Stuart who steadfastly and stoutly declared, "Did you see that,
Mama and Papa? That was God up there in Heaven, switching on his
torch to have a closer look at Gabriella and Nicholas."

Graeme's eyes twinkled merrily at Julie as he murmured, "Now who
are we to doubt or question such erudite and sage words of wisdom?"

Julie had a different opinion. "I think my Gran came down for a
look."

On the third day of the babies lives, Graeme brought several daily
newspapers to the hospital, both national and local. To Julie's surprise,

Graeme had inserted identical proclamations in the Birth Notice columns of each of them!

Each read:

"McKENZIE; Air Commodore Graeme McKenzie, Mrs Julie McKenzie, Lauren and Stuart McKenzie proudly announce the twin births of Nicholas Grant (5lbs. 4ozs.) and Gabriella Angelique McKenzie (5lbs) on June 6th, 2000. All well."

The publication of the notices resulted in a deluge of mail. It became so great that for several days the local Post Office had to resort to delivering the McKenzie daily avalanche of cards and letters in the Postmaster's private car!

Graeme sought the help of his private secretary in sorting through these piles of good wishes. He asked her to do her best to single out the immediate family ones from those of complete strangers. Handing over his own and Julie's private address books to work from, he ran his hand distractedly through his hair and said, in utter and total amazement, "Have you ever seen anything like it? Anyone would think we were pop stars or something!" He wished her 'Good Luck' before dumping the latest bulging Post Office mailbag beside her desk.

On the babies fifth day, Dr Susan Blake cleared Julie to return home with them the next day. Both were feeding well, while Julie was rested but fretting, wanting to be back in her own home with Graeme and her family.

When Graeme came to visit her at the maternity annex to join her for lunch, she asked him, "Can you take me up later this afternoon, darling? Susan says it will be okay."

Graeme, surprised but pleased by her request, answered, "Yes, of course, my darling, nothing would give me more pleasure. I can be free by three. Daisy will have Lauren and Stuart in hand. The babies will stay here? Okay then, I'll collect you as close to three o'clock as I can, and we'll go for a spin, just you and me, sweetheart."

He did not question her. He knew she would explain, if and when he needed to know, although he thought he had already reasoned what was behind her request.

So it was that at three thirty that afternoon, dressed in a flying coverall over her nightgown, Julie was about to be helped aboard his plane by her husband.

She watched his face as he went through his pre-flight checks and got his clearance from the tower for take-off. He grinned cheekily at her as they taxied to the main runway, his love of flying showing in every pore of his being.

Once they reached cruising height, the cloudless sky was almost as blue as Graeme's eyes. It was then he heard Julie reciting the 'High Flight' poem, and afterwards, in a soft voice saying, "Thank you, God, for my truly wonderful husband, for Lauren and Stuart, and now for giving us two more healthy babies.

"Thank you, Gran, for watching over us for so long. Up here I feel so close to you. My cup runneth over, thank you. Amen."

Graeme smiled tenderly at his wife, acknowledging, to himself, he was right when he had surmised this was the reason she had wanted to come up here. He clasped her hand in his and kissed her palm, saying, softly and sincerely, "Roger that. That goes for me, as well. Accept my heartfelt thanks as well, Lord, Amen"

Julie smiled radiantly back at him, "I knew you'd understand, that I didn't have to spell it out in words of one syllable."

He nodded his assent and then, with a wicked grin in her direction, his eyes twinkling mischievously, he asked, "You up to a Victory roll, to celebrate our good fortune, sweetheart?"

"Yes, darling, go for it!" she replied, her eyes aglow as she accepted his challenge.

Executing the perfect manoeuvre, high in the sky, Graeme felt exhilarated. He glanced over at her, promising himself that one day very soon he would give her flying lessons.

At mid-morning the next day, with the help of the redoubtable Sergeant Wyberg, they took their babies home.

The indomitable Sergeant asked Daisy, "Blimey! Where did all of this stuff come from? There are enough flowers to start a florists shop, enough cards and letters to keep the Post Office busy for a week, and enough baby gear for my Guv'nor and his missus to start two Nursery shops! No wonder the Hospital wanted Mrs Mac to go home, she was occupying enough space for four women!"

CHAPTER 115

During the next week, a great deal of planning and organizing took place to cope with having two new-born babies in the house.

At one four a.m. feeding, Graeme sleepily told Julie, "It's a safe bet that those who sleep like babies don't have any!"

Trying to laugh through her tiredness, Julie was grateful that her easy-going husband still maintained his natural sense of humour. When he announced that he had hired Sister Collins to come and take a night shift duty, three times a week, she confessed she had never felt so tired in her life—the two babies never seemed to be awake or want to feed at the same times!

After valiantly attempting to breast-feed for the first week, Julie had to finally admit defeat and, with Rose Collins's help, had weaned them onto bottle-feeding during their second week.

Daisy broached the subject of getting a 'daily', to come and help with the housework, asking them to meet a local widow from her church group. A couple of days later, Julie and Graeme accepted Daisy's recommendation, and Pat Warner became a welcome addition to their ever growing household.

Suddenly it was a day away from their first Wedding Anniversary, and Graeme decreed, "We are going to be stepping out, even if it has to be an early dinner. We are going out together, alone, dressing-up, candlelight dinner and 'the works', my darling, Julie."

He twirled Julie around in his arms, declaring, "Daisy and my parents have agreed to share the time between them, so that you and I, my darling wife, can go and celebrate one wonderful year together."

June 21st, 2000 dawned cloudless. Graeme declared, "Today, being our first Wedding Anniversary, and deemed to be our 'paper' Wedding Anniversary, Julie, my love, what better present could I give you than this."

With a theatrical flourish, he swept a mock Elizabethan bow. Julie's eyes opened wide as he revealed a beautifully framed enlargement of T.P.'s, family 'sunbeam' photo.

The two babies looked as though they had indeed been kissed by an eternal presence. Behind them, the faces of Julie, Graeme, Lauren and Stuart were cast in a dreamy, artistic and surreal backdrop, being just mere bit players to the main event.

It was a breath taking family portrait.

Julie gazed at it, uttering just one word, an awestruck and appreciative, "Wow!"

Graeme murmured, "No wonder T.P. wants to enter it in this year's competition. I asked him for a suitable photo to present to you this morning, and he had it sent direct to my office. He made a request that he would dearly like to borrow it back for the big competition."

With a smile of absolute delight, Julie said, "What a wonderful gift, my darling. It's truly magnificent. I feel honoured and very happy for him to exhibit it."

Graeme hung the photograph in the entrance hall, straight away. Daisy wiped an errant tear from her cheeks and huskily said, "It's so beautiful. You all look like angels around a modern Nativity scene."

When Julie's in-laws arrived for lunch, their immediate reaction was to stand stunned in admiration for several minutes. Then they requested a copy for themselves.

Julie told them, "Graeme is upstairs bathing Nicholas—Lauren is also there feeding Gabriella. The rest of the household workforce, Daisy and I, are just about ready with lunch."

Grant McKenzie whispered gleefully to Alicia, "This I've got to see! My son, the eminent Air Commodore, bathing my two week old grandson."

"Go ahead, dear, hurry," Alicia urged, "I'm hot on your heels!"

They crept up the stairs and peeped around the door of the nursery. Here they witnessed their 'Big Brass' son, his sleeves rolled up, attired in a large plastic apron, gently bathing and talking to his infant son. The charming domestic scene was complete with Lauren gently rocking in the nursing chair, cuddling and feeding Gabriella her formula bottle.

Glancing up as he heard them approach, Graeme smiled at his parents, "Guess you never thought you'd see me in this role, eh, folks? I love it. It's my job whenever I'm home. Come and see how this chap is filling out, Nana and Gramps."

Alicia gently took Gabriella from Lauren's arms, and began to 'burp' her youngest granddaughter, after dropping a kiss onto Lauren's forehead. Lauren hugged her grandmother, saying, "It's always nice and peaceful up here. Papa and I love doing this together."

Gently drying his son, powdering and dressing him as competently as though he had been doing it all his life, Graeme handed the little boy to his father. "Here you are, Gramps, hold on to this little rascal, while I heat his bottle and then you can feed him. Lauren, honey, go and round up Stuart, get him washed up for lunch and I'll check in with Mama, to see if she needs any help."

Temporarily left alone in the nursery with the twins, Alicia and Grant McKenzie exchanged fond smiles. "This has been the very best year of my life, Grant," sighed Alicia. "Have you ever seen him so happy, so contented, or so domesticated? I would never have believed it could have happened to our son, or that we should have become such an integral part of his life again. I love it!"

Rocking his grandson soothingly in his arms, Grant McKenzie murmured, "I relish every second, Alicia, my dear. My only regret is that they had to wait so long before finding each other again. Still, no use crying over spilt milk, we have them now and that's all that matters. Aah, here comes your Papa with your lunch, young Nicholas, m'lad."

Graeme grinned happily at the lovely picture before going to welcome Julie's brother, sisters and their families.

After lunch, Julie persuaded Graeme to play the piano for them. He willingly obliged as he had an almost sensual yearning to reunite with the instrument, not having touched it in nearly three weeks. He had been either too busy with the twins, or just too tired to do so.

He seated Julie beside him at the piano and announced, "I have something special to share with you, sweetheart, on this very special day. I have composed a piece of music, especially for you. It is entitled 'My Love, My Life'." He handed her a sheet of paper. "Here are the words that I have written, which explains how I feel about you. Happy Anniversary, my darling."

Julie, overcome by his gesture, rested her head on his shoulder. He began to play a gentle, seductive concerto of a melody as he recited the words.

> *"It comes in gently on the air,*
> *And playfully rustles through my hair,*
> *Curls around my head and whispers in my ear,*
> *Here I am—my love—my dear.*
>
> *It joins my spirit and my soul,*
> *And once again I feel I'm whole,*
> *Within my heart a bell will toll,*
> *And notes of happiness from my heart will roll.*
>
> *Just to know you are near,*
> *My love—my life—my dear.*
>
> *A life together we chose to share,*
> *There was no other to compare,*
> *I know that you'll always be there,*
> *I know that you for me do care.*
>
> *Just to know you are near,*
> *My love—my life—my dear.*
>
> *It comforts me across the years,*
> *Through happy moments and times of tears,*
> *To know that you are close and very near,*
> *My love—my life—my dear"*

As Graeme brought the beautiful music to a swelling climax, Julie hugged him tightly. Then, with tears coursing down her cheeks, she emotionally whispered, "Oh, my dearest, darling husband that was so beautiful. Thank you, Graeme. I love you so much."

The entire family were now loudly and enthusiastically applauding this very tender public declaration of love. As more than one lady hunted for her handkerchief, to wipe away emotional tears, Graeme signalled to Lauren to come and join them.

As Graeme gathered Julie in his arms, Lauren played their wedding day tune, 'Till'. Dancing around their lounge, their bodies moulded together, their eyes fixed upon each other, they recaptured the memories of their special Wedding Day—just one year ago.

As the final notes of the sentimental tune faded away, Graeme kissed Julie, and tenderly said, "Now, I have a final small surprise for you, Julie, dearest. We have a couple of special trees to plant, to celebrate the birth of our two babies and of our fabulous marriage."

Julie gasped as she recognised the two special trees as Sycamore trees.

Alicia took her hand, saying, "Graeme asked us to see if we could get some seeds from the original tree that you planted, what . . . thirty odd years ago? To see if we could make them germinate, well, these two have thrived. They are now nearly four months old and look how tall they are? Here you are, my dear son and daughter-in-law, it is time to plant them in your own garden, so that they can grow, healthy and strong, like your marriage and your lives together."

Looking up into her husband's blue eyes, eyes that shone with his undying love for her, Julie was overcome by the significance of what was about to happen.

The years fell away as she remembered, in vivid detail, the day she had carried that first fragile seed home so carefully in her skirt pocket before planting it.

In her mind's eye, Julie relived the moment when, busy with her task, the tall, blonde boy, the new neighbour, had approached her. He had predicted, even way back then, that one day, perhaps if the tree actually germinated and grew on the joint boundary between their homes, their own lives would someday be linked together, forever.

Looking deeply into the same incredible blue eyes of that same boy, now grown into the handsome figure of her beloved husband, Julie knew he was also experiencing the same déjà vu feeling. That he too was reliving the memory and experiencing the certain sureness of having known each other so long ago, of having been separated and of finding each other again. Finally, their union, and the amalgamation of their two spirits, which nothing, nor no-one would, or could, ever divide again.

Holding both of his hands in hers, Julie said, quietly, and with feeling, "I had begun to believe that we were the playthings of a cruel destiny that brought us together, only to cause us the greatest pain of tearing us apart once more. By the symbolic planting of these two trees, it will be as though we have come full circle. They will stand as a growing and perpetual memorial to us. Graeme Stuart McKenzie, I love you so much. I know I always have and that I always will. You and I, my darling, are now truly living our dearest dreams."

Graeme drew her body close to his and, before covering her mouth with his, murmured, "Amen to that, my darling. Dio come ti-amo, cara mia."

EPILOGUE . . . JUNE 2000

The old mother sycamore tree, the matriarch, her robes still richly green and beautifully formed, in spite of the hot dry season that had just passed, smoothed down her ruffled skirts.

A young, late evening, capricious breeze had just swished through her full-length gown of summer foliage. It had rudely upset her normal decorum, by bustling and rustling her usual, stately composure. With all the haste and boisterousness of youth, the air-born message, carried eagerly to her ears by this fickle, gossipy, warm westerly wind, had confirmed what she had already suspected for herself.

Her senses had told her that two more of her children had been replanted, with much love. They had been given the chance to start their lives by the same compassionate, human female person who had given her, their 'mother', a similar opportunity to begin her own life, over thirty years ago.

A new son and a daughter had been germinated from her last season's crop of seeds, carefully nurtured by two older pairs of gentle, caring human hands. These two fortunate youngsters had now been planted side-by-side, set to grow in a tranquil place that was already so full of love.

With a sigh of deep satisfaction, she knew that the two people, whom she had thought of with much affection over the years had, at last, found their joint destiny.

Vividly, the old mother tree recalled the grief of the lovely young, dark headed, innocent girl, who had cried at her base, as though her heart was broken. A young woman whom she had tenderly hidden and protected, by enfolding her in her lower branches on that dark, sad day, so long ago.

The same young girl who had tearfully buried, at her base, an old tin box containing a small locket, and who had sadly returned a few years later, to retrieve it when the older human couples had moved away from the district.

She also remembered the tall blonde young man, who followed the young girl a few months later. She could still hear the agony in his voice as he had whispered the girl's name. How he had laid his head upon her trunk and, in his abject despair, had beat his hands upon it, leaving behind more than a few flecks of his blood.

Since then there had been two visits by strangers, who had come to gather her seeds. She had been told about one daughter which had grown from her seed in a far distant land, but who had been cruelly slain in her youth by the enemy of all trees everywhere, lightning in an electrical storm.

The South Wind had regaled her with the brave story of how this daughter, with her last gasps, had flung her own daughter's seeds, far away from her dying body. A lone young granddaughter had survived in that far distant country, adjusting well, by all the accounts brought to her by the infrequent visitor, the South wind.

On his last visit, she had requested that he take a message to her granddaughter. "Tell her to grow well and be our southern sentinel. To be ready to report to me, whenever the young offspring of my two special people return to the country of their birth."

To her newest offspring, her message on this day was also simple, "Grow in peace and look after your new owners well. Protect them and their kin from the heat of the sun and the harshness of the winds. Guard and shield them from the rain and the snow. Know this my children; these two are very special people. Destiny had long sought them, wanting to bring them together to start an age-old Dynasty. To proudly renew and represent a partnership made aeons ago, in the Heavens above."

Julie heard the whispering in the trees all around her in the garden, as she firmed the ground around the bases of the two new Sycamore trees. She gazed questioningly into the eyes of her smiling husband, and knew that he too sensed the presence of someone, or something special, around them. Graeme inclined his head, acknowledging that he understood.

Julie gave him a loving smile and walked into the welcoming circle of his arms, to be tenderly enfolded in the only place she never, ever, wanted to leave.

Lightning Source UK Ltd.
Milton Keynes UK
UKOW040719180413

209398UK00001B/1/P